RIGHT

One 4

DIESEL

DOMINION OF BROTHERS SERIES: BOOK 5

TALON P.S. & PRINCESS S.O.

Editing: Alison Greene and Effie Vernuccio
Cover Art: Cover Creations by Princess S.O.

~ * ~ * ~ * ~ * ~ * ~

iii

![DOMINION OF BROTHERS SERIES — BY TALON PS — BY PRINCESS SO]

THE DOMINION OF BROTHERS SERIES

WRITTEN BY TALON P.S. & PRINCESS S.O.

Five Brothers at Arms share a lust for control and bondage; now they are living the BDSM lifestyle openly, and they are the very Masters who can provide satisfaction to the world of Taboo.

Plenty of people love their kink, but when the Dominion of Brothers come to New York, the Lifestyle gets a re-do with not only a boost in stimulation, their fellow Lifestylers also get a guardian. Now, the Brothers will stop at nothing to protect their friends, loved ones, and those who look to them for sexual freedom.

BECOMING HIS SLAVE

DOMMING THE HEIRESS

A PLACE FOR CLIFF

ROUGH ATTRACTION

TAKING OVER TROFIM

RIGHT ONE 4 DIESEL

TOUCHING VIDA~VINCE

SEDUCING HIS THIEF

A SLAVE TO SAVE HARPER

THE GOLDEN MASTERS' DARKSIDE

Submit your desires within the Dominion of Brothers and submerge yourself into a world of Dominance and Bliss, but get ready~

"I'm about to make you wet"

- Saburo & Princess

~ * ~ * ~ * ~ * ~ * ~

RIGHT *One of* DIESEL

THE DOMINION OF BROTHERS SERIES: BOOK 5

WRITTEN BY TALON P.S. & PRINCESS S.O.

MM / some MMfM, MMMM, & Mf / Erotic Romance / Drama / Action / BDSM – D/s / Explicit Hot Language

Diesel Gentry knows exactly want he wants. Like his brother, he wants a Unicorn, a life slave to surrender her every desire and need to him— who is, in essence and body, the very same woman his brother, Trenton Leos, already possesses. He also wants Paris Dalqeaute.

He had the sexy Fallen Angel in his domineering grip once before, but Diesel purposely let him slip through his fingers. Being a Master of Doms within the BDSM lifestyle, Diesel knew he had to set Paris free— thinking and hoping Paris would eventually come back to him, to submit to Diesel willingly, and not just because Paris' job description required it of him. After all, Paris had been hired as the director for the fetish and BDSM events down at the island resort Diesel and his brothers own. Except Paris never did return; while he proved his value to his title, he has also been using his work to hide from Diesel.

It's been a year now and Diesel's bed and life have remained empty ever since. *It's time the running stopped.*

Finding Paris isn't going to be the hard part— breaking down his walls to trust the two of them to commit to a life together is going to be the real challenge.

But even if Diesel succeeds, there is a problem with their future— what's to come threatens the lives of everyone Diesel loves— *and he doesn't even know it yet.*

~ * ~ * ~ * ~ * ~ * ~

Right One 4 Diesel is a part of a series that, until now, has been comprised of largely standalone books. In *this* next installment to the series, that readability is no longer the case. Right One 4 Diesel is not a standalone read; it is an action-packed novel that does not allow room for re-introduction of its supportive characters who were introduced in Books 1 through 4 of the Dominion of Brothers series. While it is recommended that you read all of the books in the series, Books 1 and Book 4 are needed to be able to follow along without encountering "holes" in information or plot.

~ * ~ * ~ * ~ * ~ * ~

DEDICATION

To my twin, Talon

For entrusting your stories with me to get finished.

~ * ~ * ~ * ~ * ~ * ~

A marginal, *gee-wiz thanks* to the bills, work, stress,
health issues, and computer meltdowns.
Without any of you, this book would have been finished a
year ago.
:/

~ * ~ * ~ * ~ * ~ * ~

Warning

This ebook contains sexually explicit scenes, a MM relationship, some violence, and Adult Language, which may be considered offensive to some readers. It is intended for sales and the entertainment to adults ONLY, as defined by the laws of the country in which you made your purchase. Please store your files wisely, where they cannot be accessed by under-aged readers.

However, in light of recent censorships that are but a mockup of book burning. In the most common and recently used definitions of what is deemed unacceptable offending content, it has become prudent to clarify the level of content warning here for this title. This book does NOT contain any described rape. It does NOT contain any incest, bestiality, under-aged play or sexual scenes with anyone under the legal age.

For everyone else, this book contains explicit sexual content, graphic language, and situations that some readers may NOT find objectionable. Certain side effects are bound to happen should you decide to continue reading. Symptoms may include, but not limited to: Heavy breathing, warm sensation in chest and lower regions of the body, and sudden urges to wrangle your partner towards the bedroom, {with intentions to gain a deep feeling of satedness only great sexy can bring—}. Should this happen, do not become alarmed. It is perfect natural and very beneficial end-results are likely to occur. Your partner will thank me later).

Right One 4 Diesel is a part of a series that, until now, has been comprised of largely standalone books. In *this* next installment to the series, that readability is no longer the case. Right One 4 Diesel is not a standalone read; it is an action-packed novel that does not allow room for re-introduction of its supportive characters who were introduced in Books 1 through 4 of the Dominion of Brothers series. While it is recommended that you read all of the books in the series, Book 1 and Book 4 are needed to be able to follow along without encountering "holes" in information or plot.

~ * ~ * ~ * ~ * ~ * ~

ODE TO A WORD

"You, sir, are charged with reckless misuse of words!"

"I plead the fifth."

Words always matter; they can have strength by themselves and even change the course of a soul when you string a chain of them together to create something profound and deeply emotional. And there is no limit to them. Old words, forgotten words, rare words, and very strange words. They come in different languages, and every day there are new ones. Some words even change meanings over the generations, while others have so many meanings it's hard to know if your reader will ever catch *your* meaning.

For a writer, words became the colors of an artist's paint brush used to paint murals of drama and perception for the mind and heart. So it's safe to say that true Story Tellers might sometimes stretch the meanings of a word's purpose to fulfill the projected scene he is telling, and if a word does not exist— he'll make one up.

But this *ode to a word* isn't about an author-created word (not this time, at least). Rather, it's to amend how one should appear. If you've read Becoming His Slave, then you may know where I am going with this. Yep, you guessed it, that beautiful and fragrant word: *PHALLACIO.*

Now, stop right there, I know what you're about to say: "Talon, you spelled it wrong, it's fellatio."

Well, I am here to tell you, someone was sleeping in class all those years ago and they got it wrong! They obviously weren't sleeping the day they created *cunnilingus*, so how is it that the art of oral fixation on a man's *phallus* was written down as *fellatio*? HUH? How has this wretched misspelling come to be passed down? It's not even aesthetically attractive.

And look at this:

> • *Phalex* • *Phalgastic* • *phalgun* • *phalguni* • *phali*
> •*phalic* • *phalice* • *Phaliced* • *phalick* • *phalicon*
> •*phalimous* • *phalische* • *Phalisk* • *phalker* • *Phallace*
> •*phallacio* • *Phallacious* • *Phallacity* • *phallacosity*

But *fellatio*? Talk about a word fail. But seeing how, against every argument our editor threw at me during the edits for Becoming His Slave, the word *–phallacio–* remained spelled in what should have been its correct spelling, according to its Latin word relations, and because *–pha–* is far more aesthetically pleasing to the eye than *–fe–*.

So, too, you will find I am stubborn consistently (or stubbornly consistent) in Right One 4 Diesel.

~ Talon ps

TRADEMARK ACKNOWLEDGEMENT

GLOSSARY OF CHARACTERS AND LOCATIONS

Glossary only lists characters from the previous books that are relevant to this book, as a helpful refresher, but does not list any new characters that will be introduced in Right One 4 Diesel.

MASTER OF DOMS, PATRONUS DIESEL GENTRY – *Dominion Brother – grew up with Trenton (are step brothers); owns Hyde Park Gun shop and shooting range; part owner of resort, investor of Club Pain and auction event; secretly volunteers in Project Torch to help homeless veterans; holds safety and practical methods of self-protection. Has his sights on Paris Dalqeaute. A natural linguist speaks the following languages: French, Spanish, Breton, Farsi, Chechnya, Latin, German, Mandarin, Greek, Portuguese, and Serbian.*

PARIS DALQEAUTE – *Director for BDSM & Fetish season at the island resort, underwent slave training with Trenton and Diesel; known for his Fallen Angel good looks and has a talent for food and prides himself as a master of seduction.*

~ * ~~

DOMINUS TRENTON LEOS – *Dominion Brother – owns TL Securities; part owner of island resort; investor in Club Pain; runs and operates a rotary for Doms and slaves and holds bi-annual slave auction event. Proud owner of his Life Slave, Katianna Dumas. Speaks the following languages: French, Spanish, Breton, Farsi, Chechen, Latin.*

KATIANNA AERYN DUMAS – *author of erotica, submitted Life slave to Dominus Trenton Leos.*

HEAD MASTER DANE MASTERS – *Dominion Brother – owner of Stilettos, Pink Flesh, and Club Pain; part owner of resort; investor in auction event.*

HEAD MASTER MARCUS SCRIVEN – *Dominion Brother – owner of Scriven Armored Vehicles and Services; investor in clubs and part owner in resort; shares home with Diesel in large house next door to Trenton's house.*

MASTER HARPER LANCINGS – *Dominion Brother – runs a private investigation service; investor in clubs and part owner of resort.*

VIDA (VINCE) MASTERS – *Dane Masters' younger brother.*

PYOTR LASZKOVI, Ph.D. – *a psychologist - works with veterans for trauma care, but also specializes in sexual dysfunctions due to emotional stressors. In a D/s relationship with Cliff Patterson. Has ten siblings: Jovan, Pavle, Artyom, Darko, Rury, Trofim Stanislav, Sasha, and the twin girls, Varvara and Andjela. Team Captain on the Greenwich Queens Rowing team.*

DOCTOR PAVLE LASZKOVI – *Chief Surgeon and head of the ER surgical staff at Queens Medical. Team member on the Greenwich Queens Rowing team.*

DARKO LASZKOVI – *motorcycle mechanic, engaged to Maxum St. Laurents. Team member on the Greenwich Queens Rowing team.*

MAXUM ST. LAURENTS – *CEO of financial business, one-third owner of island resort. Avid car collector. Engaged to Darko Laszkovi.*

DOCTOR SHAY LASZKOVI – *formerly Shay Wilks, engaged to Trofim Laszkovi, beneficiary for a large inheritance and under the protection of Trenton and Diesel.*

TROFIM LASZKOVI – *engaged to Dr. Shay (Wilks) Laszkovi, under the protection of Trenton and Diesel. Team member on the Greenwich Queens Rowing team.*

DETECTIVE TATE MARSHALS – *Head detective at the NYC precinct.*

HEAD MASTER RASHAWN MATISSE – *in a D/s relationship with Amelia Quinneth; son of Cardiff Matisse, board member Quinneth Global.*

TOUSSAINT LAROU – *brother to Chemène and in-law to Fambleush Boismeir who owns the erotica museum in Paris, France.*

AMELIA QUINNETH – *Heiress and VP to Quinneth Global Mgmt, Pres. of board, is Katianna's publisher, in a D/s relationship with Rashawn Matisse.*

CLIFF PATTERSON – *works as a paramedic and in a D/s relationship with Pyotr Laszkovi.*

JONAS & ANNETTE LEOS and PATRICE & NELSON (deceased) GENTRY – *Jonas & Annette are Trenton's parents. Patrice, Diesel's mother, is now polyamorous with Jonas & Annette.*

ED AND WALTER – *old 'geezers' WWII veterans that are friends of Diesel's.*

LARS MICKELS – *Trenton's attorney. Is also in the lifestyle and a slave owner.*

PIPER – *one of Trenton's long term security guys.*

PEDRO – *one of Trenton's long term security guys, married to Senita.*

WILLIAM – *Trenton's lead guy, most seniority in the company, fills in for him when needed.*

SENITA – *Trenton's & Diesel's housekeeper, married to Pedro who works for Trenton as one of his security guys.*

MERLE LONDONAIRE – *father to Sarah Londonaire who Dr. Shay Laszkovi (formerly known as Shay Wilks) was in a prearranged engagement.*

BLAINE DAVENPORT – *Dom/Handler at the island resort.*

ALAN PRIDMORE – *island resort's main director.*

LOCATIONS

CLUB PAIN – *owned by Dane Masters, downtown Manhattan.*

FIVE SOURCE SECURITIES COMPLEX:
New Hyde Park Gun Shop and Shooting Range – *Owned and operated by Diesel Gentry*
Lancings' Private Investigations – *Harper's business.*
TL Securities – *owned and operated by Trenton Leos.*
Scriven's Armored Transportation - *owned and operated by Marcus Scriven.*
Personal Offices of Dane Masters

SALIENTIS DU DELICIARUM ISLAND RESORT - *name of the Island resort which means fountain of pleasure. (or) Delicious Ejaculate; Owned by the Dominion of Brothers: Trenton, Diesel, Marcus, Harper, and Dane, Maxum St. Laurents and one other silent partner not revealed yet.*

MONTAUK GARDENS RESORT - *where the Elysian Auction is held.*

~ * ~ * ~ * ~ * ~ * ~

TABLE OF CONTENTS

~ * ~ * ~ * ~ * ~ * ~

PROLOGUE

~ * ~ * ~ * ~ * ~ * ~

ELYSIAN FIELDS ANNUAL AUCTION

Diesel stood directly behind Dominus, chewing on the side of a fingertip as he scanned the crowd in the ballroom. His trained eye observed, tagged, and rated each individual: low key— *came to watch*, medium range— *easy going* and *looking to play nice*, and red alert— *Sadists and jilted Doms on edge*. Every year was the same and the reds could be counted on one hand. But this year it seemed different. He had at least ten that were out of sorts from the rest of the crowd. Moles likely. With each new event, the pressure grew worse from local event permit offices and this year, he and Dominus were on a first name basis with the fire chief. *Never a good thing.*

"Would you stop?"

Diesel dropped his hand and glanced at his brother who'd turned to look him over.

"I'm just measuring the crowd."

"No, you're not, you're looking for *him*."

"I'm—"

"You are." Trenton cut in. "Now stop it."

Diesel sucked in a deep breath, contemplating if he needed to count to ten, then— before he could stop himself, his eyes darted out into the mass of people to zero-in on the tall, dark-headed frame. He was already craning his neck, even to a point of baited breath, waiting to catch a glimpse of the face as the man who'd caught Diesel's attention began turning around. It was equal to the amount of surging disappointment that it wasn't *him* and Diesel did his best to brush off his scoping gaze as nothing more than a casual glance. He brought his gaze around in the faux pas, running into Trenton's eyes severely leveled on him with glaring aggravation. Diesel would have argued it even now, but he was caught. His brother's pale brown eyes narrowed on him, nailing him down.

He felt a twitch of the smartass in him, entertaining the idea of wrestling Trenton down in a headlock, just to prove the bastard wrong anyway.

"You have already run a check on all flights coming in from the entire Caribbean area. You even called down to ask Alan Pritchard to confirm he was still down at the resort. Which he was. So stop looking for him."

"I didn't call—"

"Yes, you did." Trenton cut in before Diesel could even try to play one of his denial games.

Diesel only grimaced. He was good at under-the-table tactics. They just didn't work with Trenton.

His brother glanced away; his eyes, too, were scanning, but Trenton was looking for something else.

"What is it?"

"Nothing." Trenton snapped back around, "Now, I need you by my side out there."

"You say that every event."

"And when have I lied?"

Diesel wasn't going to dignify Trenton's question with a response. *Not tonight. Maybe not tomorrow night either.* He received a pointed glance for it too, but Diesel remained reticent.

"You're a mule like our father."

"Good upbringing then." Diesel chuckled with a thick layer of sarcasm and the air between them lightened. He scratched at his ear in a boyish manner, a subconscious reaction at the mention of his father. "You need to stop worrying about me." He spotted a familiar face in another one of his unintentional eye wanderings and decided it was time for some fresh energy around him before he blew off some steam by beating his brother up anyway. Choosing to run off and greet their guests was the better option, after all. "Maxum! Glad to see you made it." Diesel held out a hand and they shook, then did the same with Darko, "Darko, you keeping him in line tonight?"

Darko gave him a wicked grin. *The Laszkovi brother was foolhardy in cock heaven with his new boyfriend.*

Diesel tried to show he was happy for them, but by the same token it turned bittersweet inside; only a deep breath could will the shields up against the absence of another for whom he was feeling more so this weekend than before.

"You know," Maxum leaned in, "I didn't expect to recognize as many faces here as I do."

"Just remember, don't touch. Not even to shake hands unless they offer it first. Some take a hard offense to it." Diesel advised him and Maxum nodded.

"Don't worry, I'm his copilot to make sure he doesn't make too grievous a mistake with anyone pertaining to the etiquette of their Lifestyle." Darko interjected. He glanced around them, then back at Diesel with a questioning expression, as if he wanted to know where Diesel had stashed away a conspicuously absent face, along with the body often described as that of a fallen angel's.

Diesel headed the question off with a nod, "Something came up that required him to stay down at the resort."

"Dude, then why are *you* here?" But Darko suddenly abandoned the question, his attention reeling around when he realized his task as copilot had gone unchecked when he heard Maxum call out a familiar name.

"Amelia Quinneth. Fancy running into you here. This is the last— place— I expected—"

Diesel and Darko both spotted the heat coming from the man behind Amelia, his reposed stare meant as a warning to Maxum. Maxum didn't miss it either. It was audaciously clear he'd made just such an offense by touching someone who fell in the taboo category of *no touching* for the night. For which Maxum instantly let go of her hands and tossed his own hands down to his sides, then took a step back.

~ * ~

"I'm sorry— I-uh—" Maxum found himself at a loss for words. Not even Darko's hand slipping into his was enough to diminish the blundering feeling he felt.

4

"Oh—" Amelia's eyes lit up like wicked fires of lust and followed up with a smile, though she quickly tamped it down for *His* sake, Maxum was certain. But that didn't stop the heat from rising in his cheeks. He'd known Amelia for many years, for she was both someone he invested in as well as competed with. Finding her here as a— well— it was not among the surprises he'd prepared himself for.

Amelia leaned in, the giggle coming up as she spoke, "Don't worry, Mr. St. Laurents, I'll calm him down in a bit." She glanced over her shoulder to Rashawn Matisse, who was settling back into his refined position of control, but his eyes were bearing down on her with a warning. She rolled her lips to hide the growing smile then turned back to Maxum and reached out, clutching his arm just under the shoulders, "Perhaps though, I do think I am going to risk earning a spanking just so I can kiss those blushing cheeks of yours. They are just too scrumptious to turn down." And having said it, she did just that. Like a queen, leaving burgundy lip prints as she did.

~ * ~

Diesel tried to join them, feeling some deep admiration while watching Amelia's grace and elegance. Neither of which were marred in the slightest as she retreated to the man who watched her like a hawk and was predatorily enamored with her. His eyes scolded her playfully, but the deeper emotion, *devotion,* Diesel recognized in Rashawn's steely gaze could never be concealed by his disapproval.

Diesel's idea of *fresh air* wasn't panning out as he'd planned. *All these damned happy, languishing and possessive looks over partners was about to drive him crazy.*

He glanced at Rashawn, seeing the planning in his eyes, and at least *his* were entertaining. Diesel looked at the sultry heiress earning a full evening of discipline right before his eyes. He leaned toward her and risked speaking to her, "I'm looking forward to watching you get put over his knee at dinner time."

The mild alarm that flared in her eyes was one he'd not forget for some time. And yes, *that sudden pouty drop in her jaw was well worth breaking protocol.*

"My apologies for my rudeness, Head-Master Rashawn."

Rashawn smiled at him to show he'd rather enjoyed it himself. "Apology accepted." He kept to his candor.

Diesel almost laughed, but he just didn't have it in him. Even with seeing Amelia blossom, or to see Darko and Maxum matched so well together and now sporting new engagement rings, it made Diesel's chest feel tight. Then— out of nowhere, he felt a small hand slip into his. He glanced down, finding Trenton's Unicorn standing at his side, smiling up at him. "You are always here at the perfect time; do you know that?"

"No. That was you. You came after me and said just the right thing at the right time when I had wandered off. I haven't left Trenton's or your sides ever since. I'm always here, even at the wrong times."

She was right. She never had. But there was no way he was going to let that reality check darken his mood further. Her presence was a good thing. "There is never a wrong time with you."

She was beautiful tonight. Trenton had had a dress, designed like a cage, made for her from black mesh straps that covered little more than a wire birdcage would. One

6

strap broader than the others lay across her breasts, while the rest crisscrossed vertically and horizontally around her petite body and were trimmed with black rhinestones. An added touch of black teardrops fell around her legs from clear, almost invisible monofilament lines. And heels held to her feet by only two straps, one over dainty toes and the other around her ankles. As exotic as she looked, nothing could ever dispel his attention from her eyes. Like snow under the moon, peeking out from a thick tussle of brown wavy hair that, no matter what, always looked wind-blown or just had that well-fucked, bed-head look. This time Diesel did laugh at his thoughts a bit, because it was likely the latter of the two; knowing his brother, it was his fault her hair always looked that way. Not that Diesel would ever blame Trenton. Had she been his, he would have seen to it her hair looked about the same on a steady basis as well.

~ * ~ * ~ * ~ * ~ * ~

For Maxum, it was an odd spectacle to witness. An auction of humans that, to an outsider, would have seemed detrimental and gone against every rule of freedom. But watching the auction taking place, with Trenton Leos up on the stage like a finely crafted ringleader of decadence, left Maxum with the sense of being spun about in a bottomless sensation of surrealism. Not wrong, but definitely the epitome of unexplored taboo.

Even Diesel seemed to be in his element here, despite the contrast it held to his gun shop and self-defense classes.

Humans being auctioned off to be possessed and looked after by those who would want to be served in ways not on the standard job market. It seemed morally wrong, yet there was no black market fear lingering in the room like a stagnant haze of stale smoke one might have been expecting. Men and women perused the ballroom and hallways like any other black-tie affair, plus a little leather and eroticism thrown into the alluring mix. All was perfectly legal and in the same fashion he had witnessed countless auctions for a date with volunteered bachelors and bachelorettes. Maxum had known many of such auctions to bring in a hefty purse for an evening's cause.

At dinner, he and Darko were Diesel Gentry's guests at the main table with the remaining brothers and Darko's older brother, Pyotr. A setting where egos were laid down with napkins and replaced with laughter, even if the conversations rarely ventured far from sex.

"So come, let's see them." Diesel sent the obvious request across the table to him.

Maxum glanced along his shoulder to the man sitting next to him with a sultry bad boy look about him. It was going to be hell getting them home without making a stop or two along the way. Maybe he'd check with the concierge to see if, by some miraculous act of god, a room had become available here at the hotel that Maxum could take advantage of. Something he should have done from the start. But it'd have to wait. He wasn't about to pass up a chance to show off his new jewelry apparel.

Maxum placed his hand on the table next to his fiancé's hand, putting the engagement ring on display. The platinum band glimmered under the chandeliers with a rainbow of gemstones set in the band.

Darko reached over and added his right hand to the pile. His finger donned a dissimilar band of Tungsten steel, and in place of stones, Darko's ring was embedded with a band of rainbow-colored fiber optics inside it.

"But they don't match." Katianna leaned forward, as much as Trenton allowed, for her to get a closer look.

"Be glad you didn't see the fight we had over that little indifference." Maxum chuckled and shouldered Darko playfully.

"But why?"

"I did originally buy matching bands, but after Darko's first day of work, back from our trip to Germany, he came home fuming. That's when the fight started."

"I don't get it." Katianna looked at them both and Maxum laughed, waiting for his stubborn mate to explain himself. Even gave Darko a tap of his foot under the table to nudge him to do so.

"My hands are in grease all day and it got into the stones, which pissed me off. It was ruined in one day. When he suggested I take it off and not wear it, I punched him." Darko didn't hold back.

Not particularly the campfire story Maxum had intended to entertain their friends with, but the flabbergasted laughs weren't restrained in the least.

"You punched him?" Katianna gasped in amazement.

"Don't worry," Maxum intruded, "his bark is worse than his bite, but the make-up sex was particularly mind-blowing. After that, I got him a ring he could wear even during work that wouldn't get ruined."

"And the other ring?"

"I had it cleaned up and he now wears it on a chain from his neck." He reached over and fished it out from under Darko's shirt, letting it drop where everyone could see it. "I suppose it's as close to having a collar on him as I will ever get." He grinned, but Darko's eyes made unspoken demands and Maxum complied, sitting back in his chair and casually pulling out a chain around his own neck— dangling the match with the Tungsten ring Darko wore. His show and tell awarded him a deep kiss from Darko that nearly bent his head back on his shoulders.

~ * ~

The unvoiced *awwws* were almost as prevalent as the snickering. And Diesel found himself mirroring his brother and looking down at their mouse.

Trenton glanced at him and Diesel saw the overprotective worry in his eyes. Diesel tore his own eyes away, refusing to let Trenton see inside him any further tonight. *Enough was enough.*

"So how come we don't have Paris here? He is, after all, the event manager for the fetish season. Doesn't that require him to come up for the auction selection?" Maxum kicked up a new conversation when the kiss was over. Being part owner of the island resort, his question wasn't awkward, yet for Diesel it was. Maxum just didn't know that and managed to ask before Darko could caution him.

Diesel found himself tapping a finger on the table. A variety of excuses and arguments paraded through his brain. Each of them provided from Paris' point of view, which had led to his excusal from this evening's obligations by the board. But Diesel knew the real reason, at least in part, was Paris didn't want to come here and see *Him*.

There was just one problem with that—

Diesel wasn't done with Paris.

~ * ~ * ~ * ~ * ~ * ~

CHAPTER ONE

~ * ~ * ~ * ~ * ~ * ~

"Paris." Cayetano entered his office with a soft knock on the door.

It always struck Paris rather funny how his assistant knocked, yet walked right on in without giving Paris the benefit of actually inviting him in.

"Yes, what is it? I'm busy right now." And he was. The new submissives had just arrived from Trenton's auction. *The one he deliberately didn't go to.* He just couldn't go up there and face Diesel. The taste of the man was still too fresh, as if he'd swallowed him just yesterday, when in truth it had been a year. Had it been more like two years, Paris figured he might have had the strength to go. After all, Dominus Trenton Leos' Elysian Fields Auctions were usually held every other year. Only, demands were so high this year, what with new exotic spas opening up in Europe and on a few of the posher Mediterranean islands that boasted services for those within the lifestyle. There were also a few new private clubs opening up in major cities; all these places mimicked this resort, wanting to hire submissives as employed slaves to serve their clientele. All of which were on top of the private sector that still sought out the thrill of the auction to find the perfect submissive with whom to enter into contract. The demand was so high, the Dominus had been convinced to add a year. It certainly came in good timing for Paris— professionally that is. The Island Resort's BDSM and Fetish season last year had been such a success, they expected almost twice as many guests this year and they needed to increase the number of slaves to fill the demands.

However, going to New York for the auction meant seeing Diesel Gentry, Trenton's brother and closest confidante: The Master of Doms, the man Paris had fallen for. He wasn't ready for that face-off, so instead, he had himself exempted from the task via the board, under the guise there were too many other details for the season that required Paris' direct attention in order to accommodate such a large increase of guests and staff. Such needs far outweighed going to the auction event when it could be handled by another. The ruse had worked and he was excused. It was his assistant, Cayetano, and Valarie, another member of Paris' staff, who had been sent in his place instead.

The choice had cost Paris dearly. By not going to the auction himself, he'd lost out on two of the selections he wanted on their staff. One of them a man who would have been a gem to their collection of slaves on the island, not to mention Paris had hoped to use him as a diversion for himself as well. *One of the perks of the job*, but he hadn't been the only one looking to have the golden-haired male. The self-entered submissive's purchase price turned out to be one of the highest among the short-term slaves ever brought in.

Cayetano and Valarie had left for New York, and while both had undergone the same unique job requirement experiences as he had, they did not have Paris' knowledge of what truly delighted the eye. Paris had done his best to prep them. The two staffers were given strict instructions to bid on specific slaves from the brochure and to stay on budget. Had he gone himself, he would have been able to gauge the competition and risk the extra spending to top the competing bidder. *But nope,* too fucking scared to face the man who had the power to overwhelm him, to make him want to give everything away just to be with the man again. Hell, Paris had hardly slept with another man since then. It wasn't the same, didn't feel the same, and he didn't want them as he wanted Diesel.

"I'm very busy, so what do you need, Cayetano?" Paris reminded himself he was there.

"Yes, sir. I just got off the phone with the Masters Trenton Leos and Diesel Gentry."

Paris' eyes flicked up from the papers on his desk and locked onto the man he'd hired from the nearby island of Barbados— seconds froze as if caught in the act of something forbidden— though Paris' past with Diesel Gentry had never been shared with Cayetano. *Diesel's name again— how was it he could never escape the man?* "It's Dominus and Patronus, not Master." He corrected Cayetano, forgetting to hide his annoyance. He'd never led on about his feelings for Diesel. In fact, he'd never even spoken about his training, or who he'd gone to, to anyone here on the island. Only Alan, Paris' boss and one of the handlers, Blaine, knew and they too had kept silent about it. Though he figured that had something to do with Diesel's own machinations more than his.

"Is there a problem with the account transaction?" Paris knew there wouldn't be. He cleared the payment over the phone via wire transfer with Trenton before the slaves were loaded up on the plane, but the question posed a way out for the sudden jittering sensation he felt coming over him and thought for sure Cayetano would notice it.

Cayetano shook his head, "No, it's fine. But he mentioned something about slaves returned to him and he was bringing them down to the resort to be added to the staff serving here. Can he do that?"

Paris actually knew about the additional slaves being sent down. One of Trenton's regular clients filed bankruptcy and had his slaves surrendered back into Trenton's possession. Alan, the island's primary director, had already informed Paris of the board's approval of taking on the extras.

"Yes, it's already been approved by the board to accept them. Anything else?"

"They made reservations. They're coming down."

Paris' heart froze right along with his brain functions. *Diesel was coming here? Shit, he wasn't ready to handle this— he couldn't— how the hell would he be able to do his job professionally and act casually while Diesel's body was waltzing around the resort? With those thick cords of muscle over his chest and arms, imprinted with tattoos that not only marked his loyalty as a military soldier but also his dominance.* Paris could just envision how they would glisten under suntan oils at the pool. The tattooed pistols on the front of Diesel's hips that never failed to draw one's eyes towards the real gun. Paris was never a fan of tats, but he'd give just about anything for the chance to run his tongue over the sexy inked man right about now.

He closed his eyes, envisioning the act, licking over hip knots and those inked out guns— right down into the small nest of dark hair that circled Diesel's cock— all nine inches of length and three inches of girth.

15

Paris pulled in a long, deep breath, stifling the need to lick his lips before letting out a tantalizing sigh. Nice and slow so not to be too noticeable, reminding himself someone else was in his office. He forced on a *I have better things to deal with* look towards his assistant. "So, why bring this to me? If they want to make reservations, then let them." Now he waited because he knew there was a reason. He just needed to remind himself not to panic. That it wouldn't be nearly as big a deal as he feared.

"Well, sir, it comes with specific requests."

"Most of our clients do. Just make whatever arrangements they need and then inform staff to ensure everything is prepared. That's all."

"Except, sir, one is rather—" Cayetano hesitated. "Well, it's rather unusual. I told him you couldn't do it, but he insisted."

Paris' head did a double take right after it skipped over a few brain cells. *Wait— me?* His coping gears faltered— *he couldn't do what? What did Diesel want him to do? Okay, so he's pretty sure he knew the answer to that question, but what did Diesel say to Cayetano?* Paris cleared his throat to ward off any nervousness before he asked, "So what was it?"

Cayetano squirmed a bit before answering. "Mr. Gentry has requested a specific slave to be assigned to him during his entire stay and that in no way is the slave allowed to return to his own quarters while he is here or be given to anyone else. The slave is to remain exclusively his."

All the panic melted from his mind as Paris felt the ping of jealousy take its place. *Who the hell would Diesel be requesting to have so exclusively?* And to do it on *his* island, no doubt. "Many of our clients do, so who did he ask for?"

"You, sir."

A breeze— not even a stiff breeze, but easily one of those gentle summer ones, could have knocked Paris over when Cayetano said that. The whole world could have shut down and he wouldn't have noticed. All Paris heard was Diesel was coming to have *him*. And he already knew there would be no escaping the man's claim on him. *Oh shit— okay, now you can panic.*

"He does know you're the director here— doesn't he? Sir?" Cayetano let out a bewildered question.

Oh, Diesel knew— knew every part of what Paris did here and what he had left up *there*.

Paris had gone to New York to submit to the experience of being a slave because it was required for his job here. And while he expected to land in an orgy of several sexy men, he had not expected to land in the arms of Diesel, and that man stole something Paris didn't think existed for him.

"I tried to tell him he could not request you as his slave." Cayetano kept trying to explain his conversation with the domineering man. "But he insisted, as per our bylaws, he can and our company policy reinforces it. Said we better make good on our services or else." He shook his head with bewilderment.

Paris swallowed hard, but it was not all fear— some was because his mouth was watering. Diesel wasn't just requesting, he was making it damn clear he would not be refused, and that was just too much stimulation to ignore. To be wanted that much. Paris could just picture the man landing on the tarmac, guns out, threatening everyone in sight to hand Paris over to submit to his will or else. And if that heavy dream wasn't enough, Paris saw Diesel fucking him right there at the front doors. Bending him over and drilling right in to show everyone he was the true master of Paris Dalqeaute. *Okay, so maybe not the latter part, because Diesel didn't do anything publicly.* But it looked damn hot playing out inside his mind.

"Thank you, Cayetano. That'll be all." Paris rolled his lips, his thoughts sinking away with his will.

Desire giving way to pain.

Pain was what he was left with. Because as phenomenal as it was to be in Diesel's bed, the moment he had been kicked out was enough to destroy all the good in it. And last time it had left him with nothing to show for it but pain.

Suddenly, Paris was very aware that *that* was what he felt right now. The emptiness of wanting a man so strongly and what he would feel if he gave everything up, just to be with him one more time.

"Sir?" Cayetano was looking at him with a curious uncertainty, "So, what do you want me to do about Mr. Gentry?"

"Don't worry about it. I'll take care of it."

~ * ~ * ~ * ~ * ~ * ~

Paris barely ate his dinner, despite the dish being one of his favorites. Pan seared salmon seasoned with lime, garlic, and parmesan cheese, with a side of steamed baby asparagus, and chunks of potato soaked in a creamy butter sauce with cilantro, chives, and a splash of lemon.

It was a simple dish, something his father had taught him when he was growing up; sometimes, the best flavor came from the simplest ingredients. Yet, the first time Paris requested for Ruubos, the resort's head chef, to make the dish for him, Paris had to argue the point for over an hour before convincing Ruubos to cook it the way he wanted it. It wasn't until Paris actually rolled up his sleeves and took over the kitchen to do it himself that he got his own way with the chef. And when the dish was complete, Paris had invited Ruubos to join him. And then Paris informed him who his father had been. That was the problem with four and five star chefs— they didn't take orders from anyone, not even their own bosses when it came to how they cooked. It took being related to Chef Jean-Pierre Dalqeaute to get Ruubos' attention. Had it been Diesel giving the request, the demands would have been met from the first without contestation or criterion as the son of a renowned chef.

Paris gave up on his meal and set his fork down. He looked out into some far-off distance, across a sea and up a coastline, to the man he couldn't let go of. A man who knew control and how to get what he wanted, except Diesel was anything but a dish of simple ingredients.

Paris' focus came back to the present and to the drink being delivered to his table: A Kir Royal cocktail, a mix of crème de cassis and premium champagne. He fished out the wedges of lime and lemon with a finger, squeezed them into the bubbly then tipped his glass up, gulping it down in a few swallows. It didn't come close to doing what he wanted it to. A Kir Royal was merely a drink for looks and taste.

"Director?"

Paris glanced up. One of the new male subs stood at his table, ready to wait on him hand and foot— and cock, if Paris so much as demanded it. The many perks of the job came complete with first pick of any sub Paris wanted. But Paris didn't want the submissive man who stood waiting. What he did want scared the hell out of him. "Tell the bartender to pour me a shot of our best white tequila, then bring me the hot sauce and a handful of limes."

"Sir?" The man-slave looked at him, puzzled.

Paris was instantly annoyed. Annoyed by the drive to mimic the brothers. Annoyed that the act of speaking disrupted his inner brooding. Annoyed that his needs were being questioned. He may not be a Master or a Dom, but he was the Director, which rated just as high for their employed slaves. He was also equally annoyed that his thoughts, troubled as they were, were being disrupted by the slave's presence. "If I have to repeat myself, I'll turn you over to Blaine for the night."

The man-slave shivered, "Premium brand Tequila, yes, Director." And he scurried off as quickly as he could.

Blaine wasn't really that bad, but he certainly had their obedience trained. He was a very attentive Dom, he liked to talk openly of how rough he liked it, and he took delight in feeding his kink when the subs needed some discipline. Exuding his presence— always touring the resort throughout the day with his red leather whip, and the way he would crack it to get their attention, was palpable even from a safe distance. It was definitely effective, even if Blaine seldom ever used it on anyone's skin, save for a teasing slap of the coils of braided leather, when the sound of it wasn't enough to get their attention.

Within a few minutes, the man-slave returned with Paris' order and dutifully knelt at his feet, risking a glance upward with hopeful wanton. Paris could read what the sub was thinking in those eyes. It didn't take much consideration really; Paris was used to seeing that look in nearly every man he'd ever encountered. The biggest trouble for them was deciding if they wanted to be the seducer or *be* seduced by Paris. For Paris, the trouble was never caring, as he never wanted to stay with anyone. He indulged in the thrill of that first attraction then moved on.

Paris ignored the look from the slave and bottomed the shot of tequila in one swig. The alcohol instantly burned in his throat and he quickly bit into one of the limes to ease the discomfort, wishing he could ease all of it.

"Would you like for me to pleasure you, Director?"

"No, thank you, Silas. That will be all." Paris' mind drifted off.

"I could wait for you in your bed—"

"No, I said!" Paris snapped. But he turned away, let his thoughts go back to where they wanted, and shut the other man out. His mind barely registered the servant's reluctance to retreat.

The table jostled, stirring Paris. He looked with every intent to scold Silas for continuing to bother him, only to find Blaine sitting across from him with a gloating grin, his usual expressive attire.

"They don't please you tonight, beautiful Paris?" Blaine waved toward the slave, still waiting only a few feet away on standby should Paris change his mind, and beckoned him to fetch another drink or something else.

Paris didn't bother to answer.

"Bring him another. And one for me as well." Blaine tossed the command to Silas before he turned his attention back to Paris, "What troubles you, Paris?" The smile vanished from Blaine's face.

Paris looked up, giving him a disgruntled look before erasing it and turning more stoic. "What makes you think anything is bothering me?"

"You're the spoiled palace prince. Beautiful, desired, and ogled by all. You radiate with it. Yet here you are, sitting like a stormy cloud who's lost his royal mantle— it's noticeable."

"I'm just tired. Nothing more."

"Don't try to sell me that shit. I'm more than just your island brute. I know the psyche, and someone has your loins all tied up in a knot with tattooed hearts on it. Wouldn't happen to be the blond golden boy you hoped to get from the auctions?"

Blaine was trying to gauge Paris' reaction with a ridiculous hypothesis, and Paris knew it. Paris had actually learned a thing or two from his training with the Dominus and Patronus. *A Dom learns his submissive by testing reactions through sensation. The good ones will even switch out the sensation to something contrasting in order to gauge their subject fully.*

"I saw on the care sheet the very slave is being brought down after all. Is that what has your thoughts bound up?" The expression on Blaine's face revealed he was spotting what he was looking for from Paris. Not that he was expecting them— not for the slave. Blaine was aware how well Paris could shut him out and never let him get in his head. However, as Blaine's expression shifted, Paris realized Blaine had somehow caught on. He was just waiting for the opportune moment to have it confirmed.

"I'm told he is being brought down by the Master of Doms, the infamous Patronus Diesel Gentry. Was he not your Master when you had to undergo the experience and training of submission?"

The flicker Paris felt in his eyes was his tell— *his tension.* It was all there. Blaine's expressions shifted again. *Bingo,* Blaine's eyes said. He leaned over the table, resting an elbow on its surface. "You're in love with him, aren't you?"

It was a lucky draw of timing that Silas returned with two shots of tequila and served each of the men. An escape from answering, not even with his denial. Paris took his shot without hesitation and downed it. Then tapped his fingers into the pool of hot sauce on his plate and licked them over before chewing on a lime.

Blaine groaned, "Watching you lick your fingers should have been like watching one of the Seven Wonders of the World go up, but instead, it was just sad."

Paris' gaze shifted away, trying as hard as he could to hide his pain, his confusion. *Total disruption.*

"But I don't know which is sadder, that you found love before I got a chance to taste you? Or that you're in love and don't even know it." Blaine rose to his feet, pausing as if contemplating Paris, a moment. "Do yourself a favor, Paris. Take it— you can't possibly lose. You've already had everything else." Blaine started to walk off, but stopped and turned back to Paris with a smile that held some of his trademark gloating, "Oh, and the Patronus will be arriving tomorrow on the ship." And then he walked off.

Paris reached over, took the shot Blaine left behind, and downed it like the others. His lips rolled in a tight press, feeling every bit of the potent alcohol burning his throat and searing the way down into his gullet. He was already feeling its effects, but it wasn't helping his mood at all. He resolved to give up and go to bed. "Return to your room in the boarding home, Silas." Then he pushed off from the table and made his way down the path toward his own quarters. A small, but attractive condo just beyond the public grounds of the resort.

He punched in his access code at the gate that sectioned off the private sector and continued on, his mind still lurking in painful memory of his time with Diesel. He desired the man like no other from the moment he laid eyes on him. Paris had even reduced himself to begging for Diesel's sexual touch when Paris had failed to seduce the man to his bed. Nevertheless, when Diesel did finally make a lover out of Paris, his time in New York was already over— and the worst part had been being sent away.

Never in his life had leaving a lover been an issue because he never stayed very long. But Diesel did something to him, something he couldn't explain. Nor did he know how to cope with the separation which, even now, he wasn't doing a very good job of handling. With his mind and his passions so focused on the man, Paris was unraveled without him. Now, Diesel was coming for him— and it would no doubt do him in again.

~ * ~ * ~ * ~ * ~ * ~

CHAPTER TWO

~ * ~ * ~ * ~ * ~ * ~

Diesel sat on the floor of their state room on the ship, being anything but a lounge addict with his legs stretching out in front of him, leaning back against the sofa. He propped up his arm while he watched Chikako open her present. Her eyes lit up like a little girl's on Christmas. So young, *too young*. He'd never been able to shake that bit of knowledge from his head, no matter how often she tempted him. And she'd tried often, ever since she came to stay at the house with him and Marcus. But each time, that little factoid pricked him in the back of his mind, and he was grateful that she was, physically, too small for him anyway. That alone spared him the guilt trip he would have suffered had she eventually lured him in an attempt to enjoy her body.

Chikako flung the box lid aside and pulled out the swimsuit ensemble. Her eyes lit up like little flames. She shot him a gleaming smile, then quickly jumped to her feet and disrobed right in front of him. She didn't pass up the chance to tease him as she did, first trying on the top and turning her hairless body toward him. She even gave her hips a little sway to test if he would look. He loved the human body, so of course he looked. He just couldn't help wishing she didn't look so much like an underage girl, because *that* bothered him. He just raised an eyebrow at her, which put an instant pout on her lips, and she went back to getting the rest of the bikini on. It was a cream-colored fabric with a pink cherry blossom print, along with a matching sarong that touched the floor. The halter-top cut worked well with her small breasts and the ruffled bottom lent the illusion of curves where she had none.

"You like it?" Diesel grinned as she twirled around in it.

Chikako nodded excitedly then dropped down next to him, leaning in for a kiss. First, just a sweet, chaste peck of her lips that lingered, then her tongue slipped out to tempt him to open for her. It wasn't the first time she had tried to do so. Sometimes he relented, but not often. He knew what and who he wanted in life, and the closer he got to Paris, the more his body burned with a hungry desire that *it* tempted his typical introverted refrain for advancements, making it a challenge to contain himself with even the smallest of temptations. He closed his eyes, letting the beast within growl and crawl towards the surface, anticipating nights of rutting with a man who could take every inch of his cock, and every drop of his stamina, and match it. His breath deepened with the vision, and for some strange reason, he let Chikako have her kiss.

He let her tongue slip into his mouth, felt the sweet softness against his tongue, wanted to lick her up, but then reality slipped back in. Chikako was not the Unicorn he wanted. Yet, that too was about to happen for him, and the excitement of it had him busting so that even the tempting kiss of a submissive had his lust rushing to the forefront.

He gently pulled away from the kiss. *Dammit,* he felt as if his control slipped, even the slightest, letting loose an ounce of his salacious thirst, and he'd run to whoever tempted him. So close to what he wanted and yet, so far away from it. It put him in dire straits and nearly in trouble with being with the wrong one. He would not ruin his plans for a full, long commitment for a short thrill right now.

Chikako's hands moved over his body, like feathers floating over the roll of hard muscles of his shoulders, then his chest, and down his abs until he caught her wrist and stopped any further descent.

"You do not want me?" She dropped her eyes in a sullen expression and pushed her bottom lip out.

Damned that lower lip trick. Too many times Chikako had seen Katianna get her way with him and Trenton with her pouty ways, and Chikako had picked up on it, using it purposely to make him feel guilty for rejecting her. It didn't work, but even now it still had him softening his grip on her arm, then letting go to caress her face, rather than push her away. "Want you? In another life, I would have been head over heels crazy about you. But we've been over this before, Chi. I can't— I'll hurt you."

"We could try other ways." She offered as she moved to kiss his neck, pushing the limit with him.

"No, we cannot." He took her shoulder and firmly pressed her to sit back properly. There were only a few days left, so it'd be a shame if they were spent with a red bottom. "Besides, you're too young for me."

"Geisha are timeless. We have no age."

"Yes, but I'm an American and we do."

"Then I thirty. Is thirty old enough?"

"You are not thirty. The doctor said that, at the most, you might be twenty-four— *might.*" The other end of the guessing game put her more realistically at, or about, eighteen when she was found during the raid to rescue Katianna. Which would now make her nineteen. With no records to trace who she was, the answer was never certain, though during her year with him and Marcus, Diesel was certain Chikako fell in the younger age bracket. Nineteen might be legal, but it was *definitely too young— for him anyways.*

Chikako had been one of many girls rescued from the black market brothel Trenton and he had taken down last year, when the ringleader dared to kidnap Trenton's own slave. All the other girls, and a few young men too, had been returned to their homes and families. Chikako, on the other hand, offered no recollection of where she was from or who she was. She only offered that she'd been raised in a traditional-style, modern-day geisha house, and the man intended as her *danna* had been murdered the night she was scheduled to be delivered to him. After which, she described a series of events that led her into the hands of others and passed along to Nikolai Kirshnov, who'd then kept her drugged most of the time. During the police investigation, Chikako recalled hearing some of the men talk about how she was about to be sold to a new owner just days before they'd found her. With nowhere else to go, Diesel arranged to be her guardian and see to her care, never expecting her to be as much of a handful as she was.

The young Asian woman didn't give up her attempts on him. "It have been—"

"It has been—" he corrected, noting that she needed to continue her verb conjugating exercises when she had some downtime available.

"I have been almost full year since you find me. I older now." She moved a leg over his hips to straddle and rub against the erection in his pants. "I know what I want." It was almost as if she had stomped her dainty foot the way she said it. Just like when the little mouse would get mad, it was too damn cute to take it seriously.

Chikako had argued this once before, even used Pyotr and Cliff's age difference to persuade him. She went as far as trying to persuade Pyotr directly during one of her sessions with him. She'd insisted he intervene and convince Diesel to go along with her Topping from the bottom. The only thing Pyotr did do was warn Diesel she was far more aware and capable, being less naïve than she played out to be as part of her manipulative heist.

"Stop or I am going to spank you." Diesel gave his one and only warning and she immediately slunk back on her heels, but remained over his lap, "Don't sulk. It's not your fault; we just can't do it this way."

"There is other way?" She brightened suddenly.

"Not with me. This is why we are looking for a new *Danna* for you."

"*Danna* can only be found in Japan."

"Which is where geishas belong. In a culture that respects them." He reached up and ran his fingers through her hair. Long strands of black silk. *He loved how it felt in his hand.*

"You give me to another man?"

"One who is right for you, yes."

"But what of you? You don't have anyone to love. I want to stay with you."

"No, Chi. I've come to claim Paris."

"Maybe you give me to your Paris then."

29

Diesel laughed. *Yeah, like that one would work.* But Paris didn't swing both ways. The phenomenally sexy, fallen angel was gay through and through and proud of it. Nor would it improve Diesel's chances to convince Paris to stay with him if he also attempted to staple a geisha to their relationship. "No. It won't work that way."

"Do you prefer men over women?"

He knew the question was more than idle curiosity; she was gathering intelligence, looking for anything she could use for future approaches. *She should have been a spy instead of a geisha.* Since entering his life, she had been exposed to a considerable amount of sexual liberties. As for what she might have been exposed to prior to him, he didn't know or cared to know, for he knew it would all have been bad. "Not always, but on occasion they suit me better."

"And this man, Paris— you want to keep him. So he is special?"

"Yes, he's special."

"Why?"

"Because he can take everything I can give and match it— because in the short time I was with him, he touched something I didn't even know I was looking to have touched."

"So you love him?"

Diesel nodded, "I think so, that's why we're here."

"And if you don't love him?"

He grinned devilishly, "I'm keeping him anyways."

"Why?"

"Because my inner lusty demon loves him." He dropped his hands to the floor and jutted his hips up, lifting Chikako up with him before dropping them both back down. Her young heart giggled like chiming bells with his playfulness. It was a good note on which to end the discussion. "Come on, time to get you dressed. We'll be at port soon."

~ * ~ * ~ * ~ * ~ * ~

CHAPTER THREE

~ * ~ * ~ * ~ * ~ * ~

Diesel stood on the deck, as the ship's thrusters idled its massive two-hundred-foot-plus length gently towards the dock.

There, waiting for them, were several of the island's resident Dom handlers to take the submissive-slaves Trenton and he had brought down. The original contracts with their masters had been surrendered and renegotiated with new ones that served out their three months on the island. All six were signed.

Next to the island's handlers were several of the Resort's servant slaves, already in service, ready to greet and serve the guests as they came ashore. Paris was also among them, but not as a slave as he should have been, waiting to be surrendered to him. Instead, Paris stood there, professionally, as the island's BDSM and Fetish Event Director. Not even the tantalizing skin that showed through a navy mesh, tailored into a button-up dress shirt over breezy white slacks, was enough to pardon Diesel's feelings over the stance to stonewall him.

Diesel clenched his jaw. He should have known this wasn't going to work out. He'd thought, for sure, Paris' deliberate avoidance of him was a means to hide because Paris felt something and didn't know what to do with it. But Diesel realized now he had underestimated Paris' rebelliousness— it was more about rejection.

Diesel's nostrils flared with the hard exhale he forced out of his body. He'd been wrong before, but it'd just never hurt this bad all those other times. He turned heel, but a hand caught his arm, staying him.

"Deez?"

Diesel looked at the hand then to the man it belonged to, his brother. "I'll get the slaves ready." And he gently brushed Trenton's hand from his arm and tried his best not to storm off.

~ * ~

Trenton watched as Diesel headed back inside the ship, then turned his eyes down at the tiny woman at his side and tried to smile for her, but he knew it wasn't his best. He rolled his lips in for a moment, but the thought that burned on his mind was heart-wrenching to confess, "You have no idea the pain— what it does to us when you two run away."

Katianna looked up at him, and the flood of pain was evident in her moonlit eyes. *Oh, but she did know.* She was guilty of running away, too. It just may not have occurred to her that Paris was on the run as well. Only, instead of running to Florida to hide as she had, Paris did so in his work, using his job here at the resort to avoid Diesel.

Her eyes began to glisten and guilt marred her face.

"Shhh—" Trenton pulled her against his side, "I'm sorry, I shouldn't have said anything." He wrapped his arms around her possessively, as if in any minute, something was going to attempt to take her away from him, "We'll be here for him."

~ * ~ * ~ * ~ * ~ * ~

CHAPTER FOUR

~ * ~ * ~ * ~ * ~ * ~

The air was as thick as clay around Paris' chest, making it hard to breathe or even relax even the slightest as he watched Trenton step off the boardwalk with Katianna at his side. The six submissive slaves from Abidabi Husain accompanied the Dominus and his Unicorn, including the one Paris had marked as his top purchase selection from the Elysian Fields Event. All were here to be added to the employed staff of the resort and serve out a unique contract that granted them an experience of submission like no other.

As they approached, the tears that streamed down Katianna's face did not go unnoticed, and it pained Paris to know why she was crying. Trenton, however, quickly led her away, allowing no chance for her to speak to him, or for him to ask if she was okay and if he should do anything for her.

Was something wrong? Had she been miserable all this time as Trenton's life slave? They talked frequently via text and email. So, surely she would have said something then. No, she could not have because Trenton would have read them. Now she cried because Paris had been the one who told her to jump. No, that was nonsense, he knew without a doubt Trenton would never have treated her badly. But then why was she crying? He wasn't sure and then it didn't matter— his thoughts scattered when Diesel stepped up. The man Paris had desired beyond comprehension stood before him now. The intensity he exuded made Paris want to shrink away and pounce on him at the same time. But then Paris recognized the harsh glare and knew then Diesel was anything but happy to be there.

He felt the anger like a heat that seeped from Diesel's body, threatening to turn all it touched to ash. Now, Paris wanted only to vanish into nonexistence and he dropped his eyes, unable to meet Diesel's angry gaze any longer. Instead, he meted out more self-torture as he watched the man's boots march off without a word.

In the blink of a cosmic tragedy, from the moment the ship pulled into port until he watched Diesel's boots go by, Paris had felt his heart swell and become recharged, only to get slammed to the ground by the cold rejection. The emotional flip caused physical pain, ripping his breath from his lungs right along with it.

"Diesel?" Paris turned and looked at him, but Diesel didn't stop— didn't look back. Paris' chest caved. He'd rather have Diesel flip him on his back and pin him down with his boot than do this to him. *And why did he? Did Diesel not want him to surrender to him for the whole week after all?* "Don't walk away from me!" But the only one who looked back was the little oriental girl walking at the Patronus' side.

The next familiar face to come ashore was Sasha Laszkovi with his twin Asian-American lovers, Isaiah and Isaac. Paris remembered them and he quickly composed himself to shake hands and greet the island's remaining arrival of guests.

"Wow, you really do know how to fuck up a wet and wild dream, don't you?" Sasha shook his head in disbelief and walked on with Isaiah under one arm, Isaac under the other.

Their passing was followed by a tall, debonair man with a sharply attractive and gentle face who seemed vaguely familiar, or maybe it was just a charm about him that made him seem so. His face was turned to the young blond under his arm— the brat, Cliff was his name, who Paris had fucked while standing up in the gladiator contest during Marcus Scriven's Birthday Bash last year. They stopped, giving Paris more of a chance to properly welcome them than the others. "Pyotr Laszkovi, I remember now, I— I'm sorry I don't even know how to properly address you." Paris admitted.

"Pyotr will do." He wore a warmly amused smile.

Paris shook his head. *That couldn't possibly be acceptable.* And he sure as hell wasn't going to have the Dominus coming down on him for it either. "Please, it would be inappropriate."

"If you insist, *Gospodar* or Head Master will work well enough." Pyotr nudged Cliff with his shoulder, then gave a forward nod of his head towards the others, "Go on, I'll catch up."

Cliff eyed Paris suspiciously, but not once did the young man share that distrusting glance in Pyotr's direction before heading up the walkway as instructed.

Pyotr only stood before Paris quietly— calmly— as if enjoying the summer breeze that blew between them. "Sometimes we must make sacrifices for the ones we want to be with. They don't always have to remain so, but just enough to show we are willing to do so— *for them.*" Pyotr gave him a reassuring nod, then dropped his hands into the pockets of his slacks and strolled off, as gently as the breeze itself.

~ * ~ * ~ * ~ * ~ * ~

No sooner had Trenton and Katianna caught up with Diesel at their home on the far west point shore of the island, Kat was flinging herself into Diesel's arms with the tears still streaming down her cheeks. Diesel lifted her off her feet and hugged her to him.

He'd thought to ask, but then he knew better. He knew her tears were for him. Just as she wrapped her arms as far around him as she could, he knew the hug was also for him.

Katianna gave the best hugs next to Kimmi, and he'd gotten a fair share of them from Kat after Kimmi's passing. Kat held on, wrapped around his body like a kid-sized fuzzy blanket full of static that promised to cling to him for however long he needed— and until the chill left his body.

"I'm okay, Mouse." He whispered in her hair, but she didn't loosen her hug. She knew better. And frankly, it felt too good to have her in his arms. Even as Trenton brushed by with a gentle touch of his hand on Diesel's shoulder, then found his way into the living room and sat down, watching with a love only a brother knew. As if his brother's Unicorn naturally belonged in his own arms as well. Completely acceptable. And that helped. It only proved they were ready.

Diesel had always hoped to have a Unicorn— a Life Slave of his own one day. To have that intimate connection with a woman. But Trenton had already found the perfect one and Diesel doubted he could find another like her for himself. Not even Chikako could fill that part for him. But as he still held onto Katianna, he knew *she* could. And then he felt the faint touch of her lips on the base of his neck, the light kiss that sent a rocketing stream of warmth and electricity through his body. And called his libido to attention in three seconds flat. Of their own volition, Diesel's arms tightened around her and he let out a groan, knowing he wanted her just as he always had. *His Unicorn had already been found.* Now, all he had to do was lure his fallen angel in, to be with him forever, and his life would be complete in a way he never expected.

He carried Kat over to the sofa and dropped down next to his brother, but he kept her in his own lap. Only then did Katianna let go of his neck and sit back to glance at him. He wiped the tears from her eyes and bucked her chin up with a finger.

"So what happens now?" Kat sniffled.

"What did I tell you that one day in Florida? Do you remember what I said?"

Katianna's eyes flickered as she searched her memory, "One runaway at a time."

Diesel nodded and pressed a desperate kiss to her forehead, "Took some convincing to bring you back home. It will take some here as well."

~ * ~ * ~ * ~ * ~ * ~

That evening Paris took some extra effort to look alluring for Diesel— manscaping the day-old stubble and adding a touch of gel to his bangs, bringing out the razored fringe cut. He picked out a loose-fitting, white button-up shirt of a breezy fabric, letting it hang untucked over a pair of tailored, relaxed-fitting grey slacks. The final touch was a heavy splash of a crisp, clean cologne with a base note that carried an edible scent. He picked through his selection, giving each a sniff before finally deciding on Flamboyant Prive Oriflame, a daytime fruity and citrus scent brought back down to earth with solid undertones of seawater, oak-moss, and musk. It was perfect for the evening without getting too heavy. He only hoped the extra details would bring Diesel back around to notice him.

Only, when Paris arrived at the evening welcome banquet, held each evening when the cruise ships dropped off their guests, his hopes got tangled up in his throat and threatened to strangle him.

Trenton and Diesel were sitting at the large reserved table with Katianna between them, and then the Asian woman to Diesel's right. With them sat Pyotr and Cliff, but no sign of Sasha and the twins. Trenton was busy teasing Katianna with a spoonful of ice cream, letting it drip on her cleavage and licking it off while everyone was laughing at the fun.

Paris almost lost his bravado when the laughter quieted as he approached, "Dominus— Patronus— may I join you?" He asked. Trenton nodded and he took a seat across from them.

Diesel was just as quickly getting up from his seat, pulling the Asian girl with him.

"Deez?" Trenton called to him gently.

"No, I'm fine." Diesel answered coolly.

Paris watched as the man never even allowed his eyes to shift his way.

"It's time for Chikako's bath." And Diesel walked off, his hand at the girl's back to keep her moving with him, and left without a word to Paris.

Paris felt the jab. It hit hard and he glanced at Trenton, "What have I done wrong? I was there on the dock for him."

"Not for him, you weren't. You were supposed to be there, ready to be surrendered over to him as his lover. Instead, you stood there, armed with your walls up, hiding behind your job title."

"And submitting on a knee to him would have undone my walls?" Paris contested.

"No. But it would have given him permission to work at taking them down for you. Instead, you stood there with a clear Red as if you'd shouted it at him."

"And what of Diesel's title as Master of Doms, as the Patronus?"

"Deez knows how to love with them. You use yours to keep everyone away. Mainly him." Trenton slid his arms under Katianna's legs and got up, lifting her with him before setting her on her feet, "Good day to you, Director."

"Wait—" Paris called out, but it was too late. Trenton was already leaving and the rest of Paris' words came out in a whisper, "You said Diesel knows how to love with them—" Paris let out a heavy sigh. He felt completely abandoned, but he wasn't alone. He turned to look and there sat Pyotr, watching him quietly, a slight curl in his lip revealing his contentment, or amusement. Paris wasn't certain which.

Paris' attention flickered back to the direction in which he'd seen Diesel leave. His eyes followed the pebble path that led to Diesel and Trenton's house on the far point. But it was clear Diesel wasn't coming back. Paris looked back at the man sitting across from him and to Cliff, who'd turned his chair sideways so he could lean back against his lover's body, content to remain there, come hell or high water. For Paris, it seemed strange to see someone Cliff's age so patiently still, as if stillness was something he enjoyed.

"I've been told you have a way of getting what you want." Pyotr spoke up with a casual tone, "So I ask you, why is it you don't go after want you want most, Paris?"

Paris took a deep breath and let it out slowly, trying to stem back the pain he felt. "Right now, there seems to be an avalanched-size blockage between me and what I want."

~ * ~

"Avalanche is a good word. It admits you're not in control of yourself. That is where you start and you may find the only blockage is the one you've placed there." Pyotr nodded gently, "Remember, sometimes it only requires that act of showing your willingness to make a sacrifice to bridge what might seem an uncrossable fissure."

"Why must it be one sided?" Paris' question was heavily laced with his somber emotions.

Pyotr had to sympathize because most people, at the most precious moments, had the habit of getting in their own way of what they wanted. "I can only hope to reveal to you it's not. Diesel has already made his sacrifice." Pyotr could see as soon as he said it, the man didn't have any form of understanding to what that sacrifice might have been. Paris truly was the naïve spoiled brat Diesel pegged him as

41

when it came to relationships of the heart. "Last year, back in New York?" Pyotr continued, "He let you go. It was likely a great deal more distressing than you give him credit for." Just then Pyotr found himself silently self-equating the very same question of whether he could ever bring himself to let his own young man go. It forced his emotions to constrict and his arm tightened around Cliff. Whatever his decision could be if he had to, for now his hold never left Cliff's body as he gently kissed the blond hair resting just under his chin. He glanced back over to Paris, "Are you willing?

"To what— be his slave?"

"I believe the request was only for eight days." Pyotr deliberated in a way to make it sound like such a small thing to do. He shifted, nudging the young blond on the head with his chin to get his attention, "Would you like to dance?"

Cliff rolled his head on Pyotr's shoulder just enough so he could eye him with surprise, "Really?" His face brightened.

"I may be old, but I can still do a few tricks."

Cliff sat up, but his gaze caught Paris instantly and he gave him a scowl, "He's not old." He bit out defensively, "He just likes saving his energy for other activities."

Pyotr sat up, his hand urging Cliff up to his feet and lightly chiding, "*Draga*— don't be a brat." He winked at Paris. "Even the best of hearts can't promise forever, but we're willing to take however long we can have, counting each day as a blessing. The decision presented here can be summed up with one rule of advice."

"And what is that?"

"Don't give up the things you want in the long term to fill your life for what appeals to your momentary desires now." Pyotr gave him an all-knowing nod then took Cliff's hand and led his young lover out towards the dance floor for a slow rumba.

~ * ~

Paris watched them together, not even phased by the backward glance from Cliff, who seemed far more concerned that Paris might pose a threat. A firm hand from his *Gospodar*, bringing Cliff's attention back to him, quickly corrected the bratting, and Pyotr locked him there in a demanding kiss.

Seeing that man kissing as he did, should have rated among the most erotic views of all time, and in a former life would have had Paris pushing to his feet to join them. *Before meeting Diesel changed all that.* Now he sat, unmoving— his heart heavy. *Just like the night last summer, when he sat in his New York hotel room, staying on the phone and begging Diesel to come see him before his flight brought him back to the resort.*

He turned and stared back down the empty path that headed for the west shore, knowing it was the only direction he could travel.

~ * ~ * ~ * ~ * ~ * ~

Diesel had left Chikako back at the quarters where she was staying and came back to the house.

"Why are you doing this?" Katianna blocked his path when he came inside, standing rigid before him in the middle of the living room.

Diesel nodded, "He'll come around."

"No, he won't." She shook her head and Diesel could see the tears that threatened to form in her eyes.

"She's right." Trenton interjected coolly, "He sees you in charge and you just rejected him. He's begged once before, but he's not going to do it again. We talked about this. You had a plan— now stick to it."

"He changed that very plan by refusing my request this morning."

"Did you think it was going to be that easy? You were running backwards the whole time last summer with him, holding yourself out like a sugar cube to a mule. Then after a solid ride, you kicked him out of the corral. He isn't going to come prancing in just because you ordered him to. Stop stalling and stop his running!"

"I can't force him to be with me!"

"No, but you can show him you're not going to give up on him so easily on his first falter."

Diesel was pissed. The worst was, he knew Trent was right, but fuck if he was going to admit to it. *Rather, he'd simply like to punch his lights out for being right again, as always, which sounded like a much better plan.* Diesel was about to say something that'd probably head them in that direction when there was a knock on the door.

The three of them looked at the door then exchanged glances. Trenton reached around Kat's shoulder and purposely led her out on the terrace, leaving the business of the door to Diesel. "Goddammit." He growled, turning to answer it when the knocking came again.

He opened the door, but it only took one look— all the anger Diesel was ready to slug out with Trenton shot down his arm and swung the door to slam it shut. Except it didn't slam closed as he had intended when his fallen angel managed to catch it with an arm and foot.

"What is this?!" Paris barged his way in enough to stop the door from closing, raising his voice to match the rage that was trying to shut him out.

"It's called a door slamming in your face." Diesel growled sharply, "Like the one you slammed in mine."

"What are you talking about?" Paris shoved the remaining way in. "I didn't slam a door in your face! Though, yes, I see you have tried to do that to me several times since you've arrived." He snapped bitterly, not masking the show of pain he felt.

Diesel crossed the room, intent on walking away from the confrontation but stalling at the glass pane doors facing out towards the pool. He held fast, placing an arm up on the doorframe, and targeted his focus out into night's nothingness. He took a deep breath and willed his heart to settle down. *One— two— three— fuck it, I don't have the patience for counting—* "You were given a specific request. You made your choice. So why are you here?"

"I can ask you the very same question."

Diesel took another breath, letting his eyes float up to the ceiling— *counting.* His chest felt as if it were caving in. But he reminded himself that he was the Patronus. He could not lash out at Paris— not when he was angry, and not when he was hurting either. He also had to admit he was venturing in uncharted territory here. He'd never felt so strongly for one person outside of family before. But perhaps Paris, too, felt something. He was here after all.

Maybe he just didn't know what it was he felt and like the bucking bronc Paris was, the second that heart saddle began to cinch down, Paris started kicking. But even a bucking bronco knew the best feed was in the stables, not out in the pastures. *It was a start. But did he risk riding Paris down at the expense of his own heart?*

Diesel scrubbed his hand over his head, back and forth across the stubble of his buzz cut, just escaping to the sensation tickling his palm for one brief moment. He twisted, glancing over his shoulder to the man standing there, waiting for something— anything out of him. So beautifully sexy, a faint glimpse of the innocent man that hid under the wings of an impish fallen angel, the persona Diesel loved knowing was there. The innocence blinked back at him with a stare, pleading to not be abandoned to suffer through his lonely love life.

Diesel dropped his hand down and pinched at the bridge of his nose. He felt the fool— loving where there was little hope. But he couldn't stand the idea of anyone else ever having the chance of sleeping with his brat ever again. Just the thought that someone else would be swooping in quickly to take his place had a surge of base needs boiling up. Diesel closed in on Paris, grabbed him by the wrist and, with a brisk pace, pulled him out past the paned glass doors and out across the patio. The bulk of the body he towed was starkly contrasted to Chikako's or mouse's weight when he tugged them along. It called on his own will and strength to keep things in motion. He led Paris to the other side of the pool and through the set of sliding glass doors to his bedroom. And once in, he spun on Paris, wrapping himself around him, then brought their lips together.

The second their bodies touched, their lips fused into an inescapable seal. Paris' mouth instantly opened to him and

Diesel dove in, seeking out Paris' tongue in a desperate need to reacquaint himself with what was meant to be his. He tilted his head further and their kiss deepened into a seamless pool of want and belonging.

~ * ~

Paris' head swarmed with elated lust— to suddenly be in Diesel's arms again was like getting high. The strength of Diesel's arms, holding him— possessing him in their grip, and then matched with lips and a tongue so soft, so open for him. Strength and tenderness all wrapped up in one man. Paris' own arms wound around Diesel, never wanting to let go. He never wanted to be parted from this man again.

He felt Diesel's broad palms smooth their way down his back, coming around to grasp his hips, clinching them with a tight grip, then began pushing him back under the force of Diesel's body, following him with every step until Paris' back found the wall.

Diesel leaned into him with full body contact, pinning Paris to the wall while grinding the hard erection in his jeans against his own.

Paris couldn't stop the gasp from escaping his lungs. Heat and hunger pulsed from his groin, spreading out in a sensation he could not describe. However, when Diesel's lips moved to his neck, licking and sucking on the sensitive skin, Paris' whole body melted, releasing any lingering anguish. He rolled his head into the man who knew how to possess him, knew how to sate his lustful need. This was just the start of the appetizer.

"Why are you here, Paris?" Diesel whispered into his neck. The words triggered both fear and want in him. Their meaning prickled at raw emotions, only to have the breath used to speak them lure him in the way they draped over the hairs on his neck in a warm caress, and Paris couldn't formulate a response.

They were moving suddenly. Diesel's body felt like bricks as he turned them both along the wall until it was Diesel's back now resting against the wall, then Diesel's firm hands had Paris turning more to settle backwards and spoon against a hard chest. Paris felt every bit of the strength that existed in Diesel's hands as he guided him into the position he wanted him in. He felt the man's chest against his back, while Diesel's hands pressed down Paris' hips, down his legs— wrapped into his thighs— then roughly slid up to ignite every bit of Paris' hunger inside him and inside his slacks. The pads of Diesel's thumbs pressed firmly into the crease between Paris' groin and his legs— sliding up— framing a caressing path against his scrotum and cock without holding him.

Paris burned to have the man's firm, steady hands grip his cock and stroke him, and knew it would come, just not likely soon enough. For Diesel, the journey was half the pleasure; for Paris, it was torture, but no amount of prodding would alter the course of the dominant man's own lust and intentions. It came at the pace the Patronus mapped out and no other.

"Did you come here to surrender to me?"

There was the question that frightened Paris the most.

Surrender.

He wanted Diesel. He was trembling, he wanted Diesel so exuberantly; he had wanted him again and again, ever since that night in New York. Only, Paris wasn't sure he could give into Diesel's demands of submission like that ever again— and be his slave.

48

Paris could feel that little panic storm lighting up again. He'd not felt it since that time he sat in Dominus Trenton Leos' office while Patronus ordered him to strip down and surrender his wallet and hotel key over to them. Once again, he could sense it crawling out from whatever deep hiding place he'd managed to stuff it away, like some keepsake in a trinket box long since forgotten.

He glanced down his body, watching as Diesel unzipped his slacks then peeled them open. He could make out a bit of the mischievous grin on Diesel's face out of the corner of his eye as Diesel peered over Paris' shoulder and gazed down to soak up the sight of Paris' body, just as he himself had. All while Diesel's firm hands carried on with an agenda— pushing all the way down into Paris' briefs. Followed by fingers that snaked around the hardening flesh of Paris' cock and began stroking him gently while he felt a much thicker and harder cock press against his backside.

Diesel's hand moved farther down to cup his scrotum before returning to the erection that was growing fiercely behind the ever tightening fit of his clothes, made tighter by the present demand of Diesel's hand fisting around his shaft. Another lick on his cheek, a caressing slide of his tongue with a tease of suction— taunting him. "Paris— tell me you want this—"

"Of course, I want you. That's why I'm here." Paris panted.

"But do you want to surrender to what I can give you?"

Paris shook his head— not that he didn't want to submit, but he didn't know what Diesel was offering to give. He was confused. Diesel had demanded he be his slave. Only, Paris wanted to be far more than that and that was even scarier for him. *He'd never wanted to be with anyone, let alone*

49

stay with anyone before. But *surrender* and *stay* were not the same words.

Sex with Diesel would obliterate the ranks of any previous lover Paris had ever bed with. But it would be all the more painful when it was over. He wasn't sure he could handle it— not again. It'd been hard enough the first time, not knowing the feelings he had. It had confused him— ruined him.

"What do you want, Paris? Do you want me to stay— do you want to feel my cock deep inside you?" Diesel's hand pumped on him harder.

Damn, it was too much. Paris gripped his pants and shoved them down to release his cock, giving it over to Diesel's fist. He couldn't stop the moan that escaped once he was in the full grip of Diesel's clutches. He dropped his head back on Diesel's shoulder— fear and walls slipping to the seductive needs of a wanton manwhore— *he was folding. How could he possibly escape this man? He couldn't possibly refuse Diesel his service. Oh, he could surely try— but he did want Diesel inside him, wanted to be fucked like no other had ever fucked him. The first and only time such desires had scared Paris. Terrified him like no other. Yes— he could try, but not a night would pass before he'd find himself following the man around the island, licking at his boots for another chance to take him up on the offer. But dammit, he was the director of this place. How was he supposed to be the man in charge of the resorts special events* and *kneel at this man's feet in front of everyone at the same time?* The very question burned images in his mind of just how certain Paris was that Diesel had every intention to have him completely nude, exposed, and vulnerable in front of all eyes on the island. Paris knew he would not be spared or denied any of the tantalizing moments the resort had to offer, though they would be humiliating for him.

Diesel would see to it Paris was delivered to him as a slave and then exploited and nurtured to the fullest satisfaction.

No.

He could not go through with it.

"Tell me you want it and I'll stay. Say that you don't and I'll have my chopper get me tonight."

Panic struck— like a five-alarm bell— fierce and frenzied. *Diesel would leave?*

"No!" Paris whirled around in Diesel's arms, "You can't leave me." And he took over, his mouth coming over his, sucking at Diesel's lips— licking at them. He didn't even wait for them to open, forcing his way into Diesel's mouth. Paris probed for his tongue, stealing what he needed to feed his hunger for him, ate at his lips with unrelenting passion. He'd been starving for this— craved it so much, he often thought he was going to just fade into madness if he never tasted it again.

He pulled Diesel to the floor and came over him, never stopped taking the sustenance he stole from the man's mouth that allowed him such free rein, and their tongues tangled into a continued fierce duel.

The allowance given by the Dominant sparked a flame low in Paris' belly, and he was quickly engulfed with wild, running desire. The kiss ravaged the lips under Paris' hungry pursuit as he covered Diesel's mouth with his. Forcing the surging need for the other man's taste past his lips as he devoured him in one swift move.

Diesel wrenched their mouths free, his fists clinching into Paris' shirt and lifting him up enough for their eyes to meet. Paris understood that watchful, searching look.

Diesel was looking for the same reactions Blaine looked for. But he looked for far more than perhaps Blaine was capable of seeing. To recognize the unique submission that was developing within Paris.

"Damn you." Paris groaned and pushed his weight against the firm hands that had pried them apart.

"That's it— take what you need for now, Paris." Diesel offered with a heated expression Paris had never seen, but then he allowed Paris to regain the embrace of their kisses once more. "Take it now," Diesel severed the kiss once more to speak, "because the time for running away is at its end. In the morning, you'll be turned over to me, and I'm going to show you what it means to be with me, which is where you belong. With me."

~ * ~ * ~ * ~ * ~ * ~

CHAPTER FIVE

~ * ~ * ~ * ~ * ~ * ~

DAY ONE: PARIS' SURRENDER

His sleep was anything but bliss. In fact, it was entirely absent. His mind attempted to adlib a to-do list for the morning of who needed to take care of what while he surrendered to Diesel during his stay. But not even work could keep his focus. *Why couldn't he have just stayed in Diesel's room? Why did Diesel insist he return to his own room?* Diesel had even stopped him when he tried to undress them both. It was as if Diesel's intention was to make sure the night was not about sex, but rather about *want.* They had only kissed and touched. And a considerable amount of grinding on Paris' part. *Fucking Patronus.* Paris couldn't think of a time in his life where he'd lain next to a man and not had sex with him— *ever.* Except with Diesel.

Paris rubbed his eyes then and combed his hair back with his fingers, staring up at the ceiling in the darkness. He touched his lips, drawing up an old memory. The night was too long, with too many hours before he could be in Diesel's arms again— tasting his lips.

He sat up, swung his feet over the edge and just stayed there, naked, without any idea of where he was— inside or out. The moonlight spilled in through the glass walls of his bedroom, making the floor under his feet glow, and the sea breeze carried the fragrance of night jasmine through a side window. Next to Alan Pridmore, Paris likely had one of the nicest resident condos on the island. But it felt empty right now. *Lonely* was not something Paris did well.

He dropped back on the bed, once more staring up at the ceiling. Wishing for sleep or at least some solitude for his thoughts. There were still things he could do in the office to make sure all was smooth, maybe even stall his surrender— buy him some time to prepare mentally for it.

No. There was no preparing— he knew this was coming two weeks ago and he still hadn't gotten his head wrapped around it in time to surrender to the Patronus when he arrived. He'd made the fatal mistake of convincing himself Diesel would accept a gentle takeover. The blow from that had been painful. Watching Diesel walk away from him twice had been more than he could bear, so when Diesel had said he would leave, Paris gave him his surrender. The last thing Diesel asked him for before sending him to sleep in his own quarters was a word. And Paris had spoken it.

Green.

Paris flipped over in his bed, tossed his pillow to the side, and just lay there on his side, staring out the glass doors to the palm fronds dancing in the gentle wind. It was probably the hundredth time he'd done it. He couldn't sleep. Couldn't even keep his head together. *Damn. Probably should have taken something to help him sleep.*

He glanced up, looking at the clock— it was only twenty minutes later than the last time he'd looked, but it was too late for him to consider taking a sleep aid now.

54

He'd planned on getting up early, finishing off a few things in the office, making a few calls, divvying out the duties, then giving himself over to Diesel in time for lunch.

The monotonous rerun of what he needed to do in the morning finally lulled him to sleep, but whatever those details he believed he'd carefully scheduled out in his head for his morning— *none of them would happen.*

~ * ~ * ~ * ~ * ~ * ~

At precisely seven in the morning, and he knew it was seven because he'd just slapped the snooze and rolled back over with every intention of drifting back to sleep, six of the resort's Handlers barged into his room.

Paris found himself being snatched from his bed and before he had time to think clearly enough to raise hell or any other reaction, they had him on his knees— his arms bound behind his back— and still just as naked as he was when he went to bed.

"Open." One of them commanded. And while Paris did open his mouth, it wasn't to comply, it was to argue. But he never got the first word out when a ball gag was stuffed into his mouth. Next, they tied a black scarf over his face, covering not just his eyes but his whole face, like he was being abducted by terrorists or something. Despite his body's instinct to rebel, he knew it was useless to struggle with them. He had hired them for that specific job, handling the employed slaves and submissives both in training, discipline, and even administering when their needs outweighed those given with the guests they served. But Paris tried anyway, already calculating his first brat response with the whole idea of refusing to cooperate and walk when they would order him to. But it didn't work out—

They never asked. They simply flipped him face down, then lifted him. One Handler per arm and two more, one to each leg. Where the remaining other two who'd barged in were, he didn't know, but out the door he was being carried off— face down— bound, gagged, and blinded like a sacrificed pig for the roast. *Oh, and that little lost panic feeling he had mentioned? Yeah, it was alive and well—*thank you— *and he was completely consumed with it.*

Any attempt he'd made in the night to calm himself, working it out in his head as to what to expect and how he would handle it, failed him as the reality struck with his being toted off. Not even his destination was made known to him. As if the Handlers who carried him deliberately ran around the entire island twice then threw in a few hairpin turns on their route, just to spin Paris' awareness about and rendered him completely disoriented—

It was working; he couldn't tell where he was. Each time he thought he had it figured out, what he expected them to do next was never what they did.

Paris first thought they would just drag him over to the house and dump him off like a sack of potatoes before the Patronus. The Handlers would turn him over to his Master— drop him with a hard thud on his ass at Diesel's feet, who would just laugh at him with deep amusement then order him to suck his cock, and Paris would gladly do it. But they didn't do that. Not yet at least. At another point, Paris thought they were taking him to one of the playrooms— *that didn't happen either.* Frustration mounted and he began a verbal struggle against his gag.

At some point, amidst his futile struggles and muffled screaming, he did end up at the bathhouse, but he wasn't sure which one. Someone reached and peeled the scarf over his face up enough to remove the gag from his mouth, and Paris picked up on the smells wrapping around him, the tropical blend of lime, ginger and vanilla.

Alright, no need to panic. You're in the women's bathhouse. It's all still good— right? No. Where was Diesel? Why wasn't he with him? Paris' mind raced with questions and self-provided answers on what would now be expected of him as he attempted to assess his surroundings and what to expect.

He couldn't hear the Handlers around him anymore, couldn't sense if they were still nearby or not. He strained to listen. *God, if he could just see then he'd be alright.* He was on his own damn island and still he hated being blindfolded— and he felt himself coming loose at the seams. He really needed to get a grip on his mind. He knew where he was, no slave had ever been harmed here, so there was no need for him to be entirely freaked out. *You're just here along for the ride,* Paris told himself. *Yeah— tell that to the kid who's going for the roller coaster marathon and why the one hundred and fiftieth ride is just as scary and adrenalin-packed as the first.*

When he heard the tinkling chorus of young women snickering at him, Paris' minute resolve shattered and filled with instant dread. He strained his ears to hear them and anyone else in the room as his body began to shake. *Oh god, he was ready to bolt.*

~ * ~

Diesel and Trenton sat back and watched, keeping a short distance— close enough to watch the play of shivers, the little nuances that trembled in Paris' body, but far enough away that Paris would not notice their presence just yet. Diesel wanted the man totally off balance. Completely swept off his feet. And how easily it could be done when Diesel knew what to do.

Paris held within him the secret desire to be commanded, willing to serve with a greedy passion. However, Paris hated having his control and security stripped from him. Those were the best parts. The art of peeling all those things away that made enjoying Paris all the tastier.

Diesel waved his command to the girls, eight of them in total, and they all gathered around the god-sized fallen angel to lead him into the pool to wash him.

~ * ~

Hands— too many hands were instantly on his body. Small, not like a man's hands, and they matched the giggle of girlie voices that came with the invasion— *oh god, did they plan to torment him*? They pulled him back, carefully guided him into the thigh deep pool, and then eased him down into the water.

He couldn't escape the overwhelming sensation of having too many hands touching him— all sliding over his body with a slick lather bubbling on his skin like soap suds. *How many was it, two? No, there were more than that— four? Still more— why so many? For fuck's sake he wasn't dirty.* He felt the soap's slippery sensation of lathering silk and more of the heavy fragrances of lime fruitiness. Small fingers smoothed over his chest and underarms, around his waist, and his cock, which only had him cursing when he felt several sets of fingers wrapping around his shaft as they began stroking him. They washed his hair next, then pulled him down under the water and rinsed him off. That was when he felt a finger travel behind him and slide between his ass cheeks. A violation he wouldn't stand for.

Paris bolted to his feet, blasting out of the water with a roar. "Diesel!" He cried out while twisting and churning in the water, desperately warding off any further touching from the women, "Don't do this to me!" No answer came but neither did the girls. He cocked his head to listen and made out the swish of water as the invaders all apparently abandoned him. He sucked in a deep breath and let his head drop back on his shoulders as he let out a sigh of relief. "Thank you, Patronus." But he did not remain alone for long. Someone else was coming towards him in the pool. Paris stumbled back, only to bump into someone else. Firm hands locked onto his arms and held him in place, and then he felt a warm mouth close around his cock.

"Get the fuck off me." But whoever was attached to him didn't back away, instead the person continued to suck and lick over the length of Paris' shaft. He wasn't even sure if it was a man or woman. *Oh god, he wasn't sure— her or his mouth— it was almost sweet.* But he didn't want it to be good. He didn't want to enjoy this.

He strained against the Handlers and bent over as if that could stop the slave on his cock. "Stop— don't do this." Paris pleaded with god knows who, then sank down in the water. He'd drown them first. But then Paris felt a masculine hand slip between his legs, find its way along the crevice of his ass, and then began to finger the sensitive skin of Paris' hole.

Paris shot up out of the water like before, but this time the slave stayed with him, with a well-trained finger that zeroed in on its target and penetrated Paris' hole.

He instantly found himself succumbing to a skilled finger fucking while the slave's mouth continued working on his cock. The finger slipped in and out, too small to reach far, so it was just complete teasing, torture. Another set of lips came back over him; he picked up on the other body as a slave slipped between him and the one sucking his cock. A brush of her breast confirmed this one was a woman as she nestled down and started licking his balls. Her tongue hooked them into her mouth so she could suck on them lightly. One, then another, while a hand reached up to play with one of his nipples.

Paris tossed his head back. Moaning in anguish over it. He didn't want it to feel good, but his body threatened to react to it. He wanted to know where Diesel was— *was he even here? Did he know what they were doing to him?*

While Paris didn't know which slaves specifically surrounded him, he knew they were the ones who worked under him, intended for serving and pampering the resort's guests. Only, now that he'd been stripped of title and control, they were exacting their revenge on him. That's what this was— *revenge.*

He quivered and caught his breath as his release built up inside him. It didn't matter what this was, he was going to cum— his body shook and he felt his knees weakening. The muscles in his shoulders shivered beyond his control and he folded over, preparing for the unwanted explosion.

That's when he heard a loud clap. The strike of a heavy hand filled the bath hall, echoing off the tiled walls. A thick, heavy hand— *Diesel's hand.* He was going to scream at him, but under the command of the singular clap, Paris was suddenly abandoned again. The man and the women retreated from his body. No longer anyone sucking on him.

No more hands touching him. The Handlers behind him released his arms and stepped away.

Paris felt the moving water lap around his legs, but no longer were there slaves tormenting his body like a swarm of sirens. Abandoning his cock to suffer for its own need for release. He could make out the faint patter of bare feet as they filed out one by one. He bent over, letting out a moaning growl, wishing he could get his hands free to stroke his cock to its completion, picking up where the two slaves left off. Have the pleasure of finishing himself off. *Fuck, why didn't they just finish him before leaving?* Shit, it was bad enough that his body responded to the violating touch and brought him to the verge of cumming. He cursed against his teeth— worse than having them touch him was wishing they would come back and finish him now.

He cocked his head, listening. It was silent in the bathhouse. Just the soft flip flop splashing of the water against the tile sides of the pool. Some echoing, dripping noise in the surrounding drains, and he could hear voices in murmuring conversations with laughter, but they were far away. Guests at the swimming pool perhaps— or the bar.

He could make a run for it now. But then what? Where would he go?

~ * ~

Katianna did her best not to squirm in Trenton's lap as he and Diesel watched the torment of the man in the pool.

Paris had been informed they were coming down to the resort, but because he didn't give himself over as requested, *this* was happening. Though she didn't get what it was about, or what it was supposed to accomplish, other than to humiliate Paris. *She hated it.* It hurt watching what they were doing to him and she couldn't bear watching it any longer. *Trenton hadn't done this to her, so why would he and Diesel do it to Paris?* And telling him as much by shrugging away when her Dominus' hand came up to stroke her shoulder.

Trenton silently tapped her arm, expecting her to look at him. She couldn't— wouldn't— and as she twisted to fish her phone from his pocket, she deliberately shifted her gaze away from his to further her silent defiance.

Then, with phone in hand, she shifted off his lap. Taking her unruliness all the way to the threshold she knew he'd allow. If she so much as got to her feet with a show that she would walk away, he would call it to a stop. But instead, she stayed inside the permitted boundaries allotted to her and resettled down on her side, falling between his body and the arm rest of the chaise lounge, keeping her back to him and hiding away inside the tight margin to pout.

Even as the Handlers returned for whatever the next step was that Patronus had planned. All this in and out— on and off. She knew Paris wasn't liking this. She didn't like it either.

Even when she felt the kiss at the back of her head, she dug the heels of her invisible itty-bitty feet into the ground, refusing to be coaxed away from what she felt— *or* the intervention she had in mind. Her thumbs became a blur of movement over the qwerty touch pad and then she hit send. She realized, as she glanced over her shoulder at the naked body standing on the far end of the shallow bath-pool, she felt like she'd failed him. *Naked*— as in— he had no phone. *Duh, Kat, get your brain in gear! There wasn't going to be any—* She stopped in her assumed defeat, swiped the screen of her phone to her settings— a few taps later and—

— Pihng– Dihng— Dihng dihng diing—

Like music to her ears, the gentle digital tune rang out at full volume and echoed off the walls of the pool house.

Paris' head snapped in their direction and the relief in his body was evident even from here. And while she felt the full effect of the glaring glances she got from both Dominus and Patronus, Katianna didn't hide her evil plot-jamming victory grin in the least bit.

~ * ~

Paris heard footsteps entering the pool house. Heavy ones, boots, clunking across the tile.

Of all the things for him to think of at that precise moment, it was the scuff marks the boots might make on the jade tiles. But just as he heard the bodies wading into the water to retrieve him, something surprising echoed off the walls, dancing across the water to deliver a message to his ears. *They were there*— over by the guest lounges— *watching.* And the little mouse squeaked to let him know it.

He had no idea why or how he believed, but he was certain the light tune from a cell phone was Katianna's. That meant Diesel and Trenton were in fact here with him, watching him— controlling everything that was being done to him. While that wasn't totally nerve settling, it did dispel his growing concerns that he might not be safe. Because if nothing else, Paris knew damn well, Diesel would never let anyone harm or take advantage of him.

Several layers of anxiety dripped from Paris' body like the water that slid from his skin. Even as the firm hold of hands took him by the arms and guided him out of the pool, and steadied his weight as he stepped out, the weight of his own fear was not as heavy. He felt the ball gag pressing against his lips, this time awaiting his compliance. As if it'd become natural for him, Paris opened his mouth and allowed it to be set in place. His breath tried to betray him, which kicked up as the leather strap that held the gag secure was buckled behind his head. But knowing they were close-by changed that— all three of them— and it helped a small amount.

Next, two sets of hands became four and he was lifted off his feet, his head hanging forward like before— bound, blind, and silent, but now in Paris' mind, Diesel was walking behind them, monitoring it all.

~ * ~

Trenton broke off, his hand firmly on the back of Katianna's neck as he led her out of earshot. Even though he took her phone from her, she still showed no remorse for her action, outside of a show for it being a mistake. Though he knew better. He caught the defiant smile as it crept over her lips when she had done it, despite her attempt to shield her face from him.

He led her away, down one of the trails, then stepped into one of the garden gazebos overlooking a small pond. The octagon shaped structure's white columns were bleached further from the endless days of sunlight, yet its brilliant blue tile roof top defied the sun's attempts to rob it of its brilliant color. He sat down on the bench and right away, without prompting, Katianna knelt at his feet, still keeping her face hidden. "Why did you do that, mouse?"

"You're torturing him." She snapped.

"We are not. It may seem that way, but there is a reason for what we are doing."

"To what— humiliate him? Punish him for running away? What could possibly come of this?"

"Mouse—" Trenton leaned down to brush her shoulder, only she retreated from his touch again. Aside from the deviant grin he'd spied earlier, he could see her misunderstanding of what was happening had her feelings hurt. "Come up here, now." He ordered firmly, waving her up on his lap and, though reluctantly, she did as she was told. She always had. Something he never stopped admiring of her as she pushed up and let him pull her into his lap. He brushed the hair from her face, captured her chin and raised it to bring her eyes to meet his. "Katianna, do you know what it is Paris does when he gets scared or finds himself out of his element or out of control?"

She diverted her eyes and shook her head.

"He uses sex. It's his shield to keep people from getting close to him. He uses his power of seduction to cope with things not in his power. He seduces others to follow his will just to avoid what he fears the most. So the only way to get past it is to break his defense."

"You're just doing this to get back at him for what he did to you."

He let out a heavy sigh, "I know it would seem that way. What Paris did that night was wrong, but this is not revenge. Merely to break him of his destructive use of sex."

"Same thing."

"In some aspects, maybe so."

"What if you're going about it the wrong way?" She asked from under the cave of long, wavy strands of brown hair that had fallen back into her face.

"We're not. Paris is afraid of falling in love, which is why he keeps running away. Now that we have come to him, Diesel is making sure Paris doesn't use sex to shield any kind of development for himself."

"Then you are wrong."

"Why do you say that?"

"Paris isn't afraid to fall in love, he's afraid of admitting it because no one has said as much to him either. But if you are thinking this is going to convince him to be Patronus' Unicorn, it's not going to work."

"Kat, Diesel didn't come down here to make Paris his slave."

Katianna's pale eyes darted up at him and showed every bit of the alarmed pain in them, "So, Paris was right? This is just another episode of fucking and sexual torment, then Diesel goes back home and abandons Paris' heart again?"

"No, Kat. That's not what this is."

"You just said Diesel is going to break him."

"No, not Paris, just his defense shield. I promise you, Katianna, the spoiled Imp will remain very much intact."

~ * ~ * ~ * ~ * ~ * ~

All Paris could do was strain his ears to hear for any clues of his surroundings. Even a small murmur of a conversation between Diesel and Trenton would have been a gift as he was toted down any one of the three paths that led away from the pool house. The voices he did hear were drawing closer and registering in his head as the

66

white noise of dinnerware, eating, and conversation. The swirling anxiety began to seep back in— brunch at the club house.

He knew exactly where he was once his feet were set down and he was instructed to step up on a platform. It was a small vanity stage where select slaves could be put on display for the guests as they ate. Paris had designed the small shows himself. The slave often underwent shaving or became the canvas for an artist's paints. The Living Art tours Paris had been well known for in the past worked just as well here as they did at museums and elite night clubs around the world.

The arrival of hands came back, this time salving his body in oil. And Paris summoned up his ego. His body instantly responded in the way it knew it should— his shoulders broadened, and he deepened his breath to pull his chest up. Even with his hands still tied behind his back, Paris was capable of small flexes of muscles created under the will of motor control, which would put his physique on display as he stood like a prized gladiator brought inside the lanista's palace for some succulent rutting.

A pair of hands spread the oil down his hips and towards his groin, but before the fingers could get ahold of Paris' cock, there was a snap of fingers and the venturing hand quickly abandoned its destination, moving further down Paris' leg. Another small reminder that Diesel was still there watching over it all. The snap also said he wouldn't allow any further playtime on Paris' body, commanding the hands to behave and do only what they were instructed.

"Shall I shave him, Patronus?" Someone next to Paris asked. It sounded like one of the Handlers but could have just as easily been one of the larger men who served as a slave this season.

Paris tensed, but there was nothing he could say to protest it with the gag still in his mouth. But Diesel had to remember Paris didn't allow anyone to change his body. He'd spent half his life and a small fortune grooming himself to perfection with laser hair removal that took most of his hair away so his chest and legs were bare. Even around his scrotum and ass was smooth skin. Only the shallow happy trail on his lower belly remained, and he'd be damned if he was going to stand still while some slave or Handler shaved it off. It wouldn't be the same when it grew back.

"No." A firm command finally came and Paris felt relief that Diesel would honor his wishes that his body remain unaltered. "His body is perfect the way it is."

Damn right it was.

"He still has some hair here." The voice protested and Paris felt a hand glide down his lower abdomen until he had Paris' cock in his fist. The man gave it a few playful strokes before returning to the happy trail, tugging at the light dusting of hair.

"You're dismissed."

"Sir?"

Paris didn't hear a follow up from Diesel, but he knew the looks the Patronus was capable of and he knew the man had gotten his one and only warning. Paris even wondered if he'd find something on his desk, suggesting some additional training on how not to question a Master, when Paris was finally released to return to his position as Event Director.

The small stage sagged when the weight of another stepped up, and soon Paris felt the all familiar hands moving over his body slowly to enjoy every ripple of muscle, every contour of Paris' island-bronzed skin, then released the strap around his head and pulled the ball gag from his mouth.

"Deez?" Paris' meek voice whispered out his desperate hope that the strong hands he was feeling definitely belonged to Diesel.

"Yes, it's me." The answer resonated with desire despite its soft tone.

"Please don't leave me." Paris begged quietly. He dropped his head, fearful that the very request would likely secure his fate for just the opposite.

~ * ~

"Don't worry—" Diesel was still enjoying the thrilling sensation of admiring his fallen angel's body. *Had a man ever looked so groomed for sex?* "From here on, no one is going to touch you but me. You belong to me, Paris, and I won't stand to have anyone else touching you." His hands glided over oiled skin, taking in every detail and curve. He pressed one of his calloused fingertips stiffly into the crevice between Paris' ass cheeks, sliding tantalizingly over his sphincter, resulting in an unpreventable shudder from Paris.

Diesel splayed his fingers out wide; while one still teased Paris' hole, the others groped at the flesh of his ass. Then Diesel used his left hand to mirror the contact over Paris' genitals. The now flaccid cock was quick to swell again under Diesel's touch. Paris' body vacillated as to which hand it wanted to press toward first. His breath deepened, only to be torn from his lungs when Diesel pushed his finger, now slick with oil, past the tight ring of muscle, invading the sensitive walls inside. After only a few simple teasing strokes, Diesel then withdrew, though he tightened his left hand over Paris' shaft and continued to stroke him with a firm twisting grip. But again, only a few times to stoke Paris' *wants* into a heightened level, then abandon his body.

~ * ~

Paris felt Diesel's lips on his shoulder, a tender chewing of his teeth that cut through the alluring dichotomy of sensations. His mind could focus only on those lips that came closer, then Diesel's body pressed in against him and he could feel the man's warm breath on his neck.

"Turn to me so I can kiss you."

Paris' head swarmed with lust as he obeyed, turning his lips towards the commanding voice— turning just as Diesel's mouth came around, catching Paris in its hungry suction. A tongue lapping past his lips and dancing across his tongue, then gone. Just as Diesel had done with the other sensations he delivered.

"Which will it be, Paris?"

Paris gasped, his mind grappling for understanding when all he could fathom right now was need. "I don't understand."

"Tonight, you can have only one of the three sensations I just gave you a taste of. Which will it be?"

"Is there a wrong answer?"

"No, there is no wrong answer, but each comes with their own consequences. How you choose will determine how I will handle your training and conditioning."

"My conditioning?" Paris shook his head. He didn't understand. Diesel had come to have his way with him for the week. *So what was it he was supposed to be conditioned for?* Bewildering his thoughts further, both of Diesel's hands and his lips returned to the tantric connection, each hand stroking and petting while he ate Paris' lips in a soft, tempting kiss.

Paris let out a groan when he felt the thicker thumb of Diesel's one hand, instead of a fingertip, press inside his ass. And were it not for the kiss, Paris would have sent his head dropping back on his shoulders and let the dizzying spell take over him. Paris felt everything in him melting for the man he was willing to give anything for all three sensations, plus anything else Diesel could do to his body.

"What will it be, Paris?" The question was repeated in a husky breath against his cheek.

Paris couldn't choose. His body rippled each time Diesel's thumb tapped over his prostate, his cock throbbed with the need of release, but he could not imagine either without the man's kiss. But if he chose the kiss over all else, no doubt his body would rebel.

"I can't choose; I need all of you."

"And you will— eventually. How we get there is what needs to be decided."

Paris leaned into him, using his mouth to search for his Patronus' lips as he bucked his hips forward then back against the hands that coaxed his orgasm to the surface. "Diesel, please—" he gasped against him, "I need you."

"Decide."

"I can't."

"Then the decision will be made for you." And with that, Diesel's hands and his lips left Paris' body. Leaving him gasping at the loss.

~ * ~ * ~ * ~ * ~ * ~

CHAPTER SIX

~ * ~ * ~ * ~ * ~ * ~

Diesel's plans were well underway to have Paris at the mercy of his favorite meticulous playtime. He grabbed the next section of rope he'd set out for the full design he'd planned for Paris' body. This time, a dark, vibrant purple to be set against the slate gray. It was one of the nicer things about buying the higher priced silk ropes— they offered the broadest selection of color, unlike other natural fibers such as cotton, hemp, or bamboo, and as far as he was concerned, well worth the extra price. While it broke tradition of the Japanese art, he liked the colors and kept a variety of them in his collection. Still, the gray had been a tough color to find and he'd been saving it for a special moment. *Like right now.*

Having Paris stretched out on his bed again, the lines of black, gray, and purple could not have looked better on any other body or any other time. Except for maybe where he was about to tie Paris' remaining free hand. That was about to up the experience for him further. "Give me your left hand."

"Must you tie all of me up?" Paris put up a fuss while watching in his non-submissive manner, as it were.

Diesel let out a small huffing laugh, "Oh, absolutely." Not hiding the fun he was having while he wrapped a few coils of the gray rope around Paris' wrist, he precisionly placed Paris' hand on his groin, just mere inches from his cock, then lashed it in place. If Paris tried to reach, he would just barely be able to run his fingers down the shaft of his cock and little more.

"Fucking tease." More fussing came from his captive.

Had it not been for the plans for some heavy kissing, Diesel would have already stuffed a gag in Paris' mouth, but despite the minor complaints, doing so would be counterproductive.

"Have you ever had your coils get too tight to where they hurt someone?"

Diesel glanced from his task to Paris with a raised eyebrow, "Yes. I was a newbie once."

"What happened?"

"She kept shifting around. She liked to wrestle and play hard-to-pin-down, so it caused my wraps to shift and tighten in some places around her."

"Then what happened?"

Diesel was really more interested in the person he was tying up now than someone from his past. Yet, at the same time, communication between him and Paris was vital. They hadn't had nearly enough of it, for one. And secondly, because Paris was still new to all this.

Paris wasn't a true submissive, but Diesel fully intended to tie him up on a regular basis for his own fascination. So for now, he broke his pleasuring thoughts to tell the story.

"First time, she didn't use her safeword and before you ask, she thought it was wrong for her to use it. That somehow doing so would piss me off, or make her look weak. Anyways, she didn't use it and I didn't notice the ropes had shifted until her fingers started turning purple."

"What'd you do?"

"Unwrapped her right away." He answered, positioning Paris' fingers apart then thumped him when he moved them out of position.

"What do you think might have happened had you not been there to notice in time?"

Diesel's hands stopped in mid-movement of his weaving and glanced at him, "Paris, I never left the room. From the time I started the wraps to the time I took them off and started her aftercare, I was always there with her." He took a moment to test the coils of rope that now made two bands of four coils each. The first set bound Paris' left wrist to his hips, while the other bound Paris' outer two fingers to his thigh, finishing his work with one single end knot. Now he was free to soak up his handiwork. "I made mistakes as I grew, but not once have I ever walked away and placed my subbies in danger of being alone when those mistakes happened."

"How old were you then?"

Diesel pondered it and shrugged, "Twenty, maybe. A foolish age for playing around with so much responsibility, but I was a book nerd then too, so I had read up on nearly everything I could on ropes, Shibari, and circulation."

"Why do you think you were like that?"

"Why all the questions?"

Paris gave him sultry look, "Is talking forbidden?"

Diesel gave it some thought— of course it wasn't, but it was a matter of why Paris was so inquisitive. They'd never really just chatted because it was always more a contest of wits and the will of their libidos. Now that he thought about it, even if Paris was up to something, talking was always good. "No, it's not. And to answer your question, I figure it's being from a military family. Trenton and I had fathers who were both field experts in the military. They'd always do a ton of research about a place they were heading to until they knew every mouse and stone in that area." Diesel ran a heavy palm up over the coils covering Paris' body, then drifted over to catch the velvety smooth skin of Paris' cock. "Rubbed off on me, I suppose."

Paris' hiss matched that of Diesel's touch, "I can think of something else to rub against you."

"Already have much of that planned for today." Diesel growled as he moved up over Paris' body and slowly eased his weight down over him.

"Hardly fair with you still being dressed." Paris lifted his head up to close the gap from Diesel's approaching lips.

Diesel had never crash landed in such a potent kiss as he did with Paris. Hungry tongues coiled around each other as breaths hissed out their noses to brush each other's cheek. He twisted, dragging their lips together, then came back at him from the opposite angle. "This isn't about fair, it's about me enjoying your body the way I like to, right now.

"So that's all you're going to do again? Tease me all week and maybe if I'm lucky you'll fuck me on the day before you leave?" Paris' passion was suddenly cooling its jets and the kiss between them stalled out.

"It's possible. Because I want to enjoy more than just penetration with you."

Tension snapped to the surface of Paris' body. Now the heavy breath in his chest sang a different heated tune. Diesel could sense Paris' rage. That he dared to suggest he might only lie next to Paris and do nothing else infuriated him. Frustrated him.

For the first time, Paris squirmed uncomfortably against the ropes. "Look, will you just let me up?"

"No, I don't think so." Diesel gave him a slow, lazy smile. "It's been way too long since I had you in this position. Think I'll keep you here awhile."

Paris glanced away, his eyes looking over the gray and black braids wrapped around his right forearm, which was hung from a hook placed over the king-size headboard.

"Do you remember the way you used to beg me to fuck you?" Diesel continued, his voice low and intimate. "Remember the way you liked to suck my cock?"

Paris shifted against Diesel, undergoing his own internal war of want or walk away. It even affected his answer, "God, yes," Paris whispered, then sucked in a long inhale that hissed through his nose, "I can smell the hot, spicy fragrance of your thick cock—" Paris closed his eyes and pushed his head back into the pillow while he licked his lips at the thought, "I can even remember the sweetened briny taste of your prize."

Diesel was glad to have managed to pull Paris back from the angry storm of emotional wounds, but at the same time, it gave Diesel further insight that Paris was holding some heavy grudges towards him about being set loose.

The wounds were very real and would need some healing in all of this, but he couldn't accomplish it if he didn't get inside Paris' walls. For now, Diesel chose to rattle those walls with bait. "You were good at it, too," Diesel growled against his ear. "The best. I loved watching you between my legs, taking my cock with your tongue, working me to get my cum. Your tongue has a demanding way about it. It's fucking hot." Diesel dropped down to Paris' mouth with a heated intensity that made his cock wish he'd toss the plans to the wind and just get on to what they both wanted. Because, as cliché as it may have sounded, Paris was like a drug— one hit and Diesel was high as a kite, and wanting more.

~ * ~

Diesel still tasted the same as Paris remembered— spicy and delicious. It had been too long since Paris had kissed this man. He'd forgotten how potent it truly was. And how desperately he wanted to wrap around him and be consumed by him. To hell with these games Diesel wanted to play. Paris just wanted them to hide away on one of the far points of the island and just fuck for days until exhausted, sated, and starved.

It was all too much to try to resist the feel of a warm, masculine hand holding him in place with fingers spreading out over his throat. Not heavy, but merely a brushing reminder of who was in charge here, and the aggressive, hungry way Diesel devoured his mouth was driving him over the edge, right along with the muscle-bound body that ground against him. The zenith was when Diesel let out a throaty growl. Paris knew that sound, the one Deez made when he was getting close to cumming and needed to back off. And just then, Diesel pushed up on his arms to plank over him and all contact was gone.

"If I beg now, will it do me any good?"

"It always does you some good, it just won't always get you what you want."

If Paris thought about kicking up an attitude about that, the pressure of a three-inch-thick cock that came back down and ground against his own exposed shaft silenced any words. All that came out was a contented moan for more. But before the possibility could occur, a light knock on the glass pane of the rolling doors reached his ears. When they both looked, there was the small Asian girl who'd arrived to the resort with Diesel.

"You're not the only one who gives me trouble. She's like a mini you." Diesel nodded his head to the girl. He made a quick circulation check on Paris' bindings, poked his finger under each set of coils, then climbed off the bed to let her in.

That was the last calm thought Paris had. Now, he only felt heat driven fury. It was one thing to endure the onslaught of Diesel's teasing, but quite another to have succumbed and then put on the back burner in the same instance.

~ * ~

Diesel glanced at his watch, noting the time was reasonable that her afternoon schedule for acting as a centerpiece for Mr. Sakimoto and his son during lunch would be over. Except she was supposed to retire to her own room after her aftercare was completed, not here. "Chikako, you are supposed to be in your quarters."

"I is lonely, Patronus. I need you."

"Chikako, we have discussed this numerous times. I am going to have to discipline you if you keep it up."

"But this is strange place. I no feel safe. Every sound I hear out my window frightens me. I need you protection." Her dark, near onyx-black eyes continued to flicker towards the bed and the man tied there as she spoke practiced words Diesel wouldn't dare test the validity of. If a woman said she was scared, it was his responsibility to protect her. Even if there was a good chance, as was in this case, she was just making it all up. She was playing him against his own cardinal rule he couldn't break.

He fetched his cell phone from the dresser and punched his brother's number. "Hey, Trent, I still have Paris in the ropes and I have a surprise arrival." There was a slight pause and he used it to narrow his eyes down on Chikako, who put on her best *I don't know what you are talking about face*. What a handful she was. "That would be the very one— thanks." He dropped his phone back on the dresser then turned to her, "I'll spank you for this later." He promised.

Diesel spotted the anger bubbling back up in Paris and returned to his side to buffer the intrusion. He sat on the edge of the bed and ran his fingers over the fallen angel's body, petting the beast down, hoping to undo the tightness that had his whole body tensing like a plucked guitar string. "Relax, as you can see, I am still with you, Paris." Diesel made note to point out he had not left the room. Mistakes would not be made this night.

Chikako stepped closer, "You keep him tied up all night?"

"I might have to. He thinks he's still in control. I have to break him of that."

"He seems very angry."

"Yep."

"You try break him?"

"Only his walls."

"What happen when he is broken?"

"I get inside."

"You need only to fuck me to get inside." Paris growled.

"He very scary. He the one you and Dominus call the Imp?"

"Among a few other fond titles, but yes. Only, don't be frightened by him— I'll have him purring like a kitten before long." And he was grateful when Trenton finally showed up to take Chikako back to her own room. He hadn't made too many strides with Paris as it was, and Chikako's presence had pretty much undone all of that when she showed up and disrupted their time. Now he had to start all over.

Chikako's interruption had eaten up a good amount of the time Diesel had hoped to have playing with the bound body, but the amount of time he could keep Paris tied was almost up. And now he had spent the last of that just trying to talk Paris back down from his anger.

With new intentions, he snatched the silk scarf they'd used to cover Paris' eyes earlier in the day, and he climbed up over Paris' body, straddling his thighs. Just the right spot where he could press against him and push Paris' hand, still bound to his hip, a little closer to his own cock. A tantalizing way to tease the beast. Diesel laid the scarf over Paris' cock then came down, catching his own body weight on his hands on either side of Paris' head before crashing down on his lips.

"I think I chose wisely, don't you?" Diesel finally asked, after ensuring he had Paris breathless again.

"What do you mean?"

"I told you to choose one of the three sensations, but when you could not, I chose for you."

"I'd still like to get the other two." Paris still held some reserve, not getting buttered up so easily the second round.

Diesel shifted his weight to one hand and reached down between them, took up the scarf and used it to rub a new sensation over Paris' body. "One of the greatest pleasures I get from a woman is her hair. She has to have long hair so I can wrap it around my cock and masturbate with it." Diesel used the scarf to mimic what he described. He loosely coiled the length of dyed silk around Paris' hard shaft, then closed his fingers around both and began to stroke him, keeping it wrapped in the soft fabric. "This is what it feels like to me."

"You know I'm not into women." Paris tensed.

"It's just a sensation."

"Get it off of me." He bit out the words.

"Paris, it's silk. It's a sensation, nothing more."

"And I told you, no women."

"Paris, look around you. There is no one here but you and me. I am sharing a sensation I enjoy by alternate means."

Paris let out a heavy breath through his nose, but his breath deepened from the stimulation, despite any attempts to resist.

"Look around."

"Okay, there isn't anyone here. What do you want from me?"

"I want you to trust that I won't violate you."

~ * ~

Paris let out a huff. He hadn't accused Diesel of that, at least not in words. But he knew, in his head, that the moment Chikako showed up and just now, with the mention of a woman's hair, that was exactly where his thoughts were.

"Does it feel good when I do this?"

Paris felt Diesel's tongue as it lapped across his chest, a slow, exotic exploration until it found the small manly nipple and flicked it, then licked at it heavily and finished it with a small pecking kiss. "Yes—" Paris hissed, "Fuck you, yes."

Diesel reached up and brushed Paris' lip with a thumb, a soft feathery touch at first, then added pressure, caressing it until he was tugging on the plumpness of Paris' bottom lip. And when Paris opened his mouth to kiss it, Diesel pushed his thumb in to play with his tongue for a brief moment, then smoothed the wetness from that caress to his lip for the final touch. "And when I do this?"

"Yes." And then Paris felt the silk cloth around his cock again, felt the pressure of the strong hand that manipulated it. He could not deny that the sensation was mind-boggling. It felt so damn good, like floating in softness without losing any of the friction needed to come to his peak.

"Then say it, Paris. Tell me if it feels good."

"Yes." He gasped, but the confession itself was painful. As if he'd betrayed himself with the admission.

"Shhh— I got you, Paris. There's nothing wrong with feeling something wonderful. There is no real pain in that, only lies we've told ourselves."

Paris didn't see it that way and never allowed himself to feel it either. He kept all those experiences securely locked out. Only, Diesel had every intention of getting in— even if it meant burning Paris' locked house down, he was getting in. The first crack coming in the form of a soft kiss, rewarding Paris' admission. Soft and tender. No lust, just tenderness. Only assurance.

~ * ~

It was clear Paris wasn't going to let it go so easily. So it was time to break out the feathers: a short, fly swatter made of duck down. He soon had Paris writhing violently under him, which was kinda fun.

"No, stop." Paris protested and tried to jerk away from the approaching feathers.

"But I am having fun and dare I say, you might be smiling."

"I am not—" the last word getting bit out between clenched teeth. Then the next feather assault went trailing down Paris' side and the burst of laughter got away. "Stop— stop— I mean it."

But Diesel wasn't listening. The grin fighting to escape from Paris was too tempting to let it get away. His fallen angel had the most beautiful white teeth— perfection, like everything else about him, and Diesel wanted to see them revealed and beaming at him. So he twirled the duster over

Paris' belly a few times more and then traced his cock with it.

"Dammit, Diesel, ouch!"

"Ouch?" Diesel laughed, "Ouch is not a safe word."

"Can I use my safeword?"

"I didn't give you a safeword, so no."

"You know, I could have you brought up on charges to the review board and have your membership revoked."

Diesel stopped and gave Paris a speculative look, "On what grounds?"

"All resort submissives and slaves have the right to use a safeword, and any dominating personnel not respecting their safewords risk being placed under review and the membership revoked."

"Even though I'm on the board."

"Yes, even."

"You wouldn't."

Paris gave him a smug look.

"Why, you little brat." Diesel sat back on his heels on the bed, but not retreating just yet, "Okay, then use your safeword."

Paris twitched then, "I don't know what my safeword is."

"Then use the universal ones, like the resort and I always use. Red, Yellow, and Green."

Paris licked his lips, clearly unsure of his next move, "What happens if I say red?"

"We stop. I untie you and apply your aftercare until you feel safe again, then you'll be free to go."

There was another twitch, "And if I say yellow?"

"We pause and talk about why the feathers scare you, then you give me a green to proceed or a red to call it quits."

Paris nibbled on his lip thoughtfully, still not answering.

Checkmate. "Come on, Paris, use your safeword." Diesel goaded him. He deserved it, after all, for trying to challenge him this way.

Just then there was a knock on his door, and Trenton called from the other side, "*Dinner time, don't make me wait for you two.*"

Paris' eyes lit up with a sinister gleam, "Ha, it's dinner time."

"Your answer." Diesel pushed.

"Green."

Another knock came from the door, "*Let's go, we have guests joining us tonight.*"

Diesel let out a disgruntled huff, having been thwarted, but still ran the feathers down each of Paris' sides, which resulted in a loud howl from Paris before Diesel hopped up to set him free from the ropes. "Brat."

~ * ~ * ~ * ~ * ~ * ~

Once dinner was complete, guests still lingered, enjoying the resort's servant-slaves and entertainers while nibbling on tidbits of succulent tapas dishes served out along the banquette tables. The eye candy of bodies took their places, some lifted onto the tables while others took up spots on ottomans or posed on any one of the four-by-four vanity stages. They were all dressed in variations of Grecian robes or sarongs, and some were barefooted, some wore soft-soled sandals. Urns filled with oils for play and decanters of wine were passed around, as well as the platters of finger food to assist the guests to relish the scene of erotic antiquity.

In the center of it all, suspended over a table of decadent desserts, was Chikako. Sea blue and green braids of rope bound her arms in a stack of loops behind her back, while more of the same colored ropes mixed with sandy cream were used to create an intricate saddle that kept her webbed into a fixed kneeling position. Diesel had kept her covered in a silk kimono while he wove the cords around her. Once he had the aesthetically pleasing design finished in a torso-harness that accentuated her small breasts, he pushed the collar edges of her kimono open, letting it drape off her shoulders. With a bit more tugging of it aside between the rope coils, he exposed a single breast in a provocative wardrobe slip. The final touch was a cascade of seashell strands that dangled from her neck haphazardly. She made the perfect exotic centerpiece from the Far East and completely untouchable for guests.

Paris seemed distant the whole time they ate, and he kept his eyes shifted away, looking far off; even long after their dinner. Something that would have not been thought as good behavior, if Paris had been trained to be a true submissive. But Paris was not Diesel's true slave or submissive, and Diesel had to remind himself of that.

One of the island's servant-slaves attending the banquet returned with shots of platinum tequila for him and his brother, then knelt down at Diesel's feet.

Paying little mind to the slave doing what was expected of him, Diesel was about to turn his drink up when he felt Paris lean away and *that* caught his attention, because Paris *never* did that. Most times, once Paris was allowed to get his arms around Diesel, a person would not likely be able to run even a line of dental floss between them.

He set his drink back down and glanced over his shoulder at Paris. "I'm tired of your eyes wandering away when they should be on me."

Paris snapped around, but it wasn't lust burning in those eyes. Rather, they seemed dead, like doll's eyes. Paris was hiding something. Diesel glanced down to the slave at his feet. The very one Paris had wanted to purchase at the Elysian Auction. Paris had even gone through great lengths to have an increased purchase budget approved so he could win this one. Present company in view, Diesel wasn't sure how he felt about it, and he wasn't sure he wanted to find out. He reached down and traced the man's lip with a finger, "I may have you and this one suck me off while I go to sleep tonight." He told Paris.

Paris didn't answer.

Hmmm— Diesel contemplated the closed reaction from Paris. "Climb up on the table and pose for me, Paris." He turned to lock eyes with him to make sure he knew he was being serious, then followed it up with a perusing glance of Paris' hard physique made all the more ready in the black mesh shirt and second skin black PVC boy shorts he wore.

"Yes, Patronus." The lifeless expression on Paris' face seemed to soften and bore some new life under Diesel's wandering gaze as he pushed up from his chair.

"Wait." Diesel stood, pulling the scarf from the table. "Put this back on."

Paris turned to face him, and his last vision was of Diesel before the black silk was placed over his eyes and tied just as it had been earlier in the day. Sealing the need for his control to be surrendered over, even while being guided up on the table.

Without even being given any further orders, Paris sucked in a deep breath, lifted his shoulders, then took a stance like a Roman soldier on gate sentry duty. *A living breathing statue of a sexual god.* A light twitch in his leg and the corded muscles popped out enough to make every tongue in the courtyard wish to lick them.

Diesel felt the growl build inside him, wishing Paris would just drop all the walls so they could get on with some of the sexual tension they both needed to release. But no matter how much his cock ached to get inside Paris' body, he would not step past that threshold until after he'd gotten inside Paris' heart walls.

He reclaimed his chair at the end of the table and relaxed back, just enjoying his new table display. He retrieved his tequila and turned it up, letting the clean white liquor settle on his tongue before sliding down. Except when he reached for his chasers, he noticed his drink hadn't come with any. The hot sauce his brother was so fond of he could live without, but not without the limes. Especially with the new brand they were drinking these days. They'd picked up a bottle of Fortaleza Tequila earlier this year; it came off with a sweet-yet-spicy hit to the pallet that finished off briny like a salted glass rim, which was why sipping this one without a citrus chaser was just sacrilegious. "Tell me slave, did you forget the limes?" Diesel asked.

The blond snapped his eyes up, growing wide when he saw he'd made a mistake. "Yes, Patronus. I'm so sorry. I will go get some now." He jumped to his feet, finishing with a light bow of his head.

"Bring another round, and one for Dominus as well."

"Yes, Patronus."

"Might I ask?" The question was sparked behind him.

Diesel turned to see Pyotr leaning in towards him with a concerned look, not his usual amused one. "Have you had the young resort slave with you long today?

"Just during our meals so far."

"Play with him much?"

"Not really." Diesel shook his head, not thinking it was important, then returned his gaze to Paris, still standing guard on the table, "Just letting him serve me while I playfully torment Paris some more." Diesel tore his eyes from Paris to glance at Pyotr, "You want to borrow him?"

~ * ~

Pyotr studied the features of Diesel's face, then back to Paris up on the table and to what lengths Paris strained to capture every nuance and sound made from Diesel and those around him. He finally shook his head curtly, "No. Though I agree you should lend him out to someone else." Pyotr leaned over beyond his armrest, drew closer to Diesel then continued, using the back of his hand to guard his words from carrying, "If you truly wish to win Paris over, you'll have to clear out some clutter to make room for him."

"What do you mean?" Diesel's voice took a defensive tone.

"Relax, I am only trying to shed some light where needed." Pyotr nodded to him, then shifted his gaze to Paris so Diesel would follow, "Paris is very taken with you, but he won't come to you if you're preoccupied with another. More than anything, he fears he's nothing more than someone you like toying with. It's already hard enough he doesn't know how to give into his feelings, but he most definitely won't even try to surrender to them if you're just going to dump him again."

"I have no intentions of dumping him. I'm here to make him mine."

"Not in his eyes, and he's the one you have to win over. He's the one you have to convince." Pyotr paused, waiting for Diesel to look him in the eye, "The only way to do that is to clear your life for him to join you. Paris is a big man with an even bigger vanity. He needs a lot of space to occupy. He needs to know that while you may own him, he owns all your time and space."

~ * ~

Diesel snapped his attention from Pyotr to the man still displayed on the table. Ignoring even the small dish of quartered limes being offered with a fresh new glass of the platinum tequila from the returned slave.

He could read Paris' body and knew the fallen angel was zeroed in on him. Paris had done it since this began. Paris didn't look for anyone, just Diesel.

Diesel leaned over, eyes still locked on Paris— watched him— but directed his soft spoken command to the slave, who waited, on his knees, next to him. "Tell me, slave, so I may hear, what is it you would like to do, so that you may serve me?"

The man gasped, but Diesel still didn't look. "Patronus, I would do whatever you ask of me for your pleasure."

There it was. Paris' shoulders and the tendons along his neck tensed, and now Diesel could see they'd already been worked into knots. He glanced back down at the blond, then across the courtyard to the little Asian woman caught up in his ropes. Paris hadn't been distracted— he'd felt brushed off. Diesel leaned forward toward the slave again, but still watched Paris, "Very good, you are dismissed for now."

The man nodded, got up, and left as commanded. There was the faintest tilt in Paris' head. He was following the slave's footsteps. That was when Diesel saw the relaxed movement as it melted over Paris' body.

"Do you see what I see?" Pyotr asked directly, a soft tone muting his words from inquisitive ears.

"Yes. I do. Thank you." Diesel's thoughts were already well under way on how to correct this issue. He glanced over to Trenton, who was whispering his naughty nightcaps into Katianna's ear while they watched two women on one of the vanity stages undress each other as they danced. Diesel wasn't sure which filled him with more wicked decadence: Trenton and the perfect Unicorn, or the memory of Paris stripping down for him. But certainly the vision from his past had Diesel sucking in a deep breath. His teeth found his upper lip and pulled it in for the tip of his tongue to play with as he rearranged his plans concisely so he was clear on what he needed to do. *Very well*, he thought, he'd change their course, but it wasn't going to be a subtle announcement. Nor would he be the only one to speak the new rule.

It was also time to step up the plans to hand Chikako over to her new Master. "Dominus." He waited until his brother looked his way, "Could you send word to Mr. Sakimoto to meet with us tonight?"

"No acclimation period?"

"We've known him for a long time. No acclimation might protect him from Chikako summing up his soft spots too soon."

Trenton chuckled, "He'll fare a better chance of staying the Dom this way."

~ * ~

Katianna's entire body was already lit with a glowing warmth from her Dominus' attentive fingers and illicit words. One of his fonder play times, *second only to tormenting her.* A pastime he enjoyed.

"I want you to be up on the table next to Paris while I go speak with Master Sakimoto." He whispered against the shell of her ear, then kissed it to whisper more, "And I want you to drive Patronus crazy."

Another shiver seemed to ripple through her body to arrive in her cheeks as a soft blush and she nodded, letting Trenton see her *I'd be happy to* smile. She owed him as much after her cold shoulder retreat earlier in the day.

He was up out of his chair next, sweeping her up in his arms. He carried her over to the banquet table and used her dangling feet to sweep a number of dishes and decor off before setting her down on top of the table, then eased her back so her head landed between Paris' leather, shin-high motocross boots.

~ * ~

Trenton had been enjoying his playing with Kat, but Diesel's request was a good move, so he would do what was necessary to see it done. It was time his brother and his pet stopped prancing about, with more back-stepping than either were willing to acknowledge. It seemed inviting Pyotr to join them had been an excellent move on top of enjoying his company. Despite all his eloquence and professionalism, Pyotr had a perversion that could give both him and Deez a run for their money. *He did, very much, like having that man around.*

Trenton eased his mouse down on the table. She glanced up, getting a naughty view of the endowed package between Paris' legs and let out a giggle, but just as quickly wiped the smile away, "Sorry, Dominus."

He chuckled, "No, you're not." He then wagged a warning finger up at Paris, though he knew the blindfolded Imp couldn't see it. "Step on her and I will take my cane to those tender legs of yours."

"Not my ass, Dominus?" The energetic brat asked with more bravado than he should have. But it would seem the dismissal of the slave had empowered the man's confidence. Something Trenton never thought could have possibly been overshadowed in this man. "Your ass I will leave for Patronus' heavy hand."

"Apologies, Dominus." Paris' quick reality check of just what he was inviting showed like all his other emotions did. *He was still a sight to watch come unraveled and then put back together.*

Trenton let out a chuckle, finding it amusing, then winked at his brother, only to see a similar twinkle in Pyotr's eyes. *That man found pleasure in everything.* They exchanged an all-knowing smile, then Trenton left to meet with the man who would, in just a few hours, become the proud, and perhaps even cursed, owner of Chikako. But before Trenton was out of range he called a command over his shoulder. "Now, mouse." He didn't bother to look as he kept on, for he knew she would spread her legs out wide— and the husky curse he heard coming from Diesel said it'd been worth it.

~ * ~ * ~ * ~ * ~ * ~

CHAPTER SEVEN

~ * ~ * ~ * ~ * ~ * ~

DAY TWO: PARIS' SURRENDER

"Give me your hand." Diesel stood in the doorway at the front entrance of their modern architect island home with a rather smug smile on his face.

"Why? What are you going to do with it?"

"Just give me your hand and trust me."

Paris narrowed his eyes at him— not a drop of trust was in them. "That's just it, I *don't* trust you."

"I know. Which is why this is important. Now stop fussing and give me your hand before I change my mind and tie it behind your back."

"Answer the question, first."

Diesel glanced up at the ceiling and bit his tongue as he counted to ten. *God, could he be any more stubborn?* Diesel thought to himself after he reached twelve. He wiped his face with the back of his hand as he lowered his gaze back to Paris. "To hold it."

"Excuse me?"

"I want to hold your hand. It's a simple pleasure. No bondage involved, and no sex."

"I prefer the sex to stay in."

"Paris."

~ * ~

Paris remained reluctant, but reached his hand out, and Diesel clasped their fingers together and did just that. Held his hand. Before long, Diesel's thumb strummed up and down one of his fingers in a slow, thoughtless caress.

Paris remained suspicious, never let down his guard as he waited for the trap to be sprung. But there was no trap. Diesel spent the full afternoon leading Paris around by the hand. A late breakfast near the pool, then down to the beach for a swim and some sun, deliberately keeping it casual. Demonstrating— he supposed— of what an average day could be like for them, and that it wasn't all about sex or scenes. Though Paris was still hung up on the part where there wasn't *any* sex going on so far, and he thoroughly disagreed with Diesel's— *whatever he wanted to call it*. Nevertheless, Diesel stayed focused on Paris, trying to keep a light mood or, at best, a smile on his face. Only on occasion did he let his eyes wander, and then only to watch his brother threaten to dunk Katianna under the waves for splashing him.

~ * ~

It was definitely good to see those two smiling and laughing, Diesel thought. Trenton especially. Even with Kat's nightmares finally subsiding, his brother had taken a turn for the worse lately. Since Trofim's attack, actually. It bothered Diesel to no end. But for now, Trenton seemed to have been freed from his shadows and Diesel took delight in basking in it as well— with Paris, in whose arms he was presently leaning back against as they sat in the warm sand, and using Paris' hand to pleasure himself with. Because there was only so much platonic Diesel could take at one time.

He hadn't intentionally meant to look, but watching his brother, and the woman they both loved, being free and having a good time laughing, was a huge turn on. The only thing that could make it better was what he already had wrapped around him. *Paris.* And that just made it too much stimulation to turn away. The next thing he knew, he'd pushed his swim trunks down and was pulling Paris' hand over to tend to his rising needs, knowing full well Paris would not reject the unbidden command.

Diesel let out a long sigh and surrendered his body to the sensations. Then he reached up with his left arm, captured Paris by the neck and pulled him down to him, "Come here." Diesel growled under his breath just as their mouths collided, and Diesel pushed in to steal a salacious amount of tongue. Wide open and full on— Paris met him every time. He didn't have to hold back anything. The rest of his blood flowed south, filling his massive cock.

He felt Paris' grip tighten, picking up speed and igniting him even further. He broke from their kiss and let out a tight growl again, "Dammit, I can't wait to fuck you."

"We can do that right now. No waiting to be seated."

Diesel let out a laugh, "Not yet." He dropped his head forward onto Paris' shoulder and let out a heavy breath, "But don't you dare stop doing what you're doing now."

~ * ~

Paris didn't stop, but if this was all he was going to get right now, then he wasn't going to race Diesel to the finish line. With the blond dismissed and the Asian girl gone, he now had Diesel to himself. Yet, little else had changed, so Paris wasn't trusting that all was good or what his heart was hoping for. He just couldn't seem to get his heart to shut the fuck up about it either. So once again he was here, hopelessly hoping. So he might as well get some fun out of it too. It was his only defense mechanism.

He changed up his positon, slackened his grip around the thick cock, and began to massage it instead, using the heel of his palm to squeeze, then slide down and up again with glancing touches. Taunting him, like the feather Diesel had tortured him with yesterday. When Diesel's hips came rising up off the sand between his legs, pitching into his hand further, Paris gave him another rep or two of tight-fisted rapid strokes and a good flex over the mushroom cap.

Diesel was suddenly twisting around, hopping over his legs and dropping down in the sand. He caught Paris' arm and pulled him over with him, so he landed on an elbow and his side, stretched out beside him.

Paris didn't have much time to think before he was back inside Diesel's kiss, devoured in a way that invited him to cut loose. But Paris had greater access to his Patronus' body now and that knowledge took front stage in his mind— and his attentive hand.

Diesel's head fell back to the sand; he let out a heavy groan while Paris continued to pump his cock with the alacrity of an ironmonger stoking a bellows. Paris moistened his lips when all nine inches long and three inches wide stood straight up on its own virility and in all its tumescent glory.

"Beautiful," Paris whispered heatedly, slapping the lively erection so it bounced several times. A few more playful strokes of nothing more than a few fingers, brushing down the underside against the frenum, until the bulbous glans was swelling to an engorged, dark red cap. Paris knew there was no more play time, now he needed to finish his man off and quickly bent over Diesel, taking the thick cock into his mouth. There wasn't time to work his mouth to stretch out to take him, so for now Paris delivered all tongue and lips to lick and slide over the shaft that was already exuding signs it was near ready to explode.

"Fuck—" Diesel hissed, then Paris felt Diesel's hands on his shoulders, encouraging him to keep going. As much as he hated closing his eyes on the view, he did and then just lost himself in the sensation of having his favorite meal on his tongue once again. He relished the stretch in his checks due to Diesel's thickness, and soon he felt the powerful pulse against the flat of his tongue— followed by the first of several warm shots of cum to the back of his throat.

Paris let out a heated moan that vibrated against the flesh of the pulsing shaft as he swallowed down his prize. It was met with several more curses— along with *his* name.

~ * ~ * ~ * ~ * ~ * ~

After dinner, Diesel had Paris strapped down on the chaise lounge after it'd been relocated into the pool. His hands were tied behind the back of the chaise and his eyes once again covered by the silk blindfold. Making it all the more erotic to his preference for eye candy, Diesel instructed Paris to change into a crisp white, singlet tank and faded denim jeans. Paris came back wearing a pair that was embellished with a number of frayed holes that allowed tanned flesh to peek past strands of worn white threads.

The jeans had been a definite surprise to find in Paris' pristine wardrobe of top of the line fashion clothing. Regardless of whether Paris actually ever wore them or not, seeing him in the tattered garb now was mouthwatering, to say the least. Even the beautiful island-tanned skin of his abs that showed between the rolled-up hem of the white tank and faded blue denim was having an effect on his control. It was the contrast of color, not to mention the succulent skin. Looking at Paris' body, lazily relaxed back, while the water in the pool lapped up to soak his legs and darken the denim, was too fucking sexy to look at and not touch.

Diesel waded into the shallow end, fully clothed, and sat down on the edge of the lounger where Paris had a leg up and the other dropped down over one side. Diesel reached and undid his fallen angel's fly and opened the denim up to find the arched curve of his cock swelling inside the confines of his boxer briefs. Pale pink. He bit back his laughing surprise. *The man always looked good in pink.*

Diesel pushed his hand up the ripple of abs, holding back the need to lick them, savoring the moment when he planned on taking every part of this man and making him his forever. He pulled his hand back until the side of his thumb grazed the curve of Paris' erection.

"Deez?"

"Shhh, I just want to touch you for a while." He was hitting a return ball to Paris for what he'd gotten earlier out on the beach. Only with Paris, Diesel called the shots about how long this was going to last. He could draw it out as long as he wanted, work Paris' cock up, then just sit back and stare at it until it started to lean over, going flaccid. But Diesel had other plans this time.

Last night he had handed Chikako over to her new master. And he had taken Paris with him to witness her departure. The act itself was to show Paris that everyone else was being removed from Diesel, all but Paris. But whatever feelings Paris had about last night, he managed to hide them well.

The young receiver of the Unicorn-sized geisha, however, didn't even try to hide his delight for the woman his father had just purchased for him and seemed quite taken with her instantly. Chikako seemed taken as well, and yet the glint in her dark eyes was too evident to deny she was going to be a handful for the young man. But she also looked happy, so it was a done deal.

Paris had, at least, relaxed considerably after that, but he still put up a fuss when they went to bed and Diesel made no move towards sex.

Tonight's plans were to make sure Paris was willing to turn away any outside temptation of his own.

Paris chewed at his bottom lip, hissing as Diesel's heavy hand stroked him. "Is this payback torture for out on the beach?"

"Does this really feel like torture?"

"Depends."

"On what?'

"The outcome."

"I have been overly burdensome in the teasing department, haven't I?"

"Yes." Paris didn't hesitate with that answer.

Diesel chuckled then ran his hands down the length of both of Paris' legs, imagining them wrapped around his waist like vice grips. "Well, don't hold back any aggressions on my account."

Paris jerked, but his arms caught on the chair and kept him in place, "Funny, seeing I don't recall me being the one who tied myself up." It was borderline sarcasm, but the layer of temptuousness was still there.

Diesel knew he was riding a thin line between doing what he needed to get inside Paris' walls of sex-defense and outright destroying it all with the very same act. "Then I suppose it's time for a change of pace." He pushed up on a knee and reached around Paris to pull the quick release cord to the coils of wrap that kept them tight, letting them unravel and fall into the pool. No sooner was Paris freed when his arms snapped around Diesel and exerted his strength to pull Diesel down for a kiss. "Easy, big guy. I have something else for you first." And he pulled from Paris' grasp, one that didn't let go so easily.

"Here is just fine. The only thing I want is for you to fuck me, right now, then maybe let me fuck you after."

"Trust me." Diesel whispered, then reached down, grabbing Paris by the wrist, and yanked him up to his feet. Their bodies slammed together, followed by their lips.

He almost wished he didn't have to bother, but he needed to know. Needed to be sure Paris was willing to give up everyone else for him. Without breaking their bond, he started walking backwards, his heels found the steps, and he slowly brought Paris with him as he stepped out of the pool and toward the house.

The accordion glass doors of the living room had been folded into the wall earlier, leaving the house wide open to the evening sun and fresh sea air. Waiting inside was the blond man he and Trenton had brought down with them. The very same slave he'd sent away last night as well as the one Paris had been eyeing to be his own personal distraction. Now it was time to see just how much Paris was willing to let go of and if he was even capable of being resistant to personal temptations.

Diesel led Paris inside, stopped just beyond the tracks of the sliding doors, and pressed him back against the wall, where he took time to finish the heated kiss between them and even took some pleasure in grinding against him, feeling the hard cock trapped in Paris' jeans. "Mmmm, I think it's time to let that bad boy out, don't you?"

"Yes-sss." Paris readily agreed while nibbling on Diesel's lips, not wanting to give those up too soon either. Their hands were impossible to track, each taking a life of their own to grip pec muscles, biceps, and shoulders. Then veering around for some ass groping and back again. Diesel managed to remember his plans and popped the last button to Paris' jeans, then pushed them and the briefs down far enough to gain full access to the dick straining to get out. But it didn't come easy as the wet denim fought him, with every inch, to hang on to Paris' body. *Couldn't blame them, really.* As soon as he had Paris' cock out, Diesel waved the waiting slave closer and gave the silent command for him to tend to Paris' aroused cock.

Diesel tore away from the kiss at the same moment and watched the pleasure ripple over Paris' face, noticeable even with the blindfold over his eyes.

"Ah, damn, I never thought I'd experience the day you'd go down on me." Paris groaned, his hand dropping to the head at his cock. But he froze up suddenly.

In a flash, Diesel felt Paris' entire body go rigid against him and he glanced down, seeing Paris' fingers feeling out the thick hair.

"What the fuck!" Paris shoved the head from him then tore the blindfold from his eyes, finding himself still eye to eye with Diesel.

Diesel pushed the slave's mouth back over Paris' cock, urging him to take all of Paris into his throat, and then Diesel leaned into both of them, keeping Paris pinned against the wall.

~ * ~

"Get him off of me." Paris gritted out in a desperate whisper, but his body was responding and he had to fight it.

"Isn't he the slave you wanted? The one you were willing to go outside the budget to have?"

"I don't want him."

"Who do you want, Paris?" Diesel leaned in until his breath washed over Paris' cheek.

Paris kept his eyes squeezed shut as he tried to prevent his physical reaction— and enjoyment— from the hot mouth wrapped around his cock.

He fought it, knew he shouldn't confess it, but he couldn't deny it any longer either. "I only want you."

"Anyone else?"

"NO." Paris slammed his head back against the wall, hoping the pain would quell everything else.

"Not even the Dominus?"

"That's a trick question." Paris threw the accusation back at him. "Since the two of you share everything."

"You're right it is, my apologies. But will you answer it?"

Paris sighed. He couldn't deny that one, but he'd only take Trenton as a pair. "If you brought him to our bed, I would not refuse, but you would have to be with me."

Diesel pulled the slave from Paris and guided him back. "Return to Blaine and tell him I said you've earned your pleasure. One of your choice."

"Thank you, Sir. I choose to serve Paris."

"Go now or I'll send word to have Blaine beat you instead." Diesel snapped at the slave. "Paris is mine. No one can have him." And he watched as the man left without further issue. Only— when Diesel turned his attention back to Paris, he was met with Paris' fist straight across his jaw.

Diesel took a step back, having been caught completely off guard. He shot an angry glare at Paris. "What the fuck was that?"

"MY FUCKING SAFEWORD!" Paris shouted at him.

"I didn't give you a safeword!"

"It doesn't matter! I'm calling red!" Paris would have done just about anything Diesel asked of him, except act as a pawn in one of his sexual games. Something inside him couldn't have handled the pain if this was all he was to Diesel— a puppet.

~ * ~

Diesel was about to belch out yet another argumentative statement but caught himself. There was valid pain expressed behind the anger in Paris' eyes—

And then he stormed out.

Oh hell no. This is not how it's going to go, he thought and started after him.

"Let him go!"

Diesel spun around, ready for a fight, glaring at the man who had dared to give him orders—

— *even if it was his brother.* But one look at Trenton's face and the fight drained from Diesel. Never in his life had he seen Trenton look at him with disappointment as he did now. "You need to stay out of this and let me handle him."

"Not if handling him means setting him up for entrapment."

"I just want to be sure he can commit!"

"To someone who has given him nothing? Why should he?"

Diesel sucked in a hard breath and bulked up with every intention of spitting out an answer— if he was able to come up with one.

"Like what?" Trenton snapped at him. "He still thinks you're just here for a soiree and you have given him no reason to think otherwise."

The accusations took the wind out of him; he stepped to the wall and bent over until his forehead rested against it. He raised a fist and banged his knuckles into the wall—

once and then again— letting his mind go numb, then angry because, like always, Trenton was right and he was fucking this up. The punches came harder— faster— harder until suddenly something caught his fist and held tight. Preventing the next contact with the wall.

"It's okay to make mistakes, but don't make the added mistake of ignoring those you do make, and then not correcting them." Trenton spoke calmly, standing at his side, then released his arm.

Diesel stayed surrendered to the wall, not sure he could take another look like the last from Trenton. He wanted Paris in his life in a way he'd never wanted anyone else. He'd never sought anyone out like this, or been turned on his own ear as he was now. "What the fuck am I supposed to do?"

"You want all the guarantees before the start. It doesn't work that way. Not for any of us. You have to start and risk that the guarantees might not come."

Diesel stood, finally backing away from the wall. Somewhere in those simple words he found some resolve, though he wasn't sure he'd pass if anyone dared test him on that. "So what should I do?"

"Start with correcting and then finishing what you started here tonight."

Safeword. It was the second time it had come up. Paris had safeworded on him and he needed to respect it. He also had to resolve as to why it happened, and make his apologies for it.

Diesel drew in a deep breath and glanced around Trenton, half expecting Katianna would be standing there as she always did. He could use one of her hugs right about now. "Mouse, tell me of—" he stopped when he realized she wasn't there. He glanced at Trenton then stepped past him towards the bedroom, but she wasn't there either. He snapped around and looked at his brother, "Where is she?"

~ * ~ * ~ * ~ * ~ * ~

Katianna slipped quietly along the path towards the staff quarters. She slowed to spy through the few windows that were open, but so far no Paris. She really wasn't sure which was his, only that she had seen him go this way before.

The path continued to wind along groomed shrubs and under palm trees that swayed in the breeze, leading her beyond the main quarters for the staff and servant slaves until it came to a tall wrought iron gate. She glanced at the key card reader, then bit her lip as she twisted around to peer out in the darkness behind her. "You are so going to get a spanking for this, you know that, don't you?" she mumbled to herself, knowing that even though she saw or heard no one, she was as good as caught. *When* was only a matter of time. "Better make it worth it then." She swiped her card through the slot. Luck was on her side when three green lights lit up and she heard the lock click free. She knew she needed to hurry, taking only an extra amount of time to close the gate gently to prevent any clanging, and continued on along the path. Of course, it didn't occur to her until after she closed the gate that while she didn't know where Paris lived, *they* most probably did.

There were only two resident choices out here at the beach. One was a considerably larger, full-size house. Far more than she would think Paris had been given, so she headed for the second. A rather exotic, but cute bi-level adobe with windows that encompassed nearly the full exterior walls that faced towards the sea. While it was hard to see every detail in the dark, she could still note the resemblance it had to Trenton's home. *It's your home, too*, he would have reminded her, if he was with her right now.

She came around to the front to get a look inside. There were only a few soft light sconces lit in the spacious living room. Enough for safe wandering about without stubbing a toe on an end table— as she was apt to do. But there was movement in the bedroom section that was only a couple of steps higher than the rest of the condo. She saw Paris sitting down on the bed, naked, with a drink in his hands, but he didn't seem to be drinking it.

"Okay, you found him, now what?" She twisted up her lips and tried to think of something. She patted her hip for her phone, then realized she was in her nighty and it didn't come accessorized with pockets. She hadn't thought this through, obviously. She'd only known that whenever she crawled away to her hole to hide, there was no reaching her there. She needed to be lured out. And then she left while Trenton was preoccupied with Diesel.

She glanced around and found a few pebbles scattered near her feet, grabbed a few, and took aim.

Tink, tink—

The first two rocks hit somewhere, just not quite *there*. So she tried again.

Poink, tink—

"Dammit, you throw like a girl." She growled to herself as those skittered over the roof. But determined, she tried again.

Claink—

Bulls-eye! It hit the glass walls of the bedroom and the man inside snapped his head up.

Katianna took a few steps back, hoping to be in view, when suddenly a motion sensor light on the footstone of the front steps flickered on, bathing her in light. "Oops." She fidgeted, glancing around lest Trenton came looking too soon and ruined it before she managed to actually accomplish something.

So far, so good, and she glanced back to the bedroom, only Paris wasn't in it any longer. Then she saw him moving through the living room, having pulled on a pair of white, flowing lounge pants. *Damn, he looked hot.* She filed the view away for a book description then turned and darted off for the sound of surf not too far away.

When she reached the beach, she tromped through the moonlit sand and came to a stop at the water's edge, never daring to step into the dark, murky ocean. It was only a few minutes later when Paris showed up at her side.

"Kat? You okay?"

She stood silent a moment, just staring out into the water, watching how the surface rippled with the warning that monsters were hiding just under it. Some said the ocean was beautiful, and during the day she would often agree. However, at night, she couldn't because she only saw things she was terrified of.

"What scares you, Paris?" She saw him shrug out the corner of her eyes.

"Nothing, I suppose." He turned and looked at her, "What about you?"

Kat kept her eyes out there, watching and feeling the fear rising up to grip her. "Everything."

"There's nothing here to be afraid of."

"You're wrong." Memories of a night when she clung to her best friend on the back of an overturned canoe while sharks, drawn to the scent of blood that dripped from a cut, had circled around them. The images haunted her and played tricks on her eyes, making her see dark fins break the surface of the very water she stared out at. "There is always something to be afraid of. No matter where we go." Her eyes stayed glued out there, watching and waiting to see the fins again, if only to prove to herself the fear was justified.

"There are also many good things that keep you safe here too, Katianna."

She sucked in a deep breath, picking up the smell of the salty sea, of night jasmines and— of a favorite men's cologne that paired well with the sand notes perfectly. She smiled because of it. "I know. But I think you may have forgotten that yourself, right now." She turned to him finally and gave him a warm smile. "It's scary, but there is no safer place to land." The puzzled look he gave her said he didn't get it, but time was up. The cologne she smelled was Trenton's and he'd come for her.

"Jump." She whispered her advice and then turned away, leaving her past, filled with fear, to lurk away in the water without her, as she headed across the sand to the towering man who stood like a pillar, waiting on her.

~ * ~

Jump.

The very word hit a cord in him and he snapped around to say something, only to find Diesel standing there. Solid as a rock, but with an apologetic expression on his face. Paris hardened, but fought the urge to step off in another direction.

"Paris, I owe you an apology."

"No, what you owe me is some hardcore sex."

"No, I don't." Diesel stepped closer, only Paris countered with a step back. "But what I do owe you is some security that I am not trying to play a game with you. I want to have something more than just a piece of ass."

"I offered you all of my ass, not just a piece of it." Pain hit him— hit his heart. There *was* something he was afraid of and he was looking right at him. Only Paris didn't know how to deal with pain, so he did what came next, letting his anger come back up from earlier to take care of the rest. If there was no sex being offered, there was no sense for the rest. He turned and marched off, back to his condo to finish off the drink he'd left there.

"Paris, please." Diesel called after him and began to follow. "You safeworded, now let me fix that!"

Paris didn't bother trying to outrun him, perhaps some part of him wanted Diesel to follow him, but he still kept out of arm's reach.

"Hard limits?!" Diesel called to him just as Paris reached the front door to his place.

It took Paris a moment for the question to register. He was pissed and hurt. He was fighting, not actually considering rules, or limits, or that having called a safeword would actually get him Diesel's attention in a way that he could say what he felt inside— *sorta*. He hadn't actually safeworded either, it just sounded good at the moment. A fist-in-the-face was exactly what it had been.

He stood at the door, chest heaving. He wasn't ready to back down, but as he looked back at the man awaiting a reply, Paris saw he also wasn't being pushed for it. There was concern rather than anger, regret rather than pride—

"Hard limits." Diesel repeated the request for Paris.

Paris took a deep breath. "No more pushing others on me. I am perfectly capable of getting laid on my own if I want. Just not by you, it would seem. But it's not why I agreed to be with you this week. No more slaves, no more servants. Just you."

Diesel nodded, "Anything else?"

Paris looked him over. Diesel was all Dom, now. The *Patronus* instead of *Deez*, but Paris needed that part of him to be within reach if he was to go through with this, "That part you said to the slave? What you said—"

"About having Blaine beat him?"

"No, the other part. I want to hear you say it again, only say it *to* me this time."

Diesel took a step towards him, "You are mine. No one can have you." Diesel growled the words softly, but with a tone of no contestation. He took another step, then came up the steps, his hand coming up, catching Paris by the neck and holding him. Diesel leaned in and kissed his jaw, working his way down his neck with wet sensual kisses, "And I am yours."

Paris' eyes floated closed and already he was giving in. *Dammit, not yet. Not yet— not fucking yet!* And he pulled away from Diesel, his back landing on the door still partially opened from rushing out to catch up with Katianna, *which was just as out of sorts as this was*, "No others?"

~ * ~

Diesel caressed the side of Paris' face with the full cup of his hand to dispel the panic he tried to hide. "It's okay. I'm not going to force you to be touched by anyone else ever again." He leaned in with a gentle press and kissed Paris, mirroring his soft touch of Paris' cheek.

"You can't even talk about it or threaten me with it. I don't like it."

Pyotr had even warned him and he'd still done it all wrong. "No threats." Diesel agreed, realizing how badly he really had fucked up and leaned in to see if Paris would allow him another kiss.

"Except maybe Trenton?" Paris asked weakly, blocking the effort being made to restore the kiss.

The very exception caused a chuckle in Diesel. "Except maybe Trenton." He agreed and tried to kiss him again.

Paris stiffened suddenly and turned away, taking a step back to distance them. He shook his head, but it wasn't just rejection written on his face, but bewilderment, as if everything wasn't making sense.

Damn, but this man was far more complex than he had anticipated, "What is it, Paris?"

"You're asking for some commitment and saying you won't push anyone on me, but what about you? I'm not interested in being tied to your stages or pool lounges while someone else takes care of your needs. I don't get pleasure watching that— seeing you with others."

"There won't be any others for me either, Paris."

"How? Doesn't that go against being the Patronus?"

"Because there is someone else already meant for me. And that's who I want to concentrate on."

Paris turned away to hide the flash of inner pain, but Diesel hoped he'd ask. He wanted Paris to ask so he could tell him the answer, and he nearly sighed with relief when the question finally came.

"Who?" Paris whispered in the dark, not allowing himself to look in Diesel's direction.

Diesel held the answer, "Paris? Look at me." He waited as Paris turned to face him, "It's you."

~ * ~

Everything in Paris' mind screeched to a halt. He shook it off as this was just for this week, nothing more. Diesel couldn't possibly have meant what his heart was racing in hopes that it meant. Just for the week, but if that was all he could have, he wanted Diesel to himself. "No others?"

Diesel shook his head, "No others."

Paris returned to Diesel's arms and lowered his head into his neck, "Except maybe a mouse."

There was a hard sigh— *not relief*— and then the press of Diesel's head against his cheek before the answer came, "Except maybe a mouse."

But before Paris could question the saddened tone behind the answer, Diesel was over him, kissing him— silencing him.

Paris had never shared a soft and tender kiss with Diesel before. How strange it felt, but it made him melt inside. Suddenly, they were moving. One hand still holding his head, the other steering his hips, and walking him backwards into his home, then up the three steps leading to his open-spaced bedroom.

When the backs of his knees hit the bed, Diesel slowly lowered him down on it, following him in the very same motion. The chaste kisses that dotted his face and neck stripped him of his angst and resistance. If he had ever had any. Something deep inside him was changing, sensing a feeling or emotion he had never even looked for in a man. While Diesel was the cause for the emotional storm that raised hell inside him, he was now also the shield that coveted him from it.

Paris twisted more, coming around so he could kiss Diesel deeper, and was suddenly locked in his arm's embrace, holding him against his body. Their kiss deepened, and

Diesel held his weight up with one arm while the other clasped onto his shoulder, drawing him against his body.

Paris wanted to feel more of it as if to reassure his mind that this was *his* Diesel. The same man who knew how to fuck him into oblivion. His hands went up, stroking the hard rolls of Diesel's chest— felt out the taut muscles in the arms that held him with fierce abandon. *Yes, this was his Diesel and, oh god, was he in trouble. If being separated from him hurt bad enough last time, so help him, he was going to die after this, because he was falling helplessly in love with Deez.*

They spent the night together there. Diesel rubbed against Paris' body until they both burned for each other, drowning in each other's kissing and touching, bringing them both to near explosive releases. Yet, Diesel still withheld that part. Except, for the first time, Paris enjoyed the intimate frotting and didn't fuss over it— *not much, that is*.

~ * ~ * ~ * ~ * ~ * ~

CHAPTER EIGHT

~ * ~ * ~ * ~ * ~ * ~

DAY THREE

Paris was just finishing up his shower and not the least bit surprised when he saw fresh clothes had already been set out for him. A pair of tan and white rayon Pistol Pete lounge pants with a drawstring waist and a pale pink button-up shirt. Laid out on top of them was a pair of eggshell colored boxer briefs with large white block letters that spelled out D-I-E-S-E-L across the waist band. *Not in the least bit suggestive.*

The man who had selected them, however, was nowhere to be seen. Paris left the clothes untouched and defiantly strode out and into the open design kitchen to pour a cup of his morning coffee— completely naked. Half expecting to find Diesel there, he found it empty and only his French press, submerged in a pot of hot water that sat on the stove top, waiting on him. *At least the big beast remembered something about him.* He poured his coffee and leaned back on the counter, contemplating his thoughts. They hadn't even begun to settle enough for him to figure out which way was north. But perhaps one day of fighting with Diesel was enough. So he set his mug down and returned to his room to dress in exactly what Diesel had picked out for him.

"Strip for me."

The deep resonating tone of a man filled with desire came up behind Paris just as he had closed the buttons on his sleeve cuffs. He looked, finding Diesel coming up the steps to his room. "You laid out clothes for me. I thought—"

"Yes. Thank you." Diesel came over to the bed and made himself comfortable after propping up a few pillows against the headboard, "Now I want to watch you take them off."

Paris knew well how to play this game, perhaps better than his lover was expecting from him. It wasn't the first time Diesel had ordered him to strip, but then they were orders to get naked and nothing more. This time he said he wanted to watch, so Paris gave him something to watch.

Paris took a step toward the wall and leaned back on it, then slowly pulled the pink shirt up just high enough to allow a glimpse of his rippling abs underneath. He understood the sensual contrast of the pastel against dark tan skin and he used it to its full effect. He sauntered his hips in a slow dipping roll, matched to a sultry tune as if music began to play in the room, moving until he managed to get the drawstrings dangling in front of his cock to swing back and forth a few times, then letting the shirt fall back in place. He watched himself, slowly bringing his hands up as if he were modeling his hands for a fashion show and began to undo the buttons— one at a time— and with all the provocative flare he had.

He didn't look at Diesel; rather, he watched himself, looked down his body, as he slipped one hand under his shirt and rubbed against his chest muscles while the other hand finished off the last few buttons, then joined in feeling up his body before pushing his shirt open to the edges of his shoulders, opening the view to his chest for Diesel to see. Then, with both hands, he eased his touch down his chest, down his stomach to his loungers, and then began to pull the ends of the draw cord free. He licked his lips, anticipating the pleasure he was about to have, and dropped the heel of one hand to deliver some pressure to the bulge already forming under the slinky soft, rayon fabric. When the tent began to form, he pushed the waistband of his pants down, revealing his hard shaft pressing out through his briefs.

The whole thing was a seamless act of eroticism, undressing without the entertainment of a show. Just slow motions of his hands as they brushed his clothes from their proper placement to reveal his body, one tantalizing square inch at a time. Never glancing up once to see if Diesel was turned on by it. Paris knew damn well he was.

Then Paris turned it up a notch and began a full on performance of an ad-libbed version of a choreographed scene that looked far more like having sex against the wall than anything else. His pants hanging precariously on his hip knots while he held them at varying points, letting them slip down a little further at one side, and then the other, before pulling them back up. Beautiful yet masculine, slowly revealing the most wonderful body— *his.* If the act of stripping was impressive, then the body he revealed was extraordinary.

Here, in the flesh, everything was real – big meaty pecs and bulging biceps, hard, ripped abs without an ounce of fat– a chiseled back and perky bubble butt. The whole effect devoid of body hair to highlight his perfection. And he knew how to move every riveting detail like a lover should.

"Oh shit, Paris." The hissed words came from the bed, drawing Paris' attention away from himself to take in the view of yet another perfect body. For Diesel clearly was perfection on a completely different level. Arms thick with undefined muscles and broad shoulders. Each covered in military motif ink work. One of those arms was busily attached to the most beautiful cock Paris had ever laid eyes on. Diesel's chest swelled with a deep inhale, and Paris took note of the rest of Diesel's tattoos. Two old fashion-style sparrows, one to each side under his collar bones. And just under them, three stars of various sizes mirrored on each side of his chest.

Diesel's nipples were a feature all to themselves. Dark flat disks circled his small nipples, beckoning Paris to come play with them, making his tongue water. One of them was even pierced with a small barbell. Below the candy, and in perfect contour to Diesel's pec muscles, was writing under each. Paris couldn't remember what they said, but it was something about protecting those he loved.

Diesel Gentry was a soldier— a guardian through and through and a man to be reckoned with if someone so much as tried to harm those he loved. Paris knew that, knew the man wore love like a badge.

Paris licked his lips and reminded himself he was given orders. For Diesel Gentry was also the Patronus— the Master of Doms. And today Paris had agreed to serve him.

He returned to the wall until his back hit the cool surface of the mirrors there, then loosened the draw cord to his pants completely. He let them fall to pool around his ankles and then slowly, he stepped out of them, stretching his legs further out while maintaining his leaning position against the wall. He watched his own hands, moving up and back down over his body, recalling what it felt like to have Diesel do it. He couldn't stand it any longer and pushed a hand down into the eggshell colored boxer-briefs and took hold of his own cock.

It only took a few strokes and it was fully erect, crawling out of his briefs. He brought his hand up, quickly licked two fingers, then returned his hand to his cock and swept his moist fingertips over his sensitive glans. The direct contact had him sucking in a deep hissing breath, and the muscles in his groin bunched up. He was so wound up and sensitive from the last two days of teasing, it would not take him long to climax with any real attention, and he was half considering working himself over right then. Even if the command given didn't include that.

"Paris, come here."

Oh, he wasn't going to argue that one at all. Paris was at the bedside in two steps and dropped to his knees just as Diesel was swinging his legs around, dropping his feet back to the floor where Paris instantly took up residence between them. He opened his mouth and happily allowed Diesel to feed his erection to him.

He slurped the broad cap with all the wetness from his tongue to allow his lips to slide down around it as the near three-inches diameter of flesh stretched his cheeks to their fullest. Thick cocks made good eye candy, but sucking them took some ingenuity. A talent Paris had put a lot of effort into perfecting the last time he and Diesel were together. Except that was a year ago, and now Paris had to work his mouth up to take him again. But the man was every bit worth it and tasted sensational. The smooth skin had a clean creamy flavor and a healthy sweetness to the precum that started to seep out as Paris' grip took over for Diesel, who was now having his pleasure of mapping out Paris' back and shoulders under his broad palms.

There was a loud hiss over his head and then he felt Diesel's hands tighten into the shirt that still hung from

Paris' shoulders, followed by a ripping sound as Diesel tore the shirt from Paris' body.

That was a seven-hundred-dollar Tom Ford designer shirt, and Paris pulled off the thick cock to have a word about it, "You are buying me two replacement shirts after this."

"Yes, I will buy you whatever shirts you want," Diesel nearly growled, "Just shut up and suck me, dammit." The command was more a breathy plea than an order, all but the hand on the center of Paris' back pushing him back down. A thumb reached up from his other hand, finding Paris' lips and caressed them and his filled cheek as Paris returned his mouth around the waiting cock. "Oh fuck." Diesel breathed out the curse, fell back on the bed and just let Paris go to town on him.

Trying to suck every inch of Diesel's nine inches just wasn't possible. Though Paris wouldn't have minded spending the next couple of weeks— or months— or even a year or more trying to learn how. For now, though, he had to mix it up with licking and fisting to ensure every inch of Diesel's monster organ and sack got a considerable and equal amount of lavishing attention.

Paris tugged on the ever tightening sack and worked them up with a mix of pressure and feathery massage, then returned his hand back to pump the massive toy, igniting Diesel's breaths to become heavier and raspier. The sexiest sound a man could make. Like porn for the ears.

Hands were suddenly thrust in Paris' hair, fisting, wanting to pull him down further over him, but never did from years of self-restraint that no one could take Diesel's cock that way. But the need never waned and Paris yearned to satisfy it, so he yawned and took in as much of the thick cock down, as far to the back of his throat as he could, just as he felt the first pulse swell against his tongue.

"OH fuck!" The words blasted out with a considerable amount of painful groaning. Paris pulled back without actually letting the dick drop from his mouth, preferring to savor the taste rather than drown as Diesel shot a thick load of hot cum, filling his mouth until it dribbled from his lips.

Paris rolled his eyes up to watch the sexy body convulse with the violent pleasure then he went to work to clean up every drop of his prize.

Diesel fell back on the bed, boneless. His hands hardly having the strength to caress Paris' head before falling at his sides.

Paris finished sucking down the last savory drop then crawled up and overtop of Diesel. He wanted more— hell, he needed more.

Diesel managed to get his hand back up, raking his fingers through Paris' hair. At first, it seemed Diesel meant to encourage him, but then Diesel's hand fisted and yanked Paris back, pulling his head all the way down to the mattress until he was laid out on his back.

"Fuckin' son of a bitch." Paris cursed out, "Why do you keep stopping me?"

"Because you fuck like a bull in a china shop. You shatter everything in your wake so there's nothing left to go back to. That's how you keep everyone locked out so you can keep going on your way, fucking the next power outlet."

"I like power outlets—" he panted, "they suit me just fine."

"And that's where your problem lies with me, Paris. I'm not your next power outlet."

"Not to mention your ground wire is loose."

"What's that supposed to mean?"

"Nothing, you're the one using euphemisms. Are you going to now say you didn't enjoy me on your cock?"

"You know I did."

"Then where is the problem?"

"The problem is you seem to insist that sex be a requirement and nothing else gets in."

"I seem to recall not getting laid last night, but I didn't kick you out of my bed either."

Diesel opened his mouth to say something, but Paris didn't let him,

"It is my bed, my home, and I don't let one night stands or even the resort's slaves stay the night."

~ * ~

Diesel stilled a moment. As shallow and callous as the words came out, it might have been a slip on Paris' part to let Diesel see inside him. That while sex was still a prevalent demand, he was, in fact, letting Diesel get past the walls of Jericho. It was just hard to tell.

Diesel curled his arm still caught under Paris and used it to pull the enigma towards him until Paris fell over him into a kiss, letting the post bliss be restored as a way to thank Paris for the mind blowing oral attention and the exclusive entry into his home. "Then I should be thanking you for sharing something so guarded with me." He husked the compliment out between kisses, while Paris took a considerable amount of handsy liberties as part of the price. "Tell me, what will you tell Kat when she asks you what I taste like?"

Paris leaned back with a surprised look on his face. Then a short chuckle bubbled up that curled his lip into a sinister grin, "You taste like a wedding that's been crashed by a summer storm at sea," Paris answered.

Diesel chuckled, "Translation?"

"A rich, creamy dessert splashed heavily with a salty, earthy palates of flavors that are both verbose and intensely hot. I've never tasted anything like you."

"Mmmm— coming from an expert chef, that must be one hell of a compliment." Diesel rolled them over, placing Paris on his back, fisting his fingers into the thick black hair, pulling his head up to make his mouth available to him, "I think I like that." And he took him. Diesel's tongue diving in to seek out Paris'. Lapping at the savory flavor of his own essence still lingering in his kiss. He let his hand wander down the man's chest to find his cock, but was met with a surprise when he found it soaked in cum.

Diesel broke their kiss, Paris' multi-hued eyes already locked on him with an all-knowing expression. Diesel dragged a finger through the wet puddle he'd discovered, brought up a tasty sample of it, and fed it to Paris. He near groaned as he watched those swollen lips that had, just moments ago, been wrapped around his cock, now succulently sucked on his finger. When he pulled his finger free, that sinister grin turned into a full on, no regret, gloating smile. *Damn the Imp.* "You shouldn't have done that, Paris." The suggestion was cold and foreboding that it just might be punishable. "You do know I am going to have to punish you for this, right?" Zero remorse looked down at him. *What the hell was he going to do with him?*

~ * ~ * ~ * ~ * ~ * ~

CHAPTER NINE

~ * ~ * ~ * ~ * ~ * ~

Katianna was out at the pool, enjoying a swim in the tranquility of the safe waters. Here, there was never a worry of fins, and she'd been given some time to herself—supposedly to think about her actions while cooling off her skin from the spanking she got last night. Along with strict orders for her to not interfere anymore. It was a rare moment to be left alone, in the way of not being chaperoned, all but for the man she'd risked getting in trouble for. He, however, was presently tethered to a saddle bench, stationed in a shady corner of the pool deck. She knew the custom made bench well and the deviant construction that went into it. For hidden inside it was a powerful vibrator that could be programmed to turn on and off in intervals. Just enough to get her close to the edge, then stop, leaving her inflamed for far too long until the arousal waned, then it'd start all over again. *Grrrrr— it was a love-hate she had with that infernal bench.*

Paris had not only been handcuffed to it with the Patronus' new fancy colored handcuffs, but he'd also gotten a good lashing with a paddle on his ass, then about a dozen lazy horsehair floggings to his back. The worst was probably the tickling. But he also got a good deal of post care and petting. Afterwards, the four pairs of handcuffs were reduced to one, then the Patronus clipped him to the end of a leash, allowing him some room to move, though not much more than maybe five or six feet from the saddle bench he was chained to. Where Diesel had gone to now was interesting. She'd never known him to leave a scene and still leave his subject restrained. At first, he'd only gone inside, sitting down in the comfort of the living room while staring at his handy work. But when Kat finished another lap in the pool and came to the edge to catch her breath, he was gone. Now it was just her and Paris.

She swam a few more laps then finally pulled up on the edge and just swirled her feet in the water. To say it was an awkward arrangement was likely an understatement, but any other description would start to get too wordy. *Stupid writer.*

"How is that you are here alone without Dominus?"

She snapped around to see Paris looking at her. She saw he'd figured out he had more room than he thought and had since gotten off the saddle to stretch his legs. Then lying out on the chaise, just out of the shade, to sun himself. More importantly, getting his crotch off the tormenting machine. His expression anguished. She knew that look, no doubt she had worn that face a few times. Trenton knew too well how to hold out the prize for hours, even days, until her body craved it so desperately she would agree to damn near anything or cry for it as she often did. Tears worked way better than agreeing to the spankings. *Well, that is they had until last night.*

"I wanted to say I'm sorry about you getting in trouble. If you're not allowed to talk to me anymore, I understand."

"I'm allowed to talk." *Well sort of.*

"You've been pretty quiet. I wasn't sure."

She scooted across the pool's edge and climbed out, then went over to the saddle bench and leaned against it. Surprisingly, it wasn't vibrating under her. She shrugged to him, "Was it worth me getting disciplined for?"

Paris shook his head only minutely as if he wasn't sure if it was or not, unsure of what was going on around him to say it was worth anything yet. "Why'd he discipline you? I mean, it's not like you really said anything that would get you in trouble. In fact, you didn't say much at all."

She shrugged again then dropped her hands behind her and rested back further. "I think I said enough. Besides, I prefer writing to talking."

~ * ~

Paris watched her lean over and stretch her neck to the side a bit, then make a precarious glance inside the house. She was scouting— expecting them to come back any time soon, so he figured maybe a change of topic would be best, "Speaking of writing, I've been reading your books lately. I have them all." He sat up so they could talk more.

Her eyes flickered from the door to him with a beaming surprise. Like two icebergs catching the sun. He'd never seen eyes like hers before.

"You've read my books?"

He nodded. "I keep them in my quarters. Maybe Trenton will let you come by and sign them for me."

"Which one is your favorite?"

He rolled his head giving it some thought, "The latest one. The new Daeymon's Realm series. I think I'm in love with your character, Navarre. You'd never written homosexual content before. How did you learn to write that?"

She shrugged again, "I don't know. The stories just come to me. People are people; how they come together, and enjoy one another, has nothing to do with gender. What surprises me is people seem to always be surprised at my ability to write them. To me, pleasure is pleasure."

Paris grinned at the sudden philosophical reference.

"The book isn't about being gay. It's just a man who happens to be gay and meets another man. Or male in this story. The story is everything around them." She let a soft smile come over her lips and her eyes dropped as she pulled up her own story in her mind, "Navarre, because he is a Deaymon, has an insatiable appetite, so he'll fuck anything. But Aislinn is an imp and because his virginity was given to the Deaymon, Navarre falls in love with Aislinn and he is content to be with just him as long as Aislinn doesn't wander off."

"I guess I didn't see it that way."

"That's because you want it to be about being gay. Rather, it's a story with a gay character in it." She looked over at him, then her pale eyes seemed to look deeper into him than perhaps he wanted. "Is that what you are? I mean, do you see yourself as a gay man?"

"Yes, of course. It's what I am."

"And you're very confident and comfortable with knowing that about yourself. Which is healthy and good and because of it, I suspect you also automatically consider any relationship you might have with someone as being a gay one, right?"

Paris blinked at her a moment, since this seemed like a trick question to him, "Yeah, sure. Never really put a lot of thought into defining it as you just did, but I'm gay, so yes, if I were in a relationship with someone, it would be with another gay man."

"Except, Diesel isn't gay." She threw the comment out on the table just like that. "You need to know that if you want to love him the right way."

Paris was confused. Thoughts twisting in his mind to comprehend what such a statement would mean. *Was he going through all this for nothing? Would he not have Diesel when this ended?* "Then what is this? Why are you telling me this?"

"Don't misunderstand me. You're the person he wants; the one he's falling for, who just happens to be a man. What he feels and wants goes beyond just sex. Diesel is Navarre with an appetite for sex like a Deaymon. But above the need for sex, he wants only two things in life, his Imp and the Incubus. You're his Imp, the only one who can handle, as well as fulfill, his hunger— the one lover he can see himself settle down with and always be content with."

Paris grew uneasy, "And the Incubus? Who is that?"

"The Unicorn he has always desired."

"Like you are to Dominus?"

"I suppose so."

"If Diesel wants to have a Unicorn, why did he give Chikako away?" Paris rolled his back, the afternoon sun was beginning to take a toll on his back, making the sting from the flogger radiate more so on his skin. "The sun is burning my back. I need to be moved to the shade. I think Diesel forgot about me."

~ * ~

Katianna knew better than that as she glanced at him. Diesel was very aware of what he was doing to Paris and that Paris need only step back to the bench where he'd be out of the sun. She'd been lectured for the second time over Diesel's deep rooted plan, so that in the end Paris would be mentally and emotionally bound to him. But she could see that was already happening. "If I release your hands, you won't run off, will you?" That was the real question. She recalled Trenton's comment about Paris always running away, like she did.

"No." He affirmed, "I'm not going to take off. I just need to be able to move and get out of the sun."

Katianna pushed off from the bench and unclasped the silver belly chain from her waist and used the handcuff key that hung from it to set Paris free— *again.*

Paris yanked his hands back and rubbed at his wrists, but the movement was too fast and Katianna jumped.

Paris held his hands up in mock surrender, "Sorry—" he rolled his shoulders to work out some of the fatigue. "Just stiff and it feels good to move."

He rolled to his feet, walked over to the back of the house and listened in, then glanced at Kat, "He's in the shower." He went to the pool and dove in with hardly a splash. Did the man ever do anything less than perfect? He came up to the surface and the cool refreshment of the water revealed on his face that'd it done a good job of putting the fire on his back out some. The relief came out in an expressed happy groan that was reminiscent of some inner porn star moan.

She knew what that felt like too. It wasn't hurting anything watching him either. Paris was every bit the Imp she created in her book. Perfect body of contoured muscles and smooth tan skin. He was the poster boy for all those men who flocked to the gym, purely for the sake of peacocking. But she knew it first-hand that there was a heart inside there, somewhere underneath all that chiseled physique.

Paris came back up after swimming a lap underwater, his inky black hair now slicked back. He gave his head a vigorous shake, and then instantly finger combed it back into a now wet version of his razored style, before twisting around to catch his reflection in one of the glass walls to check himself. A few touch-ups, then he settled down into the water, leaning against the side of the pool with his arms stretched out along the edge. "So tell me why Chikako isn't his Unicorn."

Katianna came over and sat next to him, dropping her legs in the water, making circles with her feet and enjoying the swirling force against her skin. "He couldn't make love to her. She's too small for him and his size meant he couldn't love her body in any form. It's like holding the carrot out in front of the horse. It's right there, but always out of reach. Eventually, the horse falls over dead trying to get to it." She paused while thinking about it, but even as she'd said it, she didn't believe that had been the real reason, just an excuse she'd heard him say. "I think because she is so young too, it had an even heavier bearing on it." She added yet another excuse.

She was actually enjoying the conversation; she couldn't recall a time she had gotten into such a deep topic with anyone in years, other than Trenton or Diesel, or the occasional get-togethers with Amelia or Vida. The greatest comfort in talking with Paris was that he, despite all his size, was like her. Well, in a way, he was. At the moment, at least, he was technically a slave and at Diesel's mercy. She'd also seen him scared. Scared like her. For once, she wasn't alone in that category.

"And that's all, size and age?"

Katianna took a deep breath and sighed, thinking about it, "No. I think those were just excuses."

"Then what?"

"He didn't love her."

Paris was quiet a moment and she saw for herself that Paris had already allowed Diesel inside his walls. Right where Diesel was hoping to be.

"Do you think Diesel would be able to love me?" His gaze flickered toward her, then glanced down at the water and began to play with it, his hand under its surface. Playing it off like it was nothing. "Did Navarre actually love Aislinn? It was never fully brought forward in the book."

Katianna smiled and nodded, "He will love in his own way, but if you think of him as your gay partner, it will feel desperately one-sided and you'll be unhappy. But if you love him as a fluid man who simply stumbled on you and realized he'd found a treasure to keep as his lover, then yes, you'll feel his love."

"Like a Deaymon?"

"Yes, like a Deaymon, whose lover fucks like a bull."

"Matador is a better word." Paris corrected her with a grin, then grabbed the pool edge and hoisted himself up out of the water, dropping down next to her— delivering a puddle of water along with him. "My ankle banger is one hundred percent human."

She raised a brow at him, fighting back a huge grin, "In that case, there's lube in the night stand, the dresser, and in the buffet near the front door." She looked at him, counting out the items with her fingers seeing the lust ignite in him, "And there's other stuff in the shower."

Her ears perked up, hearing the shower water turn off, and she looked at Paris nervously, "If you tell them it was me who set you free—" she pulled her feet up on the edge to leave.

~ * ~

Paris quickly leaned across and kissed the top of her head with a quick peck before she could move away. "Don't worry, I'll never tell." He smiled and winked at her, feeling a little silly that he didn't give her credit for knowing what she was doing when she released his restraints. But the plot now thickened as he watched her disappear into the bedroom she shared with Trenton.

~ * ~ * ~ * ~ * ~ * ~

Diesel hadn't really left Paris unguarded— just loosely so. Kat was there if anything happened, and he could also see them both from the window of the bathroom. All was going according to plan when he saw the two talking.

He finished up his shower then jumped out and grabbed a towel off the rack. He'd no sooner had it tied about his waist when he glanced out to the pool and— "Dammit, mouse." He growled at the empty pool and headed out to go after them both, "I'll be spanking you myself this time—"

Diesel didn't get far when he walked right into Paris. "How the hell did you—"

The last words were knocked from his lungs when Paris grabbed him unexpectedly and slammed him against the wall, using every ounce of his body weight to press against him. The kiss was just as volatile with uncontrolled, stark raving mad hunger. Diesel managed to get an arm between them and pushed Paris back to sever their kiss, but Paris countered, stooping down and scooping up one of Diesel's legs, locking it in his arm, and right away was positioning his hips until Diesel felt Paris' cock lining up.

"Red." Diesel bit out the singular word.

"No! There is no red, no safeword." Paris growled, refusing to accept the rejection.

"Then you are one second from committing rape, Paris." Diesel got ahold of one of Paris' wrists and was ready to flip it around with a defensive move. "Think about what you're about to do, and the consequences that will follow. Because once you do it, there will be no undoing the damage. There will be nothing to salvage between us."

Every gear in Paris' head jammed up with those words. It was evident in his face how the marring expression rippled over him with pain. The intensity in his arms waned, his legs gave out under him, and they both went crashing to the floor.

"I'm sorry." Paris balled up, slammed his head against Diesel's chest and pleaded. "I just don't know what to do.

You make me crazy. You wind me up then stick me in a corner with nowhere to go. Or worse, you send me away so I can't be with you."

"Is that where you want to be, Paris?"

Paris shook his head, his forehead still collapsed against Diesel's chest, "I can't keep playing this game of yours. It hurts."

Diesel felt it too; he was hurting the man he wanted to be with, the man he wanted to let him in. But if Paris was hurting, was it possible Paris had already let him get past his walls? Or maybe Katianna was right. Perhaps the way to train his Fallen Angel was to let the raging bull in him out of the head stocks, then ride Paris out until he was exhausted.

This was going to be one painful reacquaintance for him, but he repositioned so he was straddled over Paris' folded legs and took Paris' cock in his grip, still hard and lathered with more than enough lubricant needed for what he was about to do. "Try to go easy on me. Remember, I don't bottom for anyone." And with that, he eased up and over the tip of Paris' cock. Slowly easing himself down. "But I will let you service me from the top— with a little *t*." He smirked.

Paris came awake. Every cell in him seemed to come alive, but his eyes said something far more. They acknowledged what'd been said and he understood the gift entirely. He moved in, his lips reaching for Diesel's neck. But as they both began to work together, there was more hissing than kissing. Diesel propped an arm behind him and got his feet anchored on the floor. Paris began to rock under Diesel's thighs, forward and up, with a gentle nudging— taking his time to work his shaft in further and deeper with careful pressure.

Diesel's teeth rattled as the first sensations of stretching pain seared at his hole, followed with the slathering strokes of sweeter sensations to ease down the pain of entry. He should have insisted on some foreplay, but he doubted Paris would have trusted him to follow up. This was the only way to show Paris he was capable of putting his own walls aside.

Paris' arms returned to their vice-grip hold on him, his face buried into Diesel's neck, holding on as if fearing it'd be taken away any second. But Paris didn't rush his cock while Diesel slowly acclimated his body to the invasion, one he hadn't felt in a year. It was never something he was particularly eager for or had a desire for, except with Paris he found himself willing to give. With Paris, Diesel was up for most things because it made them both happy.

Diesel shifted his body angle, leaning back further, manipulating the position of Paris' cock so that the few inches already inside his hole tapped against his prostate. The G-spot pleasure was what his body needed to accept the rest and he dropped his weight down to slowly work the remaining inches all the way inside. He dropped his head back on his shoulders, willing his body to relax, and the moan that came lost some of the painful edge to it as Paris slid in further.

Diesel wasn't the only one groaning though. Every muscle in Paris' body was drawn taut, the tension ready to snap off any second. Suddenly that second was up— Paris surged up to his feet, taking Diesel with him, riding up along the wall with one leg still caught in the clutch of Paris' right arm. And the bull ride began.

~ * ~

Paris let loose, picking up a smooth rocking pace into Diesel's ass, but with his one leg still down, access was limited. Paris wanted more. He shifted, managed to catch Diesel's other leg, and hefted him off the floor completely. The muscles in his arms and shoulders bulged as they held the weight of some 220 pounds of solid man. The strain burned up some of his need to throttle, but his strength didn't falter and he was finally able to slide all the way in. "Oh fuck, you're tight. It's amazing." Paris hissed.

"Shhhit— ah—" Diesel panted to catch his breath and kept a powerful grip on Paris' shoulder while his other hand hovered low to monitor Paris' movements.

The sheer delight had Paris groaning as he pushed in to nail Diesel to the wall. And still, he wanted more. The only way to do that was to transfer strength for exertion. So Paris had them sliding back to the floor— him sitting on his heels— Diesel came down, straddled over his lap, then he dropped a hand to the floor behind him to brace himself as he rode Paris' shuttling hips.

It wasn't long before Paris was finally able to pick up the pace, moving in a rolling wave that slapped against Diesel's body harder and faster until he had Diesel dropping back flat on the floor. Paris lifted Diesel's legs and spread them wide— and that was when he found all the *more* he was looking for.

~ * ~

"Dammit, you even fuck like a bull." Diesel groaned as his fallen angel grunted with every driving stroke of his cock deep inside Diesel's ass. His whole body was popping with explosive electricity, but he wasn't going to cum this way, "Jack me, dammit, Paris, I need to cum."

Paris instantly dropped a leg in exchange for Diesel's thick cock and began to do just as he was ordered to. *How he did it* was all part of Paris' powerhouse rhythm, stroking Diesel's hard shaft, firm and fast, in tandem with the rest of their movements.

This was one hell of a way to set loose the beast. Diesel reached up, grabbing Paris by the back of his head and pulling him down to him, "Kiss me and don't you dare stop." The commanded kiss was like everything else, hard and rough. But forgotten when Diesel felt his release coming, like a dam that had collapsed inside him, and he let out an exculpating heavy groan. Followed by the sensation of his semen on his skin— hot and frothy, spilling out between their bodies.

Paris managed to break from his grip, bolted upright, and speared him with one last thrust before releasing his own orgasm.

He could feel the splash of hot liquid on his insides, a feeling like no other, and the sensation gave Diesel the perspective only a rare few came to understand. This was what those usually under him all craved. To be filled with the hot fluids, as he let out a long agonizing cry of his ecstasy. Only this time, Diesel was the receiver. It was a strange place for him, outside of the driver's seat, but it hadn't been unpleasant. Rather, it'd been exhilarating. But now it was time to take the wheel again— *now that his bull was spent.*

~ * ~

Paris turned, deeply relaxed as he sat back on his heels, keeping his semi-hard erection still lodged inside Diesel's ass. Awash with bliss, he closed his eyes while his body regained some oxygen.

He felt Diesel's hand stroke up his chest, across sweat slicked skin, then down his arm to caress the back of his hand, "Was that what you were looking for?" Diesel asked him like he had just offered to pour caramel over his body and lick it up.

"Oh, yeah." Paris felt a shift in Diesel's leg and he opened his eyes, surprised Deez would want to move so soon. That was the last comprehensive thought he had for the next several seconds.

"Fuck!" Paris cursed just when Diesel's leg hooked him around the torso and literally sent Paris flipping backwards, slamming him to the carpeted floor. In zero moves or less, the hand that had been caressing Paris' arm now had it twisting behind his back with nothing more than the strength of Diesel's arms hooked around his, holding him like some monster vice grip, and pinned him face down on the floor under Diesel's body weight.

"Was it worth it?" Diesel snarled with a touch of gloating.

"Yes." Paris gritted out his response, despite the discomfort Diesel had him in.

"Very naughty little brat, you are."

"I loved fucking you. I'd do it again." Paris refused to repent for his actions, because it was the truth. It had been incredibly awesome. *And given to him*. But what the hell did Diesel expect from him, after teasing and tormenting him for nearly three days, but for him to fuck like an unleashed wild beast until he exploded? The only way it could have been better was if Diesel had fucked him. Though Paris had a good feeling that *that* was exactly what was about to happen next. *The alpha male had given, now he was going to have to re-assert his dominance.*

Diesel ground his still very hard cock between Paris' ass cheeks, threatening the entry there with increasing pressure. But it was no threat to Paris, and he wanted every inch of that cock stuffed up his ass.

"Was it worth risking a dry fuck?"

Paris jerked suddenly in his hold. *Shit.* The man just had this threatening way of making Paris feel helpless if he wanted him to. Never had anyone broken past Paris' slutty walls. He never felt abashed for his own actions— *until now.* "You can't blame me. Winding me up like you do, then leaving me jacked up like a race horse during rutting season. You knew I'd bolt for the finish line if I got loose." Paris lifted his head back, finding Diesel so close, and nuzzled against him while his ass did the same to the man's bulging organ. Even under the threat of being burned for it, Paris wanted him.

"Good thing I know how to jockey then, huh? Though I suspect it's going to be a bit more like riding a stag than a horse until I've tired you out."

Diesel got his knees under him so he straddled over the backs of Paris' legs and still held his arms locked behind him, "I'm going to lift you enough so you can get to your knees and you'll do just that, then move to your feet. Any resistance and it'll be a raw ride, understood?"

Paris nodded. He didn't doubt Diesel would hold true to his threat, or at least make it seem like he would, just to get Paris' full attention. Because the man didn't make idle threats, and a person or submissive was lucky to get off with a warning. Paris wanted to be fucked, but not without some lubrication. And while Diesel didn't have a gun on him, Paris felt it all the same as if it were. Like the first night when Diesel had fucked him. Paris had never cum as hard as he did that night and the days that followed.

Diesel stood and Paris felt his body being lifted just as Diesel said he would; the strength it would take the man to accomplish the feat had Paris' cock hardening all over again. No doubt about it, while Paris was strong, Diesel was stronger, and skilled in combat. Paris had no choice but to do as he was told and he pulled his legs up under him, getting to his knees, then to one foot, pushing up in unison with his captor.

Paris was reined into the bedroom and toward the bed, then with a slight pressure to his arms, Paris went back down on his knees and bent over the foot of the bed.

"Don't move."

Diesel's grip on Paris' arms loosened, moving his palms up along one arm and repositioning it out at his side. Paris flipped his head over so he could watch as Diesel was reaching for something and soon saw the length of rope and how it was already conveniently secured around the bed post. He used the loose end to tie Paris' wrist with zero resistance from him. He knew better, knew that Diesel's warning was still hanging over him if he dared him. He remained just as complacent as he watched his left arm get tied in similar fashion to the opposite post. Paris could only grin. He had never gotten into BDSM, but the bondage part didn't bother him, especially now because he was about to get exactly what he wanted from Diesel. He'd endured damn near anything the man asked or demanded of him, just to be where he was at that very moment.

Diesel's hand suddenly came down on one side of Paris' ass with a less than playful hard crack.

Maybe not that. Paris gritted his teeth, beating back the fire that stung like a bite on his ass cheek already sensitive from the paddling he got earlier.

What he felt next was the very thing that could reduce Paris into a driveling mess. Diesel's firm hands spread apart his ass cheeks, followed by a warm blow right over his sphincter hole that sent a chill up Paris' spine. He felt the hot wet tongue next. Right up the center cavity of his taint, all the way up until it reached his tail bone, and Paris let out the most submissive moan he'd ever made. Paris knew right then he was in for a romp that was going to swallow him up to test his hunger and endurance as a power bottom. The tongue that caressed his ass promised a long ride of torturous foreplay. Reminding Paris that what he had endured at the hands of the slaves Diesel commanded, was nothing compared to what the man could do to him with his own skill.

The tongue flattened against his flesh, licking and kissing its way down the right side of his ass cheek, taunting a reaction from the muscular globe all the way down to the lower crease of his glutes. The reaction was Paris pushing back against Diesel's mouth, wanting more of it. It got him a stinging smack— that landed on the opposite cheek. Paris gave himself some warning that perhaps next time he wouldn't lean back— *nah— what would be the fun in that?*

Diesel repeated the wet trail, first licking up the cleft of Paris' cheeks again, then slowed to rim his puckered hole and toy with it a moment, as if Diesel intended to push his tongue through. Paris hissed, it felt so delightful, and it took all the self-control he had to *not* push back on that tongue this time. He wasn't entirely sure if his pushing back was the trigger for the one-handed spanking he'd gotten, but he wasn't willing to gamble now. Not at the risk of losing that tongue probing, he wouldn't. It was too fucking good to brat away. He chewed at his lip, sucking in a deep breath as Diesel's tongue continued its journey. This time laving over the left globe, and if Paris had some notion that he could avoid another spanking, it was a false one as Diesel's cupped hand came cracking down over Paris' right ass cheek next.

He was pushing back next time, no doubt about it.

~ * ~

Diesel returned his attention towards Paris' ring and drove his tongue into it as he licked it into submission. His hands stroked over Paris' scrotum and the base of his cock as Diesel kept those positioned so they hung over the edge of the bed. Paris wanted Diesel to fuck him, that was a given, and Diesel was certain that Paris had it in his head that once it had started then he'd get his due right away. But Diesel had way more tricks up his sleeve than Paris was even aware of. He'd already gotten his craving for a flogging satisfied and had chivvied and vanquished Paris for days. Now Patronus planned to foreplay the man into annihilation, along with establishing a few marks of ownership. Starting right now as he bit into that succulent globe on the right side of Paris' ass.

"Ow! Fuck!" Paris howled, glancing over his shoulder. Diesel ignored him and laved his tongue right over the love bite, then closed his lips around it and sucked hard until Paris jerked away enough for him to lose the claim of flesh. But the reddish bruise was already started.

"Shit, you marked me?"

Diesel curled his lips in a devilish grin, "There will be plenty more when I'm finished with you." His eyes dropped down to the double crescent of teeth imprinted in his lover's flesh.

"No." Paris protested. "No biting or marking me. What if it's permanent?" Paris pulled on the ropes, trying to gain enough lead line so he could twist around more to glare at Diesel, doing his best to put his foot down, so to speak.

Diesel only grinned further, then went back to what he was doing, molesting Paris' backside with his tongue. That wasn't all. He palmed the perfectly tight muscles of ass— then moved up over his back, stretched further to touch his shoulders and arms, then pushed under Paris' body to roam the sides of his chest and back down— leaving no part of Paris' body untouched.

~ * ~

Paris writhed and moaned, rocking back against him. God, he enjoyed being devoured, but he really needed to be fucked right now. He was going to explode if Diesel didn't hurry up and arrive at the more brutal and somatic parts of their sexual copulation soon.

Diesel was sucking on his balls, first one and then the other, then his tongue pressed hard on the perineum nerves just behind Paris' scrotum, then back up through his cleft to lave over his *so ready* hole. Hands spread his cheeks wide, then Paris felt Diesel's tongue push against his hole and beyond the ring of muscle, sending every nerve ending into utter chaos. Paris squirmed and bucked against the tongue that now fucked him, "Damn it, Diesel, stop." Paris gasped, to his own surprise.

"Are you serious?" Diesel paused only long enough to get the question out before he began to kiss along Paris' ass while his hands messaged at them, pulling them wider apart for another assault of his tongue. "Do you really want us to stop?"

"No!" Paris made the fast correction of what he was asking for. "Just stop teasing me, please."

"This isn't teasing; this is foreplay,"

"Can we fast forward some?" He squirmed then bit into the bed covers and started humping the bed even more as he felt Diesel's tongue lick broadly over his hole, rolling over it. *Oh damn, it felt so good, but he couldn't handle the softness of it anymore.* Paris heard the chuckling behind him and didn't much care for its insinuation, "Fuck me, damn you!" *Damn him, he'd been* foreplayed *to death for three days, already.*

"Soon, brat. Soon."

There was a pause in Diesel's attentiveness, and then a thick dollop of chilled lubrication spread menacingly between his ass checks. The next level of barbaric suffering was to be finger-toyed, with Diesel making tiny circles against his greedy puckered ring, but that was all Diesel seemed inclined to do right then. Paris couldn't prevent the growling sounds he made as he did all he could to line his body against the single digit in order to do some of those push back evasive maneuvers, but to no avail. He finally gave up, surrendered his face to the bed, and just clamped his teeth down on the covers and groaned.

It was then— when he had given up— when Diesel pushed his finger in and *fuck*— the moan that came out. *Oh god, finally they were getting somewhere* and Paris pushed back onto Diesel's hand to deepen the contact. The finger turned and twirled, stroking the inner walls of Paris' rectum, delivering a healthy dose of lubrication with each re-entry.

Paris' arms curled against his ropes and he rocked back hard to receive the full penetration of Diesel's finger. It wasn't enough— too sweet and too light of a touch. "Fuck, Diesel, come on and fuck me!"

~ * ~

Diesel didn't answer. He was too busy looking over the bite mark he'd left on Paris' ass, contemplating improvements. He pumped into Paris' tight hole a while longer before adding a second finger to start working him to stretch open. Gaining a world of *fuck yeahs* from Paris as he got the horny devil ready. But not until he took a slight detour to finish that mark.

Diesel bent over, landing his mouth in the exact spot where he'd left the impression of his teeth, and began to suck against the skin.

Paris started bucking against him, too eager to remain complacent. The meaning of the word just didn't exist in Paris' world, but Diesel brought him under control by adding a third finger to the prepping and began pumping him harder and faster. Crooking his fingers to massage against Paris' prostrate while he continued to suck on the sweet round curve, drawing the blood to the surface, creating a satisfactory hickey. "Niiice." He let out a pleased approval of its outcome.

"What?" Paris snapped his head around in an unsuccessful attempt to look at his ass, but he figured it out as Diesel palmed the love bite. "You marked me? God dammit, Deez. I just told you not to mark me!"

Diesel pulled away with an equally satisfactory smile as he continued to admire his own handy work of the large reddish-purple mark. "You want me to fuck you?"

"Yes!"

"Then shut up about the hickey on *My* ass."

"Except it's *not* on your ass!"

~ * ~

Diesel's hand came down hard over the flesh of Paris' behind with the delivery of an intense sting to match the loud slap, "*This* is my property. Mine— and I'll mark and play with it as I please." Diesel announced this to him and before Paris could protest any further, Diesel was replacing his fingers with his cock.

The kiss of the broad mushroom cap was undeniable, and that first painful stretch had Paris pulling away rather than pushing onto him. He hissed out and sent orders to will his body to relax; now was not the time for it to tense up on him. Dammit, he wanted that cock inside him. The delicious stretch was both a pain and a pleasure that was impossible to put words to; perhaps one day, he might try to get a certain writer to help him, but for now all he could do was roll his hips over the intrusion, acclimating himself as Diesel slowly pushed his way in.

"OH, fuck, Deez! I love your cock inside me." Paris panted, still well aware that not all nine inches were in yet. But that didn't matter, he knew it would be soon, and once Diesel hit home the ride would begin.

~ * ~

Diesel had always had it in his head that the first time was going to be slow and tender, but he knew now that had been an unrealistic expectation. What Paris needed— what they both needed— was a no-rules— no-limits— rutting.

151

He chewed his lips as he rocked his head back on his shoulders, letting his mind go blank, save for the visceral sensation of Paris' body slowly swallowing his cock. He dropped a hand down at the small of Paris' back, in part to keep him still, and the rest just to remind himself— *not yet.* It wasn't that easy, though. Like Paris said, they were like the horse hocked up for the race. Every nerve ending zinged off the charts with heated anticipation. Knowing what his body needed, what his lust was capable of, and that the man in front of him was capable of consuming every ounce of it. The surreal experience was almost too much, and just when he thought he would not be able to hold back any longer, his cock bottomed out deep inside Paris' ass. He tightened his buttocks and curled his hips in a tense push, gaining a little more of the hot silky walls that clenched around his dick.

Paris let out several deep breaths in a moan that voiced his readiness and he gyrated his ass like a dance move against Diesel.

"Are you ready, Paris?"

"Yes-sss—" he hissed back over his shoulder.

"Are you sure, because once I get started, I may not be able to stop."

"One could only pray for such a fucking. Give it to me. You know I want it." And to be sure Diesel got the message, Paris eased forward then shoved back hard, impaling himself on Diesel's cock.

That was it, the green light given and Diesel didn't even try for a warm up on the tempo. He pulled nearly two-thirds of his length out then slammed right back in, on one smooth thrust, knocking Paris into the bed. That was the only count he'd make. The rest built up into a blur of jackhammering inside the man he'd craved to have back since the day he'd sent him away. To say it felt good to finally have him again was the world's greatest understatement, for Paris was a dream that kissed his skin in every sinful way. A sensation of euphoria before it ever happened in the physical aspect.

They both growled and cursed in unison as they met each other's throttles, creating a loud slapping sound between groin and ass that filled the room. He fucked his fallen angel, riding him hard and at a frantic pace, without need for concern that his lover could not take him. Diesel plundered his body, rutting on him like a savage beast. He banged as hard as he could, thrusting as high as he could, pulling out fully so he could penetrate him again, spearing Paris' ass with his rock-hard meat. They became unrelenting in their ferocity until at last Diesel felt the first warnings of his own spasm. "No— not yet." He halted for a second as the first thrill tried to get away from him, but his mental command to tamp it all back down managed to catch the explosion and put it back under containment. "Fuck— dammit, Paris." He growled and folded over him, pausing only long enough to be sure the threat of losing it subsided, then began rocking against Paris' body again. *Slower.*

~ * ~

Diesel's deep breaths jetted harsh and hot through his nostrils onto Paris' cheek with the edge of a growl. His hands were all over him and he felt his Patronus' excitement passing any bounds of self-control. There was only his base need. Their need— and it was being met head on.

Paris wanted desperately to reach back and grasp Diesel's hips. To pull them as they rolled up against him, to pull every inch of his cock to kiss Paris' nethers with an easy grinding rhythm that had him panting and bucking back out of control. "Fuck— yes— damn it, Deez." He tugged at the ropes, wishing the bed would break. So he could be free. Diesel interrupted his thoughts, pulling his head around and meeting with a harsh demanding kiss. Only, they were both breathing so hard he couldn't keep the kiss locked between them. "God yes— so good. Fuck, you feel so good." Paris spurred him on to keep it up.

Diesel had only slowed for a moment before the grinding and pumping started back up, and from there he showed no signs of relenting. Their bodies both now soaked in sweat and mixed with their colognes that wafted up to soak the room with their joint scents. Dark spices, white musk, and tobacco leaves mixed in with lime, salt, cocoa, and a whole lot of testosterone.

Damn it, he wished his arms were free now. But it was just like Diesel to make him the receiver, and not allowing him any powering from the bottom. Still, to have the ability to even hang on to the bed right about now would have been appreciative advantage. His balls ached and not just from being slammed into the bed. Though that too was doing a number on him and his cock.

Diesel's hand reached around to cup Paris just under the chin and pulled him up without ever backing off the rutting. Paris could feel the strain in his neck, to near breaking point, but none of that mattered when Diesel twisted Paris' head about to bring his mouth within reach again. Diesel dove in, an act that was more claim than kiss, but no less effective as it sent fresh shivers of pleasure skittering along his spine.

"Are you going to cum for me, Paris? Or are you going to be a brat and make me drag it out of you?"

The husky question brushed against his ear. And there was never any doubt what his answer was. "Drag it out of me."

There was a loud, dragon-like growl behind him, and there were no words to describe what that did to Paris, but there were a lot of chills associated with it, and then there was the sudden release of his arms. The ropes still coiled around his wrists but he was no longer tied to the posts. Then strength— like he'd never felt before— grappled around his waist, lifting him. Paris was no small man, weighing in at close to 240 pounds, yet Diesel picked him up like he was nothing, using his legs and groin to shove Paris onto the bed. Paris didn't even have half a second to respond when Diesel grabbed his ankles, and next thing Paris knew was he was being twisted and flipped to his back. What he saw when he came around was the warning expression of Diesel's impending ambuscaded lust.

Diesel moved in fast, grabbed the backs of Paris' thighs, and shoved them to where his knees were practically at his shoulders with his feet pointing to the ceiling. Then, with Diesel's knees tucked under Paris' ass, Diesel lined his cock up in one hand, grabbed the headboard with the other, and slammed home.

As if it were within the same anecdote of mechanics— action versus reaction, Paris' head slammed down into the pillow under him. His teeth fought to bite on his lips but curses bubbled up to prevent it, and his toes— he felt his fucking toes curl as that cock drove into his ass with a friction that would burn stone and water when he came.

Diesel's face was tense and focused as he drove inside Paris' hole like a locomotive. Driven by one hundred percent, grade-A Diesel fuel. It was any wonder Paris was able to stay sane from it all. Salaciously— mercilessly— the pounding continued, sending out shockwaves of immense pleasure with each hard thrust. Diesel kept a firm grip on the headboard while holding on to one of Paris' legs, keeping it pressed down to his chest.

Paris also held onto the headboard so he wouldn't get shoved into it. His other hand was flat on the bed, gathering some leverage to lift and meet Diesel's hips with every stroke that came down. In all this, Paris had managed to work the untethered leg up until he had his ankle on Diesel's shoulder, which soon became a chew toy for Diesel's growling and biting. "Yeah fuck me, goddammit. Keep fucking me." He growled out the staccato affirmation. Sweat dripped from Diesel's chin and forehead onto him. But when Diesel let go of his leg to grab his dick, Paris was done for. He tried to fight it. He tried to reach for Diesel's neck or shoulder, to pull him down, determined to steal a kiss or several. Whatever it took to get his focus away from the fist that was working him over in pace with the cock that fucked him with unyielding fervor. The tongue frenzy helped, but wouldn't for long. His balls ached, drawn up tight, and readied to fire his load any moment now.

Diesel shifted, digging his knees further under Paris, lifting his ass. Paris wrapped both legs firmly around the man's torso, and it became far too much sensation for him when Diesel's hand changed its grip on Paris' cock and focused on just the glans— that was it. "Fuck— son-of—bitch! Fuck!" Paris cried out incoherent words. He would have jackknifed on the bed if it hadn't been for Diesel's body blocking the way. "Like that— like that— fuck, I'm cu—!" He never finished the warning when Diesel folded over him, hips curling into him, and knocking them both into the headboard. Likely breaking through the wall, but it didn't matter; Paris was a slave to the white-hot explosions that shattered his mind and shot down his body like lightning, firing out his cock to wash his abs and chest with hot jets of his orgasm.

There was a tight growl that turned into an angry cry after his own, then something cracked and splintered near his head. All Paris could do was hold onto him, rock-hard like a tank, as Diesel shot his own load inside Paris' ass and shook like a man standing against a battering storm.

Diesel's arms came down around him, trying to make some feeble attempt to caress the side of his face and head as they both rode out the aftershocks, until he finally collapsed on top of Paris.

The room was quiet now, filled only by the heavy breaths they tried to catch up with. The event was anything but over— for once Diesel's breath had leveled out, whether Paris' had or not, he started all over again. The thick cock, for all its girth, didn't feel like it'd shrunk in the least.

Deez didn't pick back up to the high intensity throttle they'd just had, but it wasn't a soft lovemaking either.

Steady— firm— plunging again and again into Paris' ass. He rolled his hips, adjusted his angle to aim for Paris' prostate— and deeper. A keening cry rent the air. Paris fought against the building pressure that threatened him with madness. "Oh god, right there. Yes, fuck me. Fuck me." He was melting and shivering, his cock lengthening and hardening, ready to shoot again. Almost there. Holding on for a moment more, not wanting the ecstasy to end. Diesel picked up his pace in a full-on jackhammer. Muscles tensed— tighter— tighter—

The pleasure that was building inside him became too much to bear. Already he felt a second orgasm working its way up from the base of his spine, pouring over him like a hot wave as Diesel continued penetrating Paris' ass with a seemingly endless energy.

"Come for me, Paris." Diesel's deep voice was warm and commanding. "Come for me again and imagine what it would feel like to have my cock buried to the hilt in your ass forever. To feel me fucking you— filling you up with my cum every night."

Paris snapped. Euphoric waves washed over him.

With a low, strangled cry, Paris lost it completely, obeying Diesel's order with helpless pleasure. Heart pounding, chest clamoring for breath, he felt himself clenching around Diesel's shaft, felt his own cock spasming in that large, warm hand as his orgasm fountained out, coating Diesel's fist and the side of the bed with thick splatters of white jizz. He powered through his orgasm, relishing each hot spurt milked from his cock. Sweat beaded and rolled from his brow. His chest heaved and his body burned. He stared into Diesel's eyes, thrilled at the rapturous glimmer that looked back, but he also saw something else there. Something far deeper and, were it not for the quakes still rattling his nerves, it might have terrified him out of the bed. *But damn it was so right.*

After, Paris lay exhausted in his lover's arms, content to stay as they spooned against each other. Something he was never apt to be comfortable with. Usually, it was fuck until dawn then break away. But Diesel was his polar opposite there. Back in New York, Diesel made him stay, even on that first night when Diesel had both him and Marcena and kept them at his side, despite Paris' own jealousy and need to have the girl kicked out. Diesel, who was so strict and in control, his lust was about sharing, and it wasn't complete without sleeping tangled in one's legs. Then waking up in the morning to fuck some more.

Diesel's hands lazily roamed over the playground of ripped muscles, holding Paris pressed against him while he nuzzled at the back of his neck. "Why does it bother you that I marked you?"

Paris tried to stifle the hostile huff he felt coming on, since the question was interrupting his post-coital bliss, "I don't have tattoos. I don't have piercings, and I don't want my ass marked or branded." The huff got away from him anyway.

~ * ~

Diesel didn't feed into the animosity Paris was suddenly feeling, but he wasn't through with his questions either, "Who else has been looking down your backside?" He purposely kissed Paris' back and shoulder tenderly, awaiting the answer. He hadn't expected Paris to have been faithful in any way to him after he'd pushed him away. He wouldn't like it, but he wouldn't hold it against him either, but he was curious as to why Paris would get overly worked up about a love bite that would fade in a day or two— that is, if Diesel didn't keep it playfully renewed. And then it dawned on him that Paris hadn't answered. "Who else has seen your beautiful ass lately, Paris?"

"No one." Paris grumbled from his side of the bed.

"Really?" Diesel was actually surprised, but Paris wasn't one to lie about it either. He'd never known Paris to hold back when he might still have his touch to seduce anyone he wanted. "You mean you haven't been with anyone since you left New York?"

"I didn't say that, I just said no one back there." His newfound grumpy tone hadn't slighted in the bit.

"Then why care if I mark you?" He felt the tension roll through Paris' body, growing angry and bulking up in his arms. "Paris?" This time it was concern rather than general curiosity.

"Oh for god's sake, Diesel, why would you want to? Is it not bad enough that I'm already ruined?" The last of his fussing was buried into his pillow.

Diesel pushed up on an elbow and tried to pull Paris around to look at him, but the brat insisted on being fused with his pillow. Diesel chose not to force him from it. However, his concern grew, "Paris, did I physically injure you in any way?" He was serious about his question. "If you're hurt, you need to tell me. Please, I never wanted to injure you."

"No." Paris huffed through his pillow.

"Then what is it? How have I ruined you?"

Paris peered out from his pillow, "Can I go now?"

"No." Diesel's answer was stern and matter-of-fact. "Tell me what it is and I might let you run away."

Paris took a deep breath, but no confession came from him, nor did he fight when Diesel rolled to his back and urged Paris to curl up next to him.

"Then get over here, Brat. I still expect you to lie with me when we sleep."

~ * ~

Paris shifted to his stomach and rested his cheek over Diesel's rib cage, his arms stretching out over the man as if intending to hug Diesel to the bed. His mind drifted as Diesel's fingers stroked through his hair. Being *here* wasn't the problem, forced to endure Diesel's after sex cuddling wasn't so bad— it was being here inside that bliss and knowing that in five more days, *here* wasn't going to exist. That once again, Paris would be alone, and for the second time in his life, he wasn't going to like it.

~ * ~ * ~ * ~ * ~ * ~

CHAPTER TEN

~ * ~ * ~ * ~ * ~ * ~

Kat knew she was in trouble, the moment she stepped from the bedroom after taking her shower and changing. Standing there in the living room with his arms crossed over his chest, leaning back on the arm rest of the sofa, was Trenton, with Diesel siting on the sofa next to him. Both clearly waiting on her. Her inner flight defensive maneuver took over when she turned heel and started back to the room from which she came, but the call of her name abruptly stopped her.

"Kat." Trenton spoke with a firmness that personified him and warned her there was no tolerance for flight this time.

She fidgeted and didn't turn to look at him.

"Turn around and come here."

Damn it.

She turned and faced her Dominus. His face was as it always was when she was about to be scolded or under his specific commands. Those eyes, like Kahlua crème, dialed in on her, pinned her where she stood. He brought a hand from the tuck in his arms up to stroke over his lips as he contemplated. However, what worried her most was Diesel's expression. Not the usual amused grin he would fight to hide because he loved to watch Trenton command her; rather, he wore something very familiar to that of Trenton's mien. An intensity that bore down on her ass like a hand. Apparently, the post-coital bliss was short-lived for him.

Time to put on the coy. She ducked her chin, glanced up at Dominus through her lashes, and tucked her hands behind her back. "Did I do something wrong?" She asked meekly to heighten the effect.

"You know perfectly well what you did." His tone warned her he wasn't going to soften to her attempts.

Trenton pushed off the sofa and approached her, and if she'd had half a mind, she would have taken a good ten or more steps backwards, but she knew better than that. She was caught, and while sometimes there was room to playfully avoid her consequences— this was not one of those times, and she dared not take her eyes off him.

"You released Paris from his restraints, didn't you?"

She met his gaze as he started to circle around her, but she couldn't keep it. Trenton had eyes that, though soft in color, could undress and throttle her to a wall with a look alone. The power he yielded made her body go warm with heat and she glanced away. Adding to the pressure was that Diesel was very much a part of the inquisition.

Slowly, Trenton circled behind her, then settled his hands on her hips and whispered in her ear. "Look at Patronus and tell him." He caressed his way down her ass with a hand. Kat tensed as her skin seemed to send out phantom-like sensations, as if already burning from a spanking. She sucked in a breath— her heart careened against her chest in a painful thud. She couldn't string two words together to dodge what she didn't want to admit to. She felt Dominus's

163

hands moving behind her, and she quickly realized he was rolling her short dress up to expose her behind.

"Place your arms behind your back with your hands to elbows." He spoke. And once she did, he placed the rolled hem of her dress into her fingers to hold it in place. Next, with merely a finger, he hooked her lace panties and pulled them down. Making a small adjustment, so the lace gathered right under her butt cheeks, he then dragged his finger along the curve to tease her and warn her of what was about to come.

Now she knew she was not getting out of whatever trouble she was in for. Hardly seemed fair. *Where was Paris?*

"There was reason for Patronus' plan of action. You were told this, and you were also told not to interfere. The torment Patronus was leading Paris through was designed to break him of his bad boy persona. He likes to fuck and run. Even when he wants to stay, he's never been tamed to feel like he could." Trenton came back around in front of her now and faced her. He sent her a long, hot stare. The blaze in his eyes sizzled her skin. The deep timbre of his seductive voice resonated through her, settling right between her legs. Despite such pooling response below, her mouth went dry, making it impossible for her to answer her Dominus. The moisture she needed to make her tongue work had traveled south. She could feel her insides growing excited in anticipation, because she knew, or rather her body knew, that whatever spankings or discipline she'd get, luck would usually have her truly get nailed to the wall, just as his eyes promised, because it turned him on that much. And that was her body's undoing, because being fucked by her Dominus was the most erotic act on earth.

Trenton, along with his air of power and control, got to her like no man ever had. He merely laid his cards on the table and now waited patiently, certain he'd come out victorious eventually.

"We expect an answer from you, mouse." Patronus spoke up from where he sat. Thick arms crossed over his chest, riding the deep calm breath that steadied him.

"But you were trying to ride a bull still tied in the stock." She spoke up in haste, "The only way to tame a real bull is to ride the buck out." She tried rationalization for her defense.

"So you admit to setting him loose?" Diesel inquired.

"I—" Katianna clamped her mouth shut and fell silent. The way these two hovered around her had her severely nervous. *Just how bad had she fouled his plans with Paris? She'd already gotten one discipline for him the other night.*

Trenton tightened around her, his head pitching into a menacing tilt. "I won't tolerate dishonesty. That's your second punishable offense. I might let it slide. But one more—" He reached around and popped her ass once, then soothed his palm over the fresh sting on her skin.

Her breath hitched at the back of her throat from the contact of his firm hand. "Can I plead the fifth?"

Trenton and Diesel shared a grin. They were obviously enjoying her cornered disposition, and she instantly saw that that her attempt at dodging them wasn't going to be an option either. "Then can I barter for leniency on Paris?" Again they smiled, but with a subtle difference. There was something she had not surrendered to Trenton, something he very much desired to experience with her, but he would never cross that line. Never demand it of her. Even in the arrangement that he owned her, which she did not argue or resist in any way, he would still not dare break or even ask it unless she gave it to him.

"I already own you, Katianna. Everything you are, and have, belong to me already. There is nothing to barter for, my Unicorn."

"There is one." She spoke softly, bowing her head.

"And what is that?" His question came just as soft as her suggestion.

"My skin for your cane."

"That is your hard rule. You know I will not break that."

"No, but I can rescind the rule and submit to your desires."

Diesel was suddenly sitting forward, his attention unbreakable from her as Trenton stepped in front of her and caught her chin, pulling her eyes to look up at him, "Seems like a large gift to barter with. Your punishment would most likely be less painful."

"But longer?"

His eyes narrowed and he went back to stroking over his lips a moment while he thought it out, before finally answering, "Considerably."

"But if I give you this, all is forgiven?"

Trenton glanced over his shoulder to Diesel and a silent exchange was passed between them. The slightest flicker in Diesel's eyes said no way would he want to pass it up.

"For Paris, too." She quickly added this condition, since she seemed to have a full house in her hands. Dominus snapped around to stare at her, as did Diesel.

"For a hundred strokes at my discretion, no more and no less. Twenty-five of those you wear for your own discipline, the next fifty are your gift to me and the last twenty-five are to pay for Paris' discipline." He closed in on her and she dropped her eyes, but he soon had her looking back up at him, his eyes searching her face, "Is this what you'll give me?"

She couldn't prevent the nervous swallow. "A hundred?" She nearly squeaked.

"A hundred. No more. No less." He held her chin so that she could not look away to hide her uncertainty.

She rolled her lips, but whatever moisture she placed on them didn't register in her mind, only his eyes and the sultry yearning that blazed within them.

"Kat?"

She nodded as much as she could will herself to. "Yes, Dominus, one hundred strokes."

He released her chin and reached around to her sides, restoring her appearance by taking her dress from her fingers, letting the ruffled hem fall down around her thighs, then pulling her panties back up. He kissed her— first, soft and tender as if coaxing her into believing she'd be just fine, but then that hunger she had seen turned unbridled and his arms seized her, yanking her off the floor in a kiss so potent and demanding, it threatened to snap her head off her shoulders. *Oh damn, she loved every moment of it.* She gasped when he set her back down and released her from his kiss so she could breathe again. Of course, that was when it dawned on her to ask, "When?"

Oh, the sinister smile that curled up on his lips. The Marque De Sade had nothing on this man. "When I deem it the right time. But before we leave here, your skin will be kissed with a hundred red stripes."

Damn.

~ * ~ * ~ * ~ * ~ * ~

CHAPTER ELEVEN

~ * ~ * ~ * ~ * ~ * ~

After that night, Diesel relented on the torture he gave Paris, but neither did he let him leave his side. And the sex— was almost constant. Even when it wasn't, Paris' persistence had finally waned, settling himself down into a comfort that included cuddling.

The four of them often spent the afternoons on the beach in front of their home. Katianna got to try some snorkeling in the shallow, pristine blue waters with promises of valor from Trenton that he would not let any sea monsters sneak up on her.

Roughhousing on the beach was another frequented sport and even Pyotr and Cliff were known to drop by and watch or even get in on the playtime action. Katianna made sure to stay clear of it, watching with rolling laughter from a safe distance.

Occasionally, they gave up their private time together to wander over to the other side of the island and enjoy a few of the resort's activities and meals.

Sasha had his hands full just trying to convince his twin partners to disrobe and trade in their steampunk regalia for swim trunks. The tedious task was finally accomplished after both Isaiah and Isaac got a hard spanking from

Sasha's belt. Now, the two pranced about, showing off their red welts from the night before that went with their mineral washed, brown square-cut Speedo trunks and their steampunk goggles, which they had apparently fetched when they snuck back inside the room. Sasha swore up and down he was going to whip them again, but so far no one had seen him actually do it.

Pyotr and Cliff were usually easy to spot. Pyotr had always had a lust for voyeurism and he was taking full advantage of the island's openness while he could. They could often be found lounging, with Cliff laying back over him, near one of the pools, or watching one of the resort's seasonal BDSM scene displays. Pyotr would almost always be playing with Cliff's cock while watching others in their own intimate bonding nearby.

Today's scheduled event was the Gladiator games and Katianna did her best to keep silent about whose idea that might have been. She'd already gotten into enough trouble and had bargained away everything she had, so she was keeping clear of Diesel's troublemaker for now.

~ * ~ * ~ * ~ * ~ * ~

Diesel's attention was more on what he wanted to do to Paris' body than it was on the games. It'd only taken a round or two before he was thinking about the matches he'd watched Paris engage in back home. How the Imp stirred his loins and woke up urges that had slumbered too long.

They sat on the bleachers, watching, with Paris sitting between his legs on the riser below him, and all Diesel could do was stare at the brat's body. He felt his mouth water to images of bending down and kissing the back of

Paris' neck, just above the new chromed steel collar he'd hooked around him this morning before they came out. Or he could reach around Paris' body and feel him up and down, then repeat. He sucked in a deep breath and nearly growled as it came out as a heavy sigh. Paris didn't even look; rather, the fucking brat leaned back against him, wearing his smug smile, knowing full well it was he that was causing all this frustration in him.

"Does my Patronus need something?" Paris inquired, much like a peacock asking if an admirer liked his feathers.

"Come." Diesel stood, capturing the heavy chains that connected Paris' collar to the matching chromed shackles on his wrists and hauled him up, "I need some lunch before I feed my other appetites.

Paris stood but resisted the pull, standing steadfast, which got Diesel snapping around and locking him under a stern gaze.

Diesel saw the wicked ploy in his Imp's eyes. Always calculating, always playing the game of seduction to get what he wanted. It never ended, no matter how many times they fucked, sucked, fondled or just kissed. Paris was insatiable.

"Aren't you going to kiss me first? You know you want to."

Diesel's lips curled on one side, he wouldn't argue that. The fact was, he'd thought about putting Paris in the Gladiator matches, but decided he wanted him all to himself instead. The memory of having watched him in them before was enough to stoke his inner fires again. As for the kiss— "No." Not even Paris would move him to break his displeasure of public display. He enjoyed watching others, but he never returned the favor.

He spotted Trenton and his slave at the buffet, and he fingered the chains dangling down Paris' chest. Not a pull, just a playful swipe, followed by, "You better follow this time." And he turned and headed off to join the other two, grinning when he heard the clink of chains that said Paris was coming.

He pulled Paris to stand in front of him then wrapped around him so he could rough-hug him down along the buffet table, instructing Paris to collect his favorites and load up a plate for him. Trenton was just a few guests ahead of them, loading up his own. Occasionally pausing to tease Kat with a berry or other nibble before adding something to the plate they would share.

"Will you be putting him into the games this afternoon?" Someone behind them asked.

Diesel turned and acknowledged the guest who'd posed the question.

"No, not this time." Diesel answered the man with a mild grin.

"Oh, come now— big strapping man like him would likely do well—"

"To that I have no doubt." Diesel idly commented. He'd already seen Paris in action and scrapped with him a few times himself. He knew all good and well Paris was a champion, but now he was *His* champion and he had no intentions of sharing him with anyone. Especially for someone else's sport.

"Maybe I'll just submit a demand to have him entered. I can request any slave I wish." The interested man tried to bend his eyes around Diesel's hulking form to steal a better glimpse at Paris. The ballsy statement revealed he was not a man of the Lifestyle. Just here to indulge in a taboo he knew nothing about. It was fine, as they'd expected many such as him to come to the resort's specialized season, but he was wrong to think the rule applied to any slave or that Paris was up for guest requests.

Diesel stopped and slowly turned towards the man, further blocking the view, but he kept his tone polite. It would do him no good to piss off a paying guest. "Except privately owned slaves. He's mine."

"How extraordinary, but a shame." The guest took no insult and showed his envy with a deep smile.

"Shame?" Diesel held his tongue, but he was becoming increasingly aware of himself and his dislike of anyone having any interest in his man. It was both amusing and at times, like now, pissing him off.

"That he's private." The man shrugged and turned around, facing the bar at the end of the buffet table, waving the bartender over for a refill, "Tell me how you came to possess such a treasure?" The conversation struck up as if the man had asked about his favorite golfing stop.

Diesel's gaze moved over back towards the small arena, to the gilded bodies waiting in line for their turn in the matches, then back at the guest, "I won him in a gladiator tournament myself."

The man's grin melted and a new form of lust floated up in his eyes, "The tournament?"

"Yes, where guests volunteer for the battles. The champion gets the pick of available slaves and invites them to his home for a contracted weekend, after their contract season is completed here.

The man's smile beamed with a near snicker. "Good day, gents." He raised his refilled glass at them then headed off.

Diesel grinned and watched him walk off with a particular focus in his direction as he sought out whoever could sign him in for such a match.

Paris leaned into him, "Guy doesn't stand a chance against my gladiators."

Diesel's grin turned sinister, "But he'll get a whole new perspective on pleasure."

"Yeah, his backside perspective."

"Not to mention, I lied." Diesel kept his laugh to himself, grabbed the shot of tequila and Paris' pink champagne from the bar, and led the way over to the tables to join Trenton and Kat.

Diesel watched Paris with his cocktail, finding it rather funny that he was so particular about everything. His hair and clothes always had to be perfect, and he always wore the perfect fragrance of the moment that was a science and an art combined. Food had to be four-star or higher. Even his drinks were— over the top selections of brand and recipe. "Is there anything you do that isn't completely *gay?*"

Paris finished his flute of Fleur de Champagne Rosé, looked at him with a peculiarly amused expression on his face, then smiled. "Yeah— you."

~ * ~ * ~ * ~ * ~ * ~

Something came up in the office that, despite their arrangement, Diesel needed to let Paris take care of personally. Trenton and Katianna had disappeared, off to one of the spas. A surprise to Diesel. Trenton wasn't usually a willing participant to let anyone else provide back and foot rubs to his slave, but Katianna had somehow convinced him into one of the couples' massages. It would have been something to witness for sure, but for now he sat comfortably in one of the chairs in Paris' office, watching the man make magic with a fussing client expected to arrive for his planned vacation in the next week.

Diesel tried to use the time to read but kept going back to watching Paris work. The man was beautiful and masculine, all wrapped up into one extremely desirable package. The nicknames Fallen Angel and Imp both fitting perfectly. Yet here was another element of the man. Aside from all that ego and vanity, Paris was polished professionalism, capable of studiously charming even the most disgruntled of humans into work friendly characters of their former selves. Not one patronizing word or dismissal as he made them feel important without compromising the resort's regulations set to protect its exotic services. And Paris was all *his*. *Thank the stars and stripes for that.*

Once the emergency was extinguished and the resort had earned yet another satisfied costumer, Diesel led his man over to the dinner area to catch up with Trenton and Kat. He even allowed Paris to remain in his light heather-grey suit slacks and the red semi-sheer Armani shirt he wore while at the office. Enjoying the suit porn that hugged Paris' body like a candy wrapper, he'd most likely tear into him later, but for now the view was pretty damn good.

TALON PS

After dinner, they gathered out on the terrace at the amphitheatre for the evening play, where the slaves and the handlers acted out tales of sex, greed, and jealousy. Last night's dinner theme had been luau style, followed with a play about the Hawaiian Goddess Kapo and the Flying Pussy, filled with the high tempo excitement of fire twirlers and hula dancers; tonight's theme had been Greek food and a less rambunctious play about Aphrodite and Ares.

Afterwards, the four retreated to the home he and Trenton had always shared and gathered out by the pool.

Trenton wasted no time having his beautiful little life slave naked and stretched out over his chest where he began to work her over with his fingers to bring her to orgasm, the first of many he planned to dole out under the moonlight.

Diesel had Paris in a similar hold, both completely disrobed. The red silk shirt in pieces on the ground next to them. He was reminded at some point the wardrobe tab was going to get considerably costly for him.

They watched Trenton and Katianna in their own embrace. Their sweaty bodies glistened beneath the combination of moonlight and the glow from the tiki torches that circled the patio. Diesel's breaths deepened while watching Kat's body writhe from Trenton's touch. "Look at them, Paris." He kissed him, "Look how beautiful they are." Diesel reached around Paris and began to stroke his eager cock with the heel of his palm with illicit intent, "Do you feel like she does when I touch you?" He worked Paris' shaft until it began to grow rigid then moved his hand down to tease the nerves in his scrotum.

Paris gasped, "I don't know if it's like her pleasure, but I don't want it to ever stop."

176

"Then why did you hide from me? I sent you messages from New York. Even asked you to come up, but you never responded."

"After the training, you were finished with me. You refused to come see me at my hotel before I left. I needed to be with you, but not as your slave. But you refused."

"I had to." Diesel stopped and pulled Paris' face around to look at him, "It's very common for slaves to think they have fallen in love with their masters when they've been possessed by them and shown such freedom and pleasure. I had no choice but to let you go. I needed to know I wasn't under the same spell. But after you left, I was insane to have you back. That's when I knew I wanted you."

"So, why didn't you just dismiss it and write it off that I was over you?"

Paris' pain was evident. He'd tried every way he could to avoid Diesel, but being here now didn't make that go away and Diesel knew that too. "Because you didn't show up at the auction. If you were over me, you wouldn't have made it such a big deal. You would not have missed that auction event for the world. But instead, you kept yourself hidden from me." He kissed Paris. First, gently, then near neck-breaking while he returned his hands to their original task of teasing Paris' body and working him up until he had Paris moaning with his head thrown back against his shoulder. Diesel moved his gaze from the heavy chest of his lover to the couple on the other side of the pool, watching as Katianna's back arched and she whimpered from another orgasm. His hand quickened around Paris' cock, loving how it was near throbbing in his hand. "Come for me, Paris. Say my name."

Paris gasped. He arched, pushing his head back against Diesel, turning to find his neck and sucking at it to anchor his whirling sensations as Diesel's hands continued rubbing over his body. He loved the strong, domineering feel of his touch. Especially when matched against his own. "God, I'm so close, Diesel."

Diesel shifted so he could fondle his scrotum while he still stroked his cock— hard, dominant strokes, "Say it again."

"Diesel." It came out in a heavy breath.

"What do you want from me?"

"Dammit, I want you to fuck me and never stop!" Paris growled, and just then his groin thrust forward and his semen shot out— white frothing cream spilling out like a fountain of lust over their bodies.

Diesel reached down next to them, grabbed the bottle of lube, and spattered a large amount over his cock. He took hold of Paris' hips and lifted him over his cock with brute strength, then slowly lowered him down, letting Paris' body weight work on taking him inside. Diesel was instantly chewing on his lip as the tight sensation took over. It was like Paris was perfectly molded to him— so tight, but not so much that Diesel couldn't fit inside him. *God, he loved fucking this beautiful beast.*

He was hooked from the first time. Paris took all of him, every inch, every time he wanted it. And Paris wanted in return, his desires never waning. It was just as Katianna had described it— a demon fucking a matador. And it had been just that raw and brutish, and no matter how many times he wanted it, Paris was ready for him.

The muscles in his arms flexed as he lifted and lowered his lover over his cock, over and over again, stroked inside his walls, driving them both to an unfathomable sensation of rapture.

"God, I love being inside you." Diesel growled, his hips jutting up to deliver a deeper penetration, then rocking back into the easy rhythm, his arms continuing to hold Paris elevated to allow the oscillation. "How does that feel? Do you like how I fill every part of you?"

~ * ~

Paris hissed as Diesel demonstrated what he'd meant, letting Paris' body slide all the way down until Diesel was deep inside him, filling every part of his nethers. Diesel's movements paused, rooted deep in him, teasing him with the throbbing jerks of his cock. *Fuck yes, it felt good.* Paris had never had so much pleasure with one man before, had never known satisfaction until Diesel, but damned if the man knew too many speeds and knew, all too well, how to torture him with them.

Diesel shifted under him. When he started up again, the change in pitch and shallow slide tapped against Paris' glory-spot, catapulting him to new heights and into a barrage of panting and moaning. Diesel continued to shaft him, building him up until he was close to orgasm and then shifting again. Abandoning the oscillating directive against Paris' prostate and diving all the way in until bottoming out deep within his ass. The shift of sensations was annihilating his ability to grasp where he was and what was being done to him— first, being in the throes of pure pleasure and losing it, then being caught up in another equally pleasurable surge of ecstasy. But it was destroying him, too. Diesel had him riding an endless wave, not able to reach its crest and tumble over in elation, but forever building higher and higher— driving Paris insane, chasing after his own orgasm like a dog chasing his tail.

Diesel moved again, in a calculated rhythm, from slow to medium speed and back down to damn near stillness, letting only the throbbing pulse of his cock stimulate Paris' insides. Paris struggled against him, but Diesel's arms held their strength and gripped him, giving Paris no ground to find some control of where Diesel's body was in relation to his own.

"Dammit, Diesel, fuck me! I can't stand this." His head was spinning like he was drunk. He tossed his head, letting out a loud groan, his breath becoming ragged in the instant Diesel started thrusting up inside him, hard and domineering, using the strength of his legs and the gravity on Paris' body so they slammed into each other, finding new depths like they could melt into each other from the friction alone.

"Fuck yes." Paris growled. He was so fucking close, the sensitized channel walls exploding with flashes of pink and white electric riots firing off and traveling throughout his body, only to bounce back again with the slapping of Diesel's rock hard hips against the cheeks of his ass.

Even the image in his head of knowing this muscle-packed, hard body of a demon was the one drilling into him, it was an overload to a man's fantasies, because Diesel was very much real. Even Katianna's characterization of him wasn't so far removed and it was the biggest turn on for him that he could fantasize about the same man who was fucking him.

"You like it hard, don't you." The growled words from his alpha lover told him rather than asked.

Paris loved how it sounded, loved the deep dark tones of Diesel's voice. He'd had plenty of lovers who liked to talk, but none came close to eliciting the response from Paris as Diesel did.

He was building, he was nearly there— could feel the tightening in his scrotum, but before he could peak, Diesel shifted gears, again, dropping down into a slow grind. Returning to his former shallow penetrations that had the engorged head of Diesel's cock sliding against Paris' prostate once more. "*Oh* god, don't do this to me." Paris protested and bucked back against him, hoping to regain the deep penetration, begging for it— desperate to prevent the sensation of his release slipping away from him, but still close enough to torment his need for it.

"Easy— you like it when I fuck you slow too, don't you?"

"No, damn you. I do not." Paris fought to get the words past his heavy panting.

~ * ~

"Oh, I think you do." Diesel stopped and lifted Paris up until his cock nearly slipped out then locked his arms in place, which kept Paris hovering too far away from the full penetrating feel he so heatedly begged for. He watched the ripple of need tear across Paris' body in a twitching dance of agony. "Just look how your body responds." Diesel moved Paris, bobbing him up and down over little more than the first few inches of his shaft so it kissed in and out of his hole. Penetrating him in shallow movements, stimulating the cluster of sensitized nerves against the sphincter muscle.

"*Oohhh-gahd!*" Paris cried out with a roar, his hands snapping down to grip the chaise they were on, and with all his strength he managed to overpower Diesel's grip— pulling himself down and completely impaling himself on Diesel's cock. "Oh fuck, yeah." He groaned.

Diesel grabbed hold of Paris' shoulders and pulled him back on him, then he rolled them both together, still managing to keep his cock lodged inside his ass. He guided them up so they were both on their knees on the padded lounger. Diesel planted a foot on the deck, positioning them both for the pounding Paris had been waiting for, but Diesel still only nudged inside him with small micro strokes of his steel. He ran his hands over Paris' back, feeling the tension building in him.

~ * ~

Paris thought for sure he was going to lose his mind entirely just waiting for the delivery. The anticipation alone would have been enough to make him crazy, but the short, soft strokes were a madness he was beginning to hate.

Two deep, full sudden strokes sent him flying, gasping for more— only to receive more teasing micro movements, hardly a few inches of Diesel's cock— sinking in just far enough to tap the edges of his g-spot, but never giving the full caress.

"Oh god, please, Diesel, stop this and fuck me."

"I am fucking you, my beautiful Imp. I wanna do this for another ten minutes or more before I start pounding you and when you cum, I want to do it all over again." And he sank in deep again, stroking deep and fast until Paris was panting, and then slowing again, shifting his penetrating angle to stroke one side then the other. Another angle and in with just a few full thrusts, Paris was exploding.

Ecstasy was anything but pleasant as it tore through Paris like a violent storm ripping him apart. He cried out, some strange drawn-out roar, as if it was someone else who had voiced it. He folded over, gasping and crying— the elation so high— so tender it hurt.

"Oh god, Diesel, help me." He gasped. He could feel the muscles in his legs and his ass flexing and tightening around Diesel's cock that was still pounding into him, driving his orgasm to continue, never setting him free, caught up in the tumbling spiral of a wave, never washing up on the shore and surrendering to exhaustion— not yet, at least. His whole body trembled, his legs turned to water, and he crumbled to the lounger.

One last deep, penetrating thrust and Paris felt Diesel's cum shooting inside him. Hot fluids blasting against his back walls, fighting for its own space— the added pressure sent another ripple through him— finishing him. Everything grew dark as adrenalin washed away— draining him of everything— his strength— his energy— his sense of self. Gone.

The last thing he heard was his lover's claim when he growled the word— *Mine!*

~ * ~ * ~ * ~ * ~ * ~

CHAPTER TWELVE

~ * ~ * ~ * ~ * ~ * ~

It was their last day on the island, but far from the planned ho-hum, wrap-it-up type day. Today was special. So, when Katianna stepped out on the patio, only to be left standing solo while Trenton and Diesel stepped away down toward the beach to talk privately, chills began to creep up her spine. Not any of the good or deviant kind of chills that her Dominus was apt to bestow on her to torment her yearnings. No, these tingles were the ones that always tried to warn her to go hide her ass before it got spanked, or something of that nature. Or— there was a change about to be set in motion so she wouldn't forget the deal she made with one of those particular dominant devils standing out there, already tanned to tropical perfection. Why did they have to look so damn good while plotting at the same time?

All she could do was stand there, frozen, and stare while the two men conspired at the edge of the beach. Not even when Paris stepped out, and stopped at her side, did she take her eyes off them.

Because— *well*— it was rather odd. The two men never had cause enough that they had to step away to talk among themselves without prying ears.

She glanced up and gave Paris a worried look, "This isn't good."

~ * ~

Paris only shrugged. It might seem out of place for them, but it didn't raise any concerns with him either. Not that it'd have given him any forewarning anyway, if it had. He hadn't been around them as she had, to know how disconcerting this could be. Or the implication of it, if she was right. But if she was worried, he had a feeling that the little Mouse and he were likely the subjects, and he couldn't help himself from joking over it to ease his anxiety. "Perhaps we should make a run for it while we still can."

"Oh, you wouldn't dare think of such a thing." She scowled at him, then seemingly reconsidered his suggestion, "Would you?"

His attention went back out to the two men who'd stopped walking. Whatever they were talking about was serious. There were no hand gestures made to make the mind recall a name or detail. There was no shifting from foot to foot or glancing about to make it a casual affair. It was all very straight forward as they faced each other, then quite suddenly Diesel threw his arms around his brother in an unmatched hug. An embrace that seemed to go on far too long for the two of them, but something had been granted. And now the seal was unbreakable.

When the men started heading back, arms over each other's shoulders, Paris could sense that some arrangement had changed, "Last chance—" he whispered. Yet a glance at her and her hands that were worrying themselves said she felt it too. Dominus and Patronus had just plotted something.

She glanced back at the two, "Wouldn't matter. They hunt down their runaways."

"What do you mean?"

"Why do you think we're here? Once those two have their hearts and minds set on claiming someone, they never let go. It's forever."

He'd only been joking with Kat at first, but the more he'd watched them, and then her, he'd grown anxious. Only, her last comment flummoxed him completely. What she said had a billion undertones to it, but before Paris could spill even the first of the million questions it created, Diesel and Trenton had returned and Paris found himself snapped up in Diesel's grip, pulled in for a demanding kiss. All those previous thoughts and notions dissipated. However, the searing passion behind Diesel's heated kiss did something to him. How Diesel's tongue slipped past Paris' lips to steal a taste of their kiss— the hand that gripped the back of his head to assure the force of it didn't break his neck— the entire conversation with Kat. The dispersion and disquiet melted down his spine and finally dripped away from his body onto the stonework of the patio deck.

"Today is a special day." Diesel finally withdrew and growled rather satisfactory words.

"It is?" Paris was far more breathless than Diesel was.

Diesel only nodded. Then a yelp escaped Katianna and Paris looked just in time to see Trenton flipping her over his shoulder and toting her off.

"Come, we're going out to the pool." Diesel grinned.

Paris looked past Diesel to the pool behind him then back to Diesel and cocked up a questioning brow.

Diesel grinned deepened, "Not that pool. Over at the resort."

~ * ~ * ~ * ~ * ~ * ~

Trenton and Diesel paraded the two out to the large orchid pool for some public sunbathing.

Kat wore the new string bikini Trenton had picked out for her, along with a crocheted lace robe that hung loosely down her legs, clasped closed by a couple of simple hooks. The pool deck was crowded while three resort slaves on display occupied a small vanity stage at its center. Their Handler whipped their bodies with silver cords made of water that spurted out a handheld water wick. Kat watched with fascinated curiosity as the three slaves fought back their giggles between what was meant to look like harsh beatings. When their Handler had had about enough of their silliness, he stepped around in front of them and teased the clits of both females and the cock of the one male with the same water wick.

Kat couldn't help but clench her thighs tightly, knowing perfectly well what the wick could do to the body.

Something caught her attention from the corner of her eyes and she turned to see Pyotr and Cliff relaxing off to the side in the shade of a cluster of palms and bamboo. His ever-watchful deep blue eyes looked her way while his hands were submersed in Cliff's shorts. Kat blushed but was interrupted from any further voyeurism of her own when she heard Trenton calling her.

He had pulled three chaise lounges together, but rather than call her over to sit with him as he usually would, he'd set a fourth out opposite of the others. He waved her to stand by the singled-out chaise, just as Diesel and Paris both sat down, got comfortable, and looked at her as if they anticipated an acrobatic show or something. Instantly, she felt a fist-sized rock drop in her stomach. She shot a hot gaze over to Paris, who also watched, minus all the fluttering belly stuff she was feeling from what she could tell. Smug as a bug, he was.

"Pull your bikini bottoms off, Mouse." Trenton turned and faced her as he gave her the command.

Katianna's eyes wandered over the thick crowd of guests around the pool; most didn't even glance their way, but the few that did chance even a casual look was enough to stall her. She had long since grown accustomed to being on display for Trenton at home and at the club, and occasionally at the restaurants that provided them with a semi-private booth. Being displayed where any and all could see her was still something she wasn't easily comfortable with and, until now, she hadn't been tested to comply.

"Kat, don't make me have to repeat myself."

Her scowl was almost immediate as she reached under her rope, finding the thin cords that kept the bikini secured at her hips, and pulled them free until the bottoms came undone and fell freely down her legs to the pool deck. All the while, her attention was on the guests, putting on her best— *don't you dare look at me face*— that she could muster.

"Now hang them on the corner of the chaise."

Katianna's head snapped around to Trenton, forgetting to wipe the expression she'd put on for the pool quests, and he saw it. "So everyone can see them." He added these words firmly. The warning look he gave her had her scooping them up, perhaps even stomping her foot once or twice while doing so, and then she hung them on the back of the chaise on the side turned to the pool as told. Like a flag, the scantily sized cloth hung, calling to all who passed by— *hey, I am bottomless*! She did as she was told, but was sure to top it off with a fully loaded pout, bottom lip and all. Which got her nowhere with him these days. His chuckling at her defiance only proved it as he finally dropped down and stretched out on the last chaise, hands placed behind his head, with Diesel to his right, and then Paris, who at least tried to hide his amusement. Though she couldn't blame him; for once, he wasn't the one pegged for the afternoon's torment for *Their* pleasure.

Trenton's warm grin glazed over her skin like honey, melting some portion of her pout, while he nodded for her to take her place on the stage he set for her. But Trenton wasn't the only one. Diesel seemed deeply focused on her as well. He even reached over, grabbing Paris' chaise and dragged it over until it butted up against his own, then helped himself to the insides of Paris' swim briefs. Couldn't blame Diesel either. The way Paris looked in them, she'd have dove in there too, if she were allowed. Trenton had picked them out. A dark, shimmering navy, square-cut low-rise briefs with the sides cut out in slots, and so form-fitted there wasn't a chance in hell they'd contain him entirely if he got hard, which looked as if that was going to be happening real soon. Of course, Diesel and Trenton were also close to indescribable eye candy. It was only good she was a writer and was up for the challenge. Diesel, for all his muscles and ink, was lickably colorific in his pair of low-rise boxer-briefs with a wide neon green waistband. The legs were crested with white, leaving the rest a dark royal blue. His, at least, had a pull-cord tie to ensure the massive bulge that filled them out remained inside.

Kat sucked in a deep breath and did a little more of that thigh tightening, because there was still her Dominus to ogle, and she didn't think any man could be sexier than Trenton. Their vacation had rewarded him with sun-kissed skin covering his firm chest, and the happy trail of black hair led her eyes down to the silver and navy, low-cut bathing suit-briefs that fit more loosely than Paris' or Diesel's did. But that pull-cord that dangled over the front edge and swung about the imprint of his cock— if only she was a kitten instead of a mouse, she might get away with pouncing.

~ * ~

Paris was fighting himself from rolling over and tackling Deez. The slow fondling and petting going on with his junk was fun when it started, but now he was ready for some more serious attention. Any attempts on his part to establish a firm grip and Diesel was quick to swat his hard cock for it. Now he sat, chewing his lip to shreds and crawling out of his seat while he endured the blissful torture.

Diesel's hand never moved beyond casual fondling. His fingers caressed over Paris' shaft then tickled around his scrotum. Slow, like a Sunday morning, and it was driving Paris insane. Even when the staffed slaves made their rounds, with a tray of summer flavored smoothies and waters, Diesel didn't stop or pick one up.

"You know, it is my birthday today. I think a view should be fitting on my special day." Diesel made a playful gesture to Trenton, though the subtle innuendo didn't fail to reach Katianna's ears.

"You're quite right." Trenton agreed, just as casually as Diesel was being, and turned his commands to Katianna,

"Mouse, I would like you to open your robe a bit." He sent her a smooth command then sipped from his ice water.

Kat's eyes surveyed the crowd that no longer paid any attention to them, then slowly drew the draping sides apart to show her legs, though she had them clamped together tightly. She was fidgeting. Every detail of the expression on her face said she knew she hadn't revealed nearly enough of what was commanded of her. Diesel twirled a finger at her in a silent command to keep going and she pulled her robe open. But she didn't volunteer to take her top off. Even when Diesel moved his fingers again, she gave him a questioning glance, as if she had nothing more to remove, with false hopes it would be enough.

Paris was new, but he knew better than that. As far as he was concerned, Kat may as well get it over and done with, otherwise they were just going to toy with her all the more.

"You did pick out the one with the hook in front, right?" Diesel prodded Trenton, who nodded with a laughing smile.

~ * ~

"Evil" was all she could think— she knew where all this was going to lead eventually, but to draw it out like this— *evil.* Again her gaze scanned the guests around the deck and in the massive pool, while her fingers came up and undid the hook between her breasts and let the bathing suit top fall open. Her perky, golden-brown breasts out for all to see. Only, fortunately for her, no one was looking, save the three men across from her.

She laid her head back, closing her eyes, pushing her thoughts to drift away until the laughing and chattering noise of people faded away. And it was just her, the sun warming her skin, and the two men who commanded her.

191

"I think I need to see more." Another taunting suggestion was made.

Kat pretended not to hear him; surely, Trenton would draw the line on Diesel's requests, at least out here. But any notion that she was safe from full exposure was shot down when her Dominus made the request a command. "Pull your feet in and open your knees for him."

Katianna's head shot up and felt her eyes grow wide as she looked at him.

"Don't give me that look. It's Patronus' birthday; do you want to be the one who has to take his spankings tonight at dinner?"

"Tuh—" Kat's mouth popped open like a fish, she was about to say he wouldn't dare, but his eyes tightened in on her, and she knew damn well he would. She threw herself back, squeezing her eyes tight to shut the world out as she slowly did what she was told. One foot, then the next— the hem of her robe fell from her thighs, and instantly she felt the warm summer breeze on her damp flesh— *Ooooh, traitor!* And her knees, rather than open involuntarily, did the opposite and clamped tightly together.

~ * ~

Paris had to admit that watching Trenton make his demands on the little Mouse was strangely turning him on. He'd watched every slave here on the island throughout last year's season and through the training for this year. He'd watched every Dom in their handling, and never did any of them affect him the way watching the Dominus direct his Life Slave did. Her defiance displayed in a silent protest only made her all the more adorable, because he knew in the end she would surrender to him, and the rewards Dominus gave her for her submission were both mind-blowing and blissfully satisfying. If it hadn't been for Diesel being with him, he might have been envious. Perhaps in a small way he still was. But only just.

"Watch it or I will put you on display too."

Paris chuckled at that empty threat. For one, Deez had already made him go through that. Blindfolded even— and he had hated it. But here and now, where he knew he was in Diesel's possession, it didn't bother him one bit. Because he knew no one else would be allowed to touch him, and he didn't care if anyone looked. Peacocking was his forte. And to prove it, he pushed up to his feet, stepped around to stand in front of his Patronus and shoved his swim trunks down. His cock sprang out, hard and hungry, because aside from Diesel's playing with him, watching Trenton master his little Mouse was turning him on. And he never got aroused about women. But the little Mouse had somehow crawled into his heart a long time ago and made a small nest for herself. She just didn't know it yet.

"I've been meaning to try you out with a cock cage."

Paris took a sudden step back, "The hell you have."

"Yes, the hell I have." Diesel dropped his feet to the sides of the chaise and sat up. He cocked his side to the side and squinted up at him, despite the brilliant sun that cast a halo around his Fallen Angel.

"I think maybe I need to add to my hard rules." Paris started backpedaling with his ideas.

"I think you need to just sit down right here—" he patted the space between his legs, "and be glad I don't have one handy to put on you."

The bit of power play was disrupted while a waiter came by with their drinks. Trenton was sticking to water at the moment, while Diesel and Paris were going light with a local brewed beer and Kat was being treated to a frozen smoothie.

Paris took his beer, sat as told, and decidedly kept quiet while Diesel reached around him and started up where he'd left off earlier, then gave Trenton a nod that it was okay to start the living view back up.

"Mouse— pull your feet up and set them on the edge of the chaise. Keep your feet up there and open your knees wide for me." With that, she nearly dropped her honeydew smoothie. She lifted her head and widened her eyes at him. "Don't give me that look. It won't hurt at all by doing what I just requested, but it will hurt if you ignore me. I want to see all of you— out here in the sunlight. You can do it on your own or I can come over there and use the belt off your robe to tie your knees open."

~ * ~

Slowly, she moved her feet to the precise instructions, all the while watching Diesel as he was watching her. She kept her knees together at first, but when he met her gaze because she'd not followed through, she knew she could no longer push the matter. Spreading her knees a tiny bit, she waited. A couple shadowed by two resort slaves walked past just behind the three men. All four paused to look and Katianna froze. Again Diesel met her gaze, then Dominus was leaning forward to stand. "Okay—" hating it, but she knew better than to disobey his orders any longer. She spread her knees wide and felt the sun hit her private parts. The sun's kiss wasn't new, but the four faces hovering behind her current audience of three were.

"Remember, there's no one here but me." Trenton's alpha tone called to her insides.

She closed her eyes, dropped her head back to shut the view away, and warmth heated her face, but she knew it had nothing to do with the sun this time.

~ * ~ * ~ * ~ * ~ * ~

LAST NIGHT IN PARADISE

Diesel watched from the doorway of their bedroom as Trenton dressed his slave. The present wrapped in a carefully selected narrow, lacey bandeau top with matching panties, and a swath of slinky fabric that hardly registered as a mini skirt hung loosely from her hips, yet never grazed an inch of her thighs. Her hair had grown longer over the year and now cascaded down past her waist in a mess of waves, concealing the cute little ass. It swayed as she moved while Trenton applied the final touches, dabbing her skin with a summer fragrance, enveloping her in green tea leaves, hyacinth, and frangipani. It was one of his favorites because he knew, throughout the night, a deep scent of Magnolia and Tuberose blooms would linger on her body. She spotted him in the mirror and her cheeks warmed with a soft smile. Those eyes. They could capture a man's soul just as she did his right now— seeing him. *She was perfect.*

Trenton turned and met his gaze. It was time.

He pushed off and walked to the patio out back. Paris was stretched out on a chaise, gloriously naked as if he was sunning, though it had gone down more than an hour ago. He looked and shot him a sultry grin. "You still have clothes on."

Diesel glanced down his body at the loose-fitting gray lounge pants and grinned at the tent between his legs. "Not for long." He chuckled and joined Paris. He dropped down between his legs, first delivering a kiss and taking several more for himself, before settling down with his back to Paris' chest, using him as his personal pillow and arm rests. *This too was perfect.*

It wasn't much longer when Trenton came out, bringing Katianna with him, along with a tray set of four small Pontarlier glasses, only slightly different from the style one might drink sherry from. But the bottle was anything but. Its green liquid captured the soft light from the sconces and tiki torches, giving away its mystery. Tonight Trenton would take them on a voyage of Absinthe.

"He still has clothes on, too." Paris mused aloud.

"Yes, and you know damn well that looking at him right now in his black boxer briefs, absent of any identification other than the cock bulging inside, is turning you on far more than if he had been naked."

"You insult me; I would most definitely be turned on if he was naked for my eyes." Paris coiled around Diesel, hugged him, then maneuvered his legs to plant his feet on top of Diesel's and inched one foot up to heel against his balls playfully.

They watched as Trenton poured a measured amount of Absinthe in each glass until the bottom bubble-like tier was filled, then topped each with a decorative silver straining spoon with a sugar cube on each spoon. The second decanter was nothing more than ice water, but it was the element for the traditional ritual: *The Louche.* Trenton used the crystal-topped decanter cork to slow the water flow, letting it drip slowly over the sugar cube so it dissolved and dripped down into the Absinthe. The result was the glowing cloudiness that would bring out the delicate flavors of the Absinthe. He could have used an Absinthe fountain for the water, but there was something about watching how well the man controlled each drop of water himself, with the patience of a Master. Delivering the distinctive *louche effect*, the same way he would deliver pleasure and pain, in the perfect ratio for the ultimate ecstasy.

With all four drinks finally created to perfection, he passed them out. Trenton's eyes never left Diesel's. Something deep and binding passed between them. They were blood brothers, had been through thick and thin. Always at each other's side and watched another's back. This moment was like that last pause for acknowledgement before taking the final concurring steps when climbing the tallest mountain. They'd concurred their lives and today was the day when they basked in the rewards. *It was perfect.*

"Salute." It almost looked as though the green fairy danced within Trenton's eyes. A deviant smile ghosted over his lips and he raised his glass, clinked against Diesel's, then to Paris, then twisted to do the same with Kat. Then— like a true lion over his own kingdom, he watched his pride drink.

The first sip hit the palate with a cool anise flavor that quickly melded with an herbal green flavor. Like having an entire summer meadow melting over his tongue after chewing down a piece of licorice. The bitter aftertaste was warded off by the sugar. Yet Kat made a retching sound that said the taste didn't win any favors with her, and Trenton was soon unwrapping something then passing it to her.

He turned and looked out into the night, lit by nothing more than a brilliant moon that was reflected back by the ocean. Trenton started up some tunes using the remote, playing one of Diesel's favorite new music discoveries. A *symphony-rock-chill-out* style group by the name of Maserati. It was ideal, keeping the energy high but freeing them to stick to their own mood for the night instead of one dictated by lyrics. Trenton adjusted the volume, and when Diesel could hear the surf down at the beach again, it too became perfect. He slid his palms up and down Paris' legs, enjoying having him wrapped around him. Eight days gone in a blink. Nevertheless, he wouldn't give them up for any others.

~ * ~

Trenton pulled Katianna to rest back against him as she sat in his lap. His hands caressing over her— down her arms— across her legs— combing through her hair with his fingers. Taking his pleasure of her as he desired. She felt helplessly adored. Invigorated and consumed at the same time. He was her cocoon, yet she felt so alive and free. An oxymoron that she had such a hard time explaining. Her. A writer— and it'd eluded her to such a degree it almost hurt that something so unique and beautiful couldn't be put to words.

"You know I love you, right?" He purred against her ear, "And I would never do anything I didn't think was right for us." The words spoken trailed down her neck until the lips that spoke them landed on her shoulder, while his fingers caressed her arm like a light tickle. She knew this and that she didn't need to answer. This was his ritual of crooning. Admiration and claim all rolled into one act of bonding. He plucked the candy stick from her mouth and closed in for a kiss. Deep and searing. He somehow reached all the way into the pit of her stomach with his claim, depositing an ember of his passion, and for the remainder of the night he would fan that passion within until it burned fiercely. "Mine." He whispered after he'd finished the kiss, "You will always be mine."

He held the sucker out, but rather than hand it over he teased her with it. "Show me."

She knew what his command called for and she stuck out her tongue to lick playfully at the candy. Cool beige eyes glowed with lust and watched her intently. Then he drew the sucker out of reach and captured her tongue between his lips, stealing the sweetness from her. It was a funny and odd position to be in, but the way he hummed around her tongue, and then those eyes— creamy brown— could she ever get tired of staring into his eyes? Certainly not. Because every time they looked into her she felt her theca grow moist, eager for his touch. He kissed her once more, then gave her the sucker back and pulled her to him again, letting her enjoy her treat.

"What do you have in your mouth?" Diesel asked, reaching for the stick caught between her lips.

"Mango sucker." She gave him a timid reply.

He grabbed it, "Give it to me."

But Katianna clamped her teeth down tight on the stick, refusing to let it be confiscated. "No." She'd had some earlier experience talking through clamped teeth a few years ago.

"Did you just tell me no?" He was rising up as if he was about to scold her.

"No?" She whimpered.

His hands moved to her arms, pulling on her, "Come here, before I punish you for that." His tone shifted to one of much deeper desire.

Katianna lifted to escape his hands but found Trenton instead, handing her over just as Diesel was pulling her to his lap. It was clear they both intended for her to go to him.

He grasped the candy stick once again and tugged at it, "Give."

Kat reluctantly surrendered her candy to him.

Diesel didn't even look at it, passing it up to Paris. "Now, kiss me."

Katianna's eyes darted towards Trenton, uncertain of Diesel's advances. He'd always been a dominant presence in her life ever since she'd been with Trenton. He'd sheltered her and watched over her with an equal possession, but she wasn't missing the undertones of desire that told his request was for far more than a playful peck on the lips. Something he'd never done before now.

"Don't look at him, look at me." Diesel's tone shifted to something more commanding, though not as firm as when he spoke to Paris. His hands tightened and pulled her to his lips and he kissed her reluctance away. His tongue probed past her lips and played with her tongue. He hummed at the sweet fruity flavor of her kiss, his hands stroking over her body in a slow motion like his tongue, tasting her curves.

He pulled free of her lips, breathing heavily, "Oh, I've been waiting for this for a long time." He chewed on his bottom lip a moment. Savoring the kiss. "Do you know what today is, Katianna?"

"Your birthday." She whispered now.

"Mmmm—" he purred, his groin shifting under her, finding that sweet spot between her legs. "And you know what he gave me?" He asked, knowing she would understand the *he* reference to Trenton.

She shook her head.

"Anything I asked for, and there's just one more thing I want."

"What is that?"

"You." His fingers dove into her hair and pulled her back to his lips, spearing her mouth with his tongue, delivering the full impact of his hunger for her until she was breathless. He eased her to sit up on him.

"For how long?"

"Until I decide to give you back—" his hand went up to caress a breast through the lace, finding the hard nipple under it and increasing the pressure of his thumb, "Perhaps I won't give you back until morning, though. Tonight, you are my Unicorn, and I intend to enjoy every inch of you to the very fullest."

His eyes seared into her and Diesel didn't have just any average set of eyes. Some might say hazel, except staring into them now, she could not agree with that assessment. The best way she knew how to describe them was as dirty blue eyes. Marine aqua blues dusted with cinnamon brown in the center, and she'd seen them change colors a hundred times since they'd met. But there was a new color burning in his eyes tonight, one she'd never seen directed towards her. *Lust.*

"Trent has described your tongue to me so many times, I swear I'd nearly cum just listening to him. Tonight, I want to know what it feels like, Kat. Tell me your answer."

She'd known all along this time would come, when they were ready, Trenton would share her with his brother and closest friend. And she always knew what her answer would be. *Could a slave be so happy and blessed to belong to two great men?* "Green." And without waiting for his commands, she slowly began to work her way down his body to grant the awaited wish.

She took her time working her way down. The absinthe already starting to do its mischief in her mind, transforming her new Patronus into a god upon whom she was requested to serve her gifted act of phallacio. A god who just happened to have two guns tattooed on his hips.

~ * ~

Paris watched in wonder as this new curve ball came into play. He hadn't expected this. Diesel was fond of Kat, even loved her, and Diesel had openly admitted that watching Trenton and Kat together was among his top favorite turn-ons. But for Trenton to actually give his Life Slave over to Patronus was a turn of events Paris never expected for any of them. Though, watching it now, it seemed the most natural. Had it been anyone else, Paris didn't think he would have been able to sit here and like any of it. But just as he himself would not refuse if Diesel gave him over to Trenton for his pleasure, he would not refuse Diesel his gift. Not to mention, Paris was intrigued how this little woman was going to manage Diesel's massive cock. Then again, Katianna came with a highly regarded seal of approval as far as mouths go, so not only was Paris watching with intrigue, he was taking notes. He watched each detail as she worked her mouth and tongue down the sides of Diesel's cock and even sucked in the flanged rim of his glans. She matched each move to the responses Diesel gave. She couldn't get more than maybe a quarter of his shaft and the broad cap in her mouth, and for the most part she didn't try to do more, instead working her talents to the outside of his cock for a better response. And those were beginning to come in waves of plenty.

Diesel's breaths became raspy and he made encouragements along the way so that she knew he was enjoying her so far.

Trenton wasn't sitting idle either, but he wasn't in any hurry to make any strides as far as his body was concerned. His left hand rested within easy reach to touch her if the separation became too unbearable, while his right hand lay over his lap, his fingertips lightly caressed the bulge there as if he wasn't entirely sure he wanted to do anything about it. But his eyes told a different story, and Paris wished he were telepathic in order to hear what lusty notes his eyes could make. Paris' attempts on the superpower trick were interrupted when Diesel's hand was suddenly reaching up to grab at his head and pull him down into a vengeful kiss, making Paris very much a part of the experience for him.

Paris reached down, smoothing his palms over Diesel's body, feeling the ripples in his stomach and the small rises of his hips as he endured the onslaught of Katianna's tongue. Paris enjoyed every nuance he captured under his hand and every moan that Diesel fed into their kiss. He might not have been the one wrapped around his favorite toy right now, but the pleasure was still as much his as it was the Patronus'.

~ * ~

Diesel thought he was going to go out of his mind. *Dammit, for a mouth that could hardly take more than the broad cap end, his cock hardly whimpered for more.* The drug effect from the Absinthe also played its part. All those books Katianna wrote and the vivid images she created within a reader's imagination were seeping into his mind. Taking shape and color. All those paranormal worlds filled with kings, demons, and gods— and here he was upon his throne with his Fallen Angel wrapped around him, keeping him earthbound, while his new Life Slave devoured his cock.

It was perfect. The one thing he had wanted since he was a young man turned out to be two things. He was determined to have them and now he did. A lover who could take him on full strength and match it, a lover who stole his heart right alongside it. And a Unicorn—

His bliss was shattered from the fairytale euphoria when something extremely cold was sliding down the shaft of his cock, and he tore from Paris' lips to glance down and see what had changed. He looked just in time to see Trenton's hand moving down the side of his chaise to tuck the glass of ice water under him where it would be safe.

Kat popped the ice cube in her mouth then went back to her phallacio, adding the cold sensation to her otherwise hot little tongue.

"Oh fuck." Diesel gasped, throwing his head back as her tongue moved the cold surface down one side of his cock then up the next, and finally brought it over the mushroom cap before she speared his hole with her now chilled tongue. His ab muscles bunched as she sucked him with the ice in her mouth. Her tongue probed the tender slit, spreading it open with the tip of her tongue, and pushed in deeper to assault the cluster of a hundred nerve endings inside the intimate slit. She circled over the wide head, laving over it with her flattened tongue, and then back to his slit, pushing in harder.

"Oh fuck." Diesel hissed, his hands fighting back the need to grab her and pull her from his cock. All his life, it had been a matter of his lovers struggling just to handle his size, attempting to suck him with the same skill they would use for a more user-friendly size. Little Mouse didn't attempt the same strategy. Yet, what she was doing was sending him through the roof.

Diesel grabbed Paris' hand, drawing it down to his hard shaft, "Stroke me, Paris—" he hissed, needing some balance to the zinging sensation this little creature was doing to him. Her mouth, while sucking on the flange of his broad cock, was licking at nerve endings that had rarely felt such attention. Now, she had him teetering on the edge of insanity. He needed to feel his cock surrounded in sensation. A harsh groveling moan escaped him when Paris' fingers wrapped almost completely around him, answering his unspoken desires.

"But careful you don't hurt her." His brain calculated some concern, knowing that once Paris' gears started turning, there was little that could grind him to a halt, especially when there would be no stopping the orgy of pleasure he intended to have tonight.

Diesel's head thrust back in reversed sequence to his hips as they bunched up, jutting forward into Katianna's mouth with the release of his semen, "Oh god, please." He begged, but he didn't complete the wish he hoped she would grant, and that was he wanted her to taste him— all of him. He had wanted her for so long, ever since Trenton had claimed she would be his. Diesel fell in love with her too, and he'd waited for this day when his brother would share her with him. Five years he'd waited for this, and it was all spilling from his cock in one frothy load of white cream. He wasn't certain she'd be able to handle him, but as his muscles twitched with aftershocks, he felt her tongue licking over him— around the broad tip of his pulsing erection still encapsulated in the warm wet confines of her mouth.

He sucked in a long breath, melting into her and being held firmly in Paris' arms, letting the two hold him, keeping him grounded to the earth, because fuck, he felt like he'd died and gone to heaven.

A shiver ran through him as she released his cock from her lips and lightly kissed every inch of his length, sending new shock waves through his nerves, ensuring he would be revitalized soon.

"Come up here, let me taste your lips now." He hooked her under her arms, dragged her up his body, and crushed her lips to his. His tongue slipping in gently, but hungrily, passing her lips and mingling with the tongue that had just brought him exquisite pleasure.

He felt like he was tumbling backwards in a Ferris wheel as they kissed, his emotions and bodily sensations swimming in a hazy pool of euphoria. He didn't want to let go, but he did so only when it was abhorrently necessary so they could both catch their breaths. After, he swung an arm up to capture Paris around the neck and pulled him down to deliver the same deep probing kiss, now saturated in his own essence and transferred to Paris.

"Tell me what I tasted like, Kat." Diesel wanted to know. He had always wanted to know ever since he heard how she had described Trenton.

Katianna kissed his chest and laved over one nipple with the flat of her tongue before answering. "Smokey and dark, like a grass fire on the Serengeti. Would you like to taste again?" Before Diesel could comprehend what her heated offering meant, she was over his cock once more, her tongue flattened out over the head, delivering a long broad lick that encircled the purple glans, slipping through the ethereal slit, giving it a slight suction and another laving lick. She grinned satisfactorily when she pulled away and moved back up his body to deliver the taste to his tongue. Diesel's mind was blown away and readily accepted the deep kiss. True to her offer, he could taste the precum on her tongue, hot and smoky—like a wild fire on the grass plains— just like she said.

"Are you happy?" She asked with the hope she hadn't failed him.

"Oh, very much so, but I'm far from finished with you. I still want to break your virginity."

Kat tipped her head up and put on a prissy smile, "My cherry was popped a long time ago." She snipped.

"Not by me, it hasn't." Diesel sat up, snatched her up and slung her over his shoulder, and then carried her inside. He sent her bouncing on the bed, then found her ankles and jerked her to edge of the bed in one brutal pull, bringing her sex firmly against his mouth so he could dive in.

Katianna screamed, instantly jackknifing on the bed, and her hands pressed against Diesel's head as she struggled to wriggle free.

"Paris, hold her down." Diesel commanded him from between her legs. He was going to have her and no amount of fighting was going to stand in his way.

Paris stepped toward the bed, but Trenton was already there and redirected him. He pointed Paris in the direction of Diesel's lap, then took up the position of holding his slave down; stretching out against the bed rest, he pulled Katianna back down.

"Trenton?" She pleaded, seeing her Dominus over her now.

"No, dammit! She's mine." Diesel growled as he lunged back onto her body the second it became accessible to him again.

"I wouldn't dream of taking your party favor away from you tonight." Trenton grinned like a deviant lion, holding his prey down for the pack to devour as he watched lazily.

Diesel plundered Kat's body, but his mind reeled, feeling out the room around him. He wanted Paris with him. *Where did he go?* Just then, he felt a hand between his legs, spreading him, then felt soft hair brush against the inside of his thighs. He tore away from the wet cunt he was lapping up to look down and there was his bratty Imp, slipping between his legs. "Paris." He dropped a hand down to touch his hair and his face. Diesel's blood coursed like flames. The savage lust he felt was about to be complete. Being swallowed up by the orgy was like being fed pure gasoline.

He shifted his legs, gave Paris more room to work, and rocked his hips while he watched his cock slide over the man's lips. *Gods, he was beautiful down there.* "That's it, Paris, I want to feel your mouth over my cock." His words rasped out, barely having control over himself. He felt like a rutting beast set loose on the two sexiest creatures in the world, and they were both his tonight while his brother watched. The convection of the three's location around him, creating a decadent liquor for his palate like nothing he had ever imagined. And he had imagined and experienced many things. Nothing came close to this, and he found he couldn't hold himself back any longer. Nor saw any reason to. He dove, face down, between Kat's legs, covered her sex with his mouth wide open, and gorged his appetite on her body. Sucking every droplet of honey from her, just as he felt Paris take a considerable amount of Diesel's cock into his mouth.

There was a strange euphoria being pleasured and pleasuring at the same time. Like flying and falling at the same time.

"Mmm. Sweet." He caught one of the petals to her entrance between his lips and tugged on it playfully before moving back, flickering his tongue around her clit with purring strokes and checking for the delicious nectar to follow.

Ohh, yeah, there it was. Dew drops. Sweet honey. He smiled at the sight then plunged his fingers into her to coat them in her silk. Then he pulled free and began to tease the rear hole.

He rocked his hips down and pumped into Paris' mouth. Felt his hands roaming over his body. The high— he could not describe it, but it was well worth the wait he'd endured. He turned his concentration back to Katianna— to the delicacy he had spread wide before him. He used his tongue to flicker, lick, and paint her flesh with his hunger. Leaving her gasping as she tried to resist. She really did try.

Paris brought him the same pleasure, teasing his cock, sucking it into his mouth, and tempting Diesel's control the same as he was tempting Katianna's, until the attention to his cock had him drawing close to his limit. He needed to feel himself fully submerged, deep inside his salaciously designed orgy. Paris preferably first. As he hoped it would always be.

"Damn." He growled, then sank his teeth into Kat's thigh and left a quickly made, small suction mark. He attempted to push to his feet except for the greedy attachment on his cock, "Paris, come up here." He heard a slight protest and felt the tightening grip of Paris' hands, not wanting to let go of his prize. *Always the brat, he was.* "Now, Paris. I want to get inside you." His growl growing more insistent.

Paris relented and wiggled out from under him. Diesel glanced at Trenton, "I want to watch you keep her wet for me." With those words alone Trenton was sitting up, yanking Kat further up the bed as he sat back against the headboard to oblige the request.

Diesel never even glanced away, watching with a heated expression as Trenton got her into position, and suddenly his fingers were buried deep inside her wet cunt. It was too much and Diesel snapped around and attacked Paris' lips with a demanding kiss, gripping the back of Paris' head with a firm hand. Demanding— self-indulgence. "I need to fuck you and I'm going to watch them while I do it."

Paris revealed his typical proud, slutty grin. Diesel had no choice but to kiss him again, just to remove that smirk from his lips. He didn't let up until he needed far more than a kiss. He just couldn't put it off any longer. He released a breathless Paris and expelled a curse of his own, "Now, damn it."

"Okay." Paris finally gasped, "Since you put it that way."

Diesel was now wearing the smirk he'd stolen from Paris, "I knew you'd see it my way."

He crawled up on the bed, stretching out crossways so he could still watch his private show and still have all the bed space Paris and he would need without concern for crashing to the floor. Paris was already climbing up over him. Hands and kisses dotted about freely without any calculated pattern, but in between such caresses, Diesel spied a new smirk on his lover's lips. No surprise, but he had to wonder how Paris' ego came with an unlimited supply. "Dance for me, Paris."

Diesel's lungs sucked in deeply, just watching Paris get into position, straddling over him like a well-practiced artist of seduction. Their eyes locked. Those dark brown eyes, like endless pools, were nearly black with lust. Paris' chest expanded, slow and languid, pumped with the adrenaline of anticipated sex. A food source neither of them had ever been able to deplete until finding each other, and they had so much catching up to do. Together, they knew they would enjoy the long, demanding ride to see it done. But there was no urgency. Vanquishing demands and aggressive devouring were spices on the plate, and rushing to the end of the meal wasn't necessary. Especially tonight.

Paris lifted up on his knees and began to rock his body in a sensuous S that spiraled from top to bottom and back up again. He popped a bottle of lube open and let a healthy amount dribble over Diesel's shaft, then worked it all around with a few hand strokes before he went back to his dance moves over him. It must have been a sight to see— Paris back in the days when he toured the globe, performing before a crowd of people, teasing his audience's eyes with his body while stripping off all his clothing, one piece at a time. *Did they see what he was seeing now?* His man moving around in the most seductive way a man could move, oblivious to the outside world as if his sultry rhythm had entranced him as well as Diesel.

Paris lowered down to grind against Diesel's body and over the slathered cock, working his own body down so the thick shaft parted his cheeks and shared the lube between them in a slick back and forth slide.

Diesel clamped down his teeth and let out a tight hiss.

Paris never reacted to it outwardly, but Diesel knew he was gauging him well. He lifted his arms around his head as he closed his eyes, still grinding his ass over Diesel's cock. Paris' own cock jutted up like a rocket and bounced about before him with an occasional tap to Diesel's belly.

With the next lift of Paris' body, Diesel stuffed his hand between them, took hold of his shaft and held it in position while Paris slowly began to lower over it. His hips moved in a figure eight gyration, cranking down over Diesel. Like taking in a screw. Funny how the analogy came into play. Yet, that's exactly what it was, as Paris' hips spiraled down and worked Diesel's cock deeper and deeper into his ass. The sensation that came with it was taking Diesel on the fast track to the edge of exploding. "Oh fuck."

A happy-as-fuck hum rang over him, and once Paris had taken every inch of Diesel's cock inside him, the dance continued, now gyrating back up, rocking forward and back. There wasn't a submissive cell in Paris' body. Not in any form as a lover. Paris knew what his body did to him with every curving— spiraling— rocking— motion. Each used in deliberate rhythm to exact a purposeful reaction from the man he rode. Paris' arms swung out then snaked back in to touch himself as part of the moving show. But that was about all the idle watching Diesel could take before becoming an active participant. He reached out, clamped onto Paris' pecs with a fierce demanding grip, and then pulled his Fallen Angel down for a strained kiss. For strained was precisely what it was when their concentration was concededly locked in other designs of their bodies. *Like the way Paris' choreographed seduction created amazing euphoria in a spellbinding wave of fucking and then trying not to cum too soon.*

Diesel mapped out every nuance of muscle in Paris' body as the man moved over him. For a man Paris' size and the amount of muscle bulk, it was amazing to see how he had the lithe movements of a vixen cat. Pure, unadulterated, sinful sex. That's what Paris was. And one hundred percent all his, because there was no way he was going to let him get away from him ever again.

He glanced over, seeing Kat and Trenton both watching. His brother's eyes intensely soaking up all that Diesel saw in his lover and perhaps more. Nothing ever seemed to escape Trenton. His lust for others' passions was unfathomable. Every seduction and kink was the man's dessert, all set on display in the shop window of a bakery, even if he didn't indulge in all of them personally. He knew them and understood them. He watched others partake and could delight in it through the very observation of them. Seeing them explored was his mastery over everyone else. Like tonight. Trenton had made this night happen. But tonight the Dominus had also lent the control over to him entirely. Diesel decided right then he wanted to exercise his rights and reached over, snatching Kat by an ankle and pulling her from her Master towards him. "Come here. I haven't tasted enough of you yet." She was no sooner moving within reach when Diesel snatched a thigh and spun her around to face Paris, so she too could watch, if she was able to sit still, as he brought her legs over his head, right over his face.

He locked one arm around her hips, fingers pressing into the small of her back, and held her firmly down over his face, while his other hand blindly sought out Paris' cock. It wasn't hard to find, even with feeling around blindly, and he soon had it as well and began to work his lover up for a finale. He wished he could see the play between the two, see the expressions on their faces while reacting to his commands, as well as feeding off each other's drowning pleasures. He could only hope it was how he imagined— what he wanted to have with them. His Fallen Angel brat and his Unicorn.

It wasn't long before the explosion came and when it hit— where the three of them went he could not say— but he doubted any of them were still on Earth. At least for a good twenty minutes or so until the high eased off, maybe even longer. Because the post-coital bliss of having those two slumped over his chest together, where he could wrap his arms around them at the same time, kept him high for much longer.

He felt someone moving on the bed, then Trenton's face came into view. His intentions clearly sketched on his face with a naughty glint in his eyes. The Dominus was not finished with him yet, and it was then Diesel perhaps realized his brother had never truly relinquished control. For the slightly up-curled smile on his face said the fucker had planned every detail of this, and thus so far, all had gone according to *His* plan. But Diesel wasn't up for arguing just now. Fine, it was the Dominus' plan, but it was Patronus who was the center of those plans, like a gluttonous pig, and very content to stay there for a while.

"You ready to try your four-way?" Trenton purred as he brushed the mop of hair aside to unbury his Mouse and rouse her with a kiss. Obviously eager to partake himself.

"Yes—" Diesel hissed, his hand now fisted into Paris' hair as he licked over his abs, teasingly close to his cock. "*Mmmm*, fuck yes."

Trenton glanced at Paris, "You understand what a service top is?"

Paris' naughty grin was back, showing he knew full well what he was being asked.

"Make no mistake with those peacock feathers of yours, you are the slave and your commands are to service your Patronus as he demands. Even if on top."

"Yes, Dominus." Without any diminish to his wiles.

"Get on your back, Trent." Diesel let out the straightforward command, pushing up from the bed.

Trenton returned to the bed, rolling to his back, and scuffed off his briefs in a clean push down his legs.

Paris didn't hold back any expressions of his enjoyment over seeing Trenton naked.

"You just stay right where you are and wait for your instructions." Trenton gave him a playful warning, which seemed to roll right off Paris with little concern. Next, Trenton was curling a finger at Katianna to join him. He shared a tender kiss with her then reclined again on the bed, laying her back over his chest, where she looked up at Diesel and Paris as they waited for them to get into position.

Diesel followed, bringing Paris onto the bed as well. He grabbed up the lube, taking some pleasure in getting everyone ready.

Trenton edged Kat over and grabbed his shaft to slather the lubricant over it, relishing some physical pleasure in the making as he watched Diesel and Paris do the same to each other while also sharing a kiss. As much as Diesel had always enjoyed watching Trenton and Mouse together, he oddly found being watched by them equally pleasurable. He'd never been one for public display, but then again, when Trenton watched, it wasn't ogling. He suspected he might have enjoyed Trenton's eyes on them, no matter what.

Diesel let out a grumble and brushed Paris' fist from his cock, "Mmmm, that's enough, I don't want to get worked up that I'm too close. I want this to last."

Paris pressed in for a full body connection and a lingering kiss, "Then our Patronus shall have what he wants."

Not another word of encouragement was needed. Had Paris protested, Diesel knew he would have refrained. But he could see in Paris' expression that he wanted this too. Not just for him, but together. He had truly found the right one for him.

Diesel got into position, tucking a knee under his brother's thigh and scissored over the other. He glanced down at their Unicorn, waiting for him with all the lust that could burn in a woman's eyes. Diesel knew— had always known— she was the right one, too. The Unicorn for them both. And with Paris finally brought in— making them four.

"Let me get inside you, baby." Trenton whispered in Katianna's ear and his hands gripped around her hips, lifting her and then easing her down on his cock. The ease in which he slid in revealed he'd done well to prep her body for this, and they both let out their own moans as his cock slid in.

Diesel closed in, lowering between Kat's legs, brushing the engorged, broad mushroom head of his cock against her soaked pudendum. He couldn't hold back any longer. He'd waited too long for this, wanting her so badly, that now he found himself unable to draw it out any longer and so began to push in, slow and easy. It would have been tight, even without Trenton already filling her backside, but now— he found himself worried that he might not fit at all. Her lips came apart with a mute gasp, then she sucked in a deep breath and let it out. Trenton murmured in her ear, talking to her so she could relax and let her body accept Diesel's cock.

He could feel her natural silk easing his way, but the extra lube helped his entry further, feeling her walls contract and tighten around him as his girth demanded them to stretch for him.

"Oh, my god—" he huffed out, "it feels incredible inside you, Kat. The perfect little Unicorn slave." His eyes closed and he breathed deeply as he sank in further. Taking his time until he was all the way to his hilt and felt his balls pressed against Trenton's. Not for a moment was Paris sitting back idle. His hands roamed over Diesel's body and he kissed him along his shoulders and neck, already in near position, grinding his cock against Diesel's ass.

Diesel couldn't wait any longer; he wanted to be indulged to the limits and beyond that. He glanced over his shoulder, "Now it's your turn to serve me, Paris." He reached around, found Paris' hips, and pulled him towards him.

~ * ~

Paris had never held back on his lust for sex, in any way or form, though it seldom sated his needs. But here and now with Diesel, Trenton and Katianna— Paris found himself almost drunk on it. And they weren't even done yet.

He let Diesel guide him and he pressed his cock against the crevice of Diesel's firm ass, teased himself a moment, then leaned away so he could spread Diesel's buttocks apart to admire the beautiful, tight hole. He maneuvered his hips so his lubed cock slid between Diesel's ass cheeks and then

217

pressed in with a gentle nudge. He rocked back and glanced down again, enthralled as he watched his Patronus' body react. How the rosette twitched— first tightening, then relaxing to let him know he was ready for him— wanting him. Paris nudged against him again, waited to feel the entrance relax, then slowly he pushed his cock past the tight ring of muscle.

~ * ~

Diesel let out a hard gasp as Paris' cock worked its way in. Paris' hands were right back to their roaming— his back— his ass— the backs of his legs, while he slowly and steadily rocked in and out with micro movements to ease his way into his ass, each motion letting him reach deeper and deeper inside.

He could feel the pressure of Kat's succulent pussy tighten around his cock as Trenton began pushing up inside Katianna with slow deep thrusts. Each one lifting her up and onto Diesel's cock. The motion simultaneously sent him pushing back against Paris, taking him in deeper until he was filled completely. He stilled— just for a moment— to float in the hazy mix of sensation, swirling intoxication, pleasure and pain. A whirlpool coiling around him, skittering over his nerves, which strangely felt like raindrops and static. They all melded with one another. The stretching bite of being penetrated eased and replaced with a delicious awakening. He let his senses soak up the crimson pleasure he felt, then he finally started the wave action among the four of them.

Paris standing behind him, holding his hips, set the tempo for everything else. At first, the strokes were slow and sensual, and he savored the friction of male flesh against male flesh. Paired with the slick cavern of the woman underneath him, as he rocked and ground inside her, he felt Trenton mirror his movements.

The room filled with a blurring echo of moaning and heavy breathing. Katianna's becoming more of a mewing as she took on both Trenton and him. Paris sounded nearly feral behind him.

Diesel was just as high as a god in his own realm for a brief moment of carnal slaking lust. He may never have it again, but this was heaven for now and he made no attempt to settle the sensation in him. He let them take over, saturating his mind and body, and willingly became lost in the connection of bodies. He rose back on his knees, tucked in tighter against the tangle of legs from Trenton and Kat, and dropped his head back. His hand already finding the back of Paris' head and pulling him in for a demanding kiss. Never pausing in any movements, never ceasing the pleasure that stormed around them.

He could have done away with the Absinthe tonight and he would have still been intoxicated. The sounds— the sensations— the scents of their bodies warming up and perfuming the room, it was all too rich not to be drowning in it.

"Fuck, yessss." He hissed when he let go of their kiss, then bent over to do the same with Katianna. It was far rougher than he should have been with her, but she didn't squirm in the least, welcoming him as he was. So he held nothing back— tasting her tongue and nibbling on her pouty bottom lip while catching his breath the moment he felt Paris slam deep inside his body. He flexed his muscles, tightened around Paris' cock, and heard a growl emanate from behind him. But Paris' control wasn't the only one reaching its limits. He could feel Trenton shudder under them and felt the muscles of his brother's thighs bunch together as Katianna grew more vocal.

How he loved the sounds she made. Small bleats and moaning purrs she tried to contain, but Trenton never allowed it. And Trenton's hand often came around, reaching between them to torment her clit and ensure all those beautiful sounds came out a little louder so they both could enjoy them. Nothing left to chance— nothing withheld.

The momentum was building until it grew more intense, and Paris pumped harder, slamming into his ass. The inciting experience of his orgy had him tumbling in a crash of waving euphoria. Each stroke— each dive, building— and climbing— setting them loose into a fucking lust they'd never been able to touch. Diesel saw it even in his brother's eyes, deeply rooted from their past. The things they had desired now coming to their full culmination. Each caught in their own expression of moaning delight. It wasn't long before they were all panting and groaning. Paris slammed into Diesel's deep channel like a rutting bull, his cock pistoning into his body, bringing Diesel closer and closer to climax.

~ * ~

"Deez!" Paris panted his warning along with what he hoped was the approach of everyone else's peak. His body melting into each driving thrust, the peristaltic wave around his cock was going to have him cumming in no time. He tightened his grip on Diesel's hips, while another hand rested at the shoulder blade to gauge his impact as he slid into Diesel's ass, sending him back into the small woman sandwiched between Trenton and them. But he couldn't slow or stop, driven by pure need to cum. "Oh damn, I'm so close." His head rocked back on his shoulders, and he let out the groan that strangled any other words from forming.

~ * ~

"Trenton?" Diesel called to his brother with a choked voice. "Oh shit— I'm not going to be able to hold back much longer." He admitted it before Trenton could even give his own answer. Diesel took a deep ragged breath, "Cum for me, Kat, while Dominus and I fill you with our release." He hammered into her with several more strokes and willed the muscles in his sphincter to tighten around Paris.

"Ah, fuck, Diesel!" Paris cried out, his hips jutting forward and Diesel could feel the release hitting inside his back walls, filling him further. Trenton and Katianna's cries joined in with Paris', filling the room with moans. Their bodies shuddered around him, and he slammed into the hot theca, as it clinched around him one last time, and let his orgasm go. His whole body locked up. His head kicked back, finding his lover's shoulder, and strong arms wrapped around him, absorbing the tidal wave of release that shattered through his body.

Diesel let out a loud roar while his cock unloaded his release inside Kat. He couldn't bring the rutting and shunting of his body to calm until he felt everything finally drain out from him. He dropped down on his elbows, catching his weight, along with Paris' too. He lay there for long moments, just feeling the cacophony of heartbeats from his chest and from the two under him. He could even feel the pounding of Paris' chest thumping against his back. He loved every bit of each sensation and didn't dare move, lest he might miss out on one instant of a heartbeat that belonged to him tonight.

He took in a long deep breath, and when he finally opened his eyes, he found Trenton looking up at him, well satisfied himself, and looking equally content with remaining a little longer.

"Damn, that was the most incredible experience I have ever had." And without another thought, he leaned in and kissed Trenton on the lips, light and firm. It was chaste and implicatively awkward, but necessary to complete his experience. He dropped his head, surrendering his forehead against Trenton, and laid a kiss against the glistening sweat that soaked Katianna's hair, "You okay in there?" He wondered, since she was caged between him and Trenton.

Pale blues peeked up at him before closing again, her response barely an audible hum followed by a warm giggle.

Diesel let out an exhausted chuckle. "Yeah, that's kinda how I feel, too." He felt a concluding caress from Trenton on his back and remembered someone else was back there too, "Paris?"

Paris responded by kissing his shoulder as he stirred above him.

"You still alive?"

"Hmm, I hope so— because that was incredible and I hope we do it again someday."

Diesel locked his content sex-filled gaze on Trenton, "I think our pets are well fed tonight." And he eased up, lifting Paris with him as they both withdrew from their respective bodily connections. Diesel crawled up further on the bed and stretched out, pulling Paris down to face him as they both lay on their sides. Paris stopped short to rest his face on Diesel's chest, pulled one of Diesel's legs over his hips, made sure they were well good and tangled, then lastly wrapped his thick arms around Diesel's waist. However, Diesel's nest of bodies wasn't complete just yet. He would have it no other way. He reached over, grabbed Katianna by the arm, and pulled her in closer for her to snuggle next to Paris, followed by Trenton taking up the opposite end.

He felt so full, so sated in a way he'd never experienced before. He'd had three-ways before, but not like this, not in such a way where one person conducted all the bodies to ensure they all came together. His mind drifting— dreaming— *the four of them.*

"So, did I satisfy you and your birthday wish?"

Diesel cracked one eye open to find Trenton looking at him with a —*know damn well he did*— look about him. *Had Trenton ever failed to meet someone's fantasies? Probably never.* He took a deep breath and let out the hard sigh, "Yes. Way better than a party at the club. And it's not over yet. Kat still has a debt to pay." He sucked in another deep breath then let it out with a long heavy sigh that made him feel like he was sinking further into the bed. He wasn't sure he could dredge up the strength to move at all, let alone get up to watch Kat submit to his brother's cane. *Not that very moment, at least.*

~ * ~ * ~ * ~ * ~ * ~

CHAPTER THIRTEEN

~ * ~ * ~ * ~ * ~ * ~

Kat woke when the heat from the cocoon of bodies became too much. It was summer, for crying out loud. The sliding glass doors, along the back wall of the house, were still wide open since they slid into their recessed hiding spots inside the wall when they first arrived and had remained so ever since.

A near constant breeze flowed through the house, carrying with it the fragrant smell of sea salt, sand, and the mix of flora and fauna. It mingled well with the myriad of male colognes that also surrounded her. She took a slow deep inhale, loving the smells of male testosterone, sweat, sex, cologne, and the sea breeze, but she couldn't stay tucked inside the hot cove of their bodies a moment longer.

Slowly and carefully, she pushed up on hands and knees, lifting off Trenton and slipping out from under Paris' arm. Then slowly inched her way backwards to the foot of the bed. Her eyes remained glued on Trenton, expecting him to stir and call her back any moment, but to her relief he didn't. Perhaps in the nest of bodies, her absence didn't quite register enough of a change to pull him from the deep sleep. Doubtful, but he was letting her roam anyway. Nevertheless, once free, she didn't hover over him either, since that would most definitely wake him. Trenton had that strange radar sense even when he was sleeping.

It felt late, though the glowing indigo numbers on the clock read only a quarter after ten.

She crept outside out onto the pool deck and waded into the pool. The cool water was a welcomed relief, but she didn't go past the first couple of steps— just enough for her legs as she sat down on the edge.

Something stirred inside her, waking the creative writer, but she wasn't sure what. Something new and unfamiliar. Far more profound than her usual stories of passions and foreboding lust. It was something about the uniqueness of her life. There was a message in there somewhere, but she couldn't quite place it. Despite her content blissfulness, the stirring made her feel like a ball of anxiety had settled in her stomach. Like the feeling one gets while reading a thriller and she was sitting on the edge of her seat, waiting with baited breath— anticipating something to jump out at her— *what's hiding behind the door?*

She twisted around, glancing back to the table where the bottle of Absinthe still sat. A suggestive murmur worked its way to the surface in her mind, and then she noticed one of the glasses had been left untouched. The cloudy green liqueur still waiting. She puzzled over it and got up to investigate closer. She traced the bottle with her fingertips; recollected each step of the earlier preparations in her head. Seeing Trenton pour four glasses. She could see Patronus and Paris holding theirs. Then her Dominus passed the next to her with a deep grin on his face. That Cheshire cat grin for which he was notorious when he was scheming with the ultimate experiences at hand.

~~ He'd taken his glass, and she saw him sniff at it as most do their wine or cognac. He had held it up to them— spoke the word, Salute. *~~*

She pressed her memory further but, for the life of her, she couldn't recall seeing Trenton drink it. The empty shot glass that had been hers was sitting next to the one untouched. She touched both. He hadn't, because he had taken hers from her hand and then pressed it to her lips for her to drink. *He* had fed her the Absinthe as he did with nearly everything else. He never picked up his own again after that.

She dropped a finger to the rim of the glass and traced it, rolling her lips in a dare. Then grabbed it and drank it down before she could change her mind or let anyone else stop her. "Ack." She slapped her hand over her mouth— snapping around to check if anyone was stirring. It was still quiet inside. She let another grimace escape her, though far more quietly this time, then went back over to the pool to sit again. Letting her settle on what was still to come. And once more felt the strange stirring inside of her.

She sat on the edge, her legs dangling in the water, swishing about to create the silky feeling as it pushed past her skin. The sensation echoed in her mind as the Absinthe began its own dance in her body. She heard the rustling of bed sheets coming from inside. Her lion king was emerging from his den.

"What are you doing out here, little Mouse?" A well-rested and sated voice asked from behind as he emerged.

"I got too hot underneath all of you."

"Are you complaining?"

She turned and offered him a smile as he sat next to her, dropping his feet into the water like hers. He hadn't even bothered pulling his briefs back on, and here he was sitting gloriously naked with a happy flaccid cock between his legs. "Just a bit, but only because it's summer." She hummed, starting to feel the swaying effects of the Absinthe kick in. She leaned into him and found a kiss waiting for her. With just a kiss, he woke things within her. A storm of emotions and sensations that whisked up like a spiraling typhoon. Maybe it was the effect of the wicked alcohol, but she doubted it. She had long since lost her reservation with Trenton. He loved her body and soul, and she worshipped him with her heart and soul. And body. She was his, and nothing in the world had made her happier than being so.

"You didn't forget, did you?' She asked when he'd released her from the kiss and he nodded.

He kissed her again then looked her directly in the eyes, "Are you ready?"

She should have been scared— no— petrified, more like it. Yet, for reasons she couldn't fathom or explain, she wasn't. Perhaps that part *was* from the liquid courage, though unimportant as well. The underlying truth was— she wanted this and she trusted him with her life. She had given it to him, after all. "Yes, Dominus." She whispered and made the conscious effort to ensure her answer gleamed in her eyes. He saw it, and she saw the reaction within him. No one could have given him a greater gift than this.

"Then let us go." His reassuring voice said it was time and everything would be as right as it ever would be. *Trust.* That's why she wasn't afraid. She trusted him implicitly. Every note and movement about the man resonated with deep understanding and controlled confidence.

Trenton pulled her to her feet and led her back inside the house, into the living room where the bench sat waiting. Like so many benches she'd seen before, this one was built into an ottoman. A more comforting match to the living room furnishings with less dungeon appeal. They even had one at the house, and while she'd been strapped to it a number of times, it'd never been used for what was about to take place.

He released her with a slight push towards the bench. His way to invite her to have a moment to acquaint herself on her own terms. She ran her hands along the leather padding while Trenton disappeared into their room. When he returned he had a dark, unembellished, cylinder-shaped leather canister in his hand. He wanted her to watch. She could see in his expression how he waited for her full attention, then he opened the canister and tipped it over. Out poured a long, dark gray cane. It was longer than his usual switch, and when he tested it in the air, it whistled and snapped with a well-defined bend from hardly a flick of his wrist. That was when she felt the first pinch of anxiety well up in her stomach. She felt warm, but she wasn't going to change her mind.

~ * ~ * ~ * ~ * ~ * ~

He must have drifted off in his love nest of bodies, because the next thing he knew he was touched awake and Trenton was standing over him with a wicked expression on his face.

"Come." Trenton spoke mildly, "The night isn't going to wait for us any longer."

Diesel found his pants on the floor and pulled them on, and then leaned over to kiss Paris awake before following Trenton out.

228

Trenton already had Katianna in place. She looked a lot calmer than he expected, so he walked over for a closer look, just to be sure. Her breathing deepened as she was well aware of what was about to happen. He leaned over and kissed the top of her head, then ran his fingers down her back, feeling her smooth skin that was about to be turned red with a hundred lashes. He glanced at Trenton and they exchanged a heated look, and Diesel that nodded he, too, was ready to see this.

That was right about when Paris stepped out of the bedroom, took one look at Katianna already strapped over the bench, then to the cane in Trenton's hand, and he flipped out.

"Wait! What the fuck are you about to do?"

"Mouse has offered her body for Trenton's cane." Diesel reached out to contain as well as to comfort Paris.

Paris shook his head, instantly refusing the answer, "No. You can't, that's her hard rule."

Trenton turned and placed his hand on Paris' shoulder to ease him, but he glanced away. "It is her hard rule, but it is also hers to change."

"But why?"

"Partly so that you wouldn't be disciplined."

"No. that's not right. I can't let her take my discipline."

Trenton had started to turn away to begin with his intentions, but came back around and leveled his gaze on the Fallen Angel, "What are you saying?"

"I talked her into setting me free, and I jumped Diesel and nearly destroyed our time together over one act. You can't cane her for my actions."

"She has agreed to take twenty-five lashes for you."

"Then I want my twenty-five lashes back."

"I like her backside better." Trenton's eyes narrowed, calculatedly plotting.

~ * ~

Paris could see the lust burning in the man's eyes. It was no mystery as to why. The cane was Trenton's extension. The purest form of desire for the Dominus. Some men liked their crowns— their trophies— or their fast cars. Trenton carried a cane and nothing more. "What if I offered to let you draw blood? You can give me the hardest beating you can mete out. Would that make me more appealing for the discipline?"

Fires lit up in the man's eyes and ebbed just as quickly, "Very well. I accept your offer."

Without freeing Katianna from her spot, Paris was laid over the bench and eased down over her. But before they could restrain him, he leaned up and kissed her on the cheek then settled back on his heels and waited as Trenton traded the straps that held her ankles and placed them around Paris' wrists.

He knew it was going to hurt, that he would feel pain in a way he had never experienced. Nonetheless, he owed it to Katianna. Not for just releasing him days ago, but for all the other times he had caused her grief. The very first time she set him loose, he jumped Diesel. That accosting had been minor, but Paris still had only thought of himself. Especially with how he acted at the auction a year ago. His selfish stunt with Cardiff had terrified her so badly he nearly cost her a blissful life with Trenton. So frightened by the scene he put on, she fainted, and when she came to, she ran away. Even then, he thought of no one but himself when he forced himself on Trenton. Now, here they were, drawing him in and binding him into their family. He owed her some form of remuneration.

He dropped his head to the small of her back, sucked in a deep breath, and braced himself for the first stroke. Knowing well when Trenton's first strike came down, he would be turned over to the sensations of pain that would cling to his skin like the heat from a branding iron.

~ * ~

Being where he was now was a dangerous place for a man like Trenton, to be offered blood through pain. He'd only been offered it once by a submissive who'd craved intense pain. She had contracted with him to be taken to her threshold. He'd then spent the five days that followed tending to her skin and her emotions. They'd also had some of the best sex. That was all before meeting Katianna. With his Unicorn, everything was better, more exquisite, and more deeply felt. Yet, he was not about to turn down the offer Paris gave him. Nor would it have been good for Paris if Trenton were to go light on the offer. Paris had several issues he had to come to terms with, one of which was that everything he did came with consequences. Some heavier than others.

He ran his fingers down the long carbon wand, letting his fingertips inspect its smooth surface. His eyes were more intent on the rise and fall of Paris' heavy breaths as his emotions built with the anticipated incoming infliction. Trenton glanced over at Diesel to read his thoughts as well.

231

Trenton felt high off the masochistic offer from Paris, but it would not pleasure him well if Diesel did not approve. Paris, after all, belonged to his brother, not him. It was also not going to pleasure either of them to draw blood on virgin skin. He waited to see if Diesel trusted him.

Diesel was stretched out on the sofa. One arm planted on the armrest with his hand scrubbing over his chin. His other laid across his lap, at the ready, anticipating the arousal as much as Paris was anticipating the pain.

"Does Paris' gift come with your permission to continue, Patronus?"

Diesel's eyes lit up like starbursts and he nearly chewed on his finger as he shifted in his seat, then adjusted his cock in his loose-fitting pajama pants. "Granted."

In a singular smooth stroke, Trenton brought the cane across Paris' skin. The long thin wand snapped across Paris' back, just below the shoulder blades and from one side to the other, clear of the lower lumbar. The first swipe of his cane left a satisfying crisp, clean red line that quickly began to welt up in a bright ribbon over Paris' skin.

He stepped in to enjoy the first welt, laying his hand over it and pausing to feel the rise of sweltering flesh. Admiring it like it was braille that spoke of long hidden, lustful longings to him. He traced the warm line with his fingertips, causing Paris to shiver under his touch. It was remarkably beautiful. This body molded to perfection and filled with ego to the brim— now a virgin turned over fully to a new experience.

Trenton acknowledged it within himself. He stood at a dangerous threshold and proceeded with controlled caution as his cane came down against Paris' skin once again. This time across his pert ass.

He made the second stroke and watched another red welt form, taking in the riveting tension that rolled over Paris' body from his shoulders to his legs. The emotional energy that pushed and pulled on him. It was clearly enough to take the man to his threshold. It confirmed to him that he would not be drawing blood tonight. He didn't need it. He had the one time, because the woman he brandished with his cane strokes, enjoyed it. Not so much for Paris. There was a difference for him. The pleasure would not be the same. Watching Paris' virgin skin being painted with red stripes was an exquisite gift in and of itself. Paris' expectations added to it. Like the colors of Patronus' ropes— how they could shift and heighten the mood. Paris didn't need to feel true pain to reach the ultimate peak because the suggestion would do it for him. In that same instant, Trenton also realized that his desire had already long since been quenched. He needed but one offer. *She would be next.*

There was no more time to pause. Paris had given him this and he would honor it. He positioned himself around the other side, leaned down to press a kiss to the back of Paris' head— then brought his cane down over the skin, crisscrossing across the first welt. This one was done in the same way he would any other cane stroke: firm, fast with a stinging bite, but nothing more. Paris would still feel his cane marks, but he would only take twenty-five strokes from Katianna's total, plus another twenty as his own price. And so rained down the next cane stroke— and then the next.

~ * ~

Diesel couldn't stand it any longer and was soon on his feet, coming up next to Paris, dropping his hand over the inflicted skin of his backside before Trenton even divvied out the last few strokes. He had to take part— had to witness the shivers that soon transformed into a cold sweat over Paris' back as his blood sugar naturally dropped and the last stroke was laid across his back.

Diesel knelt to Paris and pulled his face around to look at him. His teeth chattered and he hovered in a daze. "Do you have any idea how hard your dick is right now?" He asked Paris while he redirected his gaze to the stiff cock that jutted out from between Paris' legs and leaked with clear droplets.

Paris let out a violent shiver, "Kiss me, dammit, please." The words shuddered through clenched teeth. But when Diesel slammed into him to do just that, there were no teeth in the way for the tangle of tongues that fought to get at each other.

Trenton was right next to them and was soon releasing the leather shackles from Paris' arms. Once free, Diesel's oversized Imp was in full force all over him. *Hangry* was a good word for it. Both of them, on their knees on the carpeted floor, Paris' arms clutched around Diesel, clamped tight as the two men dueled with each other's tongues.

Diesel dropped a hand to grip around Paris' cock and gave it a good pull while reaching around Paris and feeling the hot rippled flesh of his caned back. The heat under his palm set something off inside him. *God damn*, he nearly came himself. It took next to nothing to have Paris throwing himself back in Diesel's grip and sending a cry to the ceiling as his cock jetted out white ropes of seed all over Diesel's hand and shorts. *Fuck, yes.* Even if he never had this with Paris again, he was glad to have had it now. And he owed his brother everything for the rare experience with the man in his arms.

~ * ~

It was hard to describe Diesel and Paris as Trenton watched them. Paris had all the lust and gusto of a thousand men, and when he charged, he was like a rampaging bull. But faced with Deez, Paris was a bull who ran into a wall that simply absorbed all that energy, then used it to flip the man around and fuck him until the walls of Jericho came crashing down.

If they didn't kill each other in the bedroom first, the two were going to make a beautiful couple.

He now had his own gift to take and he turned his attention to his Life slave, who still quietly waited as she, too, had turned and watched from her position. Her pale eyes sought him out and found, to her relief, that his attention had not been so absorbed as to forget what they were about to share.

He ran his hand down her smooth back. *Now it was her turn.* He traced his fingers down one leg, reattached the restraints, then did the same on the other before walking around to her front and kneeling before her, glancing in her— dilated— eyes. He dismissed it from their earlier drinks and the dim light, and perhaps from growing tired. She'd be able to sleep soon. She would be allowed to rest for however long she needed after this, until she had recovered. And he would treasure this moment until his death. "Are you ready?" He kissed each cheek then her forehead.

"Green, Dominus." She smiled softly to him, and he kissed her forehead one more time before standing and taking his place.

"Wait? What are you doing?" Paris was suddenly asking from Diesel's shoulder and pushing upright to throw a shocked look at him.

Trenton was calm. Not even a distant rumble of thunder reverberated at the edge of his words. He stepped closer to Paris, lowered a hand to touch his cheek with a light brush of his fingertips, then moved his fingers to Paris' lips— silencing him from any further outbursts, "This is her gift to me. It is something you cannot take in her place. I allowed you to assume the punishment that rightfully belonged to you, but you cannot take hers unless she offered them. She has not. So she will receive her own twenty-five lashes for her punishment. Then I will take the additional fifty she has offered to me as her gift."

"Fifty—" the word sputtered out like a jilted sigh that puffed against Trenton's fingertips.

Trenton's attention was already floating back to the smooth back and buttocks that awaited him. Just as he did with Paris, Trenton savored that first strike that placed the full length of the graphite cane across both cheeks of her ass. Her whole body jumped and pulled on her restraints. A muffled mewl lodged in her throat with her effort to prevent crying out. She understood perfectly. If she cried out, it would spoil the scene for them both. Though he would not shame her, had she cried out anyway. Her skin was her gift, as was the courage she so willfully denied was there. Tonight, it showed it truly did exist and in exquisite measure.

The remaining original twenty-five were delivered rapidly all across her ass, fast flicks of his wrist creating a snap in the rod that licked against her skin.

Red lines quickly began to spread over her curved cheeks until he delivered the final of the set across both sides at once. He paused, taking a moment to allow her to catch her breath and so he could enjoy the feel of her skin under his palm. Raised flesh radiated with erotic heat and she shivered at his touch. Her ribs heaved with her breath until she finally relaxed.

Trenton reached down, touched her face, and then lifted her chin so she could look up at him. He felt that predatory dominance in him once more, standing over her as he did just now. His blood coursed through his veins, through his heart, and down to his cock. She was his in every way. A little less than a year ago, she gave her heart and her life to him. Now she gave him this, and he realized there may not ever be another thing for him to want after this. *What was it she had said back then, when they were in Paris a year ago? An example of a word or phrase that was beautiful, purely in terms of its sound, without regard for semantics.*

Hedonism was a school of thought, which argued that pleasure was the only intrinsic good. In very simple terms, a hedonist strived to maximize net pleasure— pleasure minus pain.

Hedonism would teach us to pursue pleasure without pain, but how does one do that? How can one experience one without the other? How does one know light without first knowing darkness? To claim such experience of sensation was to say one lived in a house that consisted of a front without a back, or a top without a bottom.

Turn to those who lived in the pleasures of BDSM, regardless to what degree, and they would tell you pleasure was, and always would be, discovered and experienced to its fullest, having known pain or restraint first.

He remembered the word she had spoken that day.

He bent over and kissed the top of her head, "I love you." He whispered his vow, then came around to her side and delivered the first four of his strikes across her back the way they were meant to be delivered— hard and final.

"Stop, please!" Paris jumped up, only to be pulled back down by Diesel.

"He has to do this." Diesel told him just as Trenton delivered another four, and a small cry broke from Katianna's lips for the first time as the red lines formed across her upper back.

"Why?" Paris pleaded.

Trenton paused, looked over at Paris and waved him over. Diesel helped him up and they both came over as Trenton drew Paris' hand to Katianna's body, touching and experiencing her skin, feeling the hot raised strokes there. Trenton nearly embraced Paris in a hug as he kept the Imp's hand over her skin and whispered all the reverence that dwelled within him so Paris would know, "Because the very act of bringing together the two things I love and desire the most in this universe becomes my cellar-door."

He needed this from her. He'd resigned himself to the fact, long ago, that he would never have it, but the need to fill it had never stopped aching inside him.

He waved Paris back, looked her over, and then brought four more across her back.

Fast whip-like snaps landed across her flesh and Katianna bit down her cries. She quickly gulped in huge lungfuls of replenishing air with the short respite that came between the sets, only they came back out in slight breathy whimpers on the verge of a moan.

After each set, he paused for his own reasons— to savor each new layer of heat over the growing anger in her skin. Her beautiful tan already glowing with lovely red lashes. He touched each one, feeling the heat himself, drawing his fingers crossways along the welts. Then he kissed his fingertips as if they carried the heat of her skin with them.

RIGHT ONE 4 DIESEL

Then began again, delivering several more sets with little to no pause between them.

Katianna's arms pulled on her restraints and her chest heaved, struggling to breathe through each strike. Her expressions came out in a myriad of whimpers, moans, and mewling. She was dropping into a zone he never figured she would go. Not her. Yet she was. *How could such a gift become greater perfection?* He walked around her, his hand dragging his fingers over the map of welts until he came around her and saw her face. Her soft features were glazed over with a drifting expression that, while not a true smile, glowed like one that could only be read as pleasure. He didn't dare force her face up to look at him, as much as he wished to be sure, since doing so would yank her from the euphoria.

He moved quickly, returning to his position and delivering the next dozen. Taking her from the edge of consciousness and seeing her delivered over to the trance state from the scene. The cane strokes now were minor compared to the previous ones he'd already delivered. Now it was about adding layers and ensuring a continuation of sensation, making it complete. More sensation, not more pain. For him, *more* was not needed, having slaked the lust for it through Paris. His hand smoothed over the redness in her skin, always following each set with a finishing touch. He never did a cane or flogging without it, both for the receiver and for his own pleasure. The results were the prize of the act, and it smoothed out the sting for the submissive, transforming their pain to pleasure for them. That she had submitted to it at all had his heart swelling as much as his cock. His ultimate desire met, and though the count was not finished, he reached down to release the first restraint.

~ * ~

"No—"

Trenton's hand stopped by the faint whisper.

"Don't stop."

Trenton instantly came around and dropped down in front of her. His hand caressed her cheek and wiped the tears away. "What did you just say?"

"Don't— stop." She breathed each word out. "I want all of them."

"No, you've taken enough." He assured her as he brushed the loose falling hairs from her face and dabbed away the sweat that beaded on her forehead.

"Please." She whimpered. "You have not given me my Dominus yet."

She knew he hadn't delivered the same caning he would have given to anyone else. She had watched him so many times. Each lash was painful, and yet the arousal he had often described was actually there; some bizarre intimacy he knew how to deliver through the switch, and that he had shortened the experience with her— she was now telling him she felt cheated of the full experience with him.

Trenton was beside himself— that his Unicorn actually asked for more, and some deep nagging in his gut didn't want to give it.

"Ameno, Dominus." She whispered to him, and just then he only saw fear on her face.

"What, baby? Anything, just tell me."

"No." She shook her head, trying to keep her sudden sobs at bay, "That's *my celador.*" She managed to get the words out as she swallowed back the tears.

Trenton gazed at her, lifting her head up to look at him, "What did you just say?"

"Ameno, Dominus— it's— Latin—"

"I know what it means—" he whispered back to her, his heart pounding in his chest.

"It's my cellar door. So finish yours." She laid her head down, resting on her check. And then something spectacular happened in the vision of a smile that bloomed like a rose, opening up in a storm. Her love for him radiating as hotly as the welts on her back.

Trenton's mouth dove over hers, kissing her wildly. She wasn't afraid of the cane or the pain; she was afraid he wouldn't comply— would not finish what he'd started, so the act in itself would not be a completed one. For both of them.

My dear Master.

That was *her* cellar door.

Trenton went to his feet and stood over her, gazing down her red back and the lines that crisscrossed over it. He walked down the side of the bench, letting his fingertips drift over the welts until he was in position, and without any further delay, he gave what they had come here for. He didn't count, for the numbers were of little concern.

Rather, she expected and entrusted him to deliver her into a sub-zone. His zone— and each added stroke, both electrified and nearly sickened him.

All his life, caning had been like a drug for him, and like any drug, he was always looking forward to his next high. But not now. What might be a first for anyone, he discovered that he could actually find that last high, and that after this he would never need it again. His need to experience her this way was fulfilled.

His cane whistled in the air and snapped across dark red, angry skin. His slave writhed under each one, lost in a mindless maelstrom of sensation. A violent shiver raced over her shoulders and chased each cane stoke he made down her back and over her ass, until it passed him and caused her toes to curl.

She was so close. He forced himself to complete them for her— *his little Mouse.*

He kicked her knees further apart, letting the snap of the switch whisper against her pussy, and somewhere after another twelve or more lashes, her body bucked. His own chest heaved heavily, surging with a wild sensation, no longer needing the whip but an encompassing of her body in a different expression of claiming. Just two more landings of his cane delivered and his Unicorn came for him.

All those years he'd spent assuming that he would enjoy having his Unicorn under his cane. When Katianna finally came along and it was clear that he would not experience it due to her hard rule, he thought it would eat at him. Yet as he stood there, having had to struggle to finish the last of the lashes she'd gifted him, he realized it had not. He had ached only because he hadn't known. Now he understood the lesson of the Hedonist finding pleasure after leaving the pain behind. His Unicorn wasn't meant for his cane. That made this moment all the more precious. And he dropped the graphite reed carelessly to the floor.

Careful inspection revealed that Katianna had indeed reached sub-space. For how long he did not know, but that he had brought her to such a state was euphoric beyond any desire he'd ever asked of her and further sated their experience together. Before even the first glancing touch, he could feel the super-heated surface of her skin radiate out to greet him. Like the softest breeze, he touched her. Just his fingertips. Her scorched skin was an exquisite sensation. He kept the contact light, brushing his fingers over the curve of her ass and up along her back, but he would experience her tormented skin in spite of everything. To not do so would waste what she had given him.

The world fell quiet in that moment. Now it was just him and a jewel to be adored, worshipped until touching was not enough. He bent down and kissed her back, feeling the same heat against his lips now. Then he moved down, stepped between her legs and dropped behind her, and he brushed the back of a thigh first with his nose, then pressed his face into the round of her ass as he relished the fire that praised him for such a fine caning. He practically purred against her skin, wondering if there was enough room in his bed for him to sleep with his head pillowed by the hot globes of her ass, while still sharing the space with Diesel and Paris. He nearly chuckled then kissed her stinging flesh again before coming up and nearly running into Diesel. The look on his face was close to begging or ready to fight for a chance to feel. Trenton took his brother's hand and guided it to the very spot he'd just pressed his cheek to. There was an odd intimacy when he controlled even the hands that reached out to touch, but Diesel soon pushed a satin robe into Trenton's other hand and then lowered down behind Katianna's still restrained body to roam over her with both hands. Purring to her.

"God, it's amazing." The way his fingers flickered over each raised red welt was like looking at art— how the intricate lines told a story. Their story.

Trenton carefully laid the robe over her back and lightly moved his hands over her body, using the cool satin to calm her skin, easing her body toward broader contact without stirring her out of her distant bliss. Diesel released the straps that bound her wrists and legs, and once Trenton had worked his arm completely around her, Diesel rolled her from the bench into Trenton's arms. Slowly, gently, he carried her to the bathroom. He kissed her face over and over again so she felt him all around her— sheltering her after she had just given him everything.

~ * ~

Katianna was barely aware, like some surreal dream in a movie when she had surrendered all her will to the man she loved, and now she was floating inside his soul. Spun about by the strange, immaculate world which made her disoriented— like being in a dream within a dream. But she felt him— felt his arms, felt his lips. His deep voice wrapping all around her, keeping everything else out. Never in her life had she felt so safe, so complete, and utterly surrounded— *so loved.*

So complete.

She stared into his eyes all the while as he bathed her, using cool waters and some strange herbal tonic easing her skin, cooling it down. She only half recalled mumbling something about Paris.

"Don't worry, I won't." His response echoed from the mist that clouded her conscious.

Then her world changed from cooling water to downy-soft clouds that patted her dry, then lastly transformed to being wrapped in soft satin. Then she found herself in his arms, being carried away. For a destination she knew without asking. Forever belonging in his bed, wrapped and guarded by her Dominus.

~ * ~

Trenton watched as he hovered over her, stroked her hair away from her face, enthralled as she fell almost instantly into sleep. He had known the moment he met her she was the perfect one for him, and his feelings for her never faltered, but he'd never known what perfection could actually feel like, until now.

Satisfied with her sound asleep, Trenton got up and went back out to rejoin Diesel and Paris. And finding they were no longer in the living room, but their moans reached his ears. Before he even saw them, he heard them out on the pool deck. He paused at the door, resting back on one of the stone columns, watching as Diesel drove his cock with deep strokes into Paris' body. The two men so completely consumed with each other's needs and desire. Able to feed the hunger they shared, where none before had ever been able to do for either of them.

He should have known it would have been a man that would fill the spot for Diesel. But Deez's desires for a Life Slave had seemed to evade, even obscure the ability to fulfill this part of him. Paris was not Diesel's Unicorn; he was the insatiable lust to match his own. Something Diesel needed far more than he needed a Unicorn. But then, Trenton had the perfect Unicorn and he knew his brother loved her, nearly as much as he did himself.

They hadn't actually planned it this way. They knew they would always be together— two and two— yet four. Just like their parents had been, but not to actually share a Life Slave. Now it seemed the only natural arrangement. No one else would do. It was kind of funny how things were falling together far better than they had planned.

The cries of both men pulled Trenton from his reveries and he watched the erotic scene with Diesel and Paris. Their heads thrown back in abandoned euphoria.

He waited until they both collapsed over before approaching. He leaned over and kissed Paris on the forehead.

Paris tried to push himself up to be receptive of the Dominus' approach, but he was too exhausted and well sated to be successful at it.

"Easy— relax, Paris." Trenton caressed the side of his head. "You and Katianna have had enough tonight." He eased him back down to rest a moment, "I'm here to tend to you, this time." He looked beyond Paris' body to his brother, who had an equally satisfied and tired expression on his face, "Bring him inside so I can administer to his welts."

~ * ~

Inside, Trenton tended to Paris in the same gentle way he would for Katianna, bathing him in the cool water infused with the tonic they'd always used for post-care. Its tonic water and blend of herbs would cool Paris' skin and help it heal quickly. Diesel watched with admiration how his brother took great care of Paris as if he was his own.

"Deez?" Paris called for him. His head lobbing over, looking for him, but his eyes remaining closed. Apparently, too drained to open them up.

"I'm right here, Paris. I'm still with you." Diesel spoke from just behind Trenton, standing over them both, watching from where he leaned against the shower wall with his arms folded.

"You're not going to send me away again, are you?" He mumbled, unmoving, almost as if he were talking in his sleep.

Diesel moved to his knees next to the tub, taking Paris' outstretched hand in his, and pulled it against his side as he drew closer, "No, never again." He whispered back to him.

Paris' head rolled away, "Good." He took a deep sighing breath and slunk down further in the tub, "Because I think I'm in love with you." Another sigh and he drifted away in a deep sleep.

Paris was no small man. So it took the both of them to get him out of the tub and not jostle him around too much. But they managed to get him to the bed without jerking him from his zone. Wrapped in a satin robe that matched Katianna's, Trenton guided Paris down on the bed next to the still sleeping body of his little Mouse, then crawled in behind her as Diesel slipped in behind Paris.

Diesel lightly stroked Paris' hair, keeping his hand off his back so as not to irritate it or pull his lover from his deep slumber. He felt a little giddy and lightheaded and his chest swelled. Perhaps still feeling some of the Absinthe, or maybe it had to do with Paris telling him he was falling in love with him. Not paying attention, his fingers floated down Paris' back, he felt the raised welts under the satin— *Absinthe*— then his eyes shot up, meeting Trenton's, who was watching him. "You broke a serious rule." Diesel whispered, rather surprised at what he just realized.

Trenton's face showed his puzzlement, "How so?"

"The Absinthe. You never do a scene while high or drunk."

"And I assure you, I still haven't."

"But—" he blinked a few times, trying to recollect if he did in fact see Trenton drink anything, but it just wasn't something he ever monitored. Trent had always been the epitome of self-control. "You mean you never drank any of it?"

A confident but tired smile crept over Trenton's face, "Do you think I would ever allow you, or anyone else, to become so uninhibited and vulnerable, without someone watching over and guarding your pleasures so you can have them safely?" Trenton bowed his head and kissed the top of Katianna's head, but his eyes remained on Diesel.

Diesel relaxed, his hand finally came to rest at the small of Paris' back, and he surrendered his head to his pillow, "No, I would never think you would. Guess I owe you one, huh?"

"Not at all. This night already gave me something a Master longs for and rarely experiences." The words drifted off near the end, as if he had daydreamed them rather than spoke them. Trenton's eyes drifted over his Life slave's slumbering body, and that of Paris' too, like they were the treasure of all things to have and behold. Life didn't get any better than this.

Diesel had seen many things and experienced so much more alongside his brother. And yet, just now he felt in awe of him, while at the same time still a part of him. Perhaps some small amount of what others felt being around him was like. For Diesel, it'd always been different; Trenton was his brother in more ways than one— where one went, so did the other, but being brought here to this moment with him held something special. Trent was right— it was something few ever experienced, but the look on Trenton's face— and the odd expression— Diesel wanted to know if his brother had a word for it. "What is it?" He finally had to ask in a whispered tone.

"Perfection." Trenton whispered back, letting the word have its moment before saying anything else. "Just one more thing to do."

"What's that?"

Trenton smiled warmly, releasing a deep, relaxing sigh, "I'm going to marry her."

If Diesel's heart wasn't already swelling beyond the proportions of his chest cavity, it sure as hell did when Trenton said those words. As he watched, Trenton nuzzled against the slave he'd just announced he would marry, then surrendered his eyes to exhausted sleep. Diesel kept watching. He just wasn't ready to let go of this moment. Even if he only managed to keep his eyes open for a few seconds longer. They were his to have. For the first time in his life, his brother just said he was going to marry. *Truly now, life just didn't get any better.*

~ * ~ * ~ * ~ * ~ * ~

CHAPTER FOURTEEN

~ * ~ * ~ * ~ * ~ * ~

Paris stood in the middle of his office and looked at his desk. As if life just stopped because someone else hit the pause button. Everything still in place— nearly everything precisely just as he left it, minus a few papers that had been taken care of by his assistants over the week, replaced with a piling stack that had to wait for his return to address directly. Paris couldn't help but fear moving to the other side of his desk where his job would resume. It frightened him almost. As if once there, he would be forever tethered to it, never able to escape it or come back to this side where everything felt so damn good, because on this side, he had Diesel in his life. On that side, Diesel had been nothing more than his boss.

Never in his life had he felt so fulfilled. So satisfied. Always he had wanted more— needed more. Sometimes the hunger was painful. Now, for once, the matador was blissfully silent inside him, almost purring like a kitten. No need for bullfights or shows. Though, he hadn't a clue how a matador could purr, he did just that. Last night, when he fell asleep in Diesel's arms.

This morning, when Deez tried to rouse him up out of bed, Paris drowsily asked for a few minutes more, then when Diesel went on to take his shower, Paris snuck out alone.

Now, he just stood there, staring at his desk, letting out a heavy sigh; life was going to turn painful for him in the five steps it would take him to walk around it. He could see the empty void already, right on the other side where his leather chair was, glaring bitterly at him.

It was almost as much of a shock as it had been this morning when he stood in his own condo and looked in the mirror, dreading to see the damage to his skin, only to find none. He'd nearly run himself dizzy, chasing his backside— twisting every way he could. His arms reaching like a contortionist to get his hands to where he could feel the evidence left behind from last night's whipping. They were real, but they were nothing more than mildly raised welt strips over his skin, barely a shade beyond his tan. A few purplish marks lingered where Trenton's switch had landed more than once on the same spot, but even those would be gone in a few days.

Paris had stood there, raking his hands through his hair, replaying the night's events through his head. He had, in fact, offered his back to spare Katianna. He had felt every stroke of the long, thin graphite cane come across his skin. The sting and heat of each one burned into his memory. As did the savage lust he'd harbored once it was over. He twisted again to see his back in the reflection— so then why did he not bear the scars of it? Only smooth, faint red lines. He felt robbed of his expectation somehow.

He'd finally given up and dressed, unable to answer his own mystery, and came in to mete it out with his office next.

There was a light knock, and he glanced over his shoulder just as Diesel stepped in.

Paris snapped his attention back to the desk he had yet to return to, but he couldn't bear to look at Diesel. Paris felt him as he stepped up behind him, but Diesel didn't press against him, keeping clear of his tender back. That didn't prevent him feeling the warmth of Diesel's body as if already pressed against him. It only caused him to tense, anticipating the spine-melting sensation of Diesel's breath on his neck. The ache of waiting for it. *He hated that part.* He let out a defeated sigh, "I was going to come to you; you didn't have to come here." His voice was woeful when he tried to be accommodating. Except this was going to be goodbye and he didn't feel too accommodating for that.

"Neither should have had to happen. I already had you with me, but you slipped out while I showered."

"It's Monday and I needed to get back to work. Lingering was only going to make it harder." Try as he might, he wasn't able to hide the pain in his voice. That Diesel sounded steady as a rock made him feel all the more abandoned, and the man was standing right behind him.

"Turn around and look at me." Diesel spoke like a solid rock with a firm, gentle command.

Paris shook his head. He couldn't. "I'm not your slave anymore. I fulfilled your request. Now it's done."

~ * ~

Diesel took a deep breath; Paris couldn't make it any harder if he tried. Diesel tried to hide the pain he felt from Paris' dejection. He'd had a plan for this morning, only Paris *bee-lined* him. "Please turn around and look at me."

Paris' head turned, but it hung low, hidden under the thick shag of dark bangs, and he never took the steps to follow through with the turn. A deep breath in, and Paris lifted his head a little more, where dark multi-hued eyes glistened with pain from under the strands of black hair.

All over again, Diesel could hear Paris' voice on the other end of a phone one year ago, begging him to come to his hotel room and be with him.

"Our chopper is already here." Diesel reached for Paris, gently turned him around to face him, and brushed the hair from his eyes.

~ * ~

"So what now?" Paris didn't really want to hear the answer. What he really wanted was to grab Diesel up, drag him across the island and stuff him back into the *home of fantasies.* Maybe if he tied *Him* up, he could keep him there. Anything, so Diesel couldn't leave.

"You go back to being Director and finish out the season. You do your job."

"So that's it? You're done with me and now I go back to what I was? You didn't need to come here to tell me that."

"Until the season is over." Diesel repeated his comment calmly and suggestively.

"Yeah, and then what? What do I do with myself after that?" He was getting angry, and Diesel hadn't promised more— hadn't asked for more— Diesel had only demanded him for this week, and Paris had given it to him. Only now, Paris wanted more. *Always had. Knew it from the start, and how real the loss would be when it was over. Yet that hadn't stopped him from wanting— he wanted all of Diesel. He didn't want to go back to his old life.*

~ * ~

"Then, you come to New York and live with me." Diesel answered and waited to see how long it would take for it to register.

It took a second, but the stir in him was visible, pulling him from the anger he was planning to use to shield his other feelings, and he was staring at Diesel now— searching his eyes for some further explanation to what he just said. But then stage fright kicked in and hit that damn panic button of his.

Diesel, for all the pleasures he'd delivered, had also put Paris through considerable hell— tormented him against all his fears. Diesel had learned about him through all of it. Yes, Paris did want to be with him, but not as his slave. Not like that— not always.

"I don't think I can stay like this with you, and I can't be your submissive slave all the time."

"I'm not insisting you to be my slave. I'm asking you to be my lover, Paris." Diesel leaned in and gave him a warm, tender kiss. Offering a notion of want.

~ * ~

Paris pulled away, "And what? I sleep in the same room I stayed in before? You'd come for me when you want me?" Paris didn't even know why he was asking such outlandish questions when his body was screaming *yes— yes— yes. He'd suffer the sleeping arrangement if it meant being with Diesel.*

"No, you'd sleep in *our* room, like healthy normal boyfriends do. My significant other. That way, you're already there when I want it, when you want it— even when we don't want it— you'll still be there."

Our room— he said *ours,* not *His.*

Okay, anger gone, elation soaring, too good to be true. "What would I do? I don't know the first thing about working in New York."

"Well, I didn't think you'd have any interest in the gun shop, but Dane wants to hire some management help, especially with the new restaurant opening up soon. Trenton is in definite need of a personal assistant, and he could always use some help with the rotary and the auction event. He won't trust it to anyone. You're already part of the resort's guests and privileges. You could be a great help to him, and that alone would keep you busy. So there's plenty for you to do. However, I would not recommend you try working for both of them. They're both slave drivers." Diesel risked a smirk, hoping to offset some of the angst in Paris, "Of course, you will still be expected to return here to the resort for the BDSM and fetish seasons, though admittedly, I won't like it much, having you gone for so long." Diesel kissed him again, light and gentle. He knew it was a lot to throw at Paris, and reassurance was definitely something needed here. "If you want some time to think it over—"

"No." Paris arms snapped around him like a snare trap, pulling Diesel into his body, his mouth coming over his, kissing him hard and deep, moving his hands across Diesel's back and shoulders. Confirming, more to himself, that the man who'd just asked him to live with him, and stay with him, was actually real and not some hallucination or dream to trick him past the pain of separation.

Paris pitched back against his desk, bringing Diesel with him. He ignored the tender shot of pain he felt on his backside when he pressed against the edge of the desk, as it only further confirmed that Diesel was real. He deepened his kiss, his tongue licking inside Diesel's mouth with painful hunger until they were both out of breath.

They broke apart, gasping, elated by the union, "So we'd be equals?"

"No." Diesel shook his head with surprise, "You belong to me now. I'll always be alpha, and from time to time I'm going to remind you of it, my pet Imp."

"You know, I'm still capable of struggling against you." Paris teased him, knowing damn well it was one of the things Diesel liked best about him— that he could fuck as hard as he could take it. *His Bull* was what he called him. "But it'll just be me and you? No one else, no more slaves or submissives?"

~ * ~

Diesel brushed Paris' hair from his eyes again; it was always falling in his eyes. It was part of what gave him that Fallen Angel look about him. "Do you understand my relationship with my brother? Or that I share the same deep desire for a Unicorn— a Life Slave?" Diesel could see the mix of understanding, and the lack of it, in his lover's eyes and chose to explain further. "Trenton's folks and mine— they were swingers, they were together—" he shrugged in a carefree way. "—since before Trenton and I were born. It's kind of an unspoken expectation that he and I would do the same. And that he now possesses the perfect Unicorn— I want us to have that. For you and I to share with them? Tell me you can accept that."

~ * ~

Paris listened, and what he heard wasn't nearly as hurtful as he had braced himself for. And still, Diesel caressed his arms and watched him carefully, waiting to see if what he wanted would put a wedge between them, and he could see some concern there.

"Like last night?"

Diesel let out a tired chuckle, "Minus the Absinthe, and not always, but yes." He waited.

Paris kissed him. Diesel wanted to have his Unicorn, and Paris had known that. At times, it bothered him, but that Diesel wanted to share in it with Trenton's Life Slave was something special. Paris had watched Trenton with Katianna, and it was like watching art come alive in them. If Diesel found his Unicorn in her as well, and they would share her with him, how could he ever deny the man he loved his dream? Paris had never desired women, but he could accept a living Unicorn— *or more specifically, a mouse. She was the exception*. He nodded, "I can."

Paris felt Diesel's hand close around his wrist with something cool to the touch, and then he heard the click. He tore himself away from the kiss and looked down, discovering a thick tungsten bracelet had just been clamped over his wrist.

"And if you ever go astray on me—" Diesel reiterated, grabbing Paris' wrist and lifting it up until the bracelet was at eye level so Paris could see the inscription on it. "I will hunt you down, bind you, and lock you away in that slave room you stayed in, where I will tease and fuck you as I see fit until no one else exists for you. Am I clear?"

Paris' eyes went to the hinged ring of glossy black metal that was now locked around his wrist, turning it so he could read the inscription: *This man belongs to The*

Patronus Diesel Gentry. A deep-rooted grin of pure mischief slid over Paris' face, and he looked back at the man who'd just claimed sole ownership over him. He pulled the dominant man against him and dove for his mouth, wrapping his arm over Diesel's shoulders to keep him in place. Diesel idled back against his hold, giving him a look that said he expected a clear answer.

"Very clear, Sir." Paris smiled as Diesel indulged his need to be kissed.

~ * ~ * ~ * ~ * ~ * ~

Katianna stirred, the large empty space that had earlier been two bodies that caged her against her Dominus too vivid in her mind to dismiss. She flipped her head around and brushed her hair from her face, coming nose to nose with Trenton. She touched his face lightly with her fingertips and brushed over his lips.

Trenton sucked in a deep breath, moved, and let out a languid groan. "Mmmm, you awake?" He mumbled.

"No." She whispered back with a smile.

"Hurry back then." Some semblance of a smile came over his face before he drifted back to sleep, but his arm retracted, letting her slip away.

After relieving herself in the bathroom, she stood before the mirror and stared at her reflection in the small portal of space she created after wiping the fog from the reflective surface. She twisted so she could see her back. "Oweee." She frowned as she reached around carefully to touch the road map of red stripes across her back. All perfectly aligned, like matchsticks laid out and stacked on top of the other, climbing up her butt cheeks and upper back. While tender and still warm, it wasn't nearly as bad as she feared it would be. Still— she didn't see herself leaning back on much of anything for a few days. The steam still lingering in the bathroom wasn't being very nice to her tender skin either, and since her mouth felt dry, she figured a visit to the fridge was warranted as part of her morning escape.

Diesel and Paris were nowhere to be seen. Which was fine, since her head was so thick and cloudy, she didn't figure she could handle any morning socializing. The shade curtains were still drawn on all the windows, keeping out the intruding light of morning. She liked the quiet in the house right now. *She liked tiptoeing through, like a mouse.* The strange thought had her quietly giggling to herself, making her realize she was still a bit tipsy, not just hung over.

The cool rush of air on her skin when she opened the refrigerator door was— *wow*— like a fresh spring kiss. So with the door wide open, she dropped down cross-legged, her back to the refrigerator, and just sat there awhile, letting the cold air put the fire out on her skin. Her eyes drifted to the bottle of orange juice in the door, inviting her to refresh her palate. She grabbed it and practically drank half the bottle down before coming up for air. Her stomach growled at her for the citrus invasion and caused a sudden queasy feeling that was anything but welcomed, so she decided that perhaps she should stop while she was ahead.

She pulled her knees up and laid her head on them, just drifting away in a small escape, when she heard footsteps coming toward her. She sighed happily when bare feet appeared before her, and she glanced up the towering body and saw hands held out for her.

"That doesn't look like hurrying back to me." It was meant to scold her if it weren't for the sleepy smile on his face.

She took his hands, letting him pull her up to her feet, and he kicked the door to the fridge closed.

"Didn't your mother ever get onto you about leaving the refrigerator door open?" He joked as he led her to the bathroom.

Showering with Trenton was always an intimate moment for them, like starting the day with renewed acquaintance. So much so she often felt like she was living in a fairy tale. *Just not this morning.*

She stood quietly while Trenton washed her body, using the tonic that would help heal as well as cool the sunburn-like sensation on her back. Her head was starting to swarm around. She felt dizzy as her thoughts became increasingly foggy, and frankly, she felt like fresh roadkill. She wanted nothing more than to go back to their bed and pass out, but the shower felt refreshing too. And so did Trenton's tender post-care.

Whether he picked up on her infirmity or not, he made no demands on her, and when they both finished washing, he made her stay in the shower a little longer. He turned the overhead rainfall showerhead on to lightly drip cool water on her without further irritating her red skin, but he left the misting jets, recessed in the walls of their shower, on a warm steam setting while he got out.

Katianna turned the overhead dripping rain off and leaned into the wall, letting the misty spray seep into her, opening her pores, and hoping to detox in its warmth. Her head was so clouded now, she couldn't hold a steady thought for more than a few moments. The marble grains of the tiles swirled around like Jupiter's stormy surface, making her feel more and more like she was drunk, when all she'd had was the orange juice.

She leaned back on the tile wall and closed her eyes, only to have her thoughts bombarded by deep images of uninhibited pleasure parading through her head— *all of them*. She had slept with all three men last night. She knew this, yet if someone were to ask her to be more specific, she couldn't. It was just one big blur of writhing bodies— a drug-induced orgy, and she almost wondered if it had been wrong. *Had she acted inappropriately, allowing Diesel and Paris to have sex with her? Maybe that's why her Dominus so willingly left her in the shower without making love to her as he most often did. He was upset with her.*

She shook her head, reminding herself this couldn't be it, but she couldn't prevent the paranoid thoughts from flooding back into her mind and laying siege anyways. *They came crashing in on her, like ghosts, seeping into her head and possessing her. Each time she cleared her head of the images of four bodies tangled together, they returned and started her mental panic all over again. Like trying to sweep water away— it always trickled back.*

Trenton and Diesel both had been so quiet this morning. And Paris— Paris was already gone by the time she woke up. She had the faint memory of him kissing her goodbye, rousing her from her sleep only briefly and planting a lingering kiss on her cheek, repeating the kiss on her lips before letting her return to her dreams.

Trenton had always been overtly possessive of her, never allowing anyone else to touch her, not even his friends at the club or when he had them over as guests. Even before she surrendered to him as his Life Slave. After the kidnapping though, his possession had grown more guarded. Always fearful someone might try to take her again. Only with his brothers— Diesel, Marcus, Harper, and Dane— did she ever feel him relax. Diesel was obviously different and considerably closer than anyone else was, and she'd always assumed that one day Trenton would share her with him. But it was an assumption. It didn't mean Trenton actually had intended to share her with him last night, and especially not with Paris. Or perhaps he did, but she wasn't supposed to enjoy it as much as she did. So now he was having second thoughts about keeping her. She was ruined for him.

The arguments whirled around her head like a dust devil. Any attestation to explain them away did her no good as they cycled right back around, running her in a mental loop. Dragging her down into further remorse that she had ruined everything between them until she began to cry.

Katianna still shook her head to rattle the thoughts away from her as she cried, hoping not to succumb to her grief. She clutched her fists against her head as if that would prevent the internal argument from continuing. *Diesel would never have done anything that Trenton found offensive, and Trenton sure as hell would not have stood by quietly if he did not approve.* She reached behind her— her fingers carefully mapping out the welts in her skin. *She gave this to him, she remembered that. Had that been enough to make up for whatever else had happened?* They all had drunk the Absinthe— maybe they all had gone further than intended and now they all walked around silently, as if on the proverbial egg shells, because there was nothing they could say or do to undo what had happened between them.

The tears were coming, her mind telling her that that was what happened— they were all silently feeling regret. *Oh god.* Her mind was instantly rampant with the conclusion. *What had she done? Mistrust could rip even the most bound relations apart. She didn't want to lose her Dominus.*

Her hands floated up to cover her face, stifling the heavier sobs threatening her. She felt something drop against her arms and glanced down— horror shocked her as she discovered the platinum collar had broken. Its pieces falling between her arm and breasts.

"No." She shifted to catch the broken strand, but one of the sapphire fitted flukes fell to the tile floor and quickly headed for the drain.

"Nooooo!" She screamed, dropping to her knees, trying to catch it.

~ * ~ * ~ * ~ * ~ * ~

Trenton's heart jumped when he heard her scream and flew to the shower, throwing the frosted glass door open, "Kat?" His eyes scanned over her to find what was wrong.

Katianna was huddled down on the stone tile of the shower stall, her hands clutched against her chest, sobbing uncontrollably. Her eyes came up and pleaded with him, "I'm sorry— I'm sorry." She held out her collar, clutched in her fingers, "It broke. I don't know how."

Trenton stepped in the shower, clothes and all, scooped her up in his arms, and carried her out. He couldn't see where it had broken, even more uncertain as to how it had come off, but she was obviously upset about it. "Shhh— it's okay, Kat, we can get it fixed." He tried to console her, not entirely sure why she was coming apart as she was.

"I'm sorry." She kept on and he couldn't get her to stop. "I can't remember— but I'm sorry. Your collar broke— I'm sorry. Please don't leave me." Her sobs turned to wails as she curled into him. Her fingers finding his shirt, clutching into it, still holding on to her collar.

"Leave you?" Trenton's arm tightened around her, "What makes you think I would leave you?"

Katianna wouldn't or couldn't answer. She refused to let go of his shirt, refused to be pushed away, not even so he could look into her face. He glanced up when he heard Diesel coming in. Diesel stood there, his chest huffing as if he'd just run at full speed to reach them. He'd obviously heard Katianna's scream too and came running, just as Trenton had. His brother's eyes searched for reasons as she came unraveled in Trenton's arms, then he shook his head, giving Trenton a questioning look.

"I don't know." Trenton confessed, shooting him a worried expression.

~ * ~

Diesel sat next to Trenton, his hands stroking over Katianna's legs, helping Trenton to console her. "Mouse? Sugar, what's happened?"

Kat's head rattled in fearful withdrawal. Whatever it was, she was afraid even to admit to it. But he saw something else— her eyes still fully dilated. He grabbed her chin, forcing her head back, and lifted an eyelid with a thumb to get a clear look at her eyes, "She's still high—" he felt the skin on her forehead and around the glands of her neck. "She's hot. She may be hallucinating."

Trenton shook his head suddenly, "Dammit, she tasted like orange juice when I kissed her while we showered."

"You let her have orange juice?"

"No, but I found her treating her back to the open fridge earlier."

Diesel left them for the kitchen and pulled the door to the fridge open. His eyes scanned its contents, then pulled the nearly empty bottle of orange juice from the door. He carried it back to the bedroom and held it up for Trenton to see. The compounds of the orange juice would have boosted any narcotic effects still in her blood stream. Essentially, Katianna was high as a kite again.

Trenton kissed her face and the top of her head, whispering to her. "You haven't done anything wrong. You have only pleased me and Deez completely." He assured her as Diesel came up to confirm it with him.

There was a knock on the door and Diesel leaned in, kissing Katianna on the temple before stepping away to get it, finding Paris.

~ * ~

"I came to see you again before you left. The chopper has refueled and is ready when you are." Paris tried to look calm. While he was still reveling in the partnership proposal, this was still a day for goodbye.

"There's a problem with Katianna. We have to stay another night to make things right for her."

Paris' expression melted, "What do you mean?"

"She may have drunk too much of the Absinthe and worked herself into a panic over what took place last night."

"May I come in please?"

Diesel stepped back, allowed Paris in, then headed back toward Trenton's room. Paris followed and watched as Diesel rejoined Trenton, who sat on the bed with a sobbing Mouse curled in his arms. Paris only peeked in.

"She's convinced she has done something wrong to upset him, and we can't figure out why." Diesel answered his unspoken question.

"Because she's like me." Paris mumbled his revelation, but even Trenton heard it and looked over at him.

"When we become your slaves— we're wide awake. We're not in some fantasy to rationalize why it's happening, or that we deserve it, or we were born to it. It is what it is. You've taken us, and it's pretty fucking frightening."

"Not helping that she's hallucinating then." Diesel spoke up.

Trenton's words were only for her. Whispered against her head as he crooned to her.

"You've never slept with her, have you?" Paris asked of Diesel.

"No, last night was the first time we've shared her."

Paris felt her panicked emotions as if they were his own. He could see right through her. "That's probably what's going wrong then. She's a writer. I know, for me, a good bit of last night is a blur and it seemed to go on forever. With everyone who should have been with her, to reassure it was meant to happen, gone this morning, she probably started creating stories in her head to fill in the gaps— to explain what might have happened. But her fitful nature made her dream up the wrong things, and now the

Absinthe has them stuck in her head like little scenarios on a repetitive skip."

~ * ~

"I know how to fix it, then—" Trenton leaned over Katianna, taking her chin in his hand and bringing her up to kiss him. He'd been through it before when she had been kidnapped by Kirshnov. The only way he saved her mental state from the horrors of what she'd gone through was kidnapping her *Himself* and pulling her back into *His* world. So, if in some bizarre way she had created a world of horror and fled there, he needed to kidnap her mind and return her as his possession— by making her live through the experience again. Except tonight, it would happen without the Absinthe, and he would remind her how much she pleased him and Diesel. "Do you know how much I love you?"

She shook her head.

Trenton knew better. She knew exactly how much he loved her, but right now, she was embroiled with the green fairy of the Absinthe. "I love you so much I need to share that experience with my brother." He kissed her face several times.

"All three of us are going to make love to you right now, because we all love you very much and nothing gives us more gratification than pleasuring your body." He brought her to her feet, turning her to face Paris. He gave Diesel a look and made Katianna watch, as Diesel walked over to Paris and began to undress him.

Trenton touched and caressed her as she watched, whispered his love and affection in her ear to keep her calm.

~ * ~

Paris couldn't think of a single moment in his life when he might have spied someone who loved, or tended to a lover, with as much devotion as Trenton did with Katianna. Or to even imagine that such love would come with an equally matched sexual relationship. He was glad he was here. He was glad life had brought him to this moment; nothing else would fill him as much as this did. He stepped toward the small woman who watched him and instantly her hands shot out to grasp his arms.

"Paris," she whispered with a hushed tone, "I think we've done something wrong." Pale blue eyes looked up at him, and he could see she was still frightened for them both.

He touched her face, dragging his thumb over her pouty lips and under her jaw, lifting them to be kissed by the man standing behind her. "No, Mouse, for once we did not." He watched Trenton kiss her tenderly, and when the Dominus looked back at Paris, so did she, her eyes asking if he was certain. Paris knew he needed to help, because inside he knew this little woman was going to be the closest friend he ever had. The one who had helped deliver him into Diesel's arms and his life. He smiled and nodded to her as Trenton slowly lowered a blindfold over her eyes.

"Jump, Katianna— jump," Paris whispered. And he knew he was right, when Trenton and Diesel closed in around them. Once more turning four into one.

~ * ~ * ~ * ~ * ~ *

CHAPTER FIFTEEN

~ * ~ * ~ * ~ * ~ * ~

<u>NEW YORK: TWO AND A HALF MONTHS LATER</u>

Diesel was just locking up when Paris came down the stairs from the office complex.

Paris had finally arrived in Diesel's life and in his home. While they had gotten together for a couple self-declared holiday weekend, and for a couple *just because*, the actual moving-in step in their relationship had put the two of them into some serious honeymoon bliss with each other. Diesel had taken time off from work so they could share it together. In addition, of course with their honeymoon came some adjustments, like Paris staking some claims of his own. Some of which, Diesel's brothers took pleasure in teasing him about.

But neither of them looked back with regret.

"There's my Fallen Angel." Diesel called to his lover when he appeared at the top of the stairs that led from the office complex up front into his gun shop, which butted up against the back of the building. He felt the gleaming in his own eyes, seeing the handsome man returning to him after his first day reporting to work with Trenton. *Damn, he looked good enough to eat in his dark grey slacks and merlot-shaded dress shirt.* The one Diesel had to purchase to replace the red one he'd sort of shredded down at the resort. "So how was your first day with orientation?"

"Insane— so much needs to be done. So many things for me to learn. I should have started working with him a month ago."

"Not a chance," Diesel protested, "a month ago, you had just moved in. I needed time to assert my claim."

Paris let out a gentle laugh and when he arrived beside him he leaned in for a kiss, "And who said you were finished?" Paris teased him.

Diesel turned, snared Paris in his arms and kissed him aggressively, his tongue licking at his mouth and biting his lower lip, "Because I said you're mine." He growled, cementing his claim.

"Perhaps you'd like to remind me right now." Paris' voice thickened like caramel with the suggestion, then he attempted to steal another kiss from Diesel.

"Mmmm— not until later. We have dinner, remember? It's the grand opening for Dane's new restaurant." Diesel pushed on Paris with his body, maneuvering him backwards and around the sales counter. Teasing him by turning his head, denying him any further glimpses of his lips.

"Mmmm—" Paris hummed back, resisting the move just enough that it increased the friction of Diesel's body against his own, not entirely giving up the pursuit for more lip action. "I haven't forgotten, but I'm not opposed to slipping a quickie in before we leave."

Diesel turned to his register and pulled the moneybag, grateful he'd already finished his count because, as always,

Paris was doing a number on his body and swaying his distraction.

~ * ~ * ~ * ~ * ~ * ~

They'd all gathered at the new restaurant for a semi-private celebration dinner; the five brothers, partners, and the staff who would make it all work, were there.

Impressed didn't even begin to describe the reaction to what Dane had created. Once through the heavy dark wood foyer, the place opened up to a two-story space that was just shy of being a palace. In the center, a large shallow pool of turquoise green water was split by an intersecting stone path. A large statue of marble, carved into the likeness of two androgynous Hellenistic servants, only moderately suggestive that one was male and the other a female, stood in the pool's center. Each pouring water back into the pond, from a double-handled vessel, to keep it renewed. There was no denying the craftsmanship that went into its creation, and Paris knew right away who its artist likely was. "Cardiff made that." He whispered to Diesel, who stayed at his side while he soaked in the restaurant's décor.

"Yes, he did." He nodded, pausing to admire the sculpted masterpiece, "He came over last fall and made it especially for Dane. He insisted on creating it where it stands now."

"He isn't here now, is he?" Paris glanced around anxiously.

"No." Diesel gave him an odd glance that perhaps said he was grateful for the artist's absence.

Birds chirped happily and Paris tracked the sound to find a large caged atrium in the corner of the restaurant. Deep extending balconies lined the walls overhead, and he surmised they were likely the private rooms Dane had mentioned as a pre-emptive answer to satisfying clientele in the Lifestyle, without alienating his more common patrons and accommodating their more modest ambience standards.

The wall adornments may have been the defining factor of the restaurant's atmosphere. Tiled frescos and carved bass reliefs along the wall revealed ancient nobles, ladies, and families gathering to bathe at a public bath, with each wall having its own half-scalloped fountain. Dane hadn't missed a detail in his attempt to transport his guests back in time, including even a long banquet table that, perhaps on opening night, would be piled high with appetizers, fruits, and desserts. Overhead, while roofed, the domed ceiling had been painted a light turquoise blue, dotted with puffs of white clouds that glowed with lighting from behind and further accented lighting sconces that glowed blue, giving the entire room below the full Mediterranean Riad appearance. The only thing missing from Dane's vision tonight were the bare-breasted wine pourers he swore to have. Because tonight, they too would sit and eat with them.

They gathered around one of the larger family tables, and right away food was brought out in swarms, not just for them but for several other tables as well. The chefs came out, surveyed the plates being set, then took up places at one of the other tables. A tall gentleman with strikingly handsome features watched over them all as they passed through the doors from the back before being presented. A man Paris recognized.

Once all the dishes had been served and everyone, including the wait staff, had sat down, Dane stood and raised his glass, "To all of you who have worked hard to make this come together, to my brothers and lovers. Today is the milestone of our journey as we open the doors to *Plat du Liguiran Riad*. May she prosper so we may all prosper from her bounty. Cheers!"

"But the glasses are empty!" Someone from one of the other tables called out just as everyone else was noticing the same thing.

"Are they?" Dane quipped, not revealing any surprises that he may have slipped on a detail, and he held up his hand and snapped several times.

All eyes moved to the four stepping out from the back. Two young women and two young men, clad in short, single-shoulder pastel togas, carrying clay carafes. Their beauty revealed as if they had just stepped from the paintings on the wall. *The final touch in Dane's vision.* The four smiled proudly with their task in order as they made their way around the tables and filled everyone's wine glasses. Not a bit shamed if a corner of fabric fell away and revealed naked flesh underneath. When the glasses were filled, they shared a laugh, revealing they too had enjoyed the surprise, then grabbed their seats among the others and joined them for the dinner.

Dane grinned like a golden lord and held up his glass once again, "To the *Plat du Liguiran Riad*!"

"To the *Plat du Liguiran Riad*!" They all cheered.

Dane sat at the head of the oval shaped table, and to his right sat Toussaint, a man Paris knew from his former days when he still ran the Museum Tours of Living Dolls. To Dane's left, however, sat Vince from Trenton's office, apparently having taken Stef's place at the front desk, and he was pure androgyny. It wasn't entirely odd that he was here with them now, but to be sitting directly next to Dane was. But that's when Paris began to notice the similarities between the two. Like the same eyes and the golden to near platinum hair. But he quickly dismissed the ridiculous thought that came to mind.

Next to Vince were Trenton and Katianna, and then Harper. A few chairs were empty, then himself and Diesel, with Marcus filling the gap between them and Toussaint.

Forks and knives clinked on plates that were soon accompanied by a rising choir of humming noises, sending their compliments to the head chef. None other than Toussaint. Another round of raised glasses passed about to each other so that everyone was included for a job well done.

Each plate was served with four tender lamb chops, only lightly seasoned with garlic and shallots, over a grilled mix of vegetables in a pool of light brown gravy. The lamb entrees were sided with a potato cake that, when split open, burst forth with a smooth creamy cheese and Tzatziki sauce. When combined with the lamb, the delicate meat and sauce inspired a decadent dance on the tongue. And there was no end of appraising moans and compliments passed around.

It was an interesting atmosphere, where Paris still felt like the newbie in a sense of closeness. He'd noticed it before when he was here with Trenton and Diesel for his training, and he felt it now. To an outsider, these men seemed like lords of a fetish cult, but on the inside, it was clearly all about family.

"So how long have you been practicing?" Paris popped the question after he'd had a moment to sample everything on his plate.

"*Pssh*, about two months now." Toussaint answered with a heavy French accent, but not so much he couldn't be understood. "Trying to place our own signature to a mix of dishes that follow more of the Moroccan, Corsican, and French Riviera side of Mediterranean cousin. It's been a challenge, but we have an expansive and varied menu selected so far."

"Corsican? Why not just follow a Greek dish line?"

"*Maudire*, everyone does Greek. Besides, Corsican cuisine has so many fun flavors to play with. I cannot resist them. Plus, we'd have to change the name too." He laughed, "And Dane and I don't want to do that." Toussaint grinned as a spoiled man would.

Paris nodded his approval of the time put into the preparations and training, but glanced at Diesel, "So why have we not been in here to help eat?"

Diesel chuckled but let Dane answer all the questions so he could keep eating.

"After the critics have eaten, a local charity comes by every day and picks up the meals and takes them to a halfway house for GLBT kids and young adults who've been thrown out by family."

"I'm sure they appreciate that." Paris nodded, enjoying a great meal from another esteemed chef.

Dane just laughed, "Actually, we get lots of notes asking us if we could just make them some regular cheeseburgers for once." And they all laughed.

"So you mentioned critics?" Paris asked to keep the topic going, as food was more than just a hobby for him.

"Yes. We've held an open door policy. Any published food critic is welcome to drop by at seven and eat whatever meal we serve. No menu shopping." Dane glanced at Toussaint, looking for any correction, "We've pretty much had one almost every evening for the last four weeks now?"

Toussaint nodded his head, and finished chewing before adding in, "And we've received several four and five stars in some of the top syndicates so far."

"It's very good. I can't place the sweet and spice combination in the grilled vegetables, though."

"It's raspberries and smoked chipotle."

A grin broke across Paris' face, enjoying the surprise ingredients, "You're kidding?"

"No. You like? I believe it was one of Chef Dalqeaute's favorite trade secrets to mix fruits with hot spices."

Paris grinned and nodded.

Dane commented to Toussaint. "Paris here was also a chef."

"No, my father was." Paris quickly corrected the statement.

"Sorry. Toussaint, this here is Paris Dalqeaute— Paris, this is Toussaint Larou."

Paris looked up and grinned devilishly, "We've met."

~ * ~

Dane didn't need to learn anything more to know just what that confirmation entailed. The look in Paris' eyes alone said it all, and of course, when he glanced at Toussaint, and how his French slut hardly shrugged with a smile as he settled back into eating his meal, purely clarified it. Dane slid his attention back to his brother's newly ensnared lover, "Paris, is there anyone I know that you haven't slept with?"

Paris hardly moved, except when he uncurled a finger and pointed toward Trenton. "Or your other brothers, for that matter, but I never got the vibe they were on the menu."

"Nor shall we." Marcus harped in with a deviant grin.

Dane glanced at Trenton, who wore his arrogantly prideful grin as usual, "I hear gears turning in the boy's head." Dane knew well Trenton didn't need to be told that, but he looked as though he'd spent some time toying and taunting Paris with it.

"So now you have Toussaint and Derek," Paris chided to return the lovers back to their Master's prospects, "your cock must be very happy."

"Derek isn't mine anymore." Dane rested back, ignoring Toussaint's narrowing gaze.

"Oh? Can I ask or is that too personal?"

"It's perfectly alright. He belongs to another. He fell in love with an Amazonian and she is his Mistress now."

"HA! Tell him about your encounter with her." Diesel laughed, which quickly spread to the others.

Dane wiped the smile from his face so he could tell the story, "She marched into my office with a monologue that resembled a riot act of what her sub would not and could not do in his job from there on out. It seemed she thought her newly acquired ownership of him stretched out into

277

the club. She had quite the list of things, several of which were requirements of Derek's job title duties."

"So what did you do?" Paris grimaced at the thought of anyone having the gonads to attempt to boss any of the Dominion brothers around, but he could also see the amusement it held for them. *A Lion does not turn its head to acknowledge a pesky dog.*

"Instructed her to have a seat, while I explained how Derek had been there for four years, and as head bartender, he would continue to do his job, none of which had anything to do with sucking my cock, but he would perform the duties of a liquor manager or he would lose his job, period. Then I suggested she perhaps needed to communicate further with her subbie on what exactly was written in his contract of agreement. Because if she attempted to use him to micromanage my business again, I'd have her banned."

"Seems harsh, don't you think?" Someone else asked among the restaurant staff that was listening in from the other table.

"I run a night club. I can't afford jealous partners coming in causing scenes that don't entertain. Thing is, Derek was never mine exclusively. So, when he came to me and said he was falling in love with someone and wanted to be committed to her, he was released from any sexual or other demands by me or the club that were not part of his job as bar manager."

"Those are not the same rules for me." Toussaint was fast to clarify himself, and Dane chuckled when he leaned in and planted a kiss on the Frenchman's temple.

"Yes, Toussaint is all mine." Dane spoke proudly.

~ * ~

"So you're living with him now?" Paris was intrigued. Toussaint was a slut, just like Paris, and not one to be tied down to just one body. Though, if he were going to be, no one could argue his choice in Dane.

"Pssh, no. I tried, but I hate the long commute to the restaurant. American drivers, they are crazy. So, I have a condo here in the city now."

"You have a car?" Paris was instantly jealous.

"Pssh— oui." Toussaint answered as if it were absurd he did not.

Paris narrowed his eyes on Diesel, "I don't have a car."

"You must be losing your touch, Paris." Toussaint made the jab, hiding his humor, "I made sure the car came with the deal before I even left France."

Paris shoulder-nudged Diesel, trying to get his attention, but Diesel kept on eating, not forthright in trying to hide his own smile.

"He got an expensive car at that." Dane quipped.

"And I service you well for it, too." Toussaint loaded up a bite from his plate, then offered to feed it to Dane directly, "Tell him, Vince." Toussaint directed his comment to the androgynous man who sat to Dane's left, "Tell them how I service him well." Though Toussaint's eyes never left the man who held his lusty gaze as Dane took the offering from his fork.

~ * ~ * ~ * ~ * ~ * ~

Paris' head was zinging off the Richter scale as they rode home, with Toussaint's gripe *that it was too far a drive* repeating in his mind along the way. It was true, nearly a two-hour drive out, but there was no way he would move out of their home for a condo in the city. He'd accept the drive, but the car thing was going to be on his list of things to get soon.

Trenton was oddly quiet, and save for keeping his eyes on the road as he drove them home, he only had eyes for Katianna. He'd been staring at her all night. More than usual and hardly said more than a few words at the dinner. "So what's up with him?" Paris asked Diesel, but got no answer from him, just one of those know-all grins. *He knew, he just wasn't telling. Talk about gears moving.*

After they got home, Diesel suggested they should go for a walk out along the shore behind the house. Instead, they ended up finding a spot in the sand behind Trenton's house, and they stared out into the dark ocean and watched the early fall thunderstorm moving along far off the coast. Diesel started a small bonfire using driftwood that was lying about, making the sit-around cozy and keeping the cold sea air at bay.

Paris was leaning back on his hands while a rather fidgety Diesel leaned back on him, sitting between his legs, wearing an anxious grin. "You've been grinning all night. You want to tell me something?"

"Tonight's the night." Diesel half chuckled to himself.

"The night for what?"

"Trenton is going to tell Kat she's going to marry him."

Paris pulled at Diesel's shoulder, twisting him to look at him, "Married? As in engagement ring? Wedding? The whole nine yards, marriage?"

Diesel nodded.

"Why the hell didn't you tell me sooner?"

Diesel's face scrunched up at him, "Because he wanted it to be a surprise. You would have told her."

"Ah—" he clamped his mouth shut. He couldn't argue with that.

"You would have." Diesel chided him.

He probably would have. Ever since Kat returned home from the island, he had emailed and talked with Kat almost daily. The only reason it slowed since his own coming-home was because he hadn't left the bedroom, and Diesel, too many times. Even then, he was noted for taking a few selfies and texting them to her. Writing material, they had called it. He was even so inclined to pull out his phone and text her now, but thought better of it, because there was something else that also struck him. Like how did this affect them? *Would the four of them be different in some way?*

"Hey. This changes nothing for us." Diesel's attentive watching called Paris back from his thoughts.

Paris looked at him. *Diesel wasn't gay; Mouse had told him that,* yet the man looked at him like there was no other in the world meant to be with him. Not a sliver of doubt in those eyes. Marriage for Diesel's brother and his slave seemed like a blessing in the evolution of their relationship, and he would still be a part of it with Diesel.

Diesel's hand came up, grabbed him behind the neck and pulled him over, and they kissed. Their own small celebration for the good news. Of course, kissing Diesel was always like some small celebration.

~ * ~ * ~ * ~ * ~ * ~

"I love how it feels when you stroke me like that, but—" Trenton's moans paused a moment, as he lay in bed with his slave. "I think there's something missing."

"Missing? What do you mean?" Katianna's hand stilled. She loved touching him just before they made love, loved how his skin felt, almost velvety over hard iron.

"Well, I think it might feel even better if your hand had this on it."

And as he said it, she felt his hand over hers, then felt the distinct item being pushed down on her ring finger. Her eyes widened and she wanted to look, but he grasped her hand and pressed it against his cock, moving her grip and stroking his shaft again.

"*Mmmm*— yeah— that's it. So much better." He crooned.

Kat squirmed, trying to twist her hand more to where she could see the ring in the dark lighting of their bedroom, but his hand kept her firmly stroking his body. She lifted, but he soon had her pinned back down, keeping her from doing that as well.

"Ahh, yes— feels so good. I might even cum this way." He panted in playful banter. Then he pulled her hand up to his lips and kissed it, while his eyes twinkled from behind their laced fingers as he looked at her, and in doing so revealed the over-sized stone he had just placed there.

Katianna's mouth dropped open like a fish when she caught the sparkle of blue from the stone placed in the engagement setting, surrounded by small clear diamonds. Even in the dim lighting of the bedroom, there was no mistaking what she was seeing.

"Trenton, oh my god." She gasped her astonishment.

"Marry me." He commanded, kissing her hand again, and then rolled her to her back as he came over her. He spread her legs with his thighs and pressed his cock against her sensitive mound.

She gasped again, "I can't. I'm your slave."

"Marry me, Katianna." His hips thrust forward, and he caught his breath as he sank into the hot world that was all his own. He lowered and kissed the side of her face, hard and hungry.

Kat's head kicked back into the pillow, proffering her neck further for his ravaging, her breath catching, and her throat making it hard to get any words out. "I can't." She cried out as he drove deep inside her walls again, "I'm your slave."

"Marry me." He thrust into her again until he was at his hilt.

"Slaves aren't allowed to marry." She was panting under him.

"Then I give you permission to say yes." He stilled inside her, and let her catch her breath, so she could give him the answer he waited for.

Katianna's eyes shot up at him, dazed from this new suggestion as he began his endless lovemaking, "Do I have your permission to say no as well?" She risked the playful question.

His face pinched into a firm expression and fought back the smile that burned behind his eyes. "Absolutely not."

A warm smile melted onto her face. She'd become his slave just a year ago. Something that terrified her at first, and yet she was perfectly at ease in his life being just that. She wasn't about to have a proposal change that for her. But if he commanded her to do so, she would love nothing more than to submit to his demands. "Then your slave obeys and says yes."

~ * ~

"Say it again." His hips starting up again, driving into her— now letting his hunger take over in a rhythmic roll. He pulled her legs up and wrapped them around his waist, letting him in deeper. He kept his weight on elbows while he kissed her with such need. Rolling with deep thrusts of his cock into her sweet theca. *His Theca.*

He couldn't get enough of her. Couldn't touch her enough— couldn't taste enough. And he wanted to hear that word again.

"Yes." She let out the breathy whisper, swept away by the sensation he created as he stroked her insides, like savory friction intended to ignite a fire to life.

Trenton's own breath grew ragged, pumped from his chest as he slid into her over and over, "Say it again."

"Yes-ssss." Her muscles clamped around him as she tried to give him that sweet word just one more time before being completely swept away with her release. The tremble of her body around his cock did him in and his own release shot out and filled her. His hips hammered down over her one last time until his whole body locked up as they shared in each other's orgasm.

They lay there, resting in each other's arms long after their heavy breaths had subsided, but Kat was rather twitchy underneath him. Nowhere near ready to fall asleep in his arms, like she usually would. "You're not going to fall asleep, are you?" He mumbled against the side of her head that shook frantically in earnest answer. He let out a hard sigh, surrendering to what she needed. "Alright then. Go on." He no sooner lifted up and freed her from his bodily cage that the covers on their bed went flying, and a tiny naked woman pounced from their bed with a squeal, quickly racing out of the room.

He dropped to his back, his ears following the girly shrill sound as it traveled down the stairs, right out the back doors and across the lawn towards Deez's house.

"Paaaaaarrrrrrrriiiiiiiisssssss!"

~ * ~ * ~ * ~ * ~ * ~

CHAPTER SIXTEEN

~ * ~ * ~ * ~ * ~ * ~

Paris came in through the back, having ridden into work with Diesel, as it would likely be the usual routine for them.

Even as Paris brought up the topic of a car for himself on the way in, Diesel's only response involved pulling Paris' hand over to grope his lap, "But then you wouldn't have this." He pointed out.

That, of course, had been enough to convince Paris to drop the subject for the remainder of the ride.

Once they finally made it into work, after a short delay, Paris dropped by his office to get his computer powered up, then headed to the front lobby to check messages before Trenton arrived. Only it seemed someone else had beaten him to it. Vince was in early, the beautiful man who'd shared guarded space with Dane last night.

Paris stopped, glanced around, then cautiously approached, "Well, good morning. I'm sorry, I wasn't expecting you in for some time."

"This is actually my regular time to come in, but since you'd started working here, Trenton gave me some leeway, allowing me to devote some morning hours to help my brother out."

"Brother—?" Paris trailed off, getting hung up on the notion that the man before him still seemed strangely familiar beyond the office.

"Dane Masters?"

"Oh, how stupid of me." Paris sputtered aloud before he could rectify the comment. "I knew you looked familiar. You're not just Vince. You used to be called Vida." Paris' jaw practically dropped to the floor. He really did like the new look on Vida. *She* made an elegantly and naturally effeminate, beautiful *he*. No more of the false get-up or overdone make up and clothes. Vince's true feminine nature showed with a rather sweet, robust glow. Like he finally found his perfect *merged pronoun* side and flourished with it. Vince was so androgynous that a simple change of clothes was all it would take to trick people to think they were talking to a man or to a woman. "Do you mind me asking? I mean, would you be comfortable with me asking you something personal?"

"Sure." Vince settled in his chair and rested his chin on a closed hand, propping himself up on an elbow and graciously waited.

"You used to work at Club Pain, right?"

"Yes, that was me."

"You've changed considerably since then. Or at least here, you're much different and I guess that's my question. Is this just another side of you that I had never met last time I was here? Or did something in you change?"

"*Ahhh*— well—" it was almost a song the way the androgynous man sighed the expression out. He looked like the face of spring with the way he tilted his head to the side in a gentle rocking motion, then looked back at Paris with a twitch of his lips that made a cute little crinkle in his nose. "You see, it's funny how those profound things that come at you, to help you find yourself, sometimes come in small packages."

"How do you mean?"

"Well, I was miserable as a man and then chronically depressed as a drag queen— but then two small, completely insignificant, and totally unrelated things spoke to me, and it was like getting hit in the face with a galactic-sized epiphany." Vince paused, tucking his chin for emphasis, "But instead of pain, all my pain was gone. Now I am happy and content as a fluid feminine man *and* a masculine woman. Two faces on the same coin. So for once in my life, I'm happy rather than torn." He sighed. It was pleasant, like the kind of sound one would make after a day's work in a flower garden. The wafting fragrance of flowers on the summer breeze at the end of the day would bring triumphant accomplishment for the sowing, and the smile that came on Vince's face was light, more inward than meant for Paris, but there was definitely a radiant warmth in there.

"What were the two things that changed you?" Paris was enthralled and would ask damn near anything to keep Vince talking.

Vince blinked a moment as if he came out of a dream, "Oh well— the first came from a movie I was watching with some friends. It was *Taking Woodstock* and the actor, Liev Schreiber, who is such a man's man in reality, played this character, *Vilma*, who was a full-on cross-dresser. I loved his character. He was still very masculine, but with lots of undertones of feminine charm and heart. His heart was a woman's. If that makes sense. Vilma was so natural about it, it grabbed me. I guess it was the hippy era that did that, but he said something in the movie— *'I know what I am, isn't that enough?* —well, anyway, it stuck with me. Not that it was any large affirmation for change, but I couldn't shake it either. I just didn't know what it meant at the time. Then, like two weeks later, I'm at work at Club Pain, talking with the Mouse, and I was venting about something or other. I don't remember what it was and she asked me, quite off topic, if I ever take the *woman* off." Vince paused, his forehead puzzled over the question as he recalled that evening, and Paris saw that it really had struck a note inside the man. Paris listened quietly as he continued. "Of course, my response was *no*, so then she asked why I try so hard then. Why was my *woman* always so overly done up? No real woman does that all the time, not even for work. Why not let my hair down and just let my *woman* chill out and relax and just *be* a woman rather than a *drag queen?*" Vince paused, let out a hard sigh, and waved his hand up in a non-sequential movement, "Within minutes I was crying— and she went into a panic—"

Paris held back the chuckle in him, because yes, the Mouse knew panic like a Shakespearian play, but he didn't want to come across as laughing at Vince.

"She ran for Trenton and then Dane came. Neither of which could get me to stop crying either. I couldn't even explain *why* I was crying. Because I really didn't know. I went home and cried some more. The next day, Dane calls me up to tell me Katianna was insisting she take me out to make up for whatever pain she caused. We went shopping at all her favorite vintage shops, which were instantly mine too. Later, we went to this spa and I got the full make over and got a massage— I didn't think they'd ever get me out of there. I had this sweet little Albanian boy rubbing me down. Of course, Kat didn't get one; she said Trenton would kill anyone who touched her."

Paris had to laugh that time, because he knew that too.

"We had lunch at one of the bistros, in my new vintage Vida-Vince clothes, my new hair and new aura. While some guy tried desperately to win my attention, the two of us ate and talked about her books, about Stef wanting to leave the office to work at Dane's new restaurant once it was finished, and I went home a relaxed pretty boy. I saw myself— saw Vince— in the mirror for the first time in years and I cried then too, because I had missed him so much. I realized that day that all my pain was from abandoning *me*. I spent a few days in therapy with Dr. Laszkovi, and Dane stayed at my side with a flourish of compliments and love. And I came out the better for it. Now here I am, finally rediscovering myself rather than hiding under years of redefining or just outright hiding. A life of depression gone. I'm finally happy and have been that way ever since."

"Wow." Paris shook his head, and for a long moment, all he could do was offer a radiant smile. "Thank you for sharing that."

"It's amazing the things that come from that tiny little woman and how they can change a person."

"Yeah, it is." He agreed completely because she'd told him something once and it had changed his life too. "I just want to say, Vince, you look absolutely stunning. Just don't tell Dane I said that. He might hurt me." He started to head back for his office, but then stopped, and glanced back at Vince, "Not that you weren't a little hottie before." Paris winked and strutted off proudly after he saw the blushing grin on the man's face. It'd been worth risking the wrath of the Golden Master.

~ * ~ * ~ * ~ * ~ * ~

CHAPTER SEVENTEEN

~ * ~ * ~ * ~ * ~ * ~

Paris was still doing some exploring in the house, taking more liberties than what he'd had during his previous visit, because this time, it was now home. Diesel had even let him pick out one of the spare rooms to convert into his own personal space. Though he'd yet decided what he wanted to do with it, it was his. There were already a few weights and a workout bench downstairs in the rec room, and he really didn't need an office at the house, though it seemed that might end up being the most likely thing he would do with the new space. But for now, it was nice to know it was his.

Paris' first request was to do a little bit of feng shui rearranging, which was met with far more compliance than he expected. In fact, Diesel and Marcus seemed content to give him free rein with little fuss—

"PARIS! Where the hell is the wine cabinet?!" Marcus' voice came booming up the stairs from down below.

Except when they couldn't find something, Paris grinned to himself.

Their bedroom was another matter— rather, the closet. It was huge, but not huge enough. At least not as far as Paris was concerned, once he got a chance for some real shopping to expand his wardrobe that he would leave here whenever he had to return to the island for his seasonal job at the resort. Diesel only had enough stuff to take about a fourth of the closet, but he insisted that there was a line, and Paris was not allowed to start crushing his things together just to make more room for his own.

Paris likely had spent hours just staring into the walk-in closet with gears rolling around in his head, figuring out a way to redesign it so that it would have more space. An island bureau was one of his ideas, but that only solved part of his dilemma. He liked his clothes hung up, not folded, whenever possible. It was an issue that had yet learned a solution. So was the hulking man, who was taking liberties rummaging through one of the many suitcases still to be unpacked.

"Ah, this is the one I like."

Paris looked over his shoulder just as Diesel was toting off with one of his bottles of cologne, but soon returned— empty handed and was back at it with his riffling. It was almost as annoying as getting his hair ruffled, which also went unchallenged, despite his attempts.

Diesel popped up suddenly, a picture frame in hand and a surprised look on his face that sent his eyebrows to the top of his forehead, "Damn, Paris. Was there ever a time in your life when you weren't so incredibly sexy?"

Paris' expression turned rigidly serious, "Not a day in your life." He took the frame from his hand and returned it to the suitcase, only to have it plucked back out with an expressed warning that Diesel now laid claim to the framed photo of Paris, when he'd only been around seventeen years old or so, and walked out with it.

Paris gave up on the closet fallacy for the time being and decided to tackle the kitchen instead.

Within the hour, he had pots and dishware pulled from the cabinets, and stacked on every surface of counter and table space, as he rearranged everything to his preference. *Why the spices were four cabinets from the stove was just ludicrous. And glasses should always be handiest to the refrigerator. Pots and pans around the stove and overhead at the island. Plates and such were to be next, down the line of cabinets so that everything worked like an assembly line that took energy and flow into consideration.* He was about to tackle the dry pantry when there was a shrill cry behind him. He spun around to find an attractive Latino woman behind him. Her hands slapped up around her face and her mouth fell open like a goldfish. But he'd been partly expecting this. It was only to her fortune that Diesel had kept him happily distracted up to now. Now the kitchen had to be corrected before it drove him insane.

"*Madre de dios!* What have you done?"

Paris hardly glanced a second time over his shoulder, but he continued with what he was working on as if she didn't exist.

"What are you still doing?" Her Latino attitude rose up when she clearly didn't like that he hadn't stopped to address her.

No one ever likes relinquishing power over anything, but the kitchen? It was his now. Without contestation.

She suddenly regained some composure and sent demands at him as if she owned the house. "You do not have the right to do this! I want everything back as it was. Get out!"

Paris had to ponder this moment and rested back on the door to the pantry, saying nothing in his silent contempt. It apparently wasn't going over well with her.

She bobbed her head with an exaggerated bug-eye glare at him, "Did you not hear me? I said, get out!"

"I live here and this is my house. And you are— exactly?"

"Nooo— you stay here." She wagged a finger at him with a fist thrown on her hip, "This is the house of the Head Masters. And it's my job to take care of them and this kitchen."

"It's Senita, right?"

"Yes. And who are you?"

"Paris." He pushed off and went over to a crate of kitchen towels he'd brought down and left on the counter until he was ready for them, "And the kitchen is mine, now. You needn't worry about it."

"Oh, I don't think so."

He stopped and gave her an amused look, "Shall I mark it? I'd rather not, it's the kitchen. But I will." A fact Senita needed to learn. He would try to work with her, but he wasn't going to relinquish control over the kitchen, and her response to it seemed to suggest that war was on the horizon.

"So, you just waltz in here and start rearranging things, and you didn't stop to think that I may not approve?"

"Yes. It was all wrong and I have to have a properly aligned kitchen. The flow was choking. And no, I don't need your approval." She was about to say something. He could tell she had a rant in the making. He'd known a few Latino women and knew that once they got started, there was no stopping them. "It's not open for debate, I have everything planned to pretty much where I want it all to go, and unless I move it, it stays where it is. Excuse me." He disappeared into the pantry with the kitchen towels, then shortly popped back out, grabbed a stack of boxes, and went back.

When he was done, he came out, already feeling better about the space. Even as Senita went from cabinet to cabinet with an increasing gasp as she discovered he'd moved nearly everything. All but the large appliances.

He heard the front door open, which would be Diesel and Marcus returning from a joint errand. He'd leave Senita to them and he marched past her, off in search of the next exploration of the home. Feeling as much of his gloating pride when he overheard her suddenly venting to none other than the man who'd given him carte blanche over the kitchen.

While their futile debate went on, switching from English to a faster paced debate in Spanish, Paris went on his merry way to ponder a new item down in the living room. A curvy bench-like sofa that hadn't been there last year. Almost identical to the one in Trenton's office. It was among the many household items Paris had yet truly explored and get acquainted with since moving up. He sat in it, enjoying the buttery soft leather. It was comfy, yet it wasn't going to win any awards for most comfortable. Maybe an honorable mention for most odd piece of furniture, because it didn't match up with anything else in the entire house. It was, however, seemingly versatile, finding he could change positions or flip over, and it was still livable for lounging.

"There are two things in this house that we don't share."

Paris snapped up to find Marcus nearly glaring over him. A surprisingly fearsome expression, despite Marcus' usually carefree appearance. Like a bonus mixture of John Lennon and Johnny Depp, if one were to ignore the more subtle tones of his BDSM lifestyle. Paris responded with nothing more than an innocent blank stare and waited to hear what those *two* things might be.

"You and that chair." And without another word, Marcus walked off.

Paris' gaze followed him until he spotted Diesel at the doorway from the kitchen.

Paris' attention instantly went back to the bench-like seat he was sitting in. "Okay, so aside from it being fairly comfortable, what's with these chairs? Trenton has one just like it in his office."

Diesel shrugged off the doorjamb and came over, "Actually, Trenton has several of them, two in his house, one at the office, and another in his booth at the club now. They're called Tantra sofas."

"Oh-kay— what's a Tantra sofa?"

"They're positioning benches for having sex."

Paris' eyes shot down to the bench through his legs, rolling over the different heights on the two humps, and very quickly the endless combination of body positions were registering in his brain. "There is no way in hell I'm getting off of it now—" he grinned wickedly, "not by Marcus' definition of the word, at least."

"Tread lightly with him, Paris. Marcus is adjusting too."

"I'm not fucking with him," Paris reached out, snagged Diesel by his jeans, and pulled him over to straddle the sofa with him, "But I am definitely going to be fucking you in just a minute."

It wasn't long and the two of them were completely stripped down naked and on a direct trajectory toward the very thing Marcus had already warned against. Only Diesel was running the show right now. He'd gotten Paris repositioned so he was sitting on the lower hump facing him while Diesel sat in the dip. He had both of them worked up and as stiff as plank boards. He also had Paris dancing on his fingers. "That's it, Paris, move for me." Diesel's fingers were buried deep in Paris' hole, busily catching his prostate and driving Paris towards insanity, while Diesel slowly jacked his own dick at a pace set more to assault Paris' view than rush himself to the finish line.

Paris was slowly inching his way off the hump he sat on and further into Diesel's lap until he had their cocks coming in contact, pushing his hips forward so his own was pressing against the wide flanged head of Diesel's engorged member. Paris rolled his body in response— chewed then licked over his lips as he gasped from the annihilation taking place on his glory spot, while he kept his burning concentration on the task of getting his cock close enough to fully frot against Diesel's.

~ * ~

Diesel allowed the encroachment, enjoying the amount of energy Paris was having to exude just to gather another inch closer, but it only gave Diesel more reach to drive him insane from the inside out. Paris' cock was practically dripping like a faucet with a direct tap to his cum. He started to growl, and then Diesel felt his Imp's ass clamp down on his fingers with the impending explosion.

Paris' head kicked back and he let out several strangled sounds amidst a barrage of raspy breaths. His hips jutted forward and a thin stream of cum splattered and poured from his cock over Diesel's hand. Diesel exchanged his cock for Paris' and stroked him a few times to press him through the orgasm, then continued the fingering in Paris' ass as if he'd never gotten the release from him. "Now let's see you do it again, Paris." And Diesel worked his fingers in once and pumped into Paris' hole, tapping away at his glory spot as if he were transmitting Morse code.

"Oh fuck, just fuck me now."

"No, I'm going to milk you one more time, then I will fuck you. So, the sooner you cum again, the sooner you'll get my cock inside you."

So began Paris' rolling hips in a grind over Diesel's fingers. He reached for his cock, but Diesel was too quick and slapped it away. "Keep your hands off your cock. Try it again and I will strap your wrists down until this is over."

~ * ~

Paris was thinking long and hard on whether challenging him was a good idea, but the two digits in his ass made it hard to focus on anything for long. His body rode on the edge of oblivion, caught between the sharp blades of pain and eccentric pleasure. Every tap to his prostate sent triggers of electrical jolts through his body, locking his muscles into fits of arrest. His whole body curled and jerked, locking up because the sharp pleasure was too much. He could hardly breathe, and he sure as hell couldn't sit still. Just when he thought he couldn't stand it— when he was blind to the fact he was sliding his ass back and forth on Diesel's fingers and thrusting his cock towards his hand that stroked only himself— when he thought for certain madness was coming for him, he felt Diesel pull his fingers free. He then wrapped his grip around Paris' still throbbing cock, gave it a good tug, and stroked it over a few times. Next, Diesel had their cocks lined up side by side, and he gripped them both as much as he could.

Paris' thrusts became wild and he began to fuck Diesel's fist with all the fury and gusto he could pull up. "Ahhhhh— fuck!!" Paris nearly came off the bench. His hands gripped the sides of the bench until his knuckles turned white. What he wanted more was to force himself onto Diesel's lap and slide down that thick cock for a solid fucking. But all he could do was what Diesel allowed, violently fucking Diesel's fist several times before settling back down to the sofa hump.

"That's it, make yourself cum for me, be quick about it, and then I'll fuck you just as you asked." And Diesel reached under Paris once more to seek out his hole and go for his prostate gland.

Paris still gripped the sides of the bench, lifted his hips to let Diesel in, and then slammed down until Diesel's fist was pressed against his ass cheeks and Paris could go no further. Essentially, igniting a fiercer finger-fucking from Diesel's hand as Paris rocked back and forth.

He couldn't ease off from the sensation of his cock sliding against the thick one, both soaked with his own jizz. He felt another wave coming, and then the room seemed to tilt on him until he felt his body arching backwards over the bench, with Diesel lifting his legs, and then felt the thick cock slowly pushing in.

"Don't forget to cum for me, Paris." A husky growl spoke to him, and the moment Paris felt the stretch, and then the broad cap of Diesel's cock as it slid over his prostate, Paris was done. Every muscle in his body clamped down and he heard the loud hiss from Diesel. All Paris could do after that was shake.

It wasn't until the tremors were finally easing off that he felt the pulsing of Diesel's load hit the insides of his walls. Oh, he would have laughed, but he was simply too fucking exhausted. Paris couldn't even move, his head hung almost completely upside-down on the other end of the humped lounge sofa and his legs spread wide, still supporting the large body of his man relaxed over him. God, it felt good, too— short lived, but definitely good. He licked his lips, trying to moisten them so he could talk, "Hardly seems fair, making me cum like that until I haven't the energy to get my brains actually fucked out or return the favor."

"And to think that was only twice. I want to see you milked dry with four or five releases."

Paris just lay there. Even his brain refused to work. Oh, he heard his Patronus all right, he just couldn't come up with a damn good impish response for him, so he just lay there. Exhausted and happy under the man he was crazy over.

~ * ~ * ~ * ~ * ~ * ~

Later that day, Diesel sought out his brother.

Marcus had been on the moody side since Paris had moved in. He hadn't made any comments that would suggest what his issues were, but the timing did. Still, Marcus wasn't the easiest man to read, and Diesel had learned that half the time it was never what he thought it was. So, after having a shower and cleaning up, he decided it was time to find out why. He found Marcus in the living room, watching the news and wearing a severe scowl on his face.

"My bench is missing." He commented on the obvious, not bothering to look up at Diesel.

"Yeah. It's now been baptized several times with Paris' spunk. Don't worry, Paris is already on the website, ordering you a replacement, plus a few more for us."

"Should have kept my mouth shut."

Diesel chuckled, "I'm the one who told him what it was."

"Yeah, like he'd never figure that one out." He replied dryly.

Diesel fell silent a moment, looking his roommate over. There was something bothering him. Far more than the sofa bench. "What's wrong?"

"I'm okay."

"No, you're not, and it's not about us taking off with your bench. So out with it before I have to kick your ass for it."

Marcus took in a long deep breath then finally looked at him. It was probably the first time he dared look Diesel in the eye since Paris had moved in. "I just never thought that you'd end up with a guy." He shook his head. His face showed his despair that it even troubled him and his eyes quickly darted away again.

Diesel scrutinized him, trying to read the emotions Marcus fought to conceal. Marcus was never one to hate on sexual differences, but all the same, his comment came as a surprise. He also knew it was best to find out why his brother said it before he became too defensive. "It's not the first time I've had a man for a lover."

"I know—" Marcus blinked then matched his gaze again. "But none of them came to live with you either. Don't get me wrong here. I know you're happy with him. I know it's

302

what you want. I just never expected you to settle down with a guy, and I'm having a tough time wrapping my head around it. That's all this is." He shook his head again.

This time, Diesel understood that it was more of a disapproval of Marcus' own thoughts rather than a disapproval of Diesel's relationship with Paris.

"I guess what I'm afraid of the most is that as I reprogram my brain, I might start thinking about all those times you and I shared a woman, and that maybe you were trying to get closer to me."

"Why would you think that?"

"Because I'm an idiot, Diesel! I over process shit. You know that." He stammered.

"So you're okay?"

"Yeah." His mood seemed to momentarily brighten and he tried to force a smile, "You just surprised me, that's all."

They were silent for a long moment. Diesel could see there was more to it and wondered if perhaps Marcus felt like he was losing his family— his brothers. Marcus grew up in foster homes; he'd never had a family until he caught up with them in the Marine force. The emotions tied with the term *losing his family* had deeper implication for Marcus than it did for the rest of them. It didn't help that he'd loved twice and lost out when neither of the women returned the heart-deep commitment Marcus had felt for them. Then it struck Diesel as to why Marcus hadn't tried for a relationship with Laurel when she was staying with them after she'd been rescued, along with Kat and Chikako. As a willing slave already, she seemed to be an ideal match for him. "Why didn't you keep Laurel?"

Marcus' expression fluttered a moment. His eyes dropped to his hands in his lap, then to some unseen thing on the carpet before he raised his eyes again. "I wanted her for the wrong reasons. I figured, after all she went through, she'd only be endeared to me because I was the one who'd rescued her, and that I would be the sweetest Master she'd ever had. I wanted to keep her because I thought she needed that from me. That I was her knight in shining armor."

"So what made you change your mind?"

"I'm not that kind of Master."

"You have been in the past. For Ajmaani."

"As angry as I was with Trenton over how he held back on Katianna all those years back, I understand them now. And it wasn't just about one thing." Marcus' expression grew distant for a moment before continuing, "Remember when Harper found out Laurel had a sister? Turned out she was trying to run away from them. Being a slave was only a means to keep from becoming a victim to a pimp."

"No—" Diesel shook his head, "she was a submissive. She went through three years of training. Trent checked her references. How'd she turn out to be a runaway?"

"She might have been perfect as a slave or sub for someone, but the reasons that motivated her for why she went into it were wrong. We both know how those scenarios turn out. And that's when I realized that I didn't consider Laurel my family, and probably never would. That was wrong, too. Just like I was with Ajmaani and with Marissa." He took a deep breath, stretching, then got up, looked down at Diesel, and his expression lightened. "Just like I am now. Paris is perfect for you, and I know that." He offered his hand to him.

Diesel looked at Marcus' hand for a moment. It seemed too strange that Marcus would settle for a handshake, or that he would need to put that much distance between them, but when Diesel slid his hand into Marcus', he was yanked up to his feet and suddenly wrapped in strong arms as Marcus hugged him.

Relief. Diesel felt deep relief and he quickly hugged his brother back. "And you were not wrong about them— they were wrong for you." He conferred this bit of insight to him. *There was never anything wrong with loving someone.*

~ * ~ * ~ * ~ * ~ * ~

CHAPTER EIGHTEEN

~ * ~ * ~ * ~ * ~ * ~

The honeymoon was over, and it was time Diesel returned to his other duties, such as his presence at Club Pain. While his lifestyle, like his brother's, went far beyond the club, it was still a social hub for them, and much of its success was lent to the brothers being present. So, to mark his return to the scene, he put on a solid demonstration of shibari on the corner stage of the nightclub with none other than Paris. The clubbers and members enjoyed every strand of rope that went into the scene, and even more when they were treated to Diesel having some fun spanking him a few times before releasing his captive Fallen Angel. But it didn't slip Diesel's attention that Paris was starting to get into the spanking. He doubted the Imp would ever willingly enjoy anything harder than that, but Paris was definitely heated up with a thick, super-charged bulge in his pants while he waited for Diesel to remove the ropes. Paris' eyes burned with one word and one word only. *Pounce.* And Diesel would happily oblige him as soon as he got the ropes off and had applied aftercare. Getting that last part in was often more of a challenge than it should be when it came to Paris. But Diesel refused to skimp on it either. Not when it came to his shibari scenes.

Diesel took Paris upstairs, away from his audience, for the aftercare. Because even rubbing Paris' limbs was becoming more alluring than post-care. Before long, the treatment was completely abandoned and the two were in the private back room, rearranging the furniture and perhaps a wall or two.

While the room offered privacy, it did little to muffle the sounds they made as Diesel plowed into his lover. When they came back out to relax in the lounge, there were more than just a few snickers.

It felt good to be back at the club. He hadn't even realized how he'd missed it until now. He'd been avoiding it somewhat, worried how Paris was going to handle him as the club's Patronus. Paris was good at managing the resort and its fetish season, but he had never welcomed any part of kink for himself. Rather, Paris endured it for what he wanted. Diesel was his opposite in this sense. He loved the lifestyle. He loved the control and the sensations he felt or could make others feel through their submission to him. Paris was not a submissive. A slut perhaps, and now *His slut*, but not a submissive, which made Diesel worry he would eventually see a lifestyle he loved fade from his life.

Now, as he sat there, his cock spent and happy, Paris sat at his feet like a preening peacock, and perhaps with a dash of gloating pig added into his ego, Diesel realized it may not vanish as much as he'd feared. The earlier scene performed downstairs had been a clear indicator as Diesel had intended to bind one of Sasha's twins. That was until Paris pushed his way in and refused to allow anyone else submit to the Patronus. An honor the Fallen Angel had no intention of sharing with anyone else just yet. If he ever did at all.

Paris still didn't exactly play the part of a submissive too well, for the eyes that should have been passive and cast downward followed Diesel's every move with a burning lust, and Diesel found he couldn't bring himself to order them down to the floor. It'd have been such a waste. But the new development in Paris was a surprise, and his willingness to endure the ropes and other restraints fed Diesel's needs plenty, even when coming from a greedy bottom. Submissives surrendered because they needed someone else to be in control. Paris submitted to Diesel's own pleasures because the reward was the post-sex. Which Paris continued to boast was some of the best he'd ever had. The logic and purpose were misconstrued, but in the end they were both getting what they wanted. So like in any D/s relationships, their unique arrangement worked for them.

It was what they were for each other. Paris was his Imp, his greedy, pushy bottom, and the occasional service top when Diesel felt the itch to take the leash off of Paris and let the wild lust go like a Tasmanian devil. It was this odd concoction that made it possible for Paris to kneel at Diesel's feet and gloat with pride while Diesel sat back, content as a king with a well-sucked cock. He stopped in his ruminations, realizing the metaphor he'd just used to describe them. *He really needed to stop reading Katianna's books.* She was putting way too many ideas in his head. He almost laughed at himself as he ran his fingers through Paris' hair, even more as Paris was in constant flux and reset his black-fringed bangs to the proper style after each pass of Diesel's hand misplaced them. Perhaps there was a limit to what Paris would put up with to get what he wanted.

"You always ride your slaves that hard?" One of the newer members was asking questions that begat his newness to the BDSM world as he sat down to join him and Paris.

Diesel still ran his hands through Paris' hair, followed by Paris' hand to put it back into place. "No, just this one."

"Oh?" The member asked, surprised.

"He likes it hard. Don't you?" Diesel turned his attention to the Imp relaxed lazily on the floor between his legs, still preening.

"Yes." Paris answered hotly, pressing a kiss into Diesel's thigh and nibbled on him.

"He says that because it pleases you, not necessarily because he actually likes it."

"No, he likes it." Diesel's gaze tightened on Paris.

"How can you be so sure?" The new member continued with his questions, but Diesel didn't find them offensive. This was why he was here. Just as Dominus was— to teach. That meant answering questions more than anything. To hand down the protocols that made BDSM safe for both Doms and subs.

"Because, first and foremost, I expect him to obey and be honest. If I ask for an opinion, it means I want his *opinion, not what he thinks I want to hear.*"

"What if the slave remains silent?"

"Then the gag is *wayyyyy too* tight, because he wouldn't dream of not complying. Silence is not a rendered opinion." Diesel grinned, then he tussled Paris' hair roughly before snatching his chin and bending over to kiss him before letting him go to right his peacocking feathers. Everyone

309

else who was in earshot of the conversation laughed, which put the new Dom in a rather smug place, because perhaps it'd never occurred to him that humor was also welcomed in the lifestyle.

"BDSM isn't about laws and sex. It's about safety and honesty for shared pleasure. The sensations of pleasure are limitless, not dictated. The rules are there so you and all those involved can play and take pleasure with them in safety."

~ * ~ * ~ * ~ * ~ * ~

CHAPTER NINETEEN

~ * ~ * ~ * ~ * ~ * ~

Paris was stretched out on the sofa in the living room of their home. His head was in Diesel's lap as they watched some TV.

"You know, it'll be Christmas soon." Diesel spoke up, after having watched a commercial that reminded him of something he planned to pick up as a present for his new partner. "Anything in particular you'd like, aside from the ordinary?"

"Nothing I wear, use, or want is ordinary." Paris corrected Diesel on his particular tastes.

"I will spank you."

Paris glanced up at him, and without hesitation obliged him with his answer, "I want a car."

Diesel blinked, raising a brow. His lover didn't even skip a beat with his Santa list, "Why do you need a car when you're pretty much driven everywhere you need to go?"

Paris frowned, "Because I want my own car. It's not like I have my own personal chauffeur and I want to be able to shop or take off for lunch whenever I want. Not when someone is going somewhere or when Trenton gives me a driver to run his errands."

"And what kind of car are we talking about? An Italian or German?" Not bothering to suggest anything less. Paris had already pointed out he had high standards and rich tastes. Diesel suspected he'd have to pay Maxum a visit to get advice on the best cars and a number for a good dealer.

"Those are fine when you're on the hunt for the next fuck. I want a car that shows I already have everything I need and want. Now, I am just showing off."

"And do you?" Diesel rolled his head to its side and eyed him suspiciously, "Have everything you want?"

"Come here and I'll show you." Paris right away started twisting around on the sofa until he had his feet thrown over the back of the sofa and his head hanging over the front edge of the seat cushion. His hands grabbed at Diesel's pant legs and pulled him to move over and stand in front of him.

It was awkward, but Diesel dropped to his knees in front of the sofa, then side-stepped until he was right at Paris' face, who was instantly making quick work with the button fly on his jeans. Paris rolled his tongue over the denim, finding his way over the light bulge before he even freed the top button of his fly. Diesel already felt the anticipation ramping up inside him, launching fast shipment routes of blood rushing to his cock, dropping his hands over Paris' chest to grope and rub him down for his own palm pleasure.

Once the buttons were done away with, Paris reached around Diesel's hips and pulled him closer; when within range, he pressed his wet mouth harder against Diesel's cock still trapped inside his boxers. Paris' tongue teased over the bulging girth, and he chewed at it like a hungry animal that was gnawing to get at the meat.

Paris was an art form when it came to seducing and teasing, every lick and touch playing a part. Nothing left to chance. No touch or movement was inconsequential to his goal, just as every brush stroke of color was a vital detail to the overall painting for an artist, and Diesel loved it. He'd learned not to rush him, except on the occasion that rushing to get inside one another was part of the seduction, and they'd done plenty of that too.

But right now, Paris had something else in mind, and the only thing Diesel was going to do to change it was take off his shirt, since it was getting in the way of watching his lover.

~ * ~

Paris sucked and chewed at the hard flesh through Diesel's briefs and the jeans, now fully unbuttoned. He stroked over the bulge as it quickly hardened under his attention, then finally pulled the waistband down to expose a small amount of skin so he could lick over it with the full flat of his tongue. Teasing Diesel until it wasn't enough for himself any longer. Time to move in and make his mark on this man, pulling more of Diesel's cock into an accessible position, but not entirely free, as he resumed his licking and pressing against it while his groping hand still latched onto Diesel's firm ass. Never letting him pull away for any reason. Paris sent his free hand on a small detour, slipping up to feel over Diesel's ripped stomach then back down, finally setting his cock completely free. He darted in, tracing over the girth of cock with his tongue; his mind, however, was set on what he had in store for Diesel. Tonight, he was going to suck his lover off in a way Diesel had never been taken.

~ * ~

Diesel hissed and his hand dropped to stroke over Paris' body, which, oddly enough, still had too many clothes on at the time, but he wasn't in a position to do anything about it just yet. He let his head fall back, listening to his breath deepening in his chest and the slight pleasant sound it was making. His body reveling in the sensation his lover was delivering to him. Even the anticipation was sweet as he had a good idea of what Paris wanted to attempt. Though no one who'd tried before had never been able to take his cock fully into their mouths. Whatever accomplishment made tonight, or just the pleasure of a full-hearted effort, was enough for him, and he wouldn't fault Paris for not succeeding in his weighty endeavor. No one could take him, not even his egotistical lover. That Paris was going to try was satisfying enough, as well as giving Diesel some apprehension. He didn't want Paris hurt by the effort, neither physically nor mentally, and he was certain both could happen. While he considered Paris' seduction an art form, Paris saw himself as the godly protégé of everything lusty and desirable, and there was no one more skilled at it than him. He perhaps often thought himself as impervious to harm as well.

Paris had Diesel's cock straight out and was sucking along the underside of the hard shaft with his wet tongue, licking in broad strokes over the rising veins. Paris used his hand to mirror the motion to the topside of Diesel's erection, until both tongue and hand came over the sensitized head of his cock.

Paris' fingers closed over as much as they could, sliding in a gentle twist, moving back only to make way for Paris' mouth. Mouth wide open, he sucked in the flanged cap and sipped at the pre-cum already starting to seep from the slit.

Diesel watched for a moment as the skin under Paris' chin flexed and moved with the tongue action Diesel felt. Before long, as the head of his cock disappeared completely in Paris' mouth, it became too much and he dropped his head back on his shoulders, closed his eyes, and just surrendered to the new sensation. It wouldn't take long for his girth to wear Paris out, so he was going to bask in it as long as he could. Enjoying the suction created by Paris' mouth, and even the popping effect, as he let go, only to come back, lapping at the head again and sucking him back inside his hot, wet mouth.

Diesel's muscles bunched instantly and a harsh moan pushed past clenched teeth when he felt the firm tongue probe down into the eye slit of his cock. It circled his swelling glans several times before it returned once again and molested the sensitive hole of nerves. Diesel groaned at the change of sensation— the sheer pleasure Paris gave with his tongue was bliss. His body was melting under the euphoria.

~ * ~

Another hiss and a hard exhale told Paris all he needed to know, and he stroked faster around Diesel's cock, pumped him hard in his fist, while his tongue continued to deliver the contact that threatened to make a man go insane.

He listened to his lover's panting, listened to the pitch it made as his mouth devoured the hard steel, and just when it seemed Diesel neared a point to take control away from him, Paris yawned his throat wide and sucked the thick cock all the way in until the sheer size of it stretched his mouth. He kept his grip on Diesel's hips to guide him gently as he slowly pushed deeper into Paris' mouth.

"Oh, son of a bitch, Paris, that feels so good." Diesel gave his praise in a hiss of pleasure. "*Mmmm.*"

Paris hadn't even brought him to the best part yet.

He shifted on the sofa some, letting his head fall further back into a more accommodating position. He yawned his throat again to open up wider and quickly eased Diesel further into his mouth until the broad head of his cock hit the back of Paris' throat. He held him there, motionless— willing his muscles to relax around the thick organ invading his mouth so completely. Sucked in a deep breath that hissed passed his nostrils, then started to pull him in further—

~ * ~

Diesel tensed and pulled back. No matter what Paris was thinking, Diesel's girth was too wide for anyone's throat. Not even his Paris, who prided himself on fulfilling Diesel's hunger. Diesel wasn't about to allow Paris to harm himself in the act. "Stop. I'm too big for that." And he backed all the way out. There were plenty of other ways his lover could satisfy him, and he was always satisfied with Paris.

Paris' fingers fisted into Diesel's jeans, still draped around his hips, and pulled him back to Paris' awaiting mouth. "Come here. I'm doing this."

"You don't have to do this, Paris."

"Shut up. I want this." The muscles in Paris' arms bunched and Diesel felt the strength in them now, pulling harder. Insistently. Either he stopped combating the attempted deep throat or Paris was going to shred his jeans for trying.

Diesel couldn't explain the exquisiteness it was for him in his lover's mouth, even though it was only part of him that

316

got the direct contact, but then that was something Paris had every intention of changing tonight.

Paris' hands kept their grip on his hips, and once again Diesel was guided to pump into Paris' mouth with slow steady strokes— all the way to the back of his throat. He panted with each one as Paris' hot tongue laved over his veins and nerve endings. He reached down, grasped the base of his cock, and stroked at it while he continued to pump the rest of him over the tantric tongue that licked him.

Paris shifted once more, and as Diesel pushed in this time, Paris pulled him even deeper, and the mushroom cap of his cock slipped down the throat that waited for him, stopping only when he felt Paris' hair brush his balls. "Oh, fuck!"

The sensation was heightened further by the visible bulge in Paris' stretched throat. He dropped his hand down and lightly brushed his thumb over the extended neck. Having nearly half his length devoured in Paris' mouth was a shock, and he quickly pulled back out, fearful for his lover. Except Paris clearly wasn't having any of that, pulling tight on him again and bringing him back. Once more, Diesel found his hard erection sliding down the back of Paris' throat until his lips came in contact with the fist Diesel still had wrapped around his shaft. Even as his mind rallied to protest, his body gave in to the succulent gift that was being surrendered over to him for his own pleasure, and his cock was loving every extra inch of mouth it was receiving.

Diesel let out a loud hiss before he slid back out, "Oh fuck!"

While Paris had somehow managed to take him partially down into his throat, there was still the need for his lover to be able to breathe, and withdrawal was necessary for that.

One more dip of that and Diesel was certain he would spill. He fisted over his hard cock, bringing that wave up to the surface, knowing that was what Paris was after. *The prize.*

~ * ~

Paris licked over the crest of his cock, then took in a long breath and pulled Diesel back into his mouth once more, guiding him to pump several times at the back of his throat before easing him back out so he could breathe in the necessary oxygen. He took a moment to allow his throat to rest and he kissed Diesel's thigh fiercely through the denim, and then went back to lick and suck over the engorged glans. When Paris was through waiting, he was pulling Diesel back into range, sucking the massive rod back into his mouth, sucking on it with all the fervor of his lust. He used his tongue to lave over the turgid flesh as he probed into the eye slit, then pumped the tip of his tongue deep against the hidden bundle of nerves. The boggling sensation ended only when he sucked in the whole of Diesel's broad cap, cascaded it with the twirling sensation of his tongue, then worked it all the way down to the back of his throat. One deep breath and he pulled Diesel to sink in the rest of the way.

~ * ~

Diesel groaned loudly. The rich dance from one heightened sensation to the next, then being completely enveloped by Paris' hot, wet mouth, was too much. Diesel stroked into him several times, trying his best not to thrust, but it was a challenge and then his cock let go, and he felt the wave as it crested over his senses. He quickly pulled out, enough so Paris could get his breath, then pushed back in and delivered the full load of his release with a harsh growl. "Ahh, fuck, Paris— ahh-ahh." He pushed down into his throat once more then eased out, allowing his lover to lick up the taste of his essence.

Diesel felt his strength drain out along with his release and leaned over, catching his weight on the sofa with his arm, hovering over his lover looking up and watching him intently with a twinkle of pride gloating about on his face.

Diesel struggled for his breath, "Proud of yourself, are you?"

"Are you not?" The three simple words came out with a rough rasp, and Paris swallowed hard in an attempt to reset his bruised larynx.

"*Pride* wouldn't be my first word that comes to mind, but perhaps *devoured* would be."

Paris shifted back around on the sofa, letting his legs drop to the floor. He rested his head on the seat, but still remained under the cloak of Diesel's body, and he lazily rolled his head to the side and looked at Diesel, "So, do I get my car?" He whispered, his voice still rough.

Diesel would have chuckled if he weren't so *blown* away at the moment, "You can have anything you want from me after that, but first I'm going to get you some tea— heavy on the honey."

~ * ~ * ~ * ~ * ~ * ~

CHRISTMAS MORNING

Like two little kids on Christmas morning, Paris grabbed Katianna and they jumped into his new Bentley Mulsanna— and off they went for a joy ride.

Leaving Trenton and Diesel standing in the driveway, looking on after them.

They both stared down their street, feeling rather dismissed by their behavior, half waiting to see if they would backtrack their actions as an emergency plea of Christmas insanity, since neither had asked for permission. But so far, as they continued to stare down the empty residential street, that didn't seem to be happening.

Diesel scrubbed across his chin, his other hand firmly on his hip. "I'm thinking a good twenty-count spanking for this one."

"Yep, at least twenty." Trenton just kept staring, waiting for them to return, but it didn't appear they were doing so anytime soon. "Call Paris and tell him to get back here with her."

Diesel shifted, twisting his mouth in a peculiar expression before swiping over his face to hide his embarrassment.

Trenton just turned and glowered at him. "Well?"

"I hadn't given him that present yet." He made a slight wince.

"You mean Paris no longer has a phone? What happened to the one he had?"

Diesel scratched the back of his head, fighting back the grin, "It met with a grievous death after a round of damn good desk sex." He chewed his lip to prevent laughing in his brother's face.

Trenton returned his glare to the empty street until a smirk flashed over him and he shook his head, then glanced down to the ground as he attempted to suppress the laugh that threatened to gurgle up.

"Merry Christmas, bro." Diesel chucked sheepishly.

The laugh finally had its way with them, and Trenton swung his arm over Diesel's shoulder and hugged him, "Merry Christmas, brother."

Diesel nodded as they both enjoyed another moment of simply staring down the empty street together, "We really do spoil them too much, don't we?"

"Yep." Trenton gave a curt nod in agreement.

~ * ~ * ~ * ~ * ~ * ~

CHAPTER TWENTY

~ * ~ * ~ * ~ * ~ * ~

Diesel pulled up in front of Pyotr Laszkovi's home, where his riders were already outside, waiting on him to pick them up. "Looks like everyone's all here and ready."

"It's a big day. You'd think they'd be pacing about inside?" Maxum, who sat shotgun, glanced at him, "I'm surprised Pyotr doesn't have them running laps to work off the jitters." He tried to laugh, but not even Diesel could help him with that. It was a big day and a nerve-wracking one at that.

Diesel got out and went around the Knight Conquest to open the door and let everyone in.

"Trenton lets you drive his Knight as well now?"

A large grin turned up on Diesel's face, so maybe he could laugh at that, "Well, after sharing Mouse with me, it is hardly arguable about his SUV now, is it?"

Pyotr smiled back, and despite the good-hearted amusement, the strain was evident for them all. "I wouldn't think so." He added this comment mildly.

Trofim and Shay came up. They tried to smile, but gave up and just climbed in when Diesel nodded them to go ahead.

They were all friends, so no need to stand on formalities. Except Pyotr. He stepped in close as if to say, *yes, some formalities were necessary,* and he clasped Diesel's shoulders with firm hands. Hands that had gripped oars and pulled against elements, and even hatred, and came out champions. "Are you certain you want to go through with this?"

For Diesel, it seemed like such an odd question, but then he saw something in Pyotr. Something he couldn't recall having ever seen since knowing the man. There was fear lingering in the shadows of his eyes. Eyes that never grew dark— always clear, brilliant cobalt orbs of intuition. Now, something truly scared him and it drew out the soldier in Diesel something fierce. He reached out, grasping Pyotr's arms, locking with him and holding him as tightly, if not more so, than Pyotr held him. "I'm a soldier before anything else. And I've learned that not all enemies are found on a battlefield or behind a gun. So if this helps to protect them, I'm all in." He gave him a silent marine-*oorah* and nodded to be sure Pyotr trusted his word of honor.

"I love my family. Cliff, my brothers, and two little sisters— more than anyone else does. No one will ever stand equal to them. However, I do consider you and Trenton very close cousins." And then that genuine carefree, amused-by-all glow came back over Pyotr and chased away the shadow as if it had never existed on his face. While it, in no way, meant Diesel's task as guardian was over, it did speak volumes that Pyotr trusted him implicitly to be on duty for his family, and they'd rest easier for his protection.

They left the city and headed out for their destination, amusing themselves with the storytelling of Maxum's tactics to manage the trip without Darko glued to his side, or getting locked in a vault to prevent him from even going.

"So how *did* you manage to get out without him? Couldn't have been easy." Pyotr asked Maxum from the seat behind him.

"I'd been telling him all along the meeting is set up for tomorrow. Which Trofim nearly blew when he called yesterday to check that I was still on."

Diesel glimpsed into his review mirror and caught the nervous blush on Trofim's face.

"I didn't know." He shrugged, then Shay wrapped an arm around him and pulled him in for a hug. Perhaps as much for Shay's own good as well for Trofim's.

"It's not like I could possibly let the hot-head be present in that room. It's going to be complicated as it is. I've done my best to snoop around, but frankly, Rothschild money tends to stay strictly in Rothschild hands. They are not going to accept willingly that you're appointing me your personal accountant. And Darko is so worked up about it, he's a walking, talking, Mount Vesuvius."

"If it's better for you, we can find someone els—"

"No." Maxum cut in firmly, "I'm sorry. I don't mean to shout, but trust me, it's not better." He turned and looked over his shoulder at Shay sitting in the back seat, "It's not better for you, or anyone, to let someone else do this. You need someone on your side. Someone you can trust and can't be bought. And I assure you, nearly all men can be bought with enough money. It just so happens I have more than enough, and you *are* family." He righted himself in his seat and carried on. He occasionally glanced down his shoulder as if he still saw Shay, but more so to be sure Shay heard him clearly and understood his dedication to him was locked in. "I've had my share of dealing with underhanded financial mongers, and while the Rothschild have their secrets, they are not as secretive as they would like to be."

"But how do we know we can trust them?" Trofim asked.

"We don't." Maxum turned back again, "It's a by-invitation-only, high stakes poker game, and while you may not always see a player's tells, the money still has to be on the table. Where it goes signals who the puppet is and who's the master."

"My father was the puppet." Shay spoke lowly.

Maxum nodded, "And now they are hoping you will be too, and that's where Diesel and I come in. Because in truth, you're one of the masters and about to come into holding of a good chunk of the money pit."

~ * ~

Shay's mind continued to race about, despite Maxum's assurances. Not even the strength Pyotr carried for him and Trofim could settle him down right now. His only anchor was in the hand he held. *Trofim. His husband.* He leaned in and kissed Trofim's forehead. *His husband. God, how he loved saying that.* They'd been so eager, they rushed their plans. Also, just to get their plans arranged before Darko and Maxum's. Those two were planning an Excalibur-sized gala. Something Shay couldn't afford. It even made him laugh because he wondered if there was another gay man on the planet who could come even close to the extravagance that Darko and Maxum's wedding plans were turning into. Because the only thing missing from their plans was a tall order to Mother Nature for a real rainbow to be delivered over them as they said their vows.

Maxum had offered to foot the bill for Shay and Trofim as his gift for a new life. But that was just it, Shay's entire life had been wrapped around money. For him, it was dark and desolate. It'd done nothing but cause pain and nearly lost him the only thing in the world that brought him true happiness. *Trofim*. So, Shay didn't want a grand fiasco to show off. All he wanted was to marry the man he had always loved. And so they drove down to Atlantic City, just the family and a few friends to bear witness as Shay and Trofim said their *I do's* under the white canopy at the end of the glass-enclosed pier overlooking the ocean. Just a few feet from the very spot, hardly a year before, where he'd told Trofim he wanted to marry him. After the reception, Trofim and he had snuck out and slipped under the pier, where they fucked like happy little wet rabbits within the crashing waves of the tide. And thus far, for them, the honeymoon hadn't ended.

Except for maybe today. The jitters eating away at his stomach were putting a damper on his married life bliss.

He'd almost walked away from his inheritance. He wanted no part of it. But Trofim had made a point. If he did, they won. It would send an unforgivable signal that they not only could do what they'd done, but they could and get away with it, along with his money. Shay owed it to Trofim to see to it they didn't. His father's attack on Trofim had been all about *this* money, the Rothschild inheritance he'd never known about. Maxum was right too. They probably figured with Benjamin Wilks out of the picture, Shay would have just idled on in his life and given them their money back without a dispute.

Today they would find out otherwise. While the money would still be locked up for several more months until Shay turned thirty, he was still able to appoint his own financier to be in charge of it. That meant getting the books and the numbers on every dollar and hidden asset that was bequeathed to him. He also was allowed to set up a few gratuitous donations each quarter for tax purposes. That's where Diesel came in. Mr. Gentry was about to be named the beneficiary of those donations, with certain earmarks for the cardiac clinic at Queens Medical Center and for the cancer center that had cared for Kimmi all those years. The rest of the allotment could be put into whatever Mr. Gentry felt could use the help. Lastly, with today's visit, Shay would be naming his beneficiaries of estate, should anything happen to him or Trofim. If the Rothschild had any notions that they could resolve this with just two cheaply purchased bullets, they were wrong. Shay was going to make it known that should they try, no amount of backhanded law would be able to cover up the trail of dead it would take for their money cult to get the money back. For Shay was naming every Laszkovi in his family singularly as beneficiaries, plus all five of the Dominion brothers and Maxum St. Laurents. It gave new definitions to the phrase *hell hath no fury like a lover scorned*, and it gave Shay a little bit of victory.

They were quiet for most of the remaining hour drive until finally arriving at the law firm, where men who had no respect for life had been in charge of the undisclosed wealth inheritance to the formerly named Shay Wilks. A control that in just a few minutes would come to an end.

But if Shay thought he was walking in there and throwing them a curve ball, he discovered they had one of their own when the receptionist welcomed them.

"Good morning, Shay Wilks. If you'll have a seat, Mr. Morgan and Mr. Londonaire will be with you in just a moment."

A lump formed in his throat and he was immediately glancing to Trofim, seeing the same worried expression on his face. Shay couldn't have that. He swallowed down his own apprehension, took a deep breath, and searched for the strength he needed to exhume for them both. A steady hand came from behind him and clasped his shoulder. When he looked, it was Pyotr, with a face full of pride and certainty. Without a word, the man conferred he could do this. His brother-in-law held no doubts.

All his life, Shay had lived under the brooding shadow of a father who made every effort to prevent him from succeeding. Cut him down when Shay defied it. Now, he had a new family, and the only thing any of them did was lend support and believe in him. Nothing else rang out as much as in this moment. It was a first, perhaps, in his life. It changed him in that very moment. He felt a rush of the old Shay come back, before the darkness that nearly cost him the man beside him. Even an air of the cockiness he used to thrive under. He snatched it up— fed it and made it burn bright in his thoughts.

He glanced back at the receptionist, while scratching his temple in an act to display an air of annoyance, then gave a flippant expression like he was forgiving the receptionist for making such a blunderbuss error, "Then he will be disappointed. Next time you schedule an appointment with me, make sure you have my correct name or I'll have your job. Also, since I'm a Cardiac Surgeon, my hourly fees far exceed theirs. I will be seen now."

"I'm terribly sorry, sir—"

Shay ignored the frivolous apology, pulled his shoulders up— his arm still around his husband— and walked on back whether they were ready or not.

The meeting commenced. They didn't like Shay strolling in like he owned the place, but then again, the money was his and they soon kowtowed to him when Shay lacked any pretense that he was there as an easy pushover. Originally, it had been planned that Maxum would do most of the talking, so eventually Shay did turn the details over to him. However, Shay had realized the pre-emptive strike needed to come from him. Pyotr and Diesel were there merely to sign the witness papers and to agree to the terms he was bestowing on them, not to act as his unofficial goons. The hodge-podge dance of old money and lethargic, stuffy bags wasn't his game, but he had grown up surrounded in much of it. He had witnessed enough political puppets that he knew how to play the game. For Shay, personally, it was about the likeness of wearing a scratchy old suit he didn't care for, but did so for the family picture. Once done, he could take it off. The idea of stripping down to nothing but his stethoscope and listening to Trofim's heart would be his reward for enduring the choking tie a little longer.

Morgan was the staunchest of them. Shay could see the loathing in his eyes the entire time. Merle Londonaire, on the other hand, seemed to be beside himself. His expressions locked down too tightly to be polite. He showed no remorse, no bitterness that the plan with Benjamin Wilks had failed. While Maxum dictated to Morgan the new arrangements of money management and funding, Shay kept watching Merle. At one point, Shay thought he saw a glimpse of disappointment, like Merle had lost some fondness he held for Shay. But it was doubtful the man really felt anything. It was enough, however, that when it was all over and done with, when the I's were dotted and the T's were crossed— Shay ordered everyone out, locking his gaze with Merle, making him stay.

"This is highly irregular—" Morgan started to protest.

"Oh shut up and get out!" Londonaire snapped. It'd been the first time he'd shown any kind of emotion in the last two and half hours.

Merle remained stiff on his side of the conference table, quiet as the others filed out of the room. As soon as the door clicked shut, both had something to say.

"I can't believe you gave up Sarah for *him*."

"Is the money really so much you'd kill your own daughter for it?"

Merle was about to respond, but then Shay's question hit hard and turned him into a gaping fool. The generic retort that was on his lips evaporated. "What did you just say?"

Shay sat up, leveling his gaze on Merle, "You'll forgive me if I don't believe you didn't already know. You and Benjamin Wilks wanted this money so badly, you kept me in the dark about it, plotted for me to marry your daughter, then you were going to have her killed and pin it on me. This way, you and Ben would be named trustees and have full access to it."

Merle's head shook violently from side to side, rejecting everything Shay was saying, "No. That's not true. Londonaires have always married into the Rothschild family. That much is true. But I would never kill my own daughter for it."

Shay jumped to his feet, slapping his hands on the table and boring into Merle, "IT IS TRUE!"

Merle's face turned grey with remorse. His eyes cast downward and he remained silent. Shay returned to his chair, the heat that burned inside ebbed only a fraction, but enough that he spoke without shouting this time, "How many have you killed to get this money?"

There was a deep sigh in Merle, but he didn't look up, and when he answered, it was barely audible, "Too many."

"You or your kind haven't been arrested yet; Benjamin's death in the prison wasn't an accident, so I suppose you got all the strings you needed pulled to keep any of this from landing on your doorstep. But mark my words— someone on your side of the table has a bullet with Sarah's name on it." He got up when Merle had nothing to say and headed for the door, but stopped, glancing back at the man, now withered in old age. Hardly half the man he was just a few hours ago when Shay had first walked in. "I know Maxum will tell me how much once he's had a chance to go through it all, but you can just tell me now. How much is it all worth?"

Merle sucked in another deep breath and let out a heavy sigh before glancing up. The shadows in his face were gone, replaced with the stiff, expressionless chiseled features of a lawyer. "If everything was liquidated at today's market value— around two-hundred-seventy *billion* dollars."

~ * ~ * ~ * ~ * ~ * ~

Diesel was delivering Maxum to his home, and the sight of Darko standing in the foyer, fuming, had them both chuckling. "He is possessive— hotheaded— and intensely

331

demanding." Maxum growled, "God, I fucking love that man." He chuckled, "And I love fucking him." He leaned over and shook Diesel's hand, "Thank you for being with us today. The look on their faces— I do so love watching attorneys eat crow." He opened the door and got out— Darko stepping out as well to meet him. Maxum glanced back in and gave Diesel an aroused wink, "Looks like my ass is in trouble."

"You may be the only man who loves arguing with his man."

"Maybe, but damn, the makeup sex is spectacular." He laughed then closed the door, and was suddenly snatching Darko by the neck, pulling him in for a fierce kiss before he'd gotten the chance to sputter the first word.

Diesel still could only laugh while he watched, because the permanent scowl on Darko's face, even as they dueled within the kiss, said he wasn't going to be bought off so easily.

The show was interrupted when his phone rang. It was Paris. "Hey, babe, just getting b—"

"*Deez, oh god — we need you. Kat and I are trapped—*"

"What?" Alarm seized him as he listened, hearing more than Paris' strained voice speaking low, "Paris, where are you? What's happening?" He could hear shouting in the background of the phone, but he wasn't sure of the words— something along the lines of—

His heart froze in his chest as a gruff voice yelled for them all to get down on the ground. "Paris!"

The answer came low and soft, muttered under his breath and shaken with fear, "*They shot someone— he's dead. Hurry—*"

~ * ~ * ~ * ~ * ~ * ~

CHAPTER TWENTY-ONE

~ * ~ * ~ * ~ * ~ * ~

CCIC WORLD BANC, QUEENS, NEW YORK

Paris cowered on the floor face down, with Kat doing much the same beside him, as the men dressed in assault fatigues stood nearby. The gang of bank robbers stepped about, circling and sometimes walking between, those also faced down on the cold tile floor like Paris and Kat, to make sure everyone knew they'd make good on their threats. *To shoot.* The body of one of the duty guards laying in his own blood in the middle of the lobby said as much.

"JUST STAY DOWN AND KEEP QUIET LIKE GOOD LITTLE BABIES AND NO ONE ELSE WILL GET HURT!" One of the gunmen shouted.

Except they weren't the only ones Paris was listening to. The Bluetooth in his ear was his lifeline to Diesel, and at the moment the jeweled gadget was his most treasured Christmas gift of all. Exceeding the Bentley entirely. The robbers had searched them all with idle glances for visible cell phones and Bluetooth devices clipped to their ears. They missed Paris'. Most likely because the one Paris had was ultra-small, like one of those small hearing aids, and it also had a jeweled back, which meant, so far, it had gotten dismissed as nothing more than glam jewelry.

"*Where are you?*" Diesel's voice came over the ear bud, while at the same time Paris sensed not everything Diesel was saying was for him. Rather, he was talking to someone else on the radio or a second phone, *"Yes, getting details right now. Patch me into S.W.A.T.! Paris— I need info. Can you tell me where you are?"*

Paris lifted his head just a few inches and glanced around to make sure none of the gunmen were within ear shot, then he tucked his head away into his shoulder and whispered the answer Diesel sought, "CCIC World Banc."

"*The global bank building on 49th street.*" Diesel transferred the info to the person he had with him or on another line. *"Paris, how many are there?"*

Again, Paris risked looking and he began to count. It wasn't all that easy. He was near petrified. Katianna was just a foot from him at a slight angle. Her entire body shivered in fear that she fought to stifle, but he could still make out her feeble whimpers and it wasn't helping him with his. Nor was anyone else's for that matter. Some forty people had been ordered to the ground and none of them were alone in their fear. A woman began sobbing uncontrollably and a guy lying not far from her broke down and began begging for his life.

"I said, heads down!" One of the gunmen shouted.

Paris did as told, unsure which of them had shouted, and to whom they had spotted, but then the shrieks came from one of the women. Nearly every head in the lobby popped up to watch in whimpering horror as a gunmen dragged the young woman, in a flowered dress, out of the lobby and into one of the side offices.

As horrified as he was, Paris used the chance to scan the lobby— counting again, but when one of them was turning his way, he dropped his head down and waited. He waited one more beat then craned his head up, a micro-tilt, just enough to peer through his hair. The gunmen had shifted again, making him lose his count. He tried again, coming up with nine men, remembering that a few of them took the bank manager into the safe, plus the one who'd taken the woman out. "Eleven. Maybe a couple more, I think."

"Okay, now, listen carefully— look at their guns, Paris. I need to know what kind of guns they have on them."

Paris dropped his head down, placed his cheek on the cool tile floor and began to whisper, "Big ones, like the ones you see in movies. Like the ones you keep locked up in the wall." He paused a moment, listening for the clunk of boots on the floor, straining to hear past the whimpers and the shouting from the men. "Deez—"

"Yes, Paris."

"One of them has on a vest."

"You mean like a bullet proof vest."

"No—" he swallowed, "as in a terrorist-type packed vest."

~ * ~ * ~ * ~ * ~ * ~

FIVE SOURCE SECURITIES COMPLEX

"LET'S GO!" Trenton was shouting through the hall as he came rushing out of his office, "Marcus, pull several of the armored bank trucks out and bring them around to the shop in back! NOW!"

Marcus and Harper were instantly out of their office to answer Trenton's call, only to find Trenton pulling on his own personal gun holsters with William already behind him.

"What's happened?" Harper asked as Marcus disappeared back in his office for keys.

"We have a terrorist group at the World's bank." Trenton answered, marching for the door at the end of the hall.

"STF call?"

"No, Paris did. He and Katianna are trapped inside." Trenton paused, glancing at the men behind him, making sure they saw in his face that this was no drill. "Harper, you're with me. William, go with Marcus and grab Piper. He should be pulling into the parking lot right about now." He waved Harper to follow as he headed down the stairs into the gun shop, "Marcus, get those trucks around!" He called back over his shoulder.

Ever since Katianna had been kidnapped, Trenton had never allowed her to wander too far from sight and certainly never left alone, but sometimes his job required him to tend to it without her in his office. Diesel had always been there to fill in when he was absent. Nikolai Kirshnov was dead, but he still had men out there who might come looking for Trenton for vengeance. And now, there was also that underlying threat of someone within the government who'd been watching him with close scrutiny. Just waiting for him to step into their grasp. So his overpowering watch over Katianna had yet to ease off.

Paris had been a boon for her— for them all, really. He became a close friend for her, who just happened to be inside the shelter of their gilded cage. And it gave Trenton some peace of mind that he didn't have to be so controlling over her while maintaining it at the same time. Among the three of them, she was always watched over.

He'd had a meeting to attend and Diesel was off helping Shay and Trofim, so when Paris was looking for any excuse to take off in his new Bentley, Trenton sent Kat with him to run errands and grab some lunch. Now, he was getting the call that their stop at the bank landed them as hostages in a bank robbery. The struggle he faced was not laying blame on anyone, or regretting allowing her to go. But he'd deal with that inner war later. Right now, he just had to get her and Paris out of that bank— alive and home safely.

Harper was already at the wall, waiting as Trenton went behind the counter and tapped in the security codes for the hidden lock hold. "Bill, close up the shop for the rest of the day, but stay here in case we need you." Trenton instructed Diesel's shop employee just as the armored trucks pulled up in front of the shop.

Trenton flipped on the police scanners next to the computer, and the chatter broadcasted out into the room, with dispatch calling in Task Force and first responders to the location just a few miles down the road from where they were. The flood of police meant the advantage of silent approach was gone. That diminished the chances of a sniper getting in close enough to pick them off before the terrorists or the news had made them. On the flip side, it meant Trenton was taking his convoy of vehicles up to the front of the line.

~ * ~ * ~ * ~ * ~ * ~

EN ROUTE FOR CCIC WORLD BANC

New York Special Task Forces Chief Miles Hailey knew the moment the details began to pour in when he got the call, he was likely going to need backup on this one. A global currency bank with over forty hostages on the lower floor, not to mention those trapped in the upper floors. Something he did not want going down on the reports was not having taken every precaution to protect those people with every skilled able body available to bring the threat to an end.

Miles rode in the back of their heavily armored Task Force control vehicle, going over the building's blueprints while en route. Too many walls and windows. And the reports had calculated at least a dozen armed men inside. While he'd expect to see every available officer on the NYPD to be set within the perimeter of the scene when he got there, what he really needed were snipers. *A long range bullet with magic targeting ability.* Even in his own team, he had but only three of those. He glanced at Chuck, who wasn't just his second in command, but one of those marksmen. "I think I need to call in some friends."

Chuck only nodded. The man would always go along with what he thought was best, and if Miles thought they needed more able bodies on this one, Chuck would back him up on it.

Miles wasted no time as soon as the van came to a stop. He hopped out and went in search of the captain on the scene to inform him he was taking over. What he found instead was a heated standoff between the chief of police and none other than the head of TL Securities— Trenton Leos.

"Trenton?" Miles cut in, and that seemed to be enough to tamp the fuse burning between them. "Clairvoyance among your skills nowadays?"

"No, it's not." Trenton's stiff answer made it clear humor wasn't among the skills either. Not today, at least.

"Then why do I find it odd that you're here before I've called to ask you to come in?" The comment should have gotten a smirk from the man, since Miles had deliberately dropped the hint bomb at his feet as well as for the COP's ears. But it didn't and that worried him.

"Diesel's partner and my fiancée are inside that building among the hostages."

Trenton might as well have just told Miles —*I'm going in there to kill every last one of them, and I'll kill you too if you try to stop me*— for all the tightly controlled malice that laced each word as Trenton spoke them. And that was only half of what Miles saw darkening the man's otherwise light colored eyes. Miles drew in a deep breath, reading the unflinching features of Trenton's face, then glancing at the chief of police, then to Chuck. "So what you are telling me is that even if I hadn't planned on calling you in, I'm stuck with you?"

Trenton didn't even answer, not with words anyways. That was his way of saying he wasn't budging. Miles turned and looked at the structure of reflective glass windows. The halo of flashing police and first response lights clogged the streets reflecting off the glass. Then there was the heavy crowd of onlookers— each one of them there to bear witness of the events about to unfold. Especially if there was any fault on the Task Force's side.

Miles turned back to the man, who was far more known than perhaps he was aware of or would likely want to be. "Yeah, alright, just let me pretend it was my idea and not yours to have your men here."

Trenton nodded curtly and the COP just groaned.

"So what have you got for me?" Miles asked and right away Trenton was leading him across the street.

Miles slammed to a halt when he came around the corner and saw just *what* Trenton truly had. He glanced at the five armored bank trucks, as well as Trenton's men waiting there, including Trenton's brothers: Diesel Gentry, Marcus Scriven, Harper Lancing, and Dane Masters. The very marksmen Miles had intended to call in, but standing here, looking at them now, he couldn't help wonder how bad this would all turn out if Trenton and his brothers weren't on their side. "You sure you're not after my job?" Miles tried to make light of it. Again, Trenton didn't joke back.

~ * ~

Miles parted the sea of police cars while Trenton and his brothers brought in the armored trucks and set them up as a walled barrier. In the event that the vest Paris reported seeing one of the men wearing was just the start of the explosives the terrorists were carrying, the trucks would take most of the blast force and protect the hundreds of people who'd gathered as on lookers. Not even the memory of 9/11 had shed the public of their morbid curiosity, unaware their presence only endangered those inside all the more.

Once in position, Trenton and the others took up station on top of two of the armored vehicles, while the STF squad trucks were kept back and out of range, acting as field headquarters.

Trenton had directed Marcus to position the vehicles for a cross fire arrangement behind the police line, across from the bank. He wasn't messing around; he pulled out the big guns and set his men up properly. Aside from the five of them, six more of his employees were on-site, and he had all of them wired into each other, using throat mics with the micro ear bugs, so they could all talk hands-free and with zero interference. That was one of the primary benefits of the throat mics; they contained a small button-sized microphone that sat over the larynx bone, held in place by a Velcro collar strap. It transmitted vocal vibrations rather than sound echoes so no outside noise was transmitted.

Overhead, the news choppers had arrived.

Now the Task Force's greatest concern was just how much of a show the terrorists inside the bank were after.

Trenton, Dane, and Diesel sat up on one truck with long-range sniper rifles already in place. Trenton had additional binoculars set up on a tripod for better surveillance. Harper and Marcus, along with Brooks O'Reiley, one of Miles' men, were stationed on top of a second truck. Miles' head gunman, Chuck, was en route for a rooftop. The rest of Trenton's security team had spread out around the building, paired up with teams from the Special Task Force. They were ordered to hold their fire and not attempt to enter the building, but they could watch and report on the positions of all the gunmen inside the bank directly to Trenton and serve as aid to any hostages, should they escape.

"Hang tight, Trenton. I don't want anybody taking a shot while we got them talking on the phone. As long as they're willing to negotiate for the release of the hostages, we can't fire." Miles Hailey was talking over the comm-link. Calm and steady he was, but he had to be. Get excited on the link, and the men's fingers did the walking sometimes too fast.

"Copy that." Trenton replied, but he wasn't happy about it. Negotiations never ended well, and right now they had a clear shot on seven of the believed eleven men inside.

"*Brooks? You copy that?*" Miles called over when his man hadn't responded.

"*Yeah, I copy that.*" The deep baritone voice finally came over the link. "*How much longer we gonna play pattycake with these mo' fuckers. It's some bad news up in there. Need to just take 'em out.*" He carried on like he was talking about taking out the trash, and the chore was keeping him from something far more important.

~ * ~

"Keep the chatter down, guys." Diesel came over the link, reminding them the talk kept them from hearing commands and what was going on inside.

Diesel glanced at Trenton, who was now listening to a second ear piece, listening in on Katianna's cell phone still broadcasting from inside. At the moment, Paris was talking to her, trying to keep her calm. Diesel had the same situation going on, only with Paris' phone. For once, the big bull had paid attention to him. New York was crazy, somebody was getting robbed or shot every day, and because of his line of work with Trenton, those risks increased. He never wanted to lose Paris, and they argued over safety measures almost constantly. Paris just refused to live like it was the end of the world with a perpetrator around every corner. Diesel just wanted to make sure his man was safe, no matter what type of situation Paris was in, and that he had a plan for everything. Because there really was a bad guy around every corner.

~ * ~ * ~ * ~ * ~ * ~

Inside, Paris and Katianna still lay face down on the hard marble floor of the World Bank. It would have been their last stop before returning to the office complex just down the street. They had just walked in and she was reading a text aloud to Paris from Trenton, demanding Paris hurry it up. He'd kept her away from the office too long and her Dominus was in the mood for some playtime—

That's when it happened.

A group of men came swarming in right behind them, pulling out assault rifles. The kind Diesel kept hidden away in the shop. Scary ones. Everyone was ordered to the ground, which put Kat and Paris on the floor closer than anyone else to the front of the bank. As she dropped to the floor, following the would-be robbers' demands, her thumb instinctively hit the call back button, then tucked her phone under her so they wouldn't see it.

Paris wasn't quite as quick as she was. Then again, he wasn't as quickly frightened as she was. But when one of the robbers fired off a few rounds, blasting several planter pots into shrapnel as a warning to everyone in the room, Paris managed to voice activate his phone to call Diesel. The phone was tucked away in his pocket, but he had a Bluetooth ear-set, so small it was about the size of a large gaudy diamond hearing aid, and so far had gone unnoticed as anything but.

The flowerpot shoot-out was far from the end of the men's display. Kat hadn't seen it, she was too busy hiding face down, but her head had instinctively popped up when the single shot from a handgun went off, chased with a myriad of cries.

Kat watched in horror as one of the security guys fell to the floor with a large red stain on his back. She nearly screamed. In fact, she probably did, like all the others. That was when Paris had used the noise to cover his voice so he could talk to Diesel. She only hoped they could hear what was happening.

She struggled to keep her sobs locked inside, but occasionally, like many of the others around her, a few whimpers got away. Two of the men grabbed up the bank manager and dragged him to the back where the vault was.

Someone pleaded, "Please let us go." That's when the vest was made visible. One of the men tore off his coat, letting it drop to the floor. He held his arms akimbo, putting the vest on display— fitted with several square items like chocolate bars wrapped in silver foil, all wired together in two rows that encircled his body.

Kat's eyes had bugged out at the sight of it. The man was white; in fact, several of them were, plus two black men, and the others she wasn't really sure what their nationality was. She realized then she was just as guilty as anyone else in the world of having a stereotypical image in her head of who terrorists were or what they looked like. But it didn't dampen the sudden revelation that this was far more than just a bank robbery.

Now, she had to struggle against the panic that she may die before Trenton got to her.

Seconds turned into minutes. Minutes turned into long hours of stagnant negotiation when the police showed up, despite the one gunman, appearing to be the leader among the terrorists, vocalizing his certainty he'd prevent any silent alarms getting set off.

Hours passed. The two terrorists who had gone to the vault had since returned— the bank manager had not. What did come out were several duffle bags. Money or gold, Katianna was sure, but then there was also a small case, which seemed to be far more important than the duffle bags to two of the men. Apparently, the bags were payment for the others, while the small hard case was what the man in charge was after. Now, they just needed to find a way to get back out. *That was seven hours ago.*

"Hey, little Mouse, look at me."

Paris was trying to get Kat's attention; she was finding it hard to take her eyes off the men in the bank. She rolled her head over the floor so she could look at him, but every little sound made her flinch. It wasn't too long ago when one of the men dragged one of the bank tellers into one of the side offices and raped her, just to pass the time. Her screams had since silenced, but no one here was forgetting those shrill cries anytime soon.

Paris continued, "You just keep looking at me, okay. We're gonna be just fine."

She nodded at him, but that didn't mean she believed him. Nor did it make the fear go away. "I'm scared—" she whispered to him.

~ * ~

"I know." He was scared too, but he didn't figure agreeing with her would be much help. "Trent and Deez know what's happened— hell, they probably already have an entire army platoon out there."

She nodded again.

"You know, Diesel's never gonna let me live this down now— you know that, don't you?"

Nod.

"We still have lots of plans to go over for your wedding, right?"

Again she nodded. Now wasn't really the time to be thinking about wedding plans, but he didn't know what else to use to keep her focused on him and not the gun-toting barbarians.

"Paris—" her voice was almost a squeak as she peeked out from under the tussle of wavy light brown hair spilled out over the floor around her, hiding both her face and the cell phone connected to Trenton.

"Yeah, Mouse?" He whispered to her, still trying his best not to let his own fear overwhelm him. He knew it would not do either of them any good if she saw it.

"I don't have anyone to walk me down the aisle."

"What?"

"WHO THE FUCK'S TALKING?!" One of the men barked out as he headed towards them. The approaching terrorist waved an automatic rifle around at the six people cowering on the floor close to Paris and Kat. "I hear another word from any of ya's and I'm gonna have me some target practice."

Another of the gunmen joined him, walking around them slowly so he could intimidate them. He stepped over each one of them, one after the other, tapping their backs with the barrel tip of his rifle. Several yelped or whimpered in response. "Say— what's this?" The gunman commented when he was suddenly standing over Katianna.

Paris' eyes widened— *her ring.* They didn't even think of hiding it and there it was, all fourteen carats of it, twinkling like an ice-blue beacon on her finger.

"Nice rock." And in a flash the man slung his rifle on his shoulder and grabbed Katianna around the wrist, yanking her up.

Katianna was instantly kicking and screaming. Her captor had her off the floor by her arm with one hand, trying to pry her locked fist open with his other hand. But his attempts froze in mid-fight when he spotted the cell phone on the floor, "Fuck! KENT! They got a phone over here!"

Kent turned out to be the same leader who held the strange hard case from the vault. He'd tucked himself away, out of sight from the front plate glass windows, at one of the desks, and was on the phone with continuing negotiation talks.

Paris risked a look and saw as the words from the man holding Kat registered on the leader's face. The man cursed and hung up— ending all talks with the city.

~ * ~ * ~ * ~ * ~ * ~

The second the man had grabbed Katianna, Trenton moved from the binocular stand to his rifle and dialed in the scope for the man's head. Just as he did so, another of the gunmen inside was pulling Paris up to his knees and had the muzzle of a nine millimeter pistol flush against his temple. Trenton focused, took aim, and watched intently through his scope, as Paris cringed under the threat but did not remain entirely passive.

"*It's going to be okay, Mouse.*" They heard Paris, still talking to her.

"*I said, shut up!*" One of the gunmen inside cursed at Paris and whacked him on the head with the gun.

"Damn it, Paris, do as they say." Diesel warned him through the Bluetooth while it still went unnoticed.

"*Stations.*" Miles' voice came over the comm-link, "*It seems negotiations have ended. If— and I use the term lightly, there is a threat, and you have a clear shot on a mark— take them out.*"

"Everyone claim a target, we have a confirmation of thirteen men in there, I want seven of them down all at once. That just might get their attention." Trenton was already taking over. He wasn't going to wait for it to escalate. It had already gone too far and now Katianna and Paris were in the bastards' crosshairs.

"*This is Chuck, I got the leader dialed in. On your call.*"

"I got the guy with Kat," Diesel confirmed as he called his target.

"You certain?" Trenton whispered to him.

"Yep, he's mine." Diesel was fused with his scope, trained on the man, even as the perp jerked about, trying to keep hold of the kicking little woman.

"Then I got the one on Paris." Trenton claimed his mark.

"*Marcus has his target; vest man is lighting up my target zone.*" Marcus called out.

Dane was next. "*Dane reporting, I got the big guy dead center.*"

"*Harper reporting, I got the short one on the group of tellers.*"

"*Yeah, I got the one to his left— he's mine.*" Brooks' baritone was unmistakable.

"*Piper here, I got the dude in the office.*"

"Piper stand down. You're not allowed to fire." Trenton responded to his man. Piper was a damn good security guard, but he wasn't a marksman either.

"*Sorry, boss man, dude be goin' down. You don't wanna know what I'm seeing here.*"

"If he's still raping her—"

"*I don't know it can be calling it rape no more—*" Piper's Jamaican accent had lost its usual cheer as he reported what he was seeing, "*Pretty lady's dead.*"

Long silence.

"*I have a man in the back in sight.*" Chuck confirmed from his point.

"On my mark, then. Deez, give Paris the signal."

"Paris— we're about to take a shot. When I say duck, you and Kat need to drop as low to the floor as possible." Trenton watched through the scope of his rifle as Paris nodded once.

"*Kat? Ever play duck-duck-goose when you were a kid?*"

"*I said shut the fuck up!*" The gunman standing over Paris brought his hand back with the intention to backslap him.

"Paris! Duck!" Diesel shouted.

"NOW KAT!"

~ * ~ * ~ * ~ * ~ * ~

Inside the bank, Paris doubled over, just as Katianna's feet kicked backwards. Her heavy boots caught the man holding her in the shins. His hand let go and she fell to the floor at the same instant the surrounding plate glass walls shattered. Shards of glass went flying all around them, followed by screams and the thuds of the two gunmen, who had just been standing over them, as their bodies hit the floor. Blood and bits of brain matter splattered everywhere. The whole scene echoed with more screams from the hostages as four other gunmen went down in a likewise manner.

Paris waited until he was certain the flying debris and gunshots had stopped, but when he looked, the first thing he saw was the body lying between him and Katianna, making his stomach revolt against the lunch still digesting. The second thing he saw was Katianna about to push up on her hands and knees and see the same thing he was seeing. The last thing he wanted was for her to see the bloody hole where there had just been a skull.

Paris was instantly up on his knees, grabbed her up, and quickly pulled her away from the two bodies and into his lap as he twisted around.

"I got you, Kat." He stammered, struggling to keep the bile down as his hand covered her eyes. He'd somehow gotten her in his lap and he quickly scooted sideways across the marble floor, down along the counter wall, and took shelter behind one of the kiosks.

"Paris?" She let out a whimper.

"*Shhh*— I got you— I got you." He panted and took a deep breath to steady himself. *Oh fuck, that was the scariest thing he'd ever been through.*

Chaos broke out in the lobby, two more gunmen had their guns up and took aim, each fired off a round in random directions, and more glass exploded around the bank lobby as they shouted threats to off all the hostages for the police outside to hear.

~ * ~ * ~ * ~ * ~ * ~

Diesel and Marcus retargeted, locked on, and fired, dropping the threatening gunmen to the floor before they could follow through with their threat.

The last three in the terrorist group tossed their weapons and dropped to the floor.

"*Move! Move! Move!*"The command rang out in everyone's ears outside and the task force stormed the building, surrounding the remaining three gunmen. Followed by local PD to escort the hostages out.

Trenton and Diesel were right there when Paris came out, carrying Katianna. Katianna jumped from his arms as soon as she saw Trenton and ran to him, jumping up into his, instantly wrapping arms and legs around him, with his arms wrapping possessively around her in return, keeping her pressed against his body.

~ * ~

Diesel grabbed Paris by the shoulder, but then his other hand was behind Paris' head, pulling him in, kissing him deeply before surrendering to embrace Paris, pressing their heads together.

"Wow!" Paris' fear melted away with relief and a bit of surprise.

"What?" Diesel sounded a little more than upset.

"You just kissed me in public." Their foreheads pressed together, but Paris managed to tweak a kiss onto his lover's cheek without losing the contact between them.

Diesel let out a growl, "You're lucky I don't spank your ass in public."

"Can I just confess now, that the smallest item you gave me for a Christmas present is the greatest gift I have ever gotten?" Whether Diesel was up for another public kiss or not, Paris slammed into him and locked their lips into a kiss that spoke with all the emotion he felt right then, being alive and in the arms of the man whose predilections had protected him.

~ * ~ * ~ * ~ * ~ * ~

ACROSS TOWN

Owen Whittaker sat at the small kitchen table in his rattrap apartment, flipping through the pages of the newspaper, not really reading, but waiting for something hiding within the words to pop out and grab him. The television's live news was on, but now with all the excitement over the bank hostage situation finished, it was just background noise.

A woman newscaster was reporting live via satellite in front of the bank where the incident took place:

"After eight long hours, the standoff at CCIC World's Banc has come to an end. New York's Special Task Forces, aided by local company TL Securities, managed to take the suspects down after negotiations to free the hostages failed."

"Trenton Leos, owner of TL Securities, was first to learn of the attempted robbery when his fiancée, none other than Author Katianna Dumas, was in the bank at the time of the incident and was able to call him. Leos then notified authorities and they were able to monitor what was taking place inside through her phone—"

Owen's head snapped up at the mention of the name— *her name.*

So, that's where she had disappeared to.

Owen snatched the cheap, pre-pay cell phone from the table, punched in a number, and waited for the one on the other end to pick up.

"Yeah?"

"Guess who I just found?"

~ * ~ * ~ * ~ * ~ * ~

CHAPTER TWENTY-TWO

~ * ~ * ~ * ~ * ~ * ~

Paris felt Diesel's eyes on him like searing, hungry hands. As Patronus, without a doubt he knew what things turned Paris on, and right now, Paris was glad to be his poster Imp of desire. It was enough to tempt the Patronus' usual inhibitions of public display.

Of course, it wasn't all about the outfit he was wearing, it was more about the fact Paris just looked far better than anyone else could have ever looked in the getup. Even he was aroused by his own reflection and had purposely led Diesel out near the dance floor where he could look at them in the wall length mirrors. Deez didn't miss a beat, knowing damn well what Paris was seeking.

He stood, facing the mirror, as Diesel passed behind him in a slow gait that suggested he might walk right on past and not stop, until he stood just beyond Paris' right shoulder and turned to look at him rather than their reflection. The reflective show was for Paris' eyes as he watched Diesel's hand move over his frame and map out every detailed inch of the body his Patronus burned for. The accessory gear Paris wore was simple yet powerful, for the only amount of true clothing he had on were the black leather boy-shorts with a lace-up front and a silver padlock dangling from the tied cord. The lock wouldn't truly prevent anything if Paris' passions made him charge, but it was a playful reminder to his bull-sized ego who *was* in charge tonight.

For footwear, Paris wore a pair of motocross boots with front scales tipped in silver chrome. On his wrists, leather cuff bracelets, each with a large silver slave ring. On his upper arms he wore leather bands decorated in white rhinestones, and he wore a black collar that matched them. His chest was left bare because it was chiseled to perfection.

Paris sucked in a deep breath, pumped up on his own adrenaline, and showed his response to Diesel, who ran his hand over Paris' chest and down over his shorts, where he groped at the bulge. Though it was the one thing that couldn't be seen in his reflection, Paris' lips were instantly in his teeth, and he groaned to bite back the urge to push into the firm hand. *Oh it was what he wanted, but he wanted Diesel to do the taking tonight. The game was on—come get me.*

Diesel stepped in behind him and kissed the back of Paris' neck, then let a warm breath cascade down Paris' spine. He felt the internal trickling sensation that fell like rain drops down into his balls and even tapped at his knees. But he steeled himself. Only his breath went unchecked, like he was a fire-breathing dragon on his Master's pet chain.

"You look so fucking hot, I can almost see myself fucking you right here and now. Tell you to put your hands on the mirror and lean over. I can watch your eyes and watch the people behind us stare in awe as I feed my thick cock up your ass." And then he pressed into Paris' backside and locked his gaze on Paris' eyes as he stared back, entirely ensnared by them. He paused as if he were waiting for a response. One that couldn't come, and that's what brought their eyes to the final detail of Paris' outfit— the rhinestone and chrome spiked muzzle mask which covered the lower area of Paris' face, from his nose down to just under the chin.

Damn, Paris cursed internally. He would have bent over at the snap of the first button on Diesel's jeans, if Paris thought for one second Patronus might actually do it.

Paris watched the hand come around his hips and pull at his crotch while Diesel continued to stay pressed against his backside. Diesel's eyes never drifted away; his eyes locked Paris in place by the look alone, while Diesel's hands had their way, feeling Paris up and down. Without a doubt, they were both playing a fantasy up in their heads.

Suddenly, Diesel's grip tightened around Paris' cock through his shorts so hard it hurt, and a thick, angry bulge ground into Paris' backside, announcing the threshold had been broached.

Diesel let out a fierce growl. "Let's go." And Paris was being wrangled upstairs as fast as they could manage.

They were halfway across the VIP playroom lobby when someone called out, "Patronus Gentry!"

Paris heard another growl from Diesel. Though this one wasn't meant to be a pleasant growl, it still had Paris' balls in all kinds of aroused states and ready to explode.

"Come join me a while." The man waved them over.

Diesel's grip on his arms tightened, pulling him to a stop or Paris would have dragged them to keep going and ignore the man.

Paris didn't recognize the man who invited them over and he shot an annoyed questioning glance to his lover. Something in Diesel's expression said *he* did know who it was and it looked like their green-light race was now a hundred shades of yellow flags, waving them down to a slow caution lap around the track. For Paris, it only had him growling with disrespect, so it was a good thing his mouth was muzzled or he would have had something to say about it.

Diesel's hand became more casual but wasn't relinquishing his control of Paris, who found himself being pulled around to the sofa and then pushed to take a spot on the floor while Diesel shook the man's hand before they both sat down.

Paris wasn't going to play the subbie here and he stared directly into the eyes of the man. He saw something in his eyes, in his expression, which rubbed Paris the wrong way, and he lengthened his stare until the man flinched and glanced away. There was something about the guy Paris didn't like. A coldness, a — *goddammit, now he had Diesel harping in his head, making everyone a suspect. Expecting to find a perpetrator behind every corner or anyone wearing a coat factory suit. Trenton and Dane were both fond of suits, but they never looked like cops in theirs.*

He snapped his head around and tried to watch Sasha while he dripped wax over one of his twin subs lying back on a bench. A few other members were chatting while enjoying their cocktails. One of the Mistresses was teasing the submissive at her feet by spreading her legs and giving the young brunette a chance to peek up her Mistress' skirt.

It was quiet for a Thursday, even with the number of members gathered upstairs.

Paris found himself turning back to eye the man once more and wondered who he was. He looked like a cop and smelled like one too. And with the room being rather tame tonight, it implied they were playing safe in the mixed company.

Too safe.

Paris rolled to his knees and pushed up into Diesel's lap, rubbing his face, spiked mask and all, into the denim jeans, trying to get at the very item that should have been stuffed nine inches up his ass right now. However, he'd be damned if he was going to hide how horny he was. Not for anyone. He might not get fucked here on the sofa, but he would put on the seduction enough that *mister interruption* would either beg to join them or leave to get out of their way.

Paris' next move was to pop the top button on Diesel's pants. Ever since the bank hostage ordeal, Paris' lust, which had already been insatiable to start, became damn near unmanageable.

"You know, for the Patronus, you don't seem to have a whole lot of control over your pet." The unnamed man sitting next to them was challenging Diesel.

~ * ~

Diesel didn't falter under the jab from Ian Paul in the slightest. The New York precinct detective had recently become a paid VIP member for an agenda other than pleasure. That much, Diesel was certain of. However, that didn't mean Ian knew anything about him or Paris.

"You know, I had a Great Dane once." Diesel began to pet Paris, who was still pawing over him, keeping him worked up and ready. He liked it. It empowered him, sitting here, getting his cock rubbed down in front of a detective. It said one thing, if nothing else— it made it clear the law had nothing condemning on them, if Ian so much as decided to go from member to cop again. "Dog was housebroken and all, but he was always getting into things, chewing up my shoes, didn't heel worth a shit, and the damn thing thought he was a lap dog too. When I took it for walks, he'd get so excited he'd just want to run and he often looked like he was walking me. So I went and got a skateboard and let him pull all he wanted, like a chariot horse." Diesel reached down, grabbing Paris by the back of his head, fisting his fingers tightly in the black hair, pulling his head back and away from his straining cock. "I loved that damnedable dog, but there is no doubt I love the fact that *this* pet sucks my dick. And no one and nothing sucks me like my pet Imp here." Diesel leaned in and licked right up the center of Paris' muzzle mask. Ran his tongue up the line of spikes, then set him free and sat back, giving off a rare show of his own arrogance like a crown. "You see, to an outsider, it may seem like he's the one in control, but I assure you— he is serving me— just as I want him to."

He gave Paris a searing look, letting him know he was still going to get his ass drilled here soon, and his Imp, fluent in body talk, sat back while his eyes glimmered like lusty pigs and his chest heaved up like a mountain amped for sex that said, *can't wait.*

Whatever Ian Paul was looking for, Diesel hoped he wasn't finding it.

~ * ~ * ~ * ~ * ~ * ~

He walked through the crowded dance floor, impervious to their presence, they didn't even register as bugs to him. His eyes glued on the glass wall of the VIP booth at the end of the walkway, in the far back of the club, and the two people who'd just stepped inside. He watched through the gaps of heads intently as he took up residence against one of the columns on the opposite side of the club. Watched as the little author sat down with a computer in hand just before the glass walls changed and somehow magically frosted over, turning into a mirror and taking the view away from him.

It mocked him.

He felt the sneer creep over his lips. He'd lost her once, but he would not let her slip from his hands a second time. *No man, and certainly no magic glass, was going to keep her safe from him this time. She was his and he'd have her in his grip again, watching as her life drained away from those ghostly blue eyes.*

~ * ~ * ~ * ~ * ~ * ~

CHAPTER TWENTY-THREE

~ * ~ * ~ * ~ * ~ * ~

"So Detective Ian Paul was at the club last night." Diesel mentioned between bites from his steak.

Trenton froze in mid-bite of his own meal and glanced at his brother, "Why didn't you say anything?"

"I'm saying right now. Last night I was fucking."

"You talked to him?"

Diesel made a side glancing shrug, "Not really, but he seemed insistent that I sat with him."

"And?"

"And I don't know why you and Dane approved his application for membership." It wasn't the first time he'd voiced his disapproval.

"Because to block him would mean he'd just send one of his undercover pawns in to scope us out. Whatever he's looking for, let him. At least we'll know when he is sniffing about and not."

"Why is he sniffing about?"

Trenton paused and looked at him a moment. Reading Diesel's face more than considering his own thoughts on the matter. "I don't know why, Deez." He answered finally. And it wasn't a lie either. Trenton had no way of knowing if Det. Paul was related to any of the information Harper had uncovered or not. He could very well be linked to the investigation revolving around the murder of Nolan Carson last year. Or just a cop looking to make a case for himself. Or he was a new Dom just as he claimed to be, one who didn't know how to turn the detective-mind off. Perhaps Ian wasn't even aware that he had the two mixed up. Unless the man came to him for mentoring, it wasn't Trenton's place to tell the man how to act. "When I know more, then I will let you know."

~ * ~

Diesel let out a heavy sigh to voice his disapproval, but outside of beating the shit out of Trenton, he knew, all too well, that when his brother was being nonchalant, there was no getting a word out of him. Diesel just didn't like that, in this instance, it was him getting walled out. Usually, it was everyone else getting the *out of order* sign. All body language said, Trenton knew something. Whether it was related to the detective's nosing about, or something else entirely, Diesel knew his brother was keeping something from him.

"So why do gay men lick each other's arm pits?" Kat was suddenly changing the topic.

Katianna's question came as such a surprise, Diesel nearly choked when taking a sip from his wine, and ended up spilling some of it. "What?"

"Why do—"

"No." He tossed his palm up to stop her. "I know what you asked—" a quick glance to both Trenton and Paris, and Diesel could see they were just as surprised by the question— well, maybe Trenton and him. Paris, on the other hand, had that mischievous expression on his face, though he too was struggling with himself to not laugh aloud at her. Making it harder on Diesel to not do so as well. "I mean, why do you ask that?"

Kat was already scowling at them for even thinking of laughing at her expense, which meant she took the question seriously. Trenton seemed to be taking a fast back seat to the inquiry. He was, after all, *not* gay, and was likely using it as his get-out-free card on the discussion. That left the question on him.

"Where did you see this?" He actually had to think about this one. Paris had certainly done it to him, but it was something they usually only did when they were alone, when Paris had him all to himself. As far as he could recall, he didn't think they had done so even in front of Katianna.

"I saw guys doing it in the gay porn Paris and I were watching the other night."

She said it so matter-of-factly that, once again, Diesel was fighting back laughter. "You've been watching gay porn?" A sound clenched at the back of his throat as he managed the question.

"Kat, why are you watching gay porn?" Trenton leaned into her as he asked the more specific question.

Kat wasn't a porn type person— *at all,* and for her to outright openly admit to watching gay versions of it was hysterical. Her face blushed, despite her attempts to conduct herself, "Research." And Diesel could see she was also getting frustrated with them.

"*Uhm*— I'm not sure really, just a guy thing to enjoy a more pungent smell." Diesel was about to suggest that Paris answer that one, when she shifted, looking up at Trenton.

"Can I write that guy and ask him?"

"What guy?" Trenton and Diesel both asked in unison.

"The guy that films the porn."

Both men turned their attention sharply on Paris.

"What?" Paris shrugged hard, then shook his head, "She was curious. I showed her a couple of the websites so she could watch, then she discovered one of the *Behind the scenes* videos, and that led her to some director's video blog. The guy is hysterical and we both get a big kick out of watching him."

Diesel's arm came up off Paris' shoulders, wrapped around his head, and pulled him into a head lock, "Oh, you are so spending the entire night in servitude now."

Paris wriggled in the headlock and nipped at Diesel's manly nipple hidden under his shirt, then sucked it through the fabric.

Diesel took a deep breath, obviously enjoying the bratty assault.

~ * ~

"Yeah, like I'm gonna hate that." Paris replied, then moved up when Diesel loosened his grip around his head and Paris pushed in, not waiting for an invitation to kiss him. Paris slipped his tongue between Diesel's lips with a burning need that quickly grew more forceful. Bringing his hands up and pushing at Diesel's shoulders, Paris had him dropping down in the booth seat, switching his own position to stay over him, and never broke the kiss. Paris had to admit he was rather surprised Diesel hadn't stopped him already, which only served to amp his lust up even higher. To show his aggressive appreciations, Paris ground his groin into Diesel, shooting jolts of pleasure that raced through both of their bodies.

He broke the kiss, let out a loud fervent gasp and sucked in a lungful of air, then pushed up on his arms to hover over his lover, who merely looked up at him. No emotions stirred him, and if they did, he didn't show them. If Diesel was about to scold him for the public display, he didn't hint to that either. He simply lay there— like a mousetrap waiting to be sprung— *any minute now.*

Paris looked out into the restaurant through his bangs, seeing people eating and milling about, coming and going to the next available table, with hardly an eye glancing their way. "I could suck you off right now— it'd be the ultimate high." He growled. *It certainly would.* Although, once he started and had that thick cock in his mouth, there would be no stopping him. He loved Diesel's cock. Loved how it felt, how it tasted, and that it was his and no one else's was such a new high for him. His brain always experimenting with new recipes to enjoy him. Instead of a new lover, it was a new way to taste or feel his *one.* His only one, and no matter what, it was always good. Always satisfying. They didn't stop until they were both well sated. That knowledge, the knowing that such satiety awaited him, stirred his lust and hunger every time, and he was always ready for his lover's cock again.

He rolled his hips into Diesel again and again, kicking up a wavy rhythm.

Diesel's expression tightened only slightly, but Paris got the hint all the same. His hips froze and he leaned away, but not without at least one naughty-boy deed, and he dropped down to lick the bulge that grew behind Diesel's jeans as the result of his ministrations. *That was all his.*

"Maybe it's time to put a collar on him." Katianna only teased him with the warning as he and Diesel resumed their proper sitting positions.

"Don't think I haven't thought about it." Diesel threatened.

"Better make it one of those pronged pinch collars." Kat added.

"Hey—" Paris scowled at her, "whose side are you on?"

"Yours." She grinned.

"And why should I need a collar? Collars are for those who need to be reminded who they belong to. I don't stay off his cock long enough for him to worry over such things."

"I don't need to be reminded." She scolded suddenly.

"No, you don't, but you wear one so Trenton doesn't have to worry about the rest of the world. He'd put an electric force field around you, if he could. I just have Diesel's cock in me all the time."

Katianna blushed and tucked her face away. Paris laughed. He had no remorse, no shame in who he was or what he loved. And he loved Diesel. To the extent he was a brat about that, too.

"You're going to get in trouble, Paris." She sang.

Paris' hand instantly moved to Diesel's crotch and groped at the hard-on underneath, "Why? It's my cock. I'll enjoy it however I want. And I have lots of fantasies to fulfill now."

~ * ~

Diesel was letting his brat angel have some fun for once. But he caught the change in Trenton's face as he perked up at the suggestion of fantasies.

"I asked you once about your fantasies, and you had to think long and hard to conjure up just one fantasy. Now you have lots of them?" A brow went up on Trent's forehead with the inquiry, but underneath the amused exterior was the Dominus at work, "What are your fantasies, Paris?"

"Paris has picked up a kink for exhibitionism." Diesel answered for his lover, ending the confession with a smack of his lips and a sarcastic expression that shouted out— *Yeah, lucky me.*

Trenton didn't even bother to stifle his chuckle on that note.

Paris grinned, leaned in, and began to list off his new bank of fantasies, "I want to suck him off while he's sitting at the dinner table of a restaurant. I want him to fuck me in a theatre, up in one of the box balconies. I want to fuck him in a giant fountain, surrounded with a hundred colors of LED lights."

~ * ~

Trenton's gaze shifted from Paris back to Diesel, watching him as he sat back in the booth, his arm relaxed out on the table, the other around Paris as he listened to his lover list every detail as if they came as no surprise. They'd obviously spent some time sharing the discussion of fantasy thrills. Diesel was the kind of man that if he asked you what your fantasies were, then he intended to fulfill them. Despite the challenges that Paris' exhibitionism presented for him, Diesel sent a deliberate expression to his brother he'd resolved his withholdings in himself and intended to meet his partner's desires with open-minded amusement. Just not tonight— *obviously.*

"Would you, could you, in a box?" Katianna's voice was quietly nudging into the conversation, though she kept herself tucked away in Trenton's arms as they listened to Paris and his to-do list of naughty things.

"Would you, could you, with a fox?" Paris quipped back to her with a devilish glint in his eyes as he glanced at her.

Diesel sidled his eyes from Kat to Paris then back to Kat, while Trenton was looking down at her with a hard angle, seeing she was obviously in on this. He tugged at her hair, pulling her head back to look up at him and scolding her, "I better not catch you in any of these public fantasies of his."

"I'm not." She gasped in one of her— *it wasn't me*— kind of responses. The ones they both had learned not to trust.

"Don't worry, she's not. It's just a game we play." Paris backed her up with a serious tone.

"To tease me." Diesel quickly added.

Katianna's face turned a naughty, blushing shade of pink, confirming her innocence.

Diesel stretched his fingers out, snagged Paris' hair and tugged, just as his brother had done to Kat, "Maybe I'll look into getting one of those shock collars instead. That might slow you down some." Diesel teased his lover with the threat.

Paris wasn't folding. He dropped his head back on Diesel's arm, then rolled to look at him with his— *I am so devilishly cute*— look. "Oh, come on—" his voice turning soft and tempting, "You know you love my ass."

~ * ~

Diesel looked at him. He'd never had anyone, man or woman, challenge him with such ruthless wanton and playfulness. The Fallen Angel was a brat beyond comprehension, but always in fair fun. Paris was a network of fireworks and desire. The kind of spirit a Dom never dared to try and tame, just adjusted the saddle to ride him hard with the wind in his hair. It was new for him, but he wouldn't give Paris up for another, no matter what or who tried to tempt him. He'd often thought about their future, concerned if Paris' nonconformity would be too much that in the end, Diesel would grow weary of the ride. He saw now he never would. It'd been the lure all along, the loyal wild creature that remained wild, but forever tethered to him. *All mine*, he thought, and leaned in to proffer a couple of tender kisses to his lover's lips, one after the other, then hummed his approval of the touch, "*Mmmm*— among other parts."

"Would you, could you in a house?" Paris grinned at him, "Would you, could you, with a mouse?"

Diesel laughed, his brat always did enjoy teasing him when he could get away with it, but getting his brother at the same time proved to be too tempting for Paris to pass up.

"Your brat is going to find my cane on his ass, if he keeps it up." Trenton warned playfully.

Diesel only smiled, for there was no doubt he would enjoy it if Paris did.

~ * ~ * ~ * ~ * ~ * ~

After dinner, they made their way to Club Pain. Neither of them had been scheduled for giving any demonstration; they just needed to be present and free up Dane's hands.

One of the clubbers came up behind Diesel, just as he was getting a shot at the bar, only moments after Paris stepped away to hit the men's room.

The young man, just shy of a foot shorter with a lithe frame, leaned in to talk in Diesel's ear over the music. "Word is out you're the new jewel to catch." The young hipster spoke while using his best attempt to sound seductive in his misguided confidence.

"How is that?" Diesel hardly glanced over his shoulder at him, but leaned more into the bar and away from the hipster, making it more an effort for the young man to lean in on him. At the same time, giving even less than his own normal enthusiasm to the approach. It wasn't the first time he'd been hit on from a clubber. The young ones were the more obvious and usually the more obnoxious as well. But part of his job, as Patronus at the club, was tolerance. Paris' job, on the other hand, was not so much. So it was only a matter of seconds. *He wondered if the kid would live through this.*

"Ever heard of the website called Tap-That Hunt?"

"Can't say that I have."

"Seduce certain men for jewel points. There's an Arcane List for the crown jewels, mostly celebrities and the rich. Some just too damn good-looking in every department to pass up. Crown jewels like you." The hipster paused to lick his lips.

Diesel just scratched at his lip, wondering what was taking Paris so long to get back. He was bored and was looking forward to the entertainment of his lover's jealous streak. He knew it was there, too. Never had a doubt in his mind Paris might be so, though so far, nothing had ever come along around them to get the Fallen Angel riled up. *Surely, this would bring it to the surface. And it's only beneficial that he, as the Patronus, should observe and learn all the many facets of his lover and reluctant submissive brat.*

"My name's Brandon." The young slut walked around to stand in front of Diesel and slipped his hand up his chest.

Diesel quickly snatched Brandon's wrist in a vice grip and held it firmly away from his body. "You should step away before you get hurt." Diesel responded flatly to the young man's advances.

"I can handle you."

"No, you can't. But the one you should really be worried about—"

Paris was right there, and before the young man knew what was happening, Paris was grabbing him up and forcefully shoving him away from Diesel. "Step away, tramp! If you know what's best for you."

Brandon recovered quickly and showed no signs of being put out just yet. "You won't be around for long. We've all heard of you. The traveling hedonist cock. Only you never stay. Which means once you're out, I plan to move in, and I'm never crawling out of the Patronus' bed." Brandon flicked his lip out with his tongue at Paris and gave him a challenging wink, then turned and sauntered off.

Paris turned on Diesel, snatching the shot glass from Diesel's hand and returned it to the bar, then moved in, planting his hands firmly on the bar with an arm to either side of Diesel's body. Paris pressed against Diesel's groin, watching him with an intense flaring in his eyes. The very things Diesel knew were in there, boiling: lust, claim, and *oh yes,* the jealous streak he knew was hiding in there somewhere. In their time at the resort, he found Paris' inner turmoil that he didn't want to face being left was rooted in his own track record that he himself *never stayed.* Now, Paris had someone he never wanted to share, and it had him frightened by his own past habits. Though, even with the grounds of the relationship already well-established with a loyalty they often reinforced, it was clear Paris didn't like that some twink was even thinking of making a move on his Patronus.

Diesel could see the turmoil in his lover. While he had not invited the youth to flirt with him, it mattered none to Paris. "What do you need from me?" Paris didn't need to fear that he would wander off to play with some kid. He'd already made his decision to have Paris, and that decision meant having only him. But if Paris needed reassurance at the moment, Diesel would give whatever his lover needed.

Paris leaned in, planting a heated kiss on his lips, and pulled away just as quickly as if the touch had burned, then moved in to repeat the contact between them. "I need to mark you."

"And you think that will stop the kid from coming up to me?'

"I don't care!" Paris was clearly pissed, "You're mine, dammit."

Diesel's gaze moved across the club, finding the young man and his friend dancing together out on the dance floor. Their eyes weren't for each other; rather, they both were fixed in his direction, watching him and Paris. Diesel reached up, taking Paris' jaw in his grip, and roughly dragged a thumb over his lover's lips, "Perhaps, I can give you more than just a kiss mark on my skin." He pulled him in for a light kiss then turned Paris around, pulling him to lean back against his chest while his hands went stroking over his jealous lover. Enjoying the feel of firm muscles that made up the physique of Paris' chest and abs. He unbuttoned the silk shirt Paris wore, pulling it open to show off the tantric body candy, while Diesel kissed and licked at Paris' neck and shoulders. "Close your eyes and just feel me." He whispered into Paris' ear, deliberately directing his warm breath to spill over the sensitive nerves to elicit a chill.

Paris leaned his head back over Diesel's shoulder and turned to get his kiss from him. Diesel put on a show for him, open-mouthed and exposed tongue, licking out over Paris' lips and across his tongue. Delivering a pool of sensual entanglement before finally diving in to devour his mouth. There was more to come. A show Diesel had in store for their young audience. His one hand still stroked over the taut pec muscles of Paris' chest while he moved the other south and grasped the hardening erection in the red denim jeans his lover wore. Diesel stroked over the impression of the long shaft then gripped it, pressing the denim down around it so their watchers could see the impressive outline of Paris' cock through the pants.

~ * ~

Paris gyrated his hips into Diesel's hand, already sending his lust reeling in a thrilling dance through his body. He'd never been in a man's hands that could send him flying as easily as Diesel did, and that his lover willingly gave up his reservations little by little to feed Paris' own salacious desire for exhibition— it made everything else disappear for him.

"Come, Paris, it's time for us to meet up with your friends on the dance floor." Diesel commanded and Paris found himself being pushed towards the dance floor by Diesel's body, pressed hard against his own, walking him toward the two young men.

Diesel's hand never stopped frisking the hard cock trapped in his jeans, while the other hand roamed over his chest and pinched at his small manly nipples.

They drew to a halt when they stood before the daring slut boy, Brandon, and his friend. Brandon licked his lips. The show had obviously been a major turn on, and he looked up at Diesel with a naive anticipation.

"So, you want me to fuck you, do you?" Diesel chewed on Paris' shoulder as he asked the question to the ambitious bottom, while his lusty Fallen Angel stood tall, leaning forward just enough to heighten his imposing stance, as he glared down at Brandon.

"You won't be disappointed." Brandon swished to give further demonstration to his confidence.

Had to give him credit. But now it was time for show-n-tell, so the hipster got a reality check of what he was trying to bite off and chew. "Hmmm— and about the website you mentioned, what do you get for me? What type of points?"

"You're listed as a blue diamond— one of the few in the game and the most challenging." Brandon's friend grinned excitedly. It was a kid's game. There were many of these types of games started through social media to challenge each other, to always one up another. Some were outright dangerous.

"Do you hear that, Paris—" he husked in his lover's ear so he could hear him over the music, "You're the proud owner of a blue diamond. I wonder what you're worth?"

"Paris is a pink diamond." Brandon answered, "Easy to get, but still worth a hundred sapphires and emeralds to have."

"Mmmm, pink." Diesel kissed Paris on the ear. "And you always look good in pink, too. However, I've changed the rules up considerably, because there isn't a chance in hell I am going to let anyone *obtain* you. Easy? Not even. That should make me the proud owner of the largest and rarest diamond out there. Pink with a flare of blue, hmm?"

~ * ~

Paris leaned back on him, relishing the banter of attention he was getting, but he was keeping silent and letting Diesel have his way.

"Pull his pants down for me, Paris. Let's have a look at your game player's package."

The suggestion meant to be more cruel than seductive, and Paris quickly complied, grasping the young man's pants by the elastic waist and jerking them down and out, but Diesel was preoccupying himself by kissing on Paris, not bothering to look. "You tell me, Paris, is it worth my time?"

Paris shrugged.

"Let me see it better." Diesel nibbled on his ear.

Paris yanked the hipster closer by the waist belt he still held, and they both glanced down at the young man's exposed soft cock. He was commando under the popularly worn jockey pants. The hipsters loved the jockeys because they could sit as low on the hip as dress codes allowed without actually falling off. Brandon wore his so low on his hip bones, they revealed the hint of soft curls that nestled at the base of his shaft, which at the moment was out of the box for all to see. But for all of Brandon's cocky pride, the ambitious bottom was a far cry from the package Diesel presently held in his hands. To prove it, Diesel finally pulled Paris' pants open, releasing the button then pushing the zipper down, and then he reached in, pulling the packaged cock up to the viewable surface without exposing it completely— just enough for the immediate audience.

Paris rolled his lips in with an added slight flutter of his eyelids as Diesel palmed over his eager flesh with a lazy-like rocking in his wrist. Except, Paris wanted the slut to feel even more humiliated, so he pulled the boy's pants down further, hooking the elastic band under Brandon's scrotum. Paris toyed with him by brushing the exposed goods with the back of his hand— goods that seemed to be at a disadvantage from stage fright. Paris started to *tsk* at him, but Diesel's firmer strokes stole his intentions and his head fell back in a gasping moan. He retracted his hand and joined it with Diesel's, cupping the swollen head in his palm, and he moaned again in deliberate display of his pleasure at the Patronus' hand.

Brandon was breathing heavily, as if on the verge of pleading to jump in between them, but his blushing face betrayed his deflated charismatic flare. Now, he was simply wet behind the ears with idol worship. It was clear to Brandon he wasn't the seducer in this game. Rather, he was being toyed with, and he was aware quite suddenly how inept he was. His eyes fell suddenly to the hands of the Patronus, fondling the now unobtainable Fallen Angel— at the impressive cock stretching across the tan waist.

Diesel saw what Brandon saw. How Paris' turgid flesh pointed the way toward the lickable crescent-shaped muscles that adorned the soft roles of his hip bones, peeking just above the red denim, presently peeled back to reveal the goods and the wisp of body hair that made up the faint manscaped happy trail. Just enough to tease the senses, but not enough to dispel a traveling tongue. "Now explain to me, Brandon, why I would give up this beautiful cock for yours?" Diesel fisted around Paris' shaft, pulled it free, and stroked it one last time before letting it bounce and slap up against Paris' abs. He looked down Paris' chest to admire the cock he already owned, then to the young man who was just starting to get hard. "Call me when you grow up some. I have a few friends that like your type and might be willing to train you into a proper subbie pet." He kissed Paris and nudged him with his hips, "Onward, Imp." Diesel signaled him to head for Trenton's booth.

~ * ~ * ~ * ~ * ~ * ~

CHAPTER TWENTY-FOUR

~ * ~ * ~ * ~ * ~ * ~

"Mr. Leos, your next interview is here." Vince's voice came over the comm. His eyes flickered out of habit to the sofa, only to find his slave absent. Kat was in the back with Diesel for her lessons with him, yet seeing the empty spot still stirred a troubled spot within him.

He tapped the intercom button on his desk phone, "Send him back, please."

A few minutes passed and a small knock on his door preceded the man who entered his office.

A clean white shirt, tucked into navy slacks, and a grey tie. Simple, professional, and strangely unsubstantial. His hair was combed back with no particular style. He wasn't here to impress; rather, if he walked out now, Trenton would not have been able to offer any identifiable characteristics about the man for a line up. To some, that might have been the worst choice for a job interview, but for Trenton's team of security, undistinguished was often best. It seldom served a purpose to stand out too much. Especially for his clients, who preferred their security guards around them, yet slipping into the cracks of oblivion.

"Thank you for waiting, Mr. Clay." He shook the hand his applicant offered, then waited as he sat across from him.

"Thank you, Mr. Leos. Please, call me Oliver."

"Alright, Oliver. I see your resume seems to be in order, but I notice it doesn't really have any length of experience in the field. What brings you here today, then?"

"I've heard of your company, and you've come highly recommended as one of the top security teams in New York, as well as a respected employer."

"You have listed here you worked for an exterminator company for five years, prior to your present employment working ground security? How does that play in with your training?"

"I moved here from Seattle and didn't know anybody or have my New York state gun license. I came across that job almost right away and decided to take it so I could take my time with the additional licensing required to work security here. Ended up with a good job with benefits, so I decided to expand my schooling further into state law."

"Did you plan on going into the police service?"

"No, I kind of liked the private service side of the field, but I figured more schooling wasn't going to hurt. At least this way, I could earn my five years with the company and have a small retirement egg. I finished an associates in law before going for my CCW permit and AFQ license certification."

"Well, Oliver, it all looks good here. I still have a few other applicants planned for interviews today, so I can't make a definitive decision just yet. I'll also have to run you through a full screening. You understand."

"Of course."

"Which reminds me, I need a fingerprint from you." Trenton pulled out a print card with an ink press pad and slid both across his desk toward the man. He watched the body language, looked for the nervous twitches that sometimes cropped up when asking for prints. Not a flinch from him as he got up, rolled his thumb on the pad, then pressed it down inside the indicated box on the card. "That'll do." Trenton passed a tissue over to him. "One last question, which I ask all applicants. What makes you an excellent candidate for the position?"

Before the question could be answered, the door to his office flew open and Harper was walking in at a brisk pace, his eyes glued to the papers in his hand, stopping only when he glanced up. It clearly became evident he'd not known Trenton was conducting interviews today.

~ * ~

Harper came to a halt midway across the room, "Sorry, Trenton, I didn't—" he did a double take when he viewed the man sitting across from Trent, "—realize you weren't alone." He stared a moment, even as the other man turned and looked his way, because there was something about him. Still holding the files in one hand, Harper shot a thumb over his shoulder, only his eyes never left the stranger. "I'll come back later." He started to move away then changed his mind, "Say, do I know you from somewhere?"

The man twisted around fully in his chair and glanced at him with a blank expression, then slowly shook his head when he obviously wasn't getting the same familiarity Harper was.

Harper shook his head, apologizing quickly, "Sorry to bother you." And he left without another word, going back to his office. He dropped down behind his desk, with every intention of going back to the reports he was supposed to be finishing up, but he just sat there and stared at the door to his office. The small tickle in the back of his brain just wouldn't go away. He felt the furrow between his brows deepen further. There was something— he clicked open a couple of tabs on his computer, flicking through files in his database, expecting something to pop up at him. But nothing did.

~ * ~ * ~ * ~ * ~ * ~

Suddenly, Trenton felt uneasy. It wasn't like Harper to mistake someone. It was a detail that made him good at what he did. He knew faces— never forgot them. So what was it about this man, who was so seemingly indistinctive, that caught Harper's attention?

"Mr. Clay, my business is to safeguard people. Sometimes from some very dangerous people, and sometimes just to shield them from fans or crowds who like to get too close. So, it is invaluable that the people I send out are worthy of such trust. So, when my brother feels like he knows you, I am not going to dismiss it lightly. Perhaps you can explain."

Oliver shook his head, apparently puzzled by it as well, "What kind of work does he do?"

"He's a private detective."

Again, Oliver shook his head, but then snapped out of it. His finger coming up as if he intended to point something out of the air with it, "Has he ever cooperated with the local police?"

"He has."

Oliver leaned forward slightly and spoke under his breath, "I can't say for sure if this is why, but I used to be an informant. I didn't usually posture myself when at the precinct, but there had been a few times I was brought in to identify— certain suspects."

"An informant?"

"Former. I had a side job at the Golden Saint Yves tower. I would see things— sometimes witness terrible things pass by in the middle of the night."

~ * ~ * ~ * ~ * ~ * ~

Walls hissed from opposite directions, followed by streams of fog that obscured her already limited eyesight in the dimly lit room. "It's just a mechanical test." She reminded herself, but not even that could convince her to stop shaking. The echo of boots pounding on pavement seemed to come up behind her. She spun around, facing a dark wall. Her will slipped away more and her heart beat furiously in her chest. She clasped the Beretta Px4-Storm nine millimeter gun in both hands, not even aware her finger wasn't on the trigger.

She wanted out. She wasn't ready for this. He had such faith in her. But he was wrong. She couldn't get the gunmen out of her head.

~~ Well, lookie what we got here." A gunmen had spoken just seconds before he grabbed her arm and hauled her up off the floor. ~~

Shots fired out in rapid succession and Katianna spun around. Her heart leaped up into her throat, choking off the scream filling the room and her ears. But when the mechanical dumpster rolled out from its hiding place inside the gauntlet room, it'd startled her so much she slammed sideways into one of the moving prop mannequins. That was it. Too many emotional triggers for her, and she lost her grip on the reality that it was only a software program meant to train her to control her fears and reactions. She let out another scream and flung her arms around her head, forgetting the gun in her hand until she squeezed too hard and fired off several rounds.

~ * ~

Diesel came barging in, just as Kat was tossing the gun from her hand. It hit the ground and fired off. While he'd only loaded it with practice caps, the embedded reaction in him flinched at the idea of a ricocheting bullet.

Katianna had already gone into hysterics and attempted to squeeze herself behind a wall.

He rushed over and pulled her into his grip, then slid down the wall to the floor and just held her as tightly as he dared. He felt horrible that he'd pushed her so hard. "Shhh, it's okay. I turned the program off."

"I'm sorry. I know you thought I could do this, but I failed. And you're going to be mad at me for it." She cried within the cave of his arms.

"No, I'm not. I was wrong. I shouldn't have put you in here or tried to push you to complete the test." He pulled her in closer, as if it was possible, and he kissed the top of her head. "I'm just so afraid, Mouse. Afraid that someone will find that one split second moment you're not under Trenton's or my protection and try to hurt you or take you away." He crushed his face against the top of her head, inhaling the scent of her hair and her sweet body. He may not be on the edge of that dark place as his brother was, but he knew for certain he wouldn't be able to handle it if they lost her. The kidnapping, then the bank scare, proved it. They were both deeply in love with her, and he would do anything to protect her and Paris to keep them safe. "Just promise me, promise me if anything happens that puts you in danger, you run— you run like hell and find a place to hide. Find a hole or crawl space and hide where no one else can get to you. Silence your phone and wait for our text to come get you." He kissed the top of her head, "Promise me."

He felt her nod against him and he knew that would have to be enough. Because Trenton was going to kick his ass when he found out he'd done this.

~ * ~ * ~ * ~ * ~ * ~

CHAPTER TWENTY-FIVE

~ * ~ * ~ * ~ * ~ * ~

After the bank threat, it seemed the wedding plans for his brother and Life Slave were put on the fast track. Whatever it was, it lit a fire under Trenton's feet, and the Mouse's plans for a spring wedding were going to be on the cold side of the Goffer's calling.

Their parents had arrived, and by order of Trenton, were being hosted at Diesel's house. This led to some very naughty teasing from Paris. *That Imp just didn't know when to stop.* Paris thought he could egg him on as he did, taunting him with his bratty antics. When Diesel made the mistake of declaring a *no-sex-while-the-folks-were-there* rule, Paris accepted the challenge. Just this morning, he came strutting out of the bathroom in a new pair of briefs with the Diesel brand logo along the wide waist band. But that wasn't the part that got him in trouble as he walked past to his bureau; Diesel found himself doing a double take as Paris pushed the waistband of his briefs down entirely so as to put his perky ass on display, and written across his ass in black were the words *fuck me*.

Diesel caught him on the next peacocking pass, yanked him over his lap and spanked that ass. Gave four rapid smacks before Paris managed to twist away, but not too far where his bottom was out of reach.

Paris threatened, "I will scream if you don't stop."

Challenge accepted. Diesel smirked. Paris barely caught the curling smirk on Diesel's lips before he had him right back over his lap and face down, and Diesel brought the flat of his palm down on that *fuck me* labeled ass. He had to or he was going to do what the ass was crying out for.

Paris made good on his threat too, which didn't stop Diesel. Delivering twenty or so— or more— he didn't bother keeping count. He was just enjoying the game of bluff— and that ass. The piece of succulent flesh that belonged solely to him. *Paris' jewels were no longer on the market.*

He couldn't help but take a long moment to rub over the now warm and tender skin, and the roundness filled his palm while deviant ideas came to mind. It'd been a while since he'd tied Paris up and had some fun with him. And perhaps it was time to catch up, seeing he'd given Paris a considerable amount of room for his imp-ish ways. Now was a good time to flip the game around and give Paris a show of why he enjoyed being a brat so much. Because any moment now, Diesel was going to remind him who was his Patronus and what that truly meant.

"Huht-hmm." Paris cleared his throat.

Diesel broke from his musings and glanced at Paris, who was glaring at him from over his shoulder. Just more goading as far as Diesel was concerned. He quickly wet two fingers with his mouth then went back down to Paris' ass. This time diving for his hole. A fast pass over the rosette, and then he pushed in. Paris fully accepted the invasion and pushed back on him with a gasping sigh.

He was just as quick to drop his knees to the floor between Diesel's legs and come upright, catching Diesel by the head and drawing him in for a deep, begging kiss.

Diesel managed to keep his fingers hooked in the hole. Not by much, but he gave his man a little tickle, and that body shifted and rose with every muscle as he brought himself to a more accessible spot.

That was about the same time there was a knock on the door.

"*Paris? Does this mean we're not going shopping this morning?*" Patrice's voice came from the other side of the door.

Diesel tried not to laugh, but the look on Paris' face when he drew back was worth a thousand words and, at least, two laughs.

The expression suddenly morphed into something more along the lines of *fuck it, I'm getting laid first* and he moved in for the kill. But Diesel caught him by the shoulders and pushed him back.

"You promised to take them shopping in New York. Two women who know how to fire every type of gun I have in my shop." He nodded the rest of what that meant.

Paris' expression on his face shifted once again. This time it looked like a whole brigade of curse words was being thrown at him.

"I love you too." Diesel smirked, releasing Paris' arm, but he caught a glimpse of something black on Paris' shoulder just as he turned and vanished into the walk-in closet. Diesel glanced at his hand, finding a transfer of the writing from Paris' ass now backwards on his palm and fingers. He wasn't even aware the chuckle had gotten away from him until Paris came out, still scowling, pulling on a sleeveless muscle shirt to go with the faded-to-near-white jeans he now wore.

"What's so funny?"

"Nothing." Diesel shook his head, trying his best not to look at the transfer on Paris' shoulder and arm.

Paris turned his back to Diesel and made his final mirror-inspection, but the knocking on the door became persistent, interrupting his intentions.

"*Paris?*"

"Coming!" Paris opened the bedroom door and let Patrice in, "Just finishing getting dressed."

Diesel shot a raised brow at the both of them, as his mother freely stepped in and got an eyeful of his bedroom. His lifestyle was not unknown to his mom, but that didn't mean he wanted her taking a tour of his bedroom. It landed one of those boyish *eww mom* anecdotes in his head.

Paris grabbed some cologne from his bureau— gave himself a few spritzes then turned to Patrice. "Ready?"

Diesel's mom nodded but then stilled, her eyes zeroing in on Paris' arm, then blushed and started to giggle.

Paris followed her finger when she pointed, finding a duplicate, though slightly smudged, imprint of his backside writing. The next expression Diesel got was the best one. Eyes narrowed and his brow stitched together. Maybe some more mental curse words. Like *you bastard* and *I'm am so going to get you back for this*. His peacock feathers were obviously ruffled now.

Diesel couldn't wait. *Game on.*

~ * ~ * ~ * ~ * ~ * ~

It was hours later, and Diesel was using the chance to watch some news and get some paperwork out of the way. Luckily, he wasn't handling too much with the wedding ceremony, most of which was turned over to Pyotr Laszkovi's twin sisters: Varvara and Andjela. The girls had designed and made not only Katianna's wedding dress but also had made a dress for her maiden of honor: Vince. Plus, a custom designed suit for her gentleman of honor: Paris.

Kat had asked for a lawn wedding with dresses from the Edwardian period. The twins made it possible. Portraying everything possible for the era. The only thing missing was the Titanic. And they, well Kat in particular, felt that was for the best, mumbling something about how it sank and being a bad omen. Diesel and Trenton had done their best not to laugh at her expense.

Even though he was free of the massive planning, so many other things had fallen behind. He was way behind on reviewing some of the newest items out there for self-defense. And there had been an increased demand on survival gear he'd yet to stock, namely the Bug-Out packs and the Get-Home bags. They were ideal for the typical New Yorker who didn't have a lot of space in the studio or home to stockpile, in the case that any of the variety of threats displayed on television should have landed here in the US. They were usually on the go anyways, so the backpacks with a little bit of everything— first-aid, tools, self-defense weapons, and food to last a person a few days, or even a few weeks, depending on the situation— were the ideal preparation. Kids liked them too, just in case the zombie apocalypse happened after all. Either way, he'd let his shop fall behind on such things. So, with all but Dad out of the house, now was a good time to get on some of that, knowing Paris wouldn't have the ladies back any time soon.

The quiet didn't last long when Jonas came marching in, like he was on orders. "Deez! Where are my wives?"

He sucked in a deep breath and paused the demo video he was watching, then gave him his full attention. "Paris took them shopping. Why?"

"You ask why? Because I haven't had a damn moment's rest with either of them since we got here, that's why! I was hoping to go down to see the Intrepid Museum then take the girls out on the Clipper City tall sail." Jonas plopped down in the chair across from the sofa where Diesel sat and just looked at him directly. He stilled a moment, his eyes looking him over.

Diesel's gaze followed his, realizing what he saw. A pile of catalogs on the TV table in front of him, a shopping list scribbled on a steno pad in his lap. Beside him, a scanner radio dialed in on the Queen's police scanners. The television was on with the CNN International News as the main channel, while the weather channel was in the corner window of the screen. And then, the ten-inch tablet, on which he'd just been watching a demonstration involving the latest Maxpedition Versipack designs, still in his hand.

"How the hell do you get anything done?" Jonas shot him an exasperated look.

Diesel thought, for a moment, that *this* was nothing. Usually, he could have up to six windows of news on the television. He settled for shrugging.

Jonas' face scrunched up a bit, his nose going up, and he was clearly calculating on something. A question was forming on his tongue, but he seemed reluctant to ask it.

Diesel knew that look on him. Jonas clearly had something on his mind. "You want to know if I'm certain about this, don't you?"

"First—" Jonas still looked at him with his nose turned up slightly, and he scratched at his chin, scrutinizing, "I want to know about these bruises on your face, though they are nearly healed." Jonas waved a finger at him, as if pointing out the marks, in case Diesel forgot they were there.

Diesel chuckled, "Brotherly love spat. You want me to answer the other one now?"

Jonas shook his head with a pursed expression on his lips, "Nope. Between the two of you, you're the last of my boys I worry about whether or not you're confident in your decisions. If you're in a relationship with a man, I know it's what you want."

"It's not about whether I'm with a man, it's about being with Paris."

"Yet, Paris is a man and prejudices come with it, whether you acknowledge them or not. Trent, on the other hand, I worry about. All this slave stuff. I don't understand it, but that little one he's got— she sure is a cutie pie, and they do seem to be in love."

"Trenton waited four years before they got involved."

"They waited because she wouldn't give in to his ideas."

"That's not true. He could have had her from the very beginning. Only he knew then he'd have just been taking

392

over where someone else left off, and that's not how he wanted it to be. He wanted her to be able to freely give her life to him, not fall to him because she had no other options. It took four years for that to happen."

"Well, I still don't understand it all. It's a dangerous line you boys are balancing on. It's a thin separation of definition. A line, barely a thread thick, between slaves who want to be slaves and ones who don't."

Diesel's eyes flickered up at his father. Their lives had never been a secret with their parents, but it wasn't something they talked about over dinner either. He just didn't realize Jonas thought this of them. "That's like saying the only difference between blue and green is a drop of yellow.

"Isn't it?"

Diesel pushed back on the sofa, his thoughts weighing in heavily on him now, having never expected to go down this road with Jonas. "Is that what you think of us?"

Jonas took a deep breath and reset his attitude at the drop of a dime, just like that. "No. Of course not. I just don't understand it and I worry this is going to bring more trouble than the two of you can handle one of these days. That's all."

"When you look at Trenton and Kat, what do you see?"

Jonas took another deep breath that hinted of a chuckle, "I see two happy as ever, love-sick kids." A wry smile curled up on one side, and Diesel could tell Jonas had a firm picture of the two of them in his head, but then his face grew serious, "And I see a son who would kill anyone who tried to harm her, regardless of any consequences."

"God save the man who dares to try, because no one on earth will be able to stop him, and I'll be right there, alongside him."

Jonas seemed to get lost in thought for a moment, a slight nod rocked his movements, then he shook the daze away and glanced back to Diesel, "And what of you? Will you marry Paris one day?"

"Yeah, I suppose it'll come to that eventually."

"Yeah? Or yes?" Jonas was always about certainty.

"Yes."

"Good, 'cause he's gonna need someone to watch over him in the hospital." He mumbled this time as he pushed up from the chair.

Diesel whipped around and called after his dad before he could march off. "Hospital?"

"Yes, 'cause I'm gonna beat him to a pulp if he doesn't bring my girls back home soon." He called out as he disappeared into the kitchen.

Diesel chuckled lightly, figuring he'd better call Paris. He found his phone under the pile of catalogs and dialed Paris' phone. "Hey, Imp, you better wrap it up and bring them in. He's getting super jealous." He paused to listen a moment, then responded, "Love you too."

~ * ~ * ~ * ~ * ~ * ~

Another day passed, and Paris and Diesel were chilling out on the sofa in the living room, simply enjoying a moment of not having to do anything, which was rare for them, especially with the anticipated day getting close. Jonas had managed to salvage his plans for the Intrepid Museum and returned an hour ago, but then they immediately disappeared into some part of the house. Leaving him and Paris to their quiet bubble for a little longer.

They always seemed to be on the move— at work, at the club, at the house, at each other. Now, with Trenton and Katianna's wedding just a few days away, and family and friends already in town for the ceremony, it was a miracle they had a quiet moment at all, so they were taking extensive advantage of it while they could as they curled up on the sofa together.

Diesel rested back lengthwise while Paris had taken up residence between his legs, lying back on his chest. Both staring out the floor-to-ceiling glass window to the ocean view, watching it move in no measurable form. It was nice for a change. Diesel had his arms draped over Paris' chest, and occasionally he felt the soft caress of his manicured hands move over his arms. Which won him a kiss to the back of his head each time. Like the monkey taught to punch the button for a treat, it happened frequently. But like all good, quiet moments, it didn't last long. But, for his mom, he would make the sacrifice.

Patrice came waltzing in with a bright smile on her face, shooed Paris over, and dropped down between the two of them.

"Where's Dad and Annette?"

"They decided to go for a walk on the beach."

"And you didn't go with them?"

"And miss an opportunity to have you all to myself for a moment? *Tuh*— they can go walk. After being dragged all over the museum, my feet have had enough walking for a few days."

Diesel waved her to bring her feet up, which she gladly did with an even brighter smile. Paris repositioned himself on the sofa, pulled Diesel's mom to lean back on him, and wrapped around her in a bear hug. Diesel slipped her flats from her feet and began to give each foot a good rub.

"Ahhhh—" she sighed playfully, "you are the greatest son in the whole wide world."

She shifted her head so she could manage an upward glance at Paris, "Does he do this for you too?"

"I get all kinds of things rubbed by him." Paris proffered his signature naughty smile.

Patrice let out a surprised yelp, her cheeks turned an instant red, then she fell back into a relaxed position, beaming at her son.

"So, you're okay with this?" Diesel asked her.

"What do you mean?"

"With Paris and me?"

"Honey, of course, I'm okay with it." She pushed to sit up and her hand reached out to cup his cheek, "Do you honestly think, for all those years the four of us were together, that Jonas' and Nelson's bodies never came in contact with each other?" She gave him a wink and a warm smile, but he could also see a hint of the pain for her loss. After all these years, she still missed her husband. "Your father was a good man. A strong one and very loving." Her smile faltered a moment, and her hand moved from his cheek to her own to wipe a tear before it could fall. "Our time together was the four of us, not just them sharing Annette and me."

Diesel took his mother's hand in his, caressing it softly with a thumb.

"Besides, I know you. You love so strongly and so deeply— I knew it would take someone very special not to feel crushed under your love." Her smile warmed again, and the shadow that revealed her pain faded away.

Paris struggled to contain the supersized grin on his face, keeping clear of her line of vision. Diesel did what he could to stifle his own grin. *They kind of had that crushing each other thing down pat, actually.*

Patrice rested back against Paris' chest, seemingly willing the tension she'd let grip her fall away, "Are you as happy as you look to me?" She asked as any mother might ask.

Diesel's eyes floated up to find Paris', those deep, dark brown eyes looking back at him, filled with content, love, and lust. "Yeah—" he nodded, "I am." He'd found someone his brothers appreciated and liked. And who also got the stamped approval of his family. Such a thing could not have changed his choice, but having their support certainly made it all better. Knowing that his family had his back. He wasn't sure if he could ever be happier than he already was, but what he did know was that if he did find it, Paris would still be at his side when it happened, and they'd have it together.

~ * ~ * ~ * ~ * ~

CHAPTER TWENTY-SIX

~ * ~ * ~ * ~ * ~ * ~

Diesel stood in his room, his tux laid out and bagged, ready to take to the botanical garden where his brother and Kat's wedding would take place. It would be a good day, but the object in his hand had him in a moment of solemnness.

"What's that?" Paris asked, swooping by, going from bathroom to closet.

Paris' beautiful naked form made Diesel nearly abandon the object in his hand.

"Wait, is that what I think it is?" Paris stopped, his head practically screwed on backwards, as his eyes locked onto the bit of silver that shimmered between Diesel's fingers. Paris turned, coming about and stepped closer, holding his wrist up and displaying the bracelet that had remained locked around his wrist since the day Diesel had placed it there. "Why haven't you given it to her yet?"

"When did we have the time? You and I have been rather busy with each other."

"So?"

"No, not so. You and I— what we have— needed to come first."

Suddenly, Paris had Diesel's head in both hands and pulled him in for a passionate kiss. Then there was the bump of a cock that was slowly on the rise.

"You best stop before I have to put a cage on that. We have a wedding to go to." Diesel did his best to use the humorous threat to steer clear of the subject.

Paris let him go but didn't bother stepping back.

Brat.

Paris smiled down at the bracelet, "So, give it to her when they get back."

Those words, right there, sucked the joy from Diesel. And Paris saw it.

It was evident in the sudden shock revealed in his expression, "You can't, can you? I don't understand. What? Do you have some kind of silent laws about collaring her after she's—" he trailed off, realizing the implications of his words were very wrong.   Or so Diesel figured. Paris was learning and growing with more understanding every day they shared together. Working with Trenton obviously had some imposing guidance involved as well.

"Trenton never planned to marry anyone. Not in his entire life did he think he ever would. So for him to do so now has some kind of finality. Like freezing their bond into something that can never be altered afterwards." He threw his hands out, frustrated that he couldn't find the right words.

"Are we talking like Star Wars sci-fi stuff here and sealing their relationship in carbonite?"

"Yes. And it wouldn't seem right for me to put this on her after the fact."

"Then you have to tell him."

"No, they get married today. I have to accept that it's just something in my life that isn't going to happen for me.

"NO! Diesel! You have to tell him. If this is what you want. Wait—" he took several steps back, "Fuck, what am I saying? You have always wanted this. A Unicorn— Kat is the one you have always wanted. That didn't change even after we met. But you still have her, you can't—"

There was a rap at the door then, and Trenton poked his head through the opening. "Guys, don't do this to me. Don't have your first lovers' spat on my wedding day."

"We're not spatting." Diesel shot his brother a scowl and tucked the bracelet into his pocket.

"Trenton, he needs to—"

"Shut up, or I swear you will go to the wedding with a sore ass." Diesel warned him.

Paris snapped a saucy grin at him, "We have time for a quickie?"

"I mean, I will flip you over my knee and give you a solid spanking."

Trenton stepped all the way through and closed the door behind him. His face solidified into a determined expression. "Is there something you need to tell me?"

"Yes." Paris answered for him.

"Paris! I mean it." Diesel growled and looked at his brother, "No, I'm fine."

"What's that in your pocket, then?"

Diesel glanced down, spotting the ringed outline of the hidden object in his sweat pants. *Ten— nine— eight— Trenton wasn't budging— fuck—* he shook his head, hating this, and still his brother didn't budge. Just waited.

Diesel reached into his pocket, pulled it out, and showed it to him. A platinum bracelet embedded with two blue sapphire solitaires. One on each side of a tiny padlock that didn't entirely match the setting, but it added an industrial finality to the more finely crafted jewelry.

Trenton turned, rather surprised, "How long have you had that?"

Diesel felt uneasy, his legs jittery under him, He really didn't want to answer this question. "I picked it up a few days before your collaring ceremony. Then later, when I was having the one made for Paris— the one he's wearing, I had the lock charm on this one replaced with an authentic lock made of the same tungsten." Diesel loved his brother, and could pretty much tell what the man was thinking just from the rare expressions, the ones he usually kept concealed, on his face. For only few ever seemed to show anything but strength, lust, and determination. Right now, though, the corners of Trenton's lips were only slightly curled up, and those eyes Mouse always blushed under so often, were as brilliant as ever. *Bastard was conspiring, and it was making Diesel nervous— like cold feet kind of nervous.*

"Be sure to have it with you at the wedding." And he turned and headed out.

"What?"

"You heard me." Trenton vanished.

Paris was staring at him.

"What?" This time the question shot to his partner.

"He does that Jedi mind-trick with you too, doesn't he?" Paris waved a finger as if he detected some invisible energy transfer between them.

Diesel only narrowed his eyes— *three— two— one—*

~ * ~ * ~ * ~ * ~ * ~

Trenton knew how to make fantasies come alive. That gift apparently also included weddings. At least his own. And he looked as cool and calm as a cat. Diesel knew it, because he was standing right beside him and not feeling anything close to it. He was doing all he could not to move and fidget around too much. He was a nervous wreck, actually.

"Hey, knock it off. It's embarrassing." Marcus whispered behind him.

Diesel shot him a hard look, but it was met with only two more faces. Harper's and Dane's. All three of them looking at him with a ready chuckle. "Not a word from any of you."

It didn't make a bit of difference. What they didn't say was clearly dancing about in their eyes. *They were laughing at him.* The only thing he could do was ignore them. If only that worked for how nervous he felt.

Music started, but none of that *here comes the bride* stuff or a sappy tune off the radio. It came from none other than the twins, Isaac and Isaiah, playing a violin duet, standing off to the side and just beyond the guests. Which were many. Maybe not in celebrity status type numbers, because Trenton had drawn the line at fifty. Though, it appeared more than that had managed to get in. Columns surrounded them, draped in wisteria of lavender and white. According to the botanical garden's managers, they bloomed all year round. As did many of the plants kept safe inside the atrium. Every now and then, a flurry of butterflies would move from one spot to another. They were the magic, all the way until Vince stepped into the garden at the start of the foot path.

"Shit." A husky breath escaped one of the guys behind him. Dane, most likely. Because at that very moment, Vince was more angelic than human, transformed into Vida as if born a woman. He was wearing an Edwardian linen and lace walking dress suit; as such, Vince looked like one of many ladies of wealth who came right off the first class deck of the Titanic.

Then, behind him came Paris, who'd been just a tad more problematic to dress. Much of which had been dictated by him. But the final touch suited him well. Even with his muscular frame. His period suit was altered to a slightly more steampunk flair, with ascot tie and a double-breasted tapestry waistcoat over a white silk shirt with billowy sleeves. Diesel never got past that, because the next thing that had his attention was Paris' eyes, which were locked onto him. *Yes, this was probably going to happen.* And maybe he wouldn't take as long as he'd thought before popping the question. Just then, Paris twisted around, his attention shifting to something behind him, only half his height. It was all the suggestion either of them needed, and

Diesel found himself leaning over and attempting a glimpse, only to bump into Trenton.

Diesel glanced at his brother, doing a double take on Trenton, who was looking at him when he should have been mirroring what Diesel had been doing. He was still wearing that grin. But then Trenton's eyes shifted to the footpath. Diesel's followed, and then he saw her.

There are times in a man's life when his head says a thousand incoherent things and says nothing at all— all at once. He couldn't recall having that feeling but a few times in his entire life. That day, when he was called into Trenton's office to find he was about to be part of a training course for a Fallen Angel. It was the first time he'd seen Paris in person— and he nearly lost his composure just at the sight of him. Another time, he was sitting next to Trenton, just as Katianna stepped into the living room to begin her journey from her old life into her new one under the ownership of the Dominus.

And then it happened again— just now, when Kat came into view from behind his Fallen Angel. She was beautiful. And it wasn't just the dress, because there wasn't much of it to elaborate on. Whatever anyone was thinking she would wear for her wedding gown, it was doubtful any of them came close to guessing what she chose. But it made sense. He recalled when he'd first met her. So many years ago, now it seemed. How far they'd all come since that day at the convention that glamorized the sex industry. Kat was throwing a tantrum over not having something to wear that would stand up to what everyone else was wearing. Trenton had stepped in and gave her the confidence to wear what she liked, and nothing less. He'd done the same for this day. Three days of Mouse tantrums had been too much, and Trenton granted her permission to pick out whatever she wanted and disregard the dozen dresses being pushed at her. Just like before, what that became was a small, five-foot woman wearing something meant to go under a dress. The tea-colored, handmade lace petticoat was simple with an antique class all its own. Leaving her shoulders mostly bare, save for some sheer material that made up the undefined straps that held the dress up, while the rest of it fell to the grassy lawn and footpath under her feet. Satin bows were added at the bodice and along the ruffles, and hints of her skin could be seen through the lace. *Had he and his brother been anywhere but at a wedding, there likely would have been a considerable amount of growling from the both of them.*

She was so beautiful, Diesel hardly took notice of Pyotr Laszkovi, dressed similarly to Paris, walking her down the aisle, but it wasn't to Trenton she was presented.

It was him.

And then he felt his brother's hand on his shoulder. He looked at him. The smile gone, leaving just that confidence and determination. Trenton gave him a slight nod.

Diesel's hand floated to the pocket of his slacks, felt the bracelet he brought with him, and all the jitters left him. He became calm, The Patronus reigning inside him. It was where he was meant to be. *This is what it felt like when your life was everything you wanted it to be because you had a harmonious control over it.*

Diesel stepped forward, took her hand from Pyotr's, and held it as he paused to soak up as many minutes as he could. To savor this arrival in his life. One he would have to thank Paris for later. "Katianna Dumas, before you are given an added title of wife to Life slave, I ask you to submit to me ownership of your body, your heart, and your life. To be my Life slave in as much of the same commitment you have given yourself over to the Dominus, with me as your Patronus. To belong to us both." And he held the bracelet out, open, inviting her in.

God, he had no words, but one. Unicorn. With teary eyes, his Unicorn submitted her left wrist into the collaring bracelet. His heart soared off into the sky, his hands stayed— calm and content, as his fingers snapped the bracelet closed, then hooked the lock into place and locked it. She looked up at him, and while he may not ever be able to explain or describe what he saw, he knew it was a love no other could give. She was the sweet hummingbird who landed in a man's hands, fragile and fearless at the same time. He never knew love could hurt so much, and he leaned in to kiss her, not even close to how much he would have liked, but it would have to do for now. Then he took her hand in his and presented her to his brother.

Vince and Paris took their places behind her just as he, Marcus, Harper, and Dane stood behind Trenton, but as the ceremony began, Diesel's eyes went to Paris. Hearing the words described for Trenton and Kat, Diesel felt them for Paris. *God, he loved that man.*

~ * ~

Paris watched, taking in every detail he could. His petite friend listened to her Dominus give his self-written vows of adoration, love, and the promise to always cherish her. Yet, looking at Trenton, Paris saw they weren't just words, for the words didn't come close to what was in Trenton's eyes in that moment. Like nothing else existed around them. Paris felt like he was watching a man who was watching the birth of the heavens, with the way his eyes lit up like a million stars. He was so glad he was there to witness it. Had he not been, no one could ever have convinced him such devotion existed. And perhaps it didn't for anyone else. But he was glad he got to see it this once.

Of course, Katianna was crying already, her fingers dutifully trying to keep tears from wrecking her perfectly applied makeup. Paris risked an unceremonious glance over his shoulder to Vince, who was also in tears.

"Do you have the ring?"

Paris' attention shot back to the ceremony as Diesel handed over the wedding bands to his brother.

Diesel— the man who had forced his way into his life because he believed they belonged together. How he came to that conclusion was beyond comprehension. Paris had never been in a long relationship, let alone a deep one. But as he stared at Diesel now, Paris couldn't think of any place he'd rather be than with him. He didn't ever want to give up his lover, not for anyone or anything.

"I now pronounce you, Dominus and Life slave, now joined as husband and wife as well. You may kiss what is yours."

Paris grinned, watching the two. Trenton had to bend down quite a bit for her, and then decided suddenly it was easier just to lift her. His arms snaked around her waist as he crushed her against his chest, and then he lifted her off her feet. And in a squeal, she kicked her feet back, losing a shoe in the process. The guests loved it and laughed as the two deepened their kiss.

Paris leaned over, just enough to see Diesel on the other side of the happy couple, and smiled at him. *He wanted what they had— and he wanted it with Diesel.*

~ * ~ * ~ * ~ * ~ * ~

CHAPTER TWENTY-SEVEN

~ * ~ * ~ * ~ * ~ * ~

In the days that followed the wedding, Diesel and Paris seemed to have found a new battery cell of energy between them. Not that they had slowed in the slightest, so this heightened level led to a considerable amount of time spent at the club, for their mutual semi-private bliss. Such was not the case tonight, as Paris found.

Tonight was the night his Patronus invited Maxum St. Laurents and Darko Laszkovi to join them.

But even with their renewed energy, Diesel was still not a dancefloor kind of man. Paris' solution was to take Darko out on the floor instead. Just from watching him, Diesel countered this was more about teasing him, and it worked. Not just for him either; Maxum was sporting a well-defined erection under his suit slacks as they watched from the VIP booth. The two darkly tanned bodies gyrating into each other like a wave of liquid sex. Rolling to a beat of the music that droned on. Darko stood behind Paris, pressing his hips into Paris' ass. The two so completely into each other, like a fantasy in motion that was played out in their minds— only, their hands also shared in the expression. Darko's lips hovered ever so close to Paris' bare shoulder, never initiating first contact, just as Paris watched him over his shoulder, expecting nothing more, but obviously thinking about it.

Diesel's cock was so fucking hard; he was going to explode if he continued watching any more of this. But as he saw Maxim get up and step to the glass wall for a closer look, Diesel suddenly became concerned that the two men on the dance floor might strike up some jealousy in his friend. But then he saw Maxum's arm move. A movement that said only one thing.

Diesel pushed up from the sofa and stepped up next to him. From the corner of his eye, he could see Maxum's hand lightly fingering over the bulge that pressed against his slacks. Out on the floor, Paris and Darko shifted around and now faced one another, so close they shared each other's breath, desiring that kiss, but still not touching.

"You know— Darko's a talented kisser." Maxum spoke aloud, and the groan in his throat gave away the obvious struggle with his own lust.

"So is Paris." Diesel added. He could see the two men were definitely into each other. That they were familiar with each other's bodies made the allure all the stronger. But Diesel also knew Paris wouldn't do anything without him. He doubted Darko would either.

He rubbed at his cock, then adjusted it in his jeans, "Your place or mine?"

"Mine's closer." The answer came so fast he nearly spat it out.

"Yours it is." Diesel gritted his teeth, barely restraining his agreement. It was damn near enough he teetered on having his way right there in the middle of the club.

The two men instantly headed out, cutting straight through the crowd toward their men. The air got thicker and heavier with carnal intent, and their men saw them coming. Diesel stepped behind Paris, sliding his arms around his lover's waist and following the rhythm, his body moving in. Maxum mirrored the same motions behind Darko, and the four connected for a tantric moment. Diesel's eyes locked on Maxum just as Paris leaned back into him. *Fuck, he wasn't even going to make it out the door.*

"Let's go."

~ * ~ * ~ * ~ * ~ * ~

The lust building among the four of them had already become toxic back at the club, but now, as Diesel sat back in the plush cushions of the leather sofa, the feral base need to feel all three of them pressed against him had taken on a heightened sensation that buzzed under his skin like static. Sitting catty-corner from him was Maxum. The glass walls of the high tower suite, overlooking the cityscape below, were a licentious backdrop only Maxum could deliver to the heady mix. But it was what was standing between them and that view that truly had Diesel's cock painfully hard, making even his loose fitting jeans feel uncomfortable. He felt as the Dominus often did; he was about to entertain his host in a way that only he could provide. And it would top the spectacular backdrop. "Undress him, Paris. Give us a show." Diesel commanded, then spread his arms out over the back of the sofa, relaxing back so he, too, could soak it all in.

From the moment Paris stepped up behind Darko, reaching around his front to break the first button from his

410

shirt, sending it pinging across the floor, it would seem Maxum forgot all about the dark ale he had intended to drink. And was all about the man who'd started living with him since the start of the New Year.

~ * ~

Paris stepped around Darko, taking over the scene with the orders given. This was his stage, and he knew what to do with it. If there had ever been a moment when he feared his life with Diesel might be dull or tame in comparison to his own wild, bachelor ways prior to their commitment, he had been wrong. Diesel knew what to do and when to unleash him, and Paris had yet to look back. Not once.

But even then, he never thought Diesel might share in more than just the one-on-one carnal lust they shared outside of their companionship with Katianna and Trenton. Not that he would have regretted it, had it remained that way.

Paris and Diesel had been so into each other— kind of like being on their own honeymoon, that he'd forgotten Diesel actually had a taste for the smaller sized orgy. Perhaps because he was also so reserved that he rarely fed that fetish. Now, here he stood with the handsome bike rider, Darko Laszkovi— a near replica of his older brother, Pyotr— with orders to undress him. So, Paris wasn't about to refuse his man of his Taboo pleasures.

He slipped his arms under Darko's, drawing his hands up Darko's chest in a slow path— up the rippling ab muscles hiding under his shirt. Touch and play was for the entertainment of their men. It was a drug so intoxicating, it threatened to inebriate Paris' brain cells on the spot. It was a good thing his hands knew what to do without thought, and his fingers, one by one, opened the buttons of

Darko's shirt— then one slid in and caressed a nipple still hidden from view. The movement of his arm became an artistic suggestion of what was actually happening behind the fine cloth. Accentuated by a deep inhale from his subject.

Paris glanced, heavy-lidded, at the two men lounging back in front of them, watching— their chests sucking in deep, slow breaths. Maxum was already struggling to remind himself to drink his beer. Diesel remained forever in control of himself. "Wait until you feast your eyes on my man's cock." Paris whispered to Darko, wishing Diesel would just go ahead and whip the beautiful beast out.

Paris rolled his head against Darko's, letting his breath flow over the shell of his ear like an added whisper. Darko's hands floated to the buttons on his jeans, but Paris quickly flicked them off. "*Mmmm*— not yet."

He undid the last few shirt buttons and both hands quickly came up, grasped the fine pec muscles, defined by years of professional rowing, and he squeezed to add some rough to the sultry view. He next swept up over Darko's shoulders, scooping the shirt up with his hands and peeled it back, letting it drop down Darko's arms and to the floor.

Immediately, Paris dropped his lips to the bronze skin of Darko's shoulder, sweeping his lips across it faintly, like a paint brush. His hands trailed down Darko's arms and then took his hands in his to guide them where he wanted them— one up and reaching back to hold Paris' head, the other down to grope at Paris' own crotch. A sway of his hips was all it took to turn on a wave emotion, and their dance resumed from the club's dancefloor, while Darko's hands went to work on Paris' body as he went back to undressing Darko's. He popped the top button of his faded jeans, then the next—

—and the next.

Again, Darko's hand went down to assist, and again, Paris flicked him away.

Paris knew not to rush this— this was the eye candy Diesel loved. Paris could tell by the way Maxum had forfeited his beer for his cock— that he did too.

Paris flattened a palm over Darko's stomach, rippled and flat like the perfect washboard, then peeled the corners of Darko's jeans away. Within, a thick cock was already bulging in his briefs. Paris brushed his fingertips along the waist band, just barely grazing the engorged mushroom cap that peeked out from them. He felt the dewy drops, soaked his fingertips with the moisture, and then he brought them up to Darko's lips.

"Oh, fuck." Maxum groaned at the sight of Darko's tongue coming out to lick, then suck two of Paris' fingers into his mouth.

Darko's hands fumbled with the belt around Paris' hips, but finally managed to get it loose, and he instantly dug in and wrapped his hand around the strained rod of throbbing flesh. Paris gasped and bit down on Darko's shoulder just then, and dropped his hand down to mirror Darko's action. He pushed his hand down into Darko's jeans and took hold of the cock, pulling it free and began stroking him.

He ground his hips against Darko's ass, trapping the man's grip between them and shivered, feeling every heady wave of his lust bounding up another notch. *That was it.* Paris grabbed hold of Darko's jeans and dropped them down his legs in a flash, giving very little time for Darko to pull his legs free, before Paris was quickly walking them forward until they were both standing in front of Maxum. Paris pushed Darko over and then dove down over the exposed puckered hole.

~ * ~

Maxum's cock bobbed at the very sound of Darko's loud moan as he fell forward into his lap. Right away he searched out Maxum's mouth and swooped in for a greedy kiss, just as Paris did with Darko's ass.

Maxum gave Darko the deep wet kiss he sought out, but not for long. He had to watch some of this. He tore their mouths apart and twisted to watch the man he'd been told, on more than one occasion, had the looks of a fallen angel, who now had his face buried in his lover's ass. *God, he was gonna come just from watching it.*

~ * ~

Darko pressed against the sofa, crushing his cock, already leaking from his heightened state. He let out several more moans, one after the other, while he moved his hands down, grappling at Maxum's body, anchoring his heightened sensations while feeling Paris' tongue probing deep into his hole then flattening out, washing over it. Only to be followed with some butterfly sensation that threatened him with madness. *Fuck, it was incredible.*

He tore through Maxum's shirt without any shame for the act. It wasn't the first time he'd damaged one of his fiancé's shirts, and it certainly would not be the last. He just didn't have the patience to undo any buttons right now and did what any demanding, horny man would do— all in one full rip.

Darko sent rendered buttons scattering and bouncing across the room. He dropped his head, started licking and biting in a frenzy around Maxum's chest, then worked his way down to the cock his lover still gripped. Darko pushed Maxum's hand aside and took over the attention with his mouth.

How it happened that none of them had paid attention, but now more than one pair of hands were tugging on Maxum's slacks, then his briefs, then Paris' hand came reaching between Darko's legs and sought contact with Maxum's naked flesh. Vanishing under his bottom, and then a hiss overhead said Paris had found what he was looking for. Darko leaned forward, allowing Paris full, maximized reach, but lost the cock in his mouth in the process. His attempt to regain it was thwarted when Maxum grabbed Darko's head and pulled him up for a kiss.

"Stop. You are going to make me cum too soon." There was growl from Darko's lips.

"Why should you worry? I'll make you cum again, even if you do." But then Maxum's eyes weren't on him, they were riveted off to the side.

Darko followed his gaze, finding Diesel stepping up, his clothes missing, and *oh fuck,* the cock jutting out from his tattooed body was unlike anything Darko had ever seen. For he had never seen Diesel undressed before. He caught a glimpse of the foil pack in Diesel's fingers before he vanished behind Paris. Now all Darko could do was surrender to the tongue that continued to molest his hole, and he became entrapped in the eyes of the man he loved as they both became drunk with the evening.

~ * ~

Diesel stepped up behind Paris and pulled him up on his knees, then reached around him, taking his time rolling the condom on his Fallen Angel, who was reveling in the seductive act Diesel was allowing him to put on. Paris nearly went limp, falling back against him, dropped his head back on Diesel's shoulder, and felt his lips press against his neck. Paris hummed as Diesel stroked him a few times to assure the condom held. He reached out and drew a finger over Darko's well soaked sphincter, then switched it out for his thumb, padded over it teasingly, then pushed in.

He hooked the man, feeling his hot insides, then pulled out and positioned Paris into place. He watched over Paris' shoulder, enjoying the view, and then using his own hips pressed against Paris' ass, he pushed him forward, sinking Paris' cock into Darko's body.

~ * ~

Darko did all he could just to catch his breath as his body stretched to accommodate the thick cock sliding its way inside his body. "Oh fuck." He breathed the words out, only to get swallowed up by Maxum, who was clearly enjoying this. The deviant grin on his face said as much. *Fucking sex addict he was, but then again, so was he.* But where Darko liked hard and raw, Maxum liked to string his orgasms out and torture him. Said it was like watching a painting have an orgasm. *Whatever.* All Darko knew right then was Paris' cock was a good measure bigger than Maxum's, and it felt amazing as it was slowly stuffed inside him.

"Mmmm, you're beautiful." Maxum hummed, "I don't get to see you so overwhelmed too often."

"Shut up and get your ass over here, so I can get inside you." Darko growled. He had every intention of making Maxum feel just as overwhelmed as he did.

"Mmmm, I love it even more when you're hangry."

Darko was going to say something, but suddenly Paris was passing a condom forward, then he felt the Fallen Angel's hot breath tickling his neck behind his ear.

"Keep it clean. I plan to swallow every inch of you, later."

Oh, that just did it for him. Darko snatched the condom, tore the foil open in his teeth, and quickly wrapped himself. He hooked Maxum's legs and yanked his ass to the edge of the sofa, gave him a few gentle nudges, then slowly began to push in.

Paris didn't really give him much time. Or, perhaps it was Diesel, because his balls had just barely made contact with Maxum's skin and suddenly Paris slammed into his own backside. There was a chorus of growls and moans, and a chaotic rhythm bumped and gyrated each of them, all daisy-chained together in a blissful fuck-fest of four.

~ * ~

Paris was in slut city heaven, sandwiched between Diesel and Darko, taking the thick cock deep in his ass while he sank into Darko's. Paris let out a string of growls and heavy groans he knew was sure to spur Diesel on, and likely the other two as well.

He rolled his body like he was moving on the dance floor— gyrating back and forth— taking and giving. Diesel hardly had to move, but did so occasionally to slam in deep. A deliberately deviant shove for Paris, for being as thorough as he was in the pleasure zones that fed and satisfied Diesel's tasty taboos as completely as he did. Or, so Paris told himself. He dropped his head back and stole a kiss from Diesel then tore away, pulled Darko back and passed the kiss to him. It didn't stop until Maxum came out the winner of the prized kiss.

~ * ~

Diesel monitored them all. He wasn't looking for the long, drawn out scene— rather, he wanted to slam them with an intense euphoria to boggle the mind and sate the cock. The top sensations, and plenty of them. No savoring right now— he wanted their senses spun around and drunk on lust. The chain was a nice warm up, but it was time to move them all around.

He eased out of Paris, gave him a slight pull on his shoulder, and when he looked, Diesel rolled his head to indicate the other end of the sofa. He obviously didn't need to say anything else. The devilish curl in Paris' lips said he knew what to do.

Diesel discarded the condom into the waste basket, then rolled a fresh clean one on, tossing another packet to Maxum this time. Paris took his place on the end of the sofa, placing his head on the very edge, and hiked a leg on the back, opening himself up for Maxum.

Diesel waved Darko to him, taking a moment just to enjoy touching his body and looking him over. He let his gaze drift over to Maxum and watched his wealthy friend do much the same to Paris, just before Maxum returned the gaze to watch Diesel with Darko. "You ready for this?" Diesel asked Maxum.

"Are you kidding?" Darko cut in, "I'm engaged to a dirty, little pervert. Of course he's ready." Darko chuckled. "But go easy on me. I've never had the likes of your size before."

"I'll be gentle— for a bit." Diesel smirked then turned Darko around, guiding him to rest his knees down on the sofa, one on each side of Paris' head.

"If only I had known ahead of time. I would have set up camera equipment so I could watch this over and over again later."

"I knew you were a pervert." Darko growled at Maxum's comment. A little bit of apprehension, over the cock that was about to fuck him, showed on his face.

Maxum leaned forward, caught Darko by the neck, and pulled him over for a kiss. It was brief, as Paris moved under Darko and began his seduction with his tongue, while Diesel lined up behind him and began working his way inside Darko's hole.

Diesel watched over Darko's body as Maxum turned his attention to Paris now. A nice touch when Maxum took Paris' legs and folded them in until his knees nearly touched his shoulders. It must have created a happy groan, because Darko suddenly let out a slight one of his own. That could only come from Paris' talented mouth. Such splendor also helped Darko from tensing up as Diesel continued slowly to work his cock inside.

Paris had loosened him up, but for Diesel's girth, Darko was still tight.

"Oh fuck, that cock's huge. God damn it." Darko cursed with a heavy breath.

Maxum was already pumping into Paris, but he still had the advantage of leaning over Paris' folded legs and kiss Darko whenever Maxum felt like it. At least up until his brain cells weren't able to make such conducive decision making.

The room had warmed, becoming aromatic with the scent of sweat, cologne, and sex. The wide layout of the room, bordered with the glass walls that looked out over the city some fifty floors or more below, only added to the intoxicating ambience, creating some god-like euphoria to the whole pile of sex. Diesel had to admit, he understood now why Maxum liked it here so much.

Diesel's bottoming out in Darko's ass was announced with a loud *oh fuck,* yet Darko had somehow managed enough brain function to drop down into a sixty-nine with Paris and sucked on the Fallen Angel's cock.

Maxum was leaning back, sitting on his heels. His knees tucked in all the way under Paris' ass, and his cock throttled all the way into Paris' hole, allowing Darko some head room and granting himself a view of his own to watch.

Diesel was able to see it all and began to ride the Laszkovi ass that had been turned over to him, adding his own pleasure into the mix.

A cacophony of sounds was added to the sensual sights and scents created by the fucking and sucking foursome. A blur of moans, groans, gasping breaths, and curses. And from the sound of them, none of them were going to last much longer, so it seemed futile to try.

The only thing that slowed him for a moment was the glancing lick Diesel felt from Paris' naughty tongue as it reached for Diesel's undercarriage. The holdup didn't stop him long though. He wanted to let loose and soon did so, picking up speed in his hips as he pistoned into Darko.

It soon became impossible for the man to remain on Paris' cock. But Maxum picked up the slack, taking Paris' cock in his hand and began fisting him. Darko at least managed to deliver some intermittent licks to the hard flesh, still red and angry when it hadn't been allowed to cum earlier.

Maxum dropped his head back, losing his ability to watch any longer, his own control succumbing to the overwhelming pleasure they all felt.

Paris' hand appeared from under the pile, grabbing for a hold on Darko's hips and pulling him down to him again. The moan that escaped Darko told it all, and Diesel began pushing in even harder, essentially forcing Darko to fuck Paris' mouth.

Maxum was suddenly pushing up on his knees, lifting Paris' legs with him in an arm lock. His hips slammed against Paris' ass, and then Diesel heard his lover's deep throaty approval escape from under everyone, just seconds before his cock shot out white cords of seed over his abs, and most likely onto Darko's face.

The whole carnal scene was followed with a cry from Maxum, like he was fighting his way to the top of a mountain, and his victory cry was as much pain as it was pleasure.

Darko's peak came next. He barely managed to hold himself up on extended arms, his back arching then humping over, as he growled out with a hard shudder.

Only Diesel was left, and he had no intentions of stopping either. He rode Darko's quake out, pawed over him to enjoy every nuance of the man's quivers, while his cock took immense pleasure in the clamping muscles of Darko's inner walls. It almost did Diesel in, but he held out for his intentions. To send Darko into sexual madness for the pleasure of his partner.

Diesel kicked a knee up on the back of the sofa, catching his weight with his hand placed there as well. Now, his cock pitched forward into Darko's body, giving an added angle toward his prostate wall and an additional inch, before bottoming out inside him again.

"Oh fuck!" Darko gasped, unable to rise back up now that Diesel was bent over him. The pounding never slowed. Locking them both in a whirlwind that was slamming them both in sexual bliss.

"Fuck yes." Diesel growled over him. And then he felt something quite unexpected. A moist finger around the base of his cock. Fumbling at first, trying to make contact in all the movement, but then pushed into Darko's already stretched hold.

"Oh, fuck, fuck, fuck!" Darko nearly heaved with the curses. And even Diesel let out a few as well. Just the one finger alone tightened a space that already fit like a vice around his cock. Now he could feel the knuckle of Paris' finger grind against the sensitized nerve endings that raced alongside the hard underside ridge of his cock. Only, Diesel knew that wasn't *all* Paris was after. He was after Darko's glory spot.

~ * ~

Darko gripped the back of the sofa. The muscles in his arm flexed, becoming corded as he held on so he wouldn't topple over. His own breath was somewhere between a growl and a hyperventilating plea, "Fuck! Make him stop!"

The sensation the two men were forcing him to endure had his mind spinning frantically, with everything heightening to a whirlwind of erotic pleasure that he could not grasp. He reached out, caught Maxum by the neck, and forcibly pulled his lover to him as he slammed their mouths together in an attempt to anchor himself.

~ * ~

Maxum gladly took the kiss, but then ripped away from him and took Darko's head in both hands, holding him out so he could watch his lover come part. Darko's deep cobalt-blue eyes rolled back while frantic moans rode out on heavy gasps for air. Each sound climbed up a note, and with a little less air, as Darko rode up the coil of energy Diesel and Paris worked him over with until it peaked. Maxum absorbed it all as he watched this sculpted body of his favorite man melt before him in pure unadulterated ecstasy.

Diesel's head launched back on his shoulders and he let out a roar, just as Darko let out a sound that couldn't be described. *It was a fucking beautiful sound.*

There was some considerable mixing of kissing and fawning after that. Then, the four men miraculously managed their way to the bedroom and collapsed in a tangle of legs and arms on the expansive sized bed, unable to discern which limb belonged to what lover. Nor did it matter, as they all drifted off into post-coital bliss, every need fed and every lust slaked.

~ * ~ * ~ * ~ * ~ * ~

CHAPTER TWENTY-EIGHT

~ * ~ * ~ * ~ * ~ * ~

Paris found Diesel downstairs in what was part gym, part recreation room, and part dungeon. To Diesel and Marcus, the last two were used for the same thing. Paris, however, didn't agree. Nevertheless, Diesel was down here, and it was more the sounds Paris heard that had drawn him down to investigate.

The large TV screen mounted on the wall was on, displaying a full out scene between a Dom and submissive. Only, the man watching from the love seat didn't seem to be doing so for the sake of self-pleasuring, as he scribbled something down on a steno pad. Paris knew those body signs by heart. The very same actions when he watched self-defense tactic tapes. Diesel was studying it, like he was watching a documentary on the sci-fi channel or something. And next to the TV, on the stereo unit shelf, sat a stack of DVD cases, all waiting their turn.

"What's this?"

Diesel glanced over his shoulder from where he sat, "Interview tapes for the resort."

"You're doing my job now?"

"Nooo— I'm doing my job."

"We agreed I was still going to keep my job at the resort, though."

"And you are. But one of our Dommes isn't returning this coming season due to health issues, and I have to find a replacement."

Paris dropped down beside him, snatched the remote from his hand, and clicked the pause button. "That is still a detail of my job."

Diesel grabbed the remote back and hit play, "Not when it requires hiring the Dominant players, it isn't."

"Since when?" Paris tried to grab it back, only to get countered with an evasive movement.

Diesel blocked him, "Since you still haven't grasped the full inner understanding of the play between the Dom and sub."

"I know the rules."

"I'm not talking about the rules. I am talking about spotting a Dom who knows how to take their subject to a level of release when the sub surrenders themselves completely and just allow themselves to feel what the Dom deems them to need."

"I don't get it."

"Precisely. Which is why you are not the one selecting the replacement."

"Then explain it to me." Paris was a control freak about his job and every aspect of it. He didn't like being intercepted, even by the man who was essentially his boss, without proper reasoning. And even still, he didn't like anyone doing *his* job for him.

"It's not something that can be explained or can be pulled from a book. It's something to be experienced."

Paris stiffened. They'd broached this topic before. Diesel was, in every sense and definition of the phrase, a Master of Doms, and he enjoyed his role. He had a need for it, just like his enjoyment of orgies, except the need to dominate was something he required. The other was a choice, and Paris had not been so willing to help fulfil the need. "I can't. I like pleasure, not pain."

"There is pleasure within the pain."

"That's bullshit; a sub submits to satisfy the Dom, but there isn't any pleasure in it, not with the whips and stuff."

"How can you be certain?" Diesel asked, turning the emphasis on Paris and giving him a chance to explain his rejection that such an experience might actually exist for some.

"No one really gets off on getting smacked and caned."

"I assure you, for some, they do."

"How?"

"Endorphins. Do you remember much from your experience with Trenton's cane?"

"Yes and no. I had the shot of absinthe, so I was tripping."

"The Absinthe was merely to help you and Katianna let go of your anxieties. A step we don't encourage often, but in highly controlled environments, it can be allowed. Your submission had already been given well before we started drinking, which allowed the exception. Do you remember pain?"

"Yes and no."

"Do you remember pleasure?"

"Yes."

"See?"

"That proves nothing."

"Then let me prove it again. This time without the Absinthe. Just you and me."

"What do I have to do?

"Submit to me. Let me take you to a place you've never truly been."

Paris' head now rattled with what Diesel was saying. It was true he didn't understand. He couldn't grasp what people desired in it, but if there was pleasure to be obtained, he wanted to know what it was. He wanted to experience it. So he nodded.

"What do you say?' Diesel asked. His voice was steady and calm— even gentle.

"Green."

"Thank you. Now you may go over there to the weight machine, undress, and then take a seat on the bench, facing into the tower."

Paris sucked in a deep breath, tried to dispel his sudden apprehension, and went to the bench. There was nothing fancy about it, other than it having pretty much all the latest workout options one could buy in an all-inclusive workout tower. It was also brand new, having bought it himself when he'd moved in. So, he knew there were no hidden surprises in its mechanical design. Nothing that was suddenly going to entrap or enclose him. Yet, he somehow felt as if it could, just because Diesel would tell it to.

He'd just finished putting his clothes on the nearby chair and sat down as directed, when Diesel came up beside him with half a dozen colored handcuffs in his hand.

"You think I need that many?" Paris looked at them then to Diesel.

"The first set is for you." He answered him then locked the green one around Paris' wrist, letting its mate dangle. "The rest are for me."

"I don't get it. You mean, you're going to wear them?"

"You know better than that. I like the colors, but I also like the sound they make when they clang against each other." And to prove his point, he moved the five still in his hand so they slid against each other, creating a distinct sound of skidding metal, while their mates clanked from the movement. "So the first set is for restraint, and the rest are aesthetic, for my pleasure."

Oddly, Paris found the sound alluring as well. Some madness he had started to develop that made him enjoy bondage. He nodded then. Diesel just looked at him, waiting for the spoken agreement. Paris nodded again, "Green."

And from there, Paris was fitted with two more sets of handcuffs. One orange, the other purple. Then up his arm went, as Diesel hooked all three of the mates to the cuffs around Paris' wrist to the straight bar that hung over his head, from the braided steel cable that ran into the machine, along its hoists, then down to the stack of weights that were locked in their station.

Next was his left arm. A red, a yellow, and a blue cuff. Up they went, until both of his arms were suspended by six loosely fitted handcuffs that gleamed in a rainbow of colored chrome.

"Breathe deep and steady, Paris."

Paris suddenly sucked in a deep breath and let it out. He hadn't realized he'd been holding it until then, but sure enough he had been. His mind tracking the movements of his man. Worrying over what was next. He felt Diesel's hand on his arms, sliding down in a gentle connection, then falling behind his neck, holding him there firmly.

"Remember, nothing is going to happen to you that you haven't already agreed to before. No harm is going to come to you." Diesel spoke behind him. Then his hand moved down his back. A calming touch. Paris knew that touch, he'd felt it many times. He'd also watched the Patronus touch others as he prepped the subs at the club to become entangled in his web of silk ropes. Diesel was right, it wasn't anything he hadn't seen before. He'd even submitted to the rope binding art. But there had never been any pain. The one time Paris had allowed that was down at the resort last summer. So again, nothing he hadn't felt before, yet somehow this time felt different. It was just the two of them. No audience, not even Trenton or Kat. Just him and his Patronus.

His feet were pulled out behind him so his knees hovered just over the floor. It pitched his body weight slightly forward, and he became more reliant on the bar overhead to hold him upright. He felt soft leather shackles placed on his ankles, then heard the distinct sound of more handcuffs. A couple of tugs and snaps to one leg, then repeated to his other. He twitched a leg, heard the clink of cuffs against cuffs, and realized Diesel had used a few more to bind the shackles together.

"Breathe deep and steady." Another reminder came from his Patronus, and Paris did what he could to obey.

It was strange to say the least. An odd feeling came over him now, just as before, when he'd turned himself over to Diesel's ropes. The stripping away of power. Or freedom of movement. As each step was meant to take more and more away from him.

"Just breathe and feel, Paris."

That was what he always said. It's what he meant. And it was exactly what began. The loss of mobility somehow locked Paris away to rely heavily on his other senses. What he couldn't see, he tracked with his ears. What he couldn't hear often shimmered over his skin in a reassuring touch, that Patronus was still there and still in control. *Nothing was going to happen that he didn't want to happen.* Paris' only role was to feel. *Oh, and to breathe.*

He felt a mix of soft and coarse hairs on his back. A horse tail flogger most likely, then the first whip across his flesh landed. Just the slightest sting, then another and another. Patronus repositioned each flogging swish a little higher— a little lower— from left to right and back again. Fast, then a few slow swats with a little more power to them, until Paris' back began to feel a solid sheen of sting. Not painful, but a slow and steady migration over what may have been fifteen or so minutes into discomfort.

When it stopped, he was rewarded with the connection of Diesel's hands. He slid his palms around, petting Paris, savoring the warmth radiating from his skin.

"It's a good start. Now we move to the next."

That statement was soon followed with the loud snap of leather. The involuntary jump in Paris' back was unpreventable, even when he heard it the second time.

SNAP.

Then he felt it— a wide strap of leather slid across his back. A glancing taste that was meant more to instigate intimidation. The combination of sound and introductory feel was all part of the game. It amped Paris' senses up higher. Everything inside him kicking into red alert that what was about to happen was going to be excruciating. He pulled on the handcuffs, making them rattle and clank overhead. His back arched as if he could crawl away out of range. Even though nothing happened. Just the slow smooth slip and slide of the wide leather strop over his back and shoulders.

"Breathe and feel." Patronus reminded him, and Paris had no sooner forced himself to take the breath that he felt the first strike.

It was nowhere near the strike of pain he'd prepared for. Just a slap on sunburned skin.

And then he felt it again.

The second strike came from the other direction. Like lazy slaps of a soft flat noodle over his skin, doing nothing more than building another slow layer of red burning on his back. He felt warm, and after another fifteen minutes or so of the easy slaps from the strop, it stopped, and once more he felt Diesel's hands. Only this time, Paris felt removed. Like he wasn't entirely attached to his body. He felt it, yet again— he didn't. Or it wasn't actually him. Just him, pretending he felt it as he listened to someone else at the club surrendering to Trenton or Dane's dominance.

A fist closed into Paris' hair at the back of his head and yanked his head back. His Patronus coming over to steal a kiss from him, and it was the best kiss Paris could recall in a while. Hungry and barbaric.

He was released, then the fist relaxed to grip the back of Paris' neck. The small gesture of claim he was accustomed to. It spoke more than words to him and strangely always comforted him.

"Again, Paris."

The hand was gone and the strop returned to his back. This time, a little harder, and the strikes more rapid. One, then another, and another, and another. He couldn't count them. He was glad he was never told to do so, or he would have failed. Sensation became everything, and the strikes of leather blurred into one another. No longer discernable. Just the radiation that spread out from his back and over the rest of his body. He broke out into a sheen of sweat and became lightheaded, and then Paris became strangely aware of his cock, slapping on the bench like a bat. He glanced down, seeing it jutting from his body. *Bounce— bounce— bounce—*

A small pool of precum under it.

His body swayed, creating more of the music from the steel handcuffs on his arms and his feet as he shifted about. His back turned into a plate of fire, and he had no recollection as to how it happened. It was as if he'd slept through some of it somehow. Awakened only because his cock and balls demanded it of him as he rocked his hips back and forth, grinding himself down on the bench to *rub* out a little more contact— just a little more friction to take him over the edge.

He felt drunk with the melee of pain, rattling metal, stinging heat, and the sounds of his own gruff moans and heavy breaths. Even the scent of his own sweat, heating his cologne, turned him on further. Making the stormy mix of it all culminate into a pleasure he'd never experienced before.

"Oh god, I don't understand!" Paris cried out.

"Yes, you do." The whipping stopped and Diesel was suddenly there, at his ear. His arms wrapping around Paris, holding him. Diesel took hold of Paris' cock, and it hardly took any effort, just a few strokes of Patronus' fist, tightening around Paris' shaft, and Paris came in his hand.

~ * ~ * ~ * ~ * ~ * ~

CHAPTER TWENTY-NINE

~ * ~ * ~ * ~ * ~ * ~

Trenton and Katianna hadn't been home more than a week since they returned from their honeymoon. But the trip had made her spoiled, and no sooner had they gotten back, she was in trouble with him and he was withholding her orgasms from her as punishment.

She'd even suffered through a full demonstration scene Thursday night at Club Pain, and still he did not free her from her torment. Even surrendering at his feet Friday for the entire night, hoping to gain some redemption, had not bought her favoritism or an early pardon.

Now, here it was Tuesday of the following week, and she was in agony. Hell, she was willing to hump the sofa arm if she thought she could get away with it, but Trenton wouldn't even let her go with Paris when he went out to run the daily errands. Something he normally let her do. *Being grounded sucked. So what, if last time, when she was on body restrictions, she'd gone and purchased a pocket vibe? Damned if he didn't catch her before she could put it to good use anyway. And he tortured her with it as part of her added-on discipline. That was after he gave her twenty-five spankings with his bare hand. It was hardly fair such things were held against her this time.*

Trenton was focused on his work, trying to catch up after their two-week-long vacation. He simply didn't notice when she texted Paris, from her regular spot on the sofa with her laptop and stack of notebooks, to request an emergency *save-your-BFFL* toy.

She and Paris had grown so close since he moved home with Diesel, and he was her best-friend. Her girl-friend and guy-friend all rolled into one. They often cuddled up together wherever they were, and she would read to him her latest story additions. He even gave her lots of new ideas when they were out shopping, which seemed to be practically all the time.

Paris loved to shop, and he also loved to cut up as they did. The man knew no shame and took considerable pleasure in bringing both men and women to sheer crimson with his words or public actions of teasing. Playfulness he had to express when he had the chance to counter his time with Diesel, who didn't tolerate public displays of affection. Though Diesel had relaxed some, allowing a few kisses from time to time, those were never enough for the lusty Paris, who thrived on shock and awe. His peacock feathers were simply too brilliant.

But, Paris wasn't just her best-friend; he was also her partner in crime. Together they managed to scheme behind their Masters' backs to look out for each other's needs— well, for hers at least, Paris had a way of just breaking the bonds and pouncing on Diesel for what he wanted when Diesel held out for too long. Katianna had no such luck. Even her pouting was losing its power over the Dominus.

She felt the muted buzz under her leg, where she had safely tucked her cell phone so that when the response came in, her Dominus wouldn't hear it— or so she hoped. Her eyes shifted from her computer screen to her husband on the phone, talking with someone and going over some issues while jotting down details onto a pad.

"And how long do you expect to be in the States?" Trenton asked someone on the other end. That meant a client was coming over from abroad, and they usually came with all kinds of trouble.

She fished her cell out from under her leg, keeping it flat on a notebook beside her, using her body to block the view of it from Trenton. Trenton was pulling up something on his computer, then conveying details to the person he was talking to. Coast all clear. She dropped her gaze in much the same way she would if looking up a word or detail on her cheat sheet.

Txt: Left you a present in the ladies' room— Paris

She grinned, but quickly muted it from her face, then deleted the text from her storage. *Something she had to be more mindful of, since she and Paris had learned the hard way.*

~ * ~ * ~ * ~ * ~ * ~

Diesel came up as soon as he got the text from Paris that he was back, both with lunch *and* Paris' eager *Blue-Veined Junket Pumper*— as he put it so eloquently. Clearly, Paris didn't have enough to occupy him that he had to come up with such entertaining nicknames for his peacocking erection. Nevertheless, it was perfect timing, since Diesel was hungry for his lover as well.

Diesel leaned back against the desk, letting Paris tear into Diesel's jeans to have some fun. Up until Diesel noticed the bag from a favorite adult novelty store on the file cabinet next to the desk. "You went to the Body Hut Shop?"

"Yes." Paris didn't let the question deter him from what Diesel had started, pulling his pants open and snagging Diesel's hand to caress his growing erection. "We're almost out of massage oil at the house. Some more gel and those ultra-lite condoms in your size for here at the office. Plus, I browsed over the latest toys, since I was there."

"Is that all you got?" Diesel questioned him suspiciously, already peeking inside the bag, and not seeing much of anything in it.

Paris grinned at him, "Of course not. Since when do I go in that store and only buy a few things?"

"Uhm-humm." Diesel leaned across the desk and punched in Trenton's extension on the speaker phone.

"*Yeah?*"Trenton's voice came over the phone.

"Where's the Mouse?" Diesel inquired to his brother.

They both heard the ruffling of papers as Trenton likely shifted closer toward the desk phone, "*Restroom, why?*"

Diesel kept his gaze fixed on Paris as he smirked and shook his head.

Paris was instantly making a face, "Oh, come on— you're not trying to suggest—" his exclamation trailed off. He wasn't about to say it out loud since he wasn't any good at lying. And when it came to Diesel and Trenton, Paris even knew not to try. Bad enough they were making the little Mouse suffer with some extended humor of their own, but he sure as hell didn't want to be put in the same boat. He would at least play it off, all the way up to the line, to try and protect her, or maybe, at the least, stall the Deez-Trent task force long enough that she'd get to put her emergency play thing to good use before being apprehended.

Nevertheless, Paris could see it in Diesel's face. The two of them had gotten wise to him and Kat. They were already caught and there was no getting around it.

Diesel leaned toward the speakerphone with a slight tattletale chuckle, "Paris made a stop at the Hut." He hung up then turned to Paris, "I get a free one for that."

~ * ~ * ~ * ~ * ~ * ~

Trenton jumped out of his desk chair and headed down the hall. It had not slipped his mind how Katianna had snuck behind his back to purchase a pocket finger-vibe once before, hoping to evade her assigned punishment and sneak in an orgasm. Now, she was chancing it again.

He found her in the restroom, struggling to get the package open without any success. He stopped inside the door and leaned against its frame, folding his arms over his chest. "What are you doing, Mouse?"

Katianna's eyes flared with more frustration than they did with any surprise of having gotten caught. She slammed the package on the counter with both hands then took a definitive step back. "Nothing." She pouted, pushing her bottom lip out, before muttering more, "Stupid packages are impossible to get open." Her brows dropped, shading over the pale blue eyes he loved, even when they were moody, as they were now.

He kicked off the door and stepped over to the counter to claim the package. He pulled a pocket knife from his slacks, making fast work of its protective shielding from mouse tampering. Paris had gone all out, selecting a sleek ergo-dynamic vibrator. It was an attractive toy, even by Trenton's standards. A matte black with a soft curved surface to it. It looked, even felt, high priced. Not that he minded, as long as the toy was worth it, and he knew of only one way to test it.

He collected the batteries already set out on the counter, loaded them in, and turned to face his little slave. "Stand still." He commanded then stepped closer until there was little space between them. He turned the vibrator on and held it before her, then touched it to her forehead and slowly guided it down the center of her face, along the side of her nose and over her lips, pausing to trace over each feature before continuing south. His gaze heating up just watching the trail he drew down her body— her throat— then between her breasts—

The breath that hitched in her chest was spurred on by the anticipation he created in her body. He used the vibrating wand to draw circles over her belly, and then traced over the waistband of her panties, until finally directing it to his point of destination.

Katianna let out a loud gasp as he pushed it between her thighs and drew it up to place pressure right under her clit. He drew it in and out, sawing it across her entrance, seeing it all in his mind how it pressed her wet lips open through the fabric. Seeing her little button swell. He might have to put her up on his desk after this so he could admire his handy work while he finished his paperwork for the day. After all, he wasn't expecting any clients in today.

Katianna's breath was quickening with sharp little intakes. He loved the small nuances of sound she made— it told him she was getting close. "Look at me, wife." He commanded her again, using her new title. *God, he loved calling her that.* But it did not take away from the fact she was still his. His Unicorn slave.

Pale blues, turned up at him through curled lashes, were inked out with dilated pupils. Her breath quivered and he instantly pulled the vibrating gadget from her body. He wore a sinister smile creased over his face as he enjoyed his torturing play with her body.

~ * ~

Katianna held on to the building sensation between her thighs. If she fussed now, she would lose it. Trenton's gaze drifted down her stomach and the sheer pink lace she wore, then lingered between her thighs, enjoying her suffering like a Cheshire cat gloating over a riddle that could not be solved. She squeezed her thighs together, trying to ease the ache. That only made the desire sharper. *She needed relief, not intensity.*

She shifted a hand to the lace panties that shielded her pussy and pressed in, rotated her fingers over her sensitive flesh, caught the ball of her hood piercing and tumbled it over the engorged nerves. She gasped. Euphoria rolled through her as tingles danced under her skin. The ache sweetened. *God, she was so close—*

~ * ~

Trenton snatched her wrist, holding it frozen in place with a tight squeeze, with just enough pressure to lift her fingers an inch away from her body. Teasing her with her own hand, "We've been through this before, my slave. Your orgasms are mine. I say when and how. Don't think for one second that just because I've made you my wife, you're allowed to cum without my permission."

Her eyes flared with heat, and he knew what that meant. He'd come to learn that the more depravity he caused her to suffer, the more will she got. He'd also learned just how much control over the muscles of her theca she had and how she could, at times, clamp her body into its own orgasm with only a minute amount of external stimulation. Considering he'd kept her deprived since they'd gotten back from their honeymoon, he was certain she would do so now.

Not willing to be bested by his saucy bride, Trenton swept her up, tossed her over his shoulder, stuffed the fancy vibrator into his back pocket, and carried her out to his office.

Kat wriggled in his hold, just enough to reach his back pocket, and managed to steal it back before he returned her to her feet inside his office, and thus began a game of cat and mouse until the building filled with screams and laughter.

~ * ~ * ~ * ~ * ~ * ~

Diesel almost burst with laughter when he heard Katianna's desperate screams just outside the door, but Paris was not lazy with the attention he gave to his cock, and that stole most of his body's reactive impulses. "Oh god, that's it." He gasped, his hand hovering over the back of Paris' head. "I'm so close."

But just then, the euphoria was interrupted when the phone's comm on Paris' desk buzzed.

"Ah fuck." Diesel cursed then leaned over, tapping the button for the speakerphone, "Yes, Vince, what is it?" Diesel responded, since he had Paris busy at the moment.

"Madame Deveroux is here to see Trenton, and by the look on her face— if the Mouse screams one more time, she's likely to faint."

Diesel was instantly sitting up, struggling to push Paris off him, "Shhi—" he caught the curse before it could spill out over the phone line, "Tell her we'll be up there in just a second." He disconnected the line, and bent over to give his protesting lover a kiss while he tried his best to stuff his cock back into his pants. And thankful for having worn a pair of loose fitting jeans on that day. "Go up there and talk with her. Stall her for a second."

"What do you want me to do?" They were both on their feet now, straightening their shirts.

"Ever see stuff on the queen mum?"

"Sure—"

"Treat her like that."

"She's from England?"

"No. Quebec, but she is royalty. And for god's sake, if Fergie is with her, don't offer to shake her hand or step too close; the woman is petrified of men." He grabbed Paris, jerked him against his body and planted a hard and heavy kiss on him, the pressure of his assault toppling Paris back a step and into the door behind him. Diesel's hand dropped and took Paris', pulling it to grope at the hard shaft rebelling inside his jeans. He broke their kiss with a lusty hiss, "And we are definitely going to finish this once she leaves."

Diesel and Paris both stepped from the office and headed down the hall, where Diesel pulled an instant disappearing act into Trenton's office, leaving Paris to handle their client's surprise arrival out in the lobby.

Trenton was bent over behind his desk, apparently trying to get his sneaky little slave out from under it. When Diesel stepped in, he straightened and glanced at Diesel with a wildly thrilled expression on his face.

~ * ~ * ~ * ~ * ~ * ~

Out in the lobby, Paris stepped up to greet their client, putting on his dazzling smile and coat of charisma while introducing himself. "Hello, is it Madame Deveroux?" He asked this while adding a touch of familiar French Canadian accent. "My name is Paris and I'm Mr. Leos's assistant.

The ruse didn't work and she gave him an unimpressed look, "Where is Mr. Leos? I came to see him, not you."

"I promise you that he'll be with you shortly. If you could just be patient. You see, he's a newlywed now, and they just got back from their honeymoon. He's still— distracted." Even without her disfavor, Paris kept his charm on full brilliance. After all, he didn't use it merely to solicit, but also to befriend, and it always worked— eventually.

~ * ~ * ~ * ~ * ~ * ~

Trenton had Kat sternly by the arm with every intention of escorting her out, but he stalled dead in his tracks when they heard the voices of Evangelina Deveroux and Paris just on the other side of the door.

"Trenton— I don't have any clothes on." Kat stammered, and her hand waved at her body and the scanty lace chemise she was wearing. Normally, that would have brought on a deep smile, but she was right; he couldn't possibly waltz her out in front of Mdm. Deveroux dressed like that.

"Under the desk and keep quiet."

Kat took a step, but then hesitated, "I want a full pardon."

Trenton's jaw clenched— "Ohh, you did not just try to pull a forced negotiation here, did you?" But with the knock on the door, he knew he had about three seconds to settle this, and the defiant upward chin on his Mouse's face said she was willing to stick it out.

"Fine." He gritted out, "Now, get under there."

Kat dashed for the hiding spot and quickly disappeared under the desk, "I want my orgasm as soon as she leaves."

"Don't push your—" he stopped when the office door cracked open and Paris showed his client in— a little old woman who hardly stood five and a half feet. She was dressed all prim and proper in her periwinkle dress suit. The hem of her heavy skirt fell midway below her knees, and the matching jacket was buttoned up, allowing only the scarf she wore tied around her neck to show. Her dark grey hair was freshly styled in the typical, old-fashioned roller-set curls.

Trenton had seen her dressed more casually before, but only when he'd gone out to the cottage where she lived with her female partner during the summer months.

Usually dressed in capris, and she had an endless supply of them in a variety of spring colors, worn with a blouse or smock top that was almost always white. She loved garden clogs, and as if her ensemble wasn't complete without them, she'd almost always have a pair of garden snips in her hand, along with a big floppy hat on her head. And that's how Evangelina Deveroux and her partner, Fergie Yves-Lachance, spent their days, pruning and loving their garden yard, walking on the beach, and visiting the parks and garden club. And shopping. The two loved shopping, mostly for antiques and at garden centers. Despite their fear of crowds, and people all together, they did a lot of it. Adamant to prevent their fear from getting in the way of living. They were also activists in both women's movements and veteran care.

"Madame Deveroux." Trenton stood, though he remained behind his desk, and gestured towards Diesel, who'd side-saddled a hip on the edge of his desk. He kept his hands folded over his lap, but from his own angle, Trenton could see it was a ploy to pass off the lazy boy pose as a means to hide the erection that had yet been killed. "You remember my partner, Diesel Gentry."

"Mr. Gentry." She acknowledged him curtly. Her eyes studied his disposition carefully, taking full notice of the tattoos on his upper arms that were in clear view because, as always, he was wearing a sleeveless shirt. "Still working with the Veterans?"

"Yes, Madame."

"I can't recall the name of your organization."

"Project Torch."

"Ah yes, I will have to see if I can pull together a contribution."

445

Diesel nodded, "It would be much appreciated, Madame."

"You served too, did you not?"

"Marines, and yes, Trenton and I served together."

"How many years?"

"Twelve years, Madame." It was odd how she questioned him. She knew Diesel well enough that she knew the answers to her question, yet every year she asked them again as if to see if they ever changed. Trenton knew she liked him, but perhaps his physical size frightened her to some aspect, or more likely it frightened Fergie, so each year Diesel's trustworthiness was reiterated, just to be certain he wasn't a threat. This was just speculation from Trenton's part; it was hard to say why because she didn't do it to any other of his staff, or any of the other brothers. Diesel got the special treatment.

"Hhmmm—" her lips rolled tight against each other, evidence that her thoughts ran deeply inward, but her eyes went back to his tattoos. "And you seem to have brought it home with you."

Diesel's own eyes flickered to his considerable ink work, then back to her, "Yes, I'm very patriotic about what I learned in service."

"Hhmmm." She hummed again. It was a constant habit of hers, "That's good. That's always good." Once more, he'd passed whatever test she had in mind and got her stamp of approval. It was obvious she didn't know what to make of the tattoos, but she was a big supporter for servicemen, even if the global events they were sent out to weren't in favor of public opinion.

Trenton had listened to her often. She remembered World War II from when she was a little girl. Remembered the Korean War, but none stuck with her as much as Vietnam, and what the returning veteran men and women went through when they came back. *Such despicable behavior from the American public to spit on their own soldiers.* She had often said this and rallied for their honor. She usually was up for talking about it, just not today, it would seem.

Trenton motioned toward the chair across from him, inviting Evangelina to sit. She side stepped toward it then stopped, "Do you still own the gun shop, Mr. Gentry?"

"Yes."

"Good. Wilcox has been talking about purchasing a new gun. He wants to upgrade that old fashion thing of his. He'll probably come in sometime during the week." Then she dropped down in the chair and let out a sigh, as if forcing herself to relax, "It was nice seeing you again, Mr. Gentry." She fidgeted a little, settling into the chair.

Diesel took the cue with a grin. While her tone was not at all rude, it was still her way of excusing him from the room. "Bonjour, Madame." He tipped forward then stepped out, shooting Trenton a wry glance before disappearing.

Trenton dropped down in his own seat, "I didn't know you had arrived yet. You usually call."

"Clair-Anne didn't contact you?" She roused with some tone of surprise, but still ever in her prim aristocratic voice.

"Claire-Anne?" The name didn't ring a bell with Trenton.

"Yes, she's our new house steward. Sweet girl, but she forgets things." Evangelina pursed her lips again briefly, then continued, "We keep hoping she'll get better, but knowing her, she's likely one night to forget to lock the manor up, and by the time we return from our stay here, the place will have been ransacked by thugs and thieves." Her eyes darted away and again her lips pursed together in a worrisome expression, as if she actually believed that some part of what she just said could happen. "Anyway, we're here now." She gave a dreadful sigh that confirmed she could do nothing about the imaginary ransacked home, "I was in for a little shopping, mostly just to see which stores were still around, and I happened to be in the area. So, I had Wilcox bring me by."

"I'll see if I can get someone out to you for tomorrow morning, but it just might not be one of your regulars for the first couple of days." Trenton offered, knowing it was important for them to feel secure.

"Oh no. Monday will be fine, but do see to it they aren't late. We have some deliveries arriving— and well— you know how Fergie gets." Evangelina looked away again, her eyes searching some distant place, or thought, with the tight lip.

It pained him. He knew what those looks were. Nightmares she didn't know how to let go of.

"Why don't you let me send someone out tonight? I have a new woman on staff. She's good."

"A new woman? Really? What's her name?" She was intrigued.

"Johanna Cezzari. She likes to go by Jo."

"Jo? You plucked her from the service, did you?" Evangelina knew a soldier's *Maverick* call sign when she heard one.

Trenton grinned, "Right out of the Army."

"Good for you." She nodded and her body began to show signs of relaxing. "You can tell her to come by at seven. We're usually finishing up dinner by then and will be able to show her around."

"Thank you." Trenton treated the agreement as if she were doing him a favor. And in a sense, she was. If he left them alone over the full weekend, by Monday they both would have talked themselves into such a fright, Fort Knox would not have been considered safe enough for them. He picked up his phone and buzzed Paris, "Paris, schedule Jo to report for the weekend, for Madames Deveroux and Yves-Lachance. Yes, starting tonight. Thanks." Trenton returned his attention to his client, "So, what else can I do for you today?"

"We're planning some time to visit Florida this year. We found a very nice place in Sanibel Island. Have you ever heard of it?"

"Yes, it's very beautiful there. I'm sure you'll like it." He commented absently because his attention was suddenly being redirected to the movement of his chair, realizing Katianna had a hold of his seat and was slowly inching him further under his desk.

"I hear it is quiet, though I can't comprehend why. You'd think everyone would want to go to the beach at the crack of spring and the warm weather, but they say you can find some lovely sea shells on the beach every morning. Fergie loves sea shells. Though I don't know what she plans to do with them—"

Trenton tried to stay focused on her chatter— she did love to talk, but the whisper-soft buzz coming from under his desk had more of his focus than faraway beaches. He was only thankful the buzz was little more than a mosquito, except that was only the start of his issue when he felt the vibrator being pressed against the inside of his thigh, followed by the press of her face. A tantalizing contact that only made him further removed from the conversation with Evangelina. He tilted back, just an inch, to glance down between his legs and caught a glimpse of his new bride, her hand buried between her own legs. The view caused his breath to swell and he inhaled deeply through his nose to soak up Kat's fragrance. He was going to spank her long and endlessly for this.

"— and I stopped by to make arrangements for security to travel with us. We'd like to keep our regulars, if possible. I don't know how used to traveling they are." Evangelina's chatter suddenly caught his attention, and he nearly slapped his face, in an attempt to tear himself away from the erotic event taking place at his feet, to face the woman who was waiting for his response.

"Uhm— yes, well— other than traveling with you and Fergie on your weekend get-a-ways, neither have been away for any length of time. How long do you plan to be in Florida?" He gulped suddenly, feeling Katianna's hand slipping up between his legs. He feigned a casual movement of his hand to his lap and brushed Kat's hand away.

"Two months." Evangelina answered.

"That's a lengthy trip for my people. I'll have to check with them. I'm assuming you'll want to take Catherine?"

"That would be quite nice, yes— and Lance. Fergie trusts Lance."

"That's right, from the purse robbery—" he recalled how Lance had clotheslined a would-be- snatcher and saved

Fergie's purse, when they were out shopping a little over a year ago when Lance filled in for Catherine one weekend. It was also the first time Fergie had ever requested any of Trenton's male employees to return specifically as a regular.

Below him, Katianna's hand made another attempt, and he tried to keep her advances at bay; he grabbed it, but she pushed with him and rubbed her fingers against his groin, causing him to catch his breath at her touch, and giving in to it.

"Yes, ever since he protected her from that thug who tried to take her purse. She's grown comfortable with him."

"I will certainly— see what I can do."

"Well, I only need the two."

"Madame Deveroux, please understand—" Trenton tried to keep his voice level, despite the occurrence under his desk and the hand unzipping his slacks, "I have to send four on a trip like this. This isn't a short visit you're taking to Florida. We're talking two months— that means my guys have to have someone for shift relief. They can't work around the clock for sixty days straight. Eight to ten is tops for that kind of scheduling."

"Ah yes, I suppose you're right."

"When do you plan to leave for Florida?" The back and forth was helping him resist the little mouse that had gotten into his pants, but he was still struggling to keep what he was feeling *down there* from showing *up here* on his face.

"Oh, not for another month. We just got here and plan to stay a while to freshen up our gardens, plus there are a few flower shows we want to go to before heading down. After our trip, we'll be back up for another month before returning to Montreal."

UP— down— up— how cruel words could be when they didn't even know it. Trenton licked his lips and took a deep breath, resolving to become unfazed in order to get through the rest of Evangelina's visit. "Has anything else changed? Anything new with the summer house in Montauk?"

"No, but I want a new car. Fergie and I— we don't like the limos. They're too flashy, as if we're movie stars. We're not movie stars, Mr. Leos, and we don't much like to be paraded around like them."

"Didn't you change into one of the Mercedes Executives a few years back?" He didn't have her file in front of him. Usually, he would have her info pulled so he could glance over past details and transactions. But, at the moment, he was at the mercy of his slave's wicked behavior, and he didn't dare try to stand up. Even if Kat hadn't already had his fly open, to stand with a tenting hard-on in front of Evangelina Deveroux was completely unacceptable.

"Yes, but it's still too much."

"Perhaps something more old-fashioned then?"

"What do you have in mind?"

"I believe Marcus has a Rolls Royce in the show room, and there may be a Bentley available." It was still showy by most standards, but it was old school style and she hadn't scoffed at the suggestion yet. "Why don't I have my assistant take you to see Marcus and see what he can do for you?" He buzzed Paris' desk again.

"*Yes?*"Paris' voice came over the intercom.

"Can you step in please?"

"*Yes, sir. Be right there.*"

"So, your new gentleman— what was his name again?" She asked.

"Paris— Paris Dalqeaute."

"Is he French too?"

"Yes, Madame. From Quebec, like you. He's from Saint de Monique, just outside of Montreal."

"Yes, I know where that is. Hhmm, my sister used to live there before she passed away. It's a lovely area, if you like golfing."

"Golfing?"

"Yes, they have more golf courses there than all of Canada put together, I think." She managed a chuckle to show her humor, "So, your new gentleman tells me you are newly married."

Trenton's face warmed instantly with his smile— *yes, yes, he was*. "Yes, Madame."

"How lovely. And what does your wife do for a living?"

The very question brought a sentimental grin to his face. Evangelina was always asking what people did for a living. She loved to hear what they did. Was it what they had always wanted to do, or it just turned out it was something they were good at? It was nearly always the first question she asked someone new to her. It was how they'd met. He'd self-assigned his services for a gentleman, in from England,

453

who was here for a large social event. Evangelina was there, keeping to the outside edge when she found the ballroom too crowded for her comfort. She ended up directly beside him, and after standing there, sneaking glances at him for some time, she struck up a conversation, asking what he did for a living. She was instantly intrigued when he told her he ran a personal security service. She'd begun to ask all sorts of questions. One of them was to ask if a person had to be in any real danger to hire a bodyguard. To which his answer had been no, many of his clients hired him simply to keep the crowds at bay, or just provide that added security in place of a gun. Evangelina was sold that night and came by his office the following morning to hire him. She was the fifth client to hire him on as a regular.

In her situation, no one was out to get her. Though she was one of the few living descendants of the royal family of Quebec, few would ever know that unless they, too, were from Quebec. Rather, Evangelina's problem was that she was claustrophobic, and the whole world was in too damned big of a hurry for her liking. She loved seeing the wonders of the cities and their architecture, just not the bump and rush of its crowds. Those sent her into near anxiety attacks.

Then there was Fergie, Evangelina's companion. Fergie had been gang raped a half a lifetime ago, but the emotional damage had never healed. For her, it was just yesterday. Fergie was terrified of men. All men. If a man even touched her by accident, she would often break down or, on a few occasions, had run, resulting in getting herself lost. Running was often dangerous. Put Evangelina and Fergie together, and it often made it difficult for them to go anywhere.

It'd been Trenton's first year in business, so he took on their details personally, and the two women had been with him ever since. His service had given them their lives back, showing them that despite their anxiety of public places, the two women were formidable activists and the world seemed to have prospered for it.

Trenton's memories were interrupted when he not only felt the sudden sensation of a vibrator against the crotch of his pants, but also Katianna's tongue as she licked over his now exposed cock. It had him nearly out of his seat and he struggled to contain his insufflations.

"You were going to tell me what she does?" Evangelina hadn't missed a beat.

"She'zz— she's a writer." He swallowed hard.

"Oh, a writer. What does she write?"

Trenton wasn't sure if he should to tell her, but he'd never been the type to proceed down the cautious road. "Erotic romance, but just this month, she was nominated for the Pulitzer on her newest book. Her first nonfiction: *Finding My Cellar Door.*"

There was a light knock at his office door, and then Paris stepped in, interrupting the conversation. Granting some internal relief. Thankfully, in just a few more seconds, Paris would be leading Evangelina out of the room. Then he could attack his naughty Life slave, who was presently attempting to jerk his pants from his legs. All he could do was sit there, straight-faced, and suffer through it, hoping Evangelina wouldn't notice.

"Paris, w—" Trenton almost stuttered, "w-would you please walk Madame Deveroux over to see Marcus?"

"Absolutely." Paris gave Trenton a questioning glance while his hand went out to assist Evangelina from her chair.

Trenton gave him a tight-faced expression and a stiff rattling shake of his head. But he didn't dare get up as he should have. He couldn't. Trenton's seeming rudeness didn't go unnoticed as Evangelina glanced over her shoulder at him before letting Paris lead her out.

"I'll be over to join you, sh-shortly— mm— Madame Deveroux." Trenton waved and almost choked on his words when he felt Kat's mouth envelop his cock.

~ * ~

No sooner had Paris closed the office door when they heard Trenton's exacerbated moans through the walls.

"*Oh god!*"

"He didn't get up." Evangelina scoffed her disapproval toward Paris, "That's considered rude manners, you know."

"Yes, Madame," Paris smiled cheerfully, "I'm sure he had his reasons."

"*Bad Kat!*"

They heard Trenton shouting this time and Paris did his best to stifle his laughter, but he couldn't prevent the redness that grew on his face while he could only smile. Because he knew of someone who was going to get a big spanking later.

"Hhmmm, hanky-panky reasons, I suspect." She gave him a snooty *tusk,* then allowed Paris to usher her back toward the lobby where they could go to the showroom. "So, you grew up in Saint de Monique?"

"Oui, Madame." He grinned.

"Don't flirt with me, young man. I am a far too old of a hen for your antics. Your parents, too, I suppose?"

"Yes, Madame." Paris' smile only brightened, finding her wit adorable.

"What do they do?"

"My mother was a painter, and my father a chef. I believe, in fact, he may have cooked for your sister for her birthday parties."

"*Hhmmm*, well, they were certainly cooking when they created you." Madame Deveroux made a funny and clucked out a chuckle.

~ * ~ * ~ * ~ * ~ * ~

CHAPTER THIRTY

~ * ~ * ~ * ~ * ~ * ~

That following Monday came to Trenton's office and delivered two bombs. One of those was named Johanna 'Jo' Cezzari.

"I expect my employees to knock before they come barging into my office, Johanna." Trenton spoke sternly without looking up. Vince had already buzzed back to warn him a fire in combat boots was heading his way.

"You're always putting me on the sissy jobs!" A young woman wearing a dark suitcoat over navy fatigues came stomping in. Her dark auburn hair was pulled back in a tight ponytail with not a single strand out of place. *At least part of her expected professionalism was intact.*

Trenton took in a deep, calm breath and sat back in his desk chair. He rested an arm out and motioned to the chair across from him. "Have a seat, Johanna, and you'll be professional and soften your tone with me." Trenton didn't let her unsettle his cool, but he wasn't going to allow this little storm front get out of control with free range to be disrespectful, either. Certainly not out of his control, that is. Jo had a track record for being a hot-head and bucking orders. Still, he had taken a chance on hiring her because he saw potential and didn't doubt her bravery or strength one bit. When she came to him, he wanted another female on his staff, and she was good for the job.

"You keep putting me on the babysitting jobs while the guys get the action packs. I call that discrimination."

"None of my clients are *sissy* jobs and I don't consider escorting Madames, Deveroux and Yves-Lachance *babysitting*."

"Then what do you call walking circles around two old biddies while they go shopping?"

Trenton set the inappropriate insult aside for the moment. While it would not go overlooked, he wasn't going to allow her to lead him into a pointless squabble. "Your file has you listed as having served a four-year term in Afghanistan, but perhaps that information is inaccurate, Johanna."

"It's not inaccurate. I was a FiSTer."

Trenton dropped his head back to his chair, his eyes going up to the ceiling while dictating his in-depth knowledge of what her job detail really was, "Fire— Support— Specialist— that's what you were. Your job requirement as an observer was to be acutely aware of the position and movements of friendly troops as well as those of opposing forces. Because of the strategic importance of this information, as an observer in the Army you had to qualify for a security clearance, depending on your specific position. As an observer, you were expected to be able to work independently for long periods of time and, because of the clandestine nature of your work and the frequent placement on or behind enemy lines, the ability to operate with minimal support was of great importance as some missions would have likely often lasted for days or weeks." He sat up and glared at her, "This is why you were given a job here. But tell me, Private First Class Cezzari, were you there to protect the people or just over there to prove to the guys you could pull a trigger with your dick?"

Jo's mouth gaped open, as if to respond with a quick comeback, but nothing came out and she snapped her lips shut while she mentally dug up something to say. "No one is after them. Their lives aren't in danger. Just two weakling females that don't know how to stand up for themselves."

"If only that had been true, but let me make it clear that you are never to make such a comment in front of them, especially in front of Fergie. She might have another opinion about there not being anyone after her. Especially when eight years ago, she was gang raped by nearly a dozen men in a train station. Only four of them were caught and they hardly did two months' time in lockup for it." He watched Jo's face pale as the reality of what Fergie had suffered sank in. He knew Johanna knew all too well what such a heinous act could do to a woman. Johanna Cezzari was the child-product of a rape. Her mother having been raped at the age of sixteen. But the family beliefs denied even considering an abortion. While Jo's mother did all she could to give her daughter love, Johanna was forever a reminder of the evil that happened to her, driving her mother to drink excessively.

"I only wish I had been around eight years ago so I could have *babysat,* as you so lightly put it. I might have had the chance to save her and she might have stayed teaching at Juilliard. So I don't want to hear about your hang-ups that one person's life is more important to safeguard than another's. That one fear is less acceptable than another. I don't care that you're hung up on the stitch that you need to prove yourself. But do not use it to demoralize the needs of my clients. They do not need to be in any mortal danger to hire my services. TL Securities is about peace of mind as much as it is about protection from harm. Do we have an understanding, Miss Cezzari? If we don't, you know where the door is." Trenton closed the file before him and slid it off to the side, then reached into the stack of others in the basket, leafing through several of them before pulling one from the middle of the stack and opening it up. "Often, our job is simply to be there so that people can feel safe enough to go about their day and try to feel normal. Our presence gives them their freedom to move about without fear or anxiety."

~ * ~

Mr. Leos hadn't once raised his voice or yelled at her. Firm, yes, but directly calm. Something her drill sergeants— her brother— her grandfather— hell, damn near every man she'd ever known in her life, would have been ranting and cursing at her by now. But not Trenton Leos. His tone would tighten, but she couldn't even recall a time that he'd gritted his teeth. Always cool and calculative. His self-control was astounding. He simply laid out the cards on the table; this was how it was, and either play the hand he gave or leave. It was almost impossible to egg on any further argument with him. He had some unseen way to wet the fuse with mere few words.

She might have admired it if it weren't for that bit of knowledge she had about him being a dominant or whatever he called himself— that his wife, who wasn't really his wife, but his slave. That knowledge damn near cost Jo her job once and she suffered a month's suspension. Jo hadn't been too happy when she got stuck babysitting *it.* Taking *it* around the city to run errands. The idea alone irritated Jo so much that halfway through the day she turned nasty on *the mouse. After all, why the hell should she care about some worthless, spineless woman who sold herself out as a sex slave just so some guy could get his rocks off whenever he wanted? Even if the guy happened to be Trenton Leos.*

Katianna-dumbass-Leos didn't deserve respect and the day came Jo didn't hold back her opinions, letting the insults fly. And when *it* tried to walk out on her, that's when Jo lost it. No way in hell was she going to allow *the mouse* to make her look bad with the boss man. So Jo rattled her up something awful until she relented.

Jo had gotten so angry— angry because Katianna was the direct opposite of what she expected of herself. The only good thing that happened that day was when Piper happened to step out of the building of Quinneth Lovely's Publishing and caught Jo's hand just before she was about to slap the little woman in her clutches. Or rather, even more so that neither Mr. Leos nor Mr. Gentry killed Jo that day, which could be considered the luckiest thing to happen to her in her entire fucking life. Trenton did, however, order Jo to undergo anger management counseling with some dude who was supposedly a specialist for veterans suffering PTSD and guys with sex issues. Not that she figured she had such, but the counseling sessions were private and kept from her record. So she agreed in order to keep her job. Having run herself out of everything else, TL Securities was her last chance at something she enjoyed and had been trained for.

Aware that Trenton was still waiting for her response, she sobered a bit, "She used to teach at Juilliard?"

"Yes, she was a cellist and pianist. A prodigy child. She started performing at concerts when she was nine years old."

"Were she and Evangelina already together then? I mean when it happened."

~ * ~

Trenton leaned back in his chair, contemplating, but he decided that perhaps if Johanna knew a little something about the two women it might help, not that he felt it was owed her. He expected his clients to be guarded and well looked after regardless of their past lives, but he was willing to make an exception this time, "Yes, but not full time. Fergie lived here because of the school. But they had met a few years earlier when Fergie performed at a fundraiser Evangelina held to raise money for the Wall."

"The wall, sir?"

"The Veterans' Wall, Johanna. People here have learned to give respect to veterans like you because of people like her. Like it or not, she earned your utmost respect."

"So, you're saying we have the Veterans' Wall because of Madame Deveroux?" Jo's habitual disdainful sarcasm resurfaced. It was the thing that got Johanna in trouble the most. So busy trying to find a ledge she could claim as her own, she shot down others she didn't think earned theirs.

"No, I'm saying she raised a considerable amount of money to help in its resurrection. And with that being said, I've decided to remove you from the detail."

"What? Wait— why?" Johanna was suddenly near jumping from her seat.

"Madame Deveroux deserves better care than what you are willing to give. You can switch out with Pedro or Carlos; they both have family down in Florida and they may appreciate the change in scenery."

463

"No. Pedro? Carlos? This is outrageous."

"Do you wish to resign from your position here at TL Securities?"

"I'm not one of your slaves, you know." She gritted out.

"Decidedly so, and you have every right to quit when you like. Then again, so do my slaves. They need only say the word, *red,* and it ends for them. Would you like to use a safeword, Johanna Cezzari?"

Jo threw her arms across her chest and slumped down in a heavy scowl, "No."

"Very well then. I will give you a call to let you know which of the two you'll be switching out with."

"No, wait. Please, I will take care of Deveroux."

"That is quite alright. You came in here requesting reassignment. Consider yourself now reassigned. If you have a problem with that, you can see yourself out. I run a business here and I don't have time to shuffle everyone around so you can pick the pretty jobs."

"So that's it? Do as you say or get fired?"

"No. Rather, do your job as assigned, or you can quit and go work for someone else. I'm not the only company that provides private security. The choice is all yours."

Jo slammed back in the chair, scowling deeper, scalding mad, tears swelling in her eyes. She gritted her teeth to fight them back.

Trenton leaned back in his chair and waited quietly— patiently. He could see the torrential rain of emotions in her face. Oh, if she only saw how badly her body wanted someone else to be in charge. To take over and give her what she needed, since she was so terrible about delivering it herself. She was aching to surrender to warm comforting arms and fighting it every inching step of the way. She was a strong-willed woman, much like Amelia, but sorely in need of help to feel pampered and coddled. Her strength warring with her feminine needs. *Hmmm, with whom to pair her up.* He'd have to think about that one for a while. Definitely too much fire for a casual Dom to handle, but perhaps a seasoned Master who loved challenges. *He'd managed a miracle with Amelia. Perhaps, one day, he could work one up for Johanna as well. Domme perhaps.*

~ * ~

Fuck, she was not going to do this in front of him, but damned if she was going to walk out of here like this either. Jo managed to bottle her emotions back up, losing the war on only one or two tears. Mr. Leos said nothing, not even a judgmental look or one of pity, which seemed to help. He watched as if he'd watched this with every one of his men. He was there, if they needed to talk, but if not, he just watched over them like a silent guardian until she got back to her feet and perhaps just one rung off her haughty ladder.

"May I be dismissed now?"

"*There's a call for you on line two.*" Vince came over the speaker comm.

Trenton glanced at the flashing red light waiting on him, then back to her, "Certainly."

"I mean, just for the day. I don't wanna be fired or nothing like that."

"I never said anything about firing you. Enjoy the rest of your evening. I'll see you in the morning with your new schedule."

She pushed off and headed out, grateful the mouse wasn't in there to see this. Though she was certain he sent his wife out to spare her own discomfort. Still, Jo was grateful no one else had seen her small breakdown. She was also glad he didn't say something condescending like— *why don't you just go buy yourself a pint of Ben and Jerry's, take a bubble bath, and sulk for the rest of the night.* Though, that was exactly what she planned on doing— ice cream with everything, hot bath, and lots of pouting. Alone.

~ * ~

Trenton picked up the phone call Vince had transferred to his desk, and that was when bomb number two was delivered.

~ * ~ * ~ * ~ * ~ * ~

CHAPTER THIRTY-ONE

~ * ~ * ~ * ~ * ~ * ~

Diesel was just wrapping up his women's self-defense class. He'd just handed out new handcuff keys, urging them to have at least one of the hide-a-keys on them at all times. "If you've been watching the news, there have been five more cases lately of women getting subdued by handcuffs from the perpetrator. If you look inside the buckle on the bracelet I gave you earlier, you'll see a cuff key inside it. Also, the small hairpin-sized money clips— if you look carefully you'll see one side has a cuff key end. The clips they can attach to your pocket or belt loop on your pants or on a shirt cuff. They're small, so they'll hide just about anywhere. I also have keys that fit on the end of your shoe laces if you want a few of those. You can pick them on your way— out—" he stopped his lecture when it became evidently clear his class was paying more attention to Paris than to him. For class, it wasn't going to do and he decided in under three seconds to make a point using his regular student, Regina.

He stepped up, caught her hand and twisted it until she squealed. But any counter thoughts she had were too late; he had her arm kinked behind her back, then he dropped to a knee, taking her down with him. She landed face down on the mat, her ass up in the air.

"Three!— two!— one!—" he turned his attention back to the class, "That's how long it took me to get your shorts down so I can rape you without any amount of resistance from you!" He let her go and patted her on the shoulder before pushing up while giving her a hand up as well, "It's okay to have fun in this class. I don't want you to be afraid of coming in here and learning how to defend yourself. But rape isn't funny. So you need to pay attention. Or you will be walking out with a false sense of knowing what to do. *I showed up at class* won't save you." He glanced at Paris and tossed a thumb over his shoulder to send him out. "You see, not all rapists look like thugs. They're attractive and well dressed. They have manners and they'll buy you a drink and flirt with you. Next thing you know, you've been drugged and being led away."

Paris wasn't having any of that, being excused so unceremoniously, until he got at least a small peck of a kiss, which got some giggles from the girls.

Diesel gave him the kiss then a smack on his ass, and finally Paris headed out. "Never let your guard down!" The class erupted in a clamor of yelps and giggles, but Diesel already knew what it was about. The flash of skin from a partially exposed ass reflected in the mirror on the opposite side of the room said it all. *Paris was going to have it reddened when he got home.*

~ * ~ * ~ * ~ * ~ * ~

Diesel had just finished closing up his shop and was ready for dinner. *Famished* was a good word for his stomach right about now. He'd knocked on Paris' door, only to get a one-minute signal with his ear attached to a phone, so Diesel jumped over to Trenton's to see if they were ready to go. He'd just stepped in but one look around and realized something was amiss. "Where's Kat?"

Trenton pointed down at his desk, an embarrassed look on his face. "She's under the desk?" Trenton's attention turned to the space under him, "Hey, baby, come on out now." He called her out if only to measure up the situation for Diesel.

"No!" A very pouty response came back at him from under the desk.

"That was a Mouse pout, if ever I heard one." Diesel chuckled at him and Trenton rolled his lips in with a— *I don't know what to do*— expression. This apparently wasn't as amusing to Trenton as it was to Diesel.

"Did you put her down there and now she's just defiantly refusing to come out?"

Trenton shook his head, "Come out now and get dressed so we can go eat."

"No."

"Did you just tell me no?"

"*Nooo-hoo.*" The pouting was breaking down into gradual sobbing.

Diesel watched at what'd apparently been going on for a while now. "You could just pull her out."

Trenton pushed his chair back and right away, a squeal came from under his desk, the quivering voice issuing a plea for him to stop.

"Okay, I give. What is this about?"

"I got a call from Hanze Coshneizmen—"

Diesel stiffened. He knew the name and he knew what this meant.

"I have to go." Trenton gave him a warning glance, "And my little slave has learned well. Too well, because she is completely naked and has completely submitted to me at my feet, because I told her over and over that her total submission would get her what she truly needed, and I would be very accommodating and reward her." He rolled his lips, then made a puckering smack and nodded.

Yep, this is what his brother gets for being too damn good as Dominus and picking out a Life Slave that he knew, from the very first time, had a pout that would make him fold. "Oh." Diesel bit back the urge to laugh at his brother's predicament. "Trained her well, did you?" But then his only half-felt grin melted away and his own emotions sobered. "Where and what for?"

"London, for the energy summit."

"For how long?"

"Eight days."

Diesel sucked in a long breath, "So when do we leave?"

"*We* don't. I need you to stay here by her side, and I leave in three days."

Right away, Diesel was shaking his head, "No. That ain't gonna happen. That man attracts danger everywhere he goes. You're not going it alone."

The sobbing cries doubled under Trenton's desk. "Great, Deez. Make it harder on me, why don't you? She stays and so do you. Period. That's the way it is always going to be from now on."

"This isn't over." Diesel protested. It made no difference that Trenton's expression said he was beyond finding any of this humorous anymore.

"Kat, get out here right now or I'm giving you a spanking," Trenton scolded.

"Okay." Katianna answered.

He pushed back, but Diesel didn't see her coming out. He even had half a mind to order her to stay right there so he could continue to argue the point he planned to make. Trenton was not going on alone. Not without him.

"Kat? You said you'd come out."

"No, I agreed to be spanked."

~ * ~ * ~ * ~ * ~ * ~

CHAPTER THIRTY-TWO

~ * ~ * ~ * ~ * ~ * ~

Since the first night Trenton left, Diesel took full advantage of having Katianna all to himself. Teasing and spoiling her to the extreme limits within their insatiable feeding frenzies. There was just no way of getting around it. What started every night as cuddling up together on the sofa led to Paris getting a hard-on. From there, the regular plans for movie night deviated into another bowl of popcorn forgotten.

Paris woke suddenly, realizing the small body, which should have been sandwiched between him and Diesel, wasn't there. He pried Diesel's arm from him then rolled out and went looking for her, finding her laptop on and waiting in the living room. But he found Kat in the kitchen, where he practically startled her out of her skin and what little clothing Diesel had allowed her to wear.

"You know you're not supposed to be doing that."

"I wanted a midnight snack while I did some writing."

"Let me take over." He offered and stepped to the stove top, waving her back. He tossed the metal spoon into the sink, replaced it with a wooden one, adjusted the heat then stirred the contents she'd already started. He glanced her way then was compelled to lift her up, and he placed her on the counter where she belonged. So natural that she should be there that, when she wasn't, he felt like something was out of place. And he was rather anal about keeping the place tidy and the arrangement of everything in the house. Luckily for him, neither Diesel nor Marcus fussed about it when Paris moved in and was compelled to start rearranging everything in the house. Aside from his anal retentiveness, everything had to have a Feng Shui balance. Senita had been the only one who gave him a hard time and still on going, but not even she deterred him.

The house hadn't actually been that bad; it was a vast open space and not at all crowded with furnishings, even though there were plenty in every room to accommodate a house full of guests— *or slaves*. The artistic layout was there in how everything was arranged, but the Feng Shui wasn't, and it drove Paris nuts when he had moved in. Diesel granted him free rein, as a way to let him stake some claim on the home, so that it was also his and not just feel like he was a guest in it all the time, and it had actually worked for him. Now it flowed and was comfortable.

Having Katianna over simply added to the bliss of their household.

Paris scooped the oatmeal into a bowl, stirred in some cinnamon and a touch of powdered sugar, then garnished the snack with semi-sweet chocolate morsels and grated coconut. "Voilà, the perfect, healthy, decadent comfort food." He grinned as he fed a spoonful to Katianna and watched her eyes light up.

"Did you learn how to cook from your father?" She asked after swallowing down her first bite with a hum.

"Yes, my father was a spectacular chef. And he always had me in the kitchen helping him. In my home, it wasn't about quantity but quality. And it was pretty damn good."

"And your mother? What did she do?"

"She was an artist, she painted."

"Was? She doesn't paint anymore."

"They're both gone."

"I'm sorry."

He shrugged, "Don't be. It was some time ago and these things happen."

She gave him an odd look, like she was trying to reach inside his psyche. While they talked all the time, they'd never really delved into their pasts together.

"Were you loved?" She finally asked, but then she looked practically morbid and scrambled to rephrase herself, "What I meant was, did they know— that you were gay? And were they okay with that?

Paris helped himself to the last bite, grinning around the spoon, and put on the deviant stare, "Afraid to say it, but I was an unnaturally well-loved *gay* boy." And he leaned in, delivering a peck on her cheek. "Sometimes I wonder if they didn't pray to have a gay son."

"Really?" Her eyes lit up like Broadway on opening night.

"Yeah, they were perfectly happy with me, no matter what I did."

Her lips curled up in a grin, a rare moment when her cuteness turned sultry. It didn't happen often and this one was his, "No wonder you're a brat."

They both cleaned up and wandered out into the living room. Paris made a pile of pillows at one end of the sofa, stretched himself out on it, and then pulled Kat down to sit between his legs and rest back on him while she wrote on her laptop.

He'd meant to turn on the television and maybe watch a movie, or just some good porn, but he ended up reading over her shoulder instead. It wasn't long until he was developing quite the erection. And just to be naughty, he dialed into his mental control on his groin and willed his cock to prod her back. It took more than once, but third time's the charm and he had her laughing so hard she couldn't keep writing.

It could have also had something to do with his roaming hands. Such bad boys that they were. And his goal wasn't to be a disruption, but rather to make it terribly difficult to stay focused on anything at all, except perhaps a chance to allow him to try and act out the details he'd just read.

"Paris! Stop." She giggled again, as if the sensation was almost ticklish.

"I can't help it— your writing turns me on." He nuzzled against the side of her head, while he pushed a hand down to slip between her legs like he'd always seen Diesel do, and found she was already wet. He pressed his lips against her head, closing his eyes and picturing Diesel joining them, and let out a gasp, "Damn, do you always get this wet when you write?"

"Do you always get this hard when you read?" She teased him back.

"When I'm reading your stuff? Yes. I even read to Diesel sometimes when we're just lying in bed." The memory brought a broad grin to his face, "I like to watch him give himself a hand job while I do."

She laughed and he knew he was making her blush. He always could. It was funny that way— an author who wrote some of the hottest stuff out there and slave to the Dominus, and yet Paris could make her blush at the drop of a shirt. Or pair of briefs. Either one worked wonders for him.

He pulled his fingers from her legs and held them up to see the silk on his fingertips, how it glistened like pre-cum did. He'd watched Trenton and even Diesel lick their fingers, always savoring the taste. Yet, he still couldn't fathom it, even though Kat and he had been shared numerous times in Diesel's bed.

He brushed his fingers against her lips and watched as her tongue slipped out and licked at them, then kissed them.

"Why can't I do that?" He whispered.

"Does it bother you?"

"No— I— I don't know, I guess. I just don't know what to do with it yet. I've never really had any inclination to sleep with a woman before. You may be the closest I've ever been before."

Katianna twisted, shooting a worried look over her shoulder, "Paris?" her voice filled with concern, "If sex with me disgusts you— you should tell—"

"No." Paris quickly stopped her and tightened his arms around her to keep her from pulling away. "No, Kat— it's not like that at all. I love having you in our bed, it's just my brain hasn't figured out why I find pleasure in it."

Kat wriggled free, casting him a worried glance, "I know we haven't actually gone all the way but have you ever? I mean, before me?"

Paris shrugged, a little uneasy. "You mean before Trenton and Diesel put us together?"

Her lip grimaced, "Yeah, I guess that's what I mean."

"You're the closest I've ever come. Before you, the closest scenario was back in college. My best friend was a girl then too. She really liked the ménage thing and I didn't mind sharing. Soon we were working our way up the hot-list, seducing all the jocks and sexy bad boys in the school up until I finished my degree. You'd be surprised how many straight guys will go along with it so long as there is still a girl involved. Only we never touched each other, not even a kiss. I never touched any woman beyond friendly hugs after that. Not until Deez. You're my first kiss.

She lowered her eyes, shaking her head in a slow indifferent manner.

"Kat?"

She looked up with tears in her eyes, "I'm sorry. I didn't know you felt forced to be with me. I'm certain if they knew—"

"Kat, stop." He growled out in somewhat laughing frustration and pulled her into his arms. "It may be a first but, dammit, little one, I love the hell out of you. So don't you dare go pulling away from me. I don't know how to explain it really. Everything is still very new, but the way I see it is you're one of Diesel's favorite toys and he likes sharing you with me. It makes him happy."

Pale blues peeked up at him from under thick brown lashes. They were so long it amazed him. "If it wasn't for you, I may not have let Diesel in, Besides, I've learned how to tease him back for all the times he tormented me by using you to my advantage."

"Oh my god, you really are a horrible brat."

He grinned, "I know, and completely unabashed." That brought her smile back and she dropped back, surrendering to a full cuddle. *Yeah, he really did love this one.* He figured out just how deeply the day she and Trenton were married and he wanted to be a deeper part of that. He never thought, in a million years that this was how his life would turn out, but damned if he didn't want any of it to change or disappear.

And the only way he knew how to make sure she understood, was to make her feel it. He pulled her up further on his chest, his hand tucked under her chin, and he pulled her lips to his. A tender roll of his lips over hers then they buried into her. He teased her mouth with his tongue to prompt her open. She hesitated, but he didn't give up until her lips parted, allowing him in to steal the taste of her tongue. A kiss like spring water and a lingering sweetness of cinnamon roll oatmeal and chocolate. It was a nice touch to the experience. He realized that, for once, he had her all to himself, and that made the kiss far more extraordinary. Soon she was returning the infectious kiss just as hotly as he was delivering it, and it surprised him every time. That this small little creature could pack such a powerful kiss. He pulled on her swelling lips, enjoying the pillowy feel of them turned over to him, giving him deviant thoughts on the next time he got the chance to torment his man. The intimate kiss ended and he gazed into her eyes before placing a peck on the end of her nose. "Okay?"

Katianna blushed, "Okay." And just like *he* was Trenton. He turned her around in his lap and shifted until they were both comfortable, then returned the laptop to her possession so she could write— and he could read.

It wasn't long until her petite fingers were tapping over the keys as fast as they could to keep up with her brain.

The story poured out like water from a great cataract. She truly drew from the things around her because, as the scene she created unfolded on the screen, he saw their kiss materialize within it. It was almost as hot as the real thing had been. Save perhaps for the major typos glaring at him. Antagonizing his anal side until he couldn't stand it any longer, "You misspelled that." He reached over her, trying to take over to correct the spelling error.

"Stop." She swatted at him.

"But you—"

"I know, and I'll fix it later, when my story lines slow down."

Did he mention he was anal as hell? "Make sure you leave this for me tomorrow to go over your proofreading." He growled in her ear.

"Don't you dare. I do the first proofing so that my wretched typing is translated properly."

He watched a moment longer as she typed out a good-sized paragraph and the number of jagged red underlines in the program continued popping up, "You really are bad."

"Shush." She snapped at him, trying to keep her concentration.

She typed more and he could see she was in the heat of the sex scene. Her fingers rapped against the keyboard as quickly as they could in the dim lighting. He felt the surging need in his groin, and just knowing she would be wet and ready for them was getting to be too much for him to ignore, and pretty soon he would have to drag her back to their bedroom for some more play with Diesel.

A sentence caught his attention, the spelling errors were hardly less than atrocious, but he still managed to read it. It was one of the best viewed details he enjoyed, a man surging into his lover from his cock's point of view, "God, your typing sucks. What is that? What does that say?" He knew what it was, he just wanted to hear her say it. To test whether it was better when spoken or better left being read.

"He thrust his cock deep, sliding past silk-lined walls that hugged like the finest glove crafted of sheer pleasure. Withdrawing only to surge forward again. Each stroke harder and faster until he was drilling into him. The whimpers caused by the elating friction were deliberately clutched in his man's throat. But he knew his pet wouldn't be able to hold it back much longer. Soon his lover would be growling, then his shouts would fill the room like diamonds forged by pounding lust."

"Oh—" he groaned, and his cock jolted against her back again. "God, that was hot. Stop where you are, we have to go wake up Diesel."

"I'm already up."

Paris twisted to find Diesel standing at the foot of the stairs and striding over as he scrubbed at his face and head.

~ * ~

Diesel knelt down beside the two of them; one hand absently went to stroke Paris' cheek.

"It's late, you need to come back to bed."

"Please—" Kat jumped right in there with pouting and small foot stomping. "Let me stay, just a little while longer. I just barely got started." She shot a sideways glare at Paris, then went back to her offer of pouting for points, "I'm on a roll."

Without ever losing his connection to Paris, Diesel caressed her face with his other hand then strummed her bottom lip with his thumb. *Damn, just like his brother. That pouting got him every time.*

"Take Paris, then maybe I can get some writing done." She added with a motion of her head in his direction and an elbow to his side. "Besides he needs to be fed again."

"I need to be fed." Diesel voiced gruffly, but still managed a chuckle at their playful banter.

"Please—" she begged with those pale blue eyes.

"Give me some sugar." He had to at least act like he wasn't a sucker for them all the time. *Payments of such bribery were a necessary means to maintain control.*

She leaned over and gave him a playful smack on the lips. It would do, because anything more and he'd drag her back to his bed himself. "Fine, but just a *little* longer. Paris and I both have to work tomorrow, which means you can't stay at home." He scooped her up in his arms, computer and all, lifting her so Paris could wriggle out from under her, then he set her back down on the sofa against the pillows Paris had piled up.

He left a kiss on her forehead then stepped in behind Paris and proceeded to walk him upstairs back to their room, using his own body to move him. His arms snaking around Paris' body and finding the iron rod in his shorts.

~ * ~

Upstairs, Paris yanked Diesel's boxer briefs down around his ankles in one hard jerk and left him to step out on his own while his hand wrapped around the monster-sized cock. Diesel's size never ceased to amaze him. And that it was perfectly straight with only a slight upward hook. Paris let his tongue reach out, licking across the engorged helmet, catching a hint of fluid on his tongue then sucking it in, engulfing him in his mouth and sinking down around him as far as he could. He worked his tongue around the shaft, wrapping one way, then the other, as he pulled back and sucked him back in again. His fist grasped what he could not get in his mouth and pumped him while his free hand stroked over his thighs then up around his ass, squeezed on them, and clutched him to thrust deeper into his mouth.

"Ahhh." Diesel let out a groan, but his fingers soon fisted into Paris' hair and pulled him up, "Come up here. We don't have enough nighttime for everything." And brought his mouth over Paris', delivered a deep hard kiss and ground his cock against his own.

Paris moaned into the kiss. *God, it was always good with Diesel, even when he was telling him there wasn't enough time for everything.*

"Come over here on top of me." Diesel husked to him then dropped down on his back on the bed with a slight bounce, and that alone had Paris' hips ready for throttle action.

It was rare to have a lover that flipped. Bottoms did it all the time, but Alphas like Diesel? It was unheard of. They never bottomed— except maybe Diesel and perhaps only for Paris' benefit. Sure, there were some things Diesel didn't do or so far hadn't done— like, he'd never see Diesel on his hands and knees, and he'd never gone down on him and give him oral. But laying there on his back with a leg propped open was his way of telling Paris he could have it any way he wanted tonight.

"I heard you two talking."

Paris crawled up on the bed at his legs, soaking up the offering as much as he was listening to hear what else he was going to say.

"You deserve the reward."

Paris had always needed it both ways. He loved feeling his lovers inside his ass, and he loved being inside his lovers with equal passion. That Diesel allowed this was the most incredible fusion of a mate he could have. And for the first time in his life, Paris had removed the *s* off the end of *lover.* Diesel was all he needed, and that he came with bonuses worked for him too.

Paris had often wondered about Diesel and how he still didn't see himself as gay. At first, Paris considered it denial of the label when Diesel called it a free agent of sex. Saying that he fell in love with a man was just chemistry, not preference. It baffled Paris sometimes. Did Diesel break all the rules or was he just making them up as he went along? It didn't matter, he supposed. Paris loved this man with everything he had: his heart, his soul and— oh yeah, his cock too.

Paris came over him, tucked a thigh between Diesel's legs and forced it up, then lowered to kiss him, thrusting his tongue past Diesel's lips to give him a show of what he felt and what was next. He fumbled for the hidden compartment on the headboard and pulled out the tube of gel, then sat back and poured a heavy amount into his palm. He locked gazes with Diesel and coated his fingers just as much as he did his cock, then transferred much of it to the waiting body. He slipped his fingers down between Diesel's legs, pushing between his ass cheeks, until Paris found the tight rosette. He rolled his finger over it, smeared the gel around the entrance and pressed his finger in, just a small amount, then pulled out. Paris used the rest of the gel to coat over his cock, and then stroking himself as he played with Diesel's dark entrance with a finger, sliding in and out, teasing him with the small intrusion.

Diesel pushed his head back, taking a deep breath and practically stretching before letting his body fall into a relaxed state. Lying back, watching him with a glorious grin on his face.

The problem with teasing Diesel was he liked it. He'd sit there and let you do it all night and never complain. For Diesel, it was like petting. There just was no such thing as teasing the man— *damn it.*

"You're incorrigible, you know that?"

His grin only deepened. "Figured this was what you wanted to do. What kind of Master would I be, denying my lover his choice from time to time?"

It was hard to go slow in moments like this, rare privileges that had Paris eager to dive in and plunder it, only later wishing he'd savored it. He'd figured out a technique that helped; from the waist up, it was full out unabridged passion, all the energy was up with his hands and lips, allowing the rest of him to move slowly. Even as he slid his cock back and forth, sawing between Diesel's ass cheeks, driving himself crazy, he remained at a simmering pace.

The Easter egg in all of it was feeling the surging movements coming from the man under him, who by impulse needed to take over, and struggled to keep himself passive while lying under Paris. There'd been a few times Diesel did take over, resulting in a body roll that put Paris on his back with Diesel finishing them both off in a rather domineering and explosive display. Those times usually rated among Paris' more favored nights as he was rarely able to walk the next day, and Diesel even pampered him during his bed recovery.

Not this time, he didn't think. There was a new glimmer in Diesel's eyes. One of pride and satisfaction.

"What's going on inside your head?" Paris dared to ask between kisses, as the peculiar look on Diesel's face was distracting his own carnal thoughts.

"Everything I have ever wanted has come true."

Paris' movements nearly ground to a halt, "Isn't it supposed to be bad when you reach that and there is nothing else to want?"

"No. Not at all. Now I get to experience every pleasure there is to have with you, and my brother and our Unicorn. I have a lifetime still to do it, too."

Diesel was rewarded with a deep, hounding, wet kiss for that one.

"It's only going to get better." He snuck in a bit more with a breathy growl before Paris lost his self-maintenance and pushed his cock deep inside his lover.

The room filled with a unison of gasping moans, and neither took it lying back. He rocked his body and slid up over Diesel's solid chest in a rolling motion that mirrored everything else. Then clipped deeper with a hip curl, pressing against Diesel's inner thighs. All heated up further by a pair of hands that moved to his back then lower, groping at Paris' ass and pulling him to sink even deeper. The energy between them became fervent and electric. His body felt in a way that startled him, but in a way he needed. He was starved for this. It turned him ravenous. Every time.

Oh fuck! It was like sinking into hot fucking heaven. The pleasurable surge swept over him like a tidal wave, rippling out over his entire body in every direction then back again. That was always the part that really got him. The surge out always seemed to snap or roll back in with the internal and bizarre sinking feeling. *Wow, it was ethereal.*

He rolled his hips in a constant gyration, pumping his cock inside the tight silky walls that clamped around him. Back and forth as his dick pushed to drill deeper. Summoning up deep slow tumultuous waves of nerve-splitting sensations. His body shivered— and it rattled him in the strangest tingling sensation— *oh god, he was already there.*

"Fuck, Diesel, I'm gonna cum already." Paris clenched his teeth and slowed his movements down, but he felt Diesel tighten around him, "Fuck! Don't do that." He panted. His head kicked back, letting out a chain of panting grunts, each one a high-pitched expression of pleasure so intense it sounded painful, and then he felt his body shudder. The sensation so fucking incredible he couldn't stop the need to pump harder, to find that peaked wave and let it crash over him. He couldn't hold back; he wanted this.

"Cum for me, Paris." Diesel commanded, never letting Paris forget what parts of this still belonged to the Patronus.

Paris clenched his teeth, fought the urge to follow his lover's command, but he wanted to cum. That Diesel asked for it made it nearly impossible to hold it back any longer. "It's too soon."

"Never such a thing. It happens when I want it to happen." Diesel's own breaths quickened with every stroke Paris rode him on.

"I want you to cum with me." Paris panted, still unable to stop the gyrating lure of his own hips sinking deep inside Diesel's body. The heat and muscles tightening around his shaft, wrapping around his hunger, demanding it to be sated. He thrust harder, his hand stroking Diesel's cock with each thrust, keeping the rhythm in sync with each other. *God, he felt like the whole bottom half of his body was going to explode any second.*

"Now, Paris."

Paris was going to protest, then he felt the swelling surge in Diesel's cock, felt the pulsing ripple under his grip. Diesel tossed his head back and let out a moan of exquisite pleasure. Paris didn't dare be left behind. He slammed in deep, pounding his cock into Diesel's ass, and locked when the explosion he felt haunting his needs lurched out. He cried out— his orgasm came so quickly and was so fierce, it was near pain and yet pure elation at the same time. He pressed deeper as the last of his semen filled his lover's cavern with hot fluids. Then weakening too quickly, Paris collapsed over Diesel's body and kissed him. Not even the strength for deep hungry kisses, because he was no longer hungry. As always, he was filled, completely sated with this man.

He eased out, the part he hated the most. He just liked to stay there, and often they did just that, locked into each other until it was time to start up again. But he really was completed this time, and sleep was calling fast. He fell to the sheets next to him, felt Diesel's fingers comb through his hair and his lips kiss him tenderly. That was Diesel, the cuddler. When Paris felt him get up from the bed, he didn't concern himself over it since he knew Deez would return to wash him. One of the many pampering things his fulfilling lover insisted on doing.

He wondered if there was a day they would ever grow tired of the petting or kissing. If they would eventually succumb to just a mundane ritual of sex, only so they could say they still *do it.*

A moment later, Diesel returned and Paris felt the warm wash cloth on his loins. The act itself should have gotten him hard all over again, and sometimes it did. *But did he mention he was in completely spent bliss right now?*

Yeah? Well, he meant it. Another moment and Diesel was sliding in behind him, pulling the sheets over their bodies. Thick, strong and possessive arms coiled around him, and lips lovingly kissed the back of his neck with slow teasing little pecks that tickled Paris' senses as they drifted off to sleep.

"I'm going to miss having her around when Trenton gets back." Paris whispered, pulling Diesel's arm tighter around him.

Diesel kissed his back tenderly, "Me too."

~ * ~ * ~ * ~ * ~ * ~

CHAPTER THIRTY-THREE

~ * ~ * ~ * ~ * ~ * ~

Paris was going through the mail at the table while Diesel prepared some lunch. It was one of the few meals he relinquished control over, allowing Diesel just to make a plain sandwich, even though Paris still found it hard to keep his seat and not interfere. *I mean, really, who puts yellow mustard on a sandwich with capicola and salami?*

Paris couldn't bear to watch any further and threw up the proverbial blinders, plus a hand, trying to focus down at the table while he leafed through the pile of the day's mail.

Among them was a large, legal-sized envelope from the resort, and he felt a slight cringe in his gut. It was getting close again. *Where had the year gone already?* But it was, and soon he'd have to head down for the fetish season that would remove him from Diesel's side for, at least, two months. He loved his job there, but he wasn't looking forward to doing the long distance relationship thing either. Thinking about it was worse than watching Diesel massacre lunch.

In dire need of diversion, he struck up a conversation with Diesel.

"How did you and your brothers come up with the idea for the island in the first place?"

Diesel had a lineup of deli meat bags laid out across the counter from which he was selecting, and then adding more yellow mustard, like he was icing a stacked pastry. He paused in contemplation, then his hands went into autopilot to assemble the rest of his lunch while he answered Paris' query. "Oh wow— well, I had just started dating this woman, Helena, and we were really into each other at the time. All we ever wanted to do was fuck. We went on this vacation trip to Martinique but got kicked out of the hotel—" his hands remained busy with their lunch as he talked, but his head bobbed in a comical way, "And we got a warning from the next one, and since we weren't about to slow down, the outcome was inevitable."

Paris almost laughed. That much he knew was true, at least that's how it was with them. He and Deez could fuck like banshees, and he could easily see them getting thrown out of a hotel or two— or three— for being too loud or for demolishing a wall. But the humor he saw in the image was tainted because it had been with someone other than him in it. He couldn't hate the man for having a past— lord knows he himself had a phone book of them, but Diesel was his now and he was spoiled rotten about it in the brattiest way.

"Anyway, figuring we might try doing something else for a couple of hours, we went out on this boat ride. Just some local guy and his boat really. We wanted to go to one of the small keys for a day and not be bothered by anybody. He told us about this hotel on one of them. Times were really rough, the place was down on its luck so not to expect any fancy fixings, but they'd appreciate the business. So, we checked in. And we fucked— everywhere— and no one ever said a thing."

Paris grew uneasy listening to all of this and he got up, slipped behind Diesel, and wrapped his arms around him as if he needed to reassert his claim on the man's body. And as always, Diesel seemed to expect it from him and leaned his head back, turning to kiss him, offering the reassurance Paris sought.

Security restored, Paris asked him to continue. "What next?"

"Well, it turned out the hotel was facing bankruptcy. Didn't make sense to me. It was a gorgeous area tucked inside the cove, which kept it perfectly protected from storms and surges, but it still offered a fabulous turquoise view from every window of the resort. The building itself was built nicely, and it just needed some pruning to get the jungle garden back under control. But I got it in my head that it would do really well as an all adult resort, and just let people have some freedom with their intimacy."

"That's why all the cabanas all over the island?"

"That's why. So I took the idea to Dane, who always had a head for that kind of thing, and then Trenton found the other two investors needed to make it possible. Then we bought the place."

"And the woman?"

Diesel shrugged, "We dated just short of a year. Sshe got her break in acting, landing a supporting part in a big production film. She was gone for a little over three months. When she returned home, she broke up with me after becoming involved with one of the actors from the cast."

Paris felt a ping of guilt suddenly. He, too, was about to leave, and this didn't possibly paint a very good picture for his lover. He took in a deep breath, kissed Diesel's jaw, and tightened around him. His way of saying he wouldn't do the same. "It's not going to be easy for you when I have to leave for work, is it?"

"Trenton is under orders to hog-tie my ass and see to it I don't attempt to hold you prisoner."

"I'm not going to do what she did."

"That's what she said before she left."

Paris recoiled from the body he rarely let go of, "You don't trust me?"

Diesel turned to face Paris, took him into his own arms and caressed the side of his face. "I do trust you, Paris. I just know sometimes life has a way of taking us places we didn't plan on going."

Before Paris could protest, Diesel brought his mouth over his, kissing him, silencing him like he often did. Paris broke from the kiss nearly breathless, but it had not stopped his mind from carrying on the argument, "Why would you say something like that? You make me feel like shit saying that."

"Then let me do something that will make you feel good again." Diesel growled lowly to him, turning them around and pushing Paris back against the counter, Diesel's hands opening up Paris' jeans, and to his shock, squatting down in front of him.

"What are you doing?" Paris nearly jumped out of his skin when he felt Diesel's wet mouth around his cock.

Diesel let the still flaccid member pop from his lips and he angled an upward glance at Paris, "What does it feel like I'm doing?"

"But you've never gone down on me."

"Do you fear it won't feel good?" His lips returned to surround Paris' shaft and sucked it all the way in until it hit the back of his throat. It's all it took to steal the breath from Paris, coming out in a startled gasp.

Diesel then worked his mouth, backing off with a swirl of his tongue underneath Paris' shaft. He suckled cautiously around the glans, rubbing his tongue against them. There was no real technique of his own, but Paris could tell he was trying to copy some of the moves Paris had performed on Diesel's thick cock as often as he got the chance. Maybe Deez was attempting a few *Mouse* maneuvers as well. Paris had not gotten one from her yet, so he could not attest to it; he could only speculate since they did exchange notes and technique often enough. However, coming from Diesel, it was slightly clumsy, more than a little bit awkward, and entirely perfect.

Paris couldn't help but let out a moan of pleasure as Diesel finally worked out how to swirl his tongue in a rhythm, synced up with some fist-pumping, in a way that guaranteed to completely melt his brain.

Paris dropped his head back, sending his answer to the question wayward to the copper pots hanging from the ceiling, "*Ahhh*— yes, it feels good."

He dropped his weight onto an elbow to the counter to steady himself, but then had to go back and watch Diesel. Becoming absorbed in the fact that his lover would step out of his boundaries of control to do this— to deliver such pleasure only for him.

Diesel let the thick shaft pop free of his lips and he glanced up at him, dark and sultry, and very much in control of what his intentions were. "Then let me give you this."

Paris dropped his head back, but Diesel quickly commanded him to watch, "Keep watching— don't take your eyes off of me. It may be a long time before I ever give this to you again."

Diesel jerked Paris' jeans down further on his hips, hooked his arms under Paris' thighs and then surged up, lifting him off the floor and placing him on the counter.

It was disorienting, but Diesel urged him to lie back, and that was when Diesel's sucking took on a whole new fever around Paris' cock.

Paris' hands began to roam. He stroked over his own chest and abs, circling one of his nipples then caressing his way down the ripple of muscles of his washboard stomach. He reached further, massaging his scrotum as his lover continued to take his erect steel into his mouth and suck him as he had never done before. *And dammit, his orgasm came way too soon.* All his muscles pulled tight, drew him up into a forced curling crunch, and then the coiling sensation in his balls snapped. Exploded with a euphoria that shot out in every direction. It was good and painful all together. Fucking amazing.

Diesel followed it up with a deep kiss. His tongue still bearing the taste of Paris' own essence. This was the part he would treasure for a long time, tasting his own cum on his lover's tongue. It made up for the awkwardness of lying out on the counter. "I'm too big to be stretched out on the counter like the Mouse."

Diesel broke with that possessively devilish grin of his, "Look pretty delicious to me."

494

"I always said I was good enough to eat." Paris took a deep breath and let it out. Having little strength to move, even though he felt pretty foolish lying on the counter. But he felt so damn good he couldn't bring himself to move just yet. This was a first. He didn't want it to slip away too soon. Diesel didn't seem to be in too much of a hurry to change that either. Making Paris feel all but giddy, smiling so hard it was starting to hurt.

"You look pleased."

"Oh yeah—" he let out another playful growl, stemmed with his deep smile. "Deez, it felt incredible."

"I'm surprised you're not telling me how bad I am at sucking cock." Diesel leaned down, resting his chin on Paris' chest playfully.

"Well— technically, you do." His hand sprung out to catch Diesel in case he pulled away, but he didn't. He stayed right there, happy. Not the type of gloating Paris would have expressed on his face, had it been he who'd done the pleasing. Diesel just looked happy that Paris was. It wasn't enough to tell him it was good. He pulled him closer, "But it was still incredible." Still drawing Diesel in until he had Diesel's lips at his, kissing him again as he was snaking his arms around Diesel, locking them together. "I wouldn't give you up for a trained mouth in a million years."

Diesel gave himself over, relaxing in Paris' arms, revealing he felt as content as Paris. That he'd given an act he'd never given to any man was gift enough for Paris, even if he wasn't any good at it. Paris didn't care about that last part; what he cared about was sharing the moment with the man he loved and who loved him back.

~ * ~ * ~ * ~ * ~ * ~

CHAPTER THIRTY-FOUR

~ * ~ * ~ * ~ * ~ * ~

LONDON, ENGLAND

The first two weeks in London were for the Energy Summit. Now, a demonstration of the Energy Fusion machine. It was penned The *Billion Dollar Experiment.* This would be only the second time the four-block-long and three-block-wide machine of advanced scientific technology had ever been powered up.

Standing inside a control room several feet underground, below the six story laboratory warehouse built specifically for the power system, never before had Trenton known such fear. He could handle guns and fighters, and mortars— but this thing— it was massive. Like something out of a sci-fi-gone-wrong-horror movie. Hundreds of monitor screens sat waiting to capture the event via cameras throughout the tunnels. Most filled with super conducting magnets, making up the so called *particle accelerator.* Surrounding them were several chambers, the size of church cathedrals, with specialized complex cameras designed to detect the said *particles.* Just about every available inch of space that remained was utilized to its fullest, crammed with cables, tubes, air ducts, conduits, and things he didn't know what to call. The engineers and scientists monitoring it all got around by way of small narrow tunnel passageways that zigzagged around and between sections of the vast power plant, as well as by scaffolding and catwalks. And as the test went on, the entire building structure hummed as if the main frame power *was* the building. Just one flip of a switch, and if anything went wrong, they would never know it. The incinerating results would happen too quickly for the brain to even acknowledge it. There would be only a flash of light for him and the some 500,000 city inhabitants that worked and lived in a twenty-mile perimeter. The delta end of the river Thames would be transformed into a harbor. This was without taking into consideration that some doomsday criers feared the experiment, if ever successful, would cause a black hole to form and swallow up the entire earth.

Trenton closed his eyes and prayed silently. He'd promised Katianna he'd never leave her. He told her this was just his job; it was what he did. Now, in the face of a fear he'd never met before, he understood what she felt. If he lived through tonight, he would make it up to her. Perhaps it was time to let William start taking the overseas trips, or maybe even Harper. His brother was definitely in need of redirection. It was time Harper stopped digging into the ugly world of people and started protecting them from it. That's what he was meant to do. He was a soldier. As was Trenton's job here and now. However, he had a responsibility to Katianna too, now. She had given him her life— surrendered every part of it to him. He owed it to her to stick around and take care of that gift.

"Mr. Leos!" Someone was shaking his shoulder.

Trenton looked up and blinked at the man still wearing a white lab coat.

"Wow. That was something, huh? Where'd you go? I've been standing here talking to you, calling your name for a good three minutes now."

Trenton rattled his head and looked around at the group of men, Hanze among them, watching from the other side of the room. Trenton swiped the sweat from his brow with his shirt sleeve. "You fucking scientists are insane." And the seven men broke out in laughter.

The man patted his shoulder and smiled, "Aye, that's what people have been saying since we said the earth was round."

~ * ~ * ~ * ~ * ~ * ~

The summit was over— and they'd managed to do so without removing the UK from the map. Now Trenton's client had one more stop and the closer they got to Brighton, the more nervous his client, Hanze Coshneizmen, became.

"Who are we meeting with there?" Trenton pressed. Not satisfied with the lack of details he'd been given. He didn't care to be on a job and not know what the job was.

"Some men from Belgium."

"And this is related to the summit?"

Hanze snapped his head around, glancing away. His eyes ghosted over as he stared out the car window. "Sometimes we do what we must behind the channels— in secret— because it is the only way to make change happen. Or stop it."

"Hanze, how much trouble are you in? Remember, there is a reason why the feds sent you to me. If there is something I should know, it's best you tell me now."

Hanze turned back to him, eyes devoid of life like he was dead already, "No, Mr. Leos, you're here to protect me as best you can, not get involved. You're here, because the feds can't break protocol."

Trenton knew then his trip had taken a turn for the worse. For the first time, he questioned whether he would be successful at protecting his client. He didn't like the answer. The one that gave him nothing but a door, barred shut, in his face.

Hanze fetched a handkerchief from his pocket and blotted his face nervously.

"You're sweating. Why?"

Hanze let out an equally nervous chuckle, "The test we ran earlier today was a piece of cake compared to the test I'm about to try when we get to our destination."

Trenton didn't know if that meant there was another one of those machines, out of the public eye and perhaps out of government restrictions, located down on the coast of England, or if they were about to do something entirely illegal. Whatever it was they were heading for, they went in silence until the driver pulled to a stop in what seemed like an abandoned mill of some sorts. Not nearly big enough to house anything from the capacity of Hanze's knowledge.

"Wait out here." The professor stepped from the car.

"No, I'm going wi—"

"Please—" Hanze cut him off, his hand out to stop Trenton, though his voice was soft, almost timid. "Wait out here. The real danger is out here, trying to get in." And with that, Hanze turned away and vanished into the shadows that engulfed the brick and mortar structure, absent of even a single unbroken window pane.

Trenton didn't like this at all. The hairs on the back of his neck stood on end, prickling at him. Something wasn't right and he put a text into Harper for intelligence info. Then disregarded the order his client had given him and headed inside.

He paused along the ramp that led up to the front roll doors— listening. Nothing. It was quiet. Too quiet actually. Not what he'd expect if a group of scientists had gathered for some not-so-public summit. It meant something *else*— something illegal was happening.

Trenton drew his gun, and continued up, his eyes sweeping back and forth, tracking for any movement or shadows that would give a man away. He never made it in when a voice with a deep accent that likely came from *south of the river* spoke from a blacked out shadow just to the side of the roll doors.

"Stohp 'ere, gun mahn. Dis 'ere show ain'ht for the likes uh'yew."

Trenton snapped around, aiming for someone he still could not see, but unless he was very short, he could still manage a shot.

"Naw need for dat. Naw one 'ere gonna hurt Prof. Coshneizmen." The dark shadow spoke.

There was a familiar sound coming from the dark recesses, then a round face lit up from the flame of his match and the mystery man on watch duty casually lit a cigarette. Both hands clearly visible. Just enough glow for Trenton to make out the shoulder holster and the top edge of the hand grip tucked away under the man's armpit.

"Naw worries, mate, 'eh won't be long." The mystery man shook the match out and vanished back into the darkness, save for the glowing ember at the end of his smoke, followed by a hazy trail blown toward Trenton. The watchman was too cool about the whole thing. Not wavered by Trenton's presence in the least. That alone made Trenton uneasy.

Trenton holstered his gun and started to step away, but something up above caught his attention and his eyes flickered up to the rooftop. The dark silhouette of a man patrolling. Arms held just right to announce he was carrying. Trenton didn't like it at all. Even as the sniper guard continued along the perimeters, making no eyes for him.

Whatever was going on, he and Hanze had a free ticket to it.

Trenton reluctantly returned to the car and their driver got out, came around, and held the door open for him. That was enough to piss Trenton off and he ripped the door from the driver's hand then slammed it shut. It was his only means of defiance at the moment. He turned on his heels and furthered it by leaning back on the car door. Barring it shut. Astutely making it clear he was not a silent posse here tonight and he would not be lax on his position to protect the professor.

The driver said nothing. Didn't even chance a warning glance, but he idled back on the hood and took liberty with a smoke himself.

Trenton folded his arms, taking the posture of a disgruntled man but, in fact, he was calming his core. Absorbing the details of where they were. Only two street lamps were working and they were parked under one of them. The other was further down at the end of the block where he made out the faint outline of a man walking his dog.

Parked in front of them was the only other car in front of the mill. Same make and model as the one he and Hanze had ridden in. Pre-arranged without Trenton's approval. It hadn't sat well with him then and then realization slammed into him. It was the slip he allowed that was going to be the death of them all. He should have insisted on reassigning the arrangements. Being sidelined as he'd been stripped of the control he needed to assure their safety. Someone else was making the rules— flipping the switches.

Danger was on the horizon. Or rather just inside that roll door leading into the broken mill.

More details came to him. Like the stream of traffic that seemed to encroach just a few blocks down, but not one vehicle came down their way. Above, the rooftop sniper guard never made another patrol around past his second.

The door to the second car opened and its driver climbed out. An odd gait attached to his step like a rehearsed approach to appear causal.

"You should remain in your car." The driver to Trenton's vehicle commented to the other man. His accent was definitely German or Belgian.

"Got a light, mate?" The man from the second car disregarded him and continued coming up as he pulled a pack of cigarettes from a jacket pocket.

The Belgian didn't respond and neither did Trenton for that matter. His eyes drifted back to the building.

The man from the second car shrugged, then returned the pack to his jacket. "So, bossman gonna make a lot of money on this arms deal, aye, chap?"

Trenton stilled, turning to study him carefully. "Arms deal." It was a cautious statement rather than a question.

"Yeah, you know, your guy— he gonna make out like a king for the price they're willing to pay for the whereabouts of them missing German missiles."

Not even a second could be counted in the instant it took Trenton to grab the man and pin him down to the hood of the car. "What the bloody fuck are you talking about?" Trenton growled into his ear, keeping his anger low so as not to invite anymore unwanted guests. The man struggled under him, but Trenton kept him in his hold. "Keep still and I won't dislocate your shoulder. Now cut to the facts to what's going on inside."

"Some arms dealers from the Middle East. Your guy is supposed to tip them off to the hiding place of some old WWII missiles that were never handed over to the UN."

"Fuck—" he growled, still not letting the man up. Hanze had just walked them into some deep shit. "Why here?"

"Some black market dealer from Belgium set it up. There's a boat already down at the pier, ready to take them across the channel with the location info."

Trenton pitched his body weight onto the man and chanced a look over his shoulder, expecting the moving shadows in the distance, "No, it's about to go bad. Someone else is already here. What's the local 911 number?"

"Huh?" The man's brows pinched inward, baffled by the request.

"An emergency extension? Local authorities. Police precinct number?" Trenton gritted the command out, growing frantic. He freed a hand so he could dig his cell phone out and started to call Harper—

"Zero-one-one, four-four, then eight-four-five, six-zero-seven, zero-nine-nine-nine." The man pinned down finally answered.

Trenton nearly dropped his phone and gaped down at the man, "You pulled that right off the top of your head?" And then something else the guy had said struck Trenton, "Zero-one-one is only used if you're calling from *outside* of the country. Who are you?"

"Trent?" Harper's voice came over the phone connection.

Trenton rattled his head. *Something wasn't right. Several somethings.* "Harper! Patch me through to the feds— Hanze Coshneizmen is in some trouble."

"Freeze right there!" A deep baritone command came from behind him, then Trenton felt the slow and steady press of a gun barrel against his temple. Out of the corner of his eye, Trenton saw their driver already turning around with gloved hands in the air around his head. The man Trenton had had pinned to the car slid away and straightened his coat as he stepped clear. This time, it would seem the man from the second car was the one who had the free pass.

Trenton sucked in a deep breath, carefully set his phone, still connected to Harper, on the hood of the car, and just as cautiously raised his hands up as ordered.

There was an instant clamor as police cars and armored vehicles came from around street corners, lights flashing, pulling up to create a grid around the building. Men both in uniform and in black fatigues rushed in, surrounding them. All heavily armed and looking trigger happy. *Moles always get a free pass.*

~ * ~ * ~ * ~ * ~ * ~

CHAPTER THIRTY-FIVE

~ * ~ * ~ * ~ * ~ * ~

Fifteen hours later, Diesel arrived in Brighton, England with Katianna and Paris glued to his heels. Not by his choosing, though; Paris had made it clear if Diesel left without them he'd just book another flight. As it were, it'd been Paris who'd managed to grab the walk-on flights so quickly and had already paid for three air tickets. It was hard to supersede what already been done.

Also brought with him were documents on Trenton's position. It lightened the load of charges and implications— but not enough that they were willing to set him free. There was still the matter of where he had been with Hanze and what the local authorities' intelligence had speculated what was taking place inside the abandoned mill. Turned out there was another matter that supported the detectives' decision to keep Trenton cuffed. Diesel had only caught a fleeting glimpse of the purple sock-eye one of the detectives was wearing, but it looked to be a beauty.

According to the report, when the task force came out with Hanze in hand, Trenton got more than rough with his own handlers. Even staring down a few aimed rifles, Trenton had attempted to enforce his demands that the professor be handled professionally and with care. All accomplished while cuffed and disarmed. Not surprising and perhaps even got a note of idol worship from Diesel. However, at the moment, the charges of assault on an officer were getting in the way of Diesel's attempts of bureaucracy. He'd been denied clearance to speak with Trenton. Getting only a chance wave through a window when Trenton was moved to another room for further questioning.

About the only real accomplishment Diesel had managed so far was getting Trenton informed they were there. That led to Trenton demanding to have his wife brought in where they held him, in exchange for cooperation. Surprisingly, the detectives went for it.

"Hey, baby." Trenton caressed Katianna's cheeks, despite his handcuffs, as she sat in his lap.

Her eyes dropped to the manacles and her lips rolled in to parry the laugh that may have been threatening.

"You laugh and I will still manage to spank you here and now." *God he was glad to have her in his arms. Not forgetting his brief moment of fear just two days ago.*

A grin did break free, but she nodded her admissions, "Yes, Dominus."

"Good." He leaned in and kissed her— just soft tender pecks. His fingertips never leaving her skin. It felt good to touch her. To embrace her in his arms. How different she felt to him now. More precious— more alive. Touching to assure himself she was here— *he* was alive and she was still all very much his.

"Mr. Leos, we're still waiting for the part about you agreeing to cooperate with us." The detective standing in the back spoke up, interrupting Trenton's obsession with his Unicorn.

"You have the detailed paperwork my brother brought to you. What else do you need to know?"

"Why don't you just tell us anyways?" Detective Wells remained in the chair across from Trenton, rubbing his temples, displaying that he was exhausted and clearly didn't have nearly as many answers as to what was going on as he'd have liked to have. Behind him, leaning against the wall, was a young detective. Connolly, Trenton believed the name was. There'd been so many passing in and out, and not all of them gave introductions. The one he'd pinned to the car turned out to be a Detective Cunningham, who now sat atop the small corner table next to the two-way mirror that reflected back to the one behind him. A definite headache room for anyone who had to sit here for far too long.

Trenton was still too absorbed in his Life slave. *His precious Unicorn.* "Have you any idea how much I love you?" He pulled her lips to him and simply pressed them to his face, willing time to stop right there, in this moment of perfection.

"Mr. Leos, if you would, please." Wells' lethargic impatience surfaced.

"You can wait. I've had a rather hectic day." The annoyance was bothersome more so to Trenton than he likely was to them.

"You don't say?" Wells sat up, hoping this was the start of the story. And perhaps Trenton should start talking, but talking with local PD usually led to bad shit at the end of the day. "We'd love to hear about it. Wouldn't you, boys?" Wells slathered on a layer of sarcasm just to make it perfectly clear his own annoyance was running parallel to Trenton's.

"After listening to the brainiacs and politicians of the world argue over whether a clean environment was really all that important versus more power, I then sat in a room with a bunch of mad scientists that flipped on a machine which, whenever that day comes that that monstrosity is actually successful, a black hole is likely going to form in London, and in which in two nanoseconds after that, the entire world will cease to exist. That or it will just blow up and all of England will join the likes of Atlantis at the bottom of the sea. So I think my day has been far worse than yours." His attention returned to the one who soothed him with the slightest caress of his fingertips over her skin.

"And then after that, you and Hanze went out for some arms deal dinner party." Cunningham blurted out.

"Do you know what the problem is when little police precincts try to play in the big-bad-boy games? They don't even have a clue what kind of ball they are chasing after. In the end, you've most likely only scored a point for the opposing team." Trenton lectured them with proverbial sarcasm. They earned the jab. They needed to have it shoved in their faces that they had walked into a situation far more dangerous than a local bank robbery.

Cunningham sipped at his coffee then grimaced and set it down. It was about the third time he'd done it. Maybe it was bitter, but it most definitely would have grown cold by now for all the lack of effort to do something about it since they'd brought him in here. Cunningham looked at his coffee, almost tempted to try again out of sheer habit, but finally resolved his arms to cross over his chest and ignored his cold cup of brew while Wells did all the questioning and Trenton did all the answering.

"Then tell us what the bloody arse is going on!" Wells slammed a fist on the table, causing Kat to jump.

"I was hired to accompany Professor Coshneizmen here for the summit and for the particle test."

"Why, then, are you here in Brighton?"

"After the testing, Hanze said he had a private meeting he needed to attend. Which brought us here."

"And what was the meeting supposed to be about?"

"He didn't say. I took it to mean it was top secret."

"And you didn't find it important that you should know more about it?"

"I did feel so. Nevertheless, Hanze was, in fact, brought to me by the US Federal Government. With that comes the understanding that sometimes what I want isn't always how things are going to be handled. My job was still to keep him safe."

"Why would the professor need a personal body guard? None of the other scientists who appeared at the energy summit came with any."

"Coshneizmen's family has been under threat for some time now."

"What kinds of threats?"

"His fourteen-year-old son was kidnapped barely a year ago and then sent back in pieces."

The three men coughed uncomfortably. It took Wells a moment to recover or rather to ask why. "Why would someone want to kill his family?"

"Coshneizmen's past is tied to Nazi Germany. His grandfather was a general, directly under Hitler's command. Hanze fled Germany years ago with his family to escape his family's less than stellar legacy. And it was after his son's death the Professor was referred to me for protective services."

"There weren't any generals with the name Coshneizmen. I checked." Cunningham spat out.

So they had read over the reports brought in from Diesel, but obviously nothing else. "Coshneizmen is his mother's maiden name." Trenton leveled his gaze on Wells, ignoring Cunningham.

The stern lines etched into Wells' face seemed to melt, "Then what was his real name?"

"You don't want to know his family's real name."

"I'm certain I do." Though Wells appeared to steel himself for the answer.

"Eichmann." Trenton answered with a secular tone, like he'd just dropped the executioner's blade. "He's from the Eichmann family. I'm sure you've heard of Adolf Eichmann. His job was transporting the Jewish captives. That was Hanze's great uncle."

"Jesus, Mary, and Joseph." Wells huffed and pushed up from the table. He walked around in a circle, dragged his hands down a face that hadn't seen a razor in days. It only served to prove Trenton was right. No one wants to know they have the prodigy child from one of history's most notorious war criminals in their office. Especially one who was sought after by modern day war mongers. Wells muttered something else along the lines of *Americans can't keep their shit to themselves*. But, for the moment, it seemed the questions were at an impasse until they regrouped and figured out where they stood from there. Trenton had told them they'd walked in on something too big for them and now they knew it.

Hanze Coshneizmen was a scientist specializing in nuclear fusion, but his grandfather had been a Nazi general for the Hitler regime. Like his brother, Adolf, his job had been in transport, only he moved the Nazi weaponry stash to keep it out of the hands of the enemy. Including several missiles. Hitler's V-2 rockets. According to Hanze, his grandfather didn't reveal the location of all of them when Germany surrendered at the end of the war. And there were still some six missiles unaccounted for. A king's ransom on the black market if anyone ever found them, and apparently someone thought Hanze knew just where they were.

~ * ~ * ~ * ~ * ~ * ~

Still waiting out in the lobby, Diesel was checking everyone's moods according to their postures. Several seemed too tense. The heist roundup had not been theirs, rather a surprise federal party-crashing. It had them all on edge to some degree, or flat out bewildered, because it didn't appear that anyone actually knew what was going on. *Him* included. Except Diesel had a fair amount of speculation of what it might involve. *He* knew who Hanze Coshneizmen was.

Paris was a different matter. He saw the officers that went back and forth across the room from one desk to another, taking as much curiosity with Paris and him as they were with them. If not for different reasons— "Stop. You're peacocking in front of everyone." Diesel ordered his lover to take it down a notch.

"What's wrong with some peacocking as long as I'm tethered to you?" Paris leaned in, indicating his attempts to steal a kiss.

Diesel wasn't about to encourage him right here in front of the entire precinct. "My brother is under arrest for threatening national security and you're practically performing a strip tease here, posing like a billboard."

Paris hardly even looked his way, "He's not under arrest. Just being held for questioning. Which you know he will get out of. I brought everything needed to clear him of any suspicions. They just have to act like they're the ones in charge."

"It's more than that."

"I agree. More than three."

"Th- three— wait, what?"

Paris leaned over the arm rest, dropping a hand on Diesel's thigh. His thumb in clear line of view of their watchers as he caressed his leg. Paris' other hand rubbed higher on his own leg on an obvious path for a full on self-groping, "More than three gay cops in here."

"Your gaydar tell you that?"

Paris' lips curled up on one side, "Yes."

Diesel could only sigh inwardly over Paris' vanity. No wonder he was peacocking. He left him to it, his own attention going back to the milling about.

Paperwork was being delivered to the only closed office by way of one out-of-uniform officer, with a rap to the glass door. A broad man answered and glanced over the papers, then his eyes seemed to dial in on Diesel and Paris. The large man scratched at the stubble on his face while the one who'd brought the papers talked some more. Then the man headed straight for them.

"Just brewed a fresh pot of tea, if you're interested." He made a suggestion with his head for Diesel to follow.

It was a clear invite. Not for tea, but to talk— away from watching eyes.

"I'm Sergeant Rowlinson, I promise I don't bite." He gave Diesel a nod.

Diesel let his eyes flicker in the direction of the still closed-off door of the interrogation room.

"I assure you, they're going to keep him for a while longer." The sergeant added.

"Yeah, alright." Diesel pushed up to follow, "Paris, stay with me."

Rowlinson led him down a hall— away from the rooms that held Hanze and Trenton— past about a dozen desks lined up in twos, then into a small break room where there was indeed a fresh pot of tea going. And another with coffee.

"Your boy seems to be giving you some trouble." Rowlinson smirked as he poured himself a tea.

"Got a broom closet?" Diesel went for the coffee instead.

"Not big enough for the likes of him, but I got a few of my men that would be more than happy to take him off your hands if he's too much trouble for you." It was more a joke, but there was still that lingering challenge, suggesting maybe Diesel wasn't as alpha as his stance made him to be or what his lover needed. Rowlinson was mistaken on all accounts.

"See? Told you." Paris was suddenly against his ear in all his usual exultancy.

"I have no intentions of passing off my cock-mongrel."

Rowlinson turned his head near all the way around to glance at him with a cocked eyebrow. "You call *him* a cock-mongrel?"

Diesel looked over at Paris, who was now lounging back in one of the chairs against the wall. He may as well have poured a breath over his nails and buffed them on his shirt for all the studly arrogance that was exuding from him. Just reveling in his own act.

"You didn't ask me to come in here to talk about my voyeuristic partner."

There was a heavy sigh and far more stirring in his tea than need be, given the chief hadn't added the first spoon of sugar or cream. "No. It isn't."

"So what do you say we get to that part?"

"Wish I could. But it seems all the channels are being cut off from me, with every glance."

"What a shame." Diesel offered no remorse or sympathy.

"Your boy in there? He really who he says he is?"

"Yes." Diesel looked at him directly.

"I got feds crawling all over my arse. British ones that are telling me to play good midwife and keep my mouth shut. American ones trying to infiltrate, telling me to let this Hanze fellow go and stay out of global business. I don't know who to trust. Not even in my own police station. I know someone here is paying out to the other side."

"Trust Trenton, and more people will come out alive."

"Back in September 1944, fifteen hundred of those goddamned rockets were dropped on London's head. With all this ISIL terrorist shit going on in the world, finding out there might be six more of those things out there that could soon be on the black market is enough to give any chief of police a heart attack. And I got the one person who knows where they are."

Just then one of the detectives stepped in. A cup of what looked like coffee still nearly full in his hand. He shot a sideways glance at them then went to the sink, dumped the contents, then headed to the coffee pot to pour a fresh cup.

Diesel eyed the detective carefully. Something itched at the back of his neck, but he managed to reject the impulse to rub at it. "Paris is one quarter Great Dane who never stops slobbering over me and insists he's a lap dog. He's also one quarter feline cat that ignores me when I call. One quarter bratty Imp who doesn't care about anything, as long as he's getting screwed. And the rest is pure Brahma bull 'cuz once he gets charging, there's no stopping him. If I have a weakness, it's enabling him, because it's all those things that make him give other Fallen Angels a good name."

The chief just looked at him, totally lost to what Diesel was getting at.

Diesel just went on as if he'd caught on anyways, "Yeah—" Diesel's admiration and fondness had his attention floating back to the man watching him like he might actually start charging with a final pounce. "he's actually the prime cut of breeding and a love machine, but his ego is already more than can fit into my house, so I call him a mongrel."

"Maybe you need to get a bigger house." The chief was slowly drifting back on topic.

"HA!" Diesel let out the hard laugh, "It's already 16,000 square feet. Mongrel is a lot easier." And he went over to where Paris sat, bowed over him, and kissed the gloating, prideful swelling man. He pulled back to look deep inside those rich brown eyes. Eyes that revealed there was just as much love in that dark pool of lust. "I put up with him because he's so much damn fun."

Again Rowlinson looked at him funny.

"Cock-mongrel." Diesel hoped it was enough to jar his memory.

Rowlinson chuckled, then the chuckle kept going. Soon he was rolling into a fit of laughter until that was all he could do, and he kept on laughing.

Diesel wasn't sure if it was just the way he'd said it or if Paris had given a wink or hand gesture to spur in the details, or if the sergeant was stupefied that Diesel had managed to put them right back to what they'd been talking about before cutting to the chase. Maybe Rowlinson just got an image in his head that wouldn't go away.

Whatever it was, the older man never stopped laughing to himself, and he even had to wipe away a few tears from his eyes as he sauntered off, out the door, and down the aisle of patrol desks. Even his men seemed dumbfounded that their sergeant would find something so utterly funny.

When Rowlinson vanished down the hall toward his office, the heads all turned doing a one-eighty his way. Diesel found himself staring down a row of questioning faces looking back at him. He then glanced at Paris, who only offered a hint of his wicked smile— and no shame at all. He'd done something, obviously, a shadow puppet to his own words. "You better hope Trenton is in some serious trouble or I am going to turn you over my knee, right here in this room, in front of all these cops to watch."

Paris curled his lips in for a slight lick of his tongue, like he was licking the tip of Diesel's cock. It didn't make it anywhere close to licking that self-satisfied grin off his face. *Still there.* And there wasn't a man alive, as far as Diesel could recall of, who could knock that chip off Paris' shoulder. Not even himself. *Fun— in— deed.*

~ * ~ * ~ * ~ * ~ * ~

Still inside the interrogation room, Trenton was of little help or cooperation with the questions, his focus more so on the woman in his arms. It was the wrong place for her to be, but after the night before the bust, he wanted her nowhere else.

"Mr. Leos, if we could have your attention for a moment more." Detective Connolly finally stepped away from the wall and spoke up, "We'd like to get some answers from you about this night." He was less than enthusiastic about Trenton seemingly running the show here, despite the guise of still being under.

He had to admit it was a strange arrangement, having his slave in his lap while he was handcuffed. It drew a tantalizing challenge to his senses, to assure his dominance was well intact. It all lent to his reluctant corroboration with men who had no idea who it was they had in their possession.

The door to the room swung open and another detective poked his head in, making an inclining sweep towards the mirrored wall behind Trenton.

Wells pushed up from the table and came around, "If you please." He held his arm out, inviting Trenton to stand with him at the mirror, ignoring Cunningham when he finally returned with a fresh coffee.

Trenton obliged, first hoisting Kat from his lap to the table, then joined him. A flipped switch on the wall and the mirror became transparent; a push of a button and Trenton listened as the detective in the other room posed virtually the same questions to Hanze.

Wells rapped a knuckle on the glass and Hanze twisted around in his chair and directed his attention their way.

It was uncertain if he could see them, but Hanze was no fool, he knew someone was behind the mirror, watching. He stood. Like a ghost that already knew its time was up. He was just waiting for the ferryman to come claim him.

He stepped up to the mirror, a blank stare in his eyes, looking beyond his own reflection but seeing nothing. "*There are stories a man is told as a boy. Strange fairytales that other boys are not told. He doesn't know if they are true or not, but he never forgets them.*" The German breeding resounded in his words now. Unable to escape his heritage any longer. "*I told them where to find them.*" A long pause, then he shrugged like it was nothing, "*I don't even know if the locations are true or not. I told them that as well. I only know what an old man said to me. An old war general making up fairytales, like a senile wish that their* misguided greatness might one day be revived and he would be an exalted leader once more."

"How could you ever—" one of the detectives behind him started to speak.

"Spare me your self-righteousness." Hanze spat the retort over his shoulder when one of the detective dare to try and judge him for his actions. "The governments— all of you have been handing out surplus for years. Where are the missiles the UN did take?" Hanze twisted harder to glance at the man directly to see if he had an answer. When none came, Hanze returned his eyes to the mirror. To Trenton. "None of you have ever held your child's hand after it'd been severed from their body. I wept and vomited. Then wept some more, but I touched every part of my son before I would let them cremate him."

Trenton felt the professor's grief. It slammed him hard. He'd wish he'd been working for the man sooner, that he might have been able to protect Hanze's son. But there was no point succumbing to a past he was not a part of. Still, Trenton grieved for the man's horrific loss, understanding the obsession that had driven the man to such a morbid act of affection and last rights.

"Even if the missiles are there—" he nearly cackled as you picked back up in his confession, "They'll never get the chance to excavate for them."

"Why's that? Where are the missiles?" Someone within the room asked.

"It's believed two of them were on the Nazi gold train. Buried in the tunnels under Walbrzych."

"Walbrzych? Nearly every treasure hunter, plus the Polish government, are trying to find that."

"*Which is precisely why the war dealers will never get a chance.*"

"*And the others?*"

"*Returned to Nordhausen. There were four tunnels there. Not two. All the factory workers and the tunnel diggers had been killed after the digging was complete so no one would know about them. The missiles were taken there and buried.*"

"*Is that the only place?*"

"*No.*"

"*Where else?*"

Hanze let out a low grieving sigh. His eyes glassed over as he spoke the single name. "*Auschwitz.*"

It was like the wind had been kicked from every chest in the room. "*Auschwitz was a death camp.*"

"*Yes, and it had several tunnels under it, more than what has been found. The Nazis dug tunnels under everything. Now Auschwitz is protected as a memorial for all those who died there. No one would ever be allowed to even step foot in that field, let alone dig there.*"

"*How can you be sure?*"

"*I'm not. I only know what an old man had said: Two by two. In Auschwitz, the dead watch the rest.*"

"*What made you tell them?*"

"*I told you, they killed my son. I didn't want them to kill my daughters over something that does not exist. Everyone knows the last of the V-2s were given over to the United*

States. Why else would they have approved my amnesty so easily?"

~ * ~ * ~ * ~ * ~ * ~

Diesel had just sat back down back where he'd started before the invitation for tea when Rowlinson came barging from his office, heading straight for the holding room where Trenton was. There was a look on his face, like a whole lot of trouble had just arrived, that had Diesel jumping to his feet to follow after him.

Rowlinson didn't even knock, just walked right in. So did Diesel.

"I just got some disturbing news from one of our sources—" Rowlinson started to say when Diesel's phone rang with an added alert signal. Rowlinson turned, glaring at him, but Diesel's wasn't the only one. He glanced to Trenton just as he shot away from the mirrors, lunging for his phone still sitting on table. For both of them to get called at the same exact moment only meant bad news.

They both answered.

The second Diesel's thumb tapped the speaker icon on the screen, Harper's voice was blaring out with the darkest of news, "*They're dead. I just got a call from Agent Johnson. Hanze Coshneizmen's wife and kids have been gunned down!*"

Trenton's head snapped up, eyes frozen on Diesel's face, his phone pressed against his head, "My guys! What about my guys?!"

"*Killed, too. All four— Rick, Max, Tyree, and Jo.*"

Trenton was silent for a long moment and then fear struck him hard. "They're coming! Get her out of here." He shouted to Diesel then turned to Rowlinson, "Can you get these fucking things off me?!" He held his cuffed hands up.

Katianna fed off the fear from the news and Trenton's sudden panic. Already, she was screaming to protest being sent away, jumping for Trenton when Diesel tried to pull her away.

Diesel reached for her again. "No. Kat, you have to come with me. We need to get you and Paris out of here now."

But she never heard him. She clearly wasn't going to leave Trenton when she had seen the fear on his face. The very thing and reason why Trenton had come with Hanze was happening, and Kat knew that Trenton's life was in grave danger. He'd been at the meet too. He would be able to identify several faces.

The entire room broke out in chaos as the detectives got the information from Rowlinson and tried to decipher what was happening. Trenton was shouting with relentless commands to get Kat to go, while trying to get more details from Harper.

"No, I'm not leaving—" she sobbed, "Last time you left me, you got shot, and then I was all alone in a hospital in France and no one would tell me anything! I'm not going through that hell again!"

Trenton pushed her into Diesel's arms. She flailed about, trying to get free, and then Trenton gave him the nod.

Diesel had no choice but to put her in a headlock and knock her out. "I'm sorry, baby girl, but it's for your own good." He whispered into her ear as she slowly fell limp in his arms.

"Get these goddamn handcuffs off me!" Trenton finally lost his cool and shouted at the four men who'd just stood there and done nothing but talk and bicker about what to do.

Diesel had to get Kat and Paris out of there first. Only then could he be of any help to his brother. He scooped Katianna up and exchanged a worried glance with Trenton. His brother was obviously trying to calculate the safest place to hide their family.

Detective Wells perked up with a suggestion, "We have a safehouse. Just a small flat toward Kemptown. It's not far and I can arrange to have her taken there."

"Conceal her, somehow—" Diesel glanced around then, spotting the area rug, "There! Roll her up in the carpet."

"Are you nuts?" Wells stammered.

"They don't know she's here, but if they've already gone after a family an entire ocean away, they won't stop at taking out Trenton's either."

Suddenly Trenton was free of his bonds and was snatching the rug up off the floor, then he tossed it over to Diesel, "Get her out, now!" Then he vanished out of the room.

Diesel shot a quick glance over his shoulder to the two-way mirror— on the other side of it, the agonizing face of a man who'd risked everything to try and save his family was pressed against it. He hadn't even been told yet.

Rowlinson was leaning out the door, bellowing out to his men in the main room, "Get Ed Davey up here and have him throw on a jumpsuit from one of the caretakers!"

Ed Davey turned out to be one of the precinct's undercover officers who'd found himself in a face-to-face show down with Trenton that nearly got Ed pounded into the hood of a car during the raid. Now he was posed as a janitor rather than some random guy walking his dog at night, and now set with the task of transporting Paris and Kat out of the building.

Diesel stepped over to Paris and pulled him into a hard hug. Then, so no one else could see, he slowly slipped his side arm into Paris' pants between them. He pressed his lips against Paris' head like a kiss and spoke quietly, "You remember the church we passed with the tall tower being built?" He felt the minute nod, "Go there. Directly across from it are some townhouses. One of them is vacant with scaffold-facing. Text me when you arrive and wait for me there." Another nod, and this time Diesel felt Paris' pain like a heavy weight, "You know what to do. If the cop so much as diverts the course or tries anything— shoot him." He felt the great heave in Paris' body, but it was followed with a nod. And he left, following the cop now armed with a woman rolled in a carpet and thrown over his shoulder. *By the looks of the rest of the precinct, you'd think they were at a funeral in way of the long faces they all wore. Some thought they were overreacting. They'd soon find out,* and he would whole-heartedly welcome coming across as over reactive instead of the former. But with what Harper had already told them, this might be the last time he'd see Paris, and he'd spent it handing him a gun.

"Paris! I love you!"

Paris snatched a hoodie from the back of one of the desk chairs as he passed, not caring to ask if he could, and pulled it on as he followed behind Davey. He refused to look back.

After watching Paris leave, Diesel rejoined Trenton, "Did anyone tell him?" Diesel leaned in toward Trenton and asked under his breath.

"No, not yet. But he has been told a threat was made."

Phones were already ringing off the hook within the small room. Calls coming in and more going out. Rowlinson barked to his men out in the main room and several of them shouted back as they relayed phoned-in details.

"We need a chopper so we can get him out." Trenton was taking charge, like it or not.

"Already on its way." Someone from one of the desks answered.

"Good. Get someone to watch the door to the roof. No one goes up or comes down but us."

Rowlinson nodded, done with arguing over who was in charge. Sometimes a cop, a good cop, had to know when he was out of his league.

"You're not taking him out of here without my authorization."

Trenton spun so fast that no one was prepared for it. Suddenly procuring a gun and leveling it between Connolly's eyes.

"Hey! That's my gun!" The officer that'd been walking past Trenton at that precise moment turned into him.

Diesel closed in, holding a hand out to stop the officer from making an unwise choice.

Several of the other officers, and Wells included, stood frozen with hands on their own sidearms, not tempting Trenton to pull the trigger.

"Let's all just take a step back and cool down here a second." Rowlinson spoke calmly over the nervous murmurs of the others.

Trenton ignored the suggestion, his attention locked on Connolly. "This whole screw up is your fault. Busting a gathering without even knowing who you were fucking going after. Then brought us all here to some yokel police station with a hundred witnesses and zero protection. Now, we are all in danger."

Connolly swallowed nervously. His body teetered slightly as his bravado swayed. His hands swiped at his slacks while he licked his lips before finally mustering up his response. "I have to go with him."

Trenton lowered the gun then passed it back to its owner, but stepped in close to Connolly and made it all vividly clear who was going to call the shots for the time being. "You do as I say, when I say. No calls to or from anyone until we're all safe. Understood?"

Connolly took a moment to give it some consideration then nodded. Even if a bit reluctantly, the threat was all too clear and Trenton wasn't taking applications for debate.

Wells reached out, grabbing Connolly and eased him back, giving Trenton a nod that they would comply.

"Trent." Diesel's eyes were locked on the men in the room to ensure no one would get trigger happy after the move his brother had just pulled. Trenton turned to him and they huddled together with their backs to the rest, "Do you have any ideas for a plan?"

"First to get out of the country."

"France?"

"Hmm, maybe, but perhaps better to get up to the Netherlands. Neutral ground, neutral government. Then speak with someone in the Dutch Consulate to find out who we can contact in Germany to put an end to this."

"In what way?"

"Blow the whole thing wide open. Take the responsibility off of Coshneizmen."

"And that will help him?" Diesel wasn't seeing how this was going to help Hanze. But then he saw his brother shake his head in a dreary sway. A cold and rash reality that there was little hope they would save Hanze in this, just hopes to prevent anyone actually finding the missiles. Because there were too many bad guys out there who would be all too happy to have them.

~ * ~

Within a half hour they heard the helicopter arrive.

Trenton's own personal firearms were returned to him. He made a quick check of each, pulling the clips to ensure all the rounds were there, setting one into the chambers, and then turning the safeties off.

"Diesel, you take the rear. Hanze, stay behind me, and Connolly, keep behind Hanze. Stay between Diesel and me at all times. If we get into anything, duck down. Do not run."

Connolly gave him a look of absurdity, "We're in a police station for god's sake. I doubt we're going to run into trouble here."

Trenton only eyed him, ignoring the ignorance. How such a young and inexperienced detective had been put in charge of the task wasn't adding up. Then again, he often found himself questioning the calls of federal task forces. It seemed England's was little better than the United States'.

Rowlinson hung up the phone and gave them a solid look, "They're ready for you. Officers in place."

Trenton nodded then waved Hanze, Connolly, and Diesel to follow closely.

He paused just inside the door to the stairwell, then stepped in further to glance both down and up the levels before he waved the others in. He listened as much as attempted to peek around blind corners. At this point, he trusted no one but Diesel. Not even the officers inside the building. The coast seemed clear, he gave a check over his shoulder at the others and in they proceeded.

Every level was treated in much the same way as they made their way up the six flights of stairs. Occasionally throwing a hand out to the men behind him, silently stopping them while taking a few steps ahead before giving it the all clear. The clatter from a door opening two flights down had Diesel's abrupt attention and he stepped into the rail and aimed downward, "Clear the stairwell! Last warning and then I open fire!"

"Shit! Clearing!" A response came from below and the quick exit echoed a hasty retreat.

They'd just made the fifth floor when Trenton heard a commotion going on further up. He signaled the guys to stop, then took off up the stairs on his own until he hit the top, finding the hallway in total darkness. The distinct muffled sound of someone gagged but trying to talk sent internal alarms off in his head.

He craned his neck to stretch around the last corner wall, hoping to see who or what without becoming an open target. "Officer!" Trenton called out to the man who was supposedly assigned to guard the door. The answer came in a muffled *humph* and what sounded like a shoe kicking at the door.

Trenton came up on the last step and saw the uniformed officer crumpled on the floor in front of the door he needed to exit. "Shit." He cursed, turned, and ran.

He never made it more than two steps down when he heard the gun go off below. "Deez!" Trenton shouted. Now he took the steps two at a time and skidded around the corner, finding Diesel standing in a stand off with Connolly, guns raised, and both staring down the other's barrel.

Connolly was shaking, but then Trenton saw the slight squeeze of the detective's fingers.

Trenton fired.

Connolly's hand exploded in red and slammed into the wall, firing off at the same time.

Diesel twisted away and returned fire. The bullet meant for him was now the victim of the cinder block wall while Connolly stumbled back— then slumped against the rail before tumbling down the stairs leaving a trail of blood along the way.

Trenton hurtled the remaining stairs and dropped down beside Hanze. Trenton took the bloody hand reaching to grab hold of him or anything. The exit hole in Hanze's neck wasn't something Trenton could do anything about. He could do nothing but watch the man's life fade away.

"My— my family—" but whatever it was Hanze wanted to say, the words died with him.

"Don't worry, they're already up there waiting for you." Trenton pulled Hanze's eyes closed and bowed his head. He'd never lost a man before. He wasn't sure there was anything he could have done differently that would have changed this outcome. But it did not dissipate the grief he now felt. He hadn't just lost one man, but an entire family.

~ * ~ * ~ * ~ * ~ * ~

It was still several more hours before Diesel and Trenton were able to leave the precinct building to the diverted safehouse to retrieve Kat and Paris.

They arrived at the abandoned townhouse Diesel had spotted when they'd ridden in earlier that day. It was easy to locate, even from several blocks away, when they spotted the high-rise being built behind a massive cathedral.

Rule number one— always set up a rendezvous spot upon arrival to a new area, in the event they got separated and had to hide.

They found Paris, along with undercover Officer Ed Davey, up on the third floor. Kat had somehow crawled inside a corner hutch that'd been left behind, hiding as she would under Trenton's desk. Paris sat in a weathered, rickety chair he'd dragged over next to the hutch and guarded it.

"You could have told me there was another plan." Davey commented to Diesel when they arrived.

"No. We could not." Diesel's gaze was locked on Paris' back.

"The safehouse would have been safe." Ed protested. He sounded like a man who'd stared down a barrel not too long ago.

"Tell that to the ones who were there and are now dead."

Ed's face almost melted off, "I don't understand. How did this all go wrong?"

"Connelly was a mole. Whoever made the hit had been told of the safehouse and they hit that too." Diesel let out a heavy sigh then took another step closer toward Paris.

"My partner, is he—?"

"Alive. He'd left to come looking for you just before the hit took place."

Ed let out a sigh of relief, then glanced at Paris, "He hasn't said more than two words since we got here. The man is not happy with any ideas of losing you. Had this gone wrong, I'd have feared he would have just stayed there and let himself wither away."

Trenton was squatting down in front of the cabinet and pulling it open, "Come out, little Mouse." He hadn't needed to say it twice when two little hands reached out for him. He caught her and pulled her out into his arms, then reached out only momentarily to touch Paris.

Diesel went over to join them and ran his hand over Paris' shoulders. His Fallen Angel didn't move, his hands clutching at the gun Diesel had given him, still in his grip, mindless of its purpose at the moment. Diesel slowly took it from him, returned the safety, then dropped it into his side holster. "Paris?"

Paris twisted and latched on. Thick arms packed with a fierce need circled Diesel's waist and held on for a long time. Just as Trenton held onto his Unicorn.

It was dark outside, but the mourning had already begun.

~ * ~ * ~ * ~ * ~ * ~

CHAPTER THIRTY-SIX

~ * ~ * ~ * ~ * ~ * ~

The swarm of cameras and onlookers, crowded together behind the police tape across the street, only caused the headlines of recent days to echo in Diesel's head.

~~ *No Rest for Nazi Orphans*~~

~~ *The Last of the Eichmann family take war secrets to the grave with them* ~~

It was about as close to giving any pity to Hanze as the news was going to, as if to prove that even in modern times, the world was unable to give up its pain or resentment of the past. Even though Hanze himself had nothing to do with it. He'd just been a child. One who'd spent his life trying to get out from under such shadows and give the world something good.

But what bothered him more weren't the headlines on the paper or the federal agent's photos of two girls shown dead with Jo's bullet-ridden body trying to shield them—

it was Trenton. It was watching his brother silently cope with the loss.

Upon their return, Trenton immersed himself in taking care of all the funeral details for his four men. One of whom had been Johanna Cezzari. The very one who'd been angry over her assignments. Still, she'd done her job and was killed in the line of duty, shielding the two little girls, Elsabeth and Karoline Coshneizmen, with her own body in hopes of protecting them from the onslaught of bullets. But in the end, it hadn't been enough. After getting hit with nearly a dozen bullets, the two girls were also killed while their mother Rosalind was forced to watch nearby, then killed as well.

Jo and Max had been veterans from active duty, so Diesel made the arrangements to have the National Guard present and to usher the caskets after the services. While Diesel was not allowed to give the same treatment to Rick and Tyree, Trenton made sure their families knew he did not think any less of them. They died trying to protect a family in the same way a soldier would.

Diesel wore his military dress uniform to honor the downed veterans that had once served their country, but his brother did not. Trenton represented for the two men who died doing the same job.

Paris and Kat stayed close to them, though the mood was sullen for all four.

Diesel remained ever vigilant over his brother and the darkness that surrounded him. The only anchor Trenton had was the small woman attached to his shirt, fingers curled into the fabric in a tight fist. Trenton never once pulled her from him, as if her need to cling to him was more for him than for her at the moment. And perhaps, in part, that was true. It wasn't the first time Diesel had known his brother to find comfort in that kind of connection.

Paris almost mirrored her, without the wrinkles to his uniform. Paris only stepped from his side on the occasions that Diesel spoke with some of the other officers at the wake, and even then Diesel didn't like it and would quickly call Paris back to his side. He didn't need the distance or the consideration for what others might have thought about him. He didn't care— he never had. Especially now. Not only had he a man for a lover, but also he was deeply in love with his man. There was no need for shame in that or a need to hide it.

But he did hate that Paris had to be here for this. There were some places that not even his Imp could make happier, and it only dulled the many colors that made Paris who he was.

He was all the more glad when the wake was over, though it pained him to see the stress on Trenton's face. All four of his men were going in different directions, which tore Trenton up something awful. Because it meant he couldn't follow any one of them for the burials.

Trenton stood diligently out front under the belvedere. His gaze out on the horizon while the caskets were carried out, one by one, and loaded up in their prospective hearses.

Families and friends paused to thank him for the honorary services, or just to shake his hand in tearful silence. A few hugs were exchanged. Then they all went their own ways, loaded up in the limos and cars that now lined up to follow their loved ones' final journeys.

Trenton never moved. Diesel, Dane, Marcus, and Harper were the last to approach him, but he waved them off so as not to leave the families waiting. Diesel was reluctant, but the rigid expression on Trenton's face, the clenching jaw, told him his brother was not all there. *Go now before he snapped.*

Diesel took a moment to stand at his side, regardless. He hardly had to twitch his hand and Paris' was already there, lacing his fingers in his, and then together they loaded up in a chauffeured car and rode away, headed for Johanna Cezzari's burial.

That was when Diesel cried.

~ * ~ * ~ * ~ * ~ * ~

Trenton dropped down on one of the benches and sat in silence in front of the funeral home while Katianna, his last rock in a stormy sea of emotions, knelt at his feet. Together, the two watched the four funeral brigades drive by in a somber parade.

The last vehicle remaining was his Knight Conquest, its glossy black armored body soaking up sunlight, as if remiss that someone he knew had been killed doing a job he gave them, and equally obtuse that he could not follow any one of them without dishonoring the others.

Songbirds chirped from trees, and it was just one more thing to remind him that life went on and often without a care for the loss of others. He couldn't bear it. He had been given a job to protect that family and now he had failed, and at the cost of his own.

"Kat, why don't you go inside and use the restroom before we go."

"I'm o—"

"Go." His order somber and quiet, but insistent. She was hesitant, but finally got up and headed in. He waited— stared at his truck, the epitome of protective vehicles, and yet he had not protected *them*. The upsurge of anguish became too much to keep restrained any longer and he was suddenly to his feet, his gun pulled from his shoulder holster— he aimed for the Knight and opened fire. "AAAAAAAAHHHHHHHhhhhhh!"

Bullets hit and bounced off the Knight, leaving shattered pock marks in the armor-glass coating, then ricocheting in all directions. Trenton didn't stop squeezing the trigger until the gun clicked with an empty chamber. He still wasn't finished and wasted no time, pulling another clip from his lapel pocket, reloaded, and opened fire once more until it, too, ran dry.

The outburst drained him. He crashed to his knees, folded over into a ball, until his head cracked on the pavement, where he remained and cried.

Katianna was suddenly there next to him. Wrapping around him like a soothing blanket to shield him from the storm, if only the storm had been *out there*.

~ * ~ * ~ * ~ * ~ * ~

CHAPTER THIRTY-SEVEN

~ * ~ * ~ * ~ * ~ * ~

Half an hour had passed, or perhaps an hour, and Trenton still sat there. He just couldn't bring himself to be ready to drive away. He'd at least moved back to the bench, and he spent a good amount of that time staring at the damage he'd done to his truck. When he grew tired of that, he stared at the ground at his feet where his slave sat, propped against his knee, having nodded out some time ago as she waited on him.

Trenton hardly looked up when he heard the crunch of small pebbles under footsteps, glancing only when the shadow of a man sat next to him.

Pyotr Laszkovi.

Trenton shook his head softly, trying to laugh, "Which one called you?"

Like always, Pyotr's smile was a warm welcome that spoke endlessly that all would be okay in time. That he somehow knew this for certain. "All four of them."

Trenton nodded. They had come, and they each took up the duty to follow a fallen soldier out so that none of his men were dishonored, while he stayed behind because he could not choose one over another. His fingers floated up and caressed the side of his Unicorn's face, his thoughts torn, and his heart still breaking over the loss.

"Honor me with your company." Pyotr gestured.

Again Trenton nodded, then woke his Unicorn and they followed the man.

"I'd been meaning to compliment you." Pyotr opened a new conversation.

"For?" Trenton asked as they walked along the sidewalk to a waiting car.

"Your capture of your Unicorn has resulted in some venturesome literature. Cliff and I enjoy reading together, and we've discovered that we can rarely manage one of her explicit sex scenes without having to— pause for relief. It's quite poetic."

Trenton chuckled, having finally read a few of her books. "I would hardly call her written sex scenes as poetic."

"Ah, but even raw sex between invested lovers becomes poetry. As I am sure it would be very exhilarating to watch the two of you together."

"I don't do shows."

Pyotr laughed, "I'd still watch."

"You had your chance down at the resort."

"I was— shamelessly preoccupied with out ventures of your hospitality."

Trenton held the door while Katianna got into the back seat of the burgundy Audi Quattro, then he sat up front with Pyotr. "You are as perverted as Dane."

"Ah, yes, Dane Masters. The man, whose dark side keeps him hovering at the threshold of his closet. Even in his brothers' company, he fears his most beloved and cherished dark-sided perversion to be unacceptable debauchery, and he is held imprisoned by them."

Again Trenton nodded, because it was true of Dane's withholdings, though not true that anyone of them would turn him away because of them. They already knew what Dane's desires were and they found no fault in them.

Pyotr pulled his car out of the parking lot without giving any inclination of where he was taking them. Or if he'd bring him back for Trenton's Knight later. Right now, it didn't seem important, or rather Trenton just didn't care.

"Trenton, I know you don't come to me to talk, but I hope you will at least listen."

Trenton let his eyes shift out the windows, watching without seeing as the roadside skipped by.

"You give your entire focus and dedication to protecting others. Only, sometimes, the threats are greater than ourselves and you can't save the world from itself." He paused a moment. Pyotr was good with words, but justifying death was something no one could do. "You can't burden yourself with the blame for this."

"I can and I will."

"For how long?"

"As long as it takes."

"Takes for what?" Pyotr gave him a double take as the car rolled to a stop at a traffic light.

"Until I know for certain Elsabeth will be safe and live out a long life away from all this."

"Elsabeth? Who— wait, that was one of the girls' names. But I don't understand, the newspaper said they were both killed."

"The youngest lived. Johanna's death wasn't in vain." Trenton slowly turned and looked at Pyotr, and their gazes locked, "A sacrifice not even her family will ever have the honor to know."

Pyotr ignored the car honking behind them as he sat at the green light and nodded his deep understanding to Trenton of the burden he too was now bestowed to carry.

~ * ~ * ~ * ~ * ~ * ~

CHAPTER THIRTY-EIGHT

~ * ~ * ~ * ~ * ~ * ~

"Want a drink? I need a drink." Paris stewed and marched straight for the bar when they got home from the funeral.

"Yeah, I'll take one." Diesel answered. The words took far more effort than they should have, but he was exhausted. Not just physically, but mentally as well. He just stopped dead center in the living room and began to loosen the buttons of his dress uniform. That's how tired he was. Drove all the way home and didn't think once to remove his coat— despite it being too hot for it. Now home, a drink and perhaps a swim sounded good. Curling up with Paris and napping sounded even better.

He removed his sidearm and dropped it down on the table. The clunk on the glass top had Paris spinning on his heels, the flare of agitation showing, but then he went back to pouring. When he brought one over, he seemed a notch or two even more uptight than he'd been when they walked in the door.

"Talk to me, Paris." Diesel took the drink then reached for him.

Paris stayed out of reach, "I don't want to talk." He downed his drink in one gulp. The lacking clink of ice caught Diesel's attention and he realized Paris was drinking something straight up. The amber liquid most likely whiskey or bourbon. Which meant something most definitely was wrong.

"Paris." Diesel draped his coat over the back of the sofa and continued with his shirt, then the belt, following with toeing off the spit-shined black shoes.

Paris ignored him and went back to the bar, where Diesel watched him grab Marcus' fine line whiskey. Diesel wasn't about to stop Paris. If he needed it, then he could have it. Whiskey could be replaced. Paris, however, was irreplaceable.

"Don't shut me out. Talk to me." Diesel went over to him, but Paris shrugged him off and stepped away once more when Diesel attempted to caress his shoulder.

Diesel closed his eyes and counted, reminding himself that this was just as hard on Paris as it was on him— only for other reasons. He just wasn't sure he had the energy to handle the bristling walls Paris was known for when he was fighting his own vulnerability. Not here and now, at least. Any other time would not be an issue for Diesel, but at this very moment, it was too much at once. Especially when the one man who'd always been his rock was the one who was really caving. Because sometimes even a Dom could come apart. Their strength leaves them or falters. Dominant men were not gods— still only human. Yet when Trenton fell, Diesel felt especially vulnerable himself. It was at that precise instant a thought struck him and Diesel had to question if he was, in fact, still a Dom. He still maintained his title at the club and with their associates. But what of Paris? *Stop.* He didn't need to be questioning himself over this. And certainly not now. "Hey, what do you say we just strip down and just take a dip in the pool for a bit, then spend the rest of the day in bed? Some napping, petting, and a little more napping."

"I don't know." Paris grumbled and went for a third refill of his glass.

"Maybe you should slow down."

Paris shot him a bitter glance and went right on with his intentions, "I'm more than capable of getting drunk when I want to, and I don't need your permission to do it."

"Fine then, but at least come out to the pool for a swim with me."

"I'm fine and I don't want to swim."

"Then talk to me."

Paris spun around glaring, "I said, I'm fine!"

"This is not fine."

"Leave me alone." Paris headed for the stairs, but Diesel rushed to intercept and Paris only turned to avoid being grabbed.

"Paris, I'm not going to leave you alone. I've told you before that I can't let you shut me out. We need to communicate when there is a problem."

"TALKING ISN'T GOING TO FIX THIS!" Paris shouted at him, slinging his drink, glass and all, across the room. It skipped across the carpet until it reached the marble surface of the hall, then skidded right into the back wall where it shattered. He started to head out the back, but Diesel wasn't going to let him turn away.

"Paris!" Diesel finally shouted to get his attention, "What do you want from me?"

Paris snapped around, glaring at him, and it all came pouring out like a broken dam. "I want all the gun shooting to end! I want the dying around me to end." He began pacing in a tight circle, his hands going back to his head, and he stared up at the high vaulted ceiling, clearly coming apart at the seams. There was still so much combusting inside him. He hadn't even begun to express himself, "Everywhere I look, it's death— dying— and shooting— and more shooting— AND I WANT IT TO STOP! I want my world safe again!"

"Paris, if there was a cure for the world to end killing, I'd pay for it myself and make sure every person on the planet got it. But I can't fix the hatred of men. I can only try to protect those within my reach and teach the rest to protect themselves."

"No! What if I told you I want you to sell the gun shop— that I want you to just get rid of it?"

Diesel struggled to keep his insides calm. He hurt too much to rage back at Paris. *This*— none of this was Paris' fault. Nor did anything Paris said, or wished for right now, anger him. "Closing the shop won't end the killing. Turning the television and news off— won't make bad things not exist."

"But why you?"

"Because I'm good at it. Because Trenton is good at it. Because I know he won't stop and I can't let him go out there with no one to have his back. You and Kat are alive because of what we can do."

Paris' attention snapped from the ceiling to leer back at Diesel, "What you do puts us in danger!"

"Some, yes. You could have stayed here while I went to help Trent. But then what about the bank? Did Trenton or I cause that? What of Kat's abduction? Did we do that? I'm grateful and thankful every day we were able to do something to save the both of you. Or we wouldn't be here, having this argument, right now!"

Paris twisted away, tossing his hands up then dropping them back down over his head, gripping the pain that had him agonizing from within, and his eyes pleaded with the ceiling.

"Paris, keep talking to me."

"It's just that—" he turned to face Diesel, and his tone dropped until it was nearly inaudible, "I don't want to lose you." He surrendered the admittance of his ultimate fear. "You made me fall in love with you, and now— I am gripped with this fear. I can't stand it! I don't want it anymore."

Diesel stepped in, took Paris' head in his own hands, and forced his gaze down so Diesel could look into his eyes. *Dark eyes,* and at the moment they were cold with resentment and the very fear he admitting to. Dark— no longer the warm, earthy mix of smoky gray and hazel around the rusty-red star burst; so many hues a soul could fall into them and flourish there usually. Now, there was only the storm of emotions, "I don't want to lose you either. Especially if there is something within my power to protect you."

"I need to get out of this house. I need air. I need space."

"Okay," Diesel nodded. "I'll take you to the nature park and we can just go for a long walk. Okay?"

Paris nodded timidly, so Diesel grabbed a change of clothes, his keys, and they headed out.

He took them out to Fire Island, where there was plenty of wide open space to keep on walking for however long they needed.

"I'm just not used to this." Paris said this without invitation for Diesel to dispute it. So he left it, allowing their footsteps to lead them, hopefully to some resolution in their heads as well. When they turned back, Paris finally took Diesel's hand and they walked the rest of the way as such, in silence.

When they made it back to where they'd parked, they found a picnic area not being used and claimed it for some personal time. Paris took up residence, sitting on the end of the table while Diesel stood between his legs, and they just held each other in quiet refuge.

Unfortunately, the quiet didn't last long when some uninvited company showed up.

A group of four guys ventured near, pausing when they spotted Diesel and Paris.

Diesel felt the trouble before the first word was uttered. Just the cocky stances of the one in the front and the way his posse followed along said it all— looking for trouble.

"Look at this shit. Whole world is going gay. Now a guy can't even come to the beach without having to look at a couple of faggots fucking in the park." The cocky one slurred.

"Go back to the city, monkeys!" The shortest of the four, in a blue t-shirt, called out.

Diesel dropped his forehead to Paris', took in deep breaths, and tried to ignore the rowdy comments from the gang of rednecks. It was definitely something Diesel did not need to hear. He wasn't a trigger-happy, hot tempered person; it took a lot of shit to work him over. This in itself would not have been worth him to turn his head their way. It was everything else that had happened over the last few days, which had been more than small issues for him to cope with. Not to mention, *his* life was causing injury to that *innocence* Paris kept so well tucked away. The secret window Diesel loved and treasured about his lover. Just knowing it was there was always enough for him, but finding out it was getting hurt by him now weighed heavily on his heart. He hated it because he didn't know how to stop or prevent it, and he feared the consequences if the beautiful flame inside his lover should get snuffed out.

"Didn't you hear my buddy here? He told you to get a fucking move on, faggot." The cocky one prodded further.

It put Diesel instantly to the edge of his ability to look the other way— and placed him on the overly defensive and protective side of what his actions would be. Not to mention, Diesel held zero— nada— as in negative tolerance for hate crimes. So when some oversized thug started calling his lover a faggot and threatening him in the way he approached, there were no negotiations as to what Diesel was going to do to the man. "I'm sorry for what I'm about to do."

"I know." Paris answered quietly as they watched the four men draw closer.

And then one of them made the first mistake.

Diesel caught the cocky man by the wrist just as he swung at him. He then twisted the arm inward, forcing the man to bend forward to avoid the pain of having his arm twisted backwards. Diesel locked his grip then took a step back, taking cocky man with him, then thrusted his right elbow straight back, level at the jawline of the next man in line, landing it directly in the second troublemaker's face. With no pause between, Diesel took a giant stride forward, bringing cocky-man's arm with him and in a fast twist, Diesel sent the guy flipping head over heels and crashing down hard on the ground on his back. A loud pop completed the movement leaving cocky-man screaming as he rolled to his side, clutching at his dislocated shoulder.

"DEEZ!"

Diesel spun around, spotting one of the others from the gang going after Paris. The sight of a broken beer bottle being weaved about had Diesel turning a shade of raging red. The thug's hand flashed out and suddenly Paris was jerking his head back with a hand immediately going to his face. Diesel lunged. *The thug was blessed if he lived past tonight.*

He took no chances the guy might swing again. He tackled him full on, twisting, taking the thug to the ground. Diesel came down on top of him and quickly swung his legs around, wrapping them around the thug's neck and shoulder. He clamped his leg muscles down, squeezing until the guy fell limp.

Diesel didn't even have the chance to get to his feet when the fourth in the group tried to come at him. He sent a boot out to catch the running attacker in the gut and allowed the momentum to catapult the guy up and over, crashing on his head. The guy recovered quickly but only found himself tackled back to the ground as Diesel came over him and threw punch after punch.

"Deez, its over. You can stop now!"

He heard Paris. He recognized the plea to stop, but he couldn't. *Too many had tried to threaten them. Too many had tried to kill them— kill Paris. Too many. This one would never live to be that kind of threat to anyone. Not to his Fallen Angel.*

"Diesel, stop the cops are here!"

"Freeze! Hold it right there, mister." The order came from a beat patrol.

The rage bellowed inside him to keep going— *don't stop until the threats were dead themselves.* His fist drawn back and ready to strike again.

"I said don't move." The commanding order came again.

Reaching inside him. Not as stern as a lieutenant's would, but it was enough to cut through the red rage that blinded him and Diesel slowly brought his hands up over his head, fingers splayed out to show he held no weapon.

He glanced over his shoulder and spotted two more officers coming up fast with tasers drawn. The one behind him had him under the aim of his police-issued revolver.

One of the new arrivals quickly stepped up behind Diesel with the telltale clink of handcuffs. "Keep your hands behind your head."

Diesel did as he was told, but when he heard the same orders given to Paris, the protests came roaring from him. "No, wait! He's the victim here. You can arrest me and these four hoodlums, but leave him be."

"I believe that's up for us to determine." One of the officers responded, bracing himself in case Diesel tried to get physical with him. And pointedly ordered him back on his knees.

Diesel dropped back down and to his relief, Paris was not handcuffed. So Diesel remained cooperatively quiet after that. *No cop liked being told how to do their job.*

An ambulance arrived shortly after for the four Diesel had tossed. Outside of the dislocated shoulder, Diesel knew full well he hadn't done any permanent damage, though he was headed in that direction all the way up until the police arrived. Cocky-man getting the all clear to go to jail and not the hospital started up with a slew of profanities that resulted in him and his buddies getting handcuffed as well. *Insurance to prevent a rematch.*

Diesel was finally aided to his feet and walked over to one of the squad cars waiting in the parking lot, where he was patted down and his wallet pulled. While he had two permits to carry a concealed, he was grateful he'd not had one on him at the time. Stupid, but grateful.

"Diesel Nelson Gentry." The woman officer read out his license. Then spotted his permit, "You carrying?"

He read the name tag on her uniform, "It's in the truck, Officer Rhodes."

"Which truck is yours?" She glanced slightly but not trusting to turn her back to him entirely. He was, after all, twice her size. But she looked tough enough for her job.

"White, Ford Raptor over there." He inclined his head to the beefy truck in the nearby parking lot.

"How many weapons do you have in your truck right now?"

"One in the console. The one I usually wear is under the seat, and two more in a lock-case behind the back seat."

"That's a lot of fire power. Am I going to find something you're not supposed to have?"

"No. When you run my name, you'll find I am licensed by the state and city of New York for a concealed-carry and for first responder's assistance."

"Anything else I need to know about? Been drinking tonight?"

"I had half a glass before coming out here."

"How long ago was that?"

Diesel twisted his arms behind him until he could just catch a glimpse of his watch, "Almost four hours ago."

"Alright then. Now, I'm gonna put you in the back of the car, but I'm gonna roll the windows down, cause it's hot out here tonight. But I don't want to hear no noise from you while we get all the information down."

"As you say."

And she opened up the door to her squad car and Diesel did as he was told and slid into the back seat and kept quiet while she called in his name and permit ID over the band radio. "Dispatch, this is unit two-eight-nine-seven, responding to a called in fight-in-progress inside the Robert Moss State Park. Six adult male subjects found in a physical altercation. Arrest in progress. Ambulance is present. I have subject one, Diesel Gentry, in custody—"

"Hey! Stop right there!"

Rhodes spun around when shouts broke out over at the ambulance. She abandoned the radio and took off to assist the other officers.

Diesel twisted around in the seat, glancing out the back window. He spotted Paris backing away from the ambulance then nearly jumped back just as someone was tackled to the ground. Diesel wasn't about to sit idle and he maneuvered his hands behind him. He felt out the small clip on his denim pocket, then pulled it free and used its hidden key end to unlock the cuffs. He'd just gotten his wrists free and was reaching out the window to open the door when Rhodes returned and quickly had her gun trained on him.

"I wouldn't do that if I were you, Mr. Gentry."

Diesel froze, let out a regretful sigh and then sat back, hands up in the air.

Rhodes grabbed the door handle with one hand, keeping her aim with the other and opened the door. "Step out slow and careful-like."

Diesel did as told.

"Face down on the ground, hands behind your back."

Again, he did as told.

"How'd you get loose?"

He raised his fingers behind him showing her the tiny escape key that he'd had clipped to his jeans.

Rhodes planted a knee into his back to keep him down, then cautiously took the hide-a-key from him before she returned a pair of cuffs to his wrists. "Why would you be carrying something like this on you?"

"I teach self-defense at my shop. When the handcuff assault rapes started, I started giving those out and several others like it to my class."

"You afraid someone is going to try and rape you?" The question was popped with a heavy dosage of sarcasm.

Diesel would have chuckled under better circumstances, "No, but I do find they can come in handy in certain predicaments."

"What's the name of your shop?"

"Hyde Park Gun Shop and Shooting Range."

"The one with that gauntlet training system the precincts use?"

"Same one."

"You know, this isn't the right way to use these. This could have gotten you shot." She held out the small key.

Though he could hardly lift his head well enough to see it, he knew what she was insinuating when she scolded him for it. "I was afraid for Paris. I will risk myself to protect him."

She let out a heavy huff, "Well, I'm gonna keep this for right now."

"How's Paris? Is he okay?"

"He's got a slight cut over his brow. The man who called the fight in said they'd jumped the two of you. So we're going to let him go home."

"And me?"

"I'm afraid we're gonna have to take you in. Self-defense or not, you used excessive force. Law says I have to take you in and let the judge handle it."

"Can I just see him a moment, see his face, and make sure he's okay?"

"You got any more of those keys on you?"

"No."

She patted him down anyway, and searched his wardrobe with her flashlight.

"Don't forget to look at my shoe laces." He muttered.

"I could have sworn you said you didn't have any more of these things on you."

"I don't, but I give those to my class as well and I sell them. You'll want to get in the habit of looking for them. May as well start with me."

"What do they look like?"

"Metal caps that slide right on the ends of the shoelace. Can't miss the key pin on the end once you know to look for it." That bit of info dump cost him his tactical boots.

When she felt secure he had told the truth, he was loaded back into the patrol car, unlaced shoes and all, and then allowed to speak with Paris.

Paris came over and knelt at the door, peering in through the window.

"Are you okay?"

Paris nodded then touched the small cut over his brow.

"Let me see."

Paris leaned his head over so Diesel could see for himself the damages. "Have Marcus glue it shut. Hopefully there won't be a scar. I know you'll hate that."

Paris didn't comment.

"Have Marcus come set the bail, okay?"

"Why don't I just get Trenton?"

"No!" He stopped himself, "Please. Leave my brother out of this. He's already been put through enough. Marcus can set the bail for me." Paris nodded quietly. But Diesel could see all that emotional building he'd released early was stirring. Hinting to come back. "You going to be okay?"

Paris nodded, not entirely convincing.

"I'm sorry for this. I know you needed me with you tonight."

"You didn't make these guys into assholes."

"No. I didn't." Diesel took a deep breath. It didn't matter that Paris borrowed the excuse to use for him. He still knew that Paris needed his lover with him, help him shield that vulnerable part of him and now he'd blown it. "I love you— just so's you know." He tried to force on a smile for him.

~ * ~ * ~ * ~ * ~ * ~

Diesel sat on the cold, metal bench against one wall of the holding cell he was in. Going on six hours now, it was beyond uncomfortable and his butt was going numb.

He knew it'd take some time before Marcus could get him out. Most of which was just waiting for the county jail to process him before allowing bail to check him out. But, dammit, he was hungry. After the funeral they'd all been too mentally tired to eat. Guess he should have grabbed something along the way to the park, but he hadn't planned on getting arrested. Now it was going on two in the morning and prisoners didn't get fed in holding. Not that he would have liked anything they'd served him. His stomach was spoiled with homemade meals from Paris, which was just as good as some of the top restaurants they went to.

The roll doors from processing opened and in walked a familiar face.

"Pedro, what the hell are you doing in here?" Diesel called out to him as one of Trenton's security guys was escorted up to the cell next to him by a county deputy.

Pedro plopped down on the bench on the other side of the bars, sporting some banged up knuckles of his own.

"Some *pendejo puñetero* was flirting with my Senita and I had to kick his ass." Pedro used his native Spanish tongue to call his wife's offender a dumbass wanker. But it certainly wasn't the first time a man had flirted with her. Hell, she got that most any and every time they went out. Her dark island complexion was smooth as golden honey and she had the hips a man liked to hang onto that went with her perfect bubble butt. Not to mention a perfectly balanced set of C cups. Senita was the epitome of Spanish fly on legs. She knew it and so did Pedro. So long as the flirters never went as far as putting their hands on her, the flirting was tolerated. The only man who didn't fall for her charm was Paris. And that was a war that had yet to come to an end. Now, *how* Pedro had convinced the likes of Senita to marry the likes of *him* had been the subject of a lot of prodding humor at his expense ince the day they got married. And neither Diesel nor Trenton had managed to get her to spill the truth.

"Pedro, every man this side of the Hudson has flirted with your wife. Since when did that become fighting words?"

"When we find out she is six weeks pregnant." Pedro grinned wide, "I'm going to be a pappy."

"I'll be damned. Well, congrats, dude."

"Thanks, homes." Pedro shook his head as if he was still taking it all in, "Finally, something I know I'm gonna be damn good at. We got home from the funeral and got the news. It fixed the day for us, so we'd all gone out for a few drinks for our guys and for new life, yanno? Seemed right. 'Til that asshole had to come up. I guess I was still hurting about Jo being dead. That was originally my assignment. Say, you think I can use that to plea temporary insanity?" Pedro meant it as a joke as he tried to laugh it off.

Now was not the time for them to get too sentimental about life or the job, so Diesel diverted the subject, "So you waitin' on bail?"

"*Nah*— was already out on bail, so I gotta wait to see the judge on Monday morning."

"Trenton is going to be pissed."

"Going to? He already is over the last fight. I'll get the riot act on this one and I assure you, he is the only one who scares me more than my Senita."

"Gentry! You're up." A corrections officer called out for him long before he reached the gate for the holding cell.

Diesel stood, waiting for the deputy to let him out, and he noticed the three men in the back of the same cell with Pedro. *Guess the fourth ended up getting a trip to the hospital after all.*

"Hey, Pedro, see those dudes in the back?" He motioned to them.

Pedro shot a quick glance behind him, "Yeah, what about them?"

"They hate fags." Diesel spoke, keeping the suggestive smirk off his face.

"Yeah? You don't say? Paris okay?" Pedro's tone turned dark and concerned suddenly.

"He's safe now."

"Guess we'll have to make friends." Pedro turned sinister.

"We?"

Pedro laughed, "Fifi is still getting checked in. He was with us to celebrate when it all went down— apparently he helped." He shrugged, "I don't know nothing about it."

"Be sure to tell the big *maricón* I said congratulations on becoming an uncle, will you?"

The deputy waved him to hurry it up.

"Sí. You bet." Pedro called out to him as they led him away.

"See you on Monday, then."

Diesel was escorted out to the hall, stopped at the desk where his personals were handed back over, then led out to the lobby where he found Trenton, Paris, and Katianna waiting on him.

Paris had that— *I didn't do it*— look on his face and Trenton— he had on his— *you should have known better*— look. Katianna was clas all her own, looking as though she was going to jump out of her skin if she didn't get her hug fast enough. So he went to her first. Hugs were way better than getting punched by his brother.

He scooped her up just as he approached, then closed in on Paris. Diesel didn't say anything to Trenton hoping to avoid the lecture. His arms wrapped around Paris and pulled him into the embrace. That's what he wanted most— to feel his lover's body against his. That was the only thing that was going to knock him out of his funk right now. That and the little woman who was getting squeezed between them. "Take me home."

~ * ~ * ~ * ~ * ~ * ~

CHAPTER THIRTY-NINE

~ * ~ * ~ * ~ * ~ * ~

Diesel sat at the bench press, staring out the wall of plate glass windows that looked out over the pool and back deck, not even seeing them. The muscles in his arms burned, pumped to the maximum strain, and yet had not come close to burning away any of the smoldering emotion bottling up inside him. He'd even added another twenty-five pounds and nothing. Pent up. Strained. He wasn't even sure why. It had been days since the funeral. Trenton's Knight had already been sent up to Toronto for new side panels. Their names had been replaced in the headlines by something new. Yesterday, a judge cleared him for justifiable self-defense, no fines, no probation. He hadn't even had to convince the judge of it. He just walked in and the decision was made to absolve him. And life was slowly returning to what should have been normal. Yet here he was, feeling completely dislodged. What happened in Brighton, was bad. But then, those sorts of things did happen in Trenton's company, and Diesel was as much aware of it when going in and reasoned it was why he kept the gun shop running. He certainly didn't need the money, but bad people needed to be wary of good people. Even if it was only a slight wariness. It's when there was none that all of society became doomed to be nothing but a victim.

All this he knew, and he was perfectly at ease with it. This was not what had him locked up inside.

The fight in the park wasn't it either. Just a few locals with too much liquid courage in them to think with some common sense, and not enough training to back up their own smoke. An inconvenience, and really bad timing on their part. But they were lucky it'd been him. He could have killed them without a second's thought. Lucky for them indeed that while they were who they were, *He* was who *He* was.

He sucked in a deep breath then pitched his head back, expelled it to the ceiling, then stared up at it.

> ~~ *He saw a replay of himself in the holding cell and the few chuckles he'd shared with Pedro and a few of the officers that were there. He then saw himself holding Paris' hands as they walked out of the county jail but then dropped it when he saw all the bullet marks on the side of Trenton's Knight. "What the fuck?" He'd asked. But his brother only tensed his jaw, refusing to answer and got in behind the wheel.* ~~

Diesel closed his eyes and let the rest of the image slip from his mind, like smoke cast away by a strong sea breeze. Like the one pushing dark gray clouds to blot out the sun that mirrored in the pool water outside his home. "You know what it is."

"What'd you say?" The question came out of nowhere.

Diesel twisted, glancing over his shoulder just as Paris was coming down the staircase. Diesel gave him a slight shake of his head, "Nothing. Just thinking out loud."

"Mmmm, I see, so you were thinking about me— *aaaand* maybe about finishing what we started in the park." Paris came up alongside him, reaching down to feel over Diesel's pumped arms. "Niiice. And your legs?"

"I wasn't working out." Diesel set his eyes back out the window, fighting his worst to keep the pressure valve sealed.

"I can think of other ways to burn energy."

The words seemed to fade from him as he stared out, looking at nothing— seeing nothing— hearing nothing— but feeling— *Everything.*

Something brushed his cheek, but it barely registered. More clouds moving into the world out there, reflecting his insides. He must have caught a virus from the Unicorn.

A sound muffled and distorted tried to speak to him, but he couldn't break his stare from what he was seeing within himself.

It made sense now. More so than it ever had his entire life. For every time things went bad out there, the need for control over a scene became a necessity for his insides. A walk-through of therapy. Why Trenton's control over Kat was so intensified compared to who he was four years ago.

Patronus.

"Not anymore." The words whispered from his breath.

"DEEZ!"

Diesel snapped around and stared at Paris. Seeing him for the first time.

"What the fuck? I'm trying to talk to you and you're ignoring me."

Diesel still stared. The sudden look on Paris' face was irksome.

"And you're still ignoring me. I don't know if you've caught on lately, but it was still just a couple days ago when shit was still going bad and I need to be the center of your attention right now."

The wrong words. And the cork exploded.

"Did you think life was always going to be fun and fancy free?! Did you think it was going to be perfect like some romance novel?!" Diesel snapped to his feet, pitching slightly toward Paris with a hot glare. He hadn't snapped at Paris when they fought days ago, but now he couldn't rein himself back any longer.

"NO! YES! But I still fucking need you to pay attention to me! And right now, you're not!" Paris shouted.

"Interesting, since the other day you had my undivided attention and you didn't want it. You wanted to get away. Now when I am not, you're throwing tantrums."

"This isn't a tantrum. This is a demand on our relationship!" Paris bit out, obviously not liking the belittling word *tantrum*.

"And this is not how you get it from me."

"If you come with an instruction manual, then fork it up P.D.Q. Because I am not going to fuck around while you decide if I exist for you today or not considering I haven't had much of anything but you holding my hand at a funeral—!"

But whatever else Paris was going to rant about, it never got out before Diesel cut him off. "I KNOW!" He turned away, his head dropped back, and his eyes rolled to the back of his head as his feet walking him in a circle like a pacing beast until he came back around. "I know all this because I was fucking there. I went through all the shit too. Trenton going away, then getting arrested, then you and Kat being in danger— then the funeral. Then the argument— then the park— and then it was me who got arrested. I distinctly recall being present during all of it. Yes! I remember it all!"

"Yeah, you know, but that shit doesn't bother you. Ever! But for your information, it does fucking bother me. I admit it, I think life is perfect. It's about having a job I love and everyone else envies— having the latest fashion designs in my closet and wearing the most edible and spicy colognes. It's about where the frayed holes in my jeans need to be to catch your attention. It's about hearing you groan when you fuck me. And when it's not? When people are shooting at me or trying to slice my face off! I DON'T KNOW HOW TO HANDLE IT!" The last words stole every bit of breath from Paris' lungs— his chest caving as he did. And those eyes. Paris' eyes were no longer filled with lust or rage.

It was him. The vulnerable man Paris kept hidden deep inside himself. He looked like a jilted, little boy standing alone in the rain.

And then it was gone.

"I need you to pay attention to me." The brick and mortar began to rebuild around him, shelling him up inside.

It was a demand. Not a plea. The one who could have said it with a magic spell vanished too soon. Hidden away even from Diesel. It was like a slap in the face. Pure insult. "I tend to your needs. But yours are not the only ones that need my attention. I have also been lenient with all your bratting about. It's fun, but as I have said once before— there is only so much I am willing to tolerate." Diesel's hand pointed distinctly at Paris, "This is not how you will get it either. I let you be many things, but the Dom in this house, you are not."

He brushed past Paris, heading for the stairs.

They were right back where they were the other night. Same argument— only the words were different— just not the meaning of them. But Diesel knew what the problem was this time. *It was him.*

"Where the hell you going!?" Paris called after him.

"For a walk."

"In the fucking rain?!"

The shout chased after him, but Diesel didn't bother glancing back. He knew it wasn't raining. Not yet anyways. Nevertheless, he'd watched the storm work its way in. It wouldn't be long. He just wasn't going to stop for Paris at the moment.

He ran all three flights of stairs to their bedroom, half expecting Paris to come chasing after him. He didn't. That was probably for the best. He stalled in the middle of their room, looking out the sliding glass doors to the balcony. The deck wood turning spotted with the first arrival of raindrops. He dropped his head back off his shoulders and counted to ten— it wasn't Paris' fault.

He needed to find a way to settle this within himself so that he didn't attempt to take it out on him again. Perhaps a run in the cold rain would do him some good.

He grabbed a jacket and came down the stairs, down one story then the other and heading across the living room for the door when he froze.

A large muscular body posed, waiting on knees in the middle of the living room, absent his shirt and with his head pressed down to the floor.

Spread out on display before him— Diesel's silk, shibari ropes. Not just a few— at least a dozen and just how he liked them, in a variety of colors selected for both contrast and blend. Paris had about four different blues, a few blacks, and a royal purple. The contrast colors were the natural and white cotton ropes Diesel always used for kinbaku.

Diesel stepped closer. Paris had removed his shirt and placed it neatly over the back of the chair. At its base, his sneakers, belt, keys, and wallet. "You trying to Top from the bottom?"

"No, Sir, Patronus. But I see my Master of Doms is in need, so I am surrendering to him. His Fallen Angel only hopes that his Patronus will see fit that he be deserving of the center of that need's attention."

One might have thought the response still was a form of Topping. Except Paris' forehead never left the carpet floor. There had only been one other time Paris had ever folded over in total surrender. Which was the night under the table, when Diesel told Trenton to send Paris packing. At the time, there was nothing in the world Paris wanted more than to keep his job at the island resort. When Paris realized just how close he was to losing it, he'd surrendered fully. Now he was doing it again. He was afraid he was losing something he dearly wanted to keep. Diesel wasn't about to reject the submissive offer.

"Remain here." Diesel gave a firm, but low volume command.

"Yes, Patronus." The proper response came from the floor. Not *where you going?* Not *for how long?* Just *yes, Patronus.*

So Diesel headed upstairs, pulling his shirt off as he went back to *His* room.

~ * ~ * ~ * ~ * ~ * ~

Paris stayed just as commanded. His heart breaking, yet holding out for hope.

He knew what he'd done. He took things as far as Diesel allowed. And the leash turned out to be a lot longer than Paris had thought it reached.

It was perhaps too long— that when Paris demanded like a free man, at a time when he knew Diesel was under pressure of so many other things— the leash was snapped back— and then dropped. A chilling reminder of who Paris was attempting to push. Yet, he'd known no other way to tell Diesel. Only that he did need all of his attention. Like a whore who had still wanted more. Diesel's attention was Paris' addiction, and when the world got ugly, he needed it the most. He just didn't know until he saw Diesel wasn't beside him. Now, he was in agony. He didn't know what to do or even worse— where he stood. He had but only the two best bits of advice he'd ever gotten from anyone to fall back on. Albeit, *jump* didn't fit this time. But, Pyotr Laszkovi's did—

> ~~ *Remember, sometimes it only requires that act of showing your willingness to make a*

sacrifice to bridge what might seem an uncrossable fissure. ~~

There was a rustle crossing the carpet, then suddenly Paris felt the peculiar touch—

~ * ~

Patronus squatted down in front of Paris' bowed body and caressed his cheek with a gloved hand to acknowledge his submission. "Your safewords are Red, Yellow, and Green. Do you understand?"

The submitted Fallon Angel nodded.

"Sit up and tell me."

Paris slowly pushed up on his heels and looked at him. His face gave Patronus the answer before he said it. *I want this.* "I understand, Patronus."

"Good." Patronus motioned his head, indicating to the sofa, "Go sit in the center of the loveseat."

Paris pushed up, but stopped when he noticed the leather pouch Diesel held in his hand "What's in the bag?"

Diesel stood and dropped the bag on the coffee table, the slight clink of metal from within put a smile on his face, "Sit, Paris. You will discover what is in the bag when I am ready to show you."

Paris bowed his head and then followed the instructions given. Patronus watched, let the movement of this beautiful man touch his desires, then turned and made his way back upstairs. This time walking along the balcony that over looked the living room, running down along one side wall to the back of the large spacious room. At its end, a long cord of rope hung from an anchor in the ceiling just behind the cluster of lights over the center of the living room, its end tied to a cleat on the rail. He loosened it, then let it all drop straight down, sweeping in right behind the sofa where Paris sat. Next, Diesel switched on the cam-light mounted on the wall and adjusted the angle until it spilled over Paris' body. Once back downstairs, he adjusted the room lighting, leaving the rest of the room in dim soft tones to better accentuate the object of his desire to truly be in the spotlight of his attention. *And soon enough, he was going to have His Fallen Angel flying in the air.*

For a long moment, he stared at the man who waited before him. Like a painter might do— staring at his blank canvas, seeing the artwork before actually beginning. Once he got the image designed in his head, he grabbed a long five-foot staff of bamboo from a closet and brought it over.

"You cut off the sleeves to the shirt I bought you." Paris broke his silence.

The white shirt he had changed into was, indeed, the very one Paris just mentioned. Minus the sleeves as of five minutes ago. That's what he had gone up to do. *Change.*

Now, instead of sweat pants and the worn t-shirt he'd had on earlier, he was properly dressed as the *Patronus* should be. His favorite pair of black leather pants with the lace up front. The white shirt Paris had given him, which he really did love, but it'd required some personal tailoring to make it perfect. The final touch was his favorite pair of gloves. Soft lamb skin that cloaked his hands like a pitch black second skin. He'd even splashed on a bit of cologne, delivering a full package of himself to heighten the experience for his subject.

He stepped in, taking Paris' jaw in his gloved grip and forced him to meet his gaze. "Do not talk unless I ask you a question or give you permission." Patronus warned with a tight grit to his words. He shifted his hold, forcing his thumb over Paris' lips, pushing them to open then grazing over his teeth, almost daring him to bite, "Does it piss you off that I have?" He knowingly smirked down at Paris. It was among one of the first things Diesel had ever said to Paris back when they first met; he'd asked the very same thing of another expensive designer shirt. Now it was more an amusing reminder of who they were to each other in this moment. Because just like last time he asked, he was about to strip Paris of all his control.

There was the barest hint of a curl in Paris' lips. A twitch that wanted so much to smile, that pride of his gloating with the memory of that day and the undeniable attraction they both felt. *So much has happened since then*. One would think a life time had gone by, but it truly had not been so long ago. Twenty-two months— just shy of two years since that day.

He rested the bamboo against the end of the sofa, then reached behind Paris' head, curled his fingers into the black hair, and pulled to bring Paris' eyes up to him, "Give me a word."

"Green, Patronus." The answer sounded like a promise of sex and so much more when he whispered it. Paris truly was the diamond's cut of pure unflawed seduction.

But Patronus was about to show him something entirely different.

He started by taking one of each of the shorter twelve foot strands of blues and purples, using them to create columns of stacked coils, using one color for each wrist. He followed it up with short strands of hemp, creating a Lark's Head single column around the tops of Paris' wrists, butted against the colored coils. He secured a safety hitch to prevent tightening and assure Paris' thumb was in proper positon so that circulation would not get cut off once he was suspended, then Patronus let the working ends drop until he was ready to weave them into the rest. He, next, made a chain of ratty appearing knots, using one of the longer bundles of hemp, running it through the five-inch stainless steel ring that hung at the end of the suspension line he'd dropped earlier, which was anchored into the ceiling. The working ends already latched around Paris' wrists were added into the configuration that looked much like a mad scientist's Jacob's Ladder, pulling Paris' arms up so they hung high overhead, but leaving a good amount of bend to the elbows.

Raindrops outside began to tap at the glass wall, but they were no longer a reflection of a brooding mood. Rather, they were the drums, which beat in cadence with Patronus' silent delight as he began to weave his silk ropes around the man who belonged to him. The tungsten bracelet on Paris' wrist bore his claim, but his ropes would reach further inside and draw Paris in. Even when the final moment of binding was brief, the act of Paris' submission could only further their design and deepen their bond. Patronus would, in fact, show Paris what it was like to be the center of His attention.

The next rope was a white coconut fiber, which was softer and more pliable than cotton yet still durable. He coiled it around in sets of twos and threes in segments down one arm, taking advantage of the bent angle of Paris' arm to create spring lines that crisscrossed over his head— from wrist to bicep.

Every inch of rope that was wrapped around Paris was paired with soft caressing. Glances of Patronus' gloved hand to reassure and comfort Paris as the process took place. Over skin— muscles— using as much precision and care as an artisan would applying gold leaf to a carved relief. To touch his silky black hair, layered in sharp razor-like edges down the back of his neck and falling over his eyes. Eyes— those, Patronus had left uncovered to follow him everywhere. Watching his hands and watching him.

Patronus remained fixated on his work, on his hands, and the ropes he wrapped around tan skin and tied into intricate looking knots. Some to hold— some to latch into another— others for the sheer aesthetic pleasure of his desires.

Now the real work began.

Paris still had his jeans on. He looked more than good, shirtless and barefooted, in the skintight, faded blue denim; he looked damn tasty. It was a spectacular contrast to the black leather love seat and the faux mink blanket he was sitting on. But as good as it appealed to Patronus' sense of sight, it would be a hindrance if he were inclined to have his way with Paris later, after he was finished with his shibari work. *Of course, he could just cut a hole in the jeans*— he paused to think about that a moment. He was acutely aware of the meticulousness Paris put into fashioning his jeans. Not one fray or hole that existed was by accident. Diesel had already run into a few issues attempting to replace a few of the shredded shirts he was guilty of mangling. *Perhaps some battles just weren't worth starting*, he laughed silently, then stepped into the task of disrobing his Fallen Angel in a manner that didn't include further wardrobe destruction.

It took far longer than it should have but, that too, only lent further to keeping Patronus in his zone. It wasn't a matter of getting from one act to the next, like a race for the finish line; it was the mechanics of each movement. He didn't just pull the jeans from Paris' legs; he had to explore the freshly exposed skin as he did. Inch by succulent tanned inch, Patronus reveled in touching and firm groping of Paris' muscles, enjoying even more the heightened breath coming from his brat's lungs as his anticipation amped up.

Even Paris' feet were sexy. It wasn't often Patronus came across men with arches. Or feet that captured his attention for that matter. Yet, Paris' did both. There was just something about them. Especially when Paris' toes curled when they were making love. Yeah, it was a pleasant thought that had Patronus snatching one of those feet up, licking it along the arch, and then gave the big toe a moment of undivided tongue attention before dropping it back to the floor. Enjoying the combined moan and chuckle from his Imp. *Lots of fun, but he didn't want to get too far off course.* The knots he had planned in his head would take some time. Time he had. His cock, however, would likely begin to disagree at some point.

Patronus kept his focus dialed in on the next lengths of rope to be added. Another blue to be intertwined with black, and then he began to construct a oven harness design that scaled Paris' entire upper torso. Blue on one side and black on the other, coming together into a spiraling mix and weaving down the center. It wasn't so much as knots— rather they were intricate weaves and overlaps made to look like fanciful artwork constructed from knots. There was also another element to it all, as he set the *bite* at its starting point then handled the working ends into the overall design in his head; he saw his and Paris' life together, from the time they met, all the way to this scene. The ropes became threads within a web that connected every encounter— every touch— winding and binding along the way.

"Patronus?"

Diesel paused and glanced at him, "Yes, you have something to say?"

"I have questions."

Diesel nodded, "Very well, ask them." And went back to the weave of coils he was working on.

"How did you learn all the shibari knots?" Paris broke the quiet.

"*Shibari* isn't about knots. It's how the knots are applied." The question in no way breaking his zone, only adding to it.

"Do the colors make a difference?"

"To some extent yes. Traditional colors are rarely used, but because shibari is about visual appeal, I like to use the brighter colors. Other applications outside of shibari are almost always done with neutral colors." He added as he reached for a length of one of the neutral bundles.

"Except you?"

Patronus let a slight chuckle slip, "I'm finished with the shibari. Now I am administering *kinbaku*." And he slipped a *bula bula* hitch over Paris' foot, secured it around his ankle, then hiked it up on the sofa and bound it to his thigh in a one-legged frogtie.

Paris sucked in a deep breath. His focus seemed to haze a bit, showing the first signs of rope drunkenness, "What does that mean?"

"To tie tightly."

"So the ropes are going to be tight when you're finished?" Paris' head lobbed a bit, and his eyes searched Patronus' face.

Patronus paused to touch Paris' cheek and then leaned in, planting a kiss on soft lips that quickly turned active to suck more of the kiss before he pulled away, going back to his work. "No." He tested the circulation in Paris' leg by pinching a toenail, then watched as it quickly went from white back to red. "To *bind tightly* refers to the act of binding, not to the end results of it. It is about the act between the rigger and the person being bound. I could tie you in ribbon but the undertaking to its completion is what binds you to me in a tight relationship. That is what kinbaku is."

"So this kin-back— whatever you called it, and shibari have different knots?"

Patronus finished the last wrap then made the finishing single knot. He sat back to look over his artwork. Paris was beautiful. Arms up, held high and loose over his head. Body bound with a woven harness of Patronus' two favorite colors. One leg spread wide and bound in place by a pole of bamboo leaning against the side of the sofa. The other folded in and bound to his body. Patronus need only to pull him out to the edge of the loveseat and the entrapped Fallen Angel was all his. Then again, Paris was his the day he'd laid eyes on him. Tonight was simply a demonstrated act to remind him of it.

"No. The knots are the same; it's the purpose of why I use them that makes the difference. If I use a particular knot for martial arts purposes, then it is called *Hojojutsu*. If the same technique is used in an artistic application, with the intent for aesthetic pleasure— it is called *Shibari*. Yet, if I used the same knot to create a sexually driven scene— then it is called *Kinbaku*.

"Sex?" It was probably the only word Paris heard out of all of it.

Patronus stood and unlaced his leathers, then freed his protesting cock from its confines. "Yes, sex. Which means no more talking." But intercourse wasn't next in line. Just a moment for him to sit back and enjoy. He stroked over his cock, feeling it thicken in his grip until his fingers couldn't touch around it any longer. The view was going to be even better once he raised the suspension line. But first he had one more thing planned out.

He went back to the coffee table, to the leather zippered pouch he set there earlier, and opened it up. "Remember when you asked me what was in the pouch?"

"Yes."

"Sounds. I bought them some time ago to use on you. Just hadn't had the chance to pull them out." He selected one from the set of eight long stainless steel implements and held it up for Paris to see, "Now, I do."

~ * ~

Oh shit— was what Paris' brain thought instantly. Paris knew exactly what sounds were and what they were for. He'd tried them once. The sensation boggled the mind and fast-forwarded him into orgasm. Like being body slammed into ecstasy but difficult when riding it out. It was a unique experience sought out by some, but not something one should do without some experience. Even down at the island, they had a Dom who was specifically experienced in the application for the pleasure of the resort's guests who wanted to have the sensation. But that bit of understanding paled in comparison when realizing his Patronus was about to use them on him. A level that had Paris' senses reeling with a nefarious mix of anxiety and elation.

"Give me a word, Paris." Patronus demanded.

Paris licked his lips, flexed his hands within the confines of the ropes, and let out a hard breath, "Green."

Patronus stepped up, sound rod and a tube of lubricant in hand. He first checked the ropes around Paris' wrists and arms. Paris dropped his head back and watched every step as his Patronus pushed a finger under the coils like it was foreplay. And in the oddest way it felt like it too. He felt lightheaded, as if he'd drank a bottle of wine when he hadn't.

His Patronus caressed his arms, taking pleasure in both skin and ribs of coiled rope, then lastly pinched Paris' fingertip and watched the results. When his expression suggested he was satisfied, he leaned over and Paris became the recipient of another heated kiss, diving in to have a taste of the emotions rising up within him as if they could be found collecting on his tongue. Perhaps they did. For the satisfied moan his Patronus made seemed to suggest that they had and it was a pleasing delicacy for him. *Damn, how it felt like his hips seemed to have a life of their own and pushed for Diesel's body.* More so for the cock that lazily jutted out towards him, poking and prodding at the edge of the sofa as Patronus got into position to insert the selected sound in Paris' cock.

Paris' teeth found his lip, and this time he consciously pushed his hips out, hoping for some contact with the monster cock that teased him with its proximity. He managed to get a glance of it against the inner thigh of his bamboo-lashed leg, but then the ropes pulled him back and it was all he got.

Now his eyes were glued to the silver rod in Patronus' fingers, how he carefully poured a line of the clear lube over it then transferred much of it to the slit of Paris' urethra by drawing the rod over the slit like a musician would draw a bow over a violin. Only, Paris doubted the violin felt as he did just now. Every muscle in his groin and his ass clenched tight with a heightened shiver. His toes curled and all he wanted was to have his cock sunk deep inside Diesel's ass right then and there. Or mouth. "Sh-shit." His teeth chattered as the cool steel continued to be drawn back and forth over his glans. He grew antsy, jumping in the ropes that held him. And that was when Patronus' hand came slapping down on Paris' hip to hold him still.

"Don't move." He warned him, then took Paris' cock in his fist, held the sound vertically over it and then slowly allowed the stainless steel rod to sink inside Paris' cock.

Paris tossed his head back and let out an exasperated moan. But the slow sinking sensation wasn't left to something so simple. His head jerking back up when he felt the back and forth slide, finding the Patronus fucking the eye of his cock with the rod of metal.

Muscles clenched and snapped in a chaotic order, left— right— behind his balls— in places he didn't know were ever within his motor control or had even existed. Most of all, the nerves along his urethra screamed with a pleasure that was too high of a crescendo for him to maintain. And when he felt Patronus ease the sound to depths that seemed to reach past his balls like it could touch his prostate, the verbal sound that came from Paris' lips were a bastardization of English expressions that were hardly recognizable. "Ohhhhhh—nnn-shheeee-iiiiite! Deez, please!"

He felt like he was falling, or perhaps he'd blacked out, since it was hard to describe. Crashing and colliding, yet an abundance of pleasure so great it was almost painful. Even the living room seemed to echo with a vocal eruption that mimicked what he felt as he came.

Somewhere in that sea of euphoria Paris felt like he was being lifted. Like floating on the air. And then he felt the ropes that bound him, catching him before he fell to the earth. Landing him perfectly against Diesel's body. That was when Paris felt that monster cock, prodding at the entry of his hole, and he gladly pushed back to take it all in. "Oh damn, fuck me, please."

"That is precisely what I intend to do to you."

The alpha tone grabbed him, letting him know he didn't have a choice in the matter, and then that sweet bite of stretch that always had Paris clamping his teeth down with a tight hiss. *Fuck yes, he loved that cock.* More so the man it was attached to, but right now he needed that cock.

"Talk to me, Paris, let me hear how much you want my cock deep inside you."

"Fuck, *yeshh*, I want you driving your thick dick all the way inside me. Every monster inch. Fuck me with that thick fucking cock."

After that, Paris wasn't entirely sure if he ever managed to get a full sentence out again. For once, Diesel had managed to bottom out in Paris' ass, and the drilling he asked for commenced as his Patronus drove his delicious rod into him without any amount of buffering. There would be no walking tomorrow. But it was worth it, feeling the demanding friction of Diesel's cock inside him, pumping endlessly, and the bruising slap of hips against Paris' ass.

Paris' entire body floated over the sofa, completely suspended in the air, allowing Patronus to stand, and there was no amount of hindrance for the drive behind each thrust until irrevocably the final command came. Paris barely heard the word as his mind became foggy with the sensations of sex— the bindings— the smell of their bodies heating up and perfuming the room with their sex, cologne, and his earlier spunk. Floating and pounding, then that word. The magical word.

"Cum for me now, you fucking brat!"

God, he hoped he did, because he felt an explosion and that was it.

~ * ~ * ~ * ~ * ~ * ~

CHAPTER FORTY

~ * ~ * ~ * ~ * ~ * ~

Diesel woke to the sounds of his growling stomach and an instant protest from the man in his arms.

"I hope you're not expecting me to get up and fix food." A happily content bottom mumbled from his pillow.

"If you can walk, then I didn't do my job well enough last night." Diesel chuckled while still nestled up against the back of Paris' head. He thought about just going back to sleep. Even though it was already afternoon, but another growl from his stomach said otherwise. He finally wrenched himself from Paris' side and crawled out to begin his search of food. "Any of that creamy yogurt-like stuff?" He bent over the bed to plant a kiss on his sleepy Fallen Angel's head.

"It's called clotted cream, and no. In fact—" Paris rolled to his back and shot Diesel a sudden glare, "that woman of yours is why."

"Who? Senita?"

"Yes. With everything that was going on, I didn't have time to do any grocery shopping myself, so I added that and a few others items to the grocery list on the fridge for her to pick up. She got everything but the items I asked her to get."

"Anything else I need to know?"

"There is some cream-filled Burrata cheese pouches in the dairy bin. Just use the microwave steamer to warm them up."

Diesel nodded, *those sounded just as good,* so he hightailed it downstairs to raid the fridge.

It wasn't long when he was coming back up, "They're gone. You eat them all?"

"No and Marcus doesn't like them, so they can't be gone."

"Well, they are and so is the bacon stuff."

Paris near jackknifed on the bed with an incredulous expression, "The toffee bacon I made right before we left for London? Marcus had eaten some of it, but there was still almost another full plate of it remaining when we got back." He plopped back down, the night's romp still taking an obvious toll on him.

Guess he did do his job right after all.

"It's her, I'm telling you, Deez. She throws out dishes I make all the time just to spite me."

"Oh, come on now, she is not."

"She is." Paris' hand was racing through his hair in a display that he was seriously frustrated by it, "What about when I caught her red-handed, adding clove spice to my braised lamb shanks. I'd had them marinating for three days and she ruined them. And the air cake soufflé I made for Kat's birthday? It was perfect when I left the house to go get the Shiraz she refused to pick up from the store when she was already out. But when I got back, it was crushed."

Diesel knocked on the wall where he stood, letting out a sigh, because while he hadn't seen it, he knew damn well Paris wouldn't ruin his own dish he'd been working and planning on for days just to set someone up. Senita was a good woman, but he couldn't refute that sometimes those Latin women could get a bug up their butts and not let up. He just wasn't used to it happening inside his own home. She also should have known better. "May have to give the kitchen back to her."

"What?" The finger raking stopped, "No! The kitchen is mine. You gave it to me and Marcus agreed."

"Yeah, well—"

"Yeah, well, nothing. It's my fucking kitchen."

"But if this doesn't stop—"

"She's the one doing this." Paris cut him off.

"Because she's been here longer than you. She thinks it's hers."

"It's mine and I'm the one sleeping with you. Don't be an Indian giver."

"Don't go there."

"It's my kitchen." The scowl took up permanent residence on Paris' face. *It was almost cute.*

"Guess I'm heading to the store, right quick then. Be back in a bit." He headed out.

"*INDIAN GIVER!*" Was shouted after him.

~ * ~ * ~ * ~ * ~ * ~

Diesel was just arriving at the store when a text came in from Paris with a list of things he deemed should have been in *His* refrigerator and weren't.

"Guess I'll have to fuck you even harder next time to make sure you don't get out of bed." He spoke aloud in response to the man who wouldn't hear it.

But Paris obviously wasn't finished. The next list sent was a grocery list for all the things he wanted put back.

Diesel was in line at the deli meats counter to get some prosciutto and something called hot cappy when he got the next text. This time a selfie shot of what was undoubtedly Paris' dick pushed into the apple pie Senita had sent over as a comfort food offering after the funeral. The next snapshot sent looked like the infamous cum shot and apple pie evidence on the glass coffee table. If Diesel had to guess, he figured Paris was leaving it behind for Senita to clean up when she came in tomorrow morning. *He might have to spank him for that one.*

He was at the butcher's block to have a ribeye roast cut and still Paris' argument to maintain his staked kitchen claim had not ended. The next several texts to come in included a three second gif of Paris' tongue licking over his lips in a suggestive tease. A second gif was a full ten seconds of watching Paris dancing naked in the kitchen, with his spent cock flopping between his legs as he gyrated his hips around. That one had Diesel's own cock twitching in his sweat pants, because he knew precisely what the move felt like when Paris reenacted it while straddled over him with his cock deep inside Paris' ass.

The dance moves were followed up with a backside selfie of Paris' ass as he bent over in front of the bathroom mirror. A hand firmly pulled a cheek aside to assure the pink rosette was winking at Diesel in the shot. That's when he gave up on the rest of the grocery list and headed for the cashier. It was there when Diesel got the grand finalé of them all. His phone rang with an alert tone. Not a text. So naturally Diesel instantly answered, "You okay? What's wrong?"

"*Ohhhh, my god*—" Paris' breathy voice came over the phone, "*I'm so close to cumming again, but I realized I needed to ask for your permission.*"

"Paris—" Diesel bit his tongue, then his lips, to stop what he was going to say while in the mixed company of less adventurous-type Hampton residents in the grocery line. He'd already gotten arrested for excessive force. He didn't want lude public behavior added to it.

"*So, can I cum, Patronus?*"

~ * ~ * ~ * ~ * ~ * ~

Paris barely got the door open to go help bring the groceries in when Diesel was on him, not even bothering with priorities. Diesel backed Paris inside the house, their mouths locked in a tangle of his searching tongue, desperate and greedy. Diesel's hands couldn't work fast enough, grasping Paris' lounge pants, peeling them down over his hips. He wrapped his fingers firmly around Paris' cock the second it sprung free and instantly stroked it before their knees hit the sofa.

Paris was trying to get Diesel's sweats down, but it was proving to be difficult with Diesel pumping his cock and using a firm rocking motion of his wrist.

"Damn it, Paris, you're not moving fast enough." Diesel wrenched himself from their kiss, just enough to bark out his frustration that there were still too many articles of clothing in the way, while pulling them both back to their feet.

"Well, which do you want first? To get undressed or fuck?"

~ * ~

"To fuck." Diesel spun Paris around then shoved him down on the sofa. He pulled a tube of gel from the side table drawer while yanking Paris' pants down further with his free hand. Once that was taken care of, his attention shifted; he pushed the front of his sweats down, letting his cock pounce out with obvious intentions, and slathered on a healthy coating of lubricant, dropped to his knees on the sofa, and then lined up behind Paris.

The succulent view of firm ass cheeks was enough to have his mouth watering, and he gave one a hard smack as a playful expression of his friskiness. Paris shot a daring glance over his shoulder at him and just for that, he had to give him another.

He spread those beautiful buttocks wide and smeared the extra gel over the tight hole. Diesel let out a groan that developed just from the anticipation of being inside of it, then pushed his fingers in. First a few strokes with one, then he added a second.

~ * ~

Paris was instantly rocking back on him until Diesel's fingers were pushed all the way inside, until there was nothing more to push. "I don't need any preliminaries after last night." Paris fussed over his shoulder. He was just as ready and hot as Diesel was ready to take him now.

Paris felt the broad tip of Diesel's cock pressing against his hole with a few careful nudges then began to push in. The groan bordering on growling, which came from Diesel, was sexy fucking music that hinted of conflicting self-control, the kind Paris loved to antagonize. Given Paris didn't share the consideration to ease in, he pushed on the sofa, nearly throwing himself backwards onto Diesel's cock, adding an additional rocking of his hips from side to side. He tossed his head and let out a pleasant moan as Diesel's cock slid for home, deep inside his hole.

~ * ~

Damn, it always felt so good inside Paris. Hot and tight, gripping his hard flesh like a fist as he sank in, until his belly was flat against the cheeks of Paris' ass. "Ah fuck, Paris—" he hissed. "You feel so good."

"Then why aren't you riding me?"

Diesel got the hint and the pounding began, knocking Paris into the back of the sofa with little chance of being able to push back.

Paris wanted it hard? Then Diesel gave it to him hard. Like a runaway train wreck. Unabated and at a frantic pace, without need for concern that his lover could not take him. He already knew Paris could. Only this time, he'd make sure Paris wasn't walking afterwards.

The plundering continued, rutting on him like a savage beast. He banged as hard as he could, thrusting as high as he could, pulling out all the way just so he could resume thrusting back in with a full puncturing penetration again. He liked how it felt and stopped just so he could play a bit. Just a small amount of drawing it out. Maybe even get Paris fussing in the process. He did so like agitating him sometimes. He pulled out until his cock fell free, this time just to nudge against the muscle ring of Paris' hole and enjoy the ravaged attempt Paris' body made to hug the glans of his own cock. "Mmmm, fuck yes."

But once having teased himself enough, he slammed all the way in, rousing a curse from Paris as well. Diesel loved the sounds that man made for him.

He regained his pace— throttling Paris' ass with unrelenting ferocity until at last he felt himself spasm. He halted for a second as the first wave of his orgasm flooded his body, then, with a yell, Diesel dropped his head back and shoved his hips home to slap against Paris' backside, pumping in a mad ride as he felt his spunk firing from his cock and filling Paris' hole.

~ * ~

Diesel collapsed onto Paris, who as good as folded over the back cushions, while he kissed the back of his neck with exhausted affection, "Did you cum? Please tell me you did." Diesel asked, out of breath.

"Are you kidding?" Paris shot a wicked grin over his shoulder, then managed a kiss to Diesel's sweaty forehead, "Marcus is going to kill us for messing up the sofas again."

Diesel suffered a glance over Paris' shoulder and saw the smeared cum all over the back of the sofa. "No worse than what you did to the coffee table." He tried to chuckle, despite feeling drained of all his energy. He reached around Paris and drew a finger through the white froth and brought it to his mouth to savor. "Mmmm." He kissed Paris' shoulder then dropped down to stretch out on the sofa, pulling Paris over him.

"Maybe I need to start more closing arguments with you over what's mine in this house."

"Why do you say that?"

"You never go after me like this."

Diesel tightened around him and licked his cheek, "Liked it, did you?"

"Yes. I like raunchy and rough with you when I can get it."

"Yeah, well, don't bother thinking you can lay any more claims on what's yours in this house. This is my house *and* Marcus' house, and everything in it, including you, belongs to me or him. You, specifically, belong solely to me. But if you want some more of this, we could skip dinner with the brothers tonight."

"Don't even think about it. We're in trouble with Trenton, too. Remember?"

Diesel pushed their bodies up until they were sitting, still not releasing Paris from his claim. "Speaking of, how is it that Trenton came to get me when I told you to leave him out of it?"

"Do you see Marcus anywhere? 'Cause if he were here, he'd be yelling at us to get off the sofa, like a pair of dogs."

Diesel just gave him a weary glance, not bothering to comment, and instead waited for Paris to finish explaining.

"So, I called Dane and *he* called Trenton."

Diesel let out a sigh, "Dane's an ass."

"Only, it didn't matter, Trenton already knew and Dane called back to simply warn me that Trent was coming and to be ready to go when he got here. Which, by the way, Trenton didn't take too well. He was pretty pissed when he came over and got me."

"How'd he find out then?"

"Cliff was in the ambulance that came to the call, he called Pyotr, and Pyotr called Trenton."

Diesel shook his head. *He should have known better to think he could bypass his brother, but he was trying to spare him any further anguish.* "What did you tell him?"

"I didn't tell him anything. He didn't even ask; he seemed to have had all the information already. Even knew where to go to bail you out."

Diesel almost laughed, realizing his brother's connections had just surprised even him, when he knew full well how extensive they were.

Diesel didn't say anything further. Instead, he made sure Paris faced him and aligned with his body and he swayed his hips back and forth to slide their spent cocks together for some post-coital frotting and heavy kissing.

~ * ~

Paris melted into it right away, adding a hungry amount of hand groping into the mix and lapping up the flavor of their kiss. He shifted to get his legs between Diesel's thick thighs to have more room for grinding. Not an easy task, given his pants were still around his knees, limiting how much he could move. Diesel wasn't waiting as he pushed up, rubbing and sliding against him. His powerful arm reaching around and taking a firm grip of Paris' ass, then just the hint of finger reaching to tease his hole.

Paris couldn't stop his own reaction as his body shifted to chase after the elusive finger.

"Stop." Diesel warned, "You're not in charge of this show." And Diesel's other hand pulled Paris down, then felt his legs coiling around his in one of those defense attack moves.

There was nothing exotic or sexy about their position except Paris couldn't fucking move. And Diesel resumed his finger teasing along the sensitized flesh of his back entry. Essentially driving him insane while the evidence of two cocks slowly growing thicker between the two of them became harder.

Just to egg Paris on even further, Diesel let out a ragged groan from his throat, as his hips pushed up. "Fuck yes, Paris."

But that's where it stopped.

~ * ~

They both froze at the sound of the sliding glass door downstairs opening and closing. Diesel tossed himself back on the sofa with a curse, his hand caressing over Paris' body, trying to muster a way to keep going without getting in more trouble with Trenton. He could hear his brother on the stairs— his impatient expression came as no surprise as Trenton reached the living room floor, came around the corner, and spotted them already engaged in a form of contained fore or post-play, but most assuredly headed for mindless pounding, despite the tangle of clothing.

"Don't even think about not going to dinner with us."

"I was just hoping for a quickie before we left." Diesel pleaded for forgiveness.

Trenton stopped, and Diesel saw his eyes drop to the spunk and food deposits on the smoky glass of the coffee table, then flash back at him, "You've already had your quickie."

"That's not mine." Diesel let out in his own defense.

Trenton just stared at him.

"Maybe shoot for two?" He winced.

"There's no such thing with you once you've shot your first load. You're good for an hour's ride on the second time around. Now, let's go."

Paris only grinned.

Diesel spotted the wicked expression and nudged him in the back. "You're not helping."

~ * ~ * ~ * ~ * ~ * ~

Once they got back from dinner, Diesel was about to lead Paris back to their own home, to give his brother and the Unicorn time alone, when Kat stopped him.

"No." Her hand reached out, taking his arm. "Don't go— anytime you and Paris aren't with us, it's like two empty voids roaming around like ghosts. I feel better when it's the four of us. Please stay— for me." Her eyes— he never could get over them. He'd never seen another set like hers, none that were human, which gave her a simple but sexy appearance, and an exotic lure all her own. There was no duplicating her. And the very reason why he gave up looking for his own Unicorn. Why look, when she was kneeling right next to him, asking him and Paris to stay? And he knew about that void feeling. He and Paris had begun to feel it themselves.

"Give me some sugar."

The instant brightness on her face when she smiled melted the last chill he was feeling; they didn't need to withdraw— they needed to be closer. That's how they, all four of them, would get past all this pain they were dragging around with them.

Kat leaned over and planted a sweet brush of her lips to his. Sweet as honey.

Trenton opened up the glass doors to the pool run and flipped a switch, causing the pool to light up in hues of aquamarine and brilliant cobalt, sending blue rippling reflections all over the living room. It was a beautiful effect.

Kat stood quietly while Trenton had his fun undressing her, then she stole away and slipped into the water with hardly a splash. Like a mermaid, she swam under its surface until she reached the other side. Trenton stood over her, walking along the pool's edge, enjoying the sight of her.

Diesel and Paris eventually joined them. Diesel sat on the edge and dropped his feet into the water, while Paris decided to take advantage of the position and began to tease him playfully, or his cock rather, before he pushed off to swim around with Kat.

How odd it seemed that it was all the more natural here in Trenton's home than in his own. Sometimes, he just felt like being more considerate of Marcus and not putting on a show. Even though Marcus had never, and likely never would, complain about it. But he had to face the fact that Trenton and he belonged together, they had given each other plenty of time to develop in their own relationships, and now it seemed to be the time to put the two together.

~ * ~ * ~ * ~ * ~ * ~

CHAPTER FORTY-ONE

~ * ~ * ~ * ~ * ~ * ~

It was a hard pill to swallow, but his company was now down four of his men. And as good as they had been, dead men could not protect his clients. A list of clients that was now growing, despite the death of Coshneizmen's family. It was their idea that TL Securities' men gave their lives in the line of duty, trying to save the family from international terrorists, that garnered most people's attention, and Trenton now had six new clients requesting his company's services. So, the time of his mourning had to be brought to an end and new security men had to be hired. Today, he'd hired three from his list of new applicants. One of whom was the non-descriptive looking man, Oliver Clay.

"Oliver, now that we have all your paperwork squared away. I want to take you to the back, where Diesel will get you set up with a sidearm, which will be your company-issued weapon, licensed both to you and to TL Securities. Plus, we'll get you started on your training." He led Oliver out of his office and into the hall to head for the gun shop.

"How long is training again?"

"Officially, it is always on going." He paused when Vince came up with a memo in hand. He read the phone message, then handed it back with a nod before picking up where he left off, "You are expected to come in once every other week for target practice, gun inspection, and updates. But for the initial training, it's thirty days before you will get your first assignment. In some cases, I may add you to a security team, depending on my clientele's needs—" he became distracted momentarily when he spotted Katianna coming in by way of the gun shop, arms weighted down with shopping bags. "Back so early?" He called to her.

Kat seemed to be more distracted by the one bag that was threatening to burst, and she was making such a poor attempt of untangling it from her arm, while still trying to maintain the other several dozen bags, that she nearly tripped herself. By the time she caught up to them, her long wavy hair hung in her face, to the extent it had to make it difficult to see.

Trenton couldn't stop the deep smile he felt, like sunshine had just walked into his life and blinded him as well, clumsy bags and all. "Mr. Clay, this is my wife, Katianna, and as with all my men, her safety will often be part of your responsibility."

~ * ~

Kat stopped struggling with her bag and looked up so as to be polite, at least. She blew out a hard breath in an attempt to knock the particularly pesky and blinding lock of hair from her eyes. Her breath died a quick death, right when her heart stopped beating, as the man with Trenton turned to face her.

The room grew dark around her, as if some evil force had crept in to devour her. She stared into that face. A face she was certain she remembered. *It couldn't be a coincidence.*

The face of the man who had tried to kill her— five— years— ago. She felt sick. The hall began to spin.

"Well— well— well, if it isn't the one who got away—" the cruel sickness of who he was rang out in the secular comment and validated her fears.

Run!

The scream bellowed up in her throat, coming up like bile, but choked out only silence as she dropped the load of bags and lunged in a back-twist for the gun shop. Feet pounding, digging into the carpet floor, and pushing off as hard as her little legs could. Her scream finally chasing after her.

~~ *No matter what— Hide! Find a place and hide.* ~~

~ * ~

Like his world had fallen into slow motion, Trenton had watched the sudden transformation in his slave's face. His only reaction was to seize the man who'd caused it. His hand shot out to grasp the man beside him, but he didn't have time to block the manifested gun grip that came down over his face.

Stars and blinding light flashed behind Trenton's eyelids. He felt his knees buckle under him, but he managed to will his hands to catch his fall. If he went down, Katianna would be running unprotected. He tightened his fist into cloth, unsure to what part of Oliver he had, but he'd be damned if he'd let go, and he used the man to pull himself back up, only to feel the brandished gun grip strike him again.

~ * ~ * ~ * ~ * ~ * ~

Diesel was out on the floor, talking with a customer and going over the long range hunting rifle, when he heard the scream coming from the offices. Within seconds, the door at the top of the stairs crashed open and out came Katianna, running in pure hysterics. Instinctively, he commanded everyone in his store to the floor, "EVERYONE DOWN!" And he pushed the man he'd been talking to down to ensure everyone understood what he meant. He wanted everyone to get down until he had a notion of what was going on. His eyes immediately searching for Paris' location, which was still at the cashier's counter. Then he ran up toward the stairs to catch Kat before she got too far.

That took all of maybe a fraction of a military second, and then his attention went back to Katianna— just as she came leaping off the top of the staircase and damn near took a bite into the tile floor.

Her feet skidded in their fight to regain traction as she catapulted herself forward and bolted out the front door before either he or Paris could get to her.

"Paris! Go after her!" Diesel bolted for the stairs. He had no idea what was going on but it obviously wasn't good, and the last time Kat went racing out of a building like her feet were on fire, it was met with a near-death collision with a vehicle. "TRENT!" he called up.

And that was when the second part of the mayhem made his appearance— gun raised, and he opened fire. The double glass, front doors to the gun shop shattered into a million pieces, sending shards everywhere and had Paris ducking for cover behind the counter again.

Diesel didn't even think, he snatched a box of ammo rounds from the nearby shelf and slammed two into the rifle he'd been demoing. But he got no further when he looked up, saw the shooter was already down the flight of steps, and Diesel now stared into the barrel of a revolver. The rifle frozen in his grip, barrel down. He splayed his fingers out in mock surrender, keeping the rifle balanced on his thumbs. Eyes locked with the gunman. The guy seemed on the nerdy side, like he was more suited for a desk job, typing data into a computer rather than standing here in a showdown. What concerned Diesel most was the guy's fucking calm disposition. He wanted to kill, and no amount of the act disturbed him.

Time stopped— only himself and the gunman standing in front of him.

Three—

Two—

One— Diesel thrust the rifle butt out and dodged right just as the revolver fired. A muzzle-flash zipped past his head just as Diesel's rifle clipped the gunman in the head. The guy stumbled, but managed to aim and fire again before even recovering his balance. He didn't miss the second time. Diesel felt the bullet bite into his left shoulder just as he was about to deliver another hard blow, hell-bent to take the gunman out. The hit forced Diesel a step back, and that was all the space the gunman needed to grab the customer who Diesel had shoved down, who still huddled nearby on the floor.

Now, with a hostage for a shield, the gunman had his escape clause.

"You're not going to shoot him," Diesel told the gunman.

"Oh no?" The gunman pushed his hostage out at arm's length. Just enough to allow the gun to come up between them, "How would you like your brain splatter?"

Diesel took a fast step back, putting his hands in the air. There was something in the gunman's eyes, cold lifeless eyes. He wasn't scared, just determined to get back after his target. *Fuck.* For whatever reason, Kat was apparently his target, and Diesel was looking at the very type of obsessive psychosis personality Harper saw every day.

The gunman began sidestepping for the door, pivoting only so much as to keep his hostage between him and Diesel.

Out of the corner of Diesel's eyes he saw Paris huddled at the edge of the counter, a 9mm Berretta Px4 Storm Type F in hand and ready to throw it his way. Diesel didn't dare give him even a hand signal. The man in front of him wouldn't miss such a movement and Diesel had already calculated the gunman saw no reason *not* to kill.

Diesel, however, danced right along with him; for every step the gunman took, Diesel countered. Keeping the space between them consistent. But when the door to freedom was on the gunman's side, the waltz changed pace. Diesel was suddenly catching the hostage being shoved into him, but his customer's life was intact for only a fraction of another second when Diesel heard the gun fire next. Blood burst from the man's right eye and mouth. And they both went down.

"SHIT! No!" Diesel cried out, but there was no time for him to grieve— Kat was out there and now, so was the gunman. *A dead gunman*— because Diesel wasn't going to let the man live out the night.

He rolled the body off and needed only look in Paris' direction when the Px4 Storm came flying straight for him. Diesel caught it in midair. That was when he heard the shouts coming from upstairs.

Diesel took off for the gunman, but what he wasn't expecting was an ambush. He hadn't even gotten out the door when the gunman or someone else was firing back into his shop. He flung himself back, crashing down into the counter, quickly kicking further back, sliding along it, and out of range to avoid getting hit again, "Paris!"

"I'm okay!" The right answer came from behind it.

"Toss me my Glock!" When he glanced up in expectation, the black chunk of gunmetal was already flying over the counter, coming his way. He caught it and pushed up to his feet, with only the minuscule hesitation when he sensed his brother's arrival. Trenton came running down the stairs and firing at will out the front door. Diesel spotted the several thick streams of blood trails down the side of his cheek from a cut just under his left eye, and more from the busted skin over the bridge of his nose. Neither slowed him down as he emptied a clip and then reloaded without missing a step on the stairs, then ran out, catching Diesel's arm along the way. The hunt was on.

But once outside, in the bright of day—

Nothing.

Diesel stood with unmatched pistols raised and ready. The gunman was gone. They both spun around, scanning every direction, but there was no sign of him— or Katianna.

"What the hell is going on, Trent?"

"I don't know, but we got to stop him before he gets to her." Trenton stood there and pointed toward the trees on the far end of the parking lot where the picnic table was.

"HEY!" They turned, seeing Harper and Marcus come running out.

"Let me have that." Diesel snatched the military rifle from Marcus' hand, trading it out for the Beretta, then tucked the Glock in the back of his pants. "Secure the building, make sure everyone inside is okay, and cover up the one dead."

Trenton glanced over his shoulder at them, "Give me some time before you call the police in."

They both nodded and Trenton and Diesel took off across the parking lot in search of the gunman.

~ * ~

Trenton couldn't catch sight of Katianna. It was a good-sized parking area, but they had the block to themselves and with Marcus Drive, a six-lane major street, in front and the interstate behind them, there wasn't much ground for her to run without running across a street. Something Trenton didn't guess she would risk repeating. So, the only other choices she had were the concrete storm-wash trenches and the woods that surrounded the complex on three sides, buffering the area from the interstate noise. They reached the far end of the lot and cut through the trees, coming out on the bank of the storm-wash. There they spotted Oliver running down its stretch, checking the storm pipes that dumped into it. *Another place Trenton knew Katianna would not choose to hide in.*

"Take him out, Diesel, but keep him talking."

"With pleasure." Diesel dropped to a knee, bringing the long-range sniper rifle up to his shoulder. Every movement in his body slow and methodically controlled. One hand gripped the trigger hilt while the other dialed in the scope, assuring he wouldn't miss. His eye narrowed notably, trained on the target, focused, and his hands held firm to the rifle. His body expanded with a deep breath, and as if time slowed in some eerie scene, Trenton watched the exhale in a thin stream and the finger that squeezed the trigger. Time shattered by the firing of the rifle and then time resumed its natural pace. Trenton looked for the results. The bullet lashed out and in the split of a heartbeat, Oliver's right leg went flying out from under him, taking him to the ground.

They closed in on him. Trenton screwed a silencer into his pistol and took another shot, with deadly accuracy, into Oliver's hand and sent the revolver he held spinning out of reach. But he wasn't giving up. Already he was pushing himself up to his knees, looking about just as they did.

As they reached him, Trenton pulled out his cell phone and called Marcus, watching with detachment as Diesel delivered several blows to their prey, then kicked the revolver further away before confiscating it.

"Marcus, bring one of the trucks around." He commanded into the phone, but his eyes were scanning the area around him. *Katianna had to be around here somewhere.*

"Why were you chasing her?" Diesel demanded as he hovered over Oliver, pressing the end of his Glock into the gunman's head.

~ * ~

He wavered slightly on his knees and grinned, tasting the blood that saturated his teeth. *It made him feel alive.* "You mean the whore that got away from me before?" He sneered, with a heavy gloat, that he was still very much alive and he would still get his chance to get her. *He would see her dead. One day soon.*

He'd hunted for her for a long time, never forgetting she was out here somewhere. At first, he'd thought for sure she was killed when she ran out in front of that truck. It wasn't until her face made the news that he realized she had survived. He'd done everything he could to get to her while she was in the hospital. Even managed to slide in as an orderly and got in her room when he was given the instructions to bathe her. But this one— his eyes diverted to the dark haired man who so foolishly just hired him on as his new security recruit— *he had watched over her like a hawk in that hospital room. Had even had the nerve to throw him out of the room when he meant to kill her while he bathed her body.*

He never got another shot to get close to her again and then she vanished. He'd seen her books pop up on the shelves, time and time again. He even read a few, but her writing tormented him. How the whore practically begged him to find her and take her. *The whore.*

~ * ~

Trenton dropped his phone back into a pocket, cracked his neck to ward away the tension that seeped into him, and he snapped a flaring gaze down at the groveling man at his feet.

Trent's hand absently went out toward Diesel, open-palmed in expectation, and wordlessly the rifle was passed over to him. He clasped it in both hands, getting a feel for its weight, then without warning, except the glaring expression that marred his face, Trenton brought it up over his shoulder then thrust the butt down, cracking Oliver directly in the face.

Oliver's body jolted under the impact, then fell back in an awkward twist, and out cold.

Trenton shifted, handed the gun back to Diesel and whirled around again, his eyes scanning. Going back to the urgent

606

search for his Katianna. *Where was she?* His searching brought him around and stopping when he noticed the blood stain on Diesel's shirt. "Shit, Deez."

"I'm okay. It's just in the shoulder. It's nothing, except Paris is gonna have the upper hand on me for a while."

"Yeah, that and Patrice is going to kill me."

"None of that matters, right now. Let's just find Kat before she gets too far."

Trenton turned around, glancing up and then down the washout once more— finding no sign of her. "Katianna!" He cried out for her.

Marcus came out of the trees, "Trent! Truck's backed in as far as she goes."

Trenton and Diesel both scooped up a shoulder of the unconscious gunman and dragged Oliver's body through the woods.

"Anyone figure out who he is?"

"Other than a man who managed to pass a record check to get a job with me? No. Not sure where Katianna ran off to, either."

They reached the truck and just as Marcus said, he'd backed into the trees as far as he could go. Marcus flung the doors open, grabbed a couple of bundles of rope he'd tossed in for good measure, and passed them over to Diesel, who made quick work with them, making sure Oliver wasn't going anywhere when he woke up. Marcus also had a ball gag and he pried the man's mouth open, popped it into place, and then fastened the strap around his head.

"Better get some first aid on those gun wounds. I don't want him dying just yet."

Marcus nodded. Then with little regard to gentleness, Marcus and Trenton tossed the now bound man up onto the floor of the truck then traded a few glances.

Trenton used the edge of his shirt to wipe off the back step to the truck. "Tuck the truck in the back of the garage and keep him gagged. We can't keep the police out of this one, but we can deny catching him."

Marcus didn't say a word. He swung the doors to the armored truck closed and locked them, without any second thoughts to the man they'd just tied up and thrown into it. He gave them both a nod, then jumped back into the cab and drove the truck away. Once it was back in the garage, it would be sitting right alongside another two dozen trucks just like it.

Diesel called Paris on the phone, "Any chance she came back?"

"*No, and I'm walking along Marcus Drive now, seeing if she went into any of the nearby shops, but so far, nothing.*"

"Ask him if she still had her phone on her when they got back." Trenton was still glancing around, looking for anything along the lines of a clue.

"Does she have her phone on her?" Diesel relayed the question to Paris.

"*I don't know. I tried calling, but she didn't pick up.*"

"She hasn't picked up." Diesel repeated the answer to Trenton.

Trenton took a deep breath "No. She wouldn't, because she would come apart, and she doesn't want her crying to give away her location. She would have kept silent."

"Text her." Diesel suggested.

Trenton pulled his phone back out and quickly texted her.

Txt: —Baby, it's safe now, we got him. Please tell me where you are— Trenton

There was a long moment before he finally got a response, but she didn't trust the message entirely.

Txt: —What's my cellar door?— Mouse

"That's my girl." He mumbled to himself that she would use a security question. Something only four people in the world knew the answer to.

Txt: —Ameno Dominus— Trenton

He typed in the answer and hit send.

Txt: —I'm under the highway overpass— Mouse

But before he could finish reading those few words, another text came in and the single word screamed out to him that something was wrong.

Txt: —Hurry— Mouse

Trenton took off in a dead run, his mind racing with every scenario that could have happened. She was under the overpass, so she could be lying under a semi-truck, but Oliver had fired off several rounds— *oh god, no*— his feet picked up pace, the soles of his feet burning from the impact— still, it wasn't fast enough.

"What's happened?" Diesel was at his side, keeping pace.

"She's under the overpass bridge." He took off back up the storm trench, heading towards the interstate, just as they made out the siren calls of the police squad heading their way.

They broke through the trees and the *whoosh* of cars and trucks sent gusts of wind swirling around them. A horn blasted at them as a passing driver panicked that they might run out into the traffic in front of them. A semi-truck's air horns added to the confusion.

Trenton reeled about, his mind stricken by thoughts of what might have happened that, for a second, he felt disoriented.

Diesel's strong hand grabbed his shoulder, steered him around to face toward the overpass bridge, and they quickly headed down the side of the interstate—

"Kat!" Trenton cried out for her as they reached the steep slope of concrete. Then, with one hand balanced in front of him, he made his way up. He reached the top support columns then the three-foot step and peered into the dark recess, but it wasn't Kat his eyes found first, it was the large sticky smear of blood on the edge of the step, smudged further by a small shoe. "Oh god—Kat!"

"Trenton—" the small feeble voice whimpered from the small dark space.

Trenton climbed up, eyes straining to see into the crevice. and only barely made out the slight movement within it. He dropped to his belly and crawled further into the tight space where she'd managed to squeeze herself into, just barely able to get his fingers around her arm. It felt wet and sticky, and she squealed when he tugged on her to come out. "Come out, Kat. I can't get to you. You gotta come out." He pleaded with her, trying to keep his own panic at bay.

He needed to see her. See with his own eyes that he wasn't going to lose her. He knew she was wounded in some way, but he didn't want to keep pulling on her until he knew where she was hurt.

"I'm afraid."

"I know, but he's gone now. You gotta come out so I can take care of you." He tried stretching in to reach her again, but she'd backed in even further. He could barely brush her arm now. "Come out, Kat."

"Trenton, that was him."

He heard the terror in her meek voice.

"Who, baby? Who was he?" He wanted her out of there now. Not knowing why she was bleeding was tearing at him. He was going to start shouting commands at her if she didn't come out on her own. Not knowing why this man had come after her was another fresh rage, and if she had the answer, he'd give her another moment, and another try, to gentle her out of the crawl space.

Sobs now bounced off the stone encasement around them, "The man who attacked me at the apartment when we first met."

Oh shit— terror, anger, rage, even hate now swirled and exploded inside Trenton's chest— which heaved with a deepening— raging breath. *Time was up.* He needed her safe in his arms, and he had to get back to the garage to make sure they didn't hand Oliver over to the police.

"Kat! Get out here now!" And when she didn't respond, "Come out here NOW, or I'll give you a *real* spanking!"

Suddenly, a hand inched out, then an arm, and the thick multiple tracks of congealed blood down her arm startled away any scolding strategy he had intended to use to get her out. He quickly clutched her arm and pulled her free in one, powerful tug.

His mouse let out a high shrill, but he didn't stop until she was completely wrapped in his arms. He rolled to his back, taking her with him, kissing her. He nuzzled his face against her head and pressed her to him until he was certain if he held on any tighter, he'd likely crush her. But he felt the hot sticky fluid on her shoulder and neck, tasted the copper on his lip when he kissed her neck. "Baby, what happened? Where are you hurt?" He rolled once more, bringing their bodies into the light that managed to stream into the tight overhead space and his eyes found the bullet wound just at the base of her neck. Just inches from her jugular vein. Everything was drenched in her blood. So much so, it was hard to tell if she was still bleeding or not. But so much had been lost already. It coated her shirt, shoulder, neck, even her collar— the etched silver and sapphire stones of her collar lost under a sticky layer of her precious blood. "DEEZ!"

~ * ~ * ~ * ~ * ~ * ~

CHAPTER FORTY-TWO

~ * ~ * ~ * ~ * ~ * ~

Trenton was screaming under his skin as he watched the paramedics prep Katianna to stabilize her while the local police detectives, along with Detective Tate Marshal, tried to question him.

Katianna's blood-caked collar was now in his hands and he used his shirt to try to wipe it clean, to find the blue stones under it all. His eyes never left his wife for one minute. The world shut out by mental walls that could not be penetrated. The darkness smelled of copper and filled his nostrils— *her copper*— *her blood.* Questions echoed in his head, muffled out by the raging beast bellowing hate and black smoke in his mind. *In his mind, he'd already killed Oliver a hundred times over.*

"Trenton!"

Trenton's attention snapped to the detective and the two cops still trying to get some answers out of him. His stare filled with the lust for blood and burned through them until one of the officers flinched with discomfort and diverted his own stare. He knew they had their questions. They had a job to do, but Trenton was less than cooperative. Right now he was focused on his Unicorn—his little mouse. *His precious Life slave.*

And the *all-points-bulletin* they would never find.

"We're ready to transport her now." One of the paramedics turned to him.

Trenton nodded and glanced at Diesel, "Send Paris with her, will you? I need to deal with the police before I take off for the hospital."

~ * ~

"Sure." Diesel's hold on Paris tightened, pulling him in closer, offering only a partial hug. There was a lot more at stake here, and it had them all on edge. What was important, first and foremost, was getting Kat to the hospital and Paris away from here as well.

"What about you? You still have a bullet in your shoulder?" Paris had just barely calmed down from that.

"I'll get them on it as soon as we can leave here." He kissed his lover, trying his damnedest not to make it sound like goodbye. "Go. Don't argue with me. Just do it." He added the command in to be sure.

Paris climbed into the back of the ambulance, but the glare he shot back at Diesel let him know he knew they were up to something and he wouldn't let the topic fade. He would demand an explanation later.

Paris hadn't been around when Katianna was kidnapped, but Diesel spoke if it often enough and of the darkness it put in all of them, especially Trenton. And it explained the Dominus' overbearing possession and protection of Katianna. Diesel had even shared with Paris how it hadn't been until they came down to the island to claim him that some of that darkness started to heal. Then, when Trenton married Kat, it seemed like it had gone away completely. Not his possessiveness of her— that never went away, but the shadows that haunted Trenton's mind and showed in his eyes seemed to have finally gone away, letting the radiant Kahlua & Cream twinkle. Kat's description always gave Diesel a slight chuckle, even now, though he'd managed to keep it to himself.

All those shadows were flooding back, and Trenton looked like a man that, in about two minutes, was going to unleash Armageddon. Hell bent on revenge. Creamy brown eyes were red now, sallow with pain and rigid hatred. Insane, like a madman's. And Diesel would follow his brother to the end of the earth, no matter where that led him.

~ * ~

"You seem rather edgy." Tate commented to Trenton, watching his leg jumping with a tweaked out rhythm, while the ambulance flipped on its lights and warning sirens before pulling out into traffic and vanishing.

Edgy? He was a rubber band wound up too tight and was going to snap with the next idiotic comment or question about how he *felt.* "You think?" Trenton rose to his feet. The fury in his eyes warning he was throwing punches at the next stupid comment that was made at him. Only the firm hold of Diesel's hand on his shoulder prevented him from doing so now. But even Diesel's cautioning grip was too much restraint for Trenton to handle and he jerked his arm from his brother's grip. "My wife is on the way to the fucking hospital with a bullet hole in her throat, and you're concerned that I'm *edgy?*"

Tate took a step back. He had good reason to do so. He and Tate had history. He knew Trenton all too well. Knew he was all control, except maybe now, and that was enough for many to want to keep some space between them and out of proximity of a swing. "Well, maybe you can explain how this guy got away from you?"

"We went over that, already." Diesel cut in, "The perp struck Trent several times to the face and head with his gun, taking him out momentarily. He then entered the gun shop by way of the offices of TL Securities and opened fire in the store, then took a hostage. I couldn't come after him without further endangering those who were still inside the shop. He shoved the hostage into me then shot him in the back of the head. After that he fled. We went out searching for him, but never found him."

"A few of the nearby offices claimed they heard shots."

Trenton thrust a pointed finger at the storefront riddled with bullet holes.

Tate flinched, as if he knew he'd just crossed the line of asking redundant questions. "Did you think to use your helicopter to search for him?" He retargeted after clearing his throat.

"If the city of New York had been willing to approve our permit application to have a permanent hanger here, I might have had that option. But as it is, it's hangered a half-hour's drive from here."

~ * ~

Tate let out a huff, knowing full well he was being played by these two. He just didn't know how to extract what he needed to know from them and not risk his front teeth. "And you have no idea where the attacker disappeared to?"

He hid none of the speculation he had. He knew better. Trenton and Diesel never allowed the bad guys to get away— ever.

"No, we don't." Trenton answered with a level tone, "My priorities went back to finding my slave. Nothing else mattered after that."

"Bullshit." That was the worst thing he could have said.

Trenton came to his feet with a fist coming up so fast that no one, not even Diesel, could have stopped in time. Tate felt the contact. A flashing red blow like a pile driver, striking his jaw, which sent him spinning on his heels then flat on his back.

Trenton was instantly swarmed with cops, thrusting him back and ordering him to the ground, which proved near impossible.

"No!" Tate called out to them, pushing back to his feet, rubbing at the bruise he felt forming already. "Let him go."

"He struck an officer."

"No, I deserved that. I was out of line." He rubbed at his jaw again. "I pushed and that's what I got." He glanced at his men and at the two who hadn't backed away from the huffing disgruntled husband. *Hell, it'd hardly been over a year since the kidnapping. He should have known not to goad him, but Trenton knew something. Something he wasn't telling—* "You never miss, Trenton." Tate locked gazes with the man, and for a brief moment there was no rage, just knowing, then slipping into something that looked like sadness.

"If that were true, Hanze Coshneizmen would still be alive." Trenton's eyes dropped and he went back to the futile job of cleaning the necklace he held.

Tate never liked it when Harper pulled rank on him. He sure wasn"t wanting to get the same crap from Trenton, but the five were as thick as thieves. And he knew he would not find out anything from them until they wanted him to. He was just wasting his time trying. Hell, he was tired. He wanted to get back to his office, file his report, and get the fuck out and go home. No doubt about that. "I'll come by the hospital tomorrow to check on her. I'll need to talk to her—" he saw the instant rage charging back up again in Trenton's eyes, powering back up like an EMP, "You'll let me know when I can talk to her." Tate directed his attention back to his men still holding Trenton. "I said let him go!" He snapped.

~ * ~ * ~ * ~ * ~ * ~

Tate and his team of men finally left, and Trenton didn't waste any time making his way into the garage toward the truck where they had Oliver stashed away. Good thing their prisoner was awake. It'd be an awful shame if he were still out cold while Trenton beat the shit out of him. But it wasn't long before Diesel, Marcus, and Harper had to pull him off of the man. And it took all three of them to do it.

Trenton didn't ease up, even when Diesel fought him to the ground. Trenton was so enraged to kill Oliver with his bare hands that he didn't see the move Diesel made to immobilize him, and he was soon wrestled into a leg lock.

"Get the fuck off me, Diesel!" He cursed.

"Not until you calm down." Diesel growled. Even though he had Trenton trapped in the grip of his legs, Diesel struggled to keep him down.

"He tried to kill Kat, god dammit!"

"I know, but she's going to be okay, and we have him in our custody. He's going to pay for this, but not if you kill him tonight."

"Ohhhhh— I haven't even begun." The dark tone promised. His eyes locked on the bloody lump on the floor of the truck, just out of reach of his feet, or he'd relent and kick Oliver Clay to death.

"Don't make me put you out."

"God dammit, Deez, if you ever loved me, you'd—"

~ * ~

"What? I'd what?!" The very notion pissed Diesel off, and he wasn't about to have this kind of heart-to-heart with him. He tightened his legs around his brother and within seconds, the blood flow to Trenton's head was cut off and he slowly slumped over.

"Fucking damn it, Diesel! Did you have to do that?" Marcus protested his disapproval.

"Ended the argument, did it not?" Diesel rolled his unconscious brother over with his boot and just slumped over himself. Hanging his head. Trenton was out, but he felt just as defeated. Not to mention, it'd taken a lot more energy than usual to take Trenton down. It wasn't that Trent was stronger, just more madness behind the eyes that usually trusted him. He hadn't really wanted to do this to Trenton. It was disheartening, but Trenton was heading for the deep end, and that wasn't good for him either. He would ask for his forgiveness for this later.

"Yeah, but—"

"But, nothing." Diesel finally pushed himself up and dragged Trenton's unconscious body from the armored vehicle and laid him out on the concrete. "Get that fucking truck out of here! When he wakes up, I'll take him to the hospital to be with Kat. Once he has his arms wrapped around her, he'll settle down some and stay put. But I can't accomplish that if we keep that guy here— besides, I really do need to get this bullet out of my shoulder."

~ * ~

Marcus nodded, though his reluctance was still evident. He'd brought the truck around and helped load the man up when called upon. But now he was beginning to see this was going to be a very bad situation. There was no out for it that would be good. But Diesel's loyalties were always with his brother first. They could all discuss the *perp* in the truck later.

Harper gave him a reassuring nod, that it'd be worked out one way or another. They just needed to stick together. Just like old times. "I'm gonna head down to the precinct to do some micromanaging down there." Harper tapped Diesel on his good shoulder, "Can't leave that man unattended or Tate's growing suspicion will just escalate."

"Where's Dane? Did I not see his car out front earlier?"

Marcus nodded, "Yeah, he came over as soon as we made the call. He's upstairs keeping Vince up there. He's pretty freaked out."

"All the more reason to get that dirtbag out of here. No sense in dragging Vince into all this. Dane would never forgive us, even if we were lucky enough he allowed us to live still."

"I'm on it." Marcus answered reluctantly; already this was wrong on a number of levels, but he'd not argued it at the start, so now he was in this hell, too. "What about him?" He indicated to Trenton, passed out on the ground.

"Just go, I'll get Dane to come down and help me get him in my truck once you two are gone. Trenton won't fight me when we're on the highway heading for the hospital, if he wakes up."

~ * ~ * ~ * ~ * ~ * ~

Paris was on him the moment he spotted the two coming up the drive to the ER waiting area. His arms wrapped tightly around Diesel, pulled them together and slammed him with demanding worry-filled kiss. He needed to feel Diesel's body embrace him like he'd never needed before. Sitting here at the hospital, waiting anxiously for the doctors to come out and say Katianna would be okay—knowing Diesel was still out there with a bullet in him—and no matter how many times Paris washed his hands, he could still see the blood.

~ * ~

"Stop, I'm okay." Diesel tried to pull back when he felt he'd granted enough of a kiss in front of everyone else watching in the waiting area.

"Don't you dare pull away from me."

621

"I'm fine, Paris, I don't need this."

"I need this. I need you."

The tone, angry and frightened, struck Diesel hard and cut like a knife in him, which superseded the pain from the bullet wound that had long since grown numb. "Okay—" he pulled Paris tight against his body, his good arm locking them together, then reached up along his back to the back of Paris' head and ushered him to rest against his neck. "Okay. I'm sorry. I'm here. I got you now."

They stayed there, wrapped around each other in silence, exchanging their souls, sealing the bond they shared.

Diesel could feel the tremble in Paris' body, deep-rooted in his bones. It wasn't the shivering panic he often created in the sexually deviant play he dished out to torment his lover from time to time. How Paris would come apart so beautifully in those final struggles, trying not to surrender to him. No, this was true nightmarish fear, and the haunting pain of what it felt like to fear losing someone. Not just once, but over and over again. Too many times in just a handful of weeks, Diesel's life had tested the enduring beauty of his Fallen Angel. At some point Diesel feared Paris would collapse under the pressure.

This is what Paris felt for him, and Diesel would not deny him his need for comfort, regardless of their audience. *They* could fuck off. *The bullet could wait a bit longer.*

"You need to get checked in." Paris mumbled into his shoulder, not relinquishing his hold just yet.

"I will. First you. When you're okay, then I'll check in."

~ * ~

Paris felt some of the weight that'd been bearing down on him slide off. It should have been the other way— that Diesel would argue with him further and put off the fact that he still had a fucking bullet in his shoulder. However, that's not how his man felt right now. Diesel had made it very clear that Paris' needs came first with him. Not that Paris ever felt denied, but it hadn't been that long ago since the last time shit happened in their lives, so he needed to be reminded of it. Plus, it just felt damn good for Deez to drop his guard, for one moment, and offer the affection, despite his usual conservative manner for public displays of it.

~ * ~ * ~ * ~ * ~ * ~

CHAPTER FORTY-THREE

~ * ~ * ~ * ~ * ~ * ~

Trenton watched through one of the portal windows of the OR doors as the surgeons continued to work on Katianna. It took every last ounce of self-control to remain where he stood and not barge in. He only did so because they had, at least, folded to his demands and allowed him this far. That and Dr. Shay Laszkovi just happened to be on shift and had pulled the strings to make it happen. While it meant he had to go through the whole process of scrubbing his hands and changing into the hospital scrubs and mask, he was here and far closer than most were ever allowed.

It unnerved him that he couldn't hear the surgical staff talking. To know if anything was life-threatening or abnormal. He could only watch the laparoscopy image relayed to the monitors hanging over their heads as Dr. Pavle Laszkovi probed Katianna's neck for torn tissue with a microscopic tube. His beautiful slave. Put to sleep on the table. Her head positioned back to keep her neck exposed, while a ventilator tube remained taped over her mouth with its opposite end attached to the machine that kept her breathing with a blue plunger. The only solace he had was the soft expression in her facial features. Even from here, he knew she was not dreaming. It would likely be the last sleep she would have that wasn't haunted by the nightmares.

~ * ~

The lab tech was coming out of the lab, just a few doors down from the operating suite she needed to head to. On the cart she pushed was a sterile encasement that held a much smaller lab-grown biological graft of tubal tissue. She twisted around like any other time, moving in auto-pilot, where she'd just back herself into the suite and pull the cart safely behind her so the doors didn't catch the incubator. More focused on the cart, she almost didn't see the man blocking the double doors to the very room she was heading for before colliding with him. "Excuse me, doctor. I didn't see you th—" she turned to make her apology and— *oh my god, the hard stare she got when he turned around.* She wasn't entirely all too sure, but she either fainted or just had an orgasm. The sexiest man she'd ever laid eyes on saw right through her, and all she could think of was she should have worn her lace bra. She quickly blinked all those disruptive thoughts away. Her job detail quickly restored, but then she didn't recognize the doctor. In fact, outside of the scrubs, she wasn't so sure he was one at all. "I'm sorry, but I don't think you should be here. I'm going to have to ask you to go to the waiting area like the others."

"*Pssst! Frida!*"

The whispered yell came from across the corridor. Frida looked and saw Shannon, who should have had the guy removed from the start, was waving to get her attention from behind the operating suite's monitoring station.

Frida shook her head in bewilderment, "What?"

Shannon was doing one of those hand slice thingies across her neck while motioning her head to the man who'd blocked Frida's path. Frida looked from Shannon to the roadblock, who'd started to pace along the two doors like a wild beast. "Sir."

He paused at each portal window, turned, then paced to the next, but never looked her way again.

Frida glanced back at Shannon, still not getting it. Then waved her off because she needed to get the graft sample into the OR. "Sir!" She called out a little louder, with more authority and, oh god, yes, those eyes— she swallowed, reminding herself to stay focused. "I need to get in there."

Without a word, he pulled the door upon and stepped aside, acting like he was allowing her safe passage, except her head near turned around backwards as she went in. Those creamy eyes followed her all the way until she crashed into something with a loud clatter.

"If you drop anything, make sure it isn't the skin segment. Our unauthorized guardian won't likely keep to the outside of the operating room any longer if you do."

"Yes, doctor— sorry, doctor." Frida quickly gathered herself and got to work.

~ * ~ * ~ * ~ * ~ * ~

Out in the waiting area, Dane sat with Vince, who was worrying his scarf to death. Dane still had his phone in hand. It'd been that way since Diesel filled him in on the details. His thumb hovered over the screen. He had a number to call for nearly every situation he wanted to make go away. Except, for this one, he didn't know who to call. He glanced over to the door that led to the operating rooms, hoping someone— anyone— would come out with some news. *Was she not going to make it* and he would have to tackle Trenton down himself if Diesel didn't get out of his own surgery soon enough? *And then, do* what *with him? Tell him it would be alright, take him out to a pasture and put him out of his misery?* His gaze dropped to his phone once more— *wishing he knew what call to make.*

The hand-wringing beside him never ceased, but it was time to put his brother's nerves to bed. He dropped his hand over Vince's and squeezed them gently. "Vince, please."

"I'm sorry—" the tear finally fell. Vince had been trying so hard to hold them back this whole time and now it was too much. "You made me go out with her and she changed my life. She made me her bridesmaid." More tears came.

Dane traded Vince's hand for his shoulder instead, wrapped his arm around it and pulled him to tuck against him, and he kissed his brother's head. "She's going to pull through."

The doors to the back swung out and a surgeon, still wearing blood-stained scrubs, stepped out. The grim look on his face was not the one they were hoping for, but he and everyone else— Vince, Marcus, Harper— they all floated up to their feet in unison as the doctor stepped up to talk to them.

~ * ~

Pavle Laszkovi walked over to the men waiting in earnest, but none stood out more so than the distressed man standing next to the tallest. Pavle knew these two. "You're here with Trenton Leos?" He asked, not figuring he was ever going to forget *that* name for a long time to come.

Every time he encountered him, the man had a way of making all those around him feel as though it was in their best interest to serve him or get blown up. This time, Mr. Leos had threatened to barge into his operation more than once, demanding what could be deemed a sports' commentary play-by-play. Then asked a hundred questions after it was over. If need be, Pavle was certain Mr. Leos could perform the most basic surgery after that little crash course in gross anatomy 101.

Dane nodded, "Yes. How is Katianna?"

"She's going to be just fine. She lost a lot of blood and will feel tired for a while, but she's going to pull through. The bullet pushed all the way through, passing between the external and internal jugulars. A small section of graft sleeving was used to strengthen the wall tissue to the internal vein, which should heal up just fine. We've moved her to the recovery room and Trenton, despite our best efforts to deny him, is also in there with her."

The signs of relief were evident, even in a man like Dane. "Thank you." He spoke softly.

It was interesting how, like another time, Dane hovered over Vince like a Doberman Pincher on guard duty. *At least this time, Pavle was delivering good news.* It wasn't always the case here at the ER, and he didn't want to know what it'd be like to give such ill news to this man. Or the one he'd left in the recovery room. But he did like how this moment brought a radiant shine back into the golden-brown eyes of one who, even in the moment of distress, was still the most beautiful androgynous man Pavle had ever set eyes on.

He watched as Dane leaned in and hugged his brother, then whispered something to him before following it with a kiss to the top of the pale blond head of hair, then walked away with only a slight side glance at Pavle.

It was the worst timing ever, but it was the one he was given and he wasn't about to pass it up. One thing about being a surgeon had taught him that time was precious. He scanned the room behind him, just to be sure the *Doberman* wasn't spying, then turned back to Vince, "I know you're worried about our friend, and this may seem in poor taste, but—" he stalled, getting caught up in him. Even how Vince's hand came up to brush the hair from his face was an act of grace, and the puffy red eyes and pink nose from bouts of crying pinned and plucked strings inside Pavle's heart, pushing him to wrap around Vince and promise him that everything in the world would be okay. It was silly, he supposed, but how could such a thing be wrong just because he felt it? "I still make a really great tea. I know this isn't a good time, but it would mean something— to me— if you'd let me take care of you."

~ * ~ * ~ * ~ * ~ * ~

Diesel finally managed to convince the doctor to move him from recovery out into another room so he could have Paris back with him. The nurses hadn't even finished rolling him in when Paris came barging through, and not two steps behind him was Dane. His tall stride was a little lighter now than it had been when they'd all arrived. He almost looked like his old self as he took up residence along one wall and leaned back like it was Friday night at the club. The golden color of his eyes was restored and matched that of his hair. But Diesel saw he was still on guard. With Trenton beyond himself, Dane naturally took over.

"You're okay." Paris, however, still sounded frantic.

Diesel cupped his face and drew him in for a kiss, "It was a shoulder wound. Non-life-threatening."

"Excuse me." Diesel's nurse tried to brush Paris aside to get in so she could plug all of Diesel's monitor tabs into the EKG next to the bed, then she added a pulse-oximeter clip to his fingertip on the same arm that had just been operated on. She finally suggested, "Perhaps he could go wait out in the waiting room."

Diesel saw Paris tense up and knew right away that wasn't about to happen, "Nah— we've been through enough today. I think I'll keep him with me for a bit." Paris inched back in, instantly sought out a kiss from him, and Diesel didn't refute him in the least. Rather, he welcomed it. He did, however, wave Paris around to the other side of the bed to give the nurse some room to work.

"Go easy on him." She gave the direct order to Paris.

She must have pegged him, right off the bat. And it had Diesel laughing until it hurt and then had to stop.

"Now, you're still feeling the local anesthesia from the surgery, so don't go trying to move around too much or you could rupture your sutures. There's a remote to your right, if you want to watch TV, and a nurse button if you need anything."

Diesel nodded, and once she stepped out of the way, he reached for Paris and pulled him back in. "Come here. I could use another kiss."

Paris was more than happy to oblige him, then settled down on the edge of the bed and held his hand, keeping mindful of the IV junction taped to it.

"How's Vince?" Diesel directed his attention to Dane.

"He's better now. Kat is out of surgery and she's going to pull through just fine. Trenton is already with her.

"She's out of recovery already?

"No." Dane said it like it was a good thing, but he didn't laugh. "How about you? How bad was it?"

"Bullet was still in and got hung up in my rotator cuff."

"Ouch."

"Ouch sums it up well. I won't be reaching over my head anytime soon. Most likely, I'll have to keep my arm taped down for about six weeks."

Dane looked to take it all in, but said nothing on it.

"What are you thinking?"

Dane's eyes flickered, as if he'd just been pulled back from some distant thoughts, and rolled his head to the side to glance his way, "I'm thinking with all that has been going on, we've been very lucky."

"You call all this lucky?" Paris snapped over his shoulder

"Yes, Paris, I do. After all, we're all still very much alive."

~ * ~ * ~ * ~ * ~ * ~

Trenton was right there when Katianna's eyes fluttered open. And all he could do was smile and thank every spiritual creator, the cosmos, and all the saints out there for those snowcapped blue eyes.

"Hey you." Her soft sweet voice barely a whisper.

"Hey, beautiful." He let out the biggest sigh of relief, planted a lingering kiss to her forehead and then sat up to look at her. "Do you remember what happened?"

She nodded. "Did you get him?"

He was about to say what he wanted her to hear, but stopped because it would be a lie. There were plenty of things he did not disclose to her for her safety or comfort, but he had never, and would never, lie to her. "He's being taken care of."

She chewed on her lip and glanced up at him with eyes filled to the brim with what he knew to be apprehension, "Do I want to know?" She asked meekly.

"No." He whispered and shook his head before offering her a soft smile, "You don't need to know about this."

Her face grew shadowed with emotions that bordered on fear and grief.

"You must trust me to do what is best to keep you safe."

She nodded then tried to shift— her face winced. A clear indication the anesthetic from her surgery was already beginning to wear off.

"The morphine is on a timer. It's set to start in about another twenty minutes. You'll feel better once it kicks in."

Her hand floated up to the large padding that was bandaged to the side of her neck. "Guess I got another scar, huh?"

"Yes. You always go for the doozies."

She tried to smile at him.

"You do realize I am going to have to punish you for this, right?"

"Why? What for?" Her expression morphed into a whole different kind of concern now.

"I did not give you permission to damage your body. Which, I will remind you, belongs to me." He tried to keep his face serious, but he loved this woman so much, and knowing she was going to be fine had his heart swelling. He was too happy to keep the firm expression, and he felt the slight curl of a smile twitch at the corner of his lips. Her own broke the surface and white teeth broke through his darkness, but her smile didn't compare to the sudden brilliance in her eyes. He loved her and she felt every drop of it.

"I'm sorry, Dominus. Will my punishment be harsh?" She honored him by playing along.

"I'm sure I will be able to figure something out."

"I'm sure you will." She whispered.

"Goddammit, I love you, Katianna." He could no longer contain it and dropped over her, delivered a deep kiss, then nuzzled with her until he heard the morphine pump beep. He gave her another kiss before she went under, and then counted down how long it took for the pain medication to take effect and return her to a sleeping state.

~ * ~ * ~ * ~ * ~ * ~

CHAPTER FORTY-FOUR

~ * ~ * ~ * ~ * ~ * ~

Paris stood at the window looking out, watching.

Six days had passed. Diesel had come home from the hospital that same day; Kat was released four days later. Yet something dark remained— foreshadowing their daily lives.

Too many times Diesel and Trenton had slipped out and gone to the armored truck Marcus had brought home. He may be new to the family and their habits, but Paris had never known Marcus to bring the trucks home. They were strictly used for jewelers, payroll, and bankroll companies. The only time he'd known of an exception to the rule was when they were used as a barricade wall during the terrorist hold-up at the World Bank. So, for Marcus to bring one home now was out of place, by its own validity. That it had stayed here since the shooting? Was something altogether different.

He'd asked Deez several times, but only got silence from him.

~~ "It's okay, we're just taking care of some things." Diesel had placated Paris during one of those questionings. ~~

Authorities were still on the hunt for the gunman, but Paris couldn't comprehend how Oliver Clay could just disappear like that. He'd even asked Harper about the investigation. Harper had a history and special interest in the case, given the man who'd attacked Kat five years ago was the same man who had killed one of Harper's clients and was wanted in the death of several more. Paris didn't even ask Trenton for permission when Harper told him that. Paris simply pulled up Oliver Clay's file and handed it over.

~~ "Thanks, I already have this." Harper handed it back.

"Is it the same guy?"

"Honestly, I'm not sure. It seems like it's him, but some things don't add up."

"What about DNA?"

"We never had anything to match him to."

"So, how do you explain him just disappearing the way Trent and Deez say it happened?"

"The same way he has eluded us all for years, Paris. This guy knows how to vanish. And you saw him yourself. There was nothing about the man that stood out from a crowd. He simply vanishes into another nobody."~~

Today's visit to the truck was different. Today he watched Harper out in the front yard, arguing with his brothers in a heated debate. Something wasn't right, and Paris was tired of being in the dark about it.

~ * ~ * ~ * ~ * ~ * ~

"GOD DAMN IT, TRENTON! I want in there right now."

"I can't let you and you know that!" Trenton blocked the doors at the back of the armored truck parked in his driveway."

"This is bullshit. That man killed a dozen women that we know of and tried to kill Kat a second time. Now I want in there to get answers."

"And if I let you do that, anything he says will become inadmissible in a court."

They all went silent, as if the plug had been pulled on the debate. It took several breaths before Harper spoke up again, "So, now you're saying you're going to turn him in?"

"No. I don't know. He hasn't said a word since we captured him. I don't know what to do with him." Trenton raked his hair back in frustration.

"You're lying!"

"He's not." Diesel chimed in.

Harper spun on Diesel, "You're just saying that to defend him!"

"You know better than that. The guy hasn't said one fucking word. He eats when we feed him, and he shits and pisses his pants whether we make facilities available or not." Diesel scrubbed over his face to mirror the same frustration his brother felt. The guy was a dead end for information.

"You get Dane to have a chat with him, yet?"

"No."

"Why the fuck not? Dane could have him talking in minutes."

"Because I don't want any more of you involved in this." Trenton barked, "Three of us are already locked in, but I could deny Marcus' knowing what I used his truck for, and Deez—

"And Deez what?" The question caught them by surprise.

All three of them spun around, and right there, standing stalk-straight and pissed off— was Paris.

"How much?" Diesel asked.

Paris glared at him, "All of it."

Diesel stepped toward him, reaching for him, "Paris, it's not what you think. Let's—"

Paris sprang back and shot a pointed finger at Diesel, "Don't you touch me right now." And he stormed off.

Diesel slumped and glanced at Harper and Trenton, but he knew there was no going after Paris. Not just yet. He also knew *this* debate wasn't over either.

~ * ~ * ~ * ~ * ~ * ~

It'd been a full day of them fighting. Over the man in the truck and little more. Paris gave his ultimatum— turn him in or they were done. Diesel never answered to it. And the truck never moved. The following day was spent in bitter cold silence. The envelope with Paris' plane tickets, waiting on the hall table, was a chilling reminder that time was up.

Diesel came up to help Paris with his repacking. For the last week, Paris had packed, and then repacked his bags, changing out items with a bizarre OCD-like ritual. But his flight was tomorrow, so it was time to settle on what he was taking and be done with it. It wasn't going to be easy. After all that had happened in the last year. Most good, even spectacular, but the darker parts had not been any small matter. And so many of them too recently. Diesel wished Paris could stay or that he could just go with him. But they had talked this out a hundred times already. It would be good for Paris to be in his job again. And get a break from all this, be spared of the man he and Trenton still held hostage in the truck outside.

He came up behind Paris and wrapped him up in his arms, but instead of his normal warm welcome, Paris stiffened in his arms. That was right about when Diesel realized Paris was packing far more than what he needed to return to the island for the BDSM and Fetish season. In fact, it looked like he was packing nearly everything. "What is this? You don't need to pack the whole house for two months."

Paris bristled, "It's not just for two months."

"What are you talking about?"

Paris wouldn't look at him as he tucked another bottle of his cologne in a pair of socks and then packed it safely away in the suitcase. "I'm not coming back."

Diesel felt like the wind had just gotten kicked out of him. "What did you just say?"

Paris said nothing more as he closed up the suitcase, locked it, then hefted it off the bed and headed downstairs with it, adding it to the others waiting at the front door. Diesel, of course, was right behind him, but talking wasn't going to change this. Arguing wasn't going to change it.

Diesel took one look at all the bags lined up, ready to go to the airport tomorrow, then snapped around to look at Paris, "Explain this now."

"I said it, already." Paris remained rigid in his stance, even his jaw was tight with emotional tension, "I'm not coming back."

"The hell you aren't. We didn't sign up for a long distance relationship. You're there for two months and that's it."

Paris shook his head. "No. I'm staying."

"Paris, please, don't make decisions like this without discussing them with me. Whatever it is, we can work this out and fix it. You know that."

"We've talked already."

"About what? What did we talk about?"

Paris spun around, grabbed the front door, and swung it open so hard that it slammed into the wall then ricocheted back closed. He opened it again and blocked it with his foot, then stabbed his finger out toward the driveway next door at Trenton's house. "THAT!— IS STILL THERE!"

Diesel's chest heaved with pain and anguish, and confusion. He couldn't bear the thought of Paris leaving him. *How the fuck had all this happened? Spiraling out of control when all they had ever tried to do was protect the ones they loved.*

"It's him or me." The ultimatum repeated.

"That's insane. Paris, that man out there has nothing to do with our relationship."

~ * ~

Paris was done with negotiations. Done being told everything had a reason. *This was his life.* "IT HAS EVERYTHING TO DO WITH IT!" He blasted out. "I came here to live with someone who loved me. A man who fights to protect people— protect me. On a deeper level, the pleasures other people enjoy, the part of the lifestyle you lead, are protected from being mutilated and bastardized into something evil. That's what you protect, who you protect. What you're doing out there— I don't even know anymore. I don't know you anymore. Who are you now?"

"Don't do this to him."

Paris snapped around, and there, walking through the door he'd left wide open, was Trenton. "You stay the fuck out of this!"

"I can't. It was my decision to do what I did, and they simply backed me like they always do." Trenton held out a yellow folder toward him, but Paris didn't accept. "Take it out on me, blame me, get pissed off and shout at me. But don't do it to Diesel. He doesn't deserve you walking out on him like this."

"Don't worry, I'm not doing it just to him. I'm doing it to you as well."

Trenton took a warning step toward Paris. The folder lowering. "What do you mean?"

"I'm taking Katianna with me."

Like a blur, Trenton was on him, grabbing Paris by the shirt and slamming him against the wall, "You're NOT taking her from me!" Papers and photos blew around the floor. Some landing face-up. The nightmare images they revealed only added to the duress around them.

"Look at you! You've gone mad!" Paris shouted right back.

"Trent! Let him go!" Diesel was now in the mix, attempting to pry Trenton's fists from Paris' shirt.

"We can't stay here like this." Paris' voice softened, but not his resolve. He refused to give in. Not this time. But then Trenton nearly collapsed against him, dropping his head against Paris' chest.

"He has tried to kill her twice already."

"And twice he has failed." Paris wrapped around Trenton and embraced him. It was the first time Trenton had ever let his walls down around him. Paris hurt, but he knew now was not the time to keep throwing punches. "Turn him in and let them lock him up forever. Let the juries and the families of the girls he killed send him to his death. But if you turn into the monster too, who are we to trust to protect us?"

Trenton suddenly dropped to his knees, and Paris went down with him, refusing to give up the protective hug he used to shield the dark emotions inside their Dominus. His eyes trailed away to one of the photos closest to them. The small frame of a body impaled on a motorcycle, bloody and twisted in such a way that whoever it was couldn't have survived.

He picked it up. He didn't want to, but he had to know who and he turned it over. His heart sank when he read Katianna's name.

Diesel was right there; he took the photo from Paris, tossed it from them and just held them both. They didn't say another word for the rest of the night. But they knew.

~ * ~ * ~ * ~ * ~ * ~

"Is it true?" She asked after they settled onto the sofa to cuddle, when Trenton had come back from Diesel's house. No television, no laptop. Just the two of them, but there was an invader. He wasn't there physically, but he was there all the same.

"Is what true, baby?" Trenton's gaze followed his fingers as they mapped out the contours of her face, and then played with her hair.

Katianna looked up at Trenton as he stroked the side of her face with the back of his hand, as if only his touching her could assure his mind that she was safely tucked away in his arms. "Do you have him out there in truck in the driveway?"

"Paris told you?"

"No, just hard to miss all the fighting going on around here. Diesel's house works like an amphitheatre. So, is it true or not?"

He let out a tired sigh, "Yes."

"Will you be turning him over to the police soon?" But she regretted the question the second she saw the pain rip across his face.

"No." He shook his head as he whispered his answer.

"Then what will you do to him?" She pressed in, tucking under his chin, and his arms wrapped around her like a reflex, holding her as if they would never let go.

"He'll die soon." He spoke over her head.

"Then how will he pay for what he did to all those women, if you don't turn him in?"

"By experiencing the same pain he inflicted on them before he dies."

"Then you've let him turn you into what he is." She leaned back against his arms and looked up into his eyes. They were so full of pain they were darkened by it— haunted by it, "You have to turn him in, Trenton."

~ * ~

Again, he shook his head, "I can't." He pressed a kiss to her forehead, "The charges won't keep him." He wouldn't lie to her, but she didn't know the dark side that had burgeoned inside him. The extent of his wrath that he would lay siege to any human for hurting her.

He was up suddenly, pacing across the floor to the far side of the living room, before turning to look at her again. *The pain that he would have to deny her this was evident, that she would even ask was like asking for mercy, and his very soul could not justify it.* "Harper has already gone over all the evidence with the district attorney— most of the evidence is no good. Too many things to lead up, there's no DNA from any of the cases, and you're the only living victim. There's no way I'm going to put you up on the stand. It would be too painful for you, and I wouldn't be able to bear it." He paced from one end of the room to the other; the uproar with Paris from earlier that night still clung to his skin, threatening to re-ignite. Not at her. This wasn't her fault. But because there was no viable solution for this— it was that which congealed into a steamy pool of stormy red in his mind and in his eyes.

"Trenton—" her voice pleaded with him.

He reeled around, "Dammit, Kat, I'm already on the brink of turning feral with all that has happened over the last year." He chewed on the edge of his thumbnail, then raked his fingers through his hair. His mind racing— finding nothing.

"Dominus."

"Don't ask this of me!" He bellowed suddenly.

~ * ~

She made no excuses for his rage or his pain, for she understood what he felt. Had she not been such a frightened person all the time, he might not have been so driven to such an extreme emotional edge. But she could not let go of this. It wasn't mercy that she asked for, or even righteousness at this point. She feared the man, feared he would come back after her. If the charges failed to convict him and put him away, or send him to the gas chamber— if he truly did get set free again, would he come for her? The very thought that such a reality could happen would likely keep her awake for many nights, even years. Waking in the cold sweats of her own nightmares and, yes, Trenton would come apart over it very quickly. But what frightened

644

her as much, if not more, was if Trenton didn't turn the man into the authorities and then they found out what he had done. Then Trenton would be arrested and she would be alone. Her shelter— her guardian— her loving Dominus would be ripped from her— and that was worse than the nightmares. That alone sent her into a tumbling panic of her own. "And what happens to me and Paris if they find out what you and Diesel have done?!" She cried out suddenly, raising her voice in a way she had never done. "What then? Paris may be able to survive on his own, but that doesn't mean he'd want to. And what of me? How will I survive?"

Trenton stilled, turning slowly to face her.

"How am I supposed to live without you?" The tears rolled from her eyes, but she wasn't finished. She was determined to spill her pain out for him, "I gave myself to you. I gave you every part of me, because I have never wanted anything more in my life than to be with you. You asked me to be yours, and you swore you'd never leave." She wasn't just crying now, she was full on sobbing. Her gut, and her chest too, heaving to breathe between the clutches of sobs. Trenton closed in on her, pulling her into his arms, but she swatted him away, "No! You tell me how I am supposed to see the justification that killing him is worth me losing you in the end!"

"We'll make sure they don't find out, Kat." He tried to pull her into his arms again.

Katianna twisted, her arms flailing out. "NO! They will find out! They always find out, because that's how it always is— the good guys get caught for taking justice into their own hands, while the bad guys always go free. It's just like how the stupid writers put it!"

Trenton finally caught her arms and clamped them behind her, pinning them in one hand while brushing her hair from her face with his other hand.

Exhausted by her own outpour, she dropped her face into his palm, her defeated emotions growing weary, "I'd rather suffer the nightmares of his going free, if it means, at least, I will always be able to wake up safely in your arms."

~ * ~

Trenton pulled her into him, let go of her arms and wrapped around her, kissing her forehead— the top of her head— her eyes— every part of her face.

His own pain had been too great that it had blinded him. Now he saw hers was equal to his. She had never yelled at him before, never screamed or raised her voice in anger. But the fear that she would lose him was just as great as his was of losing her. He let go of the deep breath he'd been holding and just held her.

He had little choice now but to give Oliver Clay up. So much abuse had been afflicted to the man, there was no way Trenton could *not* be implicated on several charges already, and he feared she would lose him anyway.

Now, he just had to tell Deez.

~ * ~ * ~ * ~ * ~ * ~

They stood in the hallway, arguing— again. Nearly the fifth argument to take place in a matter of days. This time, Trenton had called him over, and he found Trenton upstairs after having put Kat to bed.

"No, Trent, I'm not going to let you do this!" Diesel bulked up, preparing to take his brother down if he had to. *Hard enough that, come tomorrow, he'd have to watch Paris load the plane, fearing he'd keep to his previous threats and never come back. He'd have none of this about his brother going to jail because of some scum bag serial killer.* But before Diesel could attempt a move to overthrow his brother, Trenton suddenly had him.

Diesel felt his arm get wrenched, and he had no choice but to turn out of it or have his shoulder dislocated. Then he felt the impact of a leg against his ankle and down they went.

Diesel landed face down in the carpet, and the heavy weight positioned in the center of his back said Trenton had him down and the deliberation was over.

"Dammit, Deez! This is not up for discussion!"

Diesel sucked in an angered breath, "Let me go." He gritted out his version of surrender to his brother.

"I will, but if you try anything, I will knock you out." Trenton warned him, then freed him.

Diesel rolled then sat up. He got no further when Trenton grabbed his head, pulling them together until their temples touched and his brother's words grew quiet and dark.

"Dammit, Deez, there are types of darkness that once they grab a man, they never let go." He spoke low, like what he had to say was far graver a secret than knowing where Eichmann's missiles were hiding, "I can't bear to lose her. If something were to happen— I'll go into a place so black, there'd be no coming out. You'll have to put a bullet in my head."

Diesel tried to jerk away, but Trenton's grip was locked around the back of his neck like a vice. He wasn't going anywhere.

"My only hope is that you keep her safe. It's the only way to save me." The whisper so soft and pained, Diesel knew it was said only for him— no one else. Then it was sealed with the distinct press of Trenton's lips against the side of Diesel's head. *It felt like goodbye.*

Trenton released him, then pulled them both up to their feet. Diesel found himself stumbling back several steps. He turned and leaned back against the wall, looking out towards the balcony. He couldn't even bring himself to look at his brother just then. He hated this, because he knew even if he fought Trenton down on this— he would not win. *Not this time.* Trenton was alpha only by a smidgen. Diesel's advantage had always been that he could take his brother down in a physical toss— *if he cheated.* His only leverage to get his way over Trent in a dispute. But not even that was going to help now. Disregarding Trenton had just shown him his brother could render him down, if need be.

Diesel ran his hand over his head, scrubbing over the short hairs, realizing he was far overdue for a shave. He clenched his eyes closed, drumming up more anger inside from the wells to prevent his tears. Wishing more than anything he could erase what Trenton had just admitted to. But he couldn't. He turned, took a step for the stairs and stopped, shooting a half-ditch effort of a glance over his shoulder. Just not looking *at* him, "If this is how it's going to be, then I expect you and Kat to be in my bed— tonight."

"Deez—"

"I want my brother and our Unicorn as close to me as possible before you go." And with that, he trod down the stairs. He found Paris in the living room, waiting for him, waiting to know the— no— *fearing* the outcome.

Diesel closed in on him and pulled Paris into him. He wrapped his arms around Paris' head like a cage and kissed him with a deep yearning before resting his weariness, forehead to forehead.

"I love you; you know that, don't you?" Paris offered softly.

Diesel let out a hard sigh, "Yes, I do, and I am so thankful for it." He kissed his temple. "I need to take a walk— to clear my head. I'll come back to you. I promise we will spend your last night home together. I just need to purge this first."

~ * ~ * ~ * ~ * ~ * ~

CHAPTER FORTY-FIVE

~ * ~ * ~ * ~ * ~ * ~

That following morning, Diesel took Paris to the airport, keeping Katianna with him, while Trenton rode out to meet with his attorney, Lars Mickels. Harper chose to ride shotgun.

"You know, this is a very bad plan." Harper shot over to him as he brooded in the passenger seat of his Knight.

"They are all bad plans." Trenton tried to keep his focus on driving and his anger out of his foot.

"Well this is the worst of them. What about those judges?"

"What judges? What are—"

"Don't play coy with me, you know what the fuck I am talking about. You're being watched and this is just the kind of thing they are going to be looking for. You're practically throwing yourself at them."

"It's not going to come to that."

"What the fuck makes you think it won't? Have you found out more about this and you're not telling me?"

"No, of course not."

"How can I be sure?"

"I would tell you."

"Like you're telling the others?"

Trenton's foot stomped down, and it wasn't until the small silver car in front of him was having a freak session, trying to get out of his way, that he disciplined himself to back off the gas. "Whatever it is they're planning, they're not ready."

"HOW— do— you— know?"

"Because if they were, they wouldn't need a fucking excuse. They'll just make one up like they did to Shay Wilks!"

Harper was stewing, but it seemed Trenton had finally made a point that countered well enough to shut him up.

"At least let me tell the brothers."

"NO!"

"Trenton! They need to know."

"No, they don't. Not yet. The viper has yet to raise its head. If you tell Diesel and Dane now, they will start an all-out manhunt. Dane would likely re-activate. The beast will go underground and we'll never find out who's actually watching us, or why. We'll also not know which direction to watch in when they come again." Trenton pulled off the highway, crossed the intersection, and then pulled into the parking lot to his office complex and parked. He glanced at Harper with a heavy gaze, "Whatever happens, unless you are absolutely, one hundred percent certain the beast behind this has surfaced, you can't tell them."

"This sucks."

"Harper, I mean it. You keep Diesel and Dane out of this."

Harper stared out the window, watching as Lars Mickels got out of his car, looking over at them with a curiosity as to why they were not. "Fine."

~ * ~ * ~ * ~ * ~ * ~

CHAPTER FORTY-SIX

~ * ~ * ~ * ~ * ~ * ~

It took three days, and a slew of phone calls, before an agreement was arranged by means of the details, argued over excessively, as to the *hows* Trenton would turn himself over. As far as the local police were concerned, they just wanted to come in and arrest him, but detectives involved in the ongoing case against the Numbers-killer didn't want their key suspect to get lost in the translation of attacker-turned-kidnapped victim.

The first step was arranged between attorney Lars Mickels and Detective Tate Marshal, making preliminary negotiations for Trenton to bring in the detained suspect, Oliver Clay, and would then surrender himself for investigation of his conduct. By the end of the third day, Lars had a signed judge's order by way of the prosecution's arrangement, agreeing that Trenton would be released on his own recognizance during trial, and the charges would seek no more than two months' time to be served for aggravated assault by way of using forced restraint, in addition to a hefty fine, plus six months' probation.

On the fourth day, Trenton, accompanied by his attorney and his brothers, Diesel Gentry and Harper Lancing, escorted a handcuffed Oliver Clay under the claims of citizen's arrest. Trenton gave his pre-agreement statement for the record, then turned himself in.

The following morning, all arrangements were gone, and Trenton's bail was denied. *Someone else was pulling the strings, and Trenton was facing a maximum sentence.*

~ * ~ * ~ * ~ * ~ * ~

Now, four brothers gathered, along with Trenton's attorney, back at the TL Securities' office, trying to figure out what had gone wrong, and who was behind it, with heated debate. All except for Harper, who had remained quiet the entire time.

"Can the charges be overturned?" Dane asked, keeping to his formidable posture.

Lars scratched his head for the billionth time, "I'm not seeing how, other than going to trial and fighting them there. It has taken me all afternoon just to get a straight answer as to how a signed agreement with the prosecution team got tossed without warning overnight."

"And?" Diesel huffed, and he stewed behind Trenton's desk, as if sitting there would help him see what hadn't been seen so far. He reached between his legs to the space under the desk and petted the mess of hair that leaned against his knee. Paris was gone, so he had no way to send her out of the room. And frankly, he wasn't sure he'd have done so, even if Paris were there. Too many things were going wrong. Too many. And with all his years of training, he still felt helpless at the moment. He also feared that if Trenton's plea bargain had been changed, what of Oliver Clay's charges?

"The orders came from the Supreme Court." Lars made it sound like it was unbelievable. Diesel was apt to agree.

~ * ~

Harper cranked up at the mention of a Supreme Court Judge and spoke out for the first time, "Any chance you caught that name?"

Lars turned, looking at him oddly, "Name for whom?"

"The Supreme Court Judge."

Lars shifted in the chair, uncrossing his ankles and then switching them to cross again. "I'd have to look again. Why do you ask?"

Harper sucked in a deep breath that announced he had a story to tell, and it captured everyone's attention. But then he heard Trenton's instant demand in his head.

> ~~ *If Dane and Diesel start a manhunt, the beast will go underground, and we will never find out who it is.* ~~

"What do you know?" Dane turned a speculative eye on him.

Harper shook his head, disconnecting eye contact between them, "Just seemed odd a Superior Court Judge would suddenly become involved in a local issue. Might warrant some looking into, and it could lead to what Trent needs to have the whole thing thrown out."

"You may have something there. I'll start looking into it." Lars agreed.

~ * ~ * ~ * ~ * ~ * ~

Harper wasn't really going to be all that passive, so when they dispersed, he paid Trenton a visit at the county holding.

He hardly waited until Trenton was sitting across from him on the other side of the glass partition when he started up, "Trenton, you told me to keep quiet for everyone else's safety. But now yours is in jeopardy. I warned you—"

"If you blow the whistle now—" Trenton butted in, "there will be no saving me or anyone else, because you'll be blindsided by who will be coming for you."

"What are you talking about?"

"Life sentence from a Supreme Court judge? Over a vigilante case that is little more than a disgruntled husband who used excessive force and held an attacker against his will? The media would have a field day with it— not to mention the legal department." Trenton sat back a moment. His eyes darted about, as if he could read all the evidence there was before them on the floor, then he slowly leaned forward again up to the glass, "Listen to me. Oliver Clay is neither dead nor disabled. And most of all, your perp for the Number killings is in jail. I did the city a favor."

"The city doesn't like vigilantes."

"True, but the public doesn't like to see them get life for a crime they sympathize with. Not to mention, it's not even a legal maximum."

"So what are you saying?"

"I'm saying, they're testing us. They want to know if we're watching *them*."

"And what if you're wrong, Trent? What happens when it turns out you are wrong?" It took all that Harper had within himself not to bellow it out, knowing he'd draw too much attention to them. Because they were already watching. And it was that which silenced him.

"You have to trust me on this, Harper. Keep Diesel and Dane safe by keeping quiet. Play dumb and cry obscene law practices, but say nothing of the conspiracy."

Harper's face locked up. He didn't want to do this, but Trenton's eyes looked upon him— counting on him to do this.

"Promise me, Harper."

"I promise. But again, if this all goes wrong, I'm poking the bears and setting them both loose."

~ * ~ * ~ * ~ * ~ * ~

CHAPTER FORTY-SEVEN

~ * ~ * ~ * ~ * ~ * ~

Diesel sat in the dark of the living room, staring out the plate glass wall to the ocean out back. His hands mindlessly petting the long wavy hair that spilled over his lap as their Unicorn slept. He still felt as gutted now as he did earlier today.

Kat stirred when the phone rang, but thankfully didn't wake. "Hello?"

"*Deez?*" A worried voice came over the line.

Diesel's eyes fell closed and he let out the heaviest of sighs, along with his name, "Paris."

"*I'm sorry I couldn't call sooner, there was—*"

"I know. I heard and it's okay. But you don't know how good it feels to hear your voice right now."

"*I could come up. I can use the chopper to take me to Martinique, then hop a flight.*"

"No, it's okay. You need to stay there and do your job. Just talk to me right now. Tell me that in all of this, you still belong to me."

"*I seem to recall you belonging to me. Did you think I would give you up so easily?*"

"Everyone has a limit."

"*Yes. I just don't know where mine is. I don't think I have ever known limits.*" There was a long pause on the phone.

Diesel didn't so much mind, he could sit and listen to Paris think in silence all night long and be okay with that, so long as they stayed on the phone.

"*Sometimes it gets too scary, and I think maybe the line has been crossed, but I am so happy being in your life, I didn't notice.*"

"It's those damn pink gay glasses of yours." Diesel tried to laugh, but just couldn't pull it up in him, "I'm so sorry for all this. I never saw any of this coming. Had I seen it, I would have sent you away and—"

"*Yes, you did. That's why you have always insisted Kat and I took your classes and kept us supplied with things to keep us safe. You were right—*"

"About?"

"*We're alive because of you.*"

Diesel pressed the phone against his temple, mentally reaching out to touch him. His heart aching all the more.

He wanted very much to order Paris to come home, but knew that he could not.

"*I love you, Patronus.*"

"And I love you, you oversized brat."

"*How is she? How's Kat?*"

Diesel's gaze dropped to the tiny woman in his lap and caressed her cheek, then tried to wipe away a line that was creased into her forehead, "She's resting. Pyotr prescribed a mild sedative to help her sleep."

"*I'm surprised it's working, with all that is going on.*"

"It isn't by much. The nightmares are back every night and she paces around the house, fighting sleep."

"*Then how'd you get her to take the medications?*"

"Drop it in her drink or food."

"*She's too smart for that.*"

"Not when we make your famous oatmeal. She won't turn it down, even when she knows I added her meds to it."

"*So what happens now?*"

Diesel let out a heavy huff before answering. "Monday, he goes to trial."

~ * ~ * ~ * ~ * ~ * ~

QUEENS COUNTY COURTHOUSE

Monday morning, 8:00am, Trenton sat at the defendant's table, next to an empty chair where his attorney should have been, still dressed in the orange jumpsuit he'd been put into at the county jail. Whoever was calling the shots was out to play a game of humility with him, despite the fact he'd had a suit brought in for him to wear during his court appearance. Instead, he'd watched as an unnamed man took scissors to it, rendering it unsuitable. For a moment as he watched the egging display, he felt the challenge and almost allowed a slip of his emotions. It was one of his favorite suits, after all. But he knew the man standing before him was merely a puppet. *So, where was the puppet master? Close perhaps, so he could gloat.*

The room had a definitive hushed murmur that hovered around as people whispered behind their hands. Trenton's attorney, along with prosecution team, had retreated to the judge's chambers to debate over Trenton's sudden change in his plea from guilty of aggravated assault to temporary insanity. They broke the deal, so Trenton wasn't about to uphold his end of the bargain either. The prosecutor, attorney Ron Schneider, apparently hadn't expected it.

"What's going on?" Trenton heard Diesel whisper behind him.

"Not sure." Trenton answered, still keeping his eyes forward.

"So why's it taking so long, then?"

"What do you expect? They're lawyers."

"Humph."

But it wasn't much longer when the door to the judge's chambers opened, and out poured four lawyers and the judge.

"All rise!" The bailiff called out and the room broke out in a shuffle as all present complied.

"You may be seated." Judge Jonathon Harris took his own seat at the bench and called the room to order, "After a lengthy discussion and review of the preliminaries leading to the conditions of this case, I have made the decision that any statements, signed or otherwise, made by Mr. Trenton Leos, will be inadmissible throughout this trial. Any attempt, Mr. Schneider, to slip them through will be cause for a mistrial. Are we clear, gentlemen?"

It was a hard blow to the prosecution team, but a considerable boon to Trenton's defense. Both sides made their vocal agreements, though Schneider's sounded a level more reluctant than Mickels' had.

"Then let us proceed." The judge commenced.

The opening statements were made. Schneider made a grand display of Trenton's brutality and self-righteous indulgence to use his company to hold a man, not yet convicted of any crime, as his personal hostage, for a matter of seven days, before he even went to the authorities to turn him over. Schneider layered on the embellishments so heavy, he should have been awarded the Razzie for Tackiest Actor of the year.

Lars was less eloquent. Instead, he went for the heart strings over Trenton's beloved tiny wife, who nearly lost her life and now suffered endless nightmares after the killer had gone through particular and excessive lengths to come back and try again.

The defense's opening statements were followed up with testimonies from Detective Tate Marshal, then Private Investigator Harper Lancing. Schneider had attempted to block all of Trenton's brothers from being able to take the stand; he had objected to too many character witnesses. Neither was it overlooked that Diesel came with a lot of backing from the local police and his involvement with veteran outreach programs. That wasn't even factoring in his recent involvement in cancer fundraisers. Schneider just didn't want that kind of prominence on Trenton's side. Harper, however, had a *cannot-block-hall-pass,* given his involvement in the investigation and manhunt for the Numbers killer.

The direct examinations took up the first day of Trenton's trial.

The following day, Trenton showed up in an orange jumpsuit again. This time he didn't bother sacrificing another suit to his quaint silent friend, who had been there again that morning. The mystery visitor even shared an expression that may have lent he was a little disappointed that Trenton wasn't playing his game.

As the proceeding began, two of the officers on the scene were brought up on the stand, with a follow up from Det. Marshal when he was asked to return to the stand. Then, two of the witnesses who'd been inside the Gentry's Gun Shop at the time of the shooting had their turns at the stand.

Day after day, after another day, it went on. A widow bawled her eyes out as she grieved for her husband, the man who'd been killed the day of the attack. An attempt to call Oliver Clay to the stand turned into a weeklong shutdown while it was argued over from both sides. Even Harper wasn't onboard with that one; the detectives feared anything Clay said would get discredited, then inadmissible in his own trial. A risk they were not willing to take, but Lars had to play all the cards. Having Clay on the stand was not necessary, but the showy debate before the jury was. To give rise that this man was assuredly a grave threat and made all of Trenton's actions seem warranted. In the end, while the request was denied, the ploy so far was working.

Another week came, and this time Katianna was pulled to the stand against Trenton's wishes, to detail her experience. But the prosecution wasn't allowed to approach her. Rather, the judge appointed a proxy, Pyotr

Laszkovi. By the end of that day, there wasn't a dry eye in the jury box, and likely a good half of them were signing up for emotional therapy under Pyotr's Midas care.

~ * ~ * ~ * ~ * ~ * ~

Two hours after Trenton had been returned to the jail, Diesel now sat opposite him at the visitor's window.

"Where's Kat? I told you not to bring her here."

"I didn't. I sent her with Pyotr. He wanted to take her to the park for some outdoor therapy after today."

Trenton nodded. It was clear a few of his threads were worn and frayed. "It's not making any sense. They're coming at you pretty hard. It's like they're after something else."

Trenton said nothing. Neither confirming nor denying.

"Is there something you're not telling me?"

"Only speculating." Trenton gave no open offers.

"Care to tell me what it is?"

"Not until I know what it is I think I am seeing."

"You know, you used to bounce these things off me. What's changed?"

"I'm behind bars."

Diesel left shortly after. It was foolish of him to suggest Trenton talk to him about anything while there. The walls had ears. But Diesel still felt like he, too, had been brushed off.

He stopped at the register desk, picked up his personals, returned his side arm to his belt and then walked out, broodingly deep in thought. A horn blast from the street jarred his thoughts and he glanced up, only to find his beautiful Fallen Angel resting back against his truck, looking all too smug for his own good. Yet, it was amazing the magic his presence did to Diesel's insides just then. "What are you doing here?"

"I missed my boyfriend."

"I thought I told you to stay down there."

"Yes, but sixty days is way too long of a time for a brat like me to go without your arms."

"So, who's handling the office?"

"Don't worry, Cayetano and Valerie can hold the fort for one night."

"Just one night?"

"I said I missed my boyfriend. I didn't say I was giving up my position at the resort for you."

God, he loved this man. "Take me home, brat."

Paris pushed off the truck and stepped in, brushing his nose against Diesel's, "Is that an order?"

"Yeah."

Paris grinned, and then Diesel suddenly felt a hand shoved into his pocket. There was far more feeling around than his dick could usually slumber through when it came from Paris, but then the hand slipped out, heavy with a set of truck keys. "I get to drive."

"Be my guest."

Paris had come home for him. He kept saying it over and over in his head. *His fucking brat came home for him.* It was a momentary lapse in reality, and he sucked up every drop and reveled in it like a pig in mud. Held his hand as they rode home— touched it— kissed it— played with it when he could, between the few occasions when Paris needed it back so he could drive safely. And when they got home, Diesel was wrapped around him before they even walked through the door. Refusing to let go.

"Damn, it feels good to have you in my arms."

"Is this what it feels like for soldiers when they come home from the war?"

Diesel was pretty sure he nodded, but then again, he was really sure he was just glad to have Paris in his arms.

They lounged around the house in their shorts, shared a long nap, then Diesel brought Paris up to speed on the trial while Paris cooked him a *Paris specialty dinner* that even managed to draw Marcus out of his shell.

"I need to go get Katianna." Diesel started rambling aloud as he helped clear the dishes from the table. And as if on cue, the phone rang and it was Pyotr.

"Diesel, glad I caught you. I'd like to keep her overnight, if it's possible. It would give me a chance to spend some time with her tomorrow, if she has another nightmare."

"No. I appreciate you watching over her today, but I couldn't bear to have her away overnight. I'll be down in a bit to pick her up."

"Don't bother. Dane is here. I can send her back with him."

"Very well. Thank you, Pyotr."

"You're welcome, and if you need me, my door is always open."

"Thanks, but I think Paris beat you to it."

"Paris? Isn't he still away for work?"

"Yeah, but he flew home for the day."

"Well, it's doubtful I could top that kind of therapy. I'll say goodnight to you then."

"Thanks again, Pyotr." He made a quick call to Dane to verify he could bring Kat home, then with that cleared, he led Paris back out to the living room, turned the stereo on to something slow and soothing, then wrapped around Paris and just stood there.

"If this is your version of dancing, it's worse than your blow jobs." Paris teased in his ear, and the next thing Diesel knew, his arms were being repositioned, shoes toed off, then Paris carefully stepped his feet on top of Diesel's and used his hips and knees to manipulate the movement of Diesel's legs, carrying Paris with him.

"This is better?" Diesel pulled back, trying to get a glance at Paris from the awkward crowding of their bodies.

"Sure, I call it the *Topping from the bottom waltz.*"

Diesel laughed. He actually fucking laughed. He didn't think it possible, but it happened and he had Paris to thank for it, and did so by wrapping around his Fallen Angel even tighter, staying right there, attempting his horrible skills at dancing. "Damn, I love you." He whispered, probably a thousand times that night.

~ * ~ * ~ * ~ * ~ * ~

Monday, the brothers were back at court, and now it was time for Trenton to take the stand.

Schneider sashayed up to the podium, wearing an irksome expression that lifted one eyebrow up on his forehead, "It's hard to believe a man such as yourself could become temporarily insane? In fact, I think everyone here in this courtroom would agree that it's highly unlikely. Perhaps you can explain to us how this could have happened?"

Trenton didn't bother losing his cool with the prodding from the prosecuting attorney. That was his job. Trenton just never gave his emotions over to the control of others. This one especially. "Even the most skilled and highly trained individual can become emotional. It's rarer to happen, but when it does, it's like flipping a switch. It's all on or it's not."

"And what is it that you think causes this *rare* switch flipping phenomenon to take place?"

"When Oliver Clay jumped me then took off after my wife, I was able to calculate and assess, without doubt, that the man chasing after my wife had plotted this extensively by seeking out my company, and applying for a position, for the sole purpose of getting to her. Predetermined—"

"Wait! Mr. Leos, this isn't Oliver Clay's trial, this is yours. Let's go back to that word you just used. *Calculated.*" He fingers his lips to signal as if he were actually thinking, "In fact, let's use two: *Assess* and *calculate.*"

"I don't have a dictionary on hand, but I am sure my wife does; if you would like her to answer the question, I will permit it." Trenton tossed it back at him for having cut him off. The prosecutors were going to attempt, at all cost, to prevent Oliver Clay's intentions and past attempts on her life from being brought up. If they allowed it, then Trenton fared a chance to gain sympathy for his actions.

"How long did it take, from the moment you were hit in the head to the moment you went chasing after Mister Clay?"

"About five minutes or so."

"So you're telling me that in five minutes— or so— you managed to *assess* and *calculate* a conspiracy to attack your wife?"

"Conspiracies are only investigations that have either not happened yet or have not been revealed to be true. Oliver Clay did, in fact, plan this out with the attempt—"

"But, Mr. Leos!" Schneider cut him off again, "The question is— how did you manage such a conclusion in such a short amount of time?"

"I own and operate a security company. It's part of the criteria to be able to calculate situations quickly and react to the benefit of protecting our clients."

"And you got all this ability for working for yourself, shadowing rock stars and diplomats?"

"Either you haven't done your homework or you're playing dumb."

"Yes." The attorney spoke in a detached monotone that suggested his response had nothing to do with Trenton's comment and more a confirmation of the kind of response he'd thrown back at him. Schneider stepped away, acting out the part where he was lost in thought. He paused at the prosecution table then, for no reason other than his body language was all a part of his rehearsed act— he drew his finger across the glossy wood surface in such a way an observer might speculate there was information in the grains of wood. Like a fortune teller reading tea leaves. "You were in the military, too, were you not?"

"Yes. The Marines."

"How many years?"

"Twelve."

"It seems a good amount of your service in the Marines is classified. Care to tell us about it?"

"That would also be classified."

"As a reminder, Mr. Leos, you're on trial here. It might work in your favor to disclose who you are, help these people understand how you came to figure all this mess out in just a few minutes, and yet still claim temporary insanity."

"You're more than welcome to run that line by the Pentagon; however, I fear you'll just have to get used to not getting what you want."

"The validity of your training is necessary to establish how you came to be so skilled." Schneider pressed.

Trenton wasn't budging, "My military career isn't on trial. I spent twelve years in service and saw active duty. You'll have to suffice the training came with the package."

"How would you explain your temporary delusion, Mr. Leos?" It was a risky question, it opened the door to the subject the prosecution didn't want to come up, but they were trying to trap Trenton to falter on his reasons for his emotional outbursts. Trenton took the bait, but it just wasn't the answer they had calculated might come about.

"Oliver Clay killed at least twelve women. Katianna Dumas was the one who got away. He had to come back for her! And I wasn't about to let him!"

~ * ~ * ~ * ~ * ~ * ~

CHAPTER FORTY-EIGHT

~ * ~ * ~ * ~ * ~ * ~

The trial came to an end on Wednesday, coming full circle from the time it started a month ago. Trenton was sentenced to two years, then given some time served for being a first offender, leaving him with two remaining months to be served out in the Riker Island jail. In addition, a hundred thousand dollars fine, which was, at least, twice the suggested maximum fine to be paid in restitution to Queens County. Plus, six months' probation and a thousand hours to be served in therapy.

It was clear a shadow behind the curtain had attempted to get Trenton to disclose he knew they were there, but *they* failed to hook him. And when all the chances to speak of a whispered conspiracy had passed, all the trumped up charges vanished, just like the shadow that had caused them.

"You keep our Unicorn with you at all times." Trenton told Diesel directly, as the bailiff returned the shackles to Trenton's arms and legs to take him away.

~ * ~

Diesel nodded. None too happy.

While it was more or less what Trenton and his attorney had negotiated for from the start, Diesel had a hard time swallowing the pill, and a bathroom stall door suffered for it after the courtroom was dismissed.

He stepped out, his knuckles chewed up from the pounding he'd released, only to find Kat sitting out in the hall alone. "What are you doing by yourself?"

"Waiting on my Patronus."

He went to her, and then stooped down before her. His thumbs taking up refuge under her dress skirt to brush against her thighs. "Your Patronus commands you to give him some sugar."

Tears welled up in her eyes, and he knew right then it was going to be a really rough night. "Come. Let's go home. Paris left me the secret recipe for his magic oatmeal."

They started to head out, but Diesel stopped and glanced around the open foyer of the courthouse, then up along the marble stairs that wound up on either side to the upper floor. Something itched at the back of his neck. He scrubbed at it, feeling it out to get a handle on it, then suddenly he had the impulse to look behind him. It felt like someone was sneaking up behind him. It gave him the chills and he snapped around, finding no one. Just a few jurors skipping out the back and bee-lining it for the breakroom. A court clerk was squatting down, picking up her scattered papers from the folder she must have dropped. Three people, two staffers and a walking tattoo, were at the metal detectors, waiting their turn to go through. Lastly, a bailiff stepped out of the men's restroom, straightened his belt, then headed down the hall and around the corner.

Odd. He never got the itch over nothing.

~ * ~ * ~ * ~ * ~ * ~

CHAPTER FORTY-NINE

~ * ~ * ~ * ~ * ~ * ~

THIRTY DAYS LATER

Like most nights, the air was thick with a solemnness. The fact that a member of the family was missing never stopped affecting them. Even when Paris finally returned home, for Katianna, it seemed to take on even more grief as she tried to distance herself from them. It reeked of an introvert's way of letting them have some personal time. But Diesel saw the ache of loneliness that was imbued inside her, and he wouldn't have it. He was happy to have Paris home, but even they felt the strife, making the reunion bitter sweet. All this weighed on them as they waited for another month to drag by.

He dipped the natural sponge in the water and then squeezed it over Kat's shoulders to rinse the soap away. "You had a long visitation with him today."

She nodded, pulling her knees up against her and hugging them.

"What did the two of you talk about? Did you read to him?"

She hesitated with an answer, then shook her head. An odd response, as if she wasn't entirely sure what her answer actually was. "We didn't talk. Not really."

"Sometimes that's what the two of you need the most."

Pale eyes glanced up wearily at him, "What do you mean?"

"Just being there together and not needing to talk."

With the next rinse, he felt her body shivering. "Are you cold?" He turned on the faucet to add more hot water, though she shook her head that that was not the case.

"I didn't want them to take him away—" her voice near cracked. Her gaze straight forward, boring holes into the tile wall with a blank stare. "They did anyways." And then her fragile shields broke, letting out a streamer race down her cheek, followed by a hiccupping sob she tried to choke back.

"He'll be back before you know it." Diesel filled the sponge with the heated water and squeezed it over her shoulders. *He didn't believe one damn word he said. Two months might as well be two years, because that was what it was starting to feel like.*

The sobs broke loose after he said that and she dropped her cheek over her knees, eyes looking up at him, "He's mad with me."

"No, he's not. Why do you think that?"

"Because I pushed him to turn that man over to the police. And now he's sitting in prison, too." Another sobbing hiccup.

"Katianna, please don't do this. You can't come apart every time you go down to see him. It's hard on me too. And so help me, if you start crying again, I swear I'll—" he stopped because he knew he wouldn't make good on any threats.

Instead, he reached for the towel, deciding it was time just to pull her out. "Trenton isn't going to be mad with you. Horny as all hell—" he forced himself to grin, "but not mad." She almost laughed. It would have to be enough for now.

He pulled her out of the tub, wrapped her up in a large towel, and then carried her out into the living room where Paris waited for them. They really did need some time together, but now wasn't too kind to that need.

"Sit with Paris for a bit. I'll be back in to brush your hair—"

"I'll take care of her hair." Paris gave him a concerned look.

Diesel nodded, leaned in and gave him a soft, tender kiss, then went outside for a while.

He felt like he was going to jump out of his own skin. The vivid image of seeing Trenton's face earlier today when they'd gone down for visitation hour. His had a few new fresh bruises on top of a couple of old ones.

~~ *How'd you get those?*— —*Keeping the peace.* ~~

It'd not been enough, but it'd been all the answer Trenton had given him.

~~ You have to do better than this, you can't let it take you down.— — Tell that to the lion who paces behind the bars at the zoo. ~~

While Kat visited with Trenton, Diesel went to talk to some of the corrections officers. As it turned out, Trenton had pretty much said it as it was.

~~ "The jail is full of gang members, robbers, rapists, and violent thugs. It's also got the dude who ran a red light and hit a pole, the guy who is late on his child support payments, and the kid who got in a fight with a friend over a girl. Throw them to the wolves and it will turn an honest man into a lying, violent thug too. Your buddy Trenton seems to think he can defend every victim in there. The funny thing is, he's almost successful at it. ~~

Diesel dropped his head back, staring up at the night sky, counting— *one— three— five— fuck—* he just couldn't. Trenton was sitting in jail for doing what they both had done. His brother not only would bear the time, but also the criminal record, and that wasn't going to look good on his company. Diesel didn't blame their mouse for her tears, for she had been right. So had Paris. He had the same argument with Paris, and again with Harper— Dane— and even Marcus. But neither did Diesel have the self-containment to console her on her grief. His brother was locked up, feeling the bars around him like a wild animal would, and it was eating Diesel up inside. All he could do now was walk the perimeter of the homes, immerse himself in the task of protecting his family.

He headed off across the yard and walked the property around both houses, checking all the doors and windows. Then went around front and checked the eight-foot cast-iron security fence that surrounded both houses. His own house was quiet while Kat, Paris and he slept in Trent's house, and Marcus worked the club tonight. Everything checked out, and he finally felt settled enough to go back inside and turn the security system on for the night.

Paris was stretched out on the sofa, watching a movie. Katianna was curled up in his arms, sound asleep.

"How'd you manage that so soon?"

"Spiked the cider."

Diesel tried not to give a disgruntled look; he hadn't planned to sedate her unless necessary.

"She deserves at least one night without nightmares." Paris whispered, "Besides, I only gave her half of what Pyotr prescribed. The rest is just natural exhaustion."

Diesel lifted her up in his arms, carried her up to her room, and tucked her into the bed. He sat with her quietly a moment on the side of the bed, watching her sleep, and staring out into the night. He rubbed at his eyes, realizing he was tired too. He reached over to the night stand and pulled open the top drawer, eyeing the handgun kept there. He felt on edge. More so than usual. He tried to tell himself it was because of what Trenton was dealing with. Nevertheless, he reached between his legs, down the side of the bed, and slipped his fingers under the mattress, finding another. He fished the small .22 out, checked the chamber to confirm it was loaded with the safety on, then pushed it back to its hiding spot.

There was no way for him to shake the unease, because the sight of Trenton's fresh black eyes wasn't the worst news Diesel had learned today. That came after he'd already left.

Diesel went out, finding Paris in the hall, already there waiting on him. Paris took him into his arms and kissed him tenderly while Diesel rested his head against his. His mind was exhausted, too much so for sex. He just needed his lover close to him, needed his comfort.

Diesel dropped his heavy arms over Paris' shoulders and just rested there. When Paris tucked into his neck and rested on his shoulder in return, he felt half the weight of the world slip away from his shoulders. Paris was truly the best companion he could ever wish for. "Damn, I love you."

"You need sleep."

"Sleep." Diesel's tired mind only mimicked the word as if it was foreign. It's meaning almost as elusive as the act itself. "Yes, I could use some sleep."

Paris' head came up, and it was clear by the expression on his face that he knew something was up, "Then why don't you tell me what's bothering you so that you can."

Diesel looked into his eyes and could see Paris would not fight him for the details, but he was hoping he would dump the rest of that weight down, rather than take it to bed with them. He was like that. When it was time to go to bed, the clothes came off, and so did the rest of the world. "My brother is in jail, and I can't bring myself to tell her everything is going to be okay."

"Then leave that part to me."

"You can't though, because it's not okay."

"What do you mean?" Paris' eyes darted over Diesel's face, searching for the explanation. "What did Harper tell you when he called earlier?"

"Krueger signed on as his defense attorney—"

"Krueger, is that name supposed to be familiar?"

"He's one of the most vicious attorneys out there. Notorious for getting some of the worst criminals off scot-free. That bastard, Oliver Clay, will be out by tomorrow, most likely. Krueger is gonna nail Trenton hard to get his client off."

"How?"

"They're saying we caught the wrong guy. He's not Oliver Clay."

"Did you tell Trenton?"

"Are you insane? Had I told him, Trenton would have gone off the deep end. He'd get himself thrown in lockdown for the rest of his sentence. He'd lose visitation rights and never be allowed to call home to talk to Kat. I'm losing my mind, not my common sense."

"I'm sorry. I didn't mean it like that." Paris kissed him and hugged him. "Come, let us both try to get some sleep." And Diesel guided him back to Trenton and Katianna's bedroom, where they both crawled up next to her. Sleep finding them much faster than they expected.

~ * ~ * ~ * ~ * ~ * ~

CHAPTER FIFTY

~ * ~ * ~ * ~ * ~ * ~

Diesel's eyes snapped open. Something was instantly wrong. The hairs on the back of his neck danced on end, making him itch, and the skin on his arms tingled. He pricked his ears, listening to the night. Both Katianna and Paris were sound asleep next to him, and not a sound could be heard from either of them. Yet something about the room wasn't right.

The glow—

The glow from Trenton's clock was missing. His eyes darted across the room to the security panel next to the light switch. It, too, was missing the glowing key pad. Even the hum of the central air was missing.

Someone had cut the power.

And when he heard the faint clink of glass coming from one of the downstairs floors, he was certain they had an intruder, and he wasn't going to need three guesses as to whom. There wasn't a soul on the planet stupid enough to attempt breaking into this house— except, that person was still locked up, at least for another day or two.

Diesel rolled up on an elbow and reached over Paris, placing his hand over Katianna's mouth, clamping around it tightly before giving her a quick jerk to wake her.

"Shhh—" he whispered and felt her flinch, but there wasn't time to console her and she would know that. "Slowly—" he pointed her to the side of the bed. She nodded, to his relief, and he listened for their intruder while watching as she quietly slipped over the edge of the bed and disappeared underneath it. But then, quite suddenly, her hand came reaching back up, pushing the small .22 from under the mattress over to him.

Diesel pulled the gun to him, but left it as he did the same with Paris. Placing his hand over Paris' mouth before waking him.

Paris woke with a considerable jolt, but kept quiet as Diesel told him what he needed to do. He just hoped he did it.

Diesel knew Trenton would have worked out the routine with Katianna. A *what to do* for everything. For when they were in bed— or in the living room— out on the lawn— or in the truck, Trenton would have had an emergency plan for every part of the house, and he would have made sure she knew every step and count by heart.

Paris was a whole other story— no matter how many times Diesel went over the emergency plan for the shop and home, the man refused to accept that his part in the plan was to slip into a hiding place and stay out of sight until Diesel gave him the *all clear.*

"Stay here with her." He guided Paris' hand to the .22, then flipped the safety off, "It's already chambered. Do not leave this room unless I call for you."

Paris nodded against his palm.

"Do you remember the code word?"

Again Paris nodded.

"Okay. Stay hidden."

Diesel slipped from the bed, carefully pulled Trenton's Desert Eagle from the top drawer of the bureau, and then made his way out of the bedroom.

~ * ~

Only Paris didn't do what he was told, but rather stood at the bedroom door and listened. He craned his neck around the edge of the door, watching as Diesel's shadow moved down the balcony hallway, and then down the stairs. Paris had always thought he was well tuned into Diesel's presence, having fused that connection with him from spending a considerable amount of time blindfolded by the damnable dominant man so often. However, as Diesel drew away through the house, his footsteps— even his presence, slipped from awareness, and Paris could no longer track his lover's location.

Paris felt the ominous foreboding creep over him like a dark shadow reaching out to clutch at his throat. He didn't like the disconnection. He understood it— Diesel was keen on stealth. He'd been some kind of special ops for the Marines. Performing extractions and other covert secret shit. Stealth was Diesel's primary skill; so, naturally, when someone had apparently broken into the house, he would not want anyone to know where he was. Paris was vain in that sense, and he considered himself an exception to such strategy. And now, feeling it, he didn't like it.

He glanced down at the .22 in his hand. If someone was hell-bent on reaching them that they'd try breaking into their home, this was not the gun he wanted in his hand. Paris went back to the bed. He knew there was another gun. He'd watched Diesel check their placements every night.

He circled around the bed and pulled the Berretta PX4 from its hiding place in the nightstand. He set the .22 down on the floor and watched as Kat's small hand reached out, like a mouse stealing cheese. Paris kept quiet and slowly checked the gun chamber to be sure it was loaded. A hollow head copper point winked back up at him and his grip tightened as he slid it back into place with only a slight click. He took the safety off, turned, and walked right into the barrel of a gun.

Paris froze in his tracks, his focus roving from the gun, down the arm, and to the man holding it. He didn't know the face. He'd had it in his head somehow that the person they would find would be the man Trenton had beaten to a pulp. But then, all Paris had ever seen of the man was a swollen black and red face. The one he was looking at now didn't appear to have ever taken a beating. Nothing, except the eyes were the same. Filled with loathing, hatred, and evil. Not even the darkness of the room could hide the vitriol.

"What is this? Where's the girl?" The intruder's impatience was thick with a malicious intent to kill.

"What girl? There's no girl— I don't fuck women."

The intruder shifted, "What are you? Some kinda faggot?" Paris' response seemingly threw him off guard.

Paris remained stiff, but he knew how to play this game and it suddenly kicked in, becoming his coping mechanism, whether it was a good idea to antagonize an armed man or not. "The best kind. Wanna try me? You'll never go straight again." Paris used the only power he'd ever had. *Call him vain all you wanted, but he knew he was beautiful, and he knew even straight men considered him.* By fucking god, he would use it if it could help get him out of this, or at best stall the man until Diesel came back. *Where the fuck was he anyway? Why couldn't he sense where his lover was?* That alone might have been as unnerving as having this man's gun pointed at his head, except right now, the gun seemed far closer to taking away his life.

"I'm no faggot." The intruder spat the words from his mouth.

"That's what they all say, until they've had me inside them." Paris licked his lips, eyes intent on the shadowed man. His fingers tightened around the gun the intruder had not yet ordered from his grip. Only, Paris couldn't quite figure out how to get it up and take a shot without the gun he was staring down beating him to the draw.

"What's that you got in your hand?" Instantly the intruder stepped in, pressing the barrel against Paris' forehead, "Drop it now."

Paris tensed, his finger quivering. He sucked in a hard breath, but did as told, letting the Berretta drop to the floor.

"Now kick it over this way."

Paris kicked it, but he kicked it under the bed instead, and he paid for that one.

The pistol came crashing over his temple. Paris' knees buckled as a flash of white stars scattered across his brain, and down he went on hands and knees.

He felt the barrel press on his temple again as the man circled around to his side. *Oh god, this was the moment. He was going to die right here and Diesel wasn't here to prevent it.* He quaked, teeth clenching. Diesel— what he'd give to pause time, just to have one more moment with his lover. He'd not had enough time with him. He hadn't had his fill. Not that he ever thought he would. And that was much of why he loved him as completely as he did, because he always wanted to come back for more, and Diesel never denied him. *Sure, Diesel made him hold out at times until he was humping the damn furniture he was so horny, but never denied.*

Paris felt the moisture seeping into his eyes. *Fuck, was he really going to cry?*

"Whadda ya say we put your bravado to the test?" The intruder challenged him.

The comment tore Paris from his emotional demise and saw the man was actually unzipping his pants. He felt his stomach revolt, twisting with intense nausea. *Oh god, he was going to be sick.*

"Stop right there." A deep commanding order came from the hall.

Diesel!

Paris' head snapped up. *Thank god he was here.*

Diesel was keeping to the shadows of the hallway, guarding his position, but Paris could feel him— sense his body heat. He thought for sure he could actually see Diesel's body in the shadows, or Paris' mind was just playing tricks on him. Didn't matter, because he saw the taut muscles of his Patronus' chest, rippling with tension, as he held his gun locked on his target. Paris could see the

RIGHT ONE 4 DIESEL

hard, frozen stare of his face, eyes tightened— calculating every move— every flinch— every breath the gunman could possibly make. Diesel knew how to read a person's body like no other.

Paris felt the trickle of sweat make its way down his temple. He'd almost laughed, if he wasn't so fucking scared to death, because he knew Diesel wasn't sweating.

"Come out where I can see you." The intruder called to the man hiding in the darkness.

"Touch him and I will shoot you down." Diesel's dominant voice seeped out from the shadows like whirling smoke.

The gunman pressed his pistol harder against Paris' head. Paris winced. "You can't shoot me."

"But I can." The small voice came from behind.

The intruder whirled about, but it was too late.

Katianna squeezed the trigger, firing off the Berretta pointing up toward his head.

The intruder stumbled back. His mouth opened to scream— his hand frozen halfway up in an attempt to return fire, but Kat's bullet had already beaten him to it, striking him in the face. The shot was echoed by another coming from Diesel's direction. Sending the gunman to the floor.

~ * ~

"Paris!" Diesel shouted, rushing in, keeping his gun trained on the body on the floor. He gave the body a nudge with his foot, despite the hole in the gunman's face and the massive exit wound coming from his chest. He spun his attention to

Kat. Her face was splattered with blood and her eyes were as wide and white as a ghost's. "Kat."

She didn't respond, just stared at the dead body.

"Hey, Mouse, look at me."

He carefully dislodged the Beretta from her grip and tucked it away in the back of his boxer briefs, then pulled her into him. His other hand grabbed Paris and pulled him up to him as well. "You okay, Paris?"

"I'm okay." Paris buried his head into Diesel's neck, his arms locking around him with no intentions of letting go anytime soon.

Diesel pulled them both away from the body. He needed to get them out of there before they both started to freak out. His hands wrapped around Katianna's eyes and he kept Paris tightly pinned against his body. He shuffled the two out of the bedroom and out onto the balcony before dropping to his knees, keeping the two with him and holding them tight, kissing them both. Adrenaline still coursed through his body, raging under his skin, making his heart drum out a thundering tempo in his ears. The fear of losing Paris flashing through his brain had him shaking so badly he couldn't stop.

He heard a shuffle, footsteps on the staircase, and then he turned and heard the faint chirping call. "Marcus!"

"Deez!"

"Up here, it's clear." He called Marcus up, but he readied his side arm, out of line-of-sight, just in case.

He listened to the cautious steps coming up the stairs, then saw the end of Marcus' gun barrel peek around the corner, followed by Marcus' head. Diesel's *all clear* hadn't taken the guard out of the man, who stuck to protocol as he glanced around then came the rest of the way up, taking in the sight of the three of them. Diesel inclined his head toward the bedroom and Marcus continued past them, then disappeared into Trenton's bedroom.

Diesel stayed put, nudging at Paris' head, trying to get him to look up so he could kiss him, but Paris wasn't budging. Not allowing even the faintest movement that put even a wisp of hair between them. Not even for a kiss. So Diesel succumbed to kissing the top of his Fallen Angel's head instead, stroking his hair and back. His other hand still held Katianna, but when he shifted to comfort her in the same manner, she slunk to one side and he realized she'd fainted.

"How'd you get here so fast?' Diesel asked, keeping his voice down low when Marcus returned from the bedroom.

"Dane was in tonight, so I slipped out early and came straight home for once. Power was out when I pulled up."

"Shit. Our house too?"

Marcus nodded, "I was around the side checking the box when I heard the shots."

"Anything?"

"Nothing."

"Had to be off the property then."

Marcus shook his head. "Well, if he cut the power from outside, it means he brought tools. That means he's got a car nearby." Marcus gave him a nod, and they both knew they needed to check before the police arrived.

"We better go have a look around then."

Marcus nodded his agreement.

Diesel shifted, getting a foot under him and scooping Katianna in both arms, "Paris, get up. I'm taking you both downstairs."

"Shit, she's out?" Marcus exclaimed when he meant to guide Kat downstairs so Diesel could handle Paris.

Diesel looked over her unconscious body, then at him, "It's probably for the best. She shot him first."

"No shit? I know damn well Trent didn't teach her to shoot a gun, and that shot was dead on."

Diesel didn't say a word, hoping the subject would never have to come up between him and Trenton again, but, at least now, he would have a valid defense for his choice.

He carried his Mouse with his Fallen Angel, still glued to his side, and went downstairs to the living room. It took some prying, but he finally had Paris sitting down on the sofa and Kat stretched out next to him, not that Paris was entirely letting go. Diesel tried to pry Paris' grip from his shoulder again, "Paris, let go. I need to secure the perimeter."

"No. Don't you leave me." His plea was on the edge of derangement. For the second time in just a year, Paris had stared down a gun for reasons other than sexual play.

"Paris, I'm not leaving you, but I have to check a few things before the police get here. I have to keep you safe. Stay here with her. Marcus and I are going to circle around the property."

"No! Let me go with you."

"No— I want you to stay here."

"I'm going with you."

"Dammit, Paris, for once, do what I tell you." He straightened, drew away from Paris and loomed over him with a stern look. "Stay here until I come back."

~ * ~

It took everything Paris had not to follow Diesel out. Rather, Kat was the only reason why he didn't. He watched over her, for what seemed like an eternity, in the dark silence of the home. Not a sound crept through, except maybe the haunting sensation of the body upstairs turning cold.

Enjoy it while it can, 'cause *it's going to rot in hell for the remainder of eternity.* Paris' thoughts brooded. He felt the stirring in his arms, pulling him from his dark thoughts and replacing them with instant relief when he saw her pale blue eyes blinking up at him.

"Paris?" Those same eyes suddenly flooded with tears as recollection came with consciousness.

"Shhh, little Mouse, I'm fine." He shook his head, feeling tears of his own rising up. "You know, you saved my life."

Katianna sprang up, threw her arms around him, and they remained there in each other's embrace while the tears fell between them. "I need to grab some tissues."

She'd no sooner stood when, unexpectedly, the silence of the home was disrupted. A sound that made both of their hearts skip and kick up in rapid beating in their chests. It wasn't loud, or close, but there was no mistaking the sound.

Two small pops. Like a pea shooter.

Paris knew the sound from the popular gun for young ladies, and Diesel always required new gun owners to come in for a safety and target class before selling them a weapon. Paris also knew neither Diesel nor Marcus ever carried one.

Paris surged to his feet and bolted for the door. He couldn't hear anything else. The night seemed to be dead quiet, with a foreboding weight that tried to slow him down as he ran down the driveway and out onto the street. No signs of trouble to tell his head, his soul, what had happened. Not until he hit the street did he hear Marcus.

"Deez! Come on now. Stay with me!"

Paris came around the thick privacy wall of hedge trees. Another fifty yards further, under a broken street lamp was a car— behind it, Diesel's body lay on the street with Marcus kneeling over him.

"DON'T YOU DIE ON ME!" Marcus cried out.

A surge of pain rose up like a sandstorm. Paris was never even aware the scream he heard splitting through the night was his own, "*NOOOOOOOOOOOOooooooooooooo!*"

~ * ~ * ~ * ~ * ~ * ~

EPILOGUE

~ * ~ * ~ * ~ * ~ * ~

Dr. Pavle Laszkovi plopped down at the desk at the medical station in the ER at the Hampton Medical Center, where he'd been filling in for one of their chief ER surgeons. It'd been a long day and he wasn't looking forward to the long commute home. But there was a fresh new creature in his life, whose very voice had the power to brighten the end of even the most exhausting shift. "Good morning, sweetheart."

"*Hey.*" A sleepy voice answered on the other end of the phone, "*You on your way?*"

"In just a bit. Just finished up my paperwork and the shift has turned over. There's an emergency gunshot patient being rushed in by chopper, so I'm gonna hang around in case they need me."

"*I still can't believe you volunteered to fill in at a hospital all the way out in the Hamptons. Maybe I should stay with my brother the rest of the week.*"

"Are you kidding? He doesn't like me that much."

"Chopper has landed." Someone at the stationed called out.

"Gotta go. I'll be home before you know it."

"*Okay, see you soon.*"

"I'll call once I'm on the road." He no sooner hung up when the doors to the back of the ER burst open with a team of paramedics rushing in a gurney. One of the EMTs had climbed on top and was performing CPR as they rushed past.

He'd seen it before. Sometimes they came back, and sometimes they were clock-checked then marked down as DOA.

Pavle froze, his chest caving in, making it difficult to breath. The clatter of paramedics rolled by in slow motion. There'd only been one other time in his entire life as a medical doctor where time stopped in such a situation. That frightening day had been when his own younger brother had been brought into his ER, and now it did so again, when he saw who the man was they were trying to revive. "Oh no."

Two little words uttered from his lips. Words he would never recall saying until later, when the intern doctor standing next to him would bring it up.

"You know him?"

"Yes." His gaze following the team heading straight for operating room three, "Guy, get my garbs."

"Yes, doctor, right away."

TO BE CONTINUED...

~ * ~ * ~ * ~ * ~ * ~

Becoming His Slave

THE DOMINION OF BROTHERS SERIES: BOOK 1

BDSM & D/s / MF / Erotic Romance / some MM, MMF, MMM & FF / Explicit Hot Language

Katianna Dumas hovers on the edge of passion, caught up inside the exquisite eroticism she crafts as an author. Her erotic novels seduce readers with tales of new and unknown heights of pleasure to which Katianna herself, is inexperienced. That is until one night she couldn't even remember; she confessed a secret desire to Trenton Leos, who's now intent to bring her fantasy to life and lure her into his world of Dominance and Submission where he's not just any Dom, he's the Dominus. The Master of all Doms.

Life with the Dominus promises to surround her with rich, somatic passions, but therein too lies danger, and she's not sure she's strong enough to hang on. Especially when being with Him means submitting her life to Becoming His Slave.

~ * ~ * ~ * ~ * ~ * ~

Domming the Heiress

THE DOMINION OF BROTHERS SERIES: BOOK 1.5

BDSM – D/s / MF / Erotic Romance / Explicit Hot Language
Heiress Amelia Quinneth had always been known for topping from the bottom. Being CEO and owner of the family fortune and firm makes letting go of control more than just complicated. Nevertheless, submission is the one thing she desires most at the end of the day and no amount of control over her life can get her to that unobtainable bliss. That is until frustrated by lack of satisfaction, she finally reached out to Dominus Trenton Leos to be paired up with a Dom that could take charge and satisfy her needs.

However, despite her request, she never expected she would have to meet her new Dom, while remaining blindfolded for the next thirty-six hours.

Amelia's Dom turns out to be a Head-Master who quickly shows her who is in charge and strips away every layer of hers, one by one, until she found the true euphoria that comes from understanding her surrender.

Her very walls that she kept to define her fantasies have been torn down, but in order to find out who her new Master is, there is one more wall she must let go of and she's not sure she can.

~ * ~ * ~ * ~ * ~ * ~

A Place for Cliff

THE DOMINION OF BROTHERS SERIES: BOOK 2

MM / Erotic Romance / some D/s & light bdsm / Explicit Hot Language

Abandoned by his parents and left to tend to his sick sister since he was nineteen, Cliff has done little more than wonder thru his existence. That is until the Patronus Diesel Gentry sends him to meet Pyotr Laszkovi. A man nearly twice his age but his impeccable looks and debonair sexuality has Cliff falling like a love sick puppy for the man. Problem is Cliff is about two threads from coming completely undone as a human being.

Despite this Pyotr sees in him an irresistible young man who satisfies his needs like no other and is willing to be there to catch Cliff when he unravels and stay at his side during the hardest goodbye of all.

~ * ~ * ~ * ~ * ~ * ~

Rough Attraction

THE DOMINION OF BROTHERS SERIES: BOOK 3

MM / Erotic Romance / Explicit Hot Language
Like brimstone and caramel. When two men come together with a Rough Attraction that burns as fast as Nitrous Oxide in their veins, it's hard to find the cruise control and trust that they can make this last for the long run.

~ * ~ * ~ * ~ * ~ * ~

Life and relationships aren't always neat and clean, or come in perfect little packages. Maxum St. Laurents knows this all too well. After being in a four-year relationship that does everything but bring him pleasure and fulfillment, he finds himself struggling to keep working at it. It doesn't help matters that the man who satisfies every need and want he could have, is the man he is having an affair with. And for Maxum, affairs don't translate into long term relationships.

Darko Laszkovi just couldn't help himself when he spotted the handsome man ranting over a flat tire on the side of the road. Moreover, he couldn't be happier when the reward turned into an insatiable lover he hoped to keep for the long run. But, despite the rough attraction that holds them to each other like power-magnets, when Maxum struggles to let go of a relationship that doesn't work; Darko's patience and understanding that we aren't always where we want to be, gets tested to the max.

~ * ~ * ~ * ~ * ~ *

TAKING OVER TROFIM

THE DOMINION OF BROTHERS SERIES: BOOK 4

MM / Erotic Romance / Beginners in D/s / Explicit Hot Language

Trenton Leos has always been known to many as the Dominus, the man to go to for the perfect D/s match. However, Trenton and his brothers are about to find out that he and their lifestyle has become the target of a political cleansing. A shady operation with very deep pockets comes to the surface when Trenton is asked to investigate a dark secret that threatens the future of Pyotr's younger brother, Trofim Laszkovi and his lover, Shay Wilks.

~ * ~

Trofim Laszkovi would never forget how right it felt to be in Shay's Wilks' arms five years ago. But Shay's father made it abundantly clear with threats hard to ignore, that Trofim's family would pay the price if he didn't stay away from Shay. So with the help of a friend, Trofim made a career move that put him an ocean away from his family— and his heart.

Even now, having finally returned home only a year ago to the family he missed, Trofim hadn't dared allow himself to look in Shay's direction.

~ * ~

Shay Wilks has done everything he could to keep his father's plans for him at arm's length and protect his internship as a doctor from ruin by the same man. All in hopes that the only man Shay has ever loved will one-day return to him.

Now, five years later, Shay finally has another chance to be with Trofim. If only he can convince Trofim they are better together than apart as well as get out from under his father's brutal hold in time before Shay loses Trofim again— for good.

~ * ~ * ~ * ~ * ~ *

BONUS READ

touCHing viDa vinCe

THE DOMINION OF BROTHERS: BOOK 5.5

MM / Erotic Romance / Explicit Hot Language

Vida had spent a good part of his life in a whirlpool of depression and it all rooted back to his parent's rejection of him. He likely would have withered away if it weren't for his brother, Dane. His rock and chariot. The person who had touched him and made him feel so loved and adored. If only Vida could find his happy ever after with someone who also made him feel that same way Dane did.

The biggest hurdle was finding himself again. And who knew the discovery would be brought on by a little mouse?

There was something to be said about having the Dominion of Brothers as his family; they'd loved him and watched over him as he stumbled around trying to reinvent himself until finally coming to the spot they knew all along. Who he was. Now, Vince did too.

Oh, and there was also something about the handsome doctor fellow whose eyes lit up when he looked at him.

Pavle Laszkovi felt like a school kid fumbling about for the right words to ask the androgynous man for tea. He'd never laid eyes on someone so beautiful. Like an angel unspoiled by the world.

Such protection probably had a lot to do with the older brother who watched over and guarded him like a Doberman Pincher. A formidable man Pavle would have to win over if he was planning on touching Vida~Vince.

PROLOGUE

~ * ~ * ~ * ~ * ~ * ~

Vida sat at the Victorian antique vanity and stared at himself—an age went by and finally let out a self-loathing sigh.

Himself.

No makeup, not even a left over smidgen from last night. No false lashes or breast inserts—only the haunting words of what should have been a casual conversation looming around in his head like a ghost sent to torment him. He may have come out of the closet early in life, but it was still full of ghosts.

> ~~*Do you ever take your woman off?* — —*Heavens, no.*~~

He glanced at the wig still mounted carefully on the Styrofoam head, "Yet here you are putting it on every morning." He told his reflection and watched as the tear escaped him and trickled slowly down one cheek. His hand went up to the nylon on his head and pulled it off letting his own pale golden locks spill to his shoulders in a tired *bed head doo.* He closed his eyes and let more tears stream down his face. "Oh god, don't start again—" his shoulders slunk down. "This isn't healthy, you know." He looked back into the mirror and tried to concur to dismal the reflection of his self-being.

Se deep in the pit of despair he didn't even flinch when his cell phone rang.

"Yes, Dane—" he didn't even have to look at the caller ID to know it would be him. For one, no one else ever called this early in the day and two his brother was always doting on him.

"Whatever your plans are for today, cancel them. Dry your eyes and get dressed. I'll send a car in about an hour to pick you up."

Vida shook his head, "I'm really not feeling—"

"It wasn't a request." The man on the other phone stopped him. "Now be a good boy and do as I say." It was never beneath his brother to pull his head master seniority on him from time to time, not that Vida was inclined to respond to it. He wasn't a submissive— or a dom for that matter— but he wasn't willing to argue with Dane either. Somehow or another, his brother was always right and Vida took orders from him without question. Maybe because their parents had never been there to give him orders, *go do your homework*— or *clean your room— don't stay out too late.* Neither were they there to give him discipline when he didn't do those things the right way nor guidance— nor structure— not even love. Dane did all that. Oh their parents were there in body, but they acted well enough like they didn't see him, he was a ghost to their eyes and attentiveness. He could have put bullet to his head in front of them and neither of them would have bat a lash. Thus was how the ghosts got in his closet in the first place.

"Where are you taking me?" he sighed the question in the phone.

"Not me— Katianna. She's beside herself that she had hurt your feelings and she wouldn't leave either of us alone until we agreed to let her take you out to make up for it."

Oh god, he didn't want to go out and pretend to be happy. "I'll be fine. It's not necessary."

"Then you'll do it so *she'll* feel better. I'll drop by later." And the phone went dead, ending the debate.

~ * ~ * ~ * ~ * ~ *

ABOUT THE TWINS

~ * ~ * ~ * ~ * ~ * ~

We Came— We Saw— and then we made it sexy.

And that's pretty much how the Twins came to write Erotic Romances and Dark Fantasies. Both Talon PS and Princess SO have been writing together since they were kids, always challenging and competing with each other, and always each other's biggest supporters.

Writing has always been an affair creating Fictions of Dark Apocalyptic Fantasy and Film Scripts in the Action/Drama and a few Sci-Fi's. It wasn't until they began an ancient history tale that the works turned to the Erotic Genre and they've been hooked ever since.

After a life time of gathering experiences, and honing their story telling skills, they have finally starting putting them to novel size tales. So have those book moments ready, as Talon always says—

Be sure to have your reading glasses ready and block out some private time on your schedule, because—

" I'm about to make you wet

Talon ps.

~ * ~ * ~ * ~ * ~ * ~

DISCOVER THESE OTHER TITLES BY TALON PS & PRINCESS SO

~ * ~ * ~ * ~ * ~ * ~

DOMINION OF BROTHERS SERIES
Becoming His Slave
Domming the Heiress
A Place for Cliff
Un Havre pour Cliff {French Edition}
Rough Attraction
Taking Over Trofim
Right One 4 Diesel
~ * ~

QUANTUM MATES:
Pt 1~ What Torin Wants
~ * ~

DEAR SOLDIER SERIES:
Dear Soldier, With Love
Dear Soldier, With Love II: A Lost Soldier Named Grey
~ * ~

LYCOTHARIAN COLLECTION:
Bond of the Lycaon Concubine
~ * ~

TALON's KEEP COLLECTION:
Feral Dream by Talon ps, Princess so & Tom Webb
Danny's Dom by Nick Hasse
~ * ~

Muse Me Only
Inspire-Moi Seulement {French Edition}
~ * ~

THE TEDDY BEAR COLLECTION:
Their Plane from Nowhere

Big Spoon & Teddy Bear
Ivan vs Ivan
~ * ~

~ * ~ * ~ * ~ * ~ * ~
~ * ~ * ~ * ~ * ~ * ~

CONNECT AND FOLLOW THE TWINS:

WWW.TALON-PS.COM

www.ingramcontent.com/pod-product-compliance
Lightning Source LLC
Chambersburg PA
CBHW052338020726
47503CB00001B/12